The Memory of Time

C. H. Lawler

ISBN: **1530607817**
ISBN-13: **978-1530607815**

C. H. Lawler is also the author of *The Saints of Lost Things.*

On the front cover: Milam Street, Shreveport, Louisiana, in the 1920s, taken by Bill Grabill. Photo courtesy of the Noel Archives, LSU in Shreveport. Thanks to Dr. Laura McLemore.

For our ancestors who got on the boat, some of them willingly, some of them unwillingly, but all of them uncertain.

"Bridget" was the Irish immigrant servant girl who worked in American homes from the second half of the nineteenth century well into the early years of the twentieth century. They worked as cooks, maids, waitresses, laundresses, and child nurses (nannies), and so on. "Biddy" was a diminutive of Bridget.

Margaret Lynch-Brennan

The Irish Bridget

The Federal Writers' Project was founded by an act of Congress on July 27, 1935 as part of the Roosevelt administration's New Deal. Writers', editors, and historians, among others, were sent across America to record the oral histories of elderly citizens, including those born slaves and those who came as immigrants. Some have referred to the workers of the FWP as "folklorists."

Fieldworkers made about eighty dollars a month, working twenty to thirty hours a week. A majority were women.

WANTED.—A smart active girl to do the general housework of a large family, one who can cook, clean plates, and get up fine linen, preferred. N. B.—No Irish need apply

—London Times Newspaper, Feb. 1862.

You may remember her as the tall woman in the red pea coat with black buttons and the royal blue tam, a contrast to the other Manhattanites in their drab black and gray. In recent years, her hair was dyed jet black, out of time to the bags under her eyes. Her hair was still thick like it was years ago when it was naturally a luminous, raven black, just like her eyes, dark and at the same time calm and mischievous. Her smile was always the same through the decades, and, in her later years, it seemed like it was trying to push up her eyes. And you may remember the greyhound that she walked around the Upper East Side, or rather, the greyhound that walked her. Both of them placid, peaceful among the yellow rush of taxis along Fifth Avenue as she made her way to her errands, usually the Met or the deli or the synagogue. She and the dog were welcome wherever they went; people were willing to accept Francie as a 'service dog' just to have the pleasure of the woman's company.

That was my great-aunt Miriam, my grandfather's sister.

She was the kind of aunt who would fret over the placement of my yarmulke, centering it carefully and clipping it in place. Then she would take me to temple. Afterwards we would go to Patsy's, and she would let me get the Bolognese, even though it wasn't kosher, and she knew it and I knew it.

"Now tell your mother you got the chicken piccata," she would say.

She was the kind of aunt who took me out to Great Neck and taught me how to drive when I was thirteen and not old enough and paid for the repair to the bumper before my parents found out about it. The kind of aunt who regularly appeared with a new book to read and asked me about the last one she had brought me. Everything from *Tom Sawyer* and *Great Expectations* to, when I got older, Lawrence's *Lady Chatterley's Lover* and Chopin's *The Awakening*.

And then, she came and got me after my high school buddies and I found out how much beer you shouldn't drink, and she let me sleep on her bathroom floor after I puked my guts up. Then she never said a word about it, even when I said it was a stomach bug, though I'm sure that she knew better. She even made a show of washing her hands to "keep from spreading it."

She would take me to the Met, and I didn't mind a bit that she was watching me out of the corner of her eye as I looked at the nudes, and she would even point out something about them, a beauty that went far beyond any titillating rawness. She liked to quote Picasso: Art is the lie that tells the truth.

When I decided that I didn't want to be a lawyer or a doctor or an accountant like the rest of the men, and some of the women, in our family, Aunt Miriam asked me,

1

"What is it you want to be?"

"A fireman," I said.

"Well, wouldn't that be something? If it's what you want to be, then be a fireman. Don't waste who you are trying to be someone you're not."

She held a private, though heated, conversation with my father, and the matter was settled. When I graduated from the Fire Academy on Randall's Island, she pinned on my badge, smiled with pride, and patted my cheeks. My father shook my hand and kissed Aunt Miriam on the cheek. Though Levenson men are genetically programmed to be stoic, I could tell he was proud. A son just knows these things.

When the towers came down and half of my engine company was lost, and I found myself caked in soot but alive, the first person I called after Jeannie and the kids was my Aunt Miriam.

"Rise above it," she told me. "We're all going to have to rise above it. Let's not give up the high ground to these people."

The next year, in 2002 when I got the bright idea to run the New York Marathon, she rode the ferry with me out to the starting line on Staten Island and then rode it back. Then I saw her in every borough with a sign that said, *Go Patrick, I'm So Proud of You!* And below it, *Kick Some Asphalt!*

Her old arm jangled a cow bell, and she hooted as best as she could as I passed. I still have no idea how a woman almost ninety years old could navigate the subway and the crowds like she did that day, but she was there at the finish line with her sign as I tottered across with the American flag that I had carried the whole way.

We Levensons typically are a reserved bunch; we speak only when spoken to and offer a smile only in receipt of a smile. We're cordial, but reserved and very businesslike.

But my Aunt Miriam was different. She was warm, genuinely warm, and by far the aunt whose appearance at a family gathering would ensure perfect attendance by her nieces and nephews, even the ones who were in the grip of teenage angst and surliness. In our family, the explanation for her warmth was simple: she had gotten it during the time she had spent in the South like one would unwittingly contract malaria. I don't know about that, but I do know she was my favorite, and I was hers. That's how I inherited these papers, these documents. And Francie, the greyhound.

I've arranged them for you so you can read her story. So you can read all of their stories.

When I was a boy, barely a teenager, Sinatra would often see the two of us in Patsy's. Invariably, he would get up from his dining companions and come over to our table.

He would look at me and say, "Hey, Miriam, good luck keeping the girls away from this one." Then he would point at my chest and tell me I had a spot of sauce on my tie. When I looked down, he would flick my nose and then tousle my hair.

Then he would say, "How does a nice Jewish kid from Queens get an Irish name like Patrick?"

I never knew until I inherited these papers from my Aunt Miriam.

Patrick Levenson
Manhasset, NY
May 14, 2007

My dear nephew Patrick,

I'm becoming forgetful, and I want to tell you these things now, before I forget everything. Before I'm gone. And before any of that happens, as it surely will, I want you to always remember how proud I am of the man you've become.

So let me begin by saying that I had no intention of ever going there, no intention at all, whatsoever. I'd rather have been plopped down in the Amazon or Patagonia or Siberia. Anywhere but the South. Anywhere but Shreveport. Miss Fenerty called it a mongrel dog of a town, but that was when she first arrived, seventy years before I did.

I was a new journalist, freshly graduated from Barnard, with hopes of working for the Times or the Tribune or the Sun. Instead, I landed an assignment in Roosevelt's Federal Writers' Program, a used 1928 Packard that I got from my brother, your grandfather, and a map to Shreveport.

Mr. Roosevelt had given those of us in the FWP the task of interviewing the elderly, of rescuing a small bit of their history before they took it to the grave with them. The FWP gave us a battleship of a recorder made by the Presto Corporation somewhere on West Fifty-fifth Street. It used blank disks made out of some kind of lacquered material that had a pungent smell, and there was a dial and an arc with numbers on it and a needle that bounced and swept back and forth as I talked. The whole thing, case and all, weighed a ton.

Shreveport wasn't Dogpatch or Podunk like I'd expected, but really a rather nice little city, a place that was insulated to a degree from the Depression, though not completely. The first few subjects I interviewed were nonproductive, too old, too hard of hearing, too incoherent, too decrepit, or combinations of those. They were unable to tell me anything. I was becoming disheartened, thinking that none of the old people on my list would be able to tell me anything worthwhile.

Then I met Bridget Fenerty.

Her house was on Crockett Street downtown, one of the last ones remaining as Oil came barging into town in the first decades of that century. It smelled of vanilla and butter and cinnamon, but not like things baked that morning or the day before, but from things baked over the previous forty, fifty, sixty years. It instantly smelled like home to anyone who was fortunate enough to walk through her door.

I've given you all the journals and correspondence. They're arranged more or less in order. From time to time, the transcriptionist at the FWP spelled words exactly as he or she heard them or added a note in brackets when Miss Fenerty laughed, which was a beautiful, lilting sound, like the angels would laugh if you believe in angels. There are also footnotes added that shed light on certain things. I don't know who added them, someone in the FWP, perhaps. It wasn't me.

In case you ever decide to publish these papers, I've omitted the names and addresses of the newspapers that declined to hire me in 1936. I've done this in order to avoid embarrassing them in light of the long and fortunate career in journalism that I've enjoyed. I *have no animosity at this age, as I have outlived them all, so I'll let those men and their newspapers off the hook. Miss Fenerty always urged me not to abandon the high ground, and I'm not going to do it now at age ninety-two.*

The only things I haven't included are love letters that I sent and received through the years. Those will go up with my ashes. As Miss Fenerty might say, I wouldn't want you to blush and me not be there to see it. And now that I think about it, Patrick, there is a rather frank account of the night I asked your Aunt Ellie to be my Maid of Honor. I've left that in, though, if you find yourself getting embarrassed, just read it with your hands over your eyes, which is exactly the kind of whimsical advice that Miss Fenerty might have had for you. I'm too old to be embarrassed about any of it. As Miss Fenerty once told me, "St. Peter already has it in his book, and I don't give a fiddler's fart about the rest of them."

After you've read the documents, make copies if you want. I hope you do. Then I want the collection to go to the Noel Library at LSU in Shreveport. The original recordings are held by the Library of Congress, so, if you want to hear Miss Fenerty's voice, and my voice when I was a young woman, you'll have to contact them. To hear her laugh would be worth the effort. It was beautiful, even at ninety-five.

When I graduated from Barnard in 1936, my life was caught up in a whirlpool, spinning helplessly in the circumstances of the times and, I'm afraid, in a large part from my approach to them. Then I got the letter from Mr. Alsberg. From that moment on, I was set in motion, like the first domino in a line, though I had no idea where Shreveport was.

I also had no idea how that letter would change my life and that it would only take six months.

Love,

Your Aunt Miriam

Part I
Summer and Fall, 1936

June 2, 1936

As a new journalist, I feel it is fitting that I begin a journal to chronicle my career, for certainly I have great things before me, as do we all. So the speech given by the President of Barnard College told us today.

Commencement exercises were held this morning. Dr. Butler gave an address entitled, "The Decline and Fall of Morals," which bordered on a bombastic rant, his bald forehead sweating in the heat while his white mustache and arching eyebrows undulated with each point he made.

Then came the College President's address, which was the usual prattled series of platitudes and friendly admonitions, this year's version essentially the same as last year's. Elgar's *Pomp and Circumstance* blared yet again as we paraded across the stage and shook hands with the President of Barnard, the same as the class of 1935 and 1934 and so on.

Nevertheless, it was a proud moment for me and, I'm sure, for my parents as well. I thought I might be able to see them in the crowd, but all I saw was a sea of faces and shoulders in the auditorium. Four years of study boiled down to a five second walk across the stage with two handshakes: one with the Dean of the School of Journalism and one with the President of the College.

My Uncle Sol and my Aunt Gertie held a reception for me in their living room, as we no longer have the space in our much smaller apartment for a gathering of any size. Our former apartment would have been ample, but times have changed and, hence, Uncle Sol and Aunt Gertie's apartment on 32nd Street.

I made the rounds receiving the well wishes from my relatives. Polite handshakes from uncles, diminutive kisses from aunts, silent adoration from younger cousins.

"What's this?" my Uncle Sol asked me.

"My tassel. Summa cum laude," I said.

"That's an *honor*," my Aunt Gertie explained to him. "What about this?" she asked.

"A stole," I said, lifting the light blue satin with my fingers.

"You mean you stole it?" Uncle Sol joked.

"It's for being the School of Journalism's top graduate," I said.

"Ohhhh...did you hear that, Sol? Our niece is the top graduate."

"You must be a pretty smart cookie," he said.

I opened my mouth to reply, and Aunt Gertie spoke instead.

"Miriam, may I have a word with you for a moment?" She took me by the arm and led me aside.

"Tell me, Miriam. Are you still seeing the Glickstein boy?"

It wasn't what I wanted to talk about. I wanted to talk about the newspaper business and current events, Roosevelt's reelection chances in the fall, Hitler's violation of the Treaty of Versailles, anything that was big and important. But I answered her question instead.

"Yes," I said. "He's off on business. Albany, I think."

"Too bad he had to miss your big day."

Too bad all right. But anyway, it was my day and not his.

June 7, 1936

After the four-year grind of college, ending with the laurels of high achievement being placed upon my head, I think I'm entitled to a short rest of a month or so.

Try telling that to mother. Where does a person go for a little peace and quiet around here? Mother's sewing machine goes nonstop. "Can't she do that another time?" I ask her.

"Customers need their alterations done on time," she says.

I'm going to the library. It's hot as blazes in this small apartment, anyway.

June 10, 1936

After these last few days of Mother's kvetching, I'm giving in and getting started well before the end of my planned month-long respite. I've had to type my own resume, and it took me long enough. Mother has always typed my papers for me, but, with the alterations she's taken in, she claims she doesn't have time for it. I was ten minutes late for the Upper East Side Philosophy Club.

We discussed Plato. Views of some of the discussants were a bit inane (in particular, one from W. T.). Always cutting in with a quote from Immanuel Kant. Boorish.

June 13, 1936

Republican Convention in Cleveland selects Landon as pres and Knox as vice pres candidates. For some reason, two Midwesterners. I don't think they have much of a chance.

June 15, 1936

After a few days with no response, I went right down to the office of ▮▮ ▮▮ and announced who I was. The secretary told me I'd have to make an appointment.

"Tell the Editor-in-Chief that I'm here," I said. "My name was, after all, published in his very newspaper as an honored graduate." (An inability to think past certain boundaries, that's how some people wind up as secretaries.) She excused herself and then returned.

"He says you'll have to make an appointment," she said.

June 17, 1936

Finally granted an interview at ███████. The assistant editor, a Mr. █████, kept looking down at my resume and up at me as if trying to decide if I were really that person. He kept pursing his lips and tapping his pencil, asking a few perfunctory questions, stopping me in the middle of my answers, which, while they may have been a little long, were well thought out.

The whole interview didn't last nearly as long as I had imagined. Perhaps I should have held on a while before stating what I thought my starting salary should be. Live and learn.

June 19, 1936

The German boxer Max Schmeling knocked out Joe Louis today at Yankee Stadium. The whole city is glum, including Irving. I'm glad he didn't insist that I go with him.

Mother spent the afternoon pinning the wedding dress of a young bride who's getting married this weekend. There was much talk of weddings, including when mine might be. I told all three of them, the bride, her mother, and my mother, that I haven't been asked and anyway it was none of their business. Mother seemed hurt and stayed sullen the rest of the afternoon, pins sticking out of her pressed lips as she knelt and fixed the wedding dress' lacy hem in place.

June 20, 1936

Construction workers catcalling at me again like a troop of monkeys on 47th. I'll go by 48th next time.

The *Times* is full of weddings, weddings, weddings. Happy, smiling brides with wreaths and bouquets, posed looking back over their shoulders at me, their old and new last names hyphenated side by side like the titles of a double feature. Lists of parents, attendants, honeymoons, professions, and where they will live.

Irving hasn't said a thing about us which suits me fine.

June 22, 1936

Received this in the mail today.

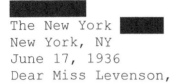

```
The New York ████
New York, NY
June 17, 1936
Dear Miss Levenson,

    Thank you for the opportunity to review your
application and meet with you.  You appear to be a
very strong candidate indeed.
    However, while your educational qualifications
are impressive, in this time of economic peril, I'm
afraid we must first consider men with families
rather than single women for our position.
    Perhaps you should try one of the periodicals
for women such as Ladies Home Journal or Good
Housekeeping.
    We wish you great success in your career.

    Sincerely,

    Thos. ██████
    Assistant Editor
    The New York ████
```

Well, perhaps Mr. ██████ should go stick his tongue in a light socket. Neanderthal.

June 25, 1936

No word from any newspaper yet. Weather: hot. I told Mother I would be looking for a job today, but instead I spent most of the day in the NY Public Library. When I got home, Mother wanted to know if I'd gotten a job yet.

No, Mother.

June 28, 1936

The Democrats chose Roosevelt again, which is no surprise. The only big news from the convention was South Carolina senator "Cotton Ed" Smith who walked out when a Negro clergyman gave the invocation. Selected as the Vice Presidential candidate was John Nance "Cactus Jack" Garner of Texas. What picturesque southern names. Oh, to be in Philly covering it all.

Dinner at Uncle Sol and Aunt Gertie's. I think they might pity us.

June 30, 1936

Though I felt like staying in out of the heat, Irving twisted my arm, and we went to see the Yankees game. We filed off the subway with the rest of humanity and then filed into the stadium with them, Irving in his straw boater and wingtip shoes, a beer in one hand and a hotdog in the other (kosher, of course). We sat down along the third base line. The sun was accosting. I kept one hand over my eyes and a program in the other, fanning myself with it.

"There he is! There he is!" he said as the teams warmed up.

"Who?" I asked.

"That new kid, DiMaggio." His finger pointed to one of the many players playing catch on the outfield grass. They all looked the same to me.

"That one?" I asked.

"Nah, that's Gehrig. Number five, next to him."

We sat in our seats in the summer sunshine and watched them stretch and warm up, young men in pinstriped uniforms white against the green grass, the murmur of the crowd barely concealing the random popping of baseballs into gloves and the crack of wood on leather as they warmed up. With the first pitch imminent, everyone rose. I stayed seated until Irving smiled and pulled me up.

He was like a child today, his hand going from the bag of popcorn to his mouth and back, and then standing up and spilling it whenever something 'momentous' happened. I've got a terrific sunburn on my arms and face.

July 1, 1936

I've expanded my search to some of the other cities in the northeast. After a few weeks of waiting (all the while enduring mother's glances and sighs at me), I received this little jewel:

The Boston
Boston, Massachusetts
June 22, 1936

Dear Madam,

The gentlemen of the New Employment Committee here at the ███ have reviewed your application carefully. We regret to inform you that there is no position available for a woman of your abilities at this time. While there are several clerical positions open, you have indicated to us, rather vehemently, that you are not interested in these.

Perhaps you will resubmit your application in the future. In the meantime, we will keep it on file in case an opening becomes available.

Until then, please accept our best wishes.

Sincerely,

███████████

Chairman,
Employment Committee
The Boston ████

July 3, 1936

Resumes sent: five (Philly, Pittsburgh, Baltimore, Providence, D.C.)
Responses: zero.

The radio says that a man shot himself at the League of Nations in Geneva today in protest of Germany's treatment of Jews. He was a Slovak and a Jew. And a journalist.

Sabbath and Fourth of July tomorrow. Irving making suggestive jokes about 'fireworks' tomorrow.

July 5, 1936

Fireworks over the Hudson last night with Irving, he with the wandering hands. A couple of smart slaps did the trick to keep them to their owner.

July 8, 1936

No word from any potential employer. I pass the time with reading and the crossword puzzles. Finished *My Antonia,* started *Beyond Good and Evil,* by Nietzsche.

A very hot week of weather.

July 9, 1936

One hundred and six degrees today. Irving and I went to the beach with the rest of New York City. A girl of no more than five almost drowned.

July 11, 1936

Triborough Bridge opened today. The WPA spent sixty million dollars to build it. Sixty million dollars for a bridge.

President Roosevelt was there for the dedication, giving the usual speech about progress and fortitude to the enormous crowd of men in straw boaters and women under umbrellas protecting themselves from the sun.

When the ribbon was cut, Irving was as giddy as a boy and insisted that we drive over it with the horde of other people. Automobiles were bumper to bumper on the pavement, and crowds were shoulder to shoulder on the sidewalks at the edges, the men and women holding their jackets on their arms and peering over the sides of the bridge.

I saw one of my classmates from Barnard there, Lillian Vilcher, a mousy girl from Schenectady with a crooked smile. I asked her what she'd been up to. She said she was there covering the opening for the *Herald Tribune.* Then she gushed that she'd just gotten to interview President Roosevelt. *The President!* She said as if he were a god.

Irving wanted to take me out to dinner, but I declined. I claimed a headache, but really I just wanted to go home. I finished Schopenhauer's *The World as Will and Representation.*

July 13, 1936

Passing down 47th Street in the heat, the chorus of jackhammers and shouts stopped as construction workers began hooting at me again, calling me a 'swell dame' with 'nice gams.' I shouldn't have, but I got into a shouting match with them. That seemed to please them even more. They apologized to my back when I walked down the street in tears.

July 15, 1936

So hot that I wish it would rain. Lots of marriage announcements in the papers. Father Coughlin on the radio attacking Jews, Communists, and FDR. Monthly on top of it.

July 17, 1936

The Upper East Side Philosophy Club meeting last night adjourned itself to a succession of bars in Midtown, the last of which was Billie's on First Avenue. I got in at 4 a.m., I'll have to admit, roaring drunk. Father was just getting up to go to work, I'm not sure where.

As I teetered in the hallway, all he said as he slipped on his shoes was, "Good morning, Miriam."

Head splitting. Writing making me nauseated.

July 18, 1936

The radio says that Spain is in a state of civil war. A general named Franco is pursuing the socialists and communists. All Irving is interested in is going to see the Yankees play the St. Louis Browns. I relented and went with him because I'll be in Chicago the next few days for an interview with The Chicago ███████.

Baseball: thirty minutes of action crammed into three hours. Irving insists on staying for the last pitch, and then there's the rush for the subway. A whole half day shot.

But I stayed because I had reluctantly accepted the train fare to Chicago from Irving, and I felt I owed it to him. I didn't want to ask Mother and Father. I don't think they have it to give, anyway.

July 20, 1936

There was talk at the UES Philosophy Club of going to Harlem to hear Father Divine speak, the Negro minister who claims to be God. A discussion ensued on the nature/existence of God. I stay undecided. Does that make me an agnostic rather than Jewish?

July 21, 1936

On the train to Chicago. Yellow cornfields all along the tracks. Plenty of blue and red "*Landon and Knox, Deeds…not Deficits*" campaign posters in the red brick small towns. The men on the main streets have jackets off and shirt sleeves rolled up. Few people venture out into the sun.

They say the heat wave is having a horrible effect, the worst on record. The bigger cities, Chicago among them, are reporting deaths from the heat.

There was a death in our building last week; I wonder if that was the reason.

July 23, 1936

Interview today with Mr. ████ at the Chicago ██████. The heat is setting records here, too, and the fan on his desk only circulated the hot air. I wore a white blouse that stuck to me, which I only noticed when I took off my jacket in the heat. I'm afraid that my makeup ran. Regardless, I felt like I was under a rubber stamp and shuffled along. I succeeded in getting an earlier train back to New York.

July 25, 1936

Back in New York and glad. The heat is here, too, but not quite as bad. Irving's gone to see the Yankees play St. Louis. Too hot for me, thank you.

The economy wheezes, and Europe is on pins and needles with Nazi aggression. Here, everyone is caught up with the Yankees and the Giants. The Roman poet Juvenal said it best two thousand years ago:

"The people no longer worry about civic duty and hope only for two things: bread and circuses."

July 26, 1936

Article in the *Times* says that most of the 1936 graduates are in jobs now. How can that be, when a candidate like me remains unemployed?

Went to Uncle Sol and Aunt Gertie's for dinner with Mother, Father, Leonard.

July 27, 1936

Papers simmering with worries of war in Europe. New York simmering in heat. This fan is little help. Any movement provokes drenching sweat.

Finishing *The Intelligent Woman's Guide to Socialism and Capitalism* by George Bernard Shaw.

July 28, 1936

I'm not your maid, Mother.

July 29, 1936

Went alone to see *Showboat*, with Irene Dunne and Allan Jones in the lead roles. The air conditioning was worth the price of the ticket. Mother is reading a new book called *Gone with the Wind*, some flowery southern romance by an author named Mitchell. The reviews are good, and some are calling for a Pulitzer. Ha.

Aug. 1, 1936

I've sent resumes to all the major papers in the east, Chicago being the westernmost city I'm prepared to live in. Even though Lillian Vilcher is working for the *Herald Tribune* and I see her name in the bylines at least three times a week, I think perhaps my being a woman is interfering with my chances. A professor at Barnard once pulled me aside and in so many words told me it might be that way.

So I tried using my initials, which almost spell out "Mr.," a thinly veiled ruse, I'm aware, but I'm getting desperate. At any rate, this Mr. ███ kept his eyes on my chest the entire interview:

███████

The Chicago ██████
Chicago, Illinois
July 24, 1936

Dear M. R. Levenson,

We thank you for your interest in the position
of reporter for our newspaper. However, we feel
that you may not be a good fit in our newsroom.
Following our meeting with you in person, we
have come to the conclusion that another candidate
may be more qualified for the position.
Thank you for your enquiry as well as for
taking the time to come all the way to Chicago in
the heat for an interview. We are privileged to
have met you. The staff all found you quite lovely
indeed.
All the newsmen here at the ███████ wish you
the best in your future endeavors.

Sincerely,

```
Wm. T. ███
Associate Editor,
The Chicago ███████
```

August 4, 1936

Mother keeps hounding me to get up and look for work. I tell her, I *am* looking for work, but no one is hiring. I've sent resumes to every major paper in the eastern United States. She says get any job, and then she whispers, "Your father and I could use some help with the bills."

Mother wants me to get a job as a waitress or a laundry girl or, God forbid, a *secretary* somewhere? Is she even aware of the prestige that a degree from Barnard carries?

August 11, 1936

Jesse Owens has now won four gold medals in Berlin. Irving is a madman in how he keeps up with it. No event is too obscure for him to follow, boxing, wrestling, rowing, badminton.

"Yessiree! Another gold for the good ole US of A!" he says as he waggles his index finger in the air and does a little turnabout dance.

August 15, 1936

Times reports a Mr. Bethea was publicly hung in Kentucky for rape. The sheriff in that county who supervised the execution is a woman. There were some 'irregularities,' and now there's an outcry calling for the abolition of the practice. Do they mean public hangings or having women as sheriffs?

When I looked closer at the byline, I saw the name of the journalist, Gracie Greenberg. I graduated four places ahead of her. I know, because I demanded that the registrar at Barnard show me our class rankings.

Mother wants me to run down to Katz' Deli for something. I yelled to her through the door that I have a headache. *A headache again?* she asks.

Yes, Mother.

August 17, 1936

A man stopped me at the corner of 52nd and Fifth Avenue and said that, with those legs and that face, you could make a fortune in tips as a waitress. He then offered me a job at the El Morocco Club on 54th.

A waitress? Please.

I declined, of course.

August 18, 1936

Father's coughing is driving me crazy. All night long. Aheh, aheh, aheh.

August 20, 1937

Topic at the UES Philosophy Club: Is pride a sin or a virtue?
A big argument ensued with my usual antagonists, who eventually stormed out. Some people just can't take criticism.

August 26, 1936

Another fight with Mother. She's been sulking all week, and finally she asks me, "Why do you sit around all day in your pajamas reading the paper? And not just one paper, all the east coast papers?"
"It is imperative that I keep up with world events, Mother," I tell her. "Do you know what that word means, *imperative?*"
"Don't get smart with me, young lady," she says, as if I were still a teenager.

Sept. 1, 1936

Irving and I had a big argument, over politics. He calls himself a Landon man and calls me Roosevelt's girl. He says Roosevelt just wants to give the country away to the 'feckless bums' as he puts it.
"Is that what you think my father is, a feckless bum?" I ask him. That put him on his heels.
"Now, now, I didn't say that," he says.
He took me for ice cream, an invitation that I grudgingly accepted. I was as cold as it was. He kept trying to make conversation. I said nothing. Serves him right.

Sept. 6, 1936

Irving took me to the Met, which was sweet because art is definitely not among his interests. He was a good sport, however, at my side through the galleries. Always gravitating to the nudes, though.

Sept. 9, 1936

Yankees clinch pennant. Irving is ecstatic as is most of New York. First time in four years, he says. Weather a little better. Mailbox empty of any viable job offers.

Sept. 12, 1936

Synagogue today with Mother and Leonard. She insisted. Father working on the Sabbath again, though I'm sure he'd rather not. After temple, I overheard Mother talking with Aunt Gertie on the temple steps. Mother's back was to me, but I heard her tell Aunt Gertie that she's given up hope on me getting a job.

Aunt Gertie said, "What about the Glickstein boy? He's no looker, but he's a nice boy and well off."

"That's our only hope," Mother said.

As if I were a piece of property, a goat or a milk cow.

They realized I was near and cut their conversation short.

Sept 17, 1936

A breezy day. The radio says that a hurricane is headed up the east coast, and there's talk of cancelling schools, etc. until after it passes. Not as many school children in our new neighborhood. I'm used to seeing droves of them this time of year, but not here in this part of the city.

Began Huxley's *Brave New World*.

Sept. 18, 1936

High winds and rain from storm offshore. I stay inside with coffee and papers. Grace Greenberg reports in the *Times* that the German Airship *Hindenburg* is sailing for America today. Maybe I'd be writing for the *Times* if I had a name with alliteration. Maybe *Louise Levenson* or *Lefty Levenson* or something like that.

Rosh Hashanah began yesterday.

Sept. 19, 1936

Missed temple today and went with Irving to see the Yankees play the Washington Senators. We've agreed not to talk politics. Mother unhappy about my missing until she found out I was going somewhere with Irving, who to her is faultless (and has money).

The Yankees won dramatically in the bottom of the ninth, which left Irving exhilarated, of course. I'd rather be among real Washington senators, the ones in suits and ties, discussing important things and not just playing a child's game.

Double header tomorrow due to rain out on Friday. Oh boy. At least the weather is more pleasant.

Sept. 20, 1936

Baseball double header: One hour of action crammed into six hours. Yankees lose first, win second. Everyone on the subway was talking about who the World Series opponent will be. Could be the Giants.

Sept. 22, 1936

Mother says she knows of a job opening at the Bergdorf-Goodman perfume counter.

I asked her, "Aren't you a little old for that kind of work?"

"I meant for you," she said.

I laughed. She didn't. She was serious, I guess.

Later, Uncle Sol dropped off some things from Katz' Deli. Latkes, knish, a salami. He means well, but it makes Mother and Father uncomfortable.

Sept 24, 1936

This was in the *Herald Tribune* today. Granted, it was buried within the pages, but still:

Young Reporter Garners Award

(Sept. 24)-The editorial staff at the Herald Tribune is proud to announce that one of our own, Lillian Vilcher, has been named the Horace Greeley Outstanding Young Journalist. The award was recently presented at the monthly luncheon of the Manhattan Journalism Society. Miss Vilcher is a 1936 graduate of Barnard College and is looking forward to her deployment to Washington in the very near future to cover the Capitol beat.

I could just scream.

Sept. 26, 1936

Yom Kippur today. Mother and Father spent the day in prayer and fasting at Emanu-El. Irving and I listened to the Yankees game on the radio. Or actually, he did. I read and pretended to listen.

Sept. 28, 1936

This city is buzzing with talk about the World Series, a 'subway series' with the Giants against the Yankees. Pictures of players are everywhere, though I only recognize two, Gehrig and DiMaggio. I guess I'll go, as Irving is insistent, and there are no prospects for employment.

Sept. 30, 1936

Father's former boss, Mr. Gaudette, died. Mother said good riddance for the way he ruined the firm and your father's good name with his chicanery.
"Now, sweetheart," Father said, "don't speak ill of the dead," Then he went to the funeral parlor to pay his respects, which was very noble after what Gaudette did to him. I asked Mother how Mr. Gaudette died.
"Oh, he drank heavily for years," she said.
Giants beat Yankees, 6 to 1 in first game of World Series. Irving is glum. Leonard is, too, but probably over a girl and not the Yankees.

Oct. 2, 1936

Yankees beat Giants, 18 to 4. Irving is happy again. Crowd was up and down, up and down, with every hit, every diving catch. Tiring.
As we were leaving the Polo Grounds, he kissed me. He had eaten a hot dog with onions, and I had to hold my breath because of his.

Oct. 3, 1936

Yankees win 2 to 1 thanks to a run in the bottom of the eighth, from what I hear. I missed it because today was the Sabbath, and Mother wouldn't allow me to miss, or at least that's what I told Irving.
Father is working double shifts somewhere. Haven't seen him in a week, though I hear him come in at night and leave in the morning. Mother waits up for him and then sees him off in the morning. When do they sleep?

Oct. 4, 1936

Yankees win 5 to 2. I have to say, Lou Gehrig's two home runs were exciting. The surge of the crowd to its feet was like a wave on the ocean. Speaking of waves, Irving accidently spilled a beer on the man in front of him.

Oct. 5, 1936

The New York Giants beat the New York Yankees in the top of the tenth. Half of New York is ecstatic; the other half is dejected. I am neither.

The newsstand on Second Avenue had a copy of the *San Francisco News* with an article about migrant workers in California entitled "The Harvest Gypsies." The article, by a man named Steinbeck, paints a deplorable picture. The workers live in filthy camps and work for next to nothing. How can things like that exist in this country?

Oct. 6, 1936

Game six and the Yankees win the series 13 to 5 icing the game with a seven run barrage in the top of the ninth. New York Yankees, World Series champs.

Yawn.

Maybe I should have been a sportswriter. It would have been easier work as there is very little thinking involved by the writer or the reader.

Irving and I went to Delmonico's to celebrate. Afterwards, we ended up at his apartment where I had to fend him off. It was like wrestling an octopus, but I did it. He said I had no idea how it hurts a man to get worked up and then put on hold.

"Well, you should have thought of that before you got all hot and bothered," I told him. I found my own way home.

Oct. 10, 1936

Friends in the UES Philosophy Club tell me that the Roosevelt Administration is hiring journalists for a project that involves interviewing the elderly and compiling their histories. They say there are positions available in other parts of the country, some of them far away, and that I should apply.

Not what I was hoping for, but it beats clerical work, and my family is driving me crazy. It's either the WPA or Bellevue.

I'm hoping for somewhere in New England or the Adirondacks. Maine, perhaps.

I received flowers from Irving. Mother seems happier about it than I am.

Oct. 17, 1936

Housebound with monthly. Maybe that's why God called for Abraham to institute circumcision, to even out the misery. Still not fair.

Oct. 22, 1936

Presidential race coming to a close. Roosevelt favored. Governor Lehman also likely to be re-elected. No senate elections for us this year. Caroline O'Day's chances are good.

Herald Tribune reports that Anne Sullivan Macy, Helen Keller's teacher, has died. She was the child of Irish immigrants and was practically blind herself. I never knew.

Oct. 28, 1936

Father is home sick, and Mother is very worried. Leonard offered to drop out of high school to work if Father can't. Mother and Father are adamantly against it.

I went for a walk in the park with Irving. It was really quite pleasant, the trees putting on yellow and orange. I was feeling very relaxed, so I told him my thoughts on Nietzsche. I think he only pretended to listen. His favorite reply was, "That's swell."

Then I told him that I was thinking of taking a job that would involve me moving away for a while. He seemed distressed and offered me a clerical position at the packing plant.

Not in a million years, Irving, I thought, though I didn't tell him.

Oct. 31, 1936

It seems there are more drunks passed out in the stairwells and on steam grates every day. I miss the old apartment and neighborhood. One rarely saw that kind of thing there, but of course times were better for everyone then. Today was the Sabbath, and I went to the synagogue with Mother and Leonard this morning. Father was too ill.

Nov. 2, 1936

The Times reports that an American, Eugene O'Neill, is favored for the Nobel Prize for literature. I personally find his work pedantic.

No word from a newspaper of any size.

(Later)
Just went for a glass of water. It's three a.m. and Mother is alone at the kitchen table. When she saw me, she dried her eyes and claimed that her allergies are bothering her.

Nov. 4, 1936
Went with Father yesterday to cast my vote for Roosevelt and Cactus Jack Garner. Irving went separately to vote, if he voted at all. Mother still hasn't registered to vote, even after almost twenty years since the ratification of the dear old 19th. The *Times* proclaims the Democrats winners in a landslide, biggest in history if you go by the Electoral College. Irving probably thinks the Electoral College is in the Ivy League.

Nov. 7, 1936

Finally, the consolation prize:

```
Federal Writers' Project
Works Progress Administration
Washington, D. C.
Nov. 1, 1936


Dear Miss Levenson,


     We are pleased to offer you a position with the
Louisiana office of the Federal Writers' Project.
We consider ourselves fortunate to have a person of
your caliber in our fold.
     You will be assigned to the city of Shreveport,
Louisiana, about two hundred miles east of Dallas,
Texas.  All the eastern positions you requested,
including New York and New England, have been
filled.
     Enclosed is a list of elderly citizens in the
area for you to contact and interview if they are
able to be interviewed.  A Presto audio recorder
```

will be sent separately. You are to become
familiar with its use and employ it in recording
the stories of any and all of the people on the
list and others as you may encounter.

Again, we are very delighted to have you and
look forward to hearing from you. We wish you the
best of luck in the field.

Sincerely,
Henry Alsberg
Director, Federal Writers' Project

Okay, Mr. Alsberg. In the absence of any other offer, I accept.

Mother, your wish is granted. I have a job now, in a place called
Shreveport, Louisiana, a thousand miles away. Are you happy?

I'll stop eating your groceries and breathing your air.

Nov. 8, 1936

Leonard and I had a big fight today, the biggest since we were little kids.
It's only logical that I should have the use of the Packard since I'll be in the
field in Louisiana. He says he needs it, and it's rightfully his because he's the
one who's kept it in running condition. I think all he wants it for is to take girls
to Coney Island and for drives out on Long Island for slap-and-tickle.

Father (who's finally well) stepped in and mediated, this after an hour of
Mother's shrieking and theatrics. I'm ready to get out of here and make my
own way, even if it is to Podunk.

Nov. 11, 1936

My departure is tomorrow, and I now have an idea what Columbus must
have felt like leaving Seville for God-knows-what. Irving hints that he has a
big surprise for me tonight. He and Father were talking when I came in from
the library, a talk that they seemed to quickly wrap up.

I was hoping to see my friends from the UES Philosophy Club before I
left, but none of them showed up last week. Very well.

Goodbye, Manhattan, Cradle of Civilization. Hello, steamy, sultry South.

Nov. 12, 1936

Ring's Rest Tourist Court
Muirkirk, MD

The family who run this place, which is really just an outbreak of tiny cabins by the side of U.S. Highway One, is a genial couple and their children. Their name is Ringe, but the name of the place is Ring's Rest. I have no idea why they dropped the E. There's an outhouse (!), and, to shower, one must go inside their home. I'll pass on the shower, but I'm afraid I can't pass on the outhouse.

Other than the trip to Chicago, I've never been across the Hudson until today. In fact, I've only left Manhattan a few dozen times, and most of those were to go to summer camp in New Hampshire. That was back in the days when father was flush with money, before the bottom dropped out.

It's been open for five years, but today was also my first time over the George Washington Bridge and my first time to actually set foot in New Jersey. Down below me, ships dotted the swath of blue water plowing V's behind them that expanded and vanished. I crossed the bridge and then circled under it to look back at Manhattan. When I was a little girl, I asked Father how it didn't sink with all the buildings on it.

"It's not a boat, Miriam," he said, and he almost smiled. "There's nothing but rock under it."

I still think of it as a boat, and today I have disembarked. Irving was there to see me off, clowning with a fake southern accent. When my parents went to check the trunk of the Packard one more time, he palmed my backside. He was still on fire from the night before.

Last night, I finally relented. I always thought my first time would be on my wedding night, carried across a hotel room threshold in a frilly wedding dress into a room full of flowers. But novelty was in the air, novelty and uncertainty, and Irving's champagne clouded everything. Irving and his champagne wooed me, and I succumbed.

He got down on one knee in the crowded dining room at the Waldorf where people in tuxedoes and evening gowns dined from fine china and crystal set on white table cloths. They all stopped eating, and I turned red from being the center of the spectacle. I put my fingers over my mouth, not from joy but from embarrassment. The waiters all stopped their crisscrossing of the room and stood by with grins on their faces and towels over their arms. All eyes were on me, including Irving's. He looked like a dog waiting for a treat.

The room became quiet, conversations trailing off into isolated clicking of silverware and then complete silence. Someone coughed, and then someone else said, *go on, say yes!*

Then music from the string quartet told me to say yes, and I did. He opened the box with the glittering ring, and the roses told me to say yes, and I did. After the clapping and cheering subsided, and everyone resumed their conversations, he asked in a whisper if he could get us a room upstairs, and the champagne told me to say yes, and I did. He registered us under the names 'Mr. and Mrs. Smones,' his nervous cross-pollination of Smith and Jones. Then he asked if I was ready, and the prospect of an easy, empty life told me to say yes, and I did.

It was my first time. He hinted apologetically that it wasn't his first time, though I'm almost positive it was. We both seemed to be trying to figure out what went where and how. It was all so sudden and certainly less than I expected, more in line with a bodily function than a romantic experience. I regret it now, not because I didn't wait until I was married, but because I don't think it was with someone I love.

Nov. 13, 1936

Perhaps the superstition about Friday the thirteenth has some credence. Last night just after midnight, south of Raleigh, I hit a deer. To save time and to save money on lodging, I had resolved to drive at night. Now I wish I hadn't.

She came out of the woods, a galloping brown flash, and she and the front right fender of the Packard intersected at the same place and same moment in time. She collided with a hollow, metallic thump. Though I was startled, I managed to slow down until I stopped at the side of the road.

The deer floundered atop the hood of the car, flopping like a fish on a boat deck, trying to get up. I sat in the car and watched her, and finally she fell from the hood, leaving a trail of red on the beige metal of the Packard.

She struggled to get to her feet and turned toward the woods from where she had come. Her legs buckled, and she wobbled a few steps. She fell forward on her front legs as if she were bowing in prayer to something in the woods, and then she collapsed on the side of the road in the glare of my headlights.

I waited behind the wheel for a while, a few moments or maybe longer, afraid of this creature that had meant me no harm. I had almost summoned the courage to get out when a buck came prancing out of the woods, and I realized that I had interrupted a courtship ritual, a romantic chase. The buck trotted over to the fallen doe, oblivious to the idling Packard, and sniffed his fallen quarry. He craned his head up and looked calmly into the headlights and into me. His antlers cast a shadow on the trees like vines in the headlight glow. He blinked and his ears changed direction, turning up and then to the side independently of each other. Then he trotted to the opposite side of the road.

He stopped again, turned to me, and then turned back. Then, suddenly, gracefully, he bounded over the fence at the edge of the woods and disappeared in a brown blur.

The Packard had been idling in a low wet chuckle the entire time, and I turned it off and waited for the doe to rise and follow. She didn't.

I got out and stood with my breath steaming out of me. The pines rose into the starlight; their shadows loomed over me in judgment. I looked up at them and then down at the victim. Her light brown fur and white underbelly were as still as if they were part of the earth. I walked up to her body, her carcass, I suppose it would be called now. Her upper legs were massive compared to the small tapered feet. Likewise, her head was small with a tiny mouth and tiny mounded white teeth in her severe overbite. My breath was smoky in the cold glare of the headlights; she had no breath, just a stare into the woods from her glassy black eyes. I was looking at her when there was a rattling sputter from down the road at my back, and a pair of headlights joined mine.

A door slammed, and a man's voice said, "Maim, yew all rot?"

"Excuse me?" I said. His accent was distinctively Carolina. He repeated himself, and I understood.

"Ma'am, you all right?"

"I'm, I'm fine," I said, though I wasn't completely sure.

The man turned to look at the doe. He knelt and put a hand to her chest, appraising her bulk with his palm. Turning his face up to mine he asked me, "Just happen?" He wore a shabby gray tweed cap. His blue eyes were lighter than his skin.

"Yes. Yes it did," I said. My heart was still racing. I felt like I was going to be sick. Then he asked me a question that I would never have anticipated having grown up in the city.

"You want her?"

I'm sure I stuttered before I finally managed to say no. I wasn't thinking what I would want her for. When I didn't say anything else, he looked back up to me.

"You mind if we take her?"

"No," I said, "You go right ahead."

He made a motion to his car, an ancient Model A that had been quietly trilling like an insect this whole time. The passenger side door opened, and out stepped a small woman with an old, thin white print dress of the same fabric that flour sacks are made. Over it she wore a tattered blue-gray sweater. She had a wool felt cloche pulled down low over her ears, and stringy blonde hair wandered out from under it. She and the man had several teeth missing. They were two dingy people who seemed to be clinging to the wreckage of their dignity in a tossing sea of misfortune, a whirlpool of tragic circumstances.

"Says we can have it," he told her.

"Thank you, kind angel," the woman said. Her glance to me was quick; she appeared reluctant to take her eyes off their bonanza. "The children could use some meat," she said.

The man pulled their Model A up ahead of the deer and shut off the engine. They lifted the animal together until the man could get it on his shoulder. He carried it forward to their car, the neck of the carcass bending and bouncing with each step as if shaking its head in an empathic 'no.' Together the man and woman hoisted it up onto the top. The woman leaned forward to look under the seat and produced a coil of rope. She held the end of it and threw the rest to the man. They stood on opposite sides of the car in the open doors and passed the rope back and forth. The steamy plume of their breathing drifted off from the headlight glow and into the dark night air. Neither of them said a word.

When they had secured the deer, the woman got back in their car, and I got back in mine. I noticed that I only had one headlight now; the other had been smashed in the collision and now hung from its mounting like an eye dangling from its socket. I started the Packard and waited for them to pull out ahead of me. The man opened his door and looked back to me. Then he ran toward me. I rolled down the window.

"God bless you, ma'am," he said, and a mist of breath trailed out into the night.

He ran back to his Model A, vaulted in, and shut the door. The old car moaned like it was trying to clear its throat without success. There was a silence, then the car rattling and failing, and then silence again. Atop their auto, the deer's head was lolled around with the spiral of its neck.

The man and the woman both exited from their sides of the car in unison, as if they had performed this maneuver more than once, more than a dozen times. The woman ran and jumped in the driver seat, and the man put his weight behind the back of the car. He lurched into the black metal as the car rocked forward and sputtered to life with a phlegmatic popping. The woman, his wife I assume, though it's possible it was his sister, idled the car and waited for the man to come forward and get in the passenger side. He took a few steps forward, looked back, and ran toward me again.

"God bless you, ma'am," he said again. His eyes were glassy, either from the cold night air or from gratitude, or from both. He scurried to the passenger door and climbed in, and they disappeared out of the sphere of light. On top of the car, the doe's tongue protruded from her mouth, and her body jostled with the vibration of the Model A.

I couldn't bear to watch it, to have to follow it and look at what I'd done, even though it was an accident, so I gave the three of them, the couple and their prize, a few minutes' head start. I pulled onto the empty road. About a mile down the road, my remaining headlight began to flicker, and then suddenly I was plunged into darkness. The road was just a pale gray path that led up to a break in the silhouette of the horizon. I pulled over and slept.

It was a long night of fitful, unsatisfying sleep. Not a single car passed in the darkness. Several times I woke and imagined that the buck had returned and was just a step from peering in my window at me. I desperately needed to relieve myself, but I held it until the gray light of dawn seeped into the world without so much as a sunrise. A lazy, absent, beamless sun.

Nov. 14, 1936

I'm parked by the side of the road and writing this by the last light of day. I'm somewhere in Georgia, between the state line with South Carolina and Atlanta. There are other cars parked around me in a clearing by the side of the highway. As the light fails, they're becoming mere shapes.

They are pilgrims like me, looking for opportunity somewhere. They are threadbare parents and children, single men alone and in groups. White and Negro. Hungry and tired.

The rain is coming down cold and hard now, and my breath is steaming up the windows. Earlier, after the rain had begun earnestly pounding the earth, I saw a white woman exit the side of their dilapidated Ford and accompany a child, a boy of six or eight or so, I'm guessing, to the edge of the clearing. The white rain beat on them, and she held her skirt over his head while he pulled down his overalls and squatted to relieve himself under a tree. When he was done, he pulled his overalls up, and they ran hand in hand back to their auto. Her hair was plastered down close to her head. They're cold and wet now, while I am only cold. I should feel lucky, but I don't.

My windows are fogged up, and the light has failed completely. I can't see any of my fellow pilgrims. Nothing to do now but shiver and sleep.

Nov. 15, 1936

Atlanta is a city in the same class as New York, a busy place, though nowhere else is New York. I miss it, but I don't miss Irving. The truth is, I've scarcely had one thought about him, let alone a fond one. The ring is in my suitcase somewhere.

I stopped at noon to bathe in a clear running stream. I couldn't stand the smell of myself anymore. I parked by the side of the road and went into the woods a hundred yards or so where the bare, gray trunks and limbs concealed me like Eve in the garden. The air was cold, and the water was even colder, but it was exhilarating to be naked in the outdoors, to feel sunlight on bare, puckering flesh. The bottom of the stream was firm and sandy, and the cold water squeezed my legs to an almost pleasant ache.

I didn't linger, though. I washed with the ten cent bar of soap, and the current took the suds downstream, weaving around tree roots and under fallen trunks like a crowd leaving a theater after a show. I dried off with my old dress and put on a clean one. Then I washed the old one and hung it up to dry in the back of the Packard. It was all done with an economy of motion spurred on by the cold. It feels good to be clean.

Nov. 16, 1936

After a late start this morning, I stopped for something to eat today in a small town in Alabama. The café was across from the courthouse where a stone soldier with knapsack, rifle, and slouch hat stared north. Parked outside were an array of automobiles, each reflecting the station and prosperity of its owner, old, new, poor, affluent. There were some wagons, too, pulled by old mules and horses who chewed and thought (thinking deeper thoughts than their masters, I should think). The eyes of the animals were hidden by blinders, spared any sideways glance at the dismal scene.

I stepped onto the porch where a man in overalls straining against a large gut sat on a bench and worked a wad of something in his mouth. He spat an amber stream into a brass spittoon, and the squirt made a metallic ring.

I opened the door to the hubbub of the lunchtime crowd. There was a whitewashed beadboard ceiling that ran the length of a room with whitewashed beadboard walls, all of it making the room feel cold despite the intense gas-driven heat and the respiring bodies. The whole place rumbled with conversation and great shaking guffaws of southern laughter, and the smoke of cigars and cigarettes tinted the air a slow-burning white. The back wall of the place was adorned with the head of a deer, and, when I saw it, I felt an odd wave of guilt push on me.

All the faces inside were white, but on a side porch there were picnic tables. Negroes were seated there in the cold with their flannel coats pulled tight around them and their hats tight to their heads. Negro women jiggled little fuzzy-headed babies on their knees and spooned bites of food into their little mouths as the babies took them in with scooping lower lips and big eyes.

The hostess, a lady great in size with a wattle like a turkey, asked me, "Ma'am, are you waitin' on a gentleman?"

"Excuse me?" I asked.

"You by yourself?"

"Yes," I replied.

"Sorry, but we can't seat unaccompanied ladies," she said.

My face betrayed my shock.

"We can offer you a sack lunch, if you want it."

A Negro busboy in a white apron was stacking dirty dishes from a table into a basket and wiping the table down. There was a scrape of a chair leg, and a man at a table near me got up and said, "She can sit with me."

He introduced himself as Mr. Dooley. He wore a red bow tie and suspenders with a starched white shirt and gray flannel trousers. His suit coat was on the back of his chair, and his hair was sickeningly sweet with pomade. His face was square and friendly, and he reminded me of a character from one of the Sunday comic strips or perhaps a composite of several of them.

The room was like an orchestra warming up, the high pitched ding of silverware on plates, tympany of cups on tables, the bass notes of chair legs on the wooden floor, woodwinds of mostly male voices in conversation. The air smelled deeply brown with the aroma of hearty food cooking, no doubt the reason for all the cars and wagons parked along the square. The turkey woman approached to take our order.

"The plate lunches are real special here," Mr. Dooley said to me.

"The plate lunch, then," I looked up and told the waitress with a smile.

"Make that two, sugar," he told her. "And two teas."

Sugar? I thought. The waitress didn't seem offended; in fact, she seemed pleased with the man's pleasantry.

"Sure, hun," she told him.

Mr. Dooley and I fell easily into a conversation, no doubt part of his training as a lawyer. His practice as an attorney elsewhere in that county takes him to the county seat once a week. He was interested in why a woman from 'up nawth' would be traveling through Alabama in the winter. I told him what my business was.

"Interviewing old folks. Don't say? I bet they'll have some tales to tell. We just lost my old granddaddy. Confederate veteran. Spent time in Camp Chase."

"Camp Chase?"

"Union prison in Ohio. Prisoner of war. Both of his brothers died in the war."

"I'm sorry to hear that," I said.

The waitress was setting down our plates. It smelled delicious.

"Well, thank you, and I appreciate your kindness. He was old, and it was his time. As for my uncles, I never knew them, obviously. It was a long time ago. But it was just yesterday to some people. You have people in the war?" he asked as he put his napkin in his shirtfront.

"No, I don't think so," I replied.

Then I thought, at the time of the American Civil War, 'my people' were still in Russia fighting the Cossacks. I must've pondered it for a moment, for his voice startled me as he continued.

"Just about everybody in this room's got a grandparent or great-grandparent that was affected by it, one way or the other." Mr. Dooley waved his fork in the air at all the people in the room as he hunched over his plate and chewed vigorously.

The table next to us fell silent as several of the men listened to one of them tell a joke, and then there was an eruption of laughter, and one of them beat his fist on the table as he chuckled uncontrollably. I heard the joke also, but I won't recount it here. It was distasteful, and in the presence of the Negro busboy, no less, like he wasn't even there. The joke wasn't funny in the slightest. Something about a watermelon.

I couldn't hold my tongue for Mr. Dooley.

"Do you think it's right? To make sport of people that way? To seat them in the cold?"

"I'll tell you something, Miss Levenson. Some of them are the nicest, purest people you'd want to meet. Honest, hardworking people. And then there're the others. Stab each other over the last piece of chicken."

"Surely you exaggerate, Mr. Dooley," I said.

He paused with a forkful of black-eyed peas in one hand and cornbread in the other, both hovering over his plate. He eyed me with a look of frustration and regret. Or maybe it was amusement.

"That's no exaggeration, Miss Levenson. I've seen it. More than once."

He seemed to have forgotten that he was eating until he looked down and saw his food. He brought the fork to his mouth and then the cornbread.

"It's a shame," he continued after he swallowed, "but it's the way it is. Keeps me in business, though. County pays me to defend them, I mean. But the actions of some of them taint them all."

"It's not fair that all should be judged on the actions of some," I said.

"Human nature, I suppose," he said. "To lump people together, that is." His fork waggled a circle in the air as if agreeing with that fact. He took a bite of cornbread and chewed thoughtfully. When the cornbread hit bottom, he glanced at me and loaded another bite of black-eyed peas on his fork, corralling it with his cornbread.

"Now I ask you, Miss Levenson. Do you think that people are treated the way they are because of how they act?"

"Or do people act the way they do because of how they're treated?" I asked him in return, and I'm afraid a little coldly. He changed the subject.

"Your pork chop's not any good?"

"I don't eat a lot of meat," I said. "Doesn't set well. Do you want it?"

"If you don't mind," he said, and I smiled and lifted my plate to him. He stabbed the meat and put it on his plate.

I watched him saw away at it, and finally I said, "Well, Mr. Dooley, I appreciate your company, but I have to get on the road again."

I stood up, and he stood up with me, pulling his napkin out of his shirt front. He took my hand graciously and nodded. The men who had enjoyed the joke at the table next to us had since gotten up and were paying at the counter. I reached for my bill, but Mr. Dooley took it from me.

"Allow me," he said, and I didn't argue. Instead I thanked him.

"Safe trip," he said, and then he added, "Watch for road work other side of Demopolis. WPA boys are puttin' in a bridge."

"Thank you, Mr. Dooley," I said, and I put on my hat and gloves. As I got to the door, I looked back. He was concentrating on the pork chop I had given him. Black faces were clearing the table where the men had been. Black faces were in the kitchen beyond the long window that bristled with order slips attached to its edges. They could cook our food and bring it to us, and then pick up the dirty dishes afterward. They just weren't allowed to eat it with us.

Nov. 17, 1936

Roads terrible. I've made very little progress, so I've decided to rest, reading an old copy of *The Good Earth*, by Pearl Buck. Crescent moon tonight like a smile standing on its end.

Nov. 18, 1936

Somewhere in east Mississippi, west of Tuscaloosa. I'm sitting on the running board of the Packard, writing this while my free hand stays warm between my knees in the folds of my dress. The black night sky is specked with bright burning stars, small but powerful, tiny but significant. Up in the cold heavens, the moon is waxing or waning, I'm not sure which. A cup of coffee would be good now, or a cigarette perhaps, if I smoked, but I'll content myself with the quiet, just the scratch of my pen across the paper of my notebook. The sound of it, and the sound of nothing else.

It's been a day of endless company towns, gangs of men in the backs of flatbed trucks, dirty, tired men on their way to or from work. Road graders puffing smoke, men with shovels, smoking like the machines they attend. Smoldering piles of debris, tree trunks and branches and stumps burning and smoking in the wake of the new roads. Children, boys mostly, watching the workers and then following the gazes of the men as they all turn to study me while I pass. All of their stares following me as they look up, watching me as I look in the mirror. Then they recede away, swallowed by the distance like a whale.

Front porches jammed with children, some with white children, some with Negro children. Old toothless grannies, either black or white, watching over them. All their feral stares watching me as I passed.

Fields and fields and fields. Furrows emanating in dirty rays out to distant tree lines where the last brown and yellow leaves cling desperately, trying not to fall and become part of the earth again. Forests of purple-gray barked pine trees and mats of copper straw beneath them. Naked oaks with gray bark and wide, antebellum style skirts of yellow, brown and orange wet leaves. Dank, dismal air. Everything wet and cold.

Nov. 19, 1936

I have to admit to quite a bit of anticipation today, as I looked forward to seeing 'The Mighty Mississippi.' As I rounded a curve and crawled over a ridge in the highway, there it was. In truth, I doubt if it's much wider than the Hudson. What I found remarkable was the expanse of sleeping cotton fields on the other side of it, recently picked bare, I take it. Ten years ago, it was a sea when the Great Flood put it all under. *The New York Times* said it was a hundred miles across here, which is hard to imagine. I'll park here tonight and watch the winter sun melt into it.

Nov. 20, 1936

I'm sitting eating a sandwich and an apple at a spot on the highway where a couple of years ago Bonnie and Clyde were shot. Finished *The Good Earth.*

(later)

Here I am, in Shreveport, checked into the Creswell Hotel, hardly the Waldorf of the South. It's situated at the very outskirts of civilization, or perhaps beyond them. No doubt I'm very near the edge of the world, the cliff that they warned Columbus he would fall off if he went too far. I'm further west than I've ever been, further west than Columbus ever went.

I saw the city from relatively far away, and I use the term 'city' loosely, as even Brooklyn and Hoboken dwarf it. From the distance, it was a collection of gray buildings and steeples set against a gray sky. Not exactly the birthplace of civilization.

The Creswell Hotel sits at the rear of downtown. There's a telephone at the desk downstairs, but none in any of the rooms, which are plain doors in a dimly lit hall. There are three floors to the hotel and a cage of an elevator operated by a garrulous man with small, low-set ears. I can't tell if he's an idiot or if he simply reflects the average intellect of the populace.

Nov. 21, 1936

I made my first foray into the wilderness today, leaving at eight in the morning. The now one-eyed Packard's hood pointed forward into the distance. I kept checking down at the map and up to the road. The weather was warm today, warm for November. In New York, it would have been warm for June.

It wasn't so much an address as directions. I followed them, stopping twice to check the map as the Packard chortled quietly. Crows cawed in the muffled distance as I looked up and down the road, checking landmarks. Then, I would get back in and set the lever in gear. The car lurched forward as the highway bent and swooped under gray-limbed trees and a white sky.

I came over a wooded rise, and there before me was an immense, flat sea of dormant cotton fields, a mile or two or more stretching all the way to where the map said the river twists quietly. I consulted the directions again, then turned at a crossroads where a whitewashed church presided over the empty fields in the cool mist. A dilapidated fence surrounded the weedy churchyard hemmed in by fields, rows of graying brown corduroy with white lint. The road narrowed from a two lane dirt thoroughfare to a single lane path, which dipped into a stretch of mud and then ascended out of it to single lane again.

I should have known not to test the mud, but, by the time I was in it, it was too late. The Packard bogged down to the axles and then spun helplessly, stirring the water into a brown the color of hot chocolate. I tried reverse, forward, reverse, forward, shifting my weight with the car, anything to gain just a little more momentum. The Packard thrashed around like a dinosaur in a tar pit.

I opened the door, and there was muddy water just below the running board. Bubbles had developed from the Packard's efforts, and they popped silently and disappeared one by one until the mud was a flat brown sheet. I sighed and swung my legs onto the seat. I pulled off my heels, hiked up my skirt, and undid my stockings from my garter and rolled them down and off.

The muddy water may have been the color of hot chocolate, but it was certainly not the temperature. I winced when my feet disappeared into the water and again when they hit the sludgy bottom. The water was to my shins. I held the hem of my dress with my right hand and balanced against the car with my left as I made my way to the back. I looked around the field in all directions. There was no one else. Just dried brown stalks dotted with specks of stray cotton. For miles.

After a few ineffective tries with one half of my body, I realized that I couldn't push well like that, holding on to my hem. I looked around again and stuffed the hem of my dress into the waist of my underwear in the front. And then I pushed. And then I cursed.

That must have done the trick. The Packard found its footing somewhere under the water. I could feel it rock up onto a ledge or a root somewhere under the water and rest there. I was exhausted, sweating in the cool damp air, leaning into the back of the Packard. I stood up and shouted into the fog, out across the empty brown cotton fields:

"*To hell with this place!*"

My shout bounced off a tree line somewhere and then was beaten down and swallowed by the mist. A crow bawled out a single caw. And then I began to shudder and shake, my will crumbling, and I cried. Leaning onto the cold beige metal with my cheek against the back window, I cried at my misfortune, I cried for the press luncheons at the White House that I wouldn't be attending, I cried for the trips I wouldn't be taking to the big cities around the world I wouldn't be visiting, I cried for the famous people I wouldn't be interviewing. I cried for my world and for myself, both of us inverted and shaken.

"What's the matter, ma'am?" a voice asked.

It startled me, and I pushed up suddenly from the back of the Packard. There was a Negro boy there in overalls atop a mule. A straw hat was low on the boy's head. He was about fourteen or so. The mule was white with black speckles over its haunches as if it had been sprayed with mud, though it was simply its coloration. The boy balanced a gun over his thighs, and about a dozen dead squirrels hung at his belt. Their large incisors were grimacing in an overbite.

I straightened and turned, still shin deep in muddy water. I'm sure my eyes were red, and my nose was swollen and running, but I said, "Nothing, I'm fine, thank you."

I wiped my nose with the back of my hand and faced him with as much pride as I could regain.

"You need any hep?"

"No," I said, and I forced out a smile with a tilt of my head. "But could you tell me where Moses Cotter lives?"

"Ol' Pop Cotter? He live bout a mile down that road you on right there." He tilted his head back to indicate a house tiny in the distance down the road where I was headed. When he did, I could see his face. It was a handsome one, despite the fact he had a lazy eye that seemed to be looking over at his straight one.

"You don't need no hep witch yo car, ma'am?" he asked me.

"No. No, I thank you for your concern, but I've gotten it unstuck."

"Awright," he said. He touched the brim of his straw hat and shook the reins. The mule wheeled around and took off at a trot. The boy and the furry mass of squirrels at his waist bounced slightly in time with the mule's canter. I looked down.

There was mud up to my knees as if my legs had been dipped in chocolate, and the front of my dress was still tucked into the front of my underwear. I looked up after him and then back down. I knew he had seen them.

The good news was that I had indeed gotten the Packard unstuck. I sat on the side of the front seat with the door open and wiped off the mud with a pair of oily rags I found in the trunk. Then I put my stockings and shoes back on and pulled the hem of my dress out of my underwear. The engine guffawed to life, and the car lurched out of the mud. The spray of it clattered off the fenders as the wheels turned. The lane ran between two fence rows like a chute.

In the middle of the brown stripes of fallow fields was a shack with a lazy plume of white smoke trailing up from a stovepipe that protruded through the roof. On the front porch were two Negro children, a boy in faded overalls that were too big, and a girl with ponytails all over her head like a little kind-faced Medusa. Their feet were bare despite the cold.

"No school today?" I asked.

"No maim, is Satty," the girl said. She seemed to be the older of the two.

"Oh," I said. I'd forgotten what day of the week it was.

"Are your mother and father home?" I asked.

"No ma'am, jess our grandmammy and her daddy."

The grandmother opened the door just then. She looked at the children and then eyed me suspiciously.

"Help you ma'am?"

"I'm here to speak with..." I reached into my satchel and checked the paper again. "Moses...Moses Cotter."

"Wuffo?"

"I'm here from the Federal Writers' Project."

"The who?" she asked with a quizzical look. She cast a look of suspicion at the light brown case of the recorder. I followed her gaze to it and said,

"Mr. Roosevelt sent me."

"President sent you?"

"Yes ma'am."

"Dixie, Looze-anna? Show nuff?"

"Yes ma'am," I said.

A smile broke on her face to reveal two rows of gapped teeth, even squares like the notches in a castle rampart.

"Come on in, den," she said.

In the front room in a rocker was an old Negro man. His eyes had slate blue rims around the pupils, and they seemed to be looking through the walls of the house, out over the dormant cotton fields and the woods and beyond that. He wasn't just old. He was ancient. He had a head of seemingly windblown bushy gray hair and an expression on his face of having just won or lost a big sum of money. It could have been either, but it was perpetually astonished-looking. On the wall above a potbelly stove was a picture of a white Jesus holding a white lamb with a shepherd's crook under his arm as he gazed sympathetically out at the black people in the room.

"Good morning," I said. "Are you Moses Cotter?" I looked at the note again. "Former slave of the Noah Cole plantation, Albany Landing, Caddo Parish, Louisiana?"

"Tha's him, but he don't hear too good," the woman said.

He looked to me, and his old eyes tried to focus. I had the idea that he only saw me as a shape.

I asked him how he was doing. He turned his tired old cloudy eyes to the woman.

"Wha? Wha she say?" he asked.

"She ask how you do," she shouted with her hand on his shoulder.

He shook his head in a slow shake like something being moved by the wind and told me, "I'm kickin', but not high. I'm flappin', but can't fly."

Then he turned silent again and resumed his startled expression. I sat down to interview him and found that the expression never changed one bit, nor did he respond to a single question, even when the woman shouted them to him. The clock on the mantle was shaped like an admiral's hat and chopped away evenly as the man and I looked at each other. His toothless jaws worked back and forth, side to side. The wind popped against the panes of glass in the window and against the cardboard that had been used to replace the broken ones. The whole arrangement looked something like a checkerboard.

I glanced down at my stockings and noticed they were mottled with mud or oil from the rags I'd used. I was calculating the price of new ones while I waited for Moses Cotter to say something.

Finally, his aimless chewing stopped, and he looked at me. He gave me an expression that begged that I listen and listen good, that it was important, serious. This is it, I thought, something from the past, something old about to be something rediscovered and new again. History was shaking the dust from itself. His old brown finger rose as his lips puckered, and then his lower lip pushed out. It was thick and cracked. Then he just said,

"White boys...don't get theyselves none."

Then he went to sleep. That was it.

The woman, an old person herself, said as if I should have known all along, "That's about all he ever say anyhow."

I thanked her, packed up the recorder, and lugged it to the Packard. The woman waved to me from the porch and thanked me for the visit.

"Careful that mud now," she said, her smile showing her notched teeth.

When I got to the mud hole, I gingerly maneuvered around it, easing past and barely clearing the fence.

Nov. 24, 1936

The city awakened today (a Tuesday) to cold mist. Down on Spring Street, a crowd was spilling out of the front door of Buckelew's Hardware. Men and women were shoulder to shoulder, pushing together politely to gain entrance. Men removed their hats as they entered. Back home in the city, Father does the same; he says it's what a man of culture does.

I joined the influx, anxious to see what the attraction was. Wet woolen garments gave the crowd a musky, animal scent. Women and some of the shorter men rose on tiptoes to see the object of everyone's curiosity. I had no idea until someone in the crowd spoke.

"Been sittin' in here seventy years. May be his last time," a man said.

"Such a shame. Hard to think of this place without him," a woman said.

"You're right, right as rain," another said.

"Who's in here?" I asked. Two women looked at me like I had just asked who the president of the United States was.

"Why, Champ Lockett," one of them said.

When we got in the doorway, my height helped me see over the cloches and bonnets of the women and the uncovered heads of the men. An old man sat in a rocking chair next to a potbelly stove. The blackened pipe rose to the high ceiling and pierced one of the embossed ceiling panels. Champ Lockett sat perfectly still in the rocker, the hook of a cane curled over his thigh just above the knee. The photographer, a Mr. Grabill, was there, taking pictures of people with the old man, who endured each pose with an exhausted smile.

A woman put her two children, a boy of eight or so and a girl slightly younger, on each side of the old man. The boy had on suspenders and a bowtie, and his hair was slicked back in that way of special occasions, the way boys get their hair fixed by mothers and aunts before their bar mitzvahs. The girl had on a nice 'Sunday' dress with a red sweater and black patent leather shoes. A bow clung to her head, tethered to a shock of her brown hair.

The children pushed out shy smiles, and Champ Lockett forced up the corners of his mouth in a weary one as they waited for the flash of the camera and the *'who's next?'* of Mr. Grabill.

"Smile big, Bobby," someone in the crowd said to the boy. "That's a gen-u-wine hero you're gettin' your picture struck with."

The boy showed more teeth, his smile looking more like a grimace than anything else. His sister blushed as her face drifted downward. A woman, their mother, I'm assuming, rushed forward to lift her daughter's chin and straighten her son's bowtie. Then she withdrew again, and the flash ripped over everything and was gone.

"Who's next?" Mr. Grabill asked loudly.

People began bumping shoulders, conversations rumbling. I believe it was you-no, you go ahead-alright, thank you kindly, and so forth. The rumble stopped when the old man spoke up. It was little more than a throat clearing. Shushes rippled through the crowd. Children were now on the shoulders of some of the men.

There was a pause, a strange, foreign silence. Even the cash register across the way fell from a waterfall of rushing numbers and into stillness. It seemed as though even the shiny new shovels and washtubs hanging on the walls were listening. Lockett's old voice strained into the quiet.

"I got something to say," he groaned. Ears and eyes were tethered to him. A child said something in a low voice, and a parent shushed him.

"I just wanted to let you all know that that day on the great redoubt in Vicksburg that..." he seemed to lose his train of thought. The tip of his old tongue darted out to wet his lips. His chest rose and fell quickly, nervously. His eyes shifted, his gaze bouncing from face to face. The crowd gathered around him, inclining their ears to his meager voice. The pot belly stove was quiet except that you could hear the wood in the stove hiss as the fire took it.

Someone in the crowd shouted, "You don't have to be so modest, sir. We all know, and we all love you for it. Three cheers for the Sergeant, the embodiment of Southern courage!"

Hats and hands were thrust into the air with each *hip hip hurrah!* Champ Lockett put his head down as the adoration of the crowd pressed in on him. His old knobby hands gripped the head of his cane. He seemed overwhelmed with emotion at the gratitude of the gathering. I moved forward in the crowd.

When I got up to the front, I told him who I was and that I'd like to interview him. His old eyes looked up to mine. The whites of them were faintly discolored. He didn't look well.

"Thank you, young miss, but I'm pretty tired. Perhaps some other time if I ever feel up to it."

A woman came through the crowd to collect him. She was impeccably dressed, with an ornate United Daughters of the Confederacy pin on the lapel of her smart felt jacket like a military medal.

"Come on, Daddy. Let's head home."

As the crowd parted for him like the sea parted for Moses, he looked back at me. The fire in the belly of the stove popped and sizzled. As he shuffled through the path in the crowd, he looked over his shoulder at me one more time and then turned away.

Nov. 25, 1936

Fairfield Avenue south of downtown is reminiscent of the Hamptons, large homes with stately yards set off the street. Fairfield Avenue is where today's subject, Savannah Wilkins, lives.

She's a woman with a pink-powdered face and crispy, sweeping blue hair like a swirl of cotton candy done up into the shape of a globe or a deep sea diver's helmet. Her eyes were theatrically done, like some Egyptian queen. She reminds me of a Japanese Kabuki dancer or the lead character from a French farce. On the chin of her dusty pink face is a small toadstool of a mole, which is about the only thing on her face that she hasn't put there herself. Her toothy smile is tall and wide and reminds me of a beaver's or the front grill of the Packard.

She informs me that she's well over a hundred and the great-granddaughter of one of the original settlers of Savannah, Georgia, hence the name. She proudly proclaims that her family was one of the founding families of the Georgia colony. I don't think she realizes it was founded as a colony for debtors, a penal colony. I held my tongue on that point. Shortly after the Civil War, her family immigrated to this county, or parish as it's called here in Louisiana.

The house is an impressive edifice, Victorian in style with a deep sweeping porch that advances down the side of the house. It's populated with white wicker rocking chairs. Under the eaves, there are hooks placed for the purpose of supporting hanging baskets. At this time of year, the hooks are empty, but I'm sure the porch is a pleasant place when the weather is warmer.

I was met at the door by Savannah Wilkins' great-granddaughter, who appeared to be no more than fifteen. She's a lovely girl with blonde hair and blue eyes, dressed as well as any Fifth Avenue shopper.

"Do come in," she said as she held the screen door open for me with the courtesy of a woman twice her age. Over the mantle was a portrait of Robert E. Lee in his gray uniform with the gold sash. On either side of the picture, there were sprays of flowers. It was more an altar than a mantle.

Miss Savannah rose and seemed particularly spry for over a hundred. The first thing she asked me was:

"What type of cocktail would you prefer, my dear?"

"I'd just prefer water," I said.

"Oh, nonsense," she fussed. Turning to her great-granddaughter, she said, "Virginia, make our guest a gimlet, would you?"

Virginia brought it to me, and frankly it was too strong to drink, so I just politely put my lips to it from time to time. Besides, it was only ten o'clock in the morning.

We sat down, and Mrs. Wilkins asked, "So what shall we talk about today?" She didn't wait for a reply. "Let's talk about Richmond in the days just before the war."

"All right," I said, and I put the blank on the Presto into circular motion. The markings at the center blurred into rings.

"Well, I was just a sweet young thing then, in those days. My father was an officer in a Georgia cavalry regiment from Savannah, and he brought us with him to the capital right after Beauregard fired on Sumter..."

I never asked her a single question. I never got the chance. She held the floor in a filibuster that would do any senator proud. Gradually, her discourse began to border on the incredible.

"...unbeknownst to his wife Varina, Jefferson Davis and I were-*how shall I say this? -paramours*. Intimates, I mean..."

I couldn't tell if this was the story of the century or a pathetic lie. I soon concluded it was the latter. It's a journalist's duty to report the truth, and this clearly wasn't it.

On she rambled.

Soon a lesser Confederate general, whose name she dropped as if it was obvious that I should know it, was included in the story, and then another. The love triangle became a rectangle, and then a pentagon. Miss Savannah was certainly a gal-about-town in her younger days, in her own mind, at least. I continued to listen as her veracity crumbled.

Her story became more and more preposterous as she merrily spun it, pausing only for a quick sip of her cocktail, so quick that I couldn't ask a question to get her off track. She was like a runaway carriage of falsehoods.

She had lounged with a sultan in his harem. She had been a consort to the King of Denmark (who as a lover was no match for the President of the Confederacy, she confided as an aside). She was with Edison when he invented the light bulb. She had smoked a peace pipe with members of the Seminole tribe, had visions, and then been forced to dance naked in the tribal lodge.

Her eyes were pale under the crust of pink powder, but they were bright and sincere. At least it was entertaining. Her granddaughter got up to get her grandmother another cocktail, and I excused myself on the pretense of helping her. I left Savannah Wilkins in the front parlor telling lies into the Presto.

In the kitchen, I asked Virginia, "She is your *great*-grandmother, isn't she?"

"No, ma'am," she said with a smile as she rattled ice into the glass. "That's my granny, she's only seventy. But she *thinks* she's ninety. Some days. Other days she thinks she's over a hundred. We just let her think whatever she wants."

The girl leaned into the hall and shouted, "Do you want a fresh lime, granny?"

From the hall, the old woman's voice was smaller in the distance:

"...so I said-*yes, please. Thank you, Virginia darling*-so I said all right but Jeff mustn't find out..."

A smiling Virginia measured gin into the tumbler as she poured another stiff one for her granny, who, if you believed her, was used to stiff ones.

"May I replenish your cocktail, Miss Levenson?" she then asked me cordially.

I held my palm up and shook my head slightly, "I'm fine, thank you."

I followed Virginia back into the parlor. She handed her granny the fresh glass and took the spent one. Miss Savannah took it carefully with two old, spotted hands. She never stopped talking, not even a hint of a pause.

Finally, I stood up. I was just wasting my time and the FWP's time. I turned off the recorder, and that made the old woman pause. She looked up. Her eyes rose in surprise and asked the question even before her mouth did.

"Can I expect you tomorrow? I have so much left I have to tell you."

I'm sure you do, I thought.

"Perhaps," I said out loud. "I'll see if I can swing by."

My little lie seemed puny and frail compared to her big muscular ones. Tomorrow is Thanksgiving, though she must have been too sauced to realize it.

As I left the house of the old socialite, General Lee was smiling his grim smile. I followed his gaze across the room where I noticed a couple of magazines on the end table.

Ladies Home Journal and *Good Housekeeping*.

Nov 26, 1936, Thanksgiving Day

Quiet TG alone. I'm back in my room at the Creswell. There's a spider that has a web in the corner of the window, outside the glass on the red brick ledge. She high steps over it as the wind moves it in and out like an eardrum. Why do I assume the spider is a she? What does she have to eat at this cold time of year? Her web is empty.

A light rain has fallen, and the headlights of cars reflect in it. The coming and going sounds like the brush of the surf on sand. It's icy, and the air is dense with cold mist. Outside my window and across the way, there's a graveyard behind the white-columned Methodist Church. The trees are bare and skeletal save for one which bristles with black leaves. I watch it, and, in a moment, the leaves take off as a whirlwind of blackbirds, elongating and bunching and elongating again, the cloud rotating on itself before they alight once more in the spiny branches of another tree. The monuments, some ringed by ornate wrought iron fences, rest pale below the swarming circus of birds. I imagine that the sleepers lying among the tangled roots beneath the monuments and trees have been granted asylum in some heaven after serving their earthly sentence in this town.

Somewhere out there, to the west over the cemetery and behind the wet gray sky, the sun is there, shining on the other side of the clouds as it settles into Texas.

I'm turning in for the night, even though it's only seven p.m. This loneliness is crushing.

Nov. 27, 1936

I drove out to an outlying town called Keatchie today to interview a subject named June Longhat. She was born, let me see if I can get this right, *Sa-Hatinu-Deet-se*. Her great-granddaughter says her great-grandmother once told her that it was in "the years that the first chimney boats came from downriver." She is reportedly one of the last native speakers of the local dialect of the Indian language, Caddo. The trouble is that she's had a series of strokes that have taken away her English, save for a few words which her granddaughter says are all impolite, and all she can courteously speak now is her first language, Caddo.

The road to Keatchie was largely unpaved and rutted in the rain, and the Packard fishtailed and bogged down. At one point, I thought for sure I would have to get out and push again, but finally the wheels found something to grip upon, and the car lurched out of the rut, spraying mud backward with a rushing sound. I was in motion again as the windshield wipers struggled against the rain which alternated between a mist and a patter.

The town of Keatchie was pleasant enough with several old and, I assume, antebellum buildings. A store, a couple of churches, some fine old homes. None of these were June Longhat's, however.

Passing through Keatchie, the road narrowed to the point that the bare limbs of the trees began to touch the side of the car as if it were moving through a crowd of curious, spiky-fingered gray people. It seemed to me that this couldn't possibly be the right path, so I stopped and checked the directions while the Packard panted thoughtfully.

Yes, it was the right road.

Finally, the little road flared open, and there it was, a house that was more a shack than anything else. The porch sagged down on one end under a tin roof that had long since transitioned from gleaming silver to a patchy, rusty reddish brown. Trash burned in a barrel, smoldering into the wet winter air. Chickens, some red and brown, some white, strutted in the scraggly yard, chuckling to themselves and rapidly casting sidelong glances around the yard and blinking against the rain. Under the porch, a dog sat up from lying on his side, eyed me indifferently, and then collapsed on his side again and sighed.

I walked up on the creaking porch, at points testing the planks with my shoe to make sure they wouldn't give way. A woman opened the door and appeared as a murky image behind the gray mesh. She opened the screen door, smiled a foolish grin, and introduced herself as Gladiola.

The inside of the house was little warmer than the outside, and I kept my coat on. On the wall was a picture of the Madonna and Child, a cheap reprint of a work by some unknown Italian artist. The house smelled of old age and things fried in grease.

June Longhat sat in a rocking chair, though it was stationary as she contemplated the floor. Her hair was silver and long, falling over the nightdress that she wore even though it was afternoon. Her eyes were thin slits above her full brown cheekbones, furrowed with a mosaic of wrinkles rising up from her cheeks.

When I introduced myself to her, she turned her eyes to me as if I were another in a long string of annoyances, and then she cast her gaze down as if she were waiting for a blow from something heavy above her. I tried to strike up a conversation as I cranked the handle of the recorder to charge it, and the old woman scarcely moved an inch. Even her respirations were minimal.

Her great-granddaughter, however, was very talkative. She is, I'm sure, starved for conversation out here on the surface of the planet Keatchie, a place more remote than the dark side of the moon. She's a lumpy girl with a large waist and small backside, and dirty bare feet despite the cold.

"You're very purty," she said.

It was a sudden, unusual thing to say, and I suppose I blushed.

"Why, thank you," I said.

She slavishly fussed over her great-grandmother, whom, after some pantomiming, we persuaded to speak into the microphone, which she did, at length. As her discourse broke into a chanting song, I asked the girl, "What is she saying?"

The girl raised her eyebrows and shook her head and with a look of regret whispered, "I ain't got a clue. I don't speak no Caddo."

The old woman continued on, now comfortably enthralled with the microphone, telling and singing all she knew. After almost two hours she began to tire, slumping down into her rocking chair with one ancient brown hand gripping the armrest like a tree root and the other gripping the microphone like a gnarled vine. I would have liked for Miss Longhat to have gone on; perhaps someone in Washington who knew a similar language could piece together what she was saying and singing. But I desperately needed a restroom break. Gladiola persuaded the old woman to take a pause, and then I had to almost pry the microphone out of her knobby hand.

I scampered out the back door to the privy. The wooden seat was cold. And down the hole...disgusting. I came back inside and packed up the recorder. The day had gotten away, and I decided to come back tomorrow. I thanked June Longhat, but I don't think she heard me. Her great-granddaughter thanked me back instead. June Longhat was slumped down in her rocker, listing to one side. She was taking great fitful gulping breaths. I gently touched her arm, and she turned her old eyes to me and then closed then again.

"She does this sometimes," Gladiola said, "she'll be all right."

I left uneasily, lugging the recorder in its bulky wooden case.

When I returned from Keatchie, there was a letter from Mother at the front desk:

Dear Miriam,

Greetings from the big city and your father, brother, and me. Everything here is exactly like you left it. Your cousin Jacob celebrated his bar mitzvah last week, and everyone asked about you. Uncle Sol and Aunt Gertie send their love. The butcher's son, Mortie, asked about you, too (again). I told him that you were officially engaged to Irving. He seemed to have a hard time hiding his rejection. Have you spoken with Irving?

I hope you're keeping the Sabbath. Do they have a synagogue there? You are keeping the Sabbath, aren't you?

Certainly you're still keeping a diary of your travels in the South, am I right? Your father and I had planned on traveling there one day. Do they still wear hoop skirts? Ha ha.

Have you developed a drawl yet? Your brother wants to know. He says he's sorry he was so sore about you taking the car. He says he understands now that you needed it to get out in the countryside there...

Well, shut my mouth, motha. Yo' letta goes on anotha fo-uh pages.

I've told mother a thousand times. Teenage girls keep diaries. Journalists keep journals. And have I spoken with Irving? I'm down here on the bottom side of the country and she's two subway stops from him, and she thinks I'll run in to him.

Irving knows what every good Jewish boy knows. You don't woo the girl, you woo the parents. Mother knows a marriage between us would lead to a job for Father and an increase in their circumstances. Once I get through this stretch, my life and my career are laid out ahead of me. Why should I be asked to sacrifice them?

Nov. 28, 1936

A clear, cold Saturday. I drove down to Keatchie to resume the interview with June Longhat. The dry, cold night wind had dried the mud, and the tires of the Packard kept falling into the ruts that were left.

As I pulled up to the little tin roof shack, Gladiola met me on the front porch to tell me that her great-grandmother died in the night. I was lugging the recorder, moving it forward with my knee and lower thigh with each step, and clutching my notebook to my chest. I stopped in the weedy front yard.

"I'm so sorry to hear that," I said, and I was. And not because I thought there was any useful information I could get from June Longhat. It was all locked away in a now-extinct dialect of Caddo, gone the way of the dodo bird and the passenger pigeon, a forgotten thing, something only to be imagined or supposed. I was sorry because I thought of this strange woman, left behind and forced to take on a new reason for living, the burden of her duty now having been lifted, sorry for this odd girl now casting about for a way to live her odd life, alone in a dilapidated house in a weedy clearing miles from anywhere.

I visited for a few minutes, expecting to see June Longhat's body laid out somewhere, but I didn't see it and didn't ask to see it. I didn't think it was my place. I stayed with Gladiola for as long as I could, which wasn't long. At last, I stood up and reached down for the recorder, trying to keep my thigh from drumming against it as I moved along to the Packard. I loaded it in the backseat and shut the door.

Gladiola called from the porch. Her smile was big and out of place for the circumstances. She was leaning into an embrace of the door jamb.

"Come back and see us, then, sometime," she said, and she waved a hearty farewell.

I backed out of the yard and moved toward the dismal lane. Chickens muttered and whooped as they scattered in my path.

Nov. 29, 1936

I'm sending Mr. Alsberg a telegram. The noise of the fire station across the street is becoming too much. I'm hoping he can find me alternate lodging.

The local paper, called the *Times*, is just as likely to headline hog and cotton prices as world events. And try to buy anything on Sunday in this town. Everything's shut down, except the churches, that is.

Nov 30, 1936

When you mention old timers in this town, his is the name that usually comes up first:

"Have you interviewed Champ Lockett? Well, wouldn't that be something if you could? Our very own hero of Vicksburg! You know he don't take visitors n'more."

I went to the library to find more information on him when really I could have asked anyone over the age of eight. Everyone knows the story, part of the lore of this place, told with starry eyes and a reverent tone.

Champ "Sergeant" Lockett, the local hero of the siege of Vicksburg, ran through a hail of bullets to gather reinforcements to close a gap and save the day. Never mind that Grant and the Federal army eventually tightened the noose around the town and forced its surrender. This city looks on the memory of that day like the silver lining of a black cloud, a sparkling diamond of a moment set among ashes, coal, and cinders.

It's commemorated on Confederate Memorial Day in June, and on the anniversary of his 'dash' in May, and on his birthday (which is in the fall sometime, I think). You would think that he made his dash over water.

School boys incorporate his daring run into their play, and songs about it are sung in pageants by tiny-voiced schoolgirls. I can only imagine the flowery praise. It all seems incongruous with a withering old man sitting still in a rocking chair at a hardware store. I suppose old age has a way of making heroes physically ordinary again.

Finding his address was easy enough: everybody knows where he lives. It's as if his house is a temple or an oracle that doesn't speak anymore. Very few have seen him, however, not in quite a few years. His appearance at Buckelew's was an unexpected bonus, as he's become quite a recluse. He still has the admiration of the people here, seventy years after the war, maybe not so much despite his shyness as because of it. Withhold something that the people want, and they'll want it even more.

He lives with his daughter, Susie Lockett Breag, the smartly dressed woman who came to collect him the other day with the Daughters of the Confederacy pin on her lapel. With the way she carried herself, chin up and her gaze over some unseen horizon, she had an air of local royalty when she came for her 'old daddy.'

They live in a house which is simpler than I expected, not a mansion with columns, but a simple white house with small square posts supporting a front porch with peeling white Adirondack chairs and bordered by weedy shrubs. Oddly enough, the house is in a neighborhood called Queensborough, like the borough in New York. She answered my knock with a smile, the same propped up smile that Savannah Wilkins sported, and I introduced myself.

"Do you think the sergeant would sit for an interview?" I asked as I balanced my recorder on my knee. I tried to prop up a smile of my own.

"I'm sorry, Daddy isn't taking visitors today," she cooed. "He's not feeling well." She said '*not*' in the way of a lot of people here, like '*naught.*'

"Do you think he'll feel up to it tomorrow?" I asked.

"Oh, I don't know," she said doubtfully. "There are very few days he feels up to anything. He's ninety-five, you know."

"Yes, I've heard," I said. "I'm collecting narratives of old people, especially notable ones like your father."

"Oh, that is so sweet of you to say. And aren't you just the prettiest thing," she gushed, "just so precious."

She backed through the door and was in the process of shutting it as she said, "Tell you what, hun. I'll tell him you came by, and, if he feels up to talking to you, we'll give you a call. Bye-bye, now."

Her face slowly disappeared into the diminishing crack of the door. As it shut, I realized that they didn't know how to contact me.

Part II
December, 1936

Dec. 1, 1936

There are perhaps half a dozen to a dozen other names on my list, but today I met someone that I intend to add to it. I came across her in, of all places, a supermarket on Line Avenue, Leon Johnson's. The self-service supermarket is still a relatively new concept here on the dim perimeter of the world, and today it was packed with housewives and their children, housekeepers on errands for their mistresses, and a few husbands sent with lists that they held and read as if they were written in Chinese. Everyone in this little backwater city must be enthralled with the idea of actually being able to handle the merchandise before buying. There I was among them, looking for a few things, though really more for the company of other human beings than anything else. My hotel room is beginning to get small.

And then there she was. A portly young Negro woman attended her patiently, carefully redirecting her.

"You need bread, Miz Biddy?"

"Yes, dearie."

The old voice was musical and mellow, even for someone her age. I asked the Negro woman, how old is she?

"Miz Biddy? Ninety-four last February."

We watched her together as she tottered over to the bread and thoughtfully looked it over, her old hands pressing into loaves to judge stale or fresh. She smiled the whole time through a face that reflected gratitude, pure gratitude at being in the presence of plenty.

"Where is she from? Her accent?" I asked the young woman.

"Miz Biddy from I-land. She came over on the boat when she was a girl."

I approached her, and the old woman turned and looked at me, and, when she did, I can only say I felt a warm sensation, like a blessing. She's a small woman with pale green eyes that must have once been a deeper green. There was a certain charm to them, and I told her so.

"My, what lovely eyes you have," I said.

She laughed and said, "That's what Little Red Riding Hood said to the wolf, or something like it. But I thank you, dear. You know," she leaned toward me and lowered her voice into a stage whisper, "They've gotten lighter as I've gotten older, and I fear I'll wake up one day and they'll be completely white, like Little Orphan Annie," she told me, pronouncing 'orphan' like 'arphan.'

"I'd like to talk to you one day," I said.

"About what?"

"About you."

"Me? And what about me, should I ask you?"

"Where you've been, what you've seen, what's happened to you."

"Well, that would take a while. I'm not sure if you know this," she leaned toward me again and said in a low voice, "but I'm an old woman. But you wouldn't know it if you looked inside. Sometimes I look in the mirror, and I can't believe it me-self."

And she laughed at her revelation.

"Only Sergeant Lockett is older, and only by a few months. He doesn't accept visitors any longer, I hear," she said. Then she smiled at me. "But I do, I most certainly do. Come for tea then," she said. "I'm home most afternoons, though this afternoon won't do. Nina's doing my hair later, or what's left of it."

Under the blue tam she wore, her old scalp had a thin atmosphere of white hair sculpted around it, a translucent fuzz just a little darker than an aura. She patted it softly.

"'Twas red at one time," she said, "thick and deep red, auburn, almost brown. Now look at it. Half of it turned white and the other half turned loose."

Nina called to her from across the way.

"You bout got everything you need, Miz Biddy?" she said.

"Yes, dear, and I thank you." She handed the loaf of bread to Nina who put it in the small basket on her arm.

Miss Fenerty gave me her address, and I wrote it down. The last house left standing on Crockett Street downtown, in between all the bigger buildings.

Dec. 2, 1936

I drove around downtown, first down Milam and then down Lake Street, until at last I found Crockett Street. As I pulled up to the house and checked the address, I realized that I could have walked had I wanted to lug the recorder.

The house was bigger than I had expected, squarely in the style of the last century with a deep porch that ran the length of the front and was screened at one end. The windows were open, and the radio inside played a tinny, nasal rendition of "I Can't Believe That You're in Love with Me." I knocked, and Nina answered the door. Past Nina, I saw her, the woman Bridget Fenerty, asleep in a chair with a book in her lap and her reading glasses perched on her button nose.

"Miz Biddy?" Nina said gently as she turned off the radio. Miss Fenerty jumped, and the book, Twain's *The Innocents Abroad*, slid off her lap and hit the floor, and she jumped again. Then she laughed at having been startled a second time. She tried to reach over her own lap for the book, but I got it for her.

"Thank you, dear," she said. "Seems I gather a little more lap every day. What is it that we'll talk about today?"

I opened the case of the recorder. At the urging of the dial I twisted, the lacquered blank began rotating. I set the lever with its stylus onto the blackness, and it began cutting a tiny groove like a plow raising up a small repeating chorus of static.

```
Federal Writers' Project,
Works Progress Administration
Transcript of Bridget Fenerty, age 94, Interviewed
and Recorded by    M. Levenson
Subsection:  Immigrant
Dec. 2, 1936
```

```
    What is it?
    What do you call it?
    A microphone?
    I'm to speak into it, am I?
    Like this?
    Hello?
    Like this, then?
    What would you like me to tell it?   My name? My
name and when and where I was born?   Very well,
then.
```

My name is Bridget Fenerty, and I was born in Ballinlough, County Roscommon, Ireland, February first, eighteen and forty-two. I was the youngest, there were five of us, total, plus Ma and Da, but I'm the only one left of all of them and have been for many, many years. There, what else is it you want to know?

Earliest memories. All right, then.

My earliest memories are of black faced sheep and wet, green ground and our stone house with a thatch roof and a fence with a wood gate. And the bog away across the field where Da said the fairies lived, and, though I never saw them, I knew it was just a matter of time before I did, the way Da could tell it. We had a dog that circled and barked at Da's heels as Da came in from work in the fields with his pipe clinched in his smile and puffing happily. He would remove it to sing as he staggered in tired from working, his boots scuffing the ground with his trouser legs stuffed in them. He had a beautiful voice, my father, and the people of the town and our part of Roscommon would ask him to sing at their weddings, and he would do it, putting on his best shirt after a long day of working. Then he would come home late and get up early in the morning to work again in the fields. But he never turned down any bride and her family, Ma said.

And I remember my parents' bed with the rope lattice bottom and the lumpy mattress and food hung from the ceiling to keep the pests out of it and how dark the room was with just a fire to light it, especially in the winter when the days seemed to last only an hour or two. And making tea over the peat fire, and Da's smile at me even though he was bone-deep tired from work. And the five of us children sleeping in front of the hearth under the thatch roof.

We were happy.

Then, when I was four or so, the potato failed us. That's what Ma said. When we dug them from the earth, they were little more than handfuls of slime, first one mound and then another and then all of them. I don't know how long it took for us to begin to starve, six months perhaps, certainly less than a year. The sheep were gone. The dog was gone. Our clothes were hanging on us so that one shirt could have fit several of us at once.

Then one night, Da and Ma held a conversation in the bed, and it was a rather warm one. I could hear them, and then Ma raised her voice, I remember it clearly, *Are we to stay here and die, then?*

The next day, we loaded up our old cart like we would do when we went into Ballimoe on Tuesdays to market and the dog would bark with excitement, but there was no dog to bark now and everything seemed so quiet.

What's that? The name of the dog? Oh, I don't remember that. Been so long, you see.

Da walked out of the door of the stone cottage, but he kept the door open. For good luck, he said, it means we'll be back. Ma stepped forward and shut it. And then we turned away and to the road.

We smaller children rode on a cart, the cart that we used to use to haul potatoes, lumpers we called them then, though now there wasn't a horse to pull it, only Da. The old horse, Barney or Barry, I can't remember his name, had vanished, just like our old dog and the sheep. Da pulled us all the way to Galway, stopping to stretch his back and mop his forehead and rest on the side of the road. Sometimes Ma would get to the front to take a turn, but Da never let her.

"Just walk alongside me, Nora, and keep me company." He smiled when he said it, as if her company along the road was all he really needed. But now I know how his body and his heart must have ached.

We sold the cart and about everything else except the clothes on our backs. The cart, the bedclothes, Da's musket, the pots that had clattered together on the way, all of it sold. Ma and Da took the money and bought us tickets to America. Ma said later it was barely enough. The last thing they sold, the item that made the difference, was our only picture, a framed picture of the Sacred Heart of Jesus.

The man in the window asked him, says, "Which boat would you be wanting? New York or Boston?"

Da says, "The cheapest one. Seven of us, we are."

"That would be to New Orleans, but it gets terribly hot there," the man says.

"Is it close to New York?" Da asked.

"Quite close, perhaps a day's journey on horseback, as I understand it," the man said. Da took it.

What a thing it was, like a building in the water with tall triangles of nets tied to the masts. It rocked gently in the fishy, salty air and made small creaking sounds. Gulls were laughing along in the distance. Everywhere was the smell of rotting wood and salt air.

It was one of the boats from New Orleans that would bring cotton from America to the factories in Liverpool and Manchester in England and then would need to be filled with something to keep the ships upright, for the journey back to America for more cotton. They could have used stones for ballast, but stones didn't pay a fare, so Irish were used. Human ballast, it was called. Human ballast for the coffin ships.

There were piles of rope and baskets of fish, fish with blank, surprised faces. My brother Patch made me laugh by imitating them, making his eyes big and drawing his jaw down, and we laughed and laughed until Ma shushed us. You know, it occurs to me now, ninety years later, that I can't recall Ma laughing once in America. Not once.

The holds of the ship had wisps of cotton all about them, and we children thought it was a grand adventure indeed, to ride on a ship, a ship with the novelty of cotton in it. Patch made a beard and moustache for himself and made me laugh by talking in an old, creaky voice like our Grandpa Kelly. Our sister Mary, Maggie we called her, gathered the loose cotton and made a doll for me out of it, binding it together with string. I still have it here somewhere, in that trunk there, I believe.

I looked out from the railing of the ship and thought how big Galway Bay was, the mudflats reaching out into it as the tide was low, but then we met the ocean, and we children who had been poking each other and laughing and shushed by Ma, well, we fell silent when we saw that endless water over the rail. We stood there quietly, all the families, only the smallest of the babies crying and whimpering as the sea took hold of the ship and made it creak and the cold Atlantic wind stung our faces. The sails high above us made sounds, snapping, fluttering, grumbling as the sea wind pushed behind them. One by one, we looked back at Auld Gray Galway and the gulls flapping above it and diving down to the water. Everyone was so quiet. We knew that this was something big, very big indeed.

Well, the boat went for Liverpool instead. Da was a decent sort of man, but when it was clear that this was England and not America, he said something, and Ma put her fingers over my ears and said "Jeems, mind your language around the children." Da was friendly with everyone, but hated the English as a rule. Ma was always a little more charitable and said that the English weren't all bad and that some of them even had souls.

There was activity again, but only for an hour or two, some quick loading and unloading and the captain exchanging papers. A rumor started that we were to be taken to work in factories in Manchester, and then someone said, no, it wasn't true. And then we were off again, into the sea, and this time there was no turning back. We passed a rocky island, a place called Fastnet Rock. Someone said, "Look, there it is. They call it the Teardrop of Ireland." It was the last any of us saw of the old country.

The days crept by as if they were mired in mud. It was slow for us children, and I'm sure it was just as bad for the adults. Overhead the sailors scampered about the rigging like monkeys, shouting short musical messages to each other that were repeated by the recipient, their hands busy with ropes as big around as a sausage, or the bigger ones as big as a man's arm. All the while, the horizon dipped and heaved, and we foolishly hoped that every rise of the ship would show us a thin gray strip of land, bumpy with trees or mountains or buildings. But no, there was always the distant flat line of a horizon that was just more ocean. And the sea kept its rhythm.

It kept the same rhythm at night as well, down in the dark in the cramped berths where, without our eyes to steady us, we could feel the rise and fall even more. You could feel your body pull against your berth with the change in the angle of the ship and smell the tobacco of the sailing men on watch on the deck above, hear their footsteps. In the darkness below, there was coughing and snoring and occasionally a suppressed chuckle and babies crying and mothers shushing them and the faintest sound of praying.

Da was a decent man, as I said. Ma said he never drank much, as is the common belief about the Irish male, though he did like to take a sociable pint now and again. Ma said he was much more likely to be carrying home a friend who was stinking drunk than to be the one carried. It's been so long, and I was so young that I have little memory of him. I only remember that he made me feel loved and cherished and that he was tired a great deal of the time. He was a man who seemed to stagger under a heavy blanket of fatigue and troubles.

He began with a cough and then stayed lying down. At first the other men tried to coax him onto the deck to take a little air. Then it was no use, and they tried to get him to at least sit up to take a little water or a small drink from a jug one of them had brought. And then one day, as the ship pitched in the sea, teetering as people would grab onto things to steady themselves, Da fell asleep.

My last memory of him was of a bundle sliding into the sea. It was about a week out from Liverpool. We were all standing wide-legged on the deck, the horizon tilting this way and that. Everything smelled damp like vomit and fish and salt-spray. The ship's captain wore bushy whiskers like this, down his cheeks and jowls, and he had bug eyes. At the time, I thought he looked like a fish, because he spent so much time at sea. That if a man spent enough time around certain animals, he began to take on their characteristics, like say if a man worked with horses, then his face got longer and his nostrils flared out. That's what I believed, but of course, I was just a girl then and a small one at that.

The captain read from a book while Ma cried, and my brother Patch and I clung to her legs, and my brother Dan and my sisters clung to each other. Other families, Irish like us, stood around, I don't know if it was out of kindness or pity or just something to break the monotony, for there was plenty of that. The sailing men went about their business, using buckets of seawater to wash the deck of the sickness and the sawdust that had been shoveled over it, and some of them sat straddled across the arms of the masts, mending sails and so forth, some of them with pipes in their mouths.

The sea heaved and fell and heaved again, and a man played a Protestant hymn on the fiddle while another sailing man held on to him and onto the mast to steady them both. The captain read one last line, "*and may flights of angels sing thee to thy rest,*" closed the book with a slap and nodded. Surely he was getting tired of the funerals and knew there would only be more. Two of the sailors tilted the wood plank and the bundle on it, Da all tied up in a canvas sheet that had been a sail, and he slid into the sea. And that was it for old Da.

Everyone looked away when the splash came up, except for me. I wanted to see where Da was going, but my mother pulled me back. I couldn't have been older than five. I thought it was a stunt by Da, that he might climb up wet from the other side of the ship, dripping and laughing at the trick he'd played on us. I didn't know I'd never see him again. I didn't know it was forever.

Later that night, it occurred to me that Da might be an angel now. I looked up to the moon, for I believed in angels then and that they needed a perch because they couldn't fly constantly forever and forever, no more than a bird could. In my little girl mind, the moon was the perch for angels, and that night I peered up at it as the timbers of the ship creaked and the sails popped in the wind and the moonlight played on the cracked, black, tossing sea. I looked for Da up there past the sails and the masts that poked into the night and toward the moon, but I couldn't see him, and I knew it must've been because it was a long way away and that he was up there, sure, just small in the distance.

I don't know what Da died of, pneumonia, perhaps. Ma always thought it was a broken heart. That if a man could no longer provide for his family, his pride and worth would leak out of him, and then his life and his heart would break and he would die. That's what Ma said.

Well, I suppose I've told this contraption quite enough for one day. Would you care for some tea?

Nina, could you bring us some tea? And bring yourself one if you like and settle with us.

Dec. 3, 1936

When the recorder was off and put away, the three of us, Miss Fenerty, Nina, and I, all sat in her parlor and took tea. Miss Fenerty asked me all about myself, as if my coming here was more about me than about her or any other old person here.

We sat there, the three of us, and had an hour or so of pleasant conversation, our three accents creating a strange invisible alphabet soup of different fonts and spellings, all kept congruent and harmonious by Bridget Fenerty's gentle stirring. If it's true that small talk is a conversation about nothing, then what we had was the opposite of that. We talked about everything. At one point as we were discussing the prospect for a hard winter, she said, "Did you know that it's summer in Rio de Janeiro?" She pronounced it *Ree-oo Dee Jan-Near-oo.*

She is simply the best conversationalist I have ever met. No one's comment is irrelevant; indeed, her reply is quickly and expertly chosen to highlight the previous one, and both seem perfect. The hour seemed like five minutes, and I could've easily spent another in their company.

I awoke at 4 a.m. after a dream that I couldn't remember, only that it was an odd combination of both wonderful and troubling. I realized that what had awoken me were the bells of the Central Fire Station across the street from the hotel, and I rose from the bed and went to my window just in time to see the fire engine pulling out of the bay and firemen scrambling onto it, pulling their oilcloth dusters around themselves and their red metal helmets on. Headed out into the cold to a call somewhere.

The engine and the sound of it receded west into the newer part of the city, and I realized I'd been dreaming of my father. We've never been close, and he's someone, I'm afraid to say, I've never given much thought to. But as I dreamed, I saw his face as he was handing out our Hanukkah gifts, his face painted with a reserved joy, a joy trying to contain itself, a pleasure trying to conserve itself.

Father is a man who still dresses before breakfast and eats in a suit and tie, even in the days after his firm failed, and he had no place to go. He dresses as if the mere act of presenting yourself is all you have to preserve a little dignity, and he leaves the house before anyone else leaves because it's an example of what a man does, he leads the way out into the world. In the months after the stock market crashed, his hours became just a little erratic, something out of the ordinary for a man of such regular habits.

Mother was suspicious, and I wonder if she thought he might have a girlfriend. Even though I was still in high school, she finally sent me out after him one day with some small piece of mail she thought he would need. I followed him through the streets of the city, shouting to him over the noise of traffic and jackhammers. His pace was rapid and at one point I thought he saw me as he turned the corner onto Sixth Avenue. But he kept going, and I lost him.

I went to his office and found the door padlocked, so I went around the corner, where I found him at a diner. There he was through the glass, and at first I didn't recognize him. His hat was on and pulled down over his face as he read the newspaper. It was open to the classifieds, and he was circling entries in red pen. I tapped on the glass, and I must have startled him, because he jumped when he saw me. Then he sighed and put down his pen. I walked down the sidewalk to the door of the diner, and he met me outside.

His chin was on his chest, and his gaze was on the sidewalk. Though he was dressed as always in a suit and tie, he acted as though he felt himself naked. As cars passed by, he glanced at them as if the drivers were pointing and laughing at him. The noises of the city, car horns and sirens and the rush of traffic, were peripheral and far away from us. I still held the letter in my hand. I don't remember what it was, something of little importance, just something Mother had given me for the pretense of following him. My father's voice crept out of him.

"The firm went under three weeks ago."

I should have told him I was sorry for him. I should have told him I was still proud of him. I should have told him he would always be my father. But instead, when he left the small, odd sphere of silence we were in and went back inside the diner, I just went home with the letter still in my hand.

And I'm sure he still dresses in a suit and tie when he goes to his job cleaning buildings at night. A proud, proud man. A man with a heart a lot like James Fenerty's must have been. Aching and ashamed.

So under the yellow light of the lone lamp in my hotel room here in the Creswell, I sat down to write him a letter. An anxiety rose in me, and, instead, I put on my robe and went down to the lobby to place a call.

The night man was reading a comic book. He picked up the phone behind the desk and placed it on the counter without looking up. The operator placed the call, and, as I waited, I was afraid that maybe my parents' phone had been disconnected, thrown overboard to help keep their household afloat, or that mother would answer the phone first and I would spend most of my call talking to her. Which I wanted to do, also, but tonight I needed to talk to my father.

The phone rang once, and I remembered what a light sleeper my father is.

"Miriam, is everything all right?"

"Yes, Father, everything's okay. I hope I'm not waking you up."

"Oh, no. I was just rising. Off to work. I've got seasonal work at Macy's unloading trucks."

"That's great," I said, though I knew it's not what he would choose to do, not what he was qualified to do. I knew that he would soon rise and fix himself, in suit and tie, and walk the thirty or forty blocks to 34th and Broadway wrapped up against the Manhattan cold because he didn't want to spend the money on the subway or the bus, money that could go to something else.

"I just wanted to tell you, thank you. Thank you for all your hard work. And how much I admire you."

There was a pause on the phone, and a honk as he blew his nose.

"Well," he said, his voice stumbling for words. "Well...you're welcome."

We spoke for a few moments, and I could hear Mother's voice in the background, "Leo, is everything all right?"

"Yes," he said. "It's just Miriam in Louisiana. Called me from Louisiana," he said with a note of wonder.

"My daughter. Calling me from Louisiana."

Dec. 3, 1936, FWP, Transcript of Bridget Fenerty

Cicero. Our dog's name was Cicero. I thought of it last night after we talked, and I wrote it down. Merry old Cicero.

We were talking about the crossing, weren't we?

The night after Da died, there was a storm, with lightning that lit up the black surface of the sea and split the sky in two with a powerful thin white streak. The sea had been calm, but it began heaving again, like this, up and down. We were all getting used to it, the motion of the sea, and I stood at the top of the ladder watching it, the sea and the dark sky and the lightning and the rain. Waves were beginning to break over the deck, and I had eased up onto it. Perhaps I wanted to check to see if Da were all right, there in the sea.

Water flashed a luminous sea green like jade and then crashed into white and fell back into the sea as the ship seemed to shrug it off like an animal trying to rid itself from something on its back. Another wave, bigger and emerald green in the moonlight, broke over the railing and slapped me, like a salty wet hand, and pushed me across the deck and into the opposite railing, and I almost went in. A sailor in an oilcloth slicker ran down the railing and grabbed me and put me over his shoulder and took me down below.

Ma took off my clothes, they were soaked, and hung them up on one of the beams below deck, and covered me up next to her, under her cloak. It took almost two days for them to dry, on account of it being so damp in the hold. I went naked most of the time. I didn't give a fiddler's fart, either. [*laughter*]

Now there was a man from Connemara in our group who had a fiddle, and at night he would entertain us with it. He played "When the Cock Crows, 'Tis Day" and "The Rocky Road to Dublin" and some others I don't recall. Everyone clapped along with him, and those who cared to danced, including my older brothers and sisters. Ma didn't, though.

A week or more passed, no one could be sure, for time was in some lower gear, and then one day someone spotted gulls, and an old man from Clare said, means there's land near, sure. And then the ship was in the river, and we took on a river pilot and a tug that belched out black smoke. On the bank there were birds, white ones, black ones, pink ones. With every bend of the river, we jammed the railings of the ship, each time disappointed with more swamp or fields. Even the marvel of another beautiful house or another alligator had lost its luster.

Until finally we saw it, New Orleans in the distance, the horizon of it furry with the masts of the sailing ships and the smokestacks of the steamers and behind them, the low square outlines of buildings and the spires and belfries of churches.

The wharves were jammed with people and carts of cotton bales, each bale seemed almost half as big as our old cottage. And the mules and horses, everywhere, mules and horses. We had expected New Orleans to be as big as Galway or Liverpool, but it was much bigger. And noisier. We could hear it; the noise of the city grew as we approached it.

There was laughing and swearing and shouting and the rumble of barrels up and down gangplanks and boat whistles and mules braying and the clop of hooves on cobblestones. Peddlers musically selling their wares in dozens of strange languages, Irish, English, and others we weren't sure of. French was one, but it would be a while before we would get acquainted with it. We couldn't tell if the city was heaven, hell, or Sodom and Gomorrah.

A man had a black bear with a wire muzzle and a red vest on him, and when the man played a tune on the pipe, the bear would dance in a circle. The man and the bear looked very similar, and it confirmed my theory that men and their animals begin to resemble each other after a time. And there were men who were as black as coffee, and that was the first time I ever saw a Negro. And stack upon stack of cotton bales, held together with iron straps. Cotton everywhere, big bales of it like enormous white cakes.

A clerk was there in a top hat and a vest with his shirt sleeves rolled up and a pocket watch in his vest pocket. He had a pen that was a long feathery thing, and he asked Ma our names. Ma told him, and the man wrote them down in the ledger. No swearing an oath to the Constitution, no saluting a flag. Just like that we were Americans. The men's velveteen britches and the women's blue cloaks and white caps set us apart, though. We still looked Irish, pasty-skinned, skinny, malnourished. Those who were once like us were now fat and sun-browned, and we took hope in that.

At the dock on Adele Street in New Orleans, we were greeted by a couple who seemed to know us, though I had never met them before. It was Ma's cousin from Ballinlough, Aunt Peg, and her husband, Uncle Jack we were told to call him. *Fáilte*, they said, welcome in Irish.

Aunt Peg was a freckled faced woman with hazel eyes and thin lips. She wore her graying auburn hair up, but strands of it kept falling down on her freckled neck, and it must have tickled her, for she had the habit of flicking her fingertips over her skin as if she felt a fly or mosquito landing there. She walked with a limp, and I believe that one leg was shorter than the other or that she had had an accident that involved her hip, though I never knew for I never saw her without the big rustle of skirts she wore about herself.

"Where's James?" Aunt Peg asked, looking up and down the levee as if he had taken a walk there. Ma shook her head, and my aunt said, there, now, dear, and Uncle Jack took off his withered stovepipe hat and said, "Well, may God rest his soul, and all the souls of the departed, then."

Aunt Peg changed the subject quickly. She looked at each of us children, taking our faces in her hands and appraising us, at last kneeling down in front of me.

"Oh, but she has Grandpa Kelly's eyes, now doesn't she?"

Ma and Aunt Peg had both been Kelly before they married.

"'Tis true," Ma said, drying her eyes and trying to smile.

This distressed me, for if I had his eyes, what did he have? Was he poking about with a stick, blind on account of me taking his eyes? I felt the jerk of my sister Colleen's hand, and we all walked along like a gaggle of geese looking about ourselves at the sights.

Well, a man approached Ma, who was a very pretty woman, about a job opportunity. Uncle took her by the hand and said, she's not the class of lady for that sort of work, and shooed the man off. We walked along in the early spring sunshine, strangers in this strange new world. It was March, and Ma remarked how pleasant and agreeable the weather was for March, and Uncle Jack says just you wait.

Just you wait, he says.

Dec. 4, 1936

I left Miss Fenerty's and returned to the Creswell. That was yesterday. This evening, the man at the desk presented me with this telegram from Mr. Alsberg:

LODGING FOUND HOUSE WPA RENTG AT REQUEST FRENCH PAINTER LEMURIER 813 STEPHENSON STREET EXPECTG YOU

At long last, nicer quarters away from the midnight wail of the fire engine. It's a good thing too, for something very unsettling has happened here at the Creswell.

I was awakened early this morning by a shriek. I scrambled into my robe, and, by the time I got to my door, several others in the hallway had gotten to theirs. Our heads poked out into the corridor. The door across the hall was open, and a man's body was lying on the bed. I could only see his legs, but I could tell from the unnatural posture and stillness of his body that he was dead. The manager was there with the master key he had used to get in the room, and he tried to console the housekeeper who had been with him when they had found the man.

The police arrived with the coroner, and the man was carried out on a gurney under a sheet. Afterward, the detective and the policeman discussed the situation, and I overhead them:

"Manager and the maid found him. Note says he just lost his job. To top it off, his wife in Dallas just left him and took their three kids," the detective, a man in a dark blue double-breasted suit, said.

"Damn cryin' shame," the policeman said. "I'll have to give 'em the call, suppose."

"Well, you're a good man for that," the detective said as he lit a cigarette and shook out the match. Then he said to us who were peeping out of our doors like prairie dogs on the plains.

"Y'all go back inside your rooms, now. Give the man a little dignity. It's all he had left."

Dec. 4, 1936,FWP, Transcript of Bridget Fenerty

Where did we leave off last time? Yes, we had just arrived on the levee.

There was a lady named Mrs. O'Brien who ran a boarding house on St. Thomas Street, where Aunt Peg and Uncle Jack Hennigan rented rooms. One part they stayed in themselves, and the other part they rented out at a small profit. That's the part we took. One room for Uncle Jack and Aunt Peg, one room for us Fenerty's, all six of us. They'd had a small cottage on Julia Street until Uncle Jack couldn't work anymore, which had been ten or fifteen years earlier, quite enough time for him to lose the calluses from his hands.

I remember so clearly first stepping into that room, the white paint peeling off the frame-and-panel door, squeaking open and tapping the wall behind it, and Uncle Jack's voice behind us, "A family from Kerry lived in here until a few days ago. Off to Texas, they are now."

There was a bed and a bureau and a small fireplace in each room but nothing to make a fire with. Four walls, a ceiling and a floor, two windows in each room. A home without a thatch roof, a first for us.

That night, men fought in the alley, and there were shouts from the crowd of "Ho!" and then another, and then a final "Ho!" and more laughter as one man went down.

"Give him some air!" someone shouted.

"Give him a beer!" another said, and then there was another roar of laughter.

We went to sleep that night, our first night in America, to the street sounds of drinking and fighting and glass breaking and laughter and shouting. Our wide eyes looked at each other in the dark.

The next day, Aunt Peg took Ma down to the C. K. O'Hara Agency, on Camp Street just opposite Lafayette Square. Mr. O'Hara arranged domestics for the well-to-do's on Prytania and St. Charles and for the Creoles across Canal Street. Maggie sat with us in our room while the sunlight slanted in. Outside, men shouted at mules and each other, and wagons rattled over cobblestones. On the river, steamboats bellowed. We sat in a circle on the floor while the breeze stirred the tattered curtains. The weather outside was bright and cool, so different from the dank chill of County Roscommon and Ireland in general. It was strange to us. We felt like we were on the moon.

Uncle Jack Hennigan woke about midmorning, and we all marveled at this, too, for we'd never seen a man keep to bed so late in the day. Da was always an early riser, by necessity. But not Uncle Jack.

Colleen was brushing my hair and telling me the story of how I was named for the patron saint of Ireland, Bridget, because I was born on her feast day, February first, and that I should be an example of a good girl always with such a name as that. I endured her piety because it was such a simple pleasure for both of us, Colleen and me. I enjoyed the gentle pull of the brush, and Colleen enjoyed grooming me like I was her pet.

He appeared in the hallway in his drawers. He was a red-faced man with graying blonde hair and whiskers that swept down from his ears and then up and over his mouth to meet in the middle, right under his nose. With all that facial hair, there still wasn't a beard. Either he shaved his chin or hair just wouldn't grow there, I never knew which. His eyes were small and shifted like he was looking for an opportunity, either to embrace or avoid. His teeth were tea-and-tobacco stained, and the incisors pitched inward, which made the ones flanking them seem to protrude outward, though I suppose they didn't.

His steps thudded on the floorboards as he came in scratching his head and his balls at the same time. Yellow-gray hair stuck out from above his ears like a housecat. His small eyes squinted against the midmorning light, and he paused in the doorway between our two rooms and looked astonished. Though it was after nine o'clock in the morning, he still smelled like a saloon.

Every Irish child knows the look of an adult who's done battle with the creature the night before, and every Irish child knows that it's the memory that's often injured by it. So it was with Uncle Jack.

"Who the feck are you?" he asked.

"Your nieces and nephews, uncle," Maggie said. "Come from old Ballinlough in Roscommon."

She was the oldest, you remember, and was in charge of us while Ma looked for work. She was about ten and having to grow up in a hurry on account of our circumstances.

"Oh yes," he said, and he looked in the bureau and then the cabinet for something. He seemed aggravated.

"Do you want us to walk with you to your work?" Dan asked. He was an earnest lad and Da's shadow when Da was off to work in the fields.

"Oh, I can't work, on account of me back," Uncle Jack said.

We would come to find out that Uncle Jack would never work again, though he would have trouble keeping up with which body part prevented him from it. It was his back, then his trick leg, then his shoulder. Or the cholera had left him weak. Or, our favorite, 'a trouble in the manly way.' He would use that one as the trump card to stop any further questions from us.

He was full of advice, Uncle Jack was:

Don't approach stray dogs, even if they're smiling at you.

When you hear hoof beats, get out of the street. Wagons and carriages here don't stop for anyone, not even children, and especially not for Irish children.

Every body of water, no matter how small, could have a snake in it, so mind yourself.

Only drink water from cisterns. Drinking water from the river or the bayou or the canal will surely give you the shits, and you don't want the shits now, do you?

No, uncle, we shook our heads solemnly.

Only eat oysters in months with an R in their name.

Stay away from lewd women of all colors.
He meant this for my brothers, Dan and Patch. At that age and being from the country, my brothers had no idea what a lewd woman was and certainly no idea what they would want to get near one for. But they were raised by Da and Ma to be polite, so they both looked concerned and nodded.

And above all, Uncle Jack said as he closed his eyes and raised his finger,

Stay away from the cray-ture.

The drink, alcohol, he meant of course.
That last bit of advice was one he could never follow himself, and I think it pained him that he couldn't. It certainly pained Aunt Peg.

Midmorning, Ma returned to check on us, and then she was off across Canal Street to work for a family named Prudhomme who lived on Dauphine, I believe it was. Maybe Rue St. Ann. Nevertheless, Aunt Peg went with her to get her set up and then was back across to report to her own employer, a family on Prytania named Carroll or Carson or something like that.

Uncle Jack left during the afternoon to see a man about employment, his spirits high and laughing a laugh that was at once boyish and sinister. He left to see about a job every day, and we soon figured it was to visit a succession of coffee houses, which were the saloons of those days. He always came in late at night from his job interviews, singing to the top of his voice.

But he was certainly right about it turning hot, Uncle Jack was. How different to come from the old country where for two months in the winter the days seemed to last an hour or two, and come to a place like New Orleans where the whole of winter itself seemed to last a month or two. Two months of winter per year in New Orleans and two months of summer per year in Ireland.

When spring came 'twas warm, and then summer came and 'twas hot.

Then summer stayed, and it got even hotter. Everything wool that we had mended additional life into was replaced with cotton and linen and so forth as soon as we could afford it. I'm sad to say that the wool clothes we had worn were used to barter with the newcomers off the boat, who had no idea of the summer heat. It was dishonest, and we knew it, but we needed the money and may God forgive us for it.

In May, Ma let the boys untuck their shirts, and, in June, she let them unbutton them. By August, when the air was at its hottest, she let them go without shirts, something she would never have allowed in Ireland. Their pale skin, as white as a fish's belly, marked them as newcomers, and they fought on account of it.

But the heat was scalding. When we complained of it, Ma would say, "Don't tell people your troubles. Most don't care, and the rest are glad you got them."

We marveled at how people could live in such a soup. The dogs of the Channel kept under the houses panting with their tongues rolled up, trying to yawn away the heat and not bothering themselves to bark at, let alone chase, the wagons that passed on the cobblestone and mud lanes of the city.

The air would be hot and wet enough to boil a potato, and then, in the middle of a sunny afternoon, clouds would gather, and the sky would open, and it would rain as hard as we had ever seen it, a rain as heavy as lead that crashed into everything and so thick you couldn't see across the alley. Then it would stop suddenly and leave a steam floating over the mud puddles and cobblestones, which were cooler now so that we could walk barefoot upon them, which is what most children in the channel did anyway for lack of shoes.

We were enrolled in school, the public schools being a new thing then. Ma worked long hours for the Prudhommes and took in mending and any other job she could find. Ma taught Maggie and Colleen mending, but I don't think she trusted me with a needle. And I couldn't sit still for very long, anyway. Patch and I were allowed to be children for a time, as we were the youngest.

There were all kinds of new sights, things that we never would have dreamed of. Theaters, steamboat calliopes, shops, music stores, carriage works, people of every possible hue with the blood of several continents in their veins and with foreign languages on their tongues. Every sense filled to overflowing. New Orleans was a wonderful place if you look at it that way. Vendors sang short little songs proclaiming the merits of what they had to sell.

Of course, it was a rough place as well, with gangs and violence, all sorts of unsavory characters coming down the river or coming up it from overseas. Women selling themselves, men, too. Saloons on every corner and their staggering patrons entering and leaving and passing out halfway in between.

But it was our home now.

Dec. 5, 1936

Yesterday, when the recorder was put away, Nina brought us tea, and we sat and talked.

"Well, 'tis a shame you can't get Champ Lockett to speak with you," Miss Fenerty said as she poured tea into her cup and then mine and then Nina's. "What a glorious adventure he had, they say."

Glar-ious, she said it.

Her hand shook a little as she replaced the teapot onto the tray, and the bottom of the pot rattled. She moved the sugar bowl to Nina and continued speaking between sips of her tea.

"I haven't seen him in ten years, perhaps. At the Confederate Memorial Day, it was. They asked him to speak, and he just stood up with his cane and waved and sat down again. He used to always be there, year in, year out, though he's never been much of a speaker. Seems a very shy man."

"My sister-in-law cleans for them, sometimes," Nina said as she put the third teaspoon of sugar in her tea. "Says Mr. Champ ain't lookin' so good."

"Well, not many can get to be our age and retain our good looks," Miss Fenerty smiled, and Nina laughed.

"Miz Biddy, you a mess!" Nina said.

And so the afternoon passed. I asked Miss Fenerty about herself when she was younger.

"I grew to be five-foot-six!" she exclaimed, with her finger nodding on five and six. "Almost as tall as you," she said. "Now, how tall are you, then?"

"Five foot nine, I believe," I said. Really I'm closer to five foot ten, but I've always been self-conscious about my height.

She's certainly shrunk to less than five feet tall now. Age has melted her, though I have the feeling that she still feels she's five foot six or that she could will herself to be that tall again at a moment of her choosing.

"I was the tallest of Colleen, Maggie, and me, but then again, Colleen didn't see adulthood. I was pretty, too, but not as pretty as Maggie. She was the prettiest girl I've ever seen."

I waited for her to expound on her sisters, but she changed the subject instead. She did it with an expression that I've noticed, a small duck of her head, an inclusive smile, a raise of her eyebrows. An expression that asks, *tell me a secret. I won't tell anyone.*

"And so where are you staying now, may I ask you?" she said.

"I'm at the Creswell Hotel now," I said. "But I'm taking a room in a house with a painter on Stephenson."

"Stephenson? That's off Line Avenue, isn't it?" she asked.

"Yes. I believe it is."

"Is this a house painter?" she asked.

"No," I said. "An artist. From France."

"Oh," she said with awe, putting the tips of her fingers near her mouth. "An artist, you say." Her mind was working. "It'll be just the two of you in the house?"

I hadn't thought of that.

"Well, then. Mind yourself in a house alone with a French artist. You know," she tilted her head forward and peered out from under her old white eyebrows as if it were time for another secret, "They have a reputation as *libertines*. They could charm the drawers off a nun, the saying in the Channel was."

"Woo, Miz Biddy!" Nina pitched forward and slapped her knees with her hands.

Miss Fenerty's expression was so whimsical that I smiled, and I felt myself smiling, as if my face was cracking open and making a sound heard only by me.

I promised her I would exercise great care with the French painter and mind myself in case he in fact turned out to be a *libertine*. Then I sat with them, and we talked for what seemed to be a few minutes. However, when I looked at the clock, it had actually been closer to an hour and a half. It had all been such a treat, I felt like I needed permission to return. I don't know why, I just did.

"Come back any time you like," she said, but she didn't smile. She didn't have to. I had heard it in her voice. I gathered the recorder, and Nina and Miss Fenerty followed me to the door.

Dec.6, 1936

This is my last entry in the journal from here at the Creswell. I'm gathering my things in my suitcase, though there isn't a lot to keep up with. This place now has the cheer of a morgue or the catacombs, dark hallways already visited by death in my short stay here and likely not the first time. A place where people go to sleep and smoke and cry and enjoy illicit love and then cry and smoke and sleep again. As much as this place saps my spirit, Miss Fenerty's lifts it. I'm off to a Sunday afternoon visit with her.

Dec. 6, 1936, FWP, Transcript of Bridget Fenerty

I see you're left handed. Well, so am I. Back in those days, it was felt by most teachers that it was an inferior way to write, with the left hand, and a sign of poor character.

Our teacher, Miss O'Rioran, was one of them. She was one of two Misses O'Riorans. They must have been identical twins, for you had one of them one year and then the very next year you had the other, and you never knew which one it was.

Each held a willow branch that could be used to administer discipline, though I can't remember either of them using it for that purpose. Though, now that I think of it, occasionally they would pop my left hand if they caught me writing with it. They mainly used it as a pointer to aid in the lesson. They would write our grammar or our spelling words or our times tables on the blackboard.

Well, it was a day when it was just getting hot, and we had been allowed a few minutes to run and play and tussle outside, what they call recess now, I suppose. We were sweaty there in our seats. My how we must have smelled. Like puppies. Miss O'Rioran was going down the times tables on the blackboard, and we were reciting them with her:

Two times three is six.
Two times four is eight.
Three times four is twelve.

The tip of the willow switch swayed like the antenna of an insect, lightly brushing against the white chalk writing. Her smiling face turning from the board to us and back again.

Well, there was a boy named Rory Murphy who was the major cause of disruptions for Miss O'Rioran. He would make noises like a cat or growl like a dog whenever she turned her back, and some of the other boys would snort at him. All would fall to silence when she turned her face back around to see who it was. Her face wasn't smiling then. He also had a small band of boys who would pick fights with the new children, calling them all sorts of names. He dipped girls' pigtails in the inkwells, stole apples and peaches off carts, that sort of thing.

It was on a day with our times tables when Rory's father appeared at the door. Mr. Murphy wore a slouching stove pipe hat, and he was carrying it in his hand. He was a short squat man in a collarless, sweat-soaked cotton shirt and suspenders. His eyes were the color of green paint thinned with turpentine, paler than the dark baggy rings around them. He spoke like it pained him to be there.

"You're having trouble with my boy, ma'am?"

Rory's face fell.

Mr. Murphy waded into the class and made his way toward the back where his son was seated. He smelled like sweat and like coffee, his father did. You could tell back then what sort of ship a man had been loading or unloading by his smell. Bananas, cotton, coffee, vinegar. A man wore the scent of his work all day and then took it home with him.

Well, Rory's eyes looked up in fear at the judgment that was about to be rendered against him. Mr. Murphy pulled his son from his seat, by the ear, and what a face Rory made. I thought his ear would come off in his father's hand. Mr. Murphy pulled him to the front of the class. Miss O'Rioran offered him the use of the willow switch.

"Thank you, ma'am, but I won't be needing it," he said as if he were declining a cup of tea.

And then Rory Murphy didn't get a whipping. And he didn't get a spanking. It was a beating he got.

Mr. Murphy jerked Rory's trousers down. His arse was just as pasty white as any other little Irish boy in the Channel. Mr. Murphy laid into it with his hand snapping on Rory's bare backside; the sound of it was like the sound of a spark, sharp and electrical. With the first few blows, his white arse was striped red from his father's fingers, and then the stripes became red circles, and then his whole arse was red from hip to hip, and it happened right there in the front of the classroom under the pictures of George Washington, the Last Supper, and the Sacred Heart.

To Rory's credit, he didn't cry once, though I thought he might bite a hole in his lip. Mr. Murphy's snapping, smacking hand continued until there were blisters forming on Rory's skin. Finally, Miss O'Rioran put her hand on Mr. Murphy's shoulder. His face and cheeks were as red as his boy's were. Mr. Murphy's hand stopped halfway back and then fell to his side before it could give another blow.

He stood there with his shoulders rising and falling slowly. His shirt was drenched in sweat, and his suspenders angled out over his broad chest and shoulders. Rory pulled his trousers up and buttoned them and scurried back to his place. The look on his face was completely different then; there was no mischief in it. He was completely vanquished. He started to sit, but winced when he tried it and remained standing. Mr. Murphy seemed to be awakening from a dream. He looked around as if seeing us for the first time.

"If any one of you other little bogtrotters needs me to tell your father you need a treatment of this sort, tell me now, for I'm headed back to the levee, and I'll see them all there shortly."

It was quiet for a moment, just the far-off noises floating in through the schoolhouse window from the levee, the remote bray-and-clop of mules and steamboat whistles. The rattle of wagons and men shouting in voices that were all a pale murmur in the distance.

"Very well," he said. "Rory, son, mind your manners for this lady who's only trying to better your station, unless you want to wind up working on the levee like your Da."

He collected his hat from Miss O'Rioran's desk, turned, and left just as quickly as he had appeared. Rory stood for the rest of class and for the rest of a week of classes, and he and the rest of us were all very well behaved indeed.

Dec. 7, 1936

Yesterday, when the recorder was turned off and packed away, she walked me to the door. Her old legs were bowed into slight curves that contrasted to the straightness of the cane that propped her up. From the porch, she smiled and waved, ducking her head forward slightly and flicking her fingers up and down like someone might wave to a small child. Nina gave a quick wave and smile and then turned to Miss Fenerty to begin bringing her inside.

I left Miss Fenerty's and turned onto Common Street, which becomes Line Avenue after a dip in and out of a valley. On the other side, I stopped at a traffic light. There was a school there, and children were playing. Even through the window glass I could hear the sound of their play in the cold, squeals and shouts. Small legs pushed out and retracted in ever higher arcs on swing sets. Small knots of children, mostly composed of either all boys or all girls, some discussing things, some chasing others, the chased ones fleeing with big smiles. In the brilliant sunshine, their shadows ran after them, and, when the children changed direction, their shadows ran from them, always tethered at their feet. Boys in two lines were throwing rocks in some kind of odd game while one dashed between.

I thought, take away their southern accents and twentieth century clothes, and they could be children of the Irish Channel. Give them New York accents, and they could be children of any Public School in the Bronx or Brooklyn or Manhattan.

There was a honk behind me, and I noticed the light was green again. I looked behind me. A woman waved apologetically with a gloved hand and a smile under her bonnet. I waved and smiled in return.

The cross streets flashed by, Merrick, McCormick, Dalzell, until finally I came to Stephenson. The neighborhood is a nice one and doesn't seem like the kind that would hold a rent house.

I parked on the street and replaced the dangling headlight back into its socket as I've become accustomed to doing. The house has two stories with a small porch like a dock that juts out into scrubby flowerbeds. I lugged my suitcase in one hand and the recorder in the other. I set them down on the porch and knocked on the door. There was no answer, so I peered into the window. The room downstairs appeared to be a living room or parlor that had been converted into an artist's studio, with paintings on easels and leaning against walls. I heard a cough upstairs, and I knew someone was home. I knocked again, this time harder.

"Jesus Christ!" a male voice upstairs shouted. "It's..." There was a pause and the small crash of objects falling on the floor upstairs. "It's eleven o'clock in the morning!"

Footsteps drummed slowly down stairs inside somewhere, and the door clicked open. A man appeared who squinted against the hard, bright winter sun. His hair was dark and cut close on the sides, the top was thicker and curly, and slick with pomade. His eyes were dark as best I could tell as he narrowed them into slits with his hand at his brow. He had a thin, Clark Gable style moustache on his upper lip. A pack of cigarettes pushed out a rectangular outline in the pocket of the royal blue silk pajamas he wore. The lapels and pockets were lined with red piping. JL was embroidered in fancy letters on the pocket.

"Who-are-you-what-do-you-want?" he muttered as he reached for the pack of cigarettes. He found one and put it to his lips.

"I'm looking for Joseph Lemurier," I said.

His face changed as if he were trying to compose himself. His voice rose above his previous mumbling, and he said, "*Oui, madame?* I am he."

He smelled sweet like apples or bourbon or maybe it was his hair pomade. Before I could decide exactly what it was, he lit the cigarette, and then everything smelled like that. I extended my hand, and he ignored it.

"I'm Miriam Levenson. Mr. Alsberg told me you would have a room for me here."

"*Entrez,*" he said. He gestured me in, and I entered lugging my suitcase and the recorder.

"*Vous parlez francais,*" I stated the obvious with a smile. I was excited to have found a small bud of culture in this town, an opportunity to use my four years of college French. French, the language of diplomacy and gentility, the language I had learned so that I could use it in Washington and the European capitals. The language I had learned so I could have conversations about art and politics with interesting people. Hearing just a word of it had rekindled my hope in some small way. That hope was quickly dashed.

"Please," he held up his hand, "We speak English." He said it dismissively, as if he didn't want his language sullied by me speaking it.

There were empty wine bottles of different sizes, green glass, purple glass, brown glass. Most of the canvases were nudes of the same dark-haired, dark-eyed woman. They perched on easels and leaned against the walls and weren't particularly good, more like high school art students might do if they were allowed to paint nudes.

His cigarette smoke mixed with the creamy smell of linseed oil and paint. Through the doorway, I saw a table in the kitchen with two plates of half-finished food and, in the sink, a stack of every conceivable dish, plate, saucer, pan, pot, all in an impossibly balanced arrangement. It seemed as if the sink held every dish in the house.

"Have a seat, *s'il vous plaît*," he said, and he gestured to a couch that had been pushed to the margin of the room to make space for easels with paintings. Opposite the settee was yet another canvas of the same voluptuous dark-eyed woman with full lips and a clownishly sultry expression.

There was the drum of footsteps on the stairs behind us. A woman in a thin, flimsy gown was gliding down the treads barefoot. The gown was of some slinky fabric, and there was the sense, the suggestion, that she was nude under it. Her black hair was in a topknot like the plumage of a bird. Her eyes were as dark as Lemurier's. She padded to the kitchen without speaking to us. As she passed us, I recognized her as the woman in the paintings.

"That is Mirlette. She is my wife, as you would say it."

There was a rustle of pots as Mirlette looked for something clean, or relatively clean, in the sink.

"Mr. Alsberg informs me that you're an artist?"

"Yes, but what is more, I am a *muraliste*," he corrected me. "The canvas is much bigger, yes."

He yelled into the kitchen to Mirlette in English, not in French.

"Mirlette, darling, get us some coffee."

Then, as an afterthought, he asked me, "You are American, you want coffee, do you not?"

I forced a smile. "Yes, I would." I didn't, but I was just trying to be cordial.

He smoked his cigarette thoughtfully as he contemplated me like a person would watch an animal at the zoo, waiting for it to perform a trick or scratch itself or yawn. We watched each other from opposite ends of the green velvet couch.

"Do you have a room for me to live in?" I finally asked him.

"It is upstairs." He threw his head in its direction. Then he added, "Have you ever done the modeling?"

I felt like a mouse must feel in the presence of a cat.

"No, never," I said.

"You should, you know. You are very beautiful." He inhaled from his cigarette, and his lower lip let the smoke escape. I smelled his pomade through it.

"I'm here to write," I said. "To listen, interview, and write."

"Most consider writing a lower art form," he said as he waggled his cigarette in the air. It seemed to whisk away the idea of writing. He was obviously trying to engage me in a debate, but I refused to take up his challenge. I had a professor at Barnard who used the same tactic.

Mirlette appeared with the coffee, a fancy silver service with nice china cups and saucers. It all seemed out of place in the near-squalor of the place. I waited for her to pour like a gracious hostess might, but she simply curled up next to Lemurier. Her gown rode up her thighs. She was naked under the gown, all right, and I kept tight eye contact with them both after that. He must have realized that I wasn't going to discuss art with him. He put out his cigarette in his empty coffee cup.

"Your room is upstairs," he said. "Mirlette will show it to you."

She looked comfortable settled into his side, but he gave her the slightest shove. She rose and lifted her arms above her head in a colossal stretch-and-yawn. Her body pressed against the thin silk. She gestured for me to follow her, and I did, up the stairs to a small bedroom.

It was small, a bed, a desk, a chair, a lamp. A window that looked out on Stephenson. No dresser, nothing else. There are, perhaps, jail cells that are better furnished. He joined us at the top of the stairs, and the three of us looked into the tiny room. He had lit another cigarette.

"It will be ten dollars," he said.

"A month?" I asked.

He blew smoke from the side of his mouth.

"For the week," he said.

I thought perhaps he had brought up my suitcase and recorder. I don't know why I thought that; courtesy, maybe. Most of the other men in this town would have. But the suitcase and the recorder were still at the bottom of the stairs. So I retrieved them, catching a whiff of the sculpture of dirty dishes in the sink in the unclean kitchen.

I've spent the evening trying to read, but instead I've listened to their loud jazz music and smelled their cigarette smoke as it permeates everything. I've resorted to opening the windows to let the cold air come in and repel the smells and sounds of this house. I'll return to see Miss Fenerty in the morning, which can't get here soon enough.

Dec. 8, 1936, FWP, Transcript of Bridget Fenerty

Rory Murphy became a municipal judge, did I tell you that last time? He was. After that day his father came to teach the lesson, the Misses O'Riorans never had a lick of trouble from him, no pun intended. But more on our life in New Orleans is what you want to know about, is it?

Maggie never went to school in America. She had gone in Ireland at the old school in Ballinlough and may have had a chance to go in the new country had Da lived. But Ma wanted us to have a house of our own, with chickens and perhaps a milking cow or a goat, and this meant that some had to work rather than attend school, and it was the oldest who had to find a living.

Maggie worked with Ma for the Prudhommes, who were having a succession of children, all born nine months and five minutes apart as they used to say in the Channel. She would come home with stories of their house across Canal Street with the expensive damask drapes and the beautiful marble mantles and the exquisite woodwork and plaster. It didn't sound like an ordinary house; it sounded like a palace. Ma never said a word about the Prudhommes' house. Perhaps she thought it was the sin of envy to mention it.

Maggie mentioned it, though, and went on at length about it. She was perfectly enthralled with it, she was. She spoke of it with such praise that you would think it was her own house, rather than her employer's. Draperies, imported rugs, dishes, silverware. To hear Maggie tell it, it was lavish.

Now, even though Uncle Jack never worked a day as far as we could tell, he was skilled at getting work for others. Yes, a paradox, I think they call it.

There was a man named Hugh McNeil who ran the work on the levee and that's who Uncle Jack spoke to for the job for Dan. Brother was put in the charge of a man named Rufus Connor who was a drayman, the class of men who took goods from the ships on the levee to merchants in different parts of the city. Agents on the levee would fill orders onto the carts, which would be loaded by Irishmen or Negroes, though never together, and the men and their carts would ferry them into the city to the businesses. It helped that Dan could drive a cart and handle animals, and I remember the proud look on my brother's face, perched up on the buckboard high above his team with his delivery behind him, barrels of molasses or sugar, or sacks of coffee destined for one of the restaurants or groceries in the city.

 Mr. Connor had a capacity for foul language that was unmatched in the city. It was said that Mr. Connor could whip a mule so hard that the mule himself would curse. Whenever mothers with small children saw him coming down the street with his wagon and his team, they would cover their children's ears or shoo them indoors into whatever shop door was closest.

He constantly harangued Dan, but Dan was a believer like Da that your work is your worth. Such a serene temperament Dan had, and he bore Mr. Connor's cursing like a saint on the gallows. He worked on Saturdays and Sundays and after school and in the summers, when he would come in at the end of a day's work, his clothes drenched to a darker shade from sweat. He would go straight to sleep, on the floor, and then be gone in the morning for more of the same.

Mr. Connor's temper was legendary and not just reserved for mules. And enough is enough, and few could bear the hailstorm of Rufus Connor's cursing. It was a day that Dan accidently let a barrel of vinegar roll off the back of a cart, and it burst on the cobblestones of Levee Street. Rufus Connor began to beat Dan with the whip he used on the mules. Dan was sitting on the cobblestones, his hands up in the vinegar-soured air to protect himself. Someone threw a brick from an alley, and it hit Mr. Connor in the chest and knocked the wind out of him. He leaned forward and put his hands on his knees. Dan scampered down the alley and never went back. Rufus Connor's mule chewed quietly; in fact, he looked pleased.

Dan found a new job, an inside job that required more thinking and less sweating. New Orleans in those days was a city of the living and the dead. What I mean is, you were either very much alive or very much dead. Perhaps it still is. Eventually, it was Death that would give Dan a boost in his career.

Dec. 8, 1936

I had to ask her.

"I threw pretty good for a girl, my brothers always said," she laughed. "Patch was there. He and Dan and I ran down the alley. We took off so fast, I'm sure all you could see of us were elbows and arseholes, as they used to say it."

I waited for Miss Fenerty to expound on death giving a boost to her brother's career, but she merrily flitted to another subject after suggesting we give the recorder the rest of the day off.

"I myself could keep talking all day, but I fear the machine would wear out," she joked.

I left her preparing for her afternoon nap and decided I would make Mother happy and go look for the synagogue. After all, tomorrow is the first day of Hanukkah, and I'll admit, I'm a little homesick. I've often heard that holidays are the hardest times to be away from home. I can see why now. In looking for the synagogue, I discovered that apparently Lemurier and I aren't the only WPA workers here.

I wandered around the riverfront, but, as much as I searched, I couldn't find it. The man at Kripinsky's Department store had told me it was on the corner of Cotton and Common, that I couldn't miss it. But there was definitely no synagogue there.

There was a young woman there who had an easel set up, and she was painting the bridge, not the new Texas Street Bridge, but the old railroad bridge. She had straight blonde hair cut to shoulder length. She was decidedly feminine in form, but her manner of dress wasn't, overalls and a white shirt with the sleeves rolled up. The shirt was mottled with paint.

"You look lost," she said, though she kept her eyes on her subject and her canvas, as she dabbed paint thoughtfully. "You look like you're looking for something."

"I'm looking for the corner of Common and Cotton," I said.

"This is *Commerce* Street," she said. She looked up. Her eyes were hazel, not quite brown and not quite green, the colors of a forest all mixed together. She smiled a row of perfect teeth. "Common Street is up the hill, all the way up." She gestured with her head in that direction.

"Your accent," I said, "you must be a Texan."

She smiled again.

"I'm afraid I am," she teased. "And your accent. You're most decidedly not from Texas."

"New York. Upper east." I still can't admit to Lower East.

There was a pause as she looked down her nose at her painting and dabbed a light blue spot in the sky. "Common and Cotton. Might you be looking for the synagogue?"

"I'm afraid I am," I said.

She wiped her hands on her overalls and extended her hand.

"Ellie Schultis," she said.

"Miriam Levenson," I said.

"What in heaven's name are you doing in Shreveport, Louisiana with an accent like that?" she asked as she turned back to her work.

"Working for Mr. Roosevelt."

She looked back to me. Her brush was tipped in a rose color and poised just over the canvas.

"Well, I'll be. Me too. Here to paint. You?"

"Here to report, to write." It sounded better than 'here to talk to old people.'

"Well, now."

I looked at the canvas, and I saw the bridge as she saw it, and what's more, as it should have been seen. Colorful, deep hues, oranges, brilliant blues.

"Where are you staying?" she asked.

"Place on Stephenson Street," I said. "You?"

"YWCA," she said gesturing somewhere off and away with her paint brush to wherever it was. There was a pause, not exactly awkward, but noticeable.

"I guess I need to go find my temple, then." I paused. "Nice to meet you."

She dabbed a small dot of rose onto the canvas, part of the sunrise over the bridge. "Nice to meet *you*," she looked up from her work and said with a smile.

As I made the corner of Commerce and Cotton, I looked down and saw that there was paint, rose colored paint, on my hand. When I looked back, I saw her looking at me. I looked away and turned up Cotton Street.

Dec. 9, 1936

I found her today sitting on the porch, rocking in the cool air and sunshine.

"Well, there you are. For the life of me, if you don't get a little prettier every time I see you," she called to me. My face broke open, and my smile and I ascended the porch steps with the recorder.

"Good morning," my smile and I said together.

"Good morning to you," she said, and she got up to open the door for us. "And Happy Hanukkah."

"How did you know I was Jewish?" I asked. She held the screen door open for me as I came through it, the recorder bouncing off my thigh as I struggled with it.

"A tall, pretty New Yorker (New *Yarker*, she pronounced it) like you with the dark hair and eyes, well, it was a hunch. I worked for a Jewish family here in the seventies and eighties. They had a daughter almost as lovely as you."

I blushed. I never blush. She moved on and changed the subject as we sat in the front parlor.

"Have you talked to Champ Lockett yet? He and I are the oldest two in town, but he's the celebrity around here."

"I tried, but no, I don't think he wants to talk," I reminded her as I set up the recorder.

"Oh, that's too bad. Quite a hero he is, they say. I guess you're stuck with me then."

I can't imagine Sergeant Lockett being better company than Miss Fenerty.

"The schoolboys here play a game they call 'Champ.' It involves two lines of boys," her old hands indicated how they were positioned, "throwing rocks and taking turns running through the lines. The teachers discourage it, but of course the boys play it anyway. They've played it for decades, for generations, even. Ever since he came back from Vicksburg."

"Why do they persist?" I asked as I opened the recorder case and checked to see that there was a fresh disk.

"Why do they persist?" she laughed. "Because they're little boys! If the teachers would just let it go, they'd tire of being hit by rocks within a week. Make it against the rules and of course they'll test them."

With my hands clasped in my lap, I pivoted in my seat from the recorder to her. I hadn't intended to, but it was a mannerism of a grade school teacher.

"Tell me more of New Orleans and the Irish Channel back then," I said.

"Very well," she said, and then she squinted as if she were trying to look into the past. Her lips were pursed, and then they broke into a smile.

Dec. 9, 1936, FWP, Transcript of Bridget Fenerty

It was the October following our arrival, and finally, the heat relented, and there was a brisk north wind that was as cool and refreshing as God's mercy. It also brought with it the sound of drums.

It was a Sunday afternoon, and Ma was preparing Sunday dinner for the Prudhommes, her paying family, and we were left in the care of our older siblings. Dan was…let me see…Dan was still working with Mr. Connor at the time, I believe, though I don't remember exactly. Colleen had rounded us up to Mass, and then afterward we had come back home again. Maggie, Colleen, and perhaps Dan were napping, but not Patch and me. We could hear the sound of the drums far across the wind, just loud enough so that if you turned your head around a little you couldn't hear it.

"Sister," Patch said to Maggie, quietly so he wouldn't wake her up. "Bridget and me are going out for a time," he said.

She mumbled, and we took this as permission. It wasn't uncommon for children our age to wander unattended in those days. We followed our ears, up St. Charles to Canal, and then up Canal to Circus Street, which, by the time I returned in the nineties, was renamed Rampart Street, I believe. Then it got louder.

We were curious. We were children, and children are curious. It's one of our strong points when we're children. The Christian Bible says we should be like children to enter the Kingdom of Heaven, but most people spend the better part of their lives trying to be grown up and sophisticated.

Well, we rounded the corner, and there we found what we were looking for and what we were warned against: Congo Square. The place where dancing and singing and shouting and some said spell-casting occurred. It seemed as though every slave in New Orleans was there, and perhaps they were, when they were allowed free time to do as they pleased on Sunday afternoons. Drums were thrumming, thumping, the hoarse wail of an instrument that looked like a hollowed out tree limb, banjos, fiddles, anything that could make a noise. Dancing in a circle, those forming the ring clapping and shouting.

The air was cool and crisp and smoky, and the ground was packed smooth by hundreds, thousands of black feet over decades of time. We pushed our way to see, and in the middle was dancing, some sort of jig we'd never seen before. I felt a slight shove on my back, and I stumbled into the ring. I looked about me, paused a moment, and then I began dancing. Patch looked at me with a big smile, and I danced over and grabbed his hand and pulled him in. And then there we were in the circle, dancing with the Africans as the ring of people was clapping and shouting and laughing at us. My red hair and Patch's sandy brown hair, plastered down sweaty to our smiling, pale freckled faces, serious looks on them. I clutched the hem of my dress in my hands and watched my feet and our shadows as they danced together, all of us. All of our dark shadows, African and Irish, dancing with the same joy.

Far across the Creole Quarter on the other side of it, the coffin ships were bringing in more Irish. But my brother and I were alive and joyful and dancing to the drums and the shouting and the handclapping, and the Africans all seemed amused with us and we were just as amused at them and ourselves as well.

And that day was a grand day altogether.

Dec. 10, 1936

Her face dissolved into a look of whimsy and enchantment as she described the dancing. Her old spotted hands clapped silently as her mind traveled back there. At last, she drifted into a sleep, and I realized that she had been on the verge of a nap when I arrived. Her ankles twitched like a dog having a pleasant dream. Nina covered her with a blanket and whispered with a smile that she would tell Miss Fenerty that I would be back another day. I carefully shut down the recorder, not wanting to bump around with it and wake Miss Fenerty. Nina helped me to the car with it and then stood on the curb and waved as I left.

I pulled down to the corner and onto Spring Street. When I stepped on the clutch, it gave way and was like stepping into thin air, like missing a step on a staircase. The gears rattled under the hood, and the Packard ground to a halt. I'll admit I was just a little flustered. I braced myself for a chorus of honking horns and shouts from the traffic behind me. What I got surprised me.

A car pulled behind and stopped. The door opened and a smartly dressed woman got out and trotted delicately up to me. She tapped on the glass with gloved hands. Her face appeared under her cloche and over the fur collar of her coat. She was pretty and middle-aged, with dark hair and eyes and porcelain skin.

"You havin' trouble?" Her voice was muted by the glass. I rolled down the window, and the cold pressed in.

"Let me help you, sugar," she said. Then she began directing traffic around us. Several people stopped their cars behind hers. A man with a too-short tie that slid down his large gut came and a Negro man in overalls. They were joined by half a dozen others who seemed to come out of nowhere. They began pushing the Packard, bodies of different shapes and sizes, different colors of skin and clothing. All of their faces contorted as they exerted themselves.

"Pull off to the side," a man in a Panama hat said. He was red in the face. I steered the car to the curb.

They stood there huffing in the cold, bright sunlight, their breath rising out of them as if they were a set of steam engines. A man in overalls put his hand on the door handle and said, "Ma'am, if you don't mind, let me take a look."

I got out, and he got in. He pushed his left foot forward, the dingy blue denim pulling tight over his knee.

"Yessum, it's the clutch all right. May take fifty dollars or more to fix it," he said. The crowd was beginning to fade away. Traffic resumed down Spring Street.

The woman in the cloche hat and fur-collared coat said, "Just leave it there. I'm sure Mr. Wray won't mind until you can come see about it. Do you need a ride?"

"Can you give me a ride to Stephenson? It's off Line Avenue."

"Sure can, sugar."

I wrestled the recorder into the back seat, almost tossing it in because of its weight. She smiled at me as I sat in the front seat with her, and we pulled into traffic. She was a pretty woman, on her way to bridge with some friends, but she said she didn't mind a bit going out of her way. My accent makes me stand out like a foghorn in an orchestra, and of course she noticed.

"My husband and I honeymooned in New York ten years ago. Such a grand place," she said as she smiled over the wheel and down Line Avenue. "We'd love to go back, but it's so hard with young children. I feel lucky to get out to bridge club."

I realized she was taking time out from her only outing, her only furlough from the monotonous business of raising children and tending house, just to help a stranger.

"I hope I'm not keeping you," I said.

"Oh, it's no bother," she smiled.

Dec. 11, 1936

With the Packard 'feeling poorly' as they say here, I took the bus downtown today. I wrestled the Presto up the steps. The big brown case slapped against the front of my thighs with hollow thumps, and the latches added a rattle to the melody. A man in a gray suit stood up and gave me his seat. He was middle-aged and handsome, with swarthy looks complete with the beginnings of a five o' clock shadow at nine o'clock in the morning. When we were downtown and at the bus stop at Common and Crockett, I stood up and brushed the wrinkles out of my dress. As I reached down for the recorder, the man picked it up and followed me down the steps with it. The bus driver waited patiently for us.

"Do you need any help with this?" he said.

"No, thank you," I said, genuinely touched. "I'm just up the street here."

"To Miss Fenerty's? Well, tell Miss Biddy that Joe Warren said hey," he said, and he ascended the steps of the bus. Through the window, I saw him sit down in the seat I had occupied and open his paper.

Today I found her reading again. Nina let me in, and there was Miss Fenerty, her glasses perched on her nose with a copy of *A Christmas Carol* in her lap. Her eyes looked up from the book and over to me, and she smiled.

"Oh, there you are, dear. I was looking forward to your visit." And when she said it, I felt the air between us warm.

"A Mr. Joe Warren said to tell you hello. I met him on the bus just now."

"Ah, Little Joe. What a pistol he was when he was a boy. He was friends with the Eaves boys I used to look after. All of those boys. Such characters! A tribe of little wild Indians, they were, delightful if you didn't let them get your goat. Here's the secret to boys..." She leaned in and her eyebrows went up, and she looked to the side as if there were someone nearby in the room who might want this piece of information, "...always get their goat first, then they won't be able to get yours."

I smiled as she chuckled.

"Dickens?" I asked her as I looked at the book in her lap.

She held it up in her old hand and said, "I always read this around Christmas time. One of my favorites. I like any story where an Englishman gets the devil and his piss scared out of him. Let me read you this."

She peered down through the small lenses to the page. The words flowered out of her mouth like a trailing vine of brogue.

"How now!" said Scrooge, caustic and cold as ever. "What do you want with me?"
"Much!" -Marley's voice, no doubt about it.

She laid an old envelope into the book gingerly to mark her place and then looked up and closed the book with a smile.

"What do you want? Much! Ha! And Marley's ghost dripping with chains on account of wanting so much! And isn't that the way of it, then? Now what were we talking about when you visited last?" she asked as she laid the book on the side table, looking under her glasses and down her small nose.

"The Channel," I reminded her, "Dancing in Congo Square. You and your brother."

Dec. 11, 1936, FWP, Transcript of Bridget Fenerty

Yes, I believe you're right, we were talking about New Orleans and the Channel, weren't we?

Across Canal Street where Ma worked were the Creole women with their crinoline skirts and their fancy bonnets and parasols and their poisonous looks at us, the Irish who were there to dig the canals and unload the ships and keep house for them with a polite *Oui, Mam'selle* and *Oui, monsieur.*

It was the only world I knew well, as I only can remember what I've already told you about Ballinlough. Ma and Maggie were working with the Prudhommes. Aunt Peg was working keeping house for a family. Dan was working for Rufus Connor. Colleen was doing mending after school. Patch and I were going to school. Everyone was working or going to school or both. Everyone except Uncle Jack. Uncle Jack didn't want anything to do with work of any sort. He drank a lot and came in late, drunk and singing:

> *Ten thousand Micks, they swung thar picks,*
> *to dig the New Canal.*
> *But the Chol-er-ay was stronger'n they,*
> *An' twoice it killed them all.*

We would hear it, Colleen, Patch and me. Ma and Maggie slept in one of the two beds in the room we rented, and we three, the younger ones, slept in the other. My older brother, Dan, slept on the floor. I'm sure they all heard Uncle Jack, too.

Colleen slept in the middle between Patch and me, to keep us from giggling and poking each other. I was six or seven, I suppose, and Patch a year older and Colleen two years older than him. She was very proper and very pious, and Patch and I were most certainly not.

Anyway, Uncle Jack Hennigan would come in late, and Patch would whisper, "Here comes Uncle Jack again, drunk off his arse."

"Don't say that," Colleen would whisper. "That's a bad word."

"What is?"

"That word."

"What? Arse?"

"Don't say it," Colleen would hiss. "Say backside or bottom, rather."

"Arse arse arse arse," Patch would whisper.

"Shhh. Mind your language," Colleen would say, trying to sound like Ma.

"Arse arse arse arse arse arrrrrrrrrrrse!" I would whisper it to her, and then Patch would join in, and we would shake and giggle until we wheezed, and poor sister was on the verge of tears.

"Feck feck feckopp," he whispered to her like a chicken might say it.

"Stop it," she moaned, and then I would join in whispering if I could stop my wheezing and snickering long enough. The rickety bed was vibrating with our pent up laughter. We only stopped because we were giggling so hard that we couldn't say anything. We didn't want to wake up Ma, as she was dead tired from work, but we did.

"Shhh, what are you children carryin' on about?" she groaned from her bed across the room. The gray darkness was tinged with the distant sounds of drunken manly revelry outside in the night streets.

Colleen: "Ma, they're sayin' bad words."

"Sweet weepin' Jaysus," Ma would say. "Could ye just be quiet for a time?"

"But Ma," Colleen whined.

Ma raised her voice into the dark air of the room we shared.

"No one use words of any sort," she thundered, and it was silent except for the sounds of carousing outside the window and the snores of Uncle Jack Hennigan in the next room. On the other side of Colleen, I could almost feel Patch smile.

But back to Uncle Jack Hennigan. He would sing late at night, coming in from drinking. You could hear him coming down the street, far away, singing it, *Ten thousand Micks, they swu-ung their picks, to dig the New Canaaaalllll....*

It would get louder as he approached. Then he would sing it as he relieved himself in the alley to the spattering on the dirt and the house and himself, leaning with his hand on the side of the house and pausing between lines as he shook himself. He would sing it as he fumbled with the door, and then in the bed in the other room that he and Aunt Peg shared, and then up to the ceiling, until it trailed into a snore and then finally he went to sleep.

He wouldn't sing it in the mornings. I suppose his head hurt then. Every morning, Uncle Jack would take the pledge to forego the drink from that day forward, a pledge that would last until noon or so. Uncle Jack's thirst slept in until then, and then it would reawaken and the two of them, Uncle Jack Hennigan and his thirst, would go for a sociable pint.

Most of the other men of the Channel were quarrelsome lot, working like beasts in the day, and at night drinking and then fighting for the pure love of it. They didn't want anything to do with the soil and farming. They wanted jobs that were independent of the earth, the earth and its potato that had betrayed them. They generally made about a dollar or so a day, loading all manner of things off the ships, goods from everywhere, and loading cotton in bales and sugar in great wooden barrels onto the ships. In the heat and the rain and the cold and the sun. Up the planks, down the planks, singing, cursing, sweating.

In their leisure hours, they would fight chickens, dogs, each other. Drinking and shouting at one another, punching each other bloody until one fell and one part of the crowd cheered and the other part cursed and the money changed hands, and then more fighting. Chickens, dogs, men. At least once, a ring was constructed, and the men had a bull fight a bear. God's own truth but it happened.

When they had fought all they wanted or could, they danced to the scratch of a fiddle, all the old tunes, dancing with each other and with the lewd women who consorted with them. We children heard it all through the window, laughter, music, singing, glass breaking, the shrieks of the women rounding into more laughter.

Well, let's turn this contraption off, then. I have something for you.

Dec. 11, Fri, later

She gave me a Christmas gift, a creamy envelope with two train tickets to New York. Then she nonchalantly turned to one of the bookcases that flanked the mantle, browsing through the vertical spines.

"Have you read much Shakespeare?" she asked as her old finger hovered over them.

"These are two tickets to New York," I said, ignoring her question.

She turned and smiled at me.

"Well, it must be hard to be away from home this time of year," she said. "They're round trip, so don't worry, I'm not trying to get rid of you."

She turned back to the wall of books and continued searching them.

"How about Stevenson? *Treasure Island.* Or *A Child's Garden of Verses.* Did you read that as a child?"

I ignored her question again.

"There are two," I said.

"Yes, so you can take whoever you like."

"Do you want to go?"

"Oh," she laughed, "I've been once, and it's a grand place entirely, but take someone else this time. Someone your own age."

Nina passed through the parlor carrying an armload of kitchen towels. I held up the tickets and said, "Nina, would you like to go to New York?"

"Now, Miss Miriam," Nina said, "Me and my husband, the reverend, we gonna have a baby." She patted her stomach. I had no idea; she's of such a size I'm sure her secret would have been concealed for some time. "Besides, it's Christmas, and we have our program, and nobody misses our program. We've got everything but a real camel."

"In my days I've known of a jackass or two you could've used," Miss Fenerty said to the wall of books as her eyes kept scanning them through her lenses.

"I expect you have," Nina said as her mouth strained against a smile.

"It would be a lovely trip even if you have to go by yourself, now wouldn't it? Maybe you could find yourself a young gentleman," Miss Fenerty said. She had given up on showing me books and was facing me, leaning forward on her cane. "Whisk him off to the city and have yourselves a time." One of her hands flew from the head of her cane to demonstrate how I might whisk him off. I stood there with the two tickets in my hand, dumbfounded.

"Well, dear, I suppose you'll need to be off to find yourself a companion to the wonderful city of New *Yark*, and won't it be just grand indeed? Certainly there must be someone around here who'd like to go."

I left the recorder at her house, in her front parlor. Even though there are a number of other names on my list, honestly I'm not concerned with them. Most of them are out of town and require the use of the car. And anyway, I've only scratched the surface with Miss Fenerty.

Dec. 12, 1936 Sat

Mother will be glad to know that I kept the Sabbath this week. B'nai Zion is a gray stone building with four Greek columns, standing at the corner of Common and Cotton, just where Ellie said it would be. Across the intersection is the Scottish Rite Temple, another handsome building. I walked up the steps of the temple in the cold and was greeted by two men in suits and yarmulkes.

"Good mawnin', ma'am," they said.

Inside, men and women sat together, and there were children and old people. Young people were eyeing and flirting, and their mothers were discouraging them, and their fathers were wishing they were young. Old men fought sleep, and old wives poked them in the ribs. Hebrew was read and spoken. Just like in New York, but with a drawl.

Rabbi Brill told a story from ten years ago at the height of the Klan when a cross was painted on the side of a synagogue in a town in Georgia. Members of the local Christian congregations were at a loss as to whether to help their neighbors remove the sign of their faith or not. Rabbi Brill said in the end they helped remove the graffiti cross and in doing so left an indelible image of their kindness and faith on the hearts of the congregation. He closed by saying that, as Jews, our kindness and faith should also be our indelible symbol.

A man of about sixty served as cantor. In the dim light, he ascended the bimah with a tallit shawl draped over his shoulders to read in a voice that was deep and gravelly and very southern, and it was strange to hear the Torah read with such an accent. It was just as odd to hear the conversations on the steps afterward:

"Y'all have a Happy Hanukah, now."

"Y'all, too. Your mama and them comin'?"

And so forth.

An older couple and I were talking when a boy of about nine or so approached us. I could tell from how the man reached out without looking to gather in the boy that he was his grandson or nephew. The man put his hand on the boy's shoulder and kept talking to me. He glanced down to the boy and broke off in midsentence when his wife asked the boy:

"Abram? What happened?"

The boy looked up to the man and smiled with a bruise that encompassed his eye.

"Let me guess. Y'all were playin' *Champ*, right?" the man asked.

The boy nodded with a grin. The man grinned back at him and then at me.

"Our grandson," he said proudly.

"Why do they still play that game?" the boy's grandmother asked. She was a pretty woman who knew how to make herself even prettier, a woman with distinctive sleepy eyes that gave her a relaxed, cosmopolitan air. Her fondness for jewelry was obvious.

"They still play it because they're not supposed to," the man said. "Same reason we did fifty years ago."

The boy saw someone, another boy his age, and darted in between grownups like a fish being returned to the water. The edge of his yarmulke flapped as he ran.

After what seemed to be two dozen or so introductions and a dozen unremembered names, I looked down Common Street. It was Saturday, of course, and over on Texas Street, the sidewalks were beginning to boil with crowds of Christmas shoppers. For some people in the surrounding villages, this is their one trip 'to town.' I walked the few blocks down to Crockett and Miss Fenerty's where I found her dusting and Nina helping. Or actually, the other way around.

"Oh, mercy! It's Miriam," Miss Fenerty exclaimed joyfully. "Nina, put us on some tea."

We talked about current events, about Hitler in Europe, about Roosevelt, about the economy. She wove our conversation like an invisible tapestry, rich and colorful, all the while sitting with the feather duster across her lap. We talked about the Klan and Father Coughlin.

"Always a finger to point at someone else to blame their troubles on, isn't it then?" she said.

Somehow, we began talking about philosophy, the transition from the Klan to philosophy seamless and natural in her telling it.

"This Kierkegaard, now who is he?" she asked with a puzzled look on her face.

"He wrote about nihilism."

"And that means the belief in nothing, am I correct?"

"Yes," I answered. It sounded silly to me now.

"Well, it's none of my business, but if you ask me, they all seem to me to be very sour people. How can you believe in nothing? Where's the joy in that? It seems to me they're all thinking very hard and getting unhappier on account of it."

She smiled at having made her point and said, "I was telling you about the Channel days, now wasn't I?"

I set the lever and its stylus down as the blank turned in a licorice-black circle.

Dec. 12, 1936, FWP, Transcript of Bridget Fenerty

Aunt Peg died in the spring of 1849, and, when that happened, Uncle Jack was despondent.

She had come home from working for her family, the Carrolls, yes, it was the Carrolls. What did I say before, the Carsons? They were the Carrolls, sure. Well, anyway, she had come in and gone straight to bed. Ma had brought her tea which Aunt Peg didn't drink. It just sat there. She left for work, Ma did, and told my brother and me we were to keep a watch on Aunt Peg. We weren't sure what for. Patch and I stood at her bedside as she slept oblivious to us. We had never seen her keep still for so long.

The day crept forward, and then night fell. Of course, Uncle Jack didn't come in until we were well to bed, singing the song about the New Canal and relieving himself in the alley and fumbling with the door. We barely woke to it. It had become a sort of drunken lullaby for us.

In the morning we woke to Uncle Jack yelling, "Get up, woman, ye'll be late for work. Get up!" Then there was a howl. It was Uncle Jack.

Aunt Peg had died in the night. I don't know what of, and I still don't. People just died then, they died young and of uncertain causes and in great numbers. I suspect for Aunt Peg it was exhaustion.

Uncle Jack's tone changed entirely.

"What'll I do now, my Peggy? What, then?" Uncle Jack moaned. "Oh, my girl, if you just wake up, I'll never take another drop, I swear, I swear it to you." We gathered in the doorway as he pulled Aunt Peg's lifeless body to himself, and he wept so that I thought he would die, too, and we would bury the two of them together. I've never seen a grown man so upset, before then or since then.

But Uncle Jack didn't die, and we buried Aunt Peg by herself. He knelt in front of the wooden cross on her grave, running his hands through his hair.

"What'll I do now, Peg? What, then?" he said.

Well, I'll tell you what Uncle Jack Hennigan did: he drank even more. We wouldn't see him for days at a time, and then he would come in and look for Ma with his hat in his hand and staring at the ground, wanting to apologize for his absence and his drunkenness. He smelled horrible, rancid, filthy, a shade better than death.

"'Twas only me and me battles with the cray-ture."

The drink, he meant, of course. Ma was working for the Prudhommes, and it was just Patch and me at home on the Saturdays he came around, the older ones of us working, and Ma herself working. By that night, Uncle Jack Hennigan was drunk again, carousing with anyone who had a penny and sleeping it off somewhere, likely on the levee on the bales of cotton where so many slept then who didn't have a roof. When it rained, many would sleep under the shop awnings or stagger off to the cemeteries and pry up the slabs of granite or open the doors to crypts and sleep off their drunk there out of the rain. The dead sleeping with the dead drunk.

Well, do you think that's enough for today?

Dec. 13, 1936

Quiet Sunday. The weather was mild today, and it's hard to believe it's winter here, too. I rode the Louisiana and Line Avenues trolley downtown, a few white churchgoers in the front, a few black churchgoers in the back. On Southern Avenue was a beautiful building that spilled across a large lot with trees and gardens. I asked someone what it was. The St. Vincent's Convent, someone said.

Downtown, I alighted from the bus as the bells of the Presbyterian, Methodist, Baptist, and Catholic churches all competed to be heard. I wandered around looking in shop windows and then stopped to visit the Packard, disabled on Spring Street. Finally, I ended up at the courthouse looking at the Confederate monument rising up from the lawn.

As I looked up at the towering man in granite, I heard a man's voice nearby. It was a father and son. Like me, they were looking up at the statue. The father had his hands in his pockets. The boy had his hands at his eyebrows, shielding away the glaring sun. Stony Sergeant Lockett stared north.

"Well, there he is, Johnny, Champ hisself," the man said with the tone of a tour guide. "It was at Vicksburg, the Yankees had us bottled up against the river, but we wouldn't let em in." The man's hands swept in an arc to describe the battle lines. "Well, the Oh-hiya boys was knockin' hard and was about to punch a hole in our lines, when there goes Champ, Champ Lockett, fella you see there up on that pedestal. He run through the lines," the man's hand pushed forward as if initiating a handshake or a dive, "through a deep ravine" his hand dove and rose, "with bullets swarmin' like bees," his hands shook in the air around an unseen globe in front of him, "over to get the Alabama boys to close up the gap. Saved the day, is all he did. Got himself captured for his troubles, but he saved the day." The man put his hands in his pockets again.

The boy cocked his head and looked back up into the sky at the statue.

"Who are these men, daddy?" the boy asked of the busts at each corner under Champ Lockett.

"Generals and such," the man said.

"But what are their names?"

"Oh, Lee and another'n. Best we head on to church now."

They made their way down Texas Street up the hill and then vaulted the steps of the Methodist Church. The service had begun, and, when the door opened to let them in, it let out a stiff blast of organ music and muffled it again as it shut.

After that, for lack of anything else to do, I rode trolleys for a while. The Allendale, the Highland, the Southern Avenue. Just before noon, I thought to buy candles to celebrate Hanukkah on Stephenson Street tonight (by myself), but then I realized you can't buy things like that here on Sunday. The shops are closed.

Around noon, I got back on the L&L trolley to head home down Line Avenue, and there she was again, Ellie, leaving the Baptist church in a simple print dress with a sweater over it. Her threadbare-gloved hands held a Bible near her hip. A navy blue ribbon held her yellow hair. Her step is distinctive, slightly pigeon toed.

I got up from my seat and tried to get her attention through the window, but she didn't see me. She turned on Travis, probably on her way back to the Y. I pressed my cheek into the cold glass as she got smaller. Several other people turned to see the object of my gaze.

When I got back to Stephenson and was in my room, there was a call. I could hear the phone outside my door on the landing; it was startling, as we rarely receive phone calls. But Lemurier answered it with his customary greeting in accented English: "Hello-who-is-it-what-do-you-want?"

A voice buzzed and crackled on the other end. Through the static, I could easily hear New York. It was Irving. Lemurier handed me the phone as if it were a dead animal.

"Who is that man?" Irving's small voice wanted to know. He sounded angry and hurt, and I guess I don't blame him. I explained to him that it was one of my housemates, a man and his wife (I stretched the truth on that one-I don't think they're actually married) and that we were sharing a house to defray expenses.

Irving exploded. "I'll pay your rent. I'll buy you a goddam house," his faraway voice rose out of the phone. My voice rose to match his. Irving may be obtuse, but he's never cursed at me.

"I can make my own way on this, Irving," I yelled into the phone, and I hung up. I sat shaking in a chair on the landing. The phone sat smugly beside me. After a few minutes, it rang again. This time rather than Angry Irving, it was Contrite Irving, gushing with apologies, though I could tell he still wasn't pleased with my housing arrangements. We made a conciliatory peace. He told me he loved me; I told him I loved him. He told me he missed me; I told him I missed him. It got syrupy sweet after that; I endured it.

As I hung up, I thought, how did he get my phone number? The operator? Mr. Alsberg? Mother?

Dec. 13, 1936, FWP, Transcript of Bridget Fenerty

It was on Ash Wednesday, the year that they rebuilt the St. Louis Cathedral in the square[1] that I first met Ned Hennessy. I was eight, and he was nine, as far as he knew, though he led a rather, shall I say, *unregimented* life as a boy. Much like Huck Finn, he was, and I was a girl version of Tom Sawyer.

My sister Colleen and I had just left St. Patrick's on Camp Street. She insisted that we go get ashes, so we did. Then we made our way home down Camp, she very satisfied with herself, and me very relieved to have gotten my ashes and then gotten out of there. Everyone was walking down the street with the smudge on their foreheads, going about their business and being reminded of their own ashes only when they saw them on someone else. It was a day that hinted at spring, the air smelling brown and green and sweet, and the flowers on the verge of bursting but not quite, only green pods. The leaves in the trees and the grass were lime green and new.

It had been a long Mass, as it generally was with Colleen, with no room

---

[1] 1850

for daydreaming or craning one's neck around to see who else was there and which old men were drunk or sleeping or both, there like me, only because they were in the custody of a determined female.

"Pay attention, Bridget," Colleen would whisper as the priest droned in Latin and swung incense around. Altar boys stood around him in their frilly vestments, surely equally bored and equally under duress imposed by a pious mother somewhere in the church, beaming red, white, and yellow with pride.

Piety was my sister Colleen's strong suit. Even though she was just a little older than me, she was forever dragging me by my hand to church. We never missed a holy day of obligation, no matter how obscure the saint whose feast day it was. She was devout and righteous, Colleen was, a pious little thing that won the admiration of the older women and nuns at St. Patrick's on Camp Street. Anyone could see she was surely headed for life in the convent.

Oh, but how we tormented poor Colleen, Patch and I! On Palm Sundays, we tickled the back of her neck with the blessed branches and made her swat at them thinking it was a fly. I once told her that the top of St. Alphonsus looked like a turnip. Of course, I did it to get her goat, which it did.

"Don't say that," she said. "It's the house of our Lord."

"Well, it does," I said nonchalantly. "A great big turnip. Upside down. Look! See it? The root of it is at the top. Perhaps St. Alphonsus is the patron saint of turnips!" She would exhale in exasperation as I smirked. What a fine pastime, needling Colleen and her righteousness.

She would drag me to confession and insist that I go first while she sat on the pew nearest the confessional and chanted the Rosary just loud enough that Father and I could hear her. Then she would waltz into the confessional after me and appear pristine in comparison to me and my sins. So I decided to do Colleen's confessing for her.

Old Father Mullon was a balding man with a small cloud of white hair around his shiny scalp. We sat down in the dark with the partition between us, the righteous on one side, the sinner on the other. There was the customary pause, and then he asked me through the screen if I had examined my conscience.

"Aye, Father," I said.

"What is it you have to confess to God, then?" he asked.

I usually confessed a few paltry sins. I called my brother a name. I lied to my teacher, Miss O'Rioran. I had a bite of ham on Friday not thinking what day it was. But then I would think about Colleen sitting outside of the confessional there on the pew with her shining array of non-sins, all along the lines of, "I fell asleep praying the Rosary," or "I had but a penny to give the cripple man on Poydras," or the like.

So I told Father Mullon some really good articles, sins worthy of confession, on Colleen's account.

"Father, I confess to you that I kicked me brother in the shins for callin' me an arse, and for that I'm truly sorry. But my sister, Colleen, ach, what a black conscience she must have! I don't really think she has the heart to tell ye all of it."

Then I outlined her iniquities as Father tried to butt in and stop me. Stealing apples off the carts at St. Mary's Market. Taking the Lord's name in vain, and in all sorts of imaginative combinations, which I gave him examples of, of course. And the Roman feasts of meat on Fridays. What shame! I paused when I thought I had dug the hole deep enough.

"You know, my child, 'tis also a sin to lie," he said.

"Oh, 'tis one, sure, Father," I would say, not realizing that it was me he was calling a liar. "And she can tell a lie and would surely do it when the truth would serve her better."

He declined to absolve me of kicking my brother in the shins for calling me an arse until I had done further reflection, and I was excused, and I couldn't have given a fiddler's fart one way or the other. As I exited, Colleen entered the booth with her lace doily on her head, and I whispered to her, "He knows all of it on you, you know."

Yes, sister loved the church as Christ himself did. Perhaps it was the theater of it she liked, all for free, which was the right price for so many then. Mother attended Sundays if she was done with her family, her paying family, that is, and Colleen took great pride in shooing and nagging my brother and me into decent enough shape for Mass.

What was it, now? Oh yes, Ned Hennessy.

Well, walking home from Mass on this Ash Wednesday, Colleen was giving me a lecture on living a good life, which included regular prayer, receiving all the sacraments, and temperance, and above all, not picking my nose in church. I was holding my shoes and walking barefoot and enjoying the coolness of the cobblestones under my soles, getting ready for Colleen to scold me about being barefoot, which she did.

"Well," I replied, "Jesus Christ didn't wear shoes, did he, sister?"

"That's different, Bridget," she said. "They didn't wear them then. They wore sandals."

"But they weren't shoes, then, were they? Sandals aren't the same as shoes. You could see their toes, plain as day, you could. But wasn't it so, then?"

Just then, we round Julia Street, and I see two boys fighting. They were fighting in the style of little boys, wild punches that put their own selves on the ground, where they quickly got up, and then headlocks, and then punches into headlocks, and then shedding headlocks and tripping the other. One boy straddled the other and was laying into him.

As I got closer, I could see that it was the Hennessy boy, Ned Hennessy, who had my brother Patch on the ground. I ran toward them, without thinking, my threadbare dress pulled against my little body by the wind as I ran, the doily that Colleen had put there flying off. I was only eight or nine then, my bare feet stirring up clods of mud.

I pulled the boy off Patch and threw him to the ground and straddled him. I started hitting him until his nose was bloody. He cried, and snot and blood came out of his nose, and he begged me to stop. I could hear Colleen from far away shrieking for me to stop, and finally I did. My little chest rose and fell and rose, again and again as I sat across my brother's attacker. Patch pulled me off the boy, who kept bawling up to the sky with his palms cradling his nose. Patch shielded him from me, oddly protecting the boy who had been tormenting him. Over Patch's shoulder, I used the language I'd heard the men in the alley use after they'd been drinking:

"Keep yer feckin' hands off me brother, unless ye be wantin' more of the same."

I don't know who was mortified the most, Patch, Colleen, or Ned Hennessy.

"Sister, sister," Patch kept saying. He would rather have taken the beating than the ridicule of having his little sister do his fighting for him. Patch handed Ned his hat and told him, "Not a word of this. To anyone, you understand?"

Ned wiped his bloody nose on his forearm and nodded, then wiped it again on the other forearm. It would have been equally embarrassing for either of them. Colleen shrieked again when Ma came home.

"Ma, Ma, Ma," she said, "Bridget's been fighting and swearing."

Ma's face was drooping with fatigue as she sat on the side of her bed and removed her stockings and shoes.

"What is it she said?" Ma asked while she rubbed the pain out of her feet.

Colleen whispered it into Ma's ear. Ma stopped rubbing her feet and looked at me.

"And where did ye learn such language, then?" Ma asked. Her mouth twisted a little, and I believe she was trying to suppress a smile. Her shoes and stockings were off, and her feet were propped on the bed frame. Colleen looked very righteous and satisfied, and I could've killed her.

"Listening to the men in the alley," I says.

"Well," Ma says, "fetch the soap. Yer mouth is filthy." [*Laughter*]

Curiously, Ned and I became friends after that. Perhaps he admired a strong female. But boys are like that; they can fight one moment and then lay down the grudge and be fast friends afterward, laughing it all off with their arms clamped around each other's shoulders. And so of course, that's exactly what we became. Best friends.

Dec. 14, 1936

Last night, the cold returned. This morning, I walked down to Line Avenue hugging myself against it, and then I waited for the Louisiana and Line Avenues trolley. It pulled up, the tether on top like an antenna reaching for the wires that fed it in sparks. I got on with several others, each of us dropping our fares in the box, a nickel and a penny, a heavy plunk and a light click. The driver, a man in a cap and bowtie, pulled the door shut with a semicircular sweep of a handle. The bus was full, and a nicely dressed man in a suit and hat got up and gestured for me to take his seat. As I turned to sit down, I saw her again.

She was in the very back seat, sitting among the Negroes there. Her cloche was pulled down on her head, but I knew it was her from the fine blonde hair that pushed out from under the hat's edges. She wore the same sweater from the day before over the same plain cotton dress, a light summer color and evidently one of the few she owns. Everyone here, like New York, is in darker colors. Everyone who can afford it.

She was sketching in a pad, flanked by two Negro men, one old and one young who sat looking off in two directions away from her. The windows were foggy from the cold air, and I doubt they could see much.

Another man, a white man who was sitting near the front, went to the back of the trolley and said, "Miss, you don't have to sit back here. You can have my seat."

She looked up from her sketch and said, "I believe I can sit anywhere I like, thank you," and she returned to her sketch. The Negro men looked around nervously, putting their hands in their laps, casting glances to Ellie and looking out the window, anywhere but at her and the man offering his seat. The older man inched away from her in his seat.

"Really, miss," the man said, and he reached for her hand. She pulled it back.

"I thank you, but I have a perfectly fine seat here. Now go on, please sir."

The man gave up and steadied himself on the silver poles against the motion of the trolley as he made his way to the front again where he sat down. Ellie looked at me and smiled, and then looked back down to her sketch.

The trolley stopped at Olive and then Jordan and then went under the railroad underpass into downtown. People got on and got off, but the trolley stayed generally full. When we pulled in front of the courthouse, the side facing Texas Street, the side with the Confederate monument, I looked back to see her putting her sketches in her satchel. As this is the end of the line, most

97

of us got off.

I waited for her there. I was looking at the soldier on the monument, and past him to the white-only and colored drinking fountains. The stone soldier was surrounded by the busts of four other men, Beauregard, Lee, and Jackson, whom I recognized as Confederate generals, and Henry Watkins Allen, governor at the time of secession. Before the monument itself, a woman in a flowing robe is sculpted. The sign says she represents Clio, the muse of history, writing in her book. There's also a plaque there, *Dedicated May 1, 1906, United Daughters of the Confederacy.*

"That's Champ Lockett on the pedestal," her voice said behind me. "I asked when I got here. They say the sculptor used his picture from when he was young. The committee insisted he be used. A Texan sculpted it, out of Texas granite."

She was next to me, the girl Ellie, the painter, the artist. We studied his face, his profile. It was poised looking north, as they all are here, on every courthouse lawn in every town in every parish and county in every Southern state. Looking north at the enemy. Perhaps they should be looking around them.

"From an artistic standpoint, it's really very well done. What do you think he's thinking?" I asked.

"Probably trying to decide what he hates worse, Yankees or pigeons."

I laughed, and she smiled. "I think pigeons are more of an immediate threat right now," I said.

"In case of pigeons, I guess he prays for rain."

We walked together down Marshall to a diner that caters to lawyers and judges and their clerks and secretaries. In the window, drawn in tempera paint, was a crude Santa with a cotton ball beard, next to a reindeer that had the proportions of a mule with tree branch-like antlers and a large red nose. The waitress, a woman of no more than eighteen, brought us two coffees. Ellie took hers black.

"Can I see what you were sketching?" I asked.

She pulled her satchel from below her seat and produced a sheaf of papers. They were cream-colored, the thick sheets of paper that artists use. On them were scenes of swamps and hills and forests and cotton fields. On another were bolls of cotton, nets of fish, oil derricks, corn in great bushel baskets, mules pulling wagons of sugar cane. As I looked through them, she watched me. I could see her in the corner of my vision.

"They're ideas for a mural that's going to go on a building they're putting up at the fairgrounds. This one," she said. She produced another drawing from her satchel and slid it in front of me. It was one of those architect's renderings of a building that's to be massive and in the new Art Deco style. A very attractive edifice, I have to say.

"It'll be called the Louisiana State Exhibit Museum. The murals will go on the inside, in this recess behind these columns." She pointed to the area on the drawing with paint-spotted fingers and took a sip of coffee. Her dainty lips were pursed full on the rim of the heavy white china cup. "I can't seem to get my co-worker motivated. Every time I show him an idea, he shoots it down. He still won't get started, and he won't let me get started."

"I like these," I said, and I honestly did. They were bold but had a hidden subtlety to them. The cotton looked soft and downy. The oil derricks gleamed hard as powerfully built men in tin helmets attended them. The mules were muscular, and I could almost see their motion as they strained against the wagons of cane.

"Thanks," Ellie said as she put them back in her satchel one by one, "but he says he has something grander in mind. Now, what that is, he won't say."

After our coffee, Ellie thanked the waitress, whose name she knew was Francie, and we walked the streets of downtown. There was so much detail that I hadn't noticed. The Majestic Theater, The Strand Theater. Shops down the streets I hadn't bothered to stroll down. Shopkeepers paused from sweeping or straightening shelves to tell us good morning, or *hi-dee*, some would say.

The day had warmed up a little, and we sat on the courthouse steps on the Milam Street side, in the winter sun but out of the winter wind. We sat there with our legs stretched out, our arms to our sides and our palms pressed into the steps next to our hips. Scattered groups of lawyers and their clerks drifted up and down the steps while we talked. Their conversations followed around them and ended abruptly as the door shut on the ones going in and began abruptly with the ones coming out of the courthouse. A judge came out folding up a black robe that he tucked under his arm. We watched him head down Milam Street and stop to talk to a young man at the corner of Milam and Marshall. I couldn't hear what he said, but both he and the boy laughed.

"You have a boyfriend?" Ellie asked me.

"Yes. A fiancé, in fact. Irving. Do you?"

"I did. Jimmy. He lived on the farm next to ours in the Panhandle. In places like Ochiltree County, geography dictates romance; if you don't live close, then a couple doesn't have a chance. You'd never see each other. We were voted most handsome and most beautiful in high school and started to school in Austin after graduation. He had a scholarship to play football but washed out because he couldn't make his grades. Jimmy was made for farm work; he had no interest in physics or math or literature."

"Is that what drove you apart?" I asked. Across the street an old Negro maid dropped a bag of groceries, and a white man in a nice suit stopped to help her gather loose cans.

"That, and the black blizzard. When we got blown out, of course they did, too. Our families had to move. Daddy's kept ours together. They're in California, and I'm the only one by myself. Jimmy's family's scattered. Last I heard, he was working for the WPA somewhere, but he drinks and gambles away his paycheck in the camps. Last I heard."

She turned her face to me. The sunlight illuminated her eyes; they were translucent, hazel.

"What about you? Irving?"

"Oh," I said in such a way that it betrayed a hint of ambivalence, to her and to myself. "Irving's a swell guy. A hard worker, successful, never met a stranger, successful, successful...did I say successful?"

Ellie smiled, stood up, and brushed her palms. She extended a hand to help me up. I took inventory of the small spots of dried paint on her fingers. Rose, blue, orange, like the colors of gumballs.

"Yes, but is he *successful?*" she joked.

I stood up and brushed off my backside. Then I thought of a treasure in this town that *I* wanted to show *her*. We walked arm in arm to Crockett Street and ascended the front porch. I pulled the screen door open and knocked on the door. The curtain in the sidelight of the door pulled back, and there was Miss Fenerty's face. A smile broke on it like a sunrise. The door cracked open, and she said:

"Ah, but isn't it true, then, what they say: birds of a feather flock together! Beautiful people have beautiful friends."

I introduced them, and Miss Fenerty said, "Nina's at choir practice, so I'll make us some tea, me-self."

We had tea and sweet potato pie as Miss Fenerty told Ellie and me (and Mr. Roosevelt) about the census man's visit in what she thinks was 1850. We ended up spending the day together, and what a wonderful day it was. The town had seemed to gain promise with each street we turned down. Ellie has animated this place for me. We both came here strangers, but I had decided to remain one and she had not.

We left Miss Fenerty waving to us from the porch. Ellie and I walked to the Y, and we bid each other goodnight. When I got back to Stephenson Street, Lemurier was just emerging from his lair, hungover and dry, smelling of his bed. And then I had a strong idea who Ellie's co-worker was.

Dec. 14, 1936, FWP, Transcript of Bridget Fenerty

When I was about eight was the first time that

I remember the census man coming.[2] The tree in the alley was green, and it was just beginning to get warm, so it must have been May or so, April or May. The census man came every ten years like they still do, though they didn't ask as many questions back then. We younger children gathered around him as he made his inquiries and put down his entries:

Who is the head of the household?
How many live here?
How many go to school?
What is the occupation of everyone?

So he wrote down:

Nora Fenerty, widow, keeping house.
Maggie Fenerty, daughter, ditto.
Daniel Fenerty, son, apprentice.

He couldn't spell *daguerreotypist*, so he just wrote 'apprentice.'

Colleen Fenerty, daughter, in school.
Patrick Fenerty, son, ditto.
Bridget Fenerty, daughter, ditto.
Jack Hennigan, widower, not working.
Place of birth: Ireland. Ditto, ditto, ditto, ditto, ditto, ditto.

Yes. Yes, now I remember it so clearly. It was in the late spring on a Thursday, Ma's day off from the Prudhommes. That was the day that she did the laundry that she took in from a variety of people, mostly single men who had no woman to do it for them.

The census taker approached on an old gray nag, swaybacked and hobbling. He dismounted and shuffled through a saddlebag while the horse swished her tail and flinched flies away with her hide. He produced a ledger book and put it under his arm while he struggled to tie the mare to a tallow tree in the alley. It would have been easier if he had tied up the horse first. We all knew it, but none of us said anything.

Ma was in the alley over a washtub full of clothes, next to an iron kettle that was boiling over a wood fire. As the man approached, she stood up from

---

[2] Likely the Federal census of 1850. The Fenerty family is listed almost exactly as the subject states, living on Annunciation Street. The census taker, a man named W. H. Ormond, records the date as April 18, 1850.

the washtub with water dripping off her forearms. She stood there for a minute watching him, and we watched both of them, dogs barking and the iron kettle bubbling and boiling and the smell of the wood smoke competing with the smell of the strong lye soap.

He was a heavy man with a swallowtail coat and a striped waistcoat. He tipped his top hat to Ma and to Maggie and announced himself. I didn't hear his name though he said it; I wouldn't remember it anyway after all this time. He sat on the edge of the porch and asked his questions and wrote down the answers with a great quill of a pen, dipping the nib into a glass bottle of ink he had opened for the occasion. Ma was unimpressed, but we children were excited to have our names written in the great book of Americans, citizens of the United States of America.

When he was done with his questions, the man blew on the page to dry the ink, touching the page and then looking at his finger. The horse continued to flinch at the green flies that buzzed her gray hide, shaking her head at them occasionally. The man tipped his hat to Ma and unhitched the mare and led her down the street, Annunciation Street. Ma went back to the kettle of boiling clothes, the drawers and shirts and trousers of a dozen men.

Aunt Peg didn't make the census, of course, as this was after she died. Her dying was the beginning of Uncle Jack being sent away. It happened thusly:

Maggie was beginning to blossom, and she seemed bewildered with what nature was doing to her. She was taller by a head now than both Colleen and me, and the blouses she wore were tenting out from her bosom. Her face stayed broken out and lost its roundness, and you could tell that loveliness was about to erupt below it, which it did. She was the most beautiful woman I've ever seen.

Which was an opinion shared by many, including Uncle Jack. Perhaps because he had no outlet for his amorous inclinations, or because he was even drunker than before, or both, his hands tended to gravitate to her curves, a sly slide down the back, a quick slip of a finger over the front, a furtive palm over a breast. Maggie was bewildered about this, too. She and the rest of us had been raised to respect our elders.

"Oh, give your old Uncle Jack a kiss, now," he would cajole her in a voice between a chuckle and a growl, his smile straining against his crooked brown teeth. She would do it quickly on his cheek, holding her breath from the stench of alcohol and dirt and grime.

"Oh, and what sort of weak kiss is that, then?" he would say.

Ma was gone a great bit of the time, and so it took a while before she found out. Of course, it was Colleen who told Ma, who wasted no time confronting him. Even though she had to be at work early the next day, she waited up for him, and it was late that night that I overheard a conversation between Ma and Uncle Jack. It began low like water beginning to boil and finished like the shriek of a tea kettle.

Ma said, "You just keep your hands off her, or I'll cut your throat in your sleep, you hear? And don't think I won't, Jack Hennigan! You'll open your eyes just in time to feel the drag of the knife!"

Well, it hadn't been but a year or so that gold had been discovered in California, and that seemed an excellent incentive for Uncle Jack to leave the city, almost as good an incentive as the threat of waking to Ma's knife across his gullet. He borrowed the fare from Ma, or really Ma gave it to him to get him out of the city. She insisted, though, that we all turn out on the levee to see him off, even Maggie, as he was our only relation in America. He sailed away, still hungover, headed for the gold fields with a promise to repay the money when he had struck it rich, which was sure to happen, of course, as the gold was just jumping out of the earth and into men's pockets, to hear him tell it.

We never received a word from him, much less any money. Two or three months later, news came that the boat loaded with fortune seekers had gone down off the tip of South America, all believed lost. So Uncle Jack Hennigan was taken by the drink after all. Or, if you believe Ned Hennessy, perhaps he wasn't. It's still a mystery to me.

Dec. 16, 1936, Wed.

Fighting a cold, stayed in and slept most of the day. Wish Mother were here with chicken soup and tea. Outside my window on the street is a man sitting in a black late model Cadillac. He seems to be watching the house, or maybe the house across the street, waiting for something. He looks in the rearview mirror, then up through the windshield, then down at what looks to be notes in his lap, all the while his face is half-hidden by the sun visor which is turned to the house. He seems to be trying to be inconspicuous, a black-suited man in a black car. He's been out there for at least half an hour.

As I write this, the Cadillac has started up and is heading back toward the Fairfield Avenue end of the street. I watch it turn south onto Thornhill. Could Irving stoop so low as to have someone keeping tabs on me?

Dec. 17, 1936, Thurs.

I felt a little better today, enough to get dressed and go downstairs midmorning and look over the list of potential subjects, even though I still don't have use of the auto. With the rent due for *chez Lemurier* and the money

I'm sending home (through Mother- Father would never accept it), I don't have the funds to get it fixed. At any rate, getting it fixed would mean more time in the countryside and less time with Miss Fenerty. As I went over the list of potential interviewees, tapping it with the pencil eraser and biting my pinky nail, a habit Mother still scolds me about, there was a knock on the front door. I opened it to find Ellie waiting there. She seemed just as surprised to see me as I was to see her.

"You found me!" I exclaimed.

"Yes," she said. "Much more pleasant than who I was looking for."

"And who would that be?" I said, though I knew.

"Monsieur Lemurier. I thought you were in the Creswell. I had no idea you would be in the same house as him."

It sounded almost cautionary. She looked past me through his studio to the kitchen. The sink was piled high, as usual.

"I see he's also a sculptor."

"Yes. Dirty dishes as a medium, an artistic first. It's groundbreaking. I think he should entitle that one *Man's Struggle with His Kitchen.*"

She laughed as she took off her sweater. Lemurier keeps the house hot.

"His painting is certainly…one of a kind," she said as she looked among the canvases.

"A school of art all its own," I said.

"He violates every tenant of art that I know of. Come on," Ellie said, "Let's at least dismantle his kitchen sculpture."

I was amazed at how she attacked the kitchen problem. I could see her mind dissect it. Pots and pans, here. Plates and saucers, there. Silverware, over there. Hot water was running into the sink. Frying pan from the stovetop. Glasses in first.

"Wash or dry?" she asked me. When I didn't respond, she said, "I'll wash, you dry."

Here's the amazing thing I've discovered about washing dishes: it frees up your tongue.

"That is one lazy son of a bitch," Ellie looked over her shoulder and said. "I doubt he wipes his own ass."

There was a silence, and I wondered if Ellie thought she had gone too far. But then I began laughing, maybe less at the content and more at the Texas drawl it was delivered in. And then I thought of something else, and I began laughing even more.

"I bet…" I couldn't get the words out, "…I bet…I bet he…" I wheezed with laughter. "I bet he gets Mirlette…to do it."

Ellie leaned forward onto her forearms, her hands dripping with dishwater, and I joined her and we laughed a good five minutes. We howled with laughter, shaking violently. Ellie bent forward with her hands on her knees and started to say something, but whatever it was dissolved into a whirlwind of laughter.

We were breathless, sighing, red-faced, pushing tears off our cheeks with the backs of our hands. We had finally succeeded in gathering a little composure, when Mirlette came in the kitchen and looked in the icebox without so much as a good morning, though it was close to afternoon. She took a bottle of milk and padded upstairs with it. When she left, Ellie and I snorted again leaning into each other and shaking. Our hands together in dishwater.

It felt good to have my hands busy. It was good for my soul, as if each new dish that emerged from the soapy water announced that I was cleaner, too. We were quiet for a short while, and then I asked her as I set a glass in the cabinet, "Do you hear from your family much?"

She rinsed a saucer and handed it to me. She suddenly seemed subdued.

"Not as often as I'd like." She rinsed a couple of forks and handed them to me. "I try to send them money when I can, when I know where they are, but they're on the move a lot. This time of year, it'll probably be the canneries on the coast. The last letter I got from them smelled like fish." She scraped something off a plate into the trash under the sink. Whatever it was, it had been there a while and was completely unidentifiable.

"Will you see them?" I asked her, "for the holidays?"

She paused with the plate in her hand and looked out the window. The plate floated to the bottom of the sink and made a small underwater clack.

"No," she murmured. "Not this time. Not this year."

She chose a coffee cup from the menagerie by the sink. It was Mirlette's. I could tell because she drinks her coffee *au lait*, a light brown, though there was a ring of grayish green in it now. Next to it was Lemurier's; he drinks his black. Ellie ran a stream of water into Mirlette's cup, swirled and emptied it, and then dunked it in the dishwater.

"What about you?" she asked as she slowly twirled the dish rag in the cup. "Are you going home?"

An idea suddenly sprung inside me, like a beautiful bird landing on a limb, coursing down out of nowhere. An idea that screamed, *of course-of course-of course.*

"Wait right here," I said, and I hurriedly dried my hands. I bounded up the stairs and returned back down them with the envelope.

"I've got an extra ticket home. To New York. To the city."

She turned to me. Her blonde hair shimmered, moving like a field of north Texas wheat must move in the wind. Her eyes, not quite green, not quite brown, looked at me.

"Let's go to the city, you and I," I said, and when I did, it sounded like the best idea I'd ever had.

"New York City?" she said aloud. "New York City," she repeated herself in awe. The coffee cup was half submerged in soapy water. "Is the Metropolitan Art Museum open during the holidays?"

"Yes it is," I smiled. "Except for Christmas Day."

She left the cup in the water and hugged me, and I felt her body against mine, wiry, muscular, tested by the elements. And when she withdrew from our embrace, though she hadn't cried, her eyes were moist. As moist as her palm prints on my shoulder blades.

"When?" she asked.

"How about the day after Christmas?"

"Deal," she said as she resumed her work on the cup.

She rinsed it and handed it to me to dry. It was bright white, clean.

When we were done with the kitchen, Lemurier appeared in his silk monogrammed pajamas. He passed us without a 'hello' or a 'thank you for cleaning the kitchen.' He checked the coffee pot, which we had cleaned and set back in its place on the stove. When he found it was empty, he bellowed up to the ceiling, "*Mirlette!*"

"Will you excuse us for a moment?" Ellie asked me as she shook her hands free of water and wiped them dry on a towel.

"I'll be on the front porch," I said. "Let's go to Miss Fenerty's when you're ready."

"Okay. It'll just be a minute."

There was a conversation that grew into an argument that escalated into a shouting match that could be heard even on the porch. French-accented English in this corner versus the challenger, Texas-accented English.

The last blast was purely Texan: *"I got plenty a ideers, but if you don't like 'em, if you don't even wanna see 'em, then think a some and we'll work on 'em together. Either way, you better get the lead outta yer ass, mister…monsieur…or ain't neither one of us gonna be workin'!"*

Her footsteps stomped through the house, each one louder as she approached. The door opened, and then she emerged with her sweater in the crook of her elbow. Her smile to me was just as pleasant as before.

Dec. 17, 1936, FWP, Transcript of Bridget Fenerty

Patch and I were the only ones of us who were in school at that time. I'd made up my mind that one day I would teach school like our teacher, Miss O'Rioran, she with the warm smile and gently encouraging voice. But of course, most of us girls had decided so, and of course, most of us ended up keeping house for one family or another, and many of us married men who worked on the levee or the railroad.

I think I may have mentioned that Dan was working as an assistant to a daguerreotypist, a man named Glospere. It was a job that suited a studious and inquisitive boy like Dan, in a dark room with chemicals, developing glass plates. Dan was fascinated by the whole process, applying the solutions, watching the images float up from somewhere within the glass plates. He would come home from a day of it, pasty white like a creature that lived in a cave, and sour smelling like vinegar.

It was a new thing then, and everyone who could afford it wanted their picture made. Most of the customers just wanted pictures with loved ones, and they would pose still for long periods of time, trying not to blink. Our family and most of the other Irish couldn't afford it, though.

Monsieur Glospere's place was on St. Phillip, a street or two up from Royal in a narrow building with three stories, the lower one holding the studio itself. It had a tapestry with a country scene hung as a backdrop and a fern on a pedestal next to it. Dan would assist the subjects in their poses as Monsieur Glospere directed them:

Head up a little. A little more. Face toward me. Merci, Monsieur. Merci, Madame. They will be ready shortly. Please have a seat in the parlor, and the boy Daniel will pour you a refreshment. Merci.

Now, Monsieur Glospere had a sideline business that involved taking pictures of naked people. Dan told us in such a way that suggested it was the natural order of things, that of course if you had a camera it was only a matter of time before you would take pictures of naked people. I've often thought that if the camera was invented on a Monday, then the first pictures of naked people were likely taken on a Tuesday.

It was a big money maker for Glospere, as he would sell postcards of the procedures as *carte de visite* to sailors and river men and farmers into market for the week, who would stow them away on their person, and I'm sure hide them in some barn loft somewhere to keep them for further study in private. They were a nickel a piece, a dime for the really risky ones, which generally included one person in a very private moment, or more than one person, usually engaging each other in all sorts of recreational excitement.

Dan was there to keep up with the clothes of these people, and he saw it all. He would tell Patch and me about it, as if he was relating what he had seen at the circus, or a new song and dance he had come across at the theater. I don't think he fully appreciated what he saw. They were some of the lewd women that Uncle Jack had spoken of, though I'm not sure if Dan ever made the connection. He was a simple boy, a simple, genius of a boy.

He told us the business of it, the way it was accomplished. The ladies would arrive and, after a short chat, begin leisurely removing their clothes, all the while chatting with Monsieur Glospere, who would keep eye contact with the subject or subjects and direct Dan with short words and hand motions. The ladies smoothly combed their hair, helping one another put it up into fashionable states. At last the woman or women would be in the altogether, and Monsieur would have them pose. He would disappear under the black hood of his camera, and the flash would illuminate the tableaux.

Dan was fascinated with them, their bare breasts, the dark thick triangles below their waists, like a cluster of grapes. Some of the girls would tease Dan, cupping their breasts and shaking them at his raptured stare. Then suddenly he would realize that Monsieur was almost shouting at him. Dan would gather himself and pour the women drinks of water or champagne or absinthe, and the women would sit there in their nakedness, leisurely sipping and chatting, either completely naked or with stockings on.

In the summers when Yellow Jack came to call, Glospere's work shifted to a clientele who had no problem holding still and not blinking.

Dec. 17, 1936, later

When the recorder was turned off, the conversation folded and unfolded and refolded itself, from people posing naked in New Orleans to Mardi Gras to carnival around the world, then to carnival in Rio de Janeiro and to Brazil and the scanty dress of the beautiful people there and then to Brazil in general. Brazil is one of her favorite topics, for some reason.

Afterward, I walked with Ellie to the Y, and then took the trolley back to Stephenson Street, where I found I had received a letter from Irving. The sentiment expressed was sweet, but how can such a successful man use such atrocious grammar?

Monthly now three days late. Starting to get a little worried.

In the meantime, it's never a dull moment here on Stephenson Street. The Creswell hotel across the street from the Central Fire Station may have been more restful than the Lemuriers' house. Almost every night, there's loud music played on the phonograph. Then a loud discussion between the two of them, always in English, always escalating into shouting and the popping tinkle as dishes crash on the floor or the wall. Then there's the crying and sobbing of Mirlette, a brief lull, then what I presume is the sound of their ecstasy as they make up on the couch. At those times, I don't dare go downstairs, sure that I will see their naked or semi-naked bodies.

What I wouldn't give to hear the gentle whirring blasts of Mother's sewing machine. It would be a lullaby compared to all this. I've come to cherish these quiet mornings when they sleep in, and I can read, clean the kitchen, and drink my coffee, keep this journal. I love it almost as much as visiting with Miss F.

Dec. 18, 1936, FWP, Transcript of Bridget Fenerty

Uncle Jack may have slept with the dead from time to time, but my brother Dan worked with them. It was in the summer, the one after the river pushed a hole in the levee and flooded so much of the city. Of course, Irish were put to work putting up new levees and digging to drain the water into the canal, the Carondolet canal, not the new one. It saved a good bit of the newer part of the city.[3] Now, Dan was still working with Glospere. In the temperate months it was portraits of newlyweds and children and families, and of course on the regular appointed days, naked people and the like. In the summer months when death and sickness ascended the river to stalk the city, Monsieur went from taking portraits of the living to taking portraits of the dead.

The work was highly seasonal, as death itself was then. Winter for pneumonia and measles, summer for cholera, malaria, and, of course, yellow fever. A daguerreotypist could make a small fortune taking memorial pictures of the dead then.

I can tell you're disgusted, but it's just what it was, then. *Mori memori*, they were called. People would pose with their dead love ones, everyone taking on a wan expression, no smiling, because if everyone in the picture couldn't smile, then no one could. Dan would help Monsieur Glospere arrange them and hold them upright, Dan hidden in the picture behind the departed with a hand pressed into the person's back or with his hands just inside their shoulders or under their arms. Later, Glospere invested in an iron brace that he could strap the defunct to, and it would look as if the person were standing in a parlor, waiting on an offer of tea.

Patch and I thought it gruesome work, though we were fascinated by it, and we wanted Dan to let us come and watch, but he said it wasn't his place to arrange things such as that, no more than he could bring us in to watch Monsieur take the naked pictures.

He worked with death, Dan did, and later it occurred to me that, because he worked with the dead, then perhaps that was the reason for what happened to him. Like the man working with horses for long enough beginning to resemble a horse, you remember.

Is that the end of that one? That's all right, Miriam; no need to put on

---

[3] The subject is likely referring to the Sauvé's Crevasse. On the afternoon of May 3, 1849, the Mississippi River, swollen by spring rains, broke through the levee upriver from New Orleans and flooded much of the city for well over a month.

another of those plates-disks you call them? We'll save the rest of that story for next time.

Dec. 18, 1936, Fri

That was all she had to say about her brother Dan, and she moved the conversation somewhere else, and I followed it happily, helplessly. Only now as I sit and write this do I realize that she never told me what happened to him.

After I left Miss Fenerty's, I walked over to the Y to visit Ellie. At the front desk was a burly woman with a slight mustache that was bleached but still a mustache. She called up to Ellie's room, and in a minute I could hear Ellie's steps pattering quickly down the stairwell.

"Well, this is a pleasant surprise," she said. She put her sweater around herself without asking if I wanted to go for a walk, and we strolled in the winter air down to Texas Street.

"Today's the day, Miriam. I've got to have a sharp talk with *Monsieur*." She put her finger across her upper lip, imitating Lemurier's moustache.

"So still no progress with the mural?" I asked.

"Same," she said. "He stays drunk, sleeps until noon, and every time I propose something, he shoots it down, clicks his tongue, exhales and sighs, rolls his eyes. Every time I ask him, 'well, what do you propose?' He says, 'I am thinking, I am thinking, but it will be grand, you will see!"

"How about you?" she asked. "Do you ever interview anyone besides Miss Fenerty?'"

"I have, a few. Some helpful, some unreliable."

We sat on a bench on the courthouse square and waited for the trolley. Behind us the Confederate generals and Governor Allen stared off into the distance as Clio, the stony muse of history pointed to the quote, *Lest We Forget*. Above those of us in flesh and stone, the Confederate icon, Champ Lockett himself, loomed with this rifle, the butt of it on the stone ledge between his feet. Ellie pointed her thumb up to him.

"I hear the one to interview would be this Lockett fellow." She pronounced it *feller*, like a Texan.

"He won't talk. I'd probably get more information out of his statue than him. I don't know how lucid he is, anyway. You get to be old, that happens. Miss Fenerty is the exception. Sharp as a tack."

The trolley pulled up, an ad for *Barbasol* across its flank. We climbed the steps and deposited our fare. Clunk-click. The trolley turned from Texas Street onto Louisiana Avenue, the tether above us snapping against the lines as it reached up to them to feed the trolley. Ellie and I rode quietly. I watched her look out the window thoughtfully. I'm sure she was getting her argument, her ultimatum, ready.

We passed the Line Avenue school. A group of boys were playing a game that must surely have been 'Sergeant Lockett,' and a teacher was pacing across the school yard to stop them. As we passed, I looked back to see the boys drop their rocks and walk to the side of the brick building to spend the rest of their recess there.

Mirlette was on the front porch in a housecoat smoking when we got to Stephenson. I'm not sure, but I don't think she had much, if anything, on under it.

"Is he home?" Ellie asked.

"He is away," she said as she contemplated her cigarette indifferently. She tapped out an ash.

"Will he be back soon?"

Mirlette shrugged her shoulders and blew out a cloud of smoke.

Dec. 19, 1936, Sat.

Saturday, and I went to temple. When I arrived back home, there was a letter from Mother.

Dear Miriam,

Your father cried after you called. I've only seen him cry a handful of times in our married life, when you and your brother were born, when his parents died, and when the firm failed. What did you say to him? He wouldn't tell me. He's getting on reasonably well, but you can only imagine how it pains a man like him not to be a better bread winner. We were hoping to have you home for the new year, but you're a big girl now, I guess.

If you talk or write to Irving, please tell him to be careful in approaching your father with a job offer. He doesn't know him like I know him; your father is a proud man and likely to lash out at any offer of kindness that he perceives as charity…

And so forth. I won't tell her that I'll be in for the holidays. It'll be a surprise, a wonderful surprise. I wonder if Leonard and Irving will be as smitten with Ellie as I am.

Irving.

Still late on monthly. Trying not to worry. It terrifies me that we may be tied together forever. But then I remember that we are.

Aren't we?

Dec. 20, 1937, Sunday

I spent this morning catching up on correspondence. I wrote a letter to Mr. Alsberg, telling him of my progress, which isn't as good as I had hoped in terms of numbers of subjects, but is quality, I assured him. I wrote a letter to Mother and Father, telling them I hoped they had a Happy Hanukkah and I was sorry that I wouldn't see them for the new year (which I really am, of course). I even wrote a few lines to Irving.

Ellie came down on the trolley to Stephenson after church, and then we walked down to a park for a picnic. We had sandwiches and root beer and discussed our trip in a few weeks. The weather was pleasant in the sunshine; a picnic in Central Park this time of year would be almost impossible. We napped in the sun as we listened to children playing, the squeak of the swings, shouts of chasing. A football landed on our blanket, and I threw it to the boy who had come to retrieve it. It was a pitiful, end over end effort, and Ellie laughed.

Our spot in the sun shifted, and it became cool. Rather than move our blanket, we took the L&L back downtown to see Miss Fenerty, hoping she would make us tea, and of course, she did, and she told us a story.

Dec. 20, 1936, FWP, Transcript of Bridget Fenerty

Ned and I were enthralled with the theater, I think I've told you. We went often and paid rarely, on account of not having money, and on account of Ned knowing every backstage door, removable basement cover, overhanging-tree-limb-next-to-a-rear-balcony in the city. You think of a place you wanted to get inside, Ned Hennessy could get you in there.

We saw many of the shows then that catered to the Irish. *The Irish Immigrant*, *The Irish Tutor*, *The Irishman in China*, all similar, all straightforward, plays about a simple man who was irresistible to the ladies, honest in his dealings with others, beat upon by life and circumstances, but ultimately triumphant, which was an inspiration to us who were still being 'beat upon.' They played at the theaters that catered to the Irish then, the National, the Olympic, the Pelican. Ned could get you into any one of them, and for free. And of course, the St. Charles Theater was no exception.

It was about the time that the name of the square in the center of town was changed from the Place d'arms to Jackson Square.[4] I've no idea why they renamed it so. That same year, the St. Charles, the hotel called the St. Charles, burned. The first time, that is. The original hotel had a dome on it, like the capitol in Washington, and it was very distinctive on the skyline of the city if

---

[4] The Place d'arms was renamed Jackson Square in 1851.

you were approaching by the river, which was how most arrived then. Several other buildings burned with it. The Methodist church was one of them, it seems to me. The city was something then, a powerful thing that could regenerate itself at will. The lot was cleared, and within two months, on a spectacular March day, they started rebuilding it.

On the day they broke ground on the new St. Charles Hotel, I listened to the speeches that the men of the Board of Directors gave, with top hats and waistcoats and sashes, all full of pomp, blathering on, speeches given in French and English quoting Latin and Greek. When the ceremony broke up, I headed home.

It was then I saw the broadside posted in the letters they used then, tall letters with big, block feet, *expected in the city this month, Jenny Lind, the Swedish Nightingale, for performances at The Saint Charles Theater, Ticket inquiries should be made at the theater office on St. Charles.*[5] And there was the pointing finger used in those days to draw attention to things. Not that Jenny Lind needed any extra attention. News had preceded her. Everywhere bits of conversation around town revolved around the same topic.

"She sang for the Queen of England herself."

"Voice like an angel. The Swedish Nightingale they call her."

"Tickets are six dollars. Six dollars!"

"Well worth it I hear tell. Heavenly, they say."

Of course, no one had actually heard her sing. Hearsay was a powerful thing then, just as it is now.

Then one day, it was announced that the singer Jenny Lind's ship was in the river, two days out, and then one day out, and then she was just around the English Turn. With that piece of news, the town mobilized. Many a shop closed, and a crowd of people gathered at the levee. I'd never seen so many people in one place. It looked like the entire city had turned out to see her.

There was a great cheer from the crowd as she got off the boat at the levee, the *Eagle* or something[6] I think it was named, and then another as she got in a carriage and was driven to the Pontalba Apartments. Later, she came onto the balcony and waved to the crowd with a handkerchief, like this, and the crowd cheered even more.

"Sing for us, Miss Lind," someone shouted.

"Sing! Sing us something, ma'am!" the crowd insisted.

She just smiled and waved, and then later she went inside. Miss Lind knew how to get a crowd worked up, or perhaps it was Mr. Barnum[7], her manager at

---

[5] Newspaper reports indicate that Jenny Lind arrived in New Orleans in February, 1851.

[6] The boat was the *Falcon.*

[7] P.T. Barnum

the time, for it was weeks until she finally gave a concert, and I was there. I was nine then. Well, let's see, yes, nine or ten.

Ned Hennessy knew a back way into the St. Charles Theater, up a rickety back staircase and through a window. We tiptoed past the watchman, who was caught up like the rest, waiting for Miss Lind to take the stage and begin. Ned and I were up above and behind the stage, near the rafters. We could see the faces of the audience, smiles of anticipation in the amber gaslight, fans fluttering here and there, an occasional cough in the buzz of conversation among finely dressed ladies and gentleman. A lot of top hats and opera glasses.

And then the house lights went down, and the murmur of conversation rose and then fell and then stopped. Someone coughed one last time. The curtain pulled back and the footlights came up, and there was a man with a deeper voice, a baritone.[8] There was polite applause, and then the piano began, and he sang a few songs in Italian. I recognize them now as opera pieces. The pianoforte played along, and, after the second song, you could tell the audience was getting restless.

From above and behind the stage, we saw the back of her, the back of Miss Jenny Lind, the Swedish Nightingale, as she waited in the wings. She walked onto the stage, and the audience rose and clapped and hurrahed for her. She tilted her head to the side, and her ringlets jiggled with the small movement. The applause boiled itself down, and then there was another cough and then quiet, absolute quiet, the quiet that Jenny Lind was waiting for. She nodded to the wings, a quiver of ringlets, and the piano began again.

She sang, and I tell you, it was a voice to make the angels weep. Her range was extraordinary, the notes pure and ringing. She sang alone, and then she sang with the baritone, and everyone was in rapture. Some of the men and women kept their eyes closed in ecstasy as Jenny Lind's voice lightly hit every note, and every note, oh, but it was pure. She sang "Home Sweet Home" and "The Last Rose of Summer." With that one, both ladies and men brought big bouquets of flowers forward. Miss Lind nodded with a small bow and turned the palm of her hand from one accompanist to another. And the applause pattered louder with each gesture like the surge of a rainstorm.

And on that day, I decided I didn't want to be a teacher like the Misses O'Rioran. I wanted to sing like Jenny Lind.

The crowd gave her an ovation that seemed to last an hour, and perhaps it did, until the stage lights were extinguished and the waxy smoke of the lanterns scented the air. Everyone exited into the street, still buzzing about the Swedish

[8] Newspaper accounts indicate that Miss Lind was accompanied by the Italian baritone Giovanni Belletti and pianist Julius Benedict.

Nightingale. In the next few days, there were no fewer than half a dozen proposals of marriage for Miss Lind, all rejected. Doubloons with her picture on them were made and distributed throughout the city. She gave a dozen or so concerts during her time in New Orleans, all of them sold out at six dollars a head, which was a sum then, and then she departed and moved upriver to Natchez and Memphis, and then further north. When she left, signs and banners went up in the city proclaiming "Jenny Lind's favorite toiletry shop" and "Jenny Lind's favorite this and favorite that." The furniture and fixtures from Mrs. Pontalba's apartment were auctioned off for an enormous sum. Even Jenny Lind's chamber pot. Now who would want something such as that, I ask you?

After that night in the Saint Charles Theater, I sang around the house, and I'm sure 'twas horrible. Ma would come in from working at the Prudhommes' and put her feet up after being on them all day. And she would say as I sang to her, "Oh, but 'tis lovely," but I know now it wasn't. It was wretched, but Ma was patient. My voice became much easier to listen to later.

When she had taken all she could, she would only then tell me, "Ah, but such a fine voice as that must need some rest, now and again." And I felt very satisfied indeed to have my voice called a fine one.

Dec. 21, 1936, Monday

Monthly started today! I feel like singing like Jenny Lind!

Thank you, God. Thank you, Moses. Thank you, Christian Jesus. Thank you, Egyptian goddess of Menstruation-I can't remember your name right now- but thank you.

Best Hanukah gift I could have asked for, a menstrual cycle. Strange indeed.

The cramping is killing me, and I'm ecstatic.

Dec. 22, 1936, Tues

I awoke in the early morning hours to a rumble like thunder though rain wasn't in the forecast. I got out of bed pulling my nightgown around me against the cold of the house. Through a gap in the curtains I saw him, there across the street, sitting with his face in the glow of the dashboard. Behind him, the neighbors' nativity scene glowed as a back drop, placing his smoking silhouette among the three wise men. The red, green, and blue Christmas lights along the eves of the house across the street reflected in the cold, black shine of the Cadillac's top and hood, and on the wet street.

The window was partially rolled down, and smoke from his cigarette wandered out from the top of it, followed by his hand as he flicked an ash occasionally. He may have seen me peeking out from the curtains because he adjusted the visor lower. I had almost gotten a good look at him. I went to the bathroom, and when I came back, he was gone again.

After he left, I dozed and read until it was 'proper morning' as Miss F would say. I dressed and rode the Highland trolley out to see a man who, it was said, once herded cattle on the Chisholm Trail, then made a fortune in oil, and then moved to the city to live with his daughter as his health declined. As I neared the house, I saw a crowd of assorted ages on the front porch, men in dark suits and women in nice dresses. I set down the recorder, sat on a tree root, and opened this morning's edition of the *Shreveport Times* I had been reading on the trolley. There was his obituary on page six.

I rode the trolley back home and took an aspirin and a nap. Miss Monthly is making up for lost time.

When I woke up, I called the YWCA and left word for Ellie to call me. There's only one phone at the Y, and it's downstairs, so it took a while for her to return my call. I stayed by the phone and waited, afraid that Lemurier would awaken and demand to use it, though I don't know of anyone who would want to have much of a conversation with him or vice versa.

She called back sooner than I thought, and she sounded breathless as if she had run down the stairs.

"Hey," she said.

"Hi," I said back. "You want to go get something to eat?"

"Sure," she said. "I know a place. Meet me at the courthouse."

When the L&L trolley pulled up to the stop at the courthouse, there she was in her usual light blue dress with the sweater over it, the felt cloche ejecting a limp spray of blonde hair at its edges. Her hands were behind her back as she examined the Confederate memorial as if it were in an art museum. With the squeaky grunt of the trolley's brakes, she looked up and we smiled at each other through the window.

We sat on a park bench and waited for the Allendale bus while we gazed up at the profile of the elusive Mr. Lockett. We looked at him and he looked at us, all three of us silent. Autos crooned and growled and sputtered behind us on Texas Street with an occasional honk, which here in Shreveport is less likely to be from exasperation with someone's driving than it is to be a greeting of someone you know.

We boarded the Allendale bus. The rear half was crowded with housekeepers returning after a day of work at one house to clean and make supper all over again at their own houses. They rode quietly, enjoying the simple pleasure of being off one's feet after a day of being on them.

We rode out to a place Ellie knew in the 'west end' called Herby K's, a nondescript one-story place with a red neon sign with the green neon name of the joint (and I mean joint) written in the center. We got a pair of fifteen cent sandwiches and a couple of nickel root beers while the owner, a jowly man named Mr. Busi, teased and flirted with us. Ellie gave it right back to him, and I realized that I was smiling. Funny how when you're not accustomed to smiling much, you can feel when you're doing it. When we left, Mr. Busi was wiping down the counter.

"Merry Christmas, ladies!" he shouted.

"Merry Christmas!" we shouted back.

We caught the bus back downtown, the shadow of it protruding down the street in front of us. The last of the sunlight gave up on the day in an orange glow, and the night was quickly dark and cold, which is not to say unpleasant. Texas Street stretched all the way down to the bridge, flanked on either side by electric trumpeting angels, snowmen, and leaping reindeer. Families wandered in front of the shop windows, the smallest children on their fathers' shoulders, their small hands wrapped around the brims of their fathers' hats, the next to smallest holding on to the end of their fathers' coats.

It was cold but not brutally cold as we walked down McNeil Street and turned onto Crocket. As we reached Miss Fenerty's house, I stopped to enjoy what I saw. The square, white posts were wrapped with colorful bulbs, and in the window was a Christmas tree, loaded with tinsel, a life-size cone of silver. In the other window was something else. She had put a menorah in the window with the Christmas lights.

We knocked on the door, and it opened. In the widening crack of it, there she was with Nina, trimming the tree.

"Oh, mercy upon me, but it's two of my favorites," she said as Nina opened the door.

We leaned down for her to kiss our cheeks, and she said, "Why, wouldn't it be a grand night for hot chocolate, then? Or would ye prefer tea?"

We chose hot chocolate, and I went with Nina into the kitchen to help her. Ellie and Miss Fenerty finished with the tree.

"That woman sure loves her holidays," Nina said as she stirred the milk on the stove. "Everybody get a cake on they birthday. She even makes a cake for a boy she took care of back during the war. The *Civil* War, baby," she said tilting her head down to me. "And that's been, what now, seventy years? And he ain't even around!"

We had our hot chocolate and sang carols. Nina played on an upright piano. Miss Fenerty sang "It Came Upon a Midnight Clear" by herself, *A capella,* and it was absolutely beautiful, so beautiful I've been humming it to myself since I returned home. A Jewish girl humming a Christmas carol.

We departed with hugs on the porch, and I told Miss Fenerty I would return tomorrow. Ellie walked up to the Y. Nina and I got on the bus. We both sat in the back, to the astonished stares of the white faces in the front returning from holiday shopping.

Dec. 23, 1936, FWP, Transcript of Bridget Fenerty

It was the summer that the President died of the cholera or something like it. The papers said it was from drinking bad milk, and Ma told us that we should be careful, that if it could happen to the President of the United States, well, it could happen to anyone.[9]

I enjoyed swimming in those days; I wasn't afraid of the water at all. When the weather warmed, April or May usually, we took to the river. We would swim in it, among the boats at the edge of the broad distance with the west bank small across it. The boys would swim in their underwear, the long-handle drawers, and I would swim in my slip, but we were just eight or ten then. Usually it was me and the boys, my brothers Patch and Dan and our friend Ned Hennessy. Sometimes other girls would swim, but usually it was just us. I enjoyed the company of the boys then more than the girls.

The river was filthy with all sorts of things floating in it, but it was cooler, as it carried the water down from the north, you see. I say cooler. It was cooler until about July when nothing was cool. Everything was warm then, hot in fact. The river stunk something awful, and the heat only made it worse.

Some children would sneak into people's cisterns to cool off, even though they knew they could get into trouble over it. We did it a time or two, my brothers and Ned and me. But the fear of getting caught put a damper on the fun of swimming, so we stuck to the river for the most part.

Well, because the river smelled so bad and the cisterns were the source of trouble with the owners, Ned Hennessy hatched a plan. It was to be a grand adventure, and the four of us discussed it like generals discussing a military campaign, but, in the end, it was only Ned and me. Patch was elsewhere, and Dan was too timid to test the rules, such was his nature. But not mine.

In those days, the Pontchartrain Railway ran from Fauborg Marigny to Millenburg,[10] which was on the lake. The fare was seventy-five cents roundtrip, more than we could afford, by far. Most of the traffic was cargo, as many of the sailing ships from Mobile docked in the lake then, and freight had

---

[9] Zachary Taylor, twelfth president of the United States and the only president ever elected from Louisiana, died July 9, 1850 of an intestinal illness, blamed by some on spoiled milk.
[10] Milneburg

to be transferred to the river boats, so they brought it over the railroad down to the city and the river where the steamboats were. There was an old wooden lighthouse there on the lake and a pier that the train ran out onto to unload the ships. The locomotive that pulled the train was called Smoky Mary.

Ned had heard the water was cleaner and altogether more pleasant in the lake, and I had heard it too, and so we were anxious to see it and swim in it. We left early in the morning, slipping into a freight car jammed with casks of vinegar and enduring the stink of them. When the conductor walked through the train, we cowered down behind the barrels, blinking at each other in the darkness. And then when the train stopped at the lake, we scampered out of the back of the car with the canvas sack Ned brought. We walked down away from the railhead, our bare feet kicking at the small wavelets of water that licked at the shore until we were well away from the train and the ships.

We swam in the altogether, Ned and I did. Naked I mean. We were just children then with no thought of being timid or embarrassed or ogling each other, not even a passing glance. And I considered myself one of the boys then, anyway. Of course, our chests were identically flat at that point in our lives. We were like Adam and Eve in the garden, unaware of their nakedness. That is, before they met the serpent and became aware of themselves.

We would take turns diving off each other's shoulders, squinting away the water out of our eyes, splashing each other, prowling for shells underwater along the bottom, surfacing and wiping water out of our faces to look at what we'd brought up. Then we would rest on the sandy bank. Ned had brought a sack, and in it was a pineapple he'd gotten, stolen off a street cart, likely, and we carved it up with an oyster shell and ate it, the juice sweet and sticky on our hands and faces. We watched the birds chase the schools of trout in the lake, diving down to the water and then out with the fish bending helplessly in their mouths. I recited a rhyme that my Uncle Jack Hennigan liked to say:

A remarkable bird is the Pelly-can
His bill can hold more than his belly-can.

Ned laughed, and then we looked out across the lake to the north shore, to Mandeville where some of the well-to-dos had summer houses. I asked him what he wanted to be when he became a man, and he said he should like to be a barber, to work indoors and shave the necks of famous men like Hugh McNeil and Maunsel White, and hear all the latest news and sing with customers when everyone was in a mood for it. He asked me what I wanted to do when I became a woman.

I said I that I once thought I should like to be a teacher like the Misses O'Riorans, they with the starched dresses and the schoolbooks and the chalk and erasers and the quiet voices full of encouragement, but now I was thinking of being a singer like Jenny Lind.

Ned said, now wouldn't that be something? Both of us working indoors out of the rain and sun and having a job where we would be admired and everyone glad to see us?

Yes, I said.

Ned and I swam all day, out away from the pier, watching the train back onto the pier, load and unload the sailing ships on the lake, and then back off the pier again and head for the city. And the ships with the webs on the rigging of the masts and spars, and the shouts of the sailors on them away in the distance. We ate the last of the pineapple. By the end of the day, we were red as little Indians, we were, all over our bodies. We winced as we slid on our clothes.

We ran to the pier where Smoky Mary was belching out smoke. As we neared, the train began to move and gather speed. We gathered speed, too, supposing that it was the last train of the day. Our little legs and arms pushing away the heavy air, the air that rushed past our ears, dulling the sound of the train whistle's hooting. I outran Ned, perhaps because I knew Ma would give me a thrashing if I were late, and the sunburn on my little arse would make it extra special. I scrambled up on the last car. Ned was right behind me, huffing like Smoky Mary herself. I gave him my hand, and he pulled himself up onto the rear platform with me. We went inside and sat down in a bench seat. I'm sure we smelled like the two little sweaty children we were, and several of the passengers wrinkled up their noses and glanced back at us.

A man was punching tickets in the passenger car we were in. We, of course, didn't have one, and when he turned to one side, we slipped past him and went to the next car up. We sat in an empty seat, nervously looking over our shoulders. Sure enough, here he comes, *Ticket, please?* Punching a hole. *Ticket please?*

We kept moving up through the freight cars. There were only six or eight cars in the whole train, and soon we were near the front, Smoky Mary herself chugging along. As we got between the first two cars, at the coupling, Ned accidentally dropped his canvas sack, and it got caught on the coupling. That sack held all the driftwood we had collected; the top of the pineapple that we were going to plant in the alley and raise our own pineapples, somehow; oyster shells with shimmering greens and purples set against the smooth white insides. In short, nothing of value unless you're an eight-year-old child.

It was caught on the coupling and hanging above the tracks, so low that every so often a cross tie would bump it and cause it to kick up and twirl a little. The crossties were a blur flashing below, and the train clacked wildly over them. Clacka-clack-clack. Clacka-clack-clack. Ned tested the distance by leaning in, but he was well short of the coupling and the sack.

"Bridget, help me," he said as he leaned in. The train was swaying, the crossties ticking and popping under its weight. I took his hand in mine and braced myself on the railing, and he leaned down to get our sack of treasure. I had all his weight, and it took the length of both our little arms. With his fingertips, he managed to snag the sack. As I was pulling him in, I looked up, and there was the conductor.

I panicked and lost my grip on the metal post, and Ned and I fell between the cars. We landed on the tracks and then the cars were passing over us and we were clinging to each other, sure that God was coming to fetch us, or the pieces of us, at any moment. I wanted to slide out between cars but Ned held onto me and wouldn't let me move. The train stirred a breeze that would've been pleasant if we hadn't been so terrified.

It seemed to go on forever. At last it passed over us, and daylight and the late afternoon sky reemerged. The conductor appeared on the very rear of the train and looked down. He saw us, and we saw him. He pulled a bell, and the wheels of the train squealed and sparked, and the whole thing came to a stop. It took fifty, maybe a hundred yards or so, but the train stopped so suddenly that it shuddered along the rails and made a frightful racket. Ned and I were still too scared to move and held onto each other there between the rails, on the gravel and the crossties.

The man jumped off the back of the train and ran to us. Next thing we knew we saw him close up. He wore a cap with a bill on it, and he was right in our faces, scolding us. He pulled us up and kept scolding, which frankly in our state of terror seemed far away. As he talked, he softened and seemed relieved, though he couldn't have been as relieved as we were. He let us ride in the back car with him, and he even gave us a penny candy from his pocket that he normally would give to paying children.

When the train got back to the city, he gave us one more friendly warning. Then we ran, and Ned grabbed my hand to hurry me along. Men were lighting the lanterns along the levee so that they could keep loading and unloading the riverboats through the night. The levee was a busy place and the work went on day and night, you see. We crossed Jackson Square, and I realized that I liked the feel of my hand in his. We crossed Canal under the scaffolding of the Customhouse which was still under construction then, and then ran down Chop-tools[?] Street. Over on Camp Street, the bells of St. Patrick's rang in front of us while the ones from St. Louis rang behind us.

At the corner of Julia and Chop-tools[?],[11] we caught our breath, and suddenly he kissed me. It was a chaste little schoolboy kiss, right on my lips

---

[11] Almost certainly Tchoupitoulas Street

which were unprepared and didn't pucker a bit, but it was my first, right there at the corner, a quick, smart peck. And then he was running away down Julia with the canvas sack of treasures in his hand, the other hand pulling up his baggy trousers as his oversized brogans slapped the cobblestones. Both were just a little too big for him.

I stood there with my fingers on my lips like I was trying to feel the kiss, to put it in my pocket for later, perhaps, but then I realized the bells of St. Patrick's had stopped ringing. I ran home. The street lamps were flickering; it was dark now. It had been one of the best days of my life. And I was sure it would be the last. I thought Ma would kill me.

When I got home, I thought she would warm my little backside, but instead she clutched me and held me and I could feel her shake with weeping, and I wished it would have been a whipping instead. My skin was on fire from the sun, and I was bruised and scraped from our fall, and it hurt where she seized me, so I suppose I received my punishment.

Dec. 23, 1936

I left Miss Fenerty's and walked the shops on Texas Street looking at the Christmas displays. The air was dense and moist and cold. It seemed to be waiting for something. The rain finally squeezed itself from the gray air, surprising all of us along Texas Street. It bounced off the rounded fenders of automobiles whose wipers flicked it off their windshields. Everything bristled with the rain.

Several of us ducked under the canopy of Montgomery Ward, one and another and then another, men turning up their collars and holding folded up newspapers over their heads, women in heels splashing where the water coursed down the curb. We all were standing there, about a half dozen of us, watching the chains of water dash to the earth. Behind us in the window, two mannequins, a well-dressed boy and girl, were posed with a sled. At their feet, several inches of snowy cotton had fallen; their faces held surprised expressions.

We strangers listened for a moment as the rain spattered from the awning. Through the static of the speakers flanking the doors to Montgomery Ward, a faraway orchestra pushed out a diminutive "The First Noel." The boy and girl mannequins in the snow-cotton seemed delighted.

We all listened for a few moments, and I felt a sense of connection so strong that I'm convinced the others under that awning felt it too. Conversations began to arise from within us. Talk was about the weather and then, the holidays.

"Well, Champ, y'all light the lights last week?" one man asked another.

"Yes sir," the other man replied. I recognized him as the man at the synagogue, the man who had read from the Torah in a drawl. "Y'all have your tree up yet?"

"Gettin' it later today if the rain passes through. Kids wanted it up last week, course."

"Well, don't they always?" the Jewish man said.

I looked through the faces and found his and studied it as covertly as I could. He bore no resemblance to the hero in the hardware store. But I had to ask.

"Are you Champ Lockett's son?"

"Oh, no," he laughed, and the other man smiled. "There's certainly a lot of children in this town named for him, but not me, really. Champ's just my nickname. I used to box a little." He offered me his hand.

"Morris Taylor," he said graciously.

"Box a little?" The other man roared. "Morris there was the Hammerin' Hebrew. City champ and dang near state champ. Don't get all modest on us, all of a sudden."

"Well, I guess I did box a little," Morris said. He seemed mildly embarrassed and changed the subject.

"This is Hank Eaves, Miss-" Mr. Taylor said.

"Miriam Levenson," I said as I extended my hand.

"Pleased to meet you," Mr. Eaves said. He was younger than Mr. Taylor, young enough to be his son.

"Hank, listen, before I forget, have you been by to see mama?" Morris Taylor said.

"Went by on Monday. You?"

"Last week. I'll get by there before Christmas, though."

I didn't understand how men with different last names could be brothers. Besides, Morris Taylor seemed a good twenty years older than Mr. Eaves.

But it was possible, so I asked. In this place, it seems like anything is possible.

"Are you two related?"

"Oh, no," Mr. Taylor laughed. "We were just raised by the same woman."

He winked at Mr. Eaves and gave me a coy smile. Mr. Eaves looked at the ground and grinned.

"We'll see you, now," he said to Mr. Eaves. "Nice to meet you, Miss Levenson," he said to me, and he dashed out into the rain with his newspaper over his head. His strides in the rain were unnaturally long; each step was a splash.

I looked to Mr. Eaves, hoping he would explain, but instead he said, "Boy, howdy! But it sure come a tide, now, hadn't it?" And then he went on to expound on the weather. I listened to them both, the rain and his drawl. They were comforting somehow in the silver-wet air.

Dec. 24, 1936

Christmas Eve, and no real work was accomplished today. There are still a few names on my list that are in town and within reach of the trolley lines, but I'm still feeling under the weather. The cramps are gnawing away in there.

No sign of the black Cadillac for a couple of days. I'm trying to convince myself he was interested in the people across the street.

Toward midday, I met Ellie downtown. The streets were full of Christmas shoppers, shoulder to shoulder in some places, and it reminded me of New York but on a much smaller scale. Ellie and I were among them, but with no one to buy for and no money to do it with anyway. Each of us had only one person.

We put our money together to get Miss Fenerty an assortment of chocolates and a poinsettia. We trundled through the cold, Ellie and I, our shoulders pressed into each other to keep warm and out of a sense of camaraderie. We laughed about things, small jokes I don't remember now and honestly don't have to remember. The sense of closeness was the crux of it all.

We arrived on her front porch in the cold. It looked as though she (and Nina...mostly Nina, rather) had put up more decorations. She ushered us in and smiled as we handed her the gifts.

"Well, let me put on some tea," she said.

When she left for the kitchen, Ellie and I looked through a bouquet of Christmas cards she'd received. One from Fort Worth, Texas from a couple named Will and Leah McShan, another from a man named Randolph in Magnolia, Arkansas, another from a woman named Klara O'Mara in St. Paul, Minnesota. *Hope to get down to see you again soon*, it said. There were quite a number of cards.

She brought the tray with the teapot and the china cups and set it down. Bing Crosby was singing on the radio as she poured me a cup of tea and handed it to me with two aspirins.

"I haven't had that sort of trouble since I was in my twenties," she said, "But I've raised several generations of girls."

I don't know how she knew. Maybe it was my body language. Her old hands rotated the poinsettia to show off its best side.

"On Christmas Eve, I always think of the first family I worked for, the Prudhommes. I worked there with Maggie after Ma died that year. They were French, Creoles as they say."

The house smelled brilliant like citrus and cinnamon and evergreens. She plucked a chocolate out for herself and passed the box to me and Ellie.

"Good for lady trouble," Miss Fenerty said as she leaned on her cane and eased back down into her chair.

"The Prudhommes had a fine house in the old part of town, St. Ann Street, just up from Dauphine." She crossed the edges of her hands in an intersection, one St. Ann Street, one Dauphine.

"Perhaps Mr. Roosevelt would like to hear this one, too."

Dec. 24, 1936, FWP, Transcript of Bridget Fenerty

The Prudhommes always celebrated Reveillon, as did most of the French in New Orleans. It was the one meal of the year that Madame supervised; she would never leave it to chance. She got in the kitchen with us and set us in motion, Maggie and me, and Madame would only go to Mass at St. Louis, the cathedral, when she knew we had things running properly.

When they returned from midnight Mass on Christmas Eve, there would be oyster gumbo, rabbit or duck pies, fish all sorts of ways and so forth. There would be daube glacé, which was a seasoned beef boiled with pigs' feet to make it into a jelly, grillades and grits, buche noel, pain perdu. Big bowls of thick creamy beige eggnog, with brandy generously applied. Turtle soup, fruits of all sorts. It was one of the finest meals of the year, like Thanksgiving is nowadays.

There were pistol shots in the air at midnight in the streets, celebrating the birth of the Christ child. Indoors, excited children ran around our feet as we set the table in the lamplight that filled the rooms up to the tall ceilings. Everything was on the best silver, all in the light of the hearth and the candles, light that bounced off the exquisite molding of the fireplace and the ceiling and doorframes, the velvet curtains with gold braided sashes casting shadows that tremored in the glow. Everything smelled deep and rich against the sharp greenery we had put up with Madame as decorations.

The last thing that was brought to the table was the café brulot, which was coffee with brandy and lemon and orange peels in it. It tasted kind of like a fruitcake, and Maggie and I had to be careful not to sample too much of it or we would be useless to our family when they came back from midnight Mass.

Monsieur was the one to set the café brulot ablaze, and then he himself brought it in, his face illuminated into a golden dancing amber by the flaming bowl. When the blaze burned off the brandy and extinguished itself, the ladle was dipped into it and cups passed around for all the family, even the youngest, whom Madame would hold on her lap and help to take a small sip.

Maggie and I were at the periphery of the scene, there to gather and fetch, but Monsieur always offered us a cup, and the toast was made in French and then to us in English:

À notre santé! Et à la vôtre! Joyeux Noel!

Dec. 25, 1936

When she made the toast, I translated for Ellie as we raised our cups of tea to one another:

To our health, and to yours! Merry Christmas!

That was last night, and today of course was Christmas Day. I expected that Lemurier and Mirlette would observe it; I assumed they were Christians. If they did, they observed it smoking and napping and making noisy love in their room and napping again. It bothered me that they didn't observe it. It was as if the universe was poorly balanced if gentiles didn't celebrate Christmas.

Ellie went to services at the Baptist Church in the best clothes she has, cotton dress, corduroy coat, tattered white cotton gloves. I would have gone to church with her, not on religious reasons of course, but just so she (and I) wouldn't have had to be alone. She misses her family. She had expected to hear from them, and I think it pains her.

We made a little Christmas dinner together. Ellie roasted a chicken. We had canned green beans and cranberry sauce we had gotten at Leon Johnson's supermarket, and we talked about New York and the things we'll do in the city. We made ourselves all the holiday we could, and it was a pleasant one.

Lemurier woke up a little after noon and complained about the mess in the kitchen. Then he and Mirlette got into a fight, in English. I rarely hear him speak French, even when they fight, which is often. Finally, Ellie and I had had enough, and we took the trolley downtown. It was decorated with greenery for the season, and when we got on and paid our fare (clunk-clink) the driver wished us a Merry Christmas.

Ellie asked him if he would be able to spend time with his family and he said, yes, that 'Santee Claws' had stopped by, and that he had gotten to watch his children open the things that Santa had brought them. The trolley was mostly empty, and we sat up front and talked to him as he repeated the cycle of stopping, ringing the bell, swinging the handle in its arc to open the door and back again to close it, and then rumbling forward again to repeat it all at the next stop.

When we got off downtown we wished the stone generals and the granite governor and Sergeant Locket and Clio the muse of history all a Merry Christmas. All the shops were closed, of course, so we wandered the streets looking over the decorations. On Crockett Street, we saw the lights inside Miss Fenerty's, and we took her up on the offer she'd made us the day before to stop by 'for a little cheer.' Inside, we found her struggling to put leftovers away. She said that Nina was with her family (and why shouldn't it be so, then? Miss Fenerty said).

People had been in and out all day, she said, "but now that I've seen the two of you, I've seen all my favorites." I'm sure she's told everyone that, and I'm sure she's probably meant it to everyone.

We helped her with the dishes and the leftovers, and then again after we had eaten cold dressing and cranberry relish and turkey. We talked the rest of the afternoon about recipes for soda bread, and literature, and how to get stains out of muslin (cold water and cider vinegar, unless it's a berry stain, and then use a dilute solution of bleach, she said), and Greek and Roman history, and how to "privy train" a child (don't start too early, follow their cues), and the state of affairs in Europe, and our favorite poets, and how to make ginger snaps so that they don't stick to the cookie sheet, Shakespeare's sonnets, the merits of a cur dog over a pure-breed.

We talked about the "*city of New Yark and what a fine adventure it'll be, sure.*" At last she told us to go home and pack and return to stay at her house tonight. The station's just a few blocks down Louisiana, and she would see us up and with a breakfast in the morning.

We did it, each of us glad to be out of the gloom of our lodgings and in the warm glow of Miss Fenerty and her home. As I write this, I can hear her singing in the kitchen, the sound of green velvet, rich and comfortable. The sound like a warm bath when the afternoon is cold and rainy outside.

Dec. 26, 1936

We slept in rooms right next to each other, Ellie staying up late into the night, sitting on the edge of my bed and talking excitedly about today. At last, I was so sleepy that I fell asleep while she was still talking to me.

This morning, Miss Fenerty had made us biscuits, scrambled eggs, bacon (for Ellie), and jelly. The three of us walked down to the train station on Louisiana. Miss Fenerty's cane probed the sidewalk before her. She was surprisingly quick for ninety-four.

The train pulled in from somewhere west, Marshall, Texas, I take it, and Ellie and I got on after hugging and thanking Miss Fenerty again. She smiled and braced herself on her cane as she stood on the platform and waved to us. As the train began to huff in preparation, I worried that Miss Fenerty might slip on the hill back up to Crockett Street, but then I saw her turn and strike up a conversation with one of the station agents, a man in a billed cap who took her arm and walked her down the platform as the train slowly pulled out.

I looked at my hand as it waved and realized that I wasn't wearing my engagement ring. Not only that, I wasn't sure where it was. I had the porter pull my bag from the back of the car, frantic that I had forgotten it. I rummaged through my bag, checking every corner until I found it in the compartment I had put it in when I left New York.

The train pulled us over the Red, the bridge Ellie had painted the day I met her, so drab and rusty when not viewed through her eyes. I looked down again at my left hand resting on my right hand in my lap and my finger. I studied the ring, small icy fragments, outcroppings of crystal, the queen of a diamond set in silver pronged settings. Certainly it's worth a small fortune. Then I looked up to watch Ellie look out the window, her forehead pressed against the cold glass, resting on a layer of golden bangs. I turned the ring on my finger so that the stone was to my palm.

Toward midday as I read, Ellie said, "Look. It's the Mississippi."

I looked up from my book to see Vicksburg crawling up the hill on the opposite bank, and I thought of Champ Lockett and wondered where he was in all this. The train chugged through the iron girders as the river seemed so large and far below as to not be moving at all.

At noon, we ate lunch in the dining car with a woman and her teenage daughter who were on their way to Savannah to visit an aunt. The girl still sported the moonscape of puberty on her face and seemed preoccupied with her hair. Every time a man under the age of thirty entered our car, her eyes greeted him and fled back to us. Her mother and I chatted. I asked if she knew of any Wilkins there. The woman said that she didn't, including any Savanna Wilkins, even though the woman had grown up there all her life.

After lunch, I read a day-old copy of the *Jackson Clarion-Ledger* while Ellie sketched. She drew the people on the train, capturing their motion, their expressions, hinting at what secrets they might have and changing them with a small stroke of her pencil. The train jostled us but her hand stayed steady. I was thinking about what problem Lemurier could have with Ellie's ideas. She could look at something, capture the essence of it, and portray it perfectly. She must've been thinking about the same thing.

"Our field manager only responds to him. Lemurier can be charming when he has to be, if you can believe it. Maybe it's the accent," Ellie said as she watched her pencil shade a portion of her sketch, part of a field and a barn.

I knew exactly the scene we had passed; it was just before we reached Meridian. I remembered there being cows around the barn, but Ellie had left them out. As I was thinking that, she added them, a group around a trough with a calf among them.

"Do you think you could go over his head?"

"Maybe." She closed one eye, and her tongue touched her upper lip as she added something fine and delicate to her sketch. "I'll give it a little more time, I guess. It's best I take my quarrel straight to him. How we do it in Texas. Straight up."

We traveled in a small sphere of comfortable silence. I drifted to sleep, and, when we woke up, we were in Alabama. I stood up and stretched my arms high. There were two men across the train watching me, and it made me put my arms down quickly. They looked away and out the window. Caught looking, as the baseball radio man says.

I went to the dining car and brought us back two coffees, cream and sugar for me, black for her. She put away her sketch pad and took her coffee from me with a smile. To know how someone takes her coffee without asking: a kind of intimacy.

As the sun went down, the porter summoned us by row to the dining car. We were seated with a man on his way to Atlanta, a drummer for a paint company returning home. He was pleasant enough company, though he talked quite a bit. His hair was slicked back, and he had his napkin tucked into his shirt. There was a gap in between his front teeth that seemed to broaden when he smiled.

"You girls been friends long?" he asked.

"A few weeks," I said. It seemed strange to tell him it had just been a few weeks. It seems like longer.

The first thing he asked when he found out we were living in Shreveport was if we knew Champ Lockett.

"In Atlanta, we don't have too many of our old heroes anymore," he said as he put a bite of steak in his mouth. He mumbled down into his plate to keep from opening his mouth. "I met him once, when I was in Buckelew's on a call."

"The hardware store?" Ellie asked.

"That's right. Mr. Buckelew used to pay him to sit in there and attract a crowd," he said. "People would come in there to see him and then buy a few ten-penny nails or a mousetrap or a new shovel. Gallon of paint or two, of course."

The paint salesman went on to expound on pigments and lead compounds and things as his fork chased his food around the plate like a dog herding sheep. The talk about paint was more interesting to Ellie than to me. Shades and hues and pigments.

Well, that's enough writing for tonight. The train is rocking me to sleep here in my berth.

Dec. 27, 1936

Stopped in Atlanta today where a flurry of people got on and off, including the woman and her daughter bound for Savannah and the paint drummer.

"Say howdy to Champ Lockett for me, now," he said as he waited in the aisle in the queue to detrain. He held an old tan valise at his knee, smiling a gap-toothed smile. A stray strand of shining wet hair fell over his forehead.

After Atlanta, the train continued on through the afternoon where there were bits of snow in isolated patches in the deeper, darker places in the woods. As we were crossing into North Carolina, Ellie said, "Look there, how beautiful."

Two doe were browsing at the edge of a clearing. Behind them a gray, leafless forest receded into a tangled, black flurry of branches and trunks. I said nothing, and Ellie turned to look at me, hoping for a smile to meet hers. I gave her a weak one. It was just for a moment, and when we looked again, the doe were gone.

We rode quietly then. The sound of the engine bellowing at crossings and the ticking on the tracks had long since become background noise. I was thinking about Miss Fenerty. Ellie must have been also.

"Did she ever marry?" she asked as she sketched.

"Who?" I asked, just to make sure.

"Miss Fenerty. Do you think she ever married?"

"She was born a Fenerty. I know that much because she told me. And she's still a Fenerty. Probably not, unless she was divorced or widowed and went back to her maiden name."

Ellie twisted her head and put her tongue to her upper lip. I've noticed that she does this as puts in a crucial detail into a drawing. On the paper, two doe were emerging at the edge of a clearing.

We connected in Washington at Union Station with just enough time for dinner. We would have liked to look around if not for time considerations. Neither of us have ever been. We vowed to come back and see it all one day. We had a quick dinner in the station, and I talked Ellie into having a glass of wine, which was a big stretch for a Baptist girl. Later as we waited on the wooden benches for our next and last connection, she fell asleep, unaccustomed to wine, I'm sure. She leaned into me, and I enjoyed her body, her presence, nestled into mine. I waited to wake her until the last call for our train to New York.

As we rested, propped together, I saw Lillian Vilcher get off a train from New York, I'm sure to enjoy her new position as the junior Washington correspondent for the *New York Herald Tribune*. I sunk back into the bench and pulled my hat down over my face as she disappeared in a rush of travelers, and a grainy voice called arrivals and departures overhead. A sleeping Ellie sunk back with me. We left Washington Union just before midnight. I've finished my book with nothing else to read.

Dec. 28, 1936

I woke this morning with a sense that the train had slowed to a deliberate rhythm on the tracks beneath us. I looked in Ellie's berth and found it empty, so I went forward into the observation car. There she was. The sunlight of a New York City winter morning slanted down on the city from the south, over the rooftops patched with snow and pipes dribbling steam up into the crystal air. The boxy dark outline of the city was backlit by the morning sky, vivid and light blue.

Ellie put her face to the cold glass of the window pane and looked up and out to the city skyline. Her expression was one of wonder, pure wonder. Her head pivoted slightly as her gaze scanned the skyline, hundreds of buildings, each bigger than any she's ever seen. I pointed out the spire of the Empire State Building.

"See the tallest one, the pointed one? And over there, the other pointed one, that's the Chrysler building. And there's the Woolworth building, and there's the Singer building."

"I thought Dallas and Shreveport were big. Or the grain elevator in Perryton."

I leaned in next to her and looked out at the city. I felt like I was seeing it for the first time, too, though I've lived here all my life, except for the last month. It seems like ten years now.

We disappeared into the tunnel under the Hudson, and then the train pulled into Penn Station with a dull metal-on-metal shriek and the rumbling concussion of train couplings slamming together. Above the platforms, the ornate steel girders framed the skylights that seeped pale light into the immense space of the station. We collected our bags, though they aren't much for such a long journey.

Penn Station swarmed with people, each moving in random, unique, important directions. Men in business suits walked while reading folded over newspapers. Well-dressed women were followed by Negro porters in bellman's caps, pulling carts with mounds of luggage. Mothers held tightly to children's hands as fathers scanned the big schedule boards with dozens of places on them. Tourists from the hinterlands were rubbernecking at it all.

Ellie was one of them. I was watching her watching everyone and everything as the hollow voice called out track numbers and destinations overhead somewhere. My free hand took her free hand, and I led her down to the subway platforms as people turned sideways to dart past us down the stairs. Down in the tunnels, subway trains thundered like dragons, some moving to the station, some moving away. I never realized how noisy the city is.

A bum slept in a pile of papers near the edge of the subway platform; a policeman nudged him with his foot and told him to move away from the tracks. The man sat up in his nest and rubbed his matted eyes and beard and began gathering his grimy belongings to move away toward the wall. The clattering roar of the subway rose in the darkness of the tunnel, and Ellie held my hand tighter. The doors opened, and the crowd pressed our suitcases into our legs as we all jammed together onto the train. Ellie and I stood and held onto the overhead rail. It was slightly more of a stretch for her, as she's not quite my height.

We managed two seats and rode quietly with our suitcases jiggling in our laps. We got out on Delancey Street and emerged into the hard cold Manhattan air. On the street, Spanish, Italian, Yiddish all spewed into the air, all within a few steps. We passed a group of men, and I clearly heard the Puerto Rican slang term for vagina. Buses droned, taxis honked, drivers cursed one another.

When we got to our building, there was no doorman like our old apartment, just a scruffy lobby of unwaxed black tile and a set of stairs that were the only way up since the elevator hasn't worked since before we lived there. An old woman (I think her name is Mrs. Greenfeld) was at the mailboxes going through her mail, her stockings sagging at her ankles. She looked up without saying anything and then back down at her mail as she sorted through it as if it were a bad hand of cards.

I felt embarrassed by our building, but Ellie's face still held a look of wonder. We went up the three flights of stairs, lugging our suitcases, though mine was certainly lighter than the Presto recorder that I'd left back in Shreveport. I set my bag down and knocked on the door. Ellie set hers down and took off her cloche. Static lifted stray strands of blonde and set them down again. Behind the door I could hear the spasmodic whirring of mother's sewing machine. It paused, and there were footsteps.

"Who is it?" my mother's muffled voice asked.

"It's me, Mother..." The door opened suddenly. "...Miriam," I finished as I saw her face.

"Miriam." Mother looked as though she didn't believe it was me. She was holding a pin cushion in one hand, a felt covered ball. Her hands cradled my face, and the soft felt of the pin cushion caressed my cheek.

"Surprise!" I said as she kissed my forehead and my cheek and held my face in her hands like she used to do when I returned from camp in the summers.

"And who is your friend?" she asked.

"This is Ellie, Ellie Schultis," I said. "She's working for Mr. Roosevelt, too. She's a painter."

They grasped hands as I looked past Mother.

"Is Father home?"

"He's asleep. He worked the graveyard shift at the paper. The printing press room."

He appeared in the short hallway in his undershirt, pulling his suspenders over his shoulders.

"I thought I heard your voice," he said.

Father shook my hand, and I embraced him instead and kissed his cheek.

"You're a good man, Father," I whispered to him. He drew me to himself closer and kissed my head. It was perhaps the most emotion, the most affection, I've ever seen from him.

"This is my friend Ellie Schultis," I told him. "She's from Texas." I didn't mean to, but I said it like she was an exotic animal brought in from some strange land, like the Romans used to parade lions and tigers through the Piazza Navona.

"Howdy," she said for effect as she shook his hand.

"Hello," Father said. He patted his chest looking for his eyeglasses in his shirt pocket and realized he just had on an undershirt. He retreated to their bedroom and returned wearing a regular shirt.

"Where's Leonard?" I asked Mother.

"Working over the holidays. You just missed him. Let me clean up his room," she scurried down the hall. Her voice was small in the other room. "He moved into it when you left. I'll put clean sheets on the bed for you. He can sleep on the couch again to give you girls some privacy."

Mother put sheets on the bed, and Ellie went to help as I sat with Father. He asked me about Shreveport and its economy and culture. Was there a synagogue? Yes, I said, a very nice one. Are they conservative or reformed? he asked. Reformed, I said. How are the locals with the Jews there? Everyone seems very respectful of one another, I said.

Mother and Ellie returned, and we sat and had coffee, which seemed weaker than before I left. Maybe it was. The radio was missing, too. It used to sit on a little stand right next to the kitchen table. I know they must have pawned it, but I don't dare ask. It would embarrass them. Mother said that I was looking well and asked if I had met anyone interesting. I told her about Savannah Wilkins and Moses Cotter and about June Longhat, the Caddo woman.

"That reminds me of your bubby Levy. Never knew more than twenty words of English. Everything Yiddish except for a little Polish..."

"…her brother had a mark put on his coat at Ellis Island and was sent back to Poland," I finished the story I had heard so many times. Mother smiled at my having remembered it, and I was reminded that I have her perfect teeth. Leonard has Father's crooked ones.

"Is she still alive?" Ellie asked.

"Bubby Levy, Miriam's grandmother, died while Miriam was at Barnard," Mother said.

Like June Longhat dying with her Caddo, I thought. I wished I had visited my grandmother more often and written down her stories, tales of the Cossacks and the crossing and Ellis Island and the old ways. And all the hard work, all that hard work, to ascend to the upper east side only to fall back down to the lower east again with the Crash, right where the Levys and the Levensons started from off the boat. Father's voice startled me. He was rinsing his cup in the sink.

"Now Schultis," he said. "That's an interesting name."

"German," Ellie said. "It was Schultz a long time ago. Somebody changed it but we're not sure who."

"Germans in Texas?" Mother asked.

"Yes ma'am. Quite a number. You'd be surprised."

"We know an Irish woman in Shreveport," I said. "Miss Fenerty. She gave us our train tickets. As a gift."

"That was very generous of her. She sounds like a nice lady," Mother said.

Father kissed Mother and excused himself to go back to bed for the day. When we heard the door to their bedroom shut, Mother asked if Irving knew I was in. It was startling, like a slap on the face or a shoulder shake. I'd been expecting it, of course, but it was still a jolt. It was a valid question that I don't fault her for asking. I was aware that I'd taken off my ring again and stowed it in my suitcase.

"I wanted to surprise him, too," I managed to say.

"I'll go call him to get him to come by," Mother said hurriedly as she set her coffee cup down. "But I won't tell him you're home."

I hope my face didn't betray me. If the truth be told, which it is here in this journal, my heart sank a little on hearing his name. How awful of me, but truthfully it did. She left to go down to the grocer to call him, and he was here within half an hour. When he arrived he rushed in the door and took off his hat. We shared a kiss; my half was perfunctory, mechanical. I could feel his hands working on my waist, yearning to caress more private places. Mother introduced Ellie and Irving, and they politely shook hands. Ellie gave him a sideways, appraising look and asked him, "Yankees or Giants?"

"Yankees," Irving said.

They fell into a conversation about baseball, both looking forward to the season a few months away. Ellie is a St. Louis Cardinals fan, something I didn't know until today. They talked about their favorite players, Dizzy Dean for Ellie, Lou Gehrig for Irving, and the relative merits of Durocher of the Cardinals versus Crosetti for the Yankees at shortstop. They talked batting averages, home run hitters, curveballs, fastballs, changeups, who had the best of each. I had no idea she was such a fan.

He wanted to take us out to dinner, but I claimed fatigue for Ellie and me. Instead, he left and got take out from Katz' for us, and we ate crowded around the little kitchen table. Father woke up and ate with us before leaving for his evening shift at the newspaper. At least one of us is working at a paper, I thought.

Afterward, Irving wanted to lure me out for a walk, but I again pleaded exhaustion after our long trip. He stood in the doorway, twirling his hat in his hands, his black wool coat hanging to his knees and concealing a body that I could feel yearning for me. He left disappointed. He left me relieved.

This afternoon after he left, a little sullen, Ellie and I took a nap on the bed in Leonard's room. Despite Mother's efforts, my old room, now Leonard's (Lennie he calls himself now, which may be to impress Ellie) room has the musky smell of an adolescent male, the smell of dirty socks and sweat and confused glands. The smell of desire casting about aimlessly.

Leonard came home in the darkness from his job as a busboy. He looked tired as he undid his bowtie and the top button of his white shirt. But when Ellie emerged from the bathroom, his eyes widened and assessed her. Before I could, he introduced himself as 'Lennie.'

I write all this in the light of a full moon that hangs over the city, enough light that I don't need a lamp. Ellie sits up in her nightgown craning her head to see the Brooklyn Bridge, just a small portion of it visible between gaps in buildings. Her feet are under her, and her arms are propped on the window sill. Her breath fogs the windows which she wipes clear with her forearms. If I was any good at drawing, I would draw her here.

My dolls are still up on the shelf, and a Barnard pennant is on the wall. They both seem to be from the same, ancient era. Ellie and I are settled in, sharing the bed I had grown up in, our faces washed in moonlight, pale and timeless. The city skyline is outlined black against it and pocked with squares of light from other people's windows.

Dec. 29, 1936

We took the Fifth Avenue bus and exited before 82nd Street. I must confess it was so I could look in the window of our old house, the brownstone between Lexington and Park on 81st. Several of the businesses have closed, Mr. Bonfanti's grocery, boarded up, Mr. Spatz' florist. Some are still open, but the shopkeepers didn't seem to recognize me. They see so many people every day, and besides, it's been several years since we lived here.

At last we came to our old house. In one of the front windows there was a Christmas tree where Father used to place the menorah. In the other window, the same two granite swans flanked a planter that was filled with snow this time of year. In the spring and summer it's filled with bright flowers, or at least it used to be. I hope the new occupants still put flowers there, geraniums, petunias, something.

"Does this place mean something to you?" Ellie's voice sounded underwater for a second. I looked over to see her red cheeks and straws of yellow hair framed by her black knit cap.

"We used to live here," I said. "I used to talk to these granite swans when I was little. I wonder if there's a little girl who lives here now who talks to them," I mumbled as I peered into the windows. "Do you think granite swans get lonely for little girls to talk to?"

"I bet girls get lonely for granite swans," Ellie said, and she took my arm. We started up 82nd, and I looked back and took one last look at our old home.

On Fifth Avenue in front of the museum, a man and a child bought roasted chestnuts from a street vendor. The little boy was bundled in a coat a size too big and fidgeted as his father, a man in a gray fedora and overcoat, paid for and received the bundle. The boy stood on one leg peering behind the glass at the chestnuts roasting on the grate. The father slipped his change into his wallet and the two of them, man and boy, joined hands and walked into the park on a path between the mounds of plowed snow.

"Do you think you'll ever have children?" I asked Ellie.

"I know I've changed a lifetime of diapers and wiped an eternity of runny noses. I would be fine without them. Does that shock you?" she asked me.

"No," I said. "But I bet you would be good with them."

"I was. But a family is a lot of work, believe me. And in these uncertain times, well…"

We ascended the steps of the Met holding hands like two schoolgirls. On entering the lobby, Ellie looked up at the architecture and pulled off her hat. The knitted black cloche had small crystal drops of mist on it the size of tiny pearls. Her hair retained the shape of the cloche, blonde strands matted down, her lips parted around her open mouth as it gaped at the immense room. Echoes of conversation were far away as I watched her take it all in, columns, arches, domes, art lurking down corridors and in side chambers like hidden treasure. Marble busts of ancient forgotten men, noses missing, penises broken off, while the subjects look away stoically.

We checked our coats at the cloak room and then wandered the halls, looking at the gallery map, glancing up, consulting the map again. In almost every chamber, there was at least one thing that caught her eye. I asked her how she knew so much about art.

"I went to school in Austin for a semester," she said. "Before things got bad for us."

We passed a painting of Perseus holding Medusa's severed head. We stood contemplating it, Ellie and I.

"That Perseus, so sly," Ellie whispered. "He used a shield with mirrors on it so the Medusa would finally see herself for what she was. It scared the shit out of her, and Perseus cut off her head."

I stood looking at Medusa's frightened face, the tangle of snakes arising from her scalp all around it. When at last I looked up, Ellie was at the other end of the gallery, enthralled with something else. Before I joined her, I looked up again at the face of the Medusa, her horror at having seen herself for the first time, and I thought of the line from the Robert Burns poem, "To a Louse":

Oh, to see ourselves as others see us.

After a day at the Met, Irving met us for dinner at an Italian restaurant on Madison. I listened to them talk baseball, and she asked him all about kosher food and how it's made and the reasons for it. For a girl who grew up having to eat anything edible, I'm sure it seems strange to automatically cross things off the list out of faith or principle. Even though Ellie rested her leg comfortably against mine under the table, I caught Irving looking at her once or twice. I tried not to let it bother me. I can imagine what Miss Fenerty might say: *well, a pretty girl is part of God's creation, too, now isn't she, then? A gentleman's bound to take a look at one.*

Dec. 30, 1936

We spent the morning helping Mother around the house, going to the grocer for her, cleaning the kitchen, and so forth. Ellie surprised me (again) when she told Mother she could help her with some of the sewing, the basic things. They sat and talked as Mother watched seams disappear under the silver pressor foot, and Ellie put on buttons. Busy hands and carefree tongues.

Irving offered to get us tickets to the opera; *Carmen* was playing with Gertrud Wettergren in the title role and Charles Kullman as Don José. I know he has little interest in the arts, and it was thoughtful of him. We took him up on it.

Before the performance, he took us to a French restaurant and then afterward offered to get us a cab, but Ellie wanted to walk through the snow, so we did. The snow filtered down from the night sky, bending and whirling among the bare trees in the dark, the flakes illuminated by the city lights. Irving's gloved hand held mine.

We entered the theater, shedding our scarves and hats. I don't think Ellie was prepared for the size or beauty of it. Her head craned around as she looked up to the ceiling, and then into every corner, looking around, up to the balcony, down to the orchestra pit.

The three of us sat together, in very nice seats, I have to say, Irving reading the playbill distractedly. Meanwhile, I watched Ellie continue to take in the ornate theater, gold-trimmed frieze work, red velvet upholstery, woodwinds, strings, and brassy horns in the pit going up and down scales. The crowd murmured as they waited. Even as the orchestra was tuning up, Irving was nodding, and by the time the houselights fell and the curtain opened, he was asleep. Ellie reached over, and we held hands like sisters. Her hand felt good in mine.

When the curtain opened, I was watching her, her eyes filled with the scenery on the stage, her ears filled with the music. With the first powerful blast from Miss Wettergren's Carmen, Ellie's mouth formed an O in amazement. She looked at me and then back to the stage and then at me again.

"How can she make such a sound, such a big, beautiful sound?" Ellie whispered.

I smiled and shrugged my shoulders. I've often wondered the same thing.

"What language is this?" she said into my ear. Our faces were side by side, our cheeks almost touching.

"French," I whispered back.

"An opera about Spain, sung in French?"

"Yes," I replied.

"Wow," she mouthed. Her eyes were illuminated in the same colors as the stage, like all the faces around us. As the performance played itself out, I whispered brief translations to her, and she nodded as her face smiled into the lights and the kettle drum pounded and the orchestra soared. Escamillo, played by Ezio Pinza, sang "The Toreador Song," and the crowd clapped its appreciation. We didn't, though it was a beautifully done rendition; we kept holding hands. At the end, in the final scene in which Carmen throws down Don Jose's ring and in return he stabs her, I looked at Irving. He had slept through the whole thing.

December 31, 1936

Just a few words today. We ate bagels and lox, and cheese blintzes that Irving brought the day before. Ellie and I spent the day wandering the city. We saw a man painting portraits on Fifth Avenue by the Park, and I thought of Dan Fenerty working for Monsieur Glospere.

Head up, merci, monsieur. They will be ready shortly.

Ellie seems a little blue, and I think she may be missing her family and feeling guilty for being here instead of with them. While it's true she's not sure exactly where they are, she thought she would have heard from them over the holidays. Still, we looked for postcards of the city and sent them hoping they would find the right recipient.

Time to get ready. Tonight Irving is taking us to Time Square to ring in the New Year.

Jan. 1, 1937

Oh my. Where do I begin? My heart is racing and won't stop. Perhaps writing about it will help me calm down.

We wandered the dense crowds in Times Square to the blare of party horns and people wearing novelty glasses in the shape of 1937, everyone drunk or on their way to getting drunk. Ellie, Irving, and I were among them.

Irving took us by his office on Seventh Avenue while around the corner on Broadway people were shoulder to shoulder, huddled in the cold and watching the ball which was less than half an hour from sliding down the pole. Irving stopped at the doorway of his company's midtown office, the one they just acquired that has a small two room apartment attached. He fished the key out of his pocket as he said, "I have to make a telephone call. Need to make sure a shipment of gefilte arrived in Pittsburgh." His voice was clownish as he did a quick pivot of his head and said, "They love their gefilte in Pittsburgh!"

The door opened as he said, "You girls want to come upstairs in the warmth while I do?"

"No," Ellie answered quickly. Her drawl was a little more pronounced from alcohol. "I mean, we'll just bundle up down here and watch the crowds, won't we, Miriam?"

"Suit yourself," he said, and he ascended the stairs.

It happened so suddenly. As soon as Irving's footsteps receded on the steps, Ellie spun me to her, and she kissed me. It wasn't a Ned Hennessy quick street corner peck, either. It was like two people in the desert, taking the last pull of water from a canteen, like two people trapped under water gasping for a last breath from an air pocket. It took a moment, and, in that moment, that small, sacred moment, I realized that I was kissing her back. The crowd seemed to fade away, and all I was aware of was Ellie and our alcohol-sweet breath on each other. Then the party horns and the shouts faded back in, and then we heard the drum of Irving's footsteps on the stairs, and we separated.

Irving returned to an odd silence. He seemed not to notice, but then again, oblivion is Irving's strong suit.

"Made it! Right on time to Pittsburgh!"

We made our way down into the midst of the Times Square crowds. My head was spinning, and I would like to say it was the alcohol. That would be a more convenient explanation. But that wouldn't be the truth.

When the ball dropped at midnight, the noise of the crowd rose in a crescendo, and Irving kissed Ellie on the cheek and me on the lips, but it was a Ned Hennessy street corner peck compared to the kiss Ellie and I had shared. This time, she and I exchanged small pointed kisses on the cheek. Irving turned to Broadway and said, "Come on girls, what say let's go for cheesecake and coffee?"

As we separated behind Irving to follow him, I felt her hand, the thumb outstretched, sweep across my breast. I closed my eyes and exhaled as the noise of the crowd faded out and then back in like the sweep of the dial across a radio station.

We were subdued as we had our cheesecake and coffee. The streets were clearing of revelers, and we headed back to the midtown office. The three of us were quiet, the alcohol beginning to recede and reveal the consequences of our revelry. Ellie rested her head against the wall of the building and shut her eyes. Irving wrestled the key out of his pocket.

In the office-apartment, he gave Ellie a blanket and a pillow from a cabinet. She was asleep on the couch within a minute. I watched her slumber, the way her lips parted slightly, her eyelids peacefully closed with a rim of blonde lashes.

I was startled when Irving took me by the hand and led me to the bedroom. On the wall, a radiator thumped a metallic rhythm of heat into the room. He kissed me, and I turned my head from his breath, steeped in the smell of Cuban cigars and scotch whiskey. He kissed my neck, one side and then the other. I closed my eyes as he unbuttoned us, shaking our clothes as if that would help remove them.

We climbed under the covers. He fumbled with the prophylactic and then with himself and then with me. After a couple of wayward stabs, he found me. I was just beginning to respond when it was over, and Irving was asleep.

It wasn't the first time we were together. That was on the night before I left, at the Waldorf, when he proposed. No, tonight wasn't our first time together, but I can't help feeling it will be our last.

For I realized that the person I had been thinking of, the person who had inspired my near-ecstasy, was sleeping in the next room.

Part III
January, 1937

Jan. 2, 1937

Lennie, as he likes to be called now, is working a graveyard shift. Mother and Father wish he wouldn't but allow it since school won't be back in for another day or two. It does leave the couch open, however. I slept there last night, leaving the bed to Ellie. Mother thinks we're still hungover, but a hangover doesn't feel this bad.

Jan. 3 1937

Said goodbye to Mother, Father, and Lennie. And Irving, of course, who brushed my bottom when he thought no one was looking, but I think Mother saw it. She certainly saw me shudder.

I'm writing this in my berth on the train back to Louisiana. Ellie is in the one right below me, and I wonder if she's awake or not. All day, an invisible, stony silence sat wedged between us like a ghost child. Ellie sat looking out the window at the gray evolving countryside, the smile she had worn on the trip up to the city replaced by a neutral horizontal strip that bordered on a frown.

"I need to stretch my legs," she said at one point, and when she got up, the train lurched out of rhythm slightly, and she fell back toward me. I put my hand on the small of her back to brace her. We both felt it, how good, how delicious, how electric, my hand on the small of her back. But Ellie's chin and eyes fell to the floor, and her expression with it, and she hurried into the aisle and moved to the back of the train, her hands on the edge of each seat, bracing her steps. I looked out the window; the train clattered on. The genie is trying to push the cork out of the bottle, and I wonder if Ellie's as terrified by it as I am.

Jan. 4, 1937

Somewhere in Georgia. I spend my time reading, she spends her time sketching. We say very little to each other and avoid eye contact. It's rained all day, hard enough to make the day seem like night and send sheets of rain that cascade down the windows and obscure the countryside.

Male passengers try to engage us in conversation, a salesman from Winston-Salem, an attorney from Richmond, lightly flirting with us. I wearily try to discourage them; I think Ellie does the same. Earlier today, I watched her sleep on the seat beside me, her downy blonde hair flowing from under her black wool hat like water flowing from a spring, falling over her forehead and eyes, her head pressed into the cold glass of the window as winter scenes of snow and barns and icy streams scrolled behind her. She has a habit of tucking the fingers of one hand between her knees when she sleeps, as endearing as her slightly pigeon-toed walk. Her lips are parted slightly in sleep, a small strip of enamel-white teeth in between them. Those lips. Mine touched them, and I am not the same now.

Jan. 5, 1937

We got into Shreveport around ten o'clock at night. The city was beginning to sleep; lights in the windows of houses were winking into darkness, one by one. The train pulled into the station with a low groan, and we collected our suitcases. There was another awkward moment on the train platform.

"Thank you for taking me," she said. Then she added, "I'm sorry," and she picked up her suitcase and walked quickly, not quite a run, up Louisiana Avenue towards the Y. Her footsteps clopped away, and, when she turned the corner, they faded to nothing. I turned to walk the few steps down to the trolley stop. As I did, I resisted the urge to look over my shoulder to see her depart up Louisiana Avenue in the other direction. I was afraid she would be looking back.

I sat on the bench under the street light with my breath steaming out of me and into small, thin temporary clouds in the black night air. I waited about fifteen minutes in the cold before I realized the trolleys didn't run that late. Rather than walk the three or four miles to Stephenson and hope that Lemurier would let me in, I walked to Crockett Street instead.

The lights were on in the windows, warm, inviting subdivided rectangles of orange light, though the Christmas lights and the tree and the menorah have been taken down. I ascended the steps of her house, set down my suitcase, and knocked on the door. I was embarrassed to be showing up so late and unannounced. The creaking steps signaled her slow progress over the wood floor.

"Coming," she said in the distance. The door cracked open. Miss Fenerty was in her robe and nightgown, and her blue tam.

"Well, it's my best girl!" she said. "I was just wishing for some company, and I couldn't have had my wish granted so well! Come in, and tell me all about your trip."

She looked out onto the porch behind me. "Where is Ellie?"

"She went back to the Y," I said. I felt vacant, yes, vacant is the word.

"You left your recorder here over the holiday." She pointed to it with her cane as she made her way back to her chair. "I hope you weren't worried for it."

The gas space heater glowed blue and amber. She sat in her chair and reached down and pulled up a red mesh bag of *Gulfstream Brand Satsuma Oranges*. Her old hands pulled at the bag, and, after a weak attempt, she handed it to me.

"Will you open this, dear?"

I feigned a slight difficulty and then easily opened the bag. She reached into it and pulled out a small squatty round type of fruit grown on the coast called a satsuma. She admired it, rotating it in her old hands. At last she worked a thumbnail into a spot and delicately began removing the peel. The aroma of it, an intense, brilliant, invisible orange scent leached into the room.

"A friend always sends me a bag of these little jewels every Christmas. Well, then. Tell me about your trip to New York." New *Yark*, she said it.

"It was great to be home. Great to see my family," I said.

"Family is everything," she said with her eyes on her fingers and the satsuma. She pulled away a section and gave it to me. "And your friend, Ellie, did she enjoy the city?"

"Like a kid in a candy store," I said as I tasted the section of orange, tangy and sweet and juicy.

"'Tis grand, sure," she said, watching the operation she was performing on the fruit. "I've been there exactly once. The year nineteen-fifteen. I suppose it was on account of seeing Jenny Lind sixty years earlier that I went, if you trace it all the way to its source."

She handed me another section. I put it in my mouth, and it was like sweet, dazzling fireworks. Her head was tilted. Her thumbs pulled away the bitter orange peel from the inner sweetness.

"I sang there once, in New York, in the theater. And I could have sung in England and Europe if it weren't for my fear, a fear that began when I was a little girl. That day that I swam with my brothers and Ned was the beginning of it, if you don't count Da being slid into the sea."

There were two sections of satsuma left, and she gave one to me and ate the other one.

"Well, perhaps Mr. Roosevelt would like to hear the story. If you're not too tired from your travel, I'll tell it to you and the recorder, despite the hour. But I'll warn you now, it isn't a happy one. It was the beginning of some dark years, and they could have destroyed me, had I allowed them."

I was too tired to object. And her voice was a comfort to me.

Jan. 5, 1937, FWP, Transcript of Bridget Fenerty

    The summer heat was upon us good then, the shade only slightly more bearable than full sun. Distant objects wavered in the heat, uneven and blurry from it like they were behind

145

hand-blown glass.

It was July, and the newspapers were paying tribute to Henry Clay, who had died a few weeks earlier.[12] After the summer before and the near accident with the train, we swam in the river, as stinking as it was. I was about ten that summer. Patch a year older, and Dan a couple of years older still.

Dan was pale and soft and studious, a thinking sort of boy, and he rarely swam with us. Because it was summer, the city had thinned out, and the daguerreotype business had settled down. Later it would pick up again when the yellow jack returned and people came in to arrange death portraits, but there was a lull at that in-between time of year, and Dan had extra time.

He was the kind of boy who had the railroad timetables memorized and could tell you when any train was departing or arriving and where it was going. He knew all sorts of other things such as all thirty-one states and their capitals, the amendments to the Constitution, and so forth. Ma talked of grooming Dan for a gentleman's job, a doctor or a lawyer. She had high hopes that he would be someone who didn't have to work in the sun, sweating and huffing and cursing. He had the brain for it, and Ma was sure he would be someone who would work inside with nice clothes and nice manners. She doted on him, Ma did.

It was a day that summer, the same summer old Mr. Clay died. We were swimming off the dock where the big ocean ships were tied up. It was me and Patch and our brother Dan, and Ned and the Rafferty boy, what was his name? Oh, but it's been so long.

The five of us were swimming among the boats tied there. We would shimmy up the posts, careful to avoid splinters, and then when we got to the top we would amuse each other with comical poses and then jump or dive. The river smelled awful, of course, and the water was no longer cool, but it was wet and swimming was something to do for free, which was the right price for us Irish children. The steamboats in the river would kick up waves that we would bob in and that would lap up the pilings in the river, darkening them up to the highpoint and then receding again as we floated up and down like corks.

There was a ship tied up there with the heavy six-inch rope. On the front of it, the bowsprit, was a woman who leaned forward over the water. Her carved wooden hair flowed down to her perfectly round, carved wooden breasts. The nipples of them were almost completely worn away and her face was blank looking, and we supposed it was from the constant spray of seawater she took.

Her empty face watched us like a wooden governess as we amused ourselves with dives and jumps. We practiced holding our breath under the

---

[12] Henry Clay, statesman from Kentucky, died in June, 1852.

water whenever the St. Louis Cathedral bells chimed, staying under the whole time until they stopped. Then we would climb the pole again, carefully standing tall with our hair wet and matted down to our heads. Then we would splash into the water next to each other, making ourselves as fat as possible to bring up more water in each other's faces. Then we treaded water in a circle, our toes barely touching as we told stories to scare each other. Stories of man-eating catfish and garfish, enormous water snakes the size of sea serpents, and alligators that prowled the water off the dock, waiting with hungry jaws for drunken sailors and stray slave children, and just wouldn't they like the tasty morsel of an Irish child? And that there were sharks that swam far up the river for just such a delicacy as that. The stories were so old and so often told that none of us were scared, not enough to get out of the water, which was clear for the first inch or two but then disappeared into a green-tinted brown. But it felt cool enough for us to ignore the stink of it.

The cathedral bells chimed again, and we all went under. When we all came up, the Rafferty boy said that the woman on the front of the ship was carved under the water, too, and you could feel her legs and her private parts. Patch knew it as a joke, and so did I, but Dan was fascinated by it. For Dan, any fact, any assertion, any theory, had to be tested, verified, proven to be correct before he could believe it. Other boys would have left it at that and changed the subject. Not Dan. He had to know, and so he dove down to find out. When he did, the boys all smiled to each other, having pulled a joke on poor Dan.

We waited. Two men passed by on the levee discussing a horse that one wanted to sell the other, and then they receded with their conversation. The cathedral bells chimed the quarter hour, and we forgot to play the game of holding our breath underwater while the bells chimed. Finally, Ned took a big breath and dove under. Patch and the Rafferty boy and I waited, and I began to worry that perhaps there actually were fish in the river big enough and with the appetite for a child. Joking wasn't in Dan's nature. Bubbles spread out on the surface, and then Ned broke the surface with a gasp.

"Patch," he said, "Help."

They each took a breath and disappeared under. Now as I waited, my imagination had the river teeming with creatures that were licking their lips and working their jaws for me and for all of us. I felt something under my foot, something that grazed my big toe and I shrieked.

"What is it?" Rafferty said. He had long since shed his normal, carefree demeanor. We all had. The thing brushed against my foot again, and then again. It was wet and slimy and mushy. My foot recoiled, and then I felt it again. It was cold and moist.

And it was the bottom. That's all it was. The bottom of the Mississippi

River.

All of a sudden there was a loud splash, and Patch and Ned pulled Dan up, and at first he looked like he was sleeping, bottom lip drawn back, like this, his head leaning back to expose his pale throat. He had purple-red circles under his eyes.

"Dan, Danny boy, stop yer foolin'," Ned said.

"Wake up, Dan," Patch said. He knew like I did that Dan would never make a joke of that sort. He was much too forthright. Patch shook Dan and slapped his cheek, a tapping against Dan's smooth pale skin that repeated itself. Dan just took it. After a minute Patch looked at me and said, "Go get Ma." There was no more mirth in his face. It was as close to crying as I'd ever seen him.

I waded out of the river, and it seemed like I would never get out. My hair was wet and my slip was wet and they both clung to me. I ran across Levee Street, dodging the wagons of the draymen and the fancy carriages of the Creoles and finally making the Quarter itself and St. Ann Street. The bells of St. Louis chimed the half hour, and I held my breath hoping it would help Dan wake up. My little arms were pumping as my feet hit the paving stones. I didn't think about the possibility of broken glass or nails like you usually had to do. I weaved between two slave women who were carrying laundry baskets on their heads. One of them yelled at me in French, but I kept going. A cat, a black cat, flashed across the street, across it and down an alley, and I crossed myself. I found the house where Ma worked, and I knocked frantically.

There was an ancient gray-haired Negro doorman named Antoine who opened the door and said, "Oui, Mam'selle?"

"Is Nora Fenerty here?" I asked when I got enough breath for it.

I was dripping with river water, and he looked at me and said, "Just a minute, young miss."

I looked inside the house. Gas lamps were flickering out a dim light in the rooms kept dark to control the heat. It was a house with high ceilings, colorfully furnished, fancy chairs and armoires and tables, curtains that were blue and red and fringed in gold.

Ma came following Antoine from the back of the house.

"Bridget?" she asked when she saw me. Her face had a concerned look about it; she knew from mine that something was wrong. She walked to the door, faster with each step, untying her apron which she hung from a hat tree in the foyer by the door.

"What is it?" she asked. "Is it Patrick?"

I don't know why she thought it was Patch.

"No, Ma. 'Tis Dan. We were swimming."

The doorman held the door for her and said, "Go on, now, Nora," and we were off to the levee, Ma and me. We ran together, and I couldn't remember the two of us ever running together like that, like two school girls. Ma clutching at the buttons at the neck of her dress in one hand and the hem of her dress in the other. Shop windows flashing past us. The wind in our ears. People and carriages only shapes. When we got to the riverfront, there was a crowd of men gathered around in a circle on the bank. Old Mr. Donnelly was one, and Mr. McHugh, and several more. Ma pushed at the back of the crowd, and it parted for her.

And there was Dan. Blanched and lifeless, his head lower than his feet and pointing down the slope toward the river. One of the men, whom I didn't know, took off his hat, a rusty brown top hat and said,

"He was probably caught between the keel and the bottom. Sorry for your troubles, ma'am."

We waked Dan in one of our two rooms on Annunciation Street on a board with a coffin supplied by the Shamrock Benevolent Society. We placed candles all around his head in a circle like a halo, which is how we did it in then. The candles dripped into odd shapes, and I thought how Dan would be fascinated by the contour of the melted wax around them if he would just wake up and look at them.

We buried him in the Bayou Cemetery. In those days, women wore black for close to a year as mourning. Ma would never wear any other color again.

Jan. 6, 1937

I turned off the recorder, and we split several more satsumas, chatting on while the space heater burned blue and orange, and the night wind played against the window panes making them murmur in some other language. We listened to the wind and the window panes converse as we took turns peeling away the glossy orange skin and sharing sections. Miss Fenerty suggested we listen to the radio.

We listened to *The Chase and Sanborn Hour,* and then Jimmy Davis sang "Nobody's Darlin' but Mine," and sometime in the night I woke up alone on the couch. The radio played "Hello World, Doggone Ya," and then KWKH signed off for the night. The space heater glowed behind the ceramic grate, the only light in the dark parlor, and it was odd how it reminded me of the whimsical smile of a jack-o-lantern. Someone had put blankets on me during the night, and I knew it had been Miss Fenerty. I pulled them up around my chin, and I smiled at the cheerful scent of satsumas on my fingers.

Jan. 7, 1937

Returned to Stephenson to find the black Cadillac parked out front again. It drove off as I arrived. Inside, Lemurier was as glum as ever, and Mirlette was still like a whipped puppy.

I also have a letter from Irving. I haven't opened it. I don't want to read it right now.

Jan. 8, 1937

I thought she'd come over by now. It's hard to sleep, and I had to make myself eat a little something. I went by Miss Fenerty's today, and she asked about Ellie again. I told her I haven't seen her since we got back. She seemed puzzled. In truth, so am I.

I listened to the lullaby of her voice as she talked about Brazil again, about Emperor Pedro II, the Paraguayan war and the Revolution of 1889, things that occurred in the other half of the world in the last century, things that I'd never heard of. She seems to know everything there is to know about Brazil, a peculiar fascination. Then, like the turn of a kaleidoscope, the subject changed again.

She told me another tale of her Irish Channel days, and I have to say it did nothing to improve my mood. So sad, all of it, so sad.

I was hoping Ellie could cheer me up, so after I left Miss Fenerty's, I went over to the Y, but it was after curfew, and visitors weren't allowed. I'll go see her tomorrow.

Jan. 9, 1937, FWP, Transcript of Bridget Fenerty

Lola Montez came to town that year and did the Spider Dance at the Varieties Theater on Gravier.[13] It was a dance in which she raised her skirt and pretended to shake spiders out of her petticoats and stomp on them. It was scandalous that she lifted her skirt as high as she did, and for those seated in the front row, even more scandalous that it was all too noticeable that Miss Montez was rather cavalier when it came to the practice of wearing drawers, as the newspapers said. That may or may not have been true, of course. Not everything you read in the papers is the

---

[13] Lola Montez was a nineteenth century entertainer who, while claiming to be Spanish, was actually from Ireland. She at one time was the consort to King Ludwig of Bavaria, and he abdicated the throne for her. She subsequently left him and mysteriously appeared in the United States as a performer, most notably known for the Spider Dance of which the subject speaks. The Daily Picayune reports she landed in New Orleans on December 30, 1852 and performed at the Tom Placide's Varieties Theater for much of January 1853 before moving on to cities upriver.

truth. No offense, dear.

Every summer, the fever stalked us like a big cat in the jungle watching a village in the clearing. We always knew it was there and that it could spring upon us whenever it chose. Yellow Jack tended to take the new ones, the ones just off the boat, so we thought we were safe, or relatively safe

It all began with a loss of my appetite, that was the first symptom, and an unusual one it was, sure, for I had an appetite the equal of my brothers, and I would have been as fat as a little pig had I not been so active as I was. It was thought that Colleen and I had eaten some bad fish or drank spoiled milk like the President had, or something like that. I didn't feel like playing, and I didn't feel like eating. I had no energy at all. Ma came home with what was left of a roast suckling pig from the Prudhommes, a rare treat for us in the heat of the summer, or any other time, really, but I wanted none of it. It was then that Ma knew how sick I was.

The lost appetite was followed by vomiting and then a fever that made everything blur and swim and tilt, and I lost hours of day and hours of night. Then I couldn't tell one from the other, day and night all the same to me. Others in the city were becoming sick also, and word spread that it was Yellow Fever that had come to pay a visit on us. Tar was burned in the street, and you could smell it, black and green and bitter. Trees were chopped down, cannons fired into the swamp to stop it. All useless, of course. Now we know it was mosquitoes what brought it, but no one did then. Everyone thought it was bad air or something of the sort.

I was put to bed with Colleen who was as sick as I was, though I had little awareness of it at the time. We lay there together side by side, our little bodies sweating and rank, our hair plastered to our heads. We shivered so hard that the bed shook, and it seemed that we were in the back of a wagon being driven over cobblestones instead of a bed. We both heaved incessantly into the same basin, pulling our hair back as we made the ridiculous open-mouthed expressions of those who are retching. After a time, Colleen's vomiting turned black like coffee grounds or wet crushed coal.

Days coasted by without the names of Monday or Wednesday or the tenth, and somewhere in my delirium I thought that a saint's feast day had passed and won't Colleen be upset that she had missed it?

And then one morning, I woke to find that I was in bed by myself. I felt her absence; the bed was bigger and yawning with me in it. There was a stain, a gray pallor on Colleen's part of the bed as if someone, Ma, I'm sure, had tried to scrub away the sickness with me in the bed. I was aware for the first time in days that it was hot outside. The air was still intensely bitter with the smell of tar burning in the street. Ma was there, of course, fanning me with an old edition of *The True Delta* and waving flies away from her face with her other hand. I sat up on one elbow and rubbed my eyes. My voice was weak from disuse and hoarse from retching.

"Ma, would you see if Colleen would come and brush my hair?" I asked in little more than a whisper.

Ma looked away from the window she had been staring out, and then she sat on the side of the bed and pulled me to herself. I couldn't see her, but I could feel her weeping.

"Oh, child. Oh dear, dear child," she said as she rocked me and kissed my cheek. And then I knew. I knew.

They had buried her with two dozen others that day, a relatively light day for death in that time. The priest sent them all off together as the Negro men waited with shovels, sweating in the heat behind the families that wept in ragtag black mourning clothes. Cannons were still booming into the swamp to the north of the city, someone's idea of prevention.

Poor, pure Colleen. I can see her yet, her stitching in her lap by the window light, or at other times by the light of a candle, the needle dipping in and out of the mending she was working on. Her lips parting, bouncing lightly over her prayer, her head tilted thoughtfully as her eyes followed her hands. Surely she had been headed for the convent, and what a true, pure daughter of Jesus she would have been.

It's entirely possible to be both pious and hateful. Indeed, I've come to feel an instant distrust to someone who brandishes their faith at others like a club to make them cower with guilt. We may be called to be instruments of God, as some say, but it doesn't mean we have to be blunt instruments. Being kind and being religious aren't necessarily the same thing, Miriam, but Colleen was both. As much as I teased her, and as much as I tormented her, she was always kind to me and to everyone, and she certainly deserves a starry crown for it, and I hope she's got it. I felt sorry for how I harassed her. And so did Patch, and we vowed that we would lead lives of piety and observe all the feast days, a vow which lasted until All Saints' Day or so. We just weren't cut out for a life such as that. Few are.

Patch had also been sick the whole time. He'd gotten it right after us but then gotten better again right before I got well, which I did, as I'm sure you figured out. Maggie had worked in Ma's place and hadn't gotten sick at all, in fact. Nor had Ma. Not at that point.

The sickness continued on, though. Other families were taken by it entirely, and that summer close to ten thousand died on account of it, the Yellow Fever. Doors stayed locked; there was almost no traffic outside in the streets or on the river. It was as if the city was holding its breath. They continued to burn tar in the streets and shoot cannons into the swamps.

The Prudhommes returned from Mandeville with the first cool snap of fall and were sorry to hear of our troubles. They were kind people, the Prudhommes were. They found that Maggie had kept the house in fine shape in Ma's absence, while Ma had nursed Colleen and Patch and me. Maggie always had a gift for cleaning. Ma returned to the Prudhommes for a week or so before she began to tire.

At first, we thought it was female trouble. Maggie said that Ma had increasingly difficult monthlies, though I wasn't quite sure what those were, not having had one yet. I thought perhaps it was a special cleaning chore she had to perform once a month for the Prudhommes, like cleaning out the fireplaces or something like that. Ma took a variety of patent medicines in an attempt to function, which by the hardest she always did. *Wright's Indian Vegetable Pills*, *Holloway's Pills for Digestion*, a new one every month. Ma had even paid a visit to Madam Platen on St. Joseph Street, who advertised herself as offering help for painful menstruation and engorgement, but 'twas no use, and she continued to suffer.

People were still dying that summer and fall, but in smaller numbers with the coming cool, and the streets and the river were beginning to bustle again, as if the city was finally exhaling after its ordeal. Black was still the color people were wearing, but some were beginning to smile again. People were stopping to talk and shake hands and congratulate each other on still being among the living.

Then one morning, we found that Ma had kept to bed. It was as odd and unexpected as the sun coming up in the west or the river flowing backwards. "I'll be up in a few minutes," she would say, but then she would fall back asleep. Very unlike her, it was, of course.

In the ballads, the dying persons tell some truth to a family gathered around and promises to wait on the other side, and then they peacefully close their eyes. In reality, the dying person is incoherent, puking and writhing on a bed of sheets soaked with sweat and black with vomit. They rattle the tin basins they're heaving into and shake so hard that you think they'll flop out of the bed. And when they die, it's convulsing with eyes open into a stare, perhaps the lids drooping down a bit, but still at the heart of it, it's a stare.

And so it was with Ma.

She had a casket and a plot in the Bayou Cemetery courtesy of the Shamrock Benevolent Society, and we had a steady stream of neighbors who offered us condolences, the men taking off their dingy hats and murmuring to us, sorry for your troubles.

And so when Ma was buried, I went to work in her place for the Prudhommes with my sister Maggie. My childhood was over.

I was eleven years old.

Jan. 9, 1937

Missed the synagogue and got up early this morning to see Ellie. Girls from the YWCA were leaving in groups for the shops on Texas Street, laughing in their best clothes with their pocketbooks on their arms and their hearts light. The big girl at the desk was reading a trashy novel when I walked up. She hurriedly put it under an edition of *The Southern Baptist Herald.*

"Can you call up for Ellie Schultis?" I asked her.

"Miss Schultis moved out yesterday."

I felt the room spin around my slouching face.

"Did she say where she was going?"

"Didn't say."

As I walked out of the lobby, I saw the girl's reflection pull her novel out from under the church paper. I walked in a personal fog down Texas Street, almost stepping off the curb at McNeil Street into the path of a trolley. Somehow, I arrived at Miss Fenerty's. It seemed as good a place to go as any. She offered to resume her story, but I declined.

"Just as well," she said. "So many of the stories from that part of me life aren't happy ones. You don't look like you could bear it right now."

We just visited. She kept the conversation as light and as joyful as she could, speaking of her admiration of the Polynesian wahinis who swam naked and thought nothing of it, nothing at all, and wasn't that a carefree way to go about your affairs, with no pretense, cavorting in the naked truth? she asked me with a chuckle. She had read about it in the *National Geographic,* she said.

But her story of carefree, naked wahinis only brought a thin smile from me, and so she just said, "I don't know what it is, but if you like, we can talk about it when you're ready." I'm sure my face was long, and I was on the verge of tears, tears that I've saved until I returned to Stephenson to find Lemurier and Mirlette at each other on the couch like a couple of (amorous) wrestlers.

There's talk of snow, and everyone on the trolley was excited, like children. I'm not excited about anything. My door is locked. Love and lust are holding court downstairs. Up here it's time for the tears I've held off.

Jan. 10, 1937, Sunday

No snow, just a little cold drizzle, and everyone is disappointed. Long faces match what mine must look like.

I took the trolley downtown hoping I would see Ellie on her way into church. The Baptists filed in wrapped up in coats and shaking hands. Some of the men lingered on the front steps, finishing cigarettes and talking. I waited, looking up one side of Texas Street and down the other, but when the doors were shut, she hadn't gone in them.

I wandered over to Oakland Cemetery behind the Methodist Church. Inside the church, the organ thundered hoarsely as the Methodist voices rose, singing,

He leadeth me, he leadeth me, oh by his hand he leadeth me...

Inside the church, the hymn ended with a blast of the organ, and the pews creaked in time, I presume under the collective weight of the Methodists. I heard the minister say, "Let us pray," and then he did.

I looked through the graves of people who must have known Bridget Fenerty, people she had perhaps loved and certainly outlived. The blackbirds whirled around again in their circus-cloud, and I sat on a concrete bench and watched them. The rain began to patter on the stones, slabs, sculptures, obelisks, all that remained to mark the presence of these lives in this town and on this earth.

The rain began to pick up, and the blackbirds kept to their branches. I walked back down to the Baptist church and stood under an umbrella waiting for her to emerge. Perhaps I had missed her when she went it. Upon leaving, umbrellas flowered against the cold rain; someone held one above the minister as he shook hands with the departing congregation. None of them was Ellie. The big doors closed on my hope. A carload of Methodists cruised down Texas Street, aiming to get to Sunday dinner before the Baptists.

Neither of us had said a word about New Year's Eve. Perhaps we should have. I crossed the street after the next car.

I miss her.

How can a ten second kiss erase a friendship?

Jan. 11, 1937, Monday

I should have put the money to getting the Packard fixed, but instead I splurged and went to get my hair done in the salon of the Youree Hotel. I was hoping it would boost my spirits, and, besides, if I got the car fixed I would be faced with traveling into the countryside. I don't want any excuse to be away if she returns. I'd rather spend more time with Miss Fenerty anyway.

I sat in the waiting area looking through *McCall's* and *Good Housekeeping* and listening to the conversations of the other women. The whole place was bathed in a fluttering cackle like a henhouse. The topics may have been mundane, but they were treated very seriously. Hitler is threatening Europe, and the biggest controversy here is who puts pickles in their coleslaw and who doesn't. There's also talk of the Klan rallying, though I'm surprised to hear all the derision the Klan gets from the women here. Men with pointed heads wearing bedsheets, one woman said, and several of the other hens laughed.

In the end, I changed my mind about getting my hair done and took the trolley back to Stephenson. Lemurier was either out or still asleep. Mirlette was in the back working on a hothouse. A limb had crashed through one of the roof panels, and she was trying to position a square of cardboard over the missing pane. The air today was more pleasant than yesterday. I walked out the back door watching my feet while I picked around puddles.

She was up on a ladder using a pair of scissors to cut the cardboard to match. Her sleeves were rolled up, and, when she saw me, she hurriedly rolled them to her wrists, even though it was fairly warm. I asked her if they had a good Christmas.

"We do not celebrate holidays. He forbids it," she said up to the panel as she positioned it. "He says they are only for others to make money." I positioned myself trying to see her face. When I did, I noticed some plants with long, splayed leaves. There were some flowers there, too, a couple of nice orchids, but the majority of the plants were the same nondescript green.

"What are these?" I asked, brushing my hand over their leafy tops.

"It ease a plant called Can o' bees."

"Can o' bees?" I asked as I moved again to see her face. She kept getting down from her ladder and turning it as she rotated away from me. "Do you eat it? Say, in a salad?"

She laughed, a girlish giggle. It almost made me want to like her.

"I guess it is that you can, but one smokes it." She pronounced 'it' like 'eat.'

Then it dawned on me that these were marihuana plants. Can o' bees. *Cannabis*. Very few of the Columbia and Barnard students smoked it, but there were some. They called it reefer. One of the UES Philosophy Club members had suggested we try some, but we never did.

Her shirt sleeves had fallen down her arms as she worked over her head. There were bruises on her arms around the elbows, small circular ones like fingerprints. She turned her face up, and under her bonnet there was a faint black eye. Her smile fell and ran when she saw me looking at it.

Jan. 12, 1937, Tues.

The rain and cold have returned. I took the trolley downtown today. The city is taking down the last of the Christmas decorations. The young waitress in the diner on Marshall Street plucked Santa's cotton ball beard. The mule/reindeer had lost his tempera painted branches/antlers but kept the same indifferent look on his face as if he were resigned to his demise, that of being wiped completely away. The waitress recognized me and waved. Then, as she continued plucking Santa's beard, she shook her head no in anticipation of the question I've been asking her every time I've seen her:

Have you seen my blonde friend who was in here with me before Christmas?

The answer is one that I've gotten every time: a slow shake 'no' closing her eyes sympathetically.

Word on the courthouse square benches is that Champ Lockett is in the hospital.

"Wouldn't that be a shame?" one person says.

"He's such a treasure of our history," another says. "Our hero. Living history."

"Took a turn over Christmas, I hear," the first one says.

I walked down to Crockett Street under my umbrella. I found Miss Fenerty on the porch watching the rain drip off the eaves.

"Well, I believe all the pretty girls are about town today," she called as I approached. She was in a chair with her blue tam on her old head and a shawl over her shoulders, rocking in slow, narrow movements. It's funny, but for someone who's been called pretty her whole life, when Miss Fenerty says it, it's like being called pretty for the very first time. It's as if she's looking at something inside of me that she sees, and no one else does. Something that *I* don't even see but should.

Jan. 12, 1937, FWP, Transcript of Bridget Fenerty

I'd been on the porch of that fine house on Rue St. Ann dozens of times, but I'd never actually been inside. The Prudhommes' house, I'm speaking of. The Negro man, Antoine, who answered the door was a younger version of the one who had opened it the day that Dan drowned, and I've always assumed they were father and son. A lot of jobs in New Orleans then and perhaps now are passed down that way, through family, a father to a son or a nephew, a mother to a daughter or a niece. And with it, the older person passes down the little things he or she knows to the next in line. So 'twas with Ma and Maggie, and then with Maggie and me.

Maggie had gone to work ahead of me that day, as I was sent to buy a new dress to work in from Mr. Phillips' on Nayades Street. My old one was mended to the point that it was mostly patches, and threadbare ones at that. It was just as well that I get a new one, as I was growing at an alarming rate, long skinny legs and arms punctuated only very little by knees and elbows. I was a gangly little sapling of a girl.

The new dress was made out of muslin with a high collar that made me itch. We servants all wore one, or variations of it. Maggie was inside in the *salle à manger*, as they called it, and we were to call it, polishing and putting away silverware. Antoine was in white-trimmed black livery, a tall man with a way of walking that was so refined that his shoulders and head hardly moved at all, and he seemed to float as he showed me back to where Maggie was.

"Hello, Bridget," she said. Normally we called each other Sister, but here it was clear that there was a certain set of rules that were to be abided by, even among sisters. Her white-gloved hands seemed to work independently of her, the same way Antoine's head and shoulders worked independently of the rest of him, a sort of detachment that was necessary for efficiency.

I stood and watched her. For a girl who had grown up eating with her hands or wooden forks and spoons, she was so nonchalant with the gleaming silverware. Candlesticks, ice buckets, brass plate chargers, a complicated array of forks, one for salads, one for fish, one for deserts, a spoon for soups, a spoon for dessert. Wine glasses, champagne flutes, port glasses.

"Wash glassware first," she lectured me as her white gloves worked the white cloth into the small recesses and set them down so lightly that they hardly made a sound at all. "Then silverware, then brass and so forth."

Her lecture on what was expected of a good servant turned to what might be particularly good advice for me and me alone. She looked about herself and then dispensed it in a hushed tone.

"You're not to fart or scratch yourself in front of your master or mistress. It's to be 'oui, Madame,' and 'oui, Monsieur' and 'no, Madame' and 'no Monsieur,' ye hear? And these fingernails. Clean, they need to be clean, not like that."

I had thin crescents of dirt under my nails.

I looked at them and then at her and held the hem of my new dress and curtsied as I said sarcastically, "Oui, mam'selle." Maggie kept polishing and pretended not to notice. She finished with the last spoon and looked at herself in the bowl of it. The reflection of her face in the spoon was blonde trimmed and egg shaped. She slipped the spoon in the drawer with the others and locked the silver chest behind it. Having finished with the dining room, she moved to a bedroom and I followed her, surprised at her speed and industry.

"A smart domestic sets the fire in the stove the night before, so that all she need do the next morning is to light it. She rises an hour before her mistress who generally arises half an hour before her master."

We stood on opposite sides of an immense bed with heavy turned posts. The canopy was made of red silk that was folded into a sort of starburst pattern. I was looking up at it when a pillow hit my chest. A fresh pillow case followed it, and I caught it. We pushed the pillows into our cases. Mine was lumpy and misshapen, and Maggie took it and smoothed it into the perfect shape hers had.

"In the upstairs parlor there's a book of *coiffures* for women and girls. Consult it. The ladies of this house insist on being *au currant*."

"Concurrent?" I asked as I tucked the sheet in at the foot of the bed.

"Up to date, it means. There's another book I picked up for you at Mr. Morgan's on Exchange Alley, *The Behaviour Book: A Manual for Ladies* by Miss Leslie. Look over it in your free time."

Under Maggie's direction, I scrubbed baseboards that day, every baseboard in every room in that great big house, on my knees with a wooden bucket and a rag. She would come in with an armload of linens and inspect what I'd done.

"Here, Bridget, you missed a spot here, and here," she would gesture with her chin over her armload of laundry, and then I would hear her footsteps thud into the next room as she completed her errand. I made faces at her as soon as she left. That night I dreamed of floors and baseboards, a line of them along walls that in my dreams never ended but went on and on. In eighty years of keeping house let it never be said that I kept an unclean one, and my cooking has always been passable, but my true loves have always been my children, the ones I took care of.

At first, being little more than a child myself, they were like younger brothers and sisters, and I would occupy them with games or read to them. They had a houseful, the Prudhommes did. And I believe that helping with the children was the one thing that I was better at than Maggie, and it was what endeared me with Madame Prudhomme.

She was a beautiful woman with creamy skin and a long, elegant neck. She knew how much jewelry was enough and how much was too much, and her smile was genuine and loving, especially to her children. She appreciated the care I gave them, which I must say was also genuine and loving. There were five of them, Phillipe, Therese, Rene, Jean-Pierre, and the baby, Celestine. I can't remember who was older of Therese and her brother Rene, and they may have been twins. Celestine was just two or so when I began working for them.

Monsieur Prudhomme was a handsome man with a hairline that was beginning to recede, and he wore the high collars and tight breeches like the fashionable men did in those days. He was a sugar broker and an educated man who was friends with several of the literary types in town, so the house was always full of books, in French and Latin and English, and learned men who discussed them over glasses of port. There were voices raised in arguments and then laughter and hands on the shoulders of friends. Meanwhile, Madame entertained the wives in the ladies' parlor where they would do embroidery and gossip.

Monsieur Prudhomme was generous with lending his books to me. I believe he thought me to be an oddity, an Irish servant girl who read and who liked to read. Which I did, constantly, on my free time. The English titles, of course. The French I learned was mostly pertaining to things to cook, clean, or take care of.

When he came home after a long day at the Exchange, he always had a baguette under his arm. Madame would place Celestine in his lap, and Monsieur would accept the little girl like he was accepting first prize in a contest. Then he would sit there and hold her and read the evening paper while Madame and I spruced up the other children before supper, which Maggie and the other servants generally prepared.

They ate leisurely in seven courses, light conversation floating around the table in the evening light. Monsieur always listened to each child and commented respectfully, no matter how preposterous the child's tale was. After supper, Monsieur Prudhomme would read to them all, the little ones in his lap, the older ones at his side on the settee, all of their eyes fixed on the page that the smallest ones couldn't yet read. Occasionally, he would pause and ask one of them a question in French, something I'm sure along the lines of, "And what do you think happened next?" Or "Why do you suppose that is?" Then he would wet his finger on his tongue and turn the page and resume reading.

I would hear them as Maggie and I cleared the table of the dishes, seven courses' worth. From the kitchen, which was separate and across the courtyard, we could hear the older children playing music for their papa, one on the pianoforte, one on the harp, one on the viola, the fiddle we Irish called it. The smallest who scratched around on the thing got the same applause from their papa as the older, more accomplished ones.

In the kitchen as the dishes soaked, Maggie and I ate the leftovers savagely in one course, and I especially so. I was starting to grow and fill out in the beginnings of a womanly way. You remember that, don't you, Miriam, when you look down at your chest and you notice a couple of small buds and lower down, a few stray hairs where there weren't any before? And you say to yourself, well, what's this, then?

The Prudhommes had two song birds that were kept in a cage, and they chirped and flitted and set a happy tone for the house. I liked to watch them as they chased each other from one perch to the other. At night, they put their games aside and cuddled close to each other on the same perch, their heads pushed down into each other's necks. With the first light, they resumed their play again.

Ned would come by now and again, but there was less time to prowl, though on Thursdays we might go down and sneak into the Olympic or the Pelican for a performance, Ned holding a window open or looking out for the watchman. I was taller than he was then, by a head, such as I had grown.

We laughed with the light of the stage in our eyes as the players enacted yet another Irish morality tale in which Paddy off the boat is buffeted by the strange new world he now inhabits before finally, through his own unwitting honesty and a dash of luck and a sudden twist of fate, he overcomes it and gets the girl and true happiness. Occasionally, Ned would reach over and hold my hand, and it occurred to me that it was gaining the beginnings of a muscular roughness. Afterward, we would leave the enchanted light of the theater, the Olympic or the Pelican usually, and take a walk down to the river or up St. Charles where the lewd women were beginning their night's work and the stevedores from the levee were beginning their night's play in the fading twilight.

Gradually, though, Ned fell in with other friends. I had but one afternoon a week to spend with him, and my work in the Prudhommes was leading to a certain refinement in me so that on the one afternoon of the week we saw each other we seemed to be more and more like strangers. I suppose it was one of the reasons that he ended up leaving the city the next year.

Jan. 13, 1937

I went to bed last night thinking of how friends might become strangers if circumstances, disguised as time and distance, were to come between them. The uncertainty is making me sick. With each day that passes, it becomes more clear that she's left the city. I hope that's what it is and that nothing's happened to her. To worry about someone other than yourself. A noble burden, but still a burden. Is this what being a parent is like?

I left for Miss Fenerty's early today while *madame et monsieur* slept in (again). There was a light drizzle, and the trolley was dank with wet coats and bodies. I rode the half hour thinking of nothing and everything. When we reached Common and Crockett, the driver's voice jostled me.

"Ain't this usually your stop, ma'am?" he asked. I alighted down the ridged steps. My invisible fog followed me down Crockett.

I could see her through the front window; she was in the parlor dusting, braced on her cane. I knocked, and at first she didn't see me. When she opened the door, I asked her where Ned went.

"Ned?" The feather duster was at her side. It looked like a dead bird, a trophy, and her cane looked like a gun she might have used to bring it down.

"You said that Ned left town. Where did he go? Was he in trouble?"

"Trouble? Oh, no. Not that I was ever aware of." She turned to dust the mantel. "He left town to work as a cabin boy."

"What ever happened to him?"

She looked over her glasses at me.

"Well, Ned ended up sailing all over the world, not just the river," she seemed pleased with this fact, that Ned had seen the world, had accomplished something. But she still hadn't answered the question. What happened to Ned?

"Patch was still in town," she said as she tottered over to her chair. "He'd been turned over to Hugh McNeil to work as a stevedore on the levee, a boy becoming a man by doing man's work, a boy learning a man's language by listening to men. The cursing, the boasting. He was working for Mr. McNeil but hoping to be promoted to screwman."

"A screwman, did you say?" I asked.

"And what do you suppose that is, then?" she had a riddle on me, and she dangled it like one would tease a cat. I had no clue what she meant by screwman.

"Well it's not what you might think, some *sart* of ladies' man." She laughed, and there was a quality to it something like wind chimes or rain falling from windblown leaves after an afternoon shower.

"A screwman was a man who went down in the holds of ships that were to be off for England. They used big jackscrews to squeeze the cotton bales so they could fit more on the ship. 'Twas dangerous work; things could give way leading to crushed men and broken bones, but the pay was better because of the danger, and they had their own organization *The Screwman's Benevolent Association* to provide for those who were maimed and for their families."

She set her duster down, and we sat where we usually sat, she in her armchair, I on the settee near her. I leaned in to prepare the recorder; it has a usual seat on the ottoman.

Jan. 13, 1937, FWP, Transcript of Bridget Fenerty

It had been the better part of a month or so, and I hadn't seen Ned once the whole time. It was unusual, as Ned would usually drop by and leave an apple in the window of the kitchen out back in the courtyard, or a flower in the keyhole of the door. Ned was like a stray cat in some ways, appearing and disappearing, and I thought nothing of it, really.

Well, I was going to market one day, and, as I passed the coffee house on Erato, a man ran out after me. He had every smell about him except for the smell of soap. Most of his fragrance was that of the creature, whiskey, that is.

"Are you the girl Bridget Fenerty?" he asked as he teetered. "Friend of

Ned Hennessy?"

"Well, I am," I said.

"I've got a note for you, from the Hennessy boy hisself. He asked me if it weren't no trouble, for me to give to ye, then."

He slapped at his pockets until he found one that rustled. His stained fingers snaked into the pocket and snared the note, and he handed it to me. The note was written on white paper like the butchers used to wrap meat, grubby and worn as if he had carried it around and slept drunk with it in the pocket of his coat. I unfolded it, careful not to get my hands dirty, careful not to hold it too close to my work dress.

It said,

"Dahr Brijit,
I'm gone of to sel the revvir and prhaps the holl of the werld but ile be back shorely I will an ile see you then tho it may be sum time. Yers truly,
Ned Hennesy."

At least he could spell his own name. It was sad but inevitable that he should leave, I suppose. I knew I would miss him, and I felt a little sorry for having neglected him, my childhood best friend. But I had ceased to be a child sometime between the moment I entered the Prudhommes' door and the moment I completed the last baseboard on that first day. Now I had a little of my own money, and I could afford to walk in the front door of the theater now. But I would miss his company.

It was the same day that the president was received for a visit to the city. There was an election that day as well, for governor, I believe.[14] There was no small amount of animosity for the Irish and the Germans in those days, and native men boasted that they were true Americans, as opposed to the Irish and the Germans who were regarded as interlopers on American soil who bowed to a foreign master in Rome. They called themselves the American party, or some called them the Know Nothings.

It was a gorgeous springtime Monday, bright green and sky blue, and Maggie and I were doing laundry which was the usual state of things on Mondays. The breeze nudged and lifted the shirts and sheets and dresses on the lines we set across the courtyard to put the clothes on after they came out of the boiling kettle and the wringer. You always did the white things first, then the finer colored things and then on to the coarser things, and then on to

---

[14] The subject's memory here is likely in error. It was *former* President Millard Fillmore who visited New Orleans on March 27, 1854, according to the March 28, 1854 issue of the *New Orleans Daily Crescent*, and the elections held that day were municipal and not gubernatorial. The Democrat John L. Lewis was elected mayor.

the servants' things last.

We weren't the only servants the Prudhommes had. There were perhaps half a dozen slaves as well, two who cooked, an old Negro woman named Mathilde who was as black as anyone I'd ever seen, and her daughter whose name escapes me but who was a lighter version of Mathilde. They had a stable hand, a gardener, and assistants to these people, and of course Antoine, the son, the younger Antoine, who was Madame's right hand man and coordinated everything.

Well, on the day I got the note from Ned, Mathilde was baking bread in the kitchen across the courtyard and the light brown smell of it was heavenly on the spring breeze. There was a line of open air rooms along the courtyard in the back, and she was in the stall next to where Maggie and me were ironing the things that were dry enough. We kept three irons apiece on a metal plate over the fire and when one cooled, you set it down and got the next and kept rotating them around. It was pleasant work with the agreeable smell of the bread and the breeze and the bright spring colors. From St. Louis Street in the front of the house, we heard men singing on their way to vote.

Well, to be short about it, there was a riot that day. Some of the native men accused some other men of having voted twice, and a shove was administered into someone's chest. One shove started it all, and isn't it so, at times? The shove was met with another shove, which was answered with a fist, and then another fist joined the conversation. Men gathered, all sorts of men, men in top hats, slouch hats, bare headed, fine boots and brogans and bare feet, men in fancy waistcoats. All sort of men, all with the same insults.

"Get away from our ballot box, mick. Voting is for Americans, step away and move on."

The fighting increased like a pot boiling, there at the Seventh.[15] The fists and chokeholds swarmed about each other, and then a club joined in, and it met with a shillelagh, and then more, and then knives happened up, and they all fell silent with a pistol shot. Men scattered down alleys, and the man in charge of the precinct was left there with the ballot box in his lap, hunched over it as if it were his child. When the smoke cleared, there were two men dead. The newspapers said they were two men who were accused of voting twice.

The next year was tense, as the true Americans as they called themselves squared off against the Irish and Germans. There were insults and fights by men who claimed we bowed to the Roman dictator, men who were sure we would breed to sufficient numbers until we could hand the country over to the Pope. Paranoia works that way; people are always prepared to believe the

[15] precinct

worst from the outset.

They were troubled years. The only joy was watching the Prudhomme children grow. I spent most of my time with them and with Maggie who was working for them. I turned thirteen that year and was beginning to blossom. My body became that of a woman then and frankly I hated it, at first I did. But boys and men begin to notice you, and you know, you begin to enjoy it, the attention. You begin to look into the mirror to see what they see. And when you see it, you naturally want to see more of it. A swell in the bosom, the press outward of your hips so that your skirts wear differently, a sheen to your hair. Mine was copper red, orange-brown, auburn almost, and full. Now would you look at it, then? White and thin. Old age is never fair, it just is, and what are we to do about it, I ask you? Then came my monthly friend, as some call it. I had no idea it would come, no idea at all. Maggie told me to keep spare rags in my apron for those days of the month.

"What do you mean?" I said. "This will happen again?"

"Every month. Didn't you know?" She handed me an old kitchen towel and said, "Now fold this up and put it in your drawers."

I did it. Then I sat on the stoop in the alley with my head down and my hands between my knees in the folds of my dress. This was horrible news.

"Feck," I said.

In the heat of the summer, the city thinned out as those who had the means left and went to Mandeville or the seaside, or Europe for the very well off. The servants packed the big trunks of households moving a large part of themselves, and then we turned out on the front steps of the house to see them off as they clopped down the cobblestones in a succession of carriages. Then those of us left stayed and prayed, as was the saying then.

The Prudhommes went to Mandeville that year and to Biloxi the next, taking Antoine with them and leaving the rest of us to dodge the Yellow Fever. Maggie and I scurried around the big, silent house and readied it for a month or so of rest from its family, drawing curtains, closing off rooms, that sort of thing. Then, we ourselves relaxed. Sister and I took turns combing each other's hair in front of Madame's looking glass and trying on the dresses and hats she'd left. Perhaps she wouldn't have minded, but to ask would have been an affront. When we weren't playing dress up, I read almost every English title in Monsieur Prudhomme's library that month.

The summer I turned fourteen, I was asked to accompany them on their vacation. It was in 1856, the year that they decided to go to the new resort they'd built at a place called Last Island. It's not there anymore, and I should know, for I was there the day that the sea took it.

Jan. 14, 1937

Very little sleep last night, despite the fact that my housemates were unusually quiet.

One kiss. How is a friendship ruined in less than ten seconds with one simple kiss?

One simple, profound, beautiful kiss.

The weather is warmer today, still with rain.

Letters today from mother and Irving, and one from an address in Jackson, Mississippi to someone named Hickey, the former occupant of the house, I'm assuming. I marked it return to sender.

Light bill is past due. I thought Lemurier was paying it.

Jan. 15, 1937

Weather is cold and crisp. Lemurier seems preoccupied with the street in front of the house, getting up to look through the drawn blinds and then sitting down. He did it at least three times today. I wonder if he's noticed the man in the black Cadillac.

He and I had a discussion. It began with a conversation about the unpaid bill and somehow twisted itself into a political debate. Normally I enjoy a good spirited political discourse, but with him it was sinister and foul. We were talking about the quote from Marx, "From each according to his ability, to each according to his need."

"Yes, it is true," he said, reclining on the sofa as he lit yet another cigarette. "But for *les capitalistes* it is ' From each according to his gullibility, to each according to his greed.' One day the worker will rise up and take this country from the Rockefellers and the Mellons and the Carnegies. The puppets will break from their strings, and the puppet-masters will be left to give the show."

There's something vaguely violent about Lemurier. If he wasn't so lazy, he would be dangerous.

Monthly started. Careful what you wish for. Horrible cramps but still relieved to have one.

I'm curious about this Last Island place, so I'm going downtown despite the wrenching in my lower stomach, determined to 'soldier on.'

Jan. 15, 1937, FWP, Transcript of Bridget Fenerty

It was the year that the city put the statue of General Jackson on his horse in the square in front of the cathedral.[16] With the scare of Yellow Fever visiting the city every year with the heat, the Prudhommes fell into the habit of spending long bits of the summer at the seaside at a place called Last Island. It was new then, a place that was building up with cottages and a hotel for the well-to-dos, mostly planters from the southern parishes. The feeling was that the ocean air was a protection from the Yellow Fever. Those who could get out of the city did so in the summer months. The rest 'stayed and prayed.'

I was much better with children than my sister Maggie was. She was developing a tendency toward nervousness, and the children's antics only made it worse. I, on the other hand, was entirely at ease with them, and the more antics, the better. So, Madame Prudhomme asked that I accompany the family as a nursemaid, particularly to the youngest two, Jean-Pierre and Celestine. They were at that time, six and four, I suppose. Let me see. Yes, about that. I had long since privy-trained Celestine by that time, so, yes, she was four.

Maggie stayed in the city to do deep cleaning while the family was away. She was better at that than I was. I was worried for her, left in the city with the possibility of death from sickness. I should have been more worried about myself.

We, the Prudhommes and I, I mean, took the ferry at the end of St. Ann Street and caught the train on the far side of the river in Algiers. The children were excited, running about from one side of the train to the other, looking out into the fields of sugarcane and the swamps. The train took us to Bayou Boeuf, and from there we took a steamer out to the island. The name of the steamer was the *Star*. Yes, that's right, the *Star*. Had a big star on the iron work between the smokestacks, and the captain was an unusually tall man named Smith or Jones or something plain like that, I believe.[17]

It plowed through the bay, Call-you[18] Bay I think it was called, gulls gliding and squawking overhead and curious dolphins arching up and under and up again through the water. They had little grins on their faces that I pointed out to the children. Celestine blew them kisses. Monsieur Prudhomme had his arms around Madame, and she leaned back into him with a smile and closed her eyes as they stood at the rail of the boat.

We landed on the north side of the island, the bay side, and men gathered our trunks and put them on a wagon, and the family got in carriages to go to the Prudhommes' beach house. We came over the low ridge of the island, and there it was, the Gulf, the Gulf of Mexico. Up and down the road that stretched along the beach were the summer houses of some of the richest

---

[16] 1856

[17] Newspaper accounts name the captain of the *Star* as Abraham Smith. He reportedly stood six foot six.

[18] Caillou Bay

people in the state at the time, and indeed, it was said, the country. The governor of Louisiana had a house there, a beautiful two story thing just down from ours. The Prudhommes' house, I'm saying.

The afternoons were bright and gauzy, as if you were looking at a blue sky through cheesecloth. After a morning of playing in the surf, we slept on the porch on pallets, the children and I, while the sea brushed back and forth over the sand. Rain gathered from the Gulf and passed overhead and inland to spend itself, dropping into the marsh from towering gray clouds in shady, slanted pillars. The air was thick and soft, stirred by the gulf breeze. Naps were easy to fall into and deep.

While the children slept, Monsieur and Madame would walk hand in hand down the beach, Monsieur in his waistcoat with his trouser legs rolled up, Madame with her skirt knotted to shorten it, both of them barefoot and holding hands. They became dark spots on the horizon where the sea met the sand, then returned tiptoeing past us. I kept my eyes shut as if I were sleeping, and then Monsieur led Madame to their room and shut the door. The lock on the door to their room clattered as the bolt was thrown.

They emerged half an hour later smiling, relaxed, and it was some time later in my life that I realized that they had adjourned for a session of love, and it comforts me a measure that they enjoyed that small morsel of heaven. I hope it's the heaven they enjoy now. They were fine people.

There were carriages to rent for rides along the beach, and people bathed in the sea, groups of women swimming in the surf, wringing water out of their skirts and hair. The children rode a wooden whirligig that was on the low crest of the island, a thing like a merry-go-round is today. There was a well where the kitchen staff of the hotel kept turtles to cook, and it was a source of amusement for little Jean-Pierre, who would look at them and poke at them with a stick. At night, the children would beg me to take them to look for crabs by lantern light while the sea murmured in the darkness.

We took our meals at the hotel run by a man named Murray.[19] It had flags fluttering from the corners in the sea breeze, a constant, whipping thing that kept everyone refreshed. The afternoons were especially restful, all of us under the same tranquil spell.

Once little Jean-Pierre, just six or seven years old, said that he would like to marry me some day. I laughed and said that I thought he would make a very fine husband indeed but that he would have to be a bit older and then we'd see, that by then he would have any number of young ladies for him to choose from, and they would probably be so much prettier than me.

"But you're the prettiest girl in the city," he said in his adorable, accented

---

[19] The subject's memory is likely in error here. The Last Island Hotel was run by two brothers named Muggah.

English and then he expanded upon it, exclaiming, "In the whole wide-wide-wide world!" He put his arms out wide, and I pulled him to me and kissed the top of his little head.

Then we would lay quietly as the sea breeze pushed through the house with the sound of the surf and the gulls squeaking in the far distance. After I would put them down on their pallets, it was always just a minute or two before Jean-Pierre and Celestine would get up and come and lay with me as the afternoon light fell in a square on the floor by my bed. I fell into a habit of singing to them in a voice that was low, just above the bluster of the breeze. They would always fall asleep within a song or two, their little mouths open, their eyes like lambs'.

One afternoon, there were footsteps on the wood planks, and I saw Madame Prudhomme smiling at us from the doorway. We smiled at each other as her children nestled in to either side of me. She was letting her hair down from the chignon I'd put it in. It fell in brown waves to her shoulders; she was a gorgeous woman, in that way of gorgeous French women.

"You have a very beautiful voice, you know," she said. It was the first time anyone had told me something like that. Ma had, of course, but it was more in the spirit of charity than anything else. I looked up to the window behind us at the bright afternoon sunshine, and when I looked back to the doorway, Madame was gone.

In the evenings after dinner in the dining room of the hotel, we would walk back along the beach in the sunset breeze to the Prudhomme cottage. There Monsieur Prudhomme would read to the children in French, and then I would read to them in English, which was our arrangement in the city, in New Orleans. He wanted them to be proficient in both. It was essential for their success and well-being, he said. We read from a book of mythology, looking at all the gods, Apollo with his laurels, Zeus with his thunderbolt, Diana with her bow. Near the end of the book was Poseidon who smiled benignly upon us, riding upon a trio of enormous fish with his trident in his grip. At the time, I thought of what a grand week it had been, the ocean breeze, the lullaby of the surf, the playful pull of the current. The weather was beautiful that week.

Then, on a Saturday, the sea began to get rough. I was watching the children as the surf chased them. They giggled and shouted as they ran from the waves, and then again as they ran after the waves as they receded. A voice startled me.

"This strong east wind troubles me."

It was a man named Pugh, who was a senator or something like that, a man of great importance, though he didn't look it with his shirt sleeves and his

169

pants legs rolled up. [20]

"East wind, sir?" I asked him.

"Yes," he said, "Old sailors say that a strong east wind is the harbinger of a storm."

He lit a cigar and threw the match to the beach. The surf took it in a rush of white foam.

"I'd get those children in, Miss," he said. "It's only going to get worse."

I called to them, Jean-Pierre and Celestine. The little fellow ran for a moment with his arms up, shouting to scare a gull off the sand. With a powerful first flap of its black and white wings, it took to the air, the wind launching the bird suddenly. It coasted a little way down the beach and landed again. Looking back, I realize that the bird knew what was going to happen, knew to stay out of the sky just then. Jean-Pierre returned with the air about him of having done his duty, running and falling, then brushing his palms to rid them of sand. He and his sister were soaked, and I threw the blanket I was carrying around the two of them.

"Will you bring us back tomorrow, Mam'selle?" they asked, their hair wet against their little heads as they shivered under the blanket together.

"We'll see," I said. I turned, and the man was making his way down the beach to a group of woman who were reading under an umbrella. Just then the wind lifted the umbrella, and it tumbled end over end down the beach past us. The bonnet of one of the women followed it. The umbrella and the bonnet raced down the beach past us and out of sight.

The weather worsened by the moment, a gale that blew in from the northeast with gusts that kept increasing. The main worry for Phillipe, the Prudhomme's oldest, was that the ball wouldn't be held that night. The young people were all looking forward to it. They were generally held every Saturday night, a chance for the island's young to court one another. It was a highlight, and for many of them, the main reason for the trip out to the island. Such are the worries of the young.

Well, they held it, but the walk home at midnight was harrowing. Sand was stinging our faces and rattling against the windows of the hotel ballroom. It made a peculiar noise, the sand did, a spatter, a needling clatter. The sea, which had made a gentle sound as if it were breathing in and out, began to breathe heavier. Then it began to roar as it became a frothy white, slamming into the beach. It was frightening, angry. Agitated.

It was a long night, and the next morning was a Sunday. Monsieur read the Mass above the howl outside and the shake of the walls. We said a prayer

---

[20] Almost certainly it was Colonel W. W. Pugh, Speaker of the Louisiana House of Representatives, who in 1856 was vacationing on the island.

for protection from the storm, asking for the intercession of Saint Midder.[21] Outside, the sea was churning in a succession of waves. Water was advancing into the yard of the house, and the wind was pushing over the oleander bushes, ripping away the pink blossoms. Anything that was ripped loose of its tether didn't fall to the ground but was cast sideways by the wind.

Sometime after noon Sunday, the water had left just a thin strip of land, and there was still more out in the Gulf and in the bay. The survivors of the Johnstown flood in Pennsylvania describe a wall of water coming down the valley. That wasn't the case for us at all. It was more like a ridge that kept sliding in, one ridge after another, ridges that kept getting higher and higher, and then it was like mountain ranges of dark, salty water. The gray water was moving on the island, a world of dark gray water.

We were having to shout at each other over the wind, our faces right in each other's faces, but our voices only a whisper in the howling. Monsieur gestured toward the window and the hotel outside it. The flags at the corners of it had long since been ripped away. The waves were beating at the front steps.

Just then, there was a sudden rush of noise and light as the roof of our cottage lifted off and flew into the sky. Mrs. Prudhomme shrieked, and the children started to cry. I knelt down to Jean-Pierre and Celestine and told them not to worry, that Miss Bridget would look after them, sure. The trouble was, they couldn't hear a word I said but for the wind. It was deafening.

We decided to make for the hotel across the way, a hundred yards, perhaps. The steps of our cottage had washed away, so Monsieur Prudhomme jumped down into the water, which was up to his knees, perhaps. The oldest, Phillipe, jumped down next to him. Phillipe was about twelve or fourteen, I suppose, and I can remember how I could suddenly see the man he would be, if we survived the day, that is.

Phillipe and his father lifted us down into the water, and we joined hands in a human chain. As soon as we were all out, the cottage pivoted and fell off its brick pilings. We headed into the wind, and it pushed our hair back and made our faces seem large, though our expressions were pinched as we squinted against it. The children weren't crying anymore; they were too frightened to cry, I suppose. The waves were getting increasingly bigger, and Madame carried Celestine, her youngest, and I carried Jean-Pierre. When we were perhaps halfway to the hotel, I looked back. When I turned my head, the wind pulled my hair to its full length so that it framed my vision. Through a tunnel of whipping copper curls, I saw our cottage turning slowly and sliding toward the bay as the sea pushed it.

---

[21] Saint Médard, a French saint invoked against storms.

When we made it to the hotel, I recognized some of the men from earlier in the week. Two of them were former soldiers who had fought together in the Mexican War and entertained the other men with stories of it. They pulled us in, and then we were all huddled inside. A Mr. Hearn wrote a book years ago about Last Island and how many had danced as the hotel was dashed to pieces.[22] I was there, and it was certainly not the case. Everyone was too terrified.

We all huddled in the dining room as the walls buckled in and out like the building was breathing, struggling for air against the storm. Rain drummed against the windows, and it was almost as dark as night outside. In the dim light we all crowded together as the flashes of lightning illuminated our terrified faces. Something would crash outside, debris from other buildings rammed by the waves into our building, and there would be a collective scream from all of us.

Water was smacking into the hotel from the outside. The wind worked its way under the eaves of the roof, and, when the roof was pulled up and flew away, we were in gray daylight again. It was a deafening sound, the roof being pried away, and no one could hear the women shrieking. You could only see each other's mouths open, just before we ducked our heads and put our hands over them.

That was when Monsieur Prudhomme decided we should leave the hotel and make for somewhere else, anywhere else. A few others were also leaving at that point. The east wall of the hotel crumbled, and then the chaos elevated itself to a whole new level. Someone shouted, the *Star*, make for the *Star*. It was the boat that had ferried us to the island. Later, I found out that the captain had beached it on the island as the storm gathered and had the crew chop away everything above the hull with axes to keep the wind from blowing it out to sea. He saved quite a number that way, sacrificing his own ship, his pride.

Monsieur jumped into the water that was raking across the island and then lifted all of us one by one into it, even Phillipe, the oldest whose attempt at manliness had played itself out, and he seemed to be a child again. Even Monsieur Prudhomme seemed pasty and small against the storm. The terror in that man's eyes is something I still see, terror not for himself, but for his family. His personal horror, his anguish that he had made the choice of the seaside rather than the city and its Yellow Jack, and that he had chosen wrongly, and now he would lose what he held dearest, his family. I tell you I see it yet.

We formed a human chain again, Monsieur Prudhomme at one end and

---

[22] Lafcadio Hearn published a novel, *Chita: A Memory of Last Island*, in 1889.

Madame Prudhomme at the other. The outline of the *Star* was blurry in the wind and rain. I was on the end with Madame, with Jean-Pierre in between us and Celestine on the other side. Each wave would crash over the littlest ones' heads, and at last Madame ended up carrying Celestine, and I carried Jean-Pierre. We had to do it to keep them from drowning. The water was just too deep for them to stay above, even on the tips of their toes.

Another mountain range of water, the largest yet, pulled us up and apart from each other. Parts of houses, large timbers, whole sides of cottages, front doors, every class of wreckage was in the waves. I found myself hanging onto Jean-Pierre's little hand. Everyone else had vanished, and it was just the two of us. Another wave of saltwater hit us, and I became aware that my hand was empty. A wave lifted me high in the air, and I paddled and looked around. I couldn't make out people from any other object in the water. It all seemed the same, and then the wave dropped me and covered me over. Then it lifted me up again, salty and wet. I don't know how long I struggled, perhaps a few minutes, perhaps an hour, perhaps longer. It was as if time had slowed down or sped up or didn't exist at all.

Eighty years it's been, and I still dream of him. I still wake up in the middle of the night thinking I have his little hand and find that I'm clutching a handful of bedsheets.

No, dear, I can go on. Just give me a minute.

It's still hard to think about. For years I blamed myself, that if I'd been stronger I would have been able to hold on to him. I'm at as much peace with it now as I think I'll ever be. And it wasn't the last time a child was taken from me.

Well, then. Anyway. Yes.

The waves were picking everything up and then dropping it, and when they bottomed out I could feel sand under my feet and then nothing as I was pushed into the bay. It was a struggle to breathe, and several times I took a great gulp of seawater when I thought it was air. I was beginning to tire. The water was littered with debris, but there was nothing I could ride upon.

Just then, I spotted a large timber, one of the big sleepers of the hotel foundation, I believe it was. There was a man clinging to the far end of it, and I recognized him as one of the waiters from the hotel dining room. They wore white shirts with dark green waistcoats over them, very distinctive. It took all I had left, but I swam to it. When I got near it, a wave pushed me toward the timber, and I had to grab on tight with my fingertips to keep from going past it. It was long, and big enough around so that I could barely get my arms around it. It was slippery in the salt water, and I had to hold on to it tightly to keep from being washed off it. I called to the man on the other end.

"Have you seen the Prudhomme children?" My voice was small in the howl of the wind.

A wave doused us, and when I pushed the water and the salt out of my face, I looked down the timber, which was about as long as these two rooms here put together. The waiter had a gash in his face that I hadn't seen before, and one eye was slightly higher than the other on account of it. He was dead, of course. He slowly slid off the timber, or I suppose, the sea pulled him off. Another wave surged through us, and when I looked down the timber again, he was gone.

The waves pushed me across the bay toward the marsh, the timber poking through each rough, white surge that came up from the Gulf behind me. The whole thing would spin into the waves and then roll with me on it. I would be plunged into the black bay under the timber and everything would go silent except for the gurgle of the water. Then I would struggle to get out from under it, oddly grateful for the howl of the wind again.

I kept scanning the water for signs of Celestine or Jean-Pierre or any of the other Prudhommes, but all I saw was more water. My legs dangled from the timber into the angry bay. I found I could climb onto it from the side and keep on top of it better that way. Bodies began to float by, most of them were face down and the clothes that were left on them trailed around them like seaweed. The currents had robbed them of a lot of their clothing.

At last, I felt something under my bare feet. The surf had long since taken my shoes and most of my clothes. There was grass in the water under my feet; I felt it brush past with each wave. I could only feel it if my body was stretched out tall, and then it got easier. Gradually, I had to pull my feet up and then my knees were brushing the grass under the water. Finally, I let the timber continue on further into the marsh without me. It was nighttime then, though the day had been so dark there was little difference. In the dark, the water became knee high, and then I could feel the marsh grass under it. I sat down in it, and it was up to my waist. I was exhausted.

I sat there as the water rushed past me for I don't know how long. The wind ripped all night, the clouds dashing across the night sky. In the morning, the flood waters had receded, and the marsh was a prairie of yellow grass again. The sun was hot, and I sat there hemmed in by water and marsh grass. Everything was a blur and the sun went down and I lay down with it. The moon raced in and out of small breaks in the clouds. The sun came up and then down several times, and I lost count then. Every afternoon it rained. It spattered the mud around my head as I lay in it.

Things moved in the grass. I stood up, and there were miles and miles of knee high grass, pale yellow like straw in all directions. I was dry, so dry, so thirsty, and I desperately wanted to drink the water, but I knew it was salty and no good to drink. After a day or two, I began to imagine Uncle Jack was there warning me, *you don't want the shits, now, do you?*

No, Uncle Jack, I mumbled.

Every body of water, even the smallest puddle, could have a snake in it, I imagined him saying.

I'm afraid of snakes, I muttered, and Uncle Jack laughed and said, *well, mind yourself, then, girl.*

One moment he would be there, and the next it would be an empty stretch of yellow grass, and I knew it must be the heat and its delirium. I slept again, and when I awoke, there was a pinwheel in the sky. It was black, and it whirled around, revolving unsteadily. I squinted into the sun and saw what it really was. Feather tipped wings, serrated at the ends. Craning bald heads with monstrous beaks. They were buzzards, patiently waiting for me. My delirium had changed, and the hallucination of Uncle Jack stopped visiting me. I had given up.

Later in the day, there was a rustle in the grass, and then there he was blotting out the sun. I thought that perhaps Colleen had been right, that there was a God and that this was him, and he was coming for me. The face eased down from the sunlight, and I could see he was as black as night. He studied me there as I was sunburnt and mostly naked, dry as a chip, my lips cracked and swollen and chapped. I could barely move.

"Shhh," he said. "Hush now, missy. Don't you move nary a muscle. Just be still."

He picked me up, his big dark forearms making the marsh water tinkle as he broke the surface, and he scooped me up. So effortless.

"Shhh," he said. "Just be still, hear? Don't you waste no breath, now."

He turned, and the sunlight scalded my eyes. My eyelids were matted together, and it was hard for me to open them anyway. His footsteps swept through the water, his feet making sucking sounds as they plunged in and out of the sulfurous mud. I was powerless. The grass brushed against his legs as he waded forward until finally we came to a halt. Sitting in the middle of the marsh was one of the billiard tables from the hotel. The green felt was ripped at one corner, but it was otherwise intact, as if fishermen had put it there to unwind between catches. In fact, as he set me on it, I noticed that there were billiard balls still in the pockets.

He put me gingerly upon it, and I shielded my eyes with my hand. I couldn't tell what clothes I had on, or if I had on any at all. I tried to lift my head up but I was weak, weak as a kitten. He put his finger across his lips and told me again to be still. Then he started unbuttoning his shirt.

This is it, I thought. Surely he was going to ravish me, here far away from civilization. It wasn't an uncommon theme in those days, white women being ravished by Negroes who couldn't control themselves. Or perhaps it was the white women who couldn't control themselves, and it was the Negroes who had been led into temptation, but it was talked about in whispers nonetheless. I resigned myself to it. There was nothing I could do.

His shirt came off. His body was black and muscular and sweaty. I closed my eyes again, and then I felt his shirt cover me. It was a red and white checked gingham, and it smelled like a man's toil. I opened my eyes, and then shielded them with my hand as I looked down at it. It was so large it covered me from my neck to my knees.

"Now you stay right here. I be right back, now," he said, and he put his big hand on my forehead. He took a few steps that receded away, wet and gurgling into the watery distance.

"Wait, don't leave me," I wanted to say, but my voice was dry and ineffective and flat, not even a whisper. I was alone with the grass and the water and the sky again.

The breeze from the Gulf picked up and whistled across the yellow grass, and the angle of the sun changed a little. I was glad to be out of the water, but dry, so very thirsty. So thirsty that if I had had the strength to get off the billiard table and get down to drink the salty water, I would have. I began to hallucinate that there was a cistern across the way, rising out of the straw-colored weeds, but when I tried focusing my eyes, it disappeared.

Later I heard a noise, a paddle making a dumping sound as it plunged into the water, and then I heard him again.

"Right here, boss. They she go."

Two white men in slouch hats and neckerchiefs approached me. They looked at me thoughtfully. I looked back at them with blinking, crusted eyes. One of them had a canteen of water that smelled faintly of whiskey, as if it had held that before the water. He held it to my lips. The other one lifted up the red checked shirt and peeked under it.

"Did he touch you, ma'am?" he asked as if he wanted it to be true.

I shook my head no.

"Gentleman," I croaked. "Every bit a gentleman."

They loaded me onto the boat, a small one of perhaps twenty feet. It had an engine that looked like a kitchen stove; it belched smoke and rattled and chugged, which was a terrific racket after the quiet of the marsh. The boat had a canopy in the rear, and they put me under it. The two white men smoked and minded the tiller and looked out on the marsh while the Negro man stoked the engine. As we turned down the winding lane of water between the fields of marsh grass, there it was, a cistern. It had floated across the bay. The men talked as if I couldn't hear them.

"That's that cistern where we found them three, ain't it?" one said. He pointed at it with the long stem pipe he was smoking.

"Yeah, that's it, God rest their poor souls. That's the one."

"Twelve miles inland. All this washed up. And that girl yonder with it."

In Brashear City, they took me to the house of a doctor there. He examined me and guessed that I had been very close to dying, six hours, or less, perhaps. I woke later to see what I thought was a bird as big as a person at my bedside in the afternoon light. A lady in white, a lady whose hat reminded me of a seagull, fanned me with a palmetto branch and gave me spoonfuls of brandy while she sang to me in French. Later in the week, I would wake, and she would be praying the Rosary or tatting lace like a spider patiently spinning a web. It took me a while to realize she was a nun.

It was two days before I could make water and three before I could sit up in a chair for any length of time. Every time I opened my eyes, she was there, a figure in crisp white like a bird, a swan or a goose. As I gained my strength, I finally gained the courage to ask the question.

"The Prudhommes?" I asked.

The nun put down the lace she was working on and sat on the side of my bed. She nervously wet her lips as her eyes scanned the room, hoping to find the right words. She exhaled heavily.

"The Prudhommes are...accounted for," she said.

"Can I see them?" I asked.

She looked out the window as she judged the timing of what she had to tell me. I suppose she decided there was no putting it off.

"No, child. The sea took them all. The search party buried them on the island."

I was still too dry to cry a tear, though I desperately needed to, and I was still too weak to sob. I drifted back to sleep to the sound of the Rosary in French. It rained that afternoon, and I watched it drip from the eaves. It drummed on the roof, rushed through the downspout and into the cistern where it moved in a hollow swirl.

That's that cistern where we found them three, ain't it? I remembered the man saying.

That's when I was able to cry.

When I was well enough, a week perhaps, they put me on the train back to New Orleans with new shoes and a new white linen dress. Reporters from the papers were there at the station to get my story, but I pretended not to be able to talk, and they left without a single line from me.

It was because I was heartbroken, not mute. I had lost family all over again. They had recovered all their bodies, even the little one, the one whose hand I had lost in the water.

I never saw him again, the Negro man, the angel who saved me that day, and I haven't been in the water since. Eighty years. It still terrifies me. It comes to me in nightmares of towering waves, dark and salty. And I haven't used the word nigger once, nor have I allowed it to be used in my presence.

When I arrived back in the city, Maggie and Patch were both there to see me.

"We thought you were among the dead," Maggie said as she held me and wept. Patch's eyes were red, and, when it was his turn to hold me, I felt him shake, though he never said a word.

It fell to Maggie and me to straighten the house, or at least I hoped it would give us something to do. But Maggie had gotten everything spotless for the homecoming the Prudhommes never made, and so she and I just sat in the empty house. In the silence, the long clock ticked for no one, and the two birds chattered to themselves in their cage. I got up and watched them. One would fly from the lower perch to the upper perch, and the other would follow. Back and forth. Back and forth.

An urge came across me, and I opened the little door. One of the birds flew past my arm and out the window in a flurry of tiny wings. The other sat on the perch by my hand, his small head tilting this way and that. I reached my hand in and held my finger out. He jumped from one perch to the next and then landed on my finger. His clawed feet were like little wires. I held him up to my face, and he opened his beak and chirped. I turned to the window, and, after I stroked his head, I launched him up into the sky.

Jan. 16, 1937

"How many were on Last Island?" I asked her.
"Hundreds," she said. "Four hundred or so, they estimated."
"How many died?"
"Two hundred they think."
We sat quietly.

I left last night as she looked out the side window at the sunset. I couldn't tell if she was on the verge of sleep or wistful or just sad at the memory she had dredged up. I hope it wasn't the latter. Perhaps it would have stayed dormant if I hadn't asked her, or perhaps it's always there and just tolerated. A woman her age shouldn't have to resurrect a memory like that, only to have to bear it again. Nina saw me to the door. The winter sun fell quickly and left the world in purple and blue shadows.

Sabbath today. Mr. Levy was cantor, a beautiful voice. Mother was a Levy. I wonder if Mr. Levy and I are related, somewhere on this side of the ocean or the other. Maybe I'll ask him one day, but not today. It was cold and rainy again, and I left the temple without visiting afterward.

As I was walking down Cotton Street from the temple, I'm sure I saw the black Cadillac turn onto Edwards Street. The man's hand flicked an ash through a crack in the window; that was the giveaway. I raced under my umbrella to the corner, my heels clacking on the sidewalk, trying to catch a glimpse, a clue, a license plate maybe. When I got to the corner, I watched the reflection of the taillights streak red and away on the wet pavement. I strained my eyes to make out the plates as the Cadillac disappeared onto Milam. I could only tell that they weren't Louisiana plates. Louisiana plates are green with a pelican. These were black with white numbers.

I turned and went to Miss Fenerty's. I found her in the parlor reading the morning *Shreveport Times*. I let myself in, as she told me I could. She asked where Ellie's been. I told her I didn't know.

"Perhaps she's gone to look for her family in California," she said. "She didn't say?"

"No," I said as bravely as I could.

"Oh," Miss Fenerty said. Her mind seemed to be chewing on the fact of why she left and where she would go and when and if she might return.

I couldn't bear the short silence that followed; I was afraid that I might begin sobbing. So I reminded her, "We were talking of New Orleans last time, weren't we? What did you do after the Prudhommes?"

"Yes," she said. "It was the beginning of the Vauborel years."

Jan. 16, 1937, FWP, Transcript of Bridget Fenerty

Maggie went down to Mr. O'Hara's Agency and found us work together for a family named Vauborel. She and I worked for them soon after the Prudhommes were lost and remained with them for several years until Monsieur Alphonse went missing, which I believe was sixty-one. Yes, of course, it was sixty-one because there was talk of war at the time.

Alphonse Vauborel was an enormous man with an enormous appetite and an equally enormous temper. He had a thick moustache that curled under his upper lip as if it were being sucked into his gullet by the draft of food going down, and he stroked it and petted it like a black cat. It didn't matter if he was speaking French or English, his voice was deep and booming like a trumpeting elephant. He wore a black stovepipe hat like so many of the gentlemen of the time did, and his massive gut pushed against his black waistcoat so hard that you could almost tell the time on the watch that was hidden in its pocket. I will tell it to you plainly, then, and may God forgive me for speaking ill of the dead: he was a genuine arse.

Their house was on Toulouse Street. No matter how well lit the house was, no matter how drawn back the curtains were, the house always seemed dark, as if light were afraid to come into it, as if the light were repelled by the house. It was a place that was so devoid of levity that sometimes it was hard to catch a breath in it.

Every servant believes in his or her heart, in some way, large or small, that the house really belongs to them. They know what needs to be done. They know its faults. They know its special niches. They know how the sun slants in, and how far on the wall it reaches according to what time of year it is, like a sundial works. They know the cool recesses of it in the summer, the warm alcoves in the winter. Every spot, every crack. A house belongs, truly belongs, to the person who cares for it. But the Vauborel's house was different. I always felt the we belonged to the house, that it possessed us.

Maggie did most of the cooking and always had to prepare two meals, one for Monsieur V. by himself and one for his family. We once saw him eat an entire holiday goose at Reveillon, by himself and in one sitting, mind you. Afterward, he slept in his chair while his family tiptoed around him trying not to wake him. They were frightened of him, as he was a cruel man, Monsieur was.

He used to whip the children, scolding them in French and making them kneel on grains of rice and say the Rosary. After their beatings and when they were set kneeling in penance, he himself went for cigars and port and quadroon women and who knows what else. It was common knowledge in the city, the talk of servants in the marketplace. We took to hiding his belts so he couldn't beat his children with them as readily, hoping he would cool off a little in the moments he searched for them. He terrorized them, and his favorite instrument of terror was the church.

Every room of the house had a painting of some scowling saint, the faces of them portrayed as suffering and angry. And every room had a *predieu* in it. Monsieur Vauborel had a padded knee cushion with fancy embroidery on his, which Maggie and me were always having to mend on account of the wear it got from Monsieur's weight. Those of the others were plainer, with imprints in the cypress planks from the grains of rice he made the children kneel on in penance for some infraction of his rules. Despite Mr. Vauborel's policy of strict Lenten contrition for his family, the truth of it is, he always found a way to put on weight during Lent.

Monsieur's zeal would have easily eclipsed that of my sister Colleen, though hers was always of the good-natured sort. He insisted that Madame take the children to Mass on all the high holy days, the feast days, all of it. He himself attended less frequently.

There were two children, Monique and Guillaume, and he was forever shouting, bellowing at them and at their mother, a woman who did everything she could do to stay out of his way. The three of them were relieved when he woke up from his after-dinner table nap and went out "to take a little air" as he said. Maggie and I were just as relieved. We could all feel the air lighten and refresh when the door closed behind him.

Later, he would come back in again just as Maggie and I cleaned up at the end of the evening. His children would watch for him, his big black shadowy silhouette eclipsing the lamplights. As he approached, they would scamper from the window to some other part of the house. Then the door would open and darken with his form filling it, and he would take off his coat and shake out his umbrella, if it had been raining, or take off his scarf if it was cold. As soon as he was in the door, he would start on Madame in his bellowing voice. I can say that in the four or five years we worked for the Vauborels, I never once saw an ounce of affection between the two of them. Not a wisp of it.

One of the two of us, Maggie and me, would stay in a room upstairs to be available, and the other would go back to the room we rented in the Channel with brother. We generally alternated nights we stayed with the family. Staying with the Vauborels was considered the short straw.

Monsieur Vauborel was stingy with his books and newspapers, and I had to be sly about my reading them, the ones in English. He was an attorney, I believe, though I was never sure and never felt comfortable in asking him. I don't think Madame Vauborel even knew, but their house was a fine one, with high ceilings with beautiful plasterwork and gaslights. Mahogany furniture, fancy mantles over the fireplaces in every room, Persian carpets in all of them. The carpet in one of the upstairs bedrooms was the one we used that day, as I'll tell you. He was a good provider, Monsieur Vauborel, though there was talk around town about the amount of money he lost at the Metairie Races.

We worked for several years for the Vauborels, and during this time I grew into womanhood, filling up and out and getting the attention of the boys. Some of them were shy, some of them were bold. Some were so forward as to ask for a kiss, and sometimes they could have one and sometimes they couldn't. I was beyond the awkwardness and beginning to enjoy the attention, though I must say, I held on to my virtue despite the pull of nature inside me. And then one day, I met up with an old acquaintance whose charm gave my virtue a test.

Jan. 17, 1937, Sunday

I brought the recorder home yesterday, thinking I would inventory the disks I'd made of BF. I arrived at Stephenson to find the door locked but jazz musique playing behind it. I set the recorder down on the porch and knocked. From behind the door, there was an exasperated, "Aaaah!" I knocked again, this time harder. After a few moments, Lemurier opened it with his customary greeting:

"Who-is-it-what-do-you-want?"

I was in no mood for his haughtiness.

"If you would give me the key or at least keep it unlocked, you wouldn't have to keep answering the door," I said as I trundled the recorder in, lifting it to my waist with both hands as I opened the door fully with my back. When I rolled through the door, I saw Mirlette.

She was totally nude and appeared to be unconcerned about me seeing her. She sat on a chair in front of Lemurier's easel. Her face squinted as she lit a cigarette, cupping her hands around it and then waving the match out. A fly or something buzzed around her head, and she waved at it with her cigarette hand, the plume of smoke leaving zigzags around her head. She exhaled and reclined back on the chair again, putting one heel on the edge, completely unconcerned. Her skin was creamy and smooth, her bare breasts something beautiful and certainly worthy of a canvas or a block of marble.

The canvas before Lemurier, however, was another of his masterpieces, misshapen, grotesque, a hodgepodge of unrelated details. It was half finished, and anyone other than Lemurier would have hoped it was in the process of being erased rather than being created. He dabbed the brush at the canvas as if he expected the portrait to hit him.

He looked to Mirlette and lifted his chin up and to the side with his cigarette hand, and Mirlette followed his cue, eyeing him as she turned her head. He put the cigarette to his lips again, and then they each had one in their mouth. Lemurier snapped at her to remove hers. She took one more pull on it and peevishly blew smoke at him and set her cigarette down. I came upstairs as quietly as I could, easing the recorder carefully against the front of my thighs.

Downstairs, Lemurier is yelling for Mirlette to keep still. The rain is picking up outside. I'm trapped in here with them. I wish the car were fixed. I wish Ellie were here.

Jan. 18, 1937

Lemurier and I received our paychecks in the mail today. I held it up and admired it, the wonders of your own paycheck, drawn on a bank in Washington, D.C. and signed by Mr. Alsberg himself. I cashed it and sent a good bit of it to mother with an admonition for her not to tell Father. I told her to just put it in their account. We both know how proud he is. And, of course, I set aside that which is required as tribute to the Caesar, Joseph Augustus, the Emperor of Stephenson Street. Hopefully, he'll pay the light bill.

Now I've seen it all:

As I write this, Lemurier is outside urinating unconcerned in the backyard, a hand with a smoking cigarette on one hip and the other one on his putz. At least his back is to me.

(later)

He's returned from watering the backyard and says he wants to have a party to unveil his newest work, his masterpiece he calls it. I couldn't think of an excuse fast enough. Sometimes I wish

Jan. 19, 1937

As I was writing last night, the lights went out, suddenly and with no warning in midsentence. Apparently the light company decided we've used enough free electricity. I hoped that perhaps the 'art' debut would be cancelled, but about ten minutes later my door rattled, and it would have opened had I not locked it, as I'm in the habit of doing now. Only then was there a knock.

"It ease time," I heard Lemurier's voice say as I smelled his cigarette behind the door. He knocked again, louder this time, and it was safe to say he wasn't going away until I came downstairs. I opened the door to see his up-lit face in the light of a candle, with the orange spark of his cigarette as the only other light in the darkness. The candle threw shadows over his face and made his forehead look big and dark like Frankenstein's monster.

"Come downstairs for the debut," he said.

He waited for me to go down the stairs first, possibly in case I would return to my room and lock myself in again or possibly to gawk at my figure as I descended. It was unnerving to walk down the stairs knowing he was watching me.

Mirlette was in the dark, smoking 'Can o' bees,' holding the reefer between her thumb and forefinger. I could only see her face when she put it to her lips and pulled an orange ember to its tip. She was barefoot in a cocktail dress, sitting on a chair next to an easel with a canvas on it. A sheet was thrown over it, as if it would illuminate itself when the sheet was removed.

"Have the seat," Lemurier directed me, and I sat on the couch. He was brimming with pent up pride. He said a few philosophical words about war and mankind and existence and aggression, and when he was done, Mirlette took one more pull on her reefer and set it down in a saucer by her chair. She exhaled a cloud that glowed in the candlelight and pulled the sheet from the canvas.

It was hideous, possibly the most grotesque thing I've ever seen. The kind of image that refuses to go away when you close your eyes.

It was Mirlette, I assumed, because the subject was naked, except for a doughboy hat, puttees and boots. The nude body and its pose were that of Mirlette, but the face was skeletal with the bony, toothy grin of a skull, or of death itself.

Mirlette sat down without looking at it and picked up her reefer and pulled on it again. She put the fingers of her free hand in her hair and propped her head up with them. Her gaze was away and into the darkness of the house. Lemurier looked to me and waited for my praise. I did what I could.

"Well, isn't that something?" finally stumbled out of my mouth. My mind searched for something else to say. The candle that Lemurier held before the painting flickered. "What do you call it?"

"The Trenches of Flanders," he said proudly, and then he expounded on his use of color and perspective, and the symbolism. It was nauseating, truly it was. When he had exhausted what he had to say, he directed Mirlette to put Jazz musique on the hand cranked Victrola. Wine was poured. I have to say, it was a good bottle of wine; the price of it could have paid the light bill.

The subject of the painting may have been Mirlette, but make no mistake about it, this little soiree was clearly about Lemurier. He recited poetry, some that I recognized as Langston Hughes and some that I'm sure was Lemurier's own composition.

Mirlette listened with her leg draped over the armrest of the chair. Lemurier patted the seat next to him on the couch, and she moved over to sit there, lithe, mysterious, slinking. Her eyes are exotic like those of a jungle cat, like her movements.

I sat in a chair next to them as they passed the reefer back and forth. She was lying on the couch now, her head in his lap as he slumped down in the haze of wine and tar-smelling reefer smoke. I realized that I was filling my wine glass again. Was this the second or third time? The cold house seemed less frigid, or maybe the cold seemed less pertinent. I felt comfortable enough to ask them about their life in France and how they met. Lemurier seemed willing this time to let Mirlette talk, though it seemed mechanical, practiced, scripted.

She said that they had met in France when he was in the French army. He had been wounded twice and awarded medals for bravery. After the war, the two of them traveled France and Belgium painting murals in an effort to re-beautify post-war Europe. Lemurier slouched silently, expressionless as she told his humble, heroic life story.

When Mirlette was finished with the French version of a Horatio Alger, rags-to-riches story, she turned her gaze up at the ceiling, and he put the reefer to her lips in a way one might give a dog a treat for a trick performed. They exhaled out into a convergent cloud and stared out at the same unseen thing. He caught my stare.

"It ease a cigarette," Lemurier said. He pinched it between his thumb and forefinger and held it up like Hamlet contemplating Yoric's skull. "A magique..." his voice trailed into a whisper, "Cigarette."

He passed it to me, and I pinched it lightly, as if it might try to bite me. Its acrid smoke smelled bitter and green and crept out of the end like a cobra rising from a basket. I put it to my lips and pulled. The air buzzed with thousands of unseen, unheard conversations. The reefer made its rounds between us, each of us squinting as we pulled on it and then passing it on.

It came to me again, and the smoke from it dried my throat instantly. I coughed, and Mirlette giggled and took it from me. I waited, and it seemed nothing happened and then everything happened, though in the room nothing happened. Lemurier held court as the ember circled among us, our faces wide-eyed with drooping lids. The night sounds of dogs barking and cars passing on Line Avenue and the needle skipping on the record and the buzzing silence and the hum of the house.

"Let's have some jazz musique," Mirlette purred. She hesitated.

A moment later, she said again, "Let's have some jazz. Did I say that all ready?" She giggled again, and it sounded in my head like the notes of a bass drum.

She got up from the floor at Lemurier's feet where she had been sitting cross-legged while he stroked the nape of her neck with his fingernails. She tottered to the phonograph and pulled a record out of its paper jacket, squinting her feral, feline eyes at it, putting it down without re-sheathing it, picking up another and squinting at it and putting it on the turntable. She clumsily set the needle down on it, and it scratched loudly like a cat in an alley at night. Then, after a couple of rhythmic ticks, the smooth, nonchalant voice of Billie Holliday floated up.

Lemurier had something important to say. You could tell because he interrupted Mirlette with a sharp, *everyone shut up! I am inspired*. It was some sort on impromptu poetry.

"There's a cave in France with prehistoric drawings. Painted with the juice of berries and the blood of animals. Together, painted together that way." He pulled on the magic cigarette and added, "and rocks. Made out of clay."

The smoke curled up like a vine or a snake as he watched it. Mirlette sat on the floor before him with her head on his knee. Her gaze was watching a mile away, or farther, perhaps. He held the reefer for her, and her beautiful, full lips pulled on it. She closed her eyes and exhaled a cloud that curled up into the air.

He put his hand in his hair, and I couldn't tell if he was having a thought that troubled him or fascinated him. The record ended in rhythmic ticking, and no one had the inclination to get up and reset it or put on another record or lift a finger. It was if we were all part of the same rock formation. At last, Lemurier sat up and pulled Mirlette to her feet. He offered me his hand.

"Come to bed with us." He asked it so nonchalantly, so matter-of-factly, as if asking me to take a walk or pick something up from the grocers. I'm sure my face was horrified. I would never be far enough under the influence of any drink or magique cigarette to be intimate with someone like him.

"No," I said. "Certainly not."

Mirlette was there hanging on him, and I couldn't tell if she was complicit with his request or simply insensible from the wine and the reefer. I stumbled up the stairs, which seemed to be endless. I fell forward and crawled up the last few steps on my hands and knees. Downstairs I heard them on the couch, beginning their lovemaking without me.

That was last night. I write this now by the light of day, with my door locked, which is how I intend to sleep from now on.

I did venture down to get the mail and found a letter from mother. Father is trying to get work as a broker again but having a hard time. Mother thinks it's because his name is still tainted from the firm's failure, even though he had nothing to do with its collapse. My father's a good man; it's not fair.

No sign of the black Cadillac. No sign of Ellie, either, and I can't think of her without crying.

I'm resigned to marrying Irving and being Miriam Glickstein. It has a certain ring to it, doesn't it? Irving is a nice guy and would be a good provider, but the thought of marrying him makes me want to light up a reefer, which otherwise, I have resolved never to do again.

As I write this (still a little hungover), the long workday of arguing has begun again downstairs, and glass just broke in the kitchen I cleaned this morning, a deed that will go without a word of thanks from either of them, I'm sure.

I've got to get out of here for a while and pay the light bill while I'm out. Going out the window is tempting.

Jan. 19, 1937, FWP, Transcript of Bridget Fenerty

It was the year that a new president was set up in Washington. The one who never married.[23] No, the one after him but before Lincoln. Ah, but if you'd say it, why then we'd

---

[23] The only bachelor president of the United States was James Buchanan, inaugurated in 1857.

both know. Well, anyway, it was then that Ned Hennessy returned.

I was waiting for the trolley on Camp Street, and some men there were making a joke about the new president preferring the company of men to women. He was said to keep company with a bachelor senator from the south,[24] and that he would crawl over a naked woman to get to a man, I think they said. Several of the women present at the stop turned their heads away in disgust at the joke, but I listened closely hoping they would tell another. I turned my head, and then there he was.

What a handsome man he'd become. For one thing, he had grown into his ears, which had always seemed too big for his head, and working out of doors had turned his skin a pleasant bronze. He had grown a thick set of whiskers.

"Bridget," he said with a voice full of wonder. "You're a woman."

"'Tis the natural way of things," I said coyly as I looked away with a lifted chin and a smile, which was an Irish Channel girl's way of flirting. "A girl grows to be a woman, but isn't it the truth, then?"

"And a pretty girl grows to become a beautiful woman."

I blushed. That Ned.

"You've become a man," I managed to say.

"'Tis the natural way of things," he said as he looked me right in the face with a smile and a tilted head. I thought I would melt. But I took his arm, and we walked down Camp, ignoring the trolley as the mule pulling it came clopping up. The man driving the trolley had a Limerick accent.

"Are ye gettin' on then, me fair rosheen?"

We waved him on as Ned spoke of where he'd been in the years that we'd spent apart. He had seen Vicksburg, houses perched above churches above houses, on and on up the side of the bluff. He had seen St. Louis and Cincinnati. He had come back down to New Orleans, and then gone to sea, to Morocco, LeHavre, Liverpool. Back to New Orleans and then around the cape to San Francisco and back.

"You were in New Orleans, and you didn't come and see me?" I asked him.

"I came by once in the summer, but you were away to the seashore, they told me."

"Ah," I said, but I didn't want to ruin our reunion by recounting Last Island.

"I ran into your Uncle Jack in San Francisco," he said.

"Are you sure it was him?"

"Sure, it was him. Still looked like a tabby tomcat."

---

[24] William R. King from Alabama. President Andrew Jackson referred to Buchanan and King as "Miss Nancy" and "Aunt Fancy."

"Did you speak to him?"

"Yes, I said 'Jack Hennigan! It's me, Ned Hennessy from old New Orleans, friend of your niece Bridget and nephew Patrick.' He claimed I was mistaken. He was preaching the gospel in Portsmouth Square in San Francisco. Your Uncle Jack! The gospel! Repent, he said!"

Ned laughed at the very idea. I wasn't sure if it was him, my Uncle Jack, I mean, and to this day I have doubts it was. Uncle Jack, the Gospel, indeed. Ha.

We walked along, speaking of the old times and the times to come. And then, there at the corner of Julia and Camp, Ned kissed me. He did, and this time I melted. I don't know what seaport or river town he learned to do it in, but it made me feel weak and warm. It took all my might to keep my knees from buckling under me. It was the sort of kiss that gets in your pocket and follows you home.

He was only in a day or two before he was to leave for upriver. I told him Maggie and I were working on Toulouse Street for a family and taking a room together on Chestnut Street. I expected a letter from him on a regular basis, I told him, and he promised he would send one, if I would excuse his spelling and not think ill of its poor quality. Of course not, I said, and then I kissed him and waited for my knees to waver again.

He left in two days, bounding onto the steamer *Paul Jones,* which was bound for St. Louis. He was one of the men throwing off the lines as the boat brayed like an enormous mule and backed out into the current. We waved one to the other as I began counting the days when he would return.

Sadness makes the heart grow fonder, of course, and I gave up on other boys, and there were quite a few, to be sure. Ned would return every week or two if it was just to St. Louis he was going, and every month or two if it was to Pittsburg or Kansas City or Cincinnati. We would see each other, and he would kiss me and I would kiss him, and things would come to a boil as we would feel the hidden contours of each other. At last, I would push his hands away and tell him I would have to be Mrs. Ned Hennessy for anything further. I was just turned sixteen, old enough to be married in those days, but young enough to have notions that a man and wife should spend their days under one roof, not under separate roofs. He still had the wanderlust in him, and he couldn't give up the river completely. If only he could have gotten a city job and left the river alone. If only.

Patch was working on the levee as a stevedore and in the evenings, in my free time, the three of us got on as before, though Ned and I craved time alone, apart from him. Ned would bring me trinkets from the river towns he visited, all sorts of fancy bonnets, none of which I would ever have the occasion to wear, lest I be accused of 'putting on airs.'

"Save your money for a little house," I would tell him, "I can only wear so many nice dresses."

"Oh, but I like to see you all dressed up."

But, of course, I had nowhere to wear such finery.

The sun continued to skirt the Vauborels' house on Toulouse Street. It was a beautiful prison, a gilded cage for Maggie and me, a joyless, drab palace. We were only there to keep it tidy and keep its family fed and cleanly clothed. There was no love in it, no joy.

And in the meantime, the Vauborel children learned the art of manipulation. As they grew, they would cry to their mother about mistreatment they'd received from us or from each other, and when she was sufficiently angry and had turned her head, they giggled and grinned. Monsieur continued his bombastic ways, and we came to appreciate the days he traveled on business to Memphis and Natchez, or the afternoons he spent at the Metairie Races, or the nights he spent in the arms of the whores and mistresses he visited. It was all common knowledge that he did.

We spent four or five years working for them, and looking back, I'm sometimes amazed we lasted six months. We alternated living in the servant's quarters, a small room on the top floor with a simple cot and a nightstand, Maggie one night, me the next, even days for her, odd for me. If the family needed anything in the middle of the night, the one of us on duty was expected to rise and see to it. If either of the children was sick, we took the basin and clean linens to them. If Monsieur developed an appetite in the night, it was one of us who went to the kitchen to prepare something. I came to suspect that Maggie was included in his appetite.

It was in early summer when I was sixteen or so. There was trouble in the city, and vigilantes had thrown out the city government and set themselves up. It was only for a week or so, but I had been at the house when it happened.[25] I sent word to Maggie to stay put and not to bother coming to Toulouse Street and the Vauborels until the city's troubles were sorted out.

That night, Monsieur appeared standing at the side of my bed in the moonlight. He was big and luminous in his nightclothes, as if the moon itself had found its way into my chamber. My face was hidden by a slant of shadow, so he couldn't tell if it were me or Maggie. He was grasping himself through his nightclothes and moving his other hand over me, up over my chest and down my stomach to my private parts. It was startling, of course, and I sat straight up in bed.

---

[25] A vigilance committee was formed in 1858, ostensibly to rid the city of crime perpetrated by the lower classes, mostly Irish and German immigrants. During the first week of June, 1858, the committee took over the municipal government but was then driven out.

"Monsieur!" I said. "You must be sleepwalking, sir! Let me walk you back to your bed."

Well, of course I didn't think he was sleepwalking. I believe he was expecting to find Maggie and not me. I rose and took him by his forearm as we both pretended he had been sleepwalking. In their fancy fortress of a bed, Madame Vauborel was fast asleep, just a head in a white sleeping cap on a pillow. She was always a sound sleeper; it may have been the only time she was at peace.

As he neared the bed, his side of the bed, he palmed my breast and my arse at the same time, and I slapped his face so hard that Madame shifted in her sleep. Her face was washed in moonlight, and I could tell she was still out like a light. I dug my fingernails into his forearm, and he made a face that would have let out a scream if he hadn't wanted to wake Madame. I growled low into his ear.

"You touch me or Maggie again, and I'll cut off your *reason-for-being* in your sleep, you hear?"

He didn't say anything; he just got back in bed with Madame Vauborel. I backed out of the room all the way to my small quarters. I closed the door and set a chair tilted under the doorknob.

It was a long week until the troubles were settled and order restored. When I saw Maggie, I asked her if she had had similar experiences with Monsieur.

"He comes in sometimes at night and puts his hands on me and himself. How am I to say no?"

She was a beautiful girl, but a little naïve and complacent, not near the pistol that I was.

"You just tell him," I said, "If he throws us out, then we'll find somewhere else to work if we have to."

Monsieur paid well, I have to say, so we stayed on with the Vauborels, though I took as much nighttime duty as I could until I was sure that Monsieur was keeping to his own bed. It was just as well as Maggie was beginning to miss work anyway.

She had developed a nervousness and female problems. She took laudanum for them, and she slept a great deal. The quality of her work was beginning to suffer until it was only adequate. I would have to cover for her when she overslept, or when her monthly overwhelmed her, or when she had fits of nervousness. So much so that when Ned would come in off the river wanting to spend some time, I was frequently covering for sister. Those years, my late teens, were some of the hardest worked of my life.

They continued that way until Monsieur disappeared.

Jan. 20, 1937

I went to the library and looked it up. James Buchanan, fifteenth President of the United States. His niece was his first lady, as he never married.

The president of the United States, never married. Could it have been for lack of prospects? The most important man in the country, without a single female admirer?

Perhaps he was homosexual, though there's certainly no proof of it. Of course, they do teach us important facts like George Washington had wooden teeth, and the first Roosevelt had the Teddy Bear named after him.

The question I keep asking myself is, how could an enormous (*enarmous*, as she says it) person like Monsieur Vauborel disappear?

Jan. 21, 1937

After leaving Crockett Street, I arrived back on Stephenson to find a small measure of relief in the mailbox, mixed with a much larger portion of sorrow. I know she's okay, and I know where she's going. I got this letter from her today. It's written on the back of an invoice for produce for a place called "The Open Road Diner."

Dear Miriam,

I'm sorry I didn't say goodbye. It was a spur of the moment decision. I'm just so unbearably lonesome for my family, for Daddy and Mama, for my little brothers. So I'm on my way to California. Of course, now I'm lonesome for you. I miss you, Miriam, but I can only say it from this distance.

I can't keep taking Mr. Roosevelt's money for work I'm not doing, or I should say, not being allowed to do. I bet Lemurier won't even know I'm gone.

I've enjoyed knowing you. I hope you get to interview Sgt. Lockett soon, and I know you'll make it to a newspaper one day. You'll make a mighty fine reporter. Maybe one day when we're married and maybe have families (you, not me) we can look each other up.

Your friend,
Ellie

I know there's more to it than missing her family. Part of me says pull it together old girl, and part of me says I can't.

Jan. 21, 1937, FWP, Transcript of Bridget Fenerty

Ned wouldn't stay in town, but he didn't sail the ocean any longer, either. I suppose that was the compromise. There was talk of war in those days, and he didn't want to go abroad when it came and not be able to come home. To me, of course.

Jesus, Mary, and Joseph, but every time I saw him he was more handsome. Dark hair and dark eyes on a fair complexion freckled by the sun and a body full of muscle. When he was younger, his ears had seemed like those of an elephant, but he appeared to have grown into them as a man.

It was the year that Cornelius Horrigan was the reigning city champ, having knocked out Paddy the Bull the year before at the fork in the road that ran past Bayou St. John.[26] Ned and I were at the edge of the crowd of men, and some women, as they carried Horrigan away on their shoulders, Horrigan sweaty and smiling, his knuckles bloody. And Paddy the Bull on his knees under a live oak, stunned and bloodied with his arms limp at his sides, listening to the crowd sing Horrigan's praise as it receded away back toward town.

Ned was in from the river, and we had gone out to see it, all twenty-eight rounds. We walked arm and arm, following the crowd behind Horrigan, but Ned would delay us, saying things like 'oh, but look at this interesting tree,' and 'what sort of bird do you think that is?' and 'look, Bridget, an alligator sunning himself on the bank, doesn't he look just like a log, then?'

Then, on the banks of Bayou St. John, he spun me to him and he kissed me and he kissed my neck, and his hands were about me, between me, over me, on me and my breath was short and my knees were weak. My hands were on the back of his neck as he kissed mine below my jaw. My excitement came and washed through me like a wave and then another, and surely I would have lost all of my virtue had it not been for the clop of a carriage on the Bayou Road.

As it approached, we separated, Ned and I. I pulled my skirts from between my legs where they'd gotten pushed, and Ned adjusted his trousers, and we said hallo to the driver and noticed he had Paddy the Bull in the back, bloodied in a heap in the corner on the seat. We followed it into town, with the larger part of my virtue still intact.

I held onto it, too, though it was a struggle. Perhaps it was for Colleen's sake. I know what she would have said: Sister, pray to good St. Agnes, she of the virtue tested and proven. But then Ned would kiss me and run his hands over me, and I would pull them away from the parts of my body that he had made tingle.

"Take me to the priest," I would tell him breathlessly, tugging my clothes

---

[26] Horrigan defeated Paddy the Bull, in 1860, according to the *New Orleans True Delta*.

back into place, "and then ye can do as ye please."

But when I was alone, I would have to put my own hands where his had been. Don't look shocked, that sort of thing has always been, and it's as natural as a baby's first breath. Ah, but after all, we're made of flesh and blood then, aren't we?

At the time, there was beginning to be talk of secession and with it, war. The men who had an issue with us immigrants, Irish and Germans, found new enemies, northerners and abolitionists. Lincoln had been elected, and people were waiting for the general affairs of things to go places in a hand basket.

At the end of 1860, South Carolina excused itself from the union, and states were following it the way boys will take up a dare and fold to the pressure of their peers. Then, the following month, a committee of men met in Baton Rouge and voted. News went out on the telegraph wires that we were on our own now, and the American flag came down and a new flag, white with a red star and a pelican, went up.

I had just turned nineteen, and Patch and Ned had come around to the Vauborels to discuss taking me on the town for my birthday. For servants to have visitors come in the house, well, this was against the rules of most employers. Friends and relations of hired girls were not to be brought in the house for any reason. We weren't to treat the house as if it were ours in any way.

Well, Patch and Ned were sitting in dining room chairs, tilting back like Lords of the Manor when who should arrive unexpectedly at noon but Monsieur Vauborel.

He exploded. Patch and Ned scurried out the back door as Monsieur shouted at me and Maggie, his shouts in French and English, peppered with *Ma maison! Ma maison!* He picked up an andiron from one of the fireplaces and had Maggie and me cornered in the dining room. When he was angry, especially angry, his eyes went wild and his stare was blank like he was someplace else. This was one of those times. He held the andiron high, and he smiled under the cascade of his mustache.

"Vache!" He said under his breath, bitch in French, I'm sure you know. It was a word he used fairly frequently with us, and we knew what it meant. He swung the andiron, but it missed us and caused him to lose his balance for a moment. We could have run, brushed past him and made for the door. How differently things may have turned out if we had. But the moment for that fled as we should have, and instead we cowered into the corner as close to the wall as we could go without going through it like a ghost. He was standing right over us, and he lifted the tool over his head.

Just then there was a squeaking, crunching sound. His chest lurched forward a little as something poked out of it, like the beak of a bird poking out of a hollow in a tree trunk, except it was the tip of a blade and behind him was our brother Patch. He and Ned had heard the commotion and came back to see about us.

There was a moment of indecision, as all of us, including Monsieur Vauborel himself, contemplated the scene. He put his palm over the tip of the blade and seemed oblivious to the sharp point poking out of himself. Patch was breathing heavy as if what he had done was taxing his strength. We were all terrified. It was as if it was all happening underwater. Monsieur Vauborel looked at us and opened his mouth, and when he did, we saw the inside was bright red with blood. The andiron fell to the floor just a split second before he did, first on his knees, and then on his chest.

There was a quick, low quarrel among Maggie, Ned, and Patch about what to do next. I was too overcome to add anything to the argument. Finally, Patch pulled his knife out of Monsieur Vauborel. It was a big bowie knife, a knife of generous proportions that the stevedores used to cut ropes and what have you down on the levee. It had stuck itself in the floorboards when Monsieur Vauborel had fallen, and Patch had to put his foot on the man's back to wiggle it out. That's when the blood came out in a torrent.

"What'll we do now?" Maggie asked. The boys paced, and Patch said, over and over, "Feck, feck, feck."

Finally, Ned stopped pacing and said, "Here's what we do. Maggie, get a rug the missus isn't likely to notice gone for a while. We wrap him up in it, stow him under the house, and tonight we carry him off."

Maggie and I ran upstairs to the same room without speaking for we both knew exactly the rug, one from the spare bedroom. We pushed away the bed in the guest room and rolled the rug out from under it. It was a beautiful red and gold rug with a forest scene on it. The two of us, Maggie and me, rolled it up and carried it downstairs on our shoulders. Patch and Ned unrolled it and rolled Monsieur Vauborel up into it, while Maggie kept watch on the front porch for Madame to return from her errands or for the children to return from school. Maggie had become a nervous person after Ma died, and she tapped her foot and jiggled her knee as she waited on Ned and Patch to get Monsieur Vauborel disposed of. "Jesus, Jesus, sweet Jesus," she kept repeating.

I myself knew we had no time for nervousness. I grabbed a couple of pails of water from the cistern and some brushes. There was a proper puddle of blood now. A big man like Monsieur has a lot of it, apparently. Once Ned and Patch had him rolled up, they lifted him, huffing and puffing under his weight.

"Sister," Patch said, "you'll have to help us."

I set the pails and brushes down and took the feet end of the roll. Ned took the middle, Patch the head and shoulders. The soles of Monsieur

Vauborel's expensive boots were sticking out the end of the rug right in my face. A dark red ring had developed in the middle of the roll, a ring that was so wet that a drop of maroon blood was beginning to form. I could see it beginning to cleave itself away.

We paraded him through the house and paused at the side door until Patch gave the all clear. We lugged Monsieur and his rug down the side of the house and dropped it with a heavy sound. Then we rolled the bundle under the house.

Patch said, "We'll fetch him tonight," and then he and Ned scampered down the alley way past the cistern and onto St. Ann Street. I turned to go back inside.

Maggie was using a mop to sop up the blood. We took turns emptying the buckets outside, buckets of water that turned from crimson to pink to clear as the job got done until gradually there was only a very small amount left. Mostly it was around the slit in the floor board where the knife had gotten stuck.

That's how Madame Vauborel found us. Maggie and me were on our knees scrubbing the floors.

"Have you seen monsieur?" she asked. "He wasn't at his office. They said he would be here."

And for once, Maggie was cool.

"He said he was going to see a man about a debt, Madame, somewhere downriver," Maggie said smoothly, "that he would be back in a few days. He seemed worried, Madame," Maggie said as she looked up and pushed her hair out of her face with her forearm.

"Oh," Madame said, and then, "Is it the day for floors?"

"Bridget," Maggie said, "spilled something."

"What? Spilled what?"

"An inkwell," I said. I saw a spot near Madame V's foot and scrambled to blot it up. It was the spot that had cleaved off from the blood-stained rug. She saw the rag.

"Red ink?"

"Oui, madame," I said. "Monsieur had a well of it. Perhaps for the debt."

She looked down to the clean floor and used the toe of her shoe to examine the slit in the floorboard. An expression of mild wonder slid onto her face and then slid away, and she left for the parlor to enjoy a few quiet moments of embroidery. She was always as content with his absence as we were, perhaps more so.

Later that night, Patch and Ned came with a wagon. They retrieved Monsieur's body, and with a great deal of muffled grunting and suppressed swearing, they loaded him in and covered him with old oyster sacks. At the outskirts of town, they found a crate that had been used to hold bananas. They put Monsieur Vauborel in it with Madame's rug and turned him loose in the river, hoping it would carry him into the Gulf and oblivion. That was what we had hoped.

Jan. 23, 1937

Synagogue today. Found out the vacant lot across Cotton Street was once the home of a man named Blanchard who was governor of Louisiana. It apparently was an impressive structure with garrets and deep porches. Beginning to recognize names and faces. Mr. Taylor was cantor today. Very cold. Talk of snow again. Went by BFs.

Jan. 23, 1937, FWP, Transcript of Bridget Fenerty

Yes, it was Monsieur Vauborel we were speaking of, weren't we? Well, the truth comes out, then, doesn't it? As much as we cover it over or whitewash it, it always comes out, like a seed buried in the earth, shoots of the truth push the dirt away and strive for the sunlight. They found the trunk with him in it a week later, just past the English Turn. The banana crate with its occupant had gotten hung up in the branches of a willow. I'm sure it was an unpleasant surprise to those who opened it.

Monsieur was a man who had accumulated gambling debt and whose demeanor accumulated enemies, and it was supposed that someone had come to collect. But, as March turned to April, suspicion began to stir. For one thing, he was found in the rug, and Madame V thought she recognized it. We had bought a cheap copy from the man down on Carondelet Street and replaced the one in the guestroom. We stood by as she stood on it, examining it, lifting up the corner of it there in the spare bedroom. At last, she assured herself that it was the original. Then we exhaled, Maggie and me.

The police came and asked questions of Maggie and me and Madame. They wanted to know where my brother was, and Maggie said she didn't know. They asked me, and I said, "How should I know? He's a grown man, he is, and goes where he pleases." They left doubtful and unsatisfied.

We had all seen people die before, such were the times that there was no escaping it. Death had visited us all before, but this time it was as if we had asked him to come. As soon as Mr. Vauborel hit the floor, we all changed a little, but none of us changed more than Maggie. Perhaps it was because when he fell, his face was looking at her, and if he had died looking at one of the rest of us, all purely to chance, we would have been the one most changed. Like a game of chance, like spin the bottle, where one person gets singled out.

A funeral Mass at the cathedral was held, all pomp and prancing and farting for such a foul gentleman as Monsieur, but perhaps it was necessary for one whose feet were so mired in sin, the worst of all his own hypocrisy and self-righteousness. Strange, but I don't recall either of the children shedding a single tear for their father.

We lost our positions, of course. Madame had to let us go and, in fact, had to move out of the house on Toulouse Street to a humbler dwelling. The house and its secret were sold to a man from upriver somewhere. Maggie and I cleaned it one last time and then took down the curtains, which Madame sold with the bedclothes and most of the furniture. Monsieur had indeed accumulated a lot of debt, and Madame was left with the red ink. Her new house was a much simpler affair on the edge of town.

Maggie never worked again, not as a housekeeper, I mean. It was the beginning of her descent.

Jan. 24, 1937, Sunday

No snow, but something much better.

When I arrived for a visit with Miss Fenerty, she met me at the door.

"Oh, thank goodness you're here. There's someone upstairs who I'm sure would like to see you," she said.

I bounded upstairs hoping who it would be as Miss Fenerty looked up at me from the foot of the stairs, one hand on her cane and one on the banister. I looked in one bedroom, but it was empty. In the next bedroom, there she was. Ellie.

She was asleep, but she opened one eye and said, "Hey."

"Hey," I said back.

"Hey?" she murmured. "A month and a half and you're beginning to sound like a southerner," she smiled weakly. Then I saw her lip. It was bruised and swollen like a dark bulbous fruit. My gaze and my fingers caressed it as I asked her what happened. Then I saw that she had bruises on her throat also.

"I was headed out to California to find my daddy and my family. Money got low, and I took a job as a waitress in a diner in New Mexico. The cook at the diner had been eyeing me while I swept up. It was late at night, around closing time. The manager left, and it was just me and the cook. He locked the door and made a pass at me, and when I told him I wasn't interested, he grabbed me and pulled me into the kitchen and thought he'd have some fun with me. I put up a fight, and he gave me this lip."

"Did he...?"

Her smile bent up slowly. She put her fingers to her lip; it looked like it hurt her to smile, but it also looked like the pain was worth it.

"Let's just say that a man can't do his job with a broken tool. I left him hunched over holding himself and walked on the highway at night. After a couple of miles, a sheriff picked me up. He took me to the town doctor, who looked me over and put in the stitches. Everything's all right, just sore and looks like hell.

"They asked me if I had a place to go. I told them I just wanted to go home. They asked me where's home, and I couldn't tell him where my family was other than 'California.' The only other place I could think of was Shreveport. Here, with Miss Fenerty on Crockett Street." She hesitated. "And with you."

I brushed her blonde hair out of her eyes, hair as straight and golden as wheat and as soft as cotton. The clock's second hand on the mantle clacked by comfortingly.

"They bought me a train ticket and sat with me under the light at the station. It picked me up in the middle of the night."

She was beginning to mumble. Sleep was stalking her. In that thin sliver of a moment, a truth escaped her.

"Before I left Shreveport, I went to see a preacher. He said my feelings were amiss, and it would be an abomination if I acted on them."

I got into the bed on top of the covers next to her and held her, and I felt her breathing slacken into a quiet sleep. When I woke up later, someone had closed the door to the room. I went right back to sleep.

Jan. 25, 1937, Monday, evening

Left Miss Fenerty's this morning after sleeping as deeply as I can remember. We had added to our interview, the story of her placement with a new employer, a young couple named Burton. After she and I had tea, I went straight from there to Market Street to see about the Packard. I thought, foolishly, that maybe the Packard had healed itself. Perhaps in my elation that Ellie had returned, I thought anything was possible, even self-repairing autos.

But again, the Packard would start but not go. The engine whirred, but the gear would not engage. It struck me that I've used this expression in the past to describe someone whom I found to be peculiar or stupid.

Some men inside a machine shop, Negro and white, came out and watched me. They seemed to be happy to have the diversion. They each took compulsory looks under the hood, "mashing" on the clutch and feeling it squish underfoot, scratching heads and offering suggestions. They were a set of men sweaty from their work, even in the winter cold. A voice called out from the darkened workshop.

"You hard-legs get back to work," it said.

The men looked over their shoulders and reluctantly turned to resume working. The foreman came out and took off his hat and said, "I'm sorry for my language, ma'am, didn't see you. I do apologize."

I was half a block down Market Street when I felt an urge to run back to the big open bay of the machine shop. They were complaining, all of them, white and Negro, as one of them mimicked the foreman, who was back behind his glass enclosure and oblivious to their grousing.

"Thanks," I called into it.

"You're welcome, ma'am," their voices called back. I felt a grin creep over my face. I couldn't resist.

"*You hard-legs*," I added into the darkness.

Laughter, hearty male laughter, erupted in the darkened shop.

Jan. 25, 1937, FWP, Transcript of Bridget Fenerty

It's funny isn't it, strange, I mean, how circumstances spin, and through one small twist, everything changes.

I was standing in line at the O'Hara Agency for placement of domestics, waiting for another assignment after Madame Vauborel decided she could no longer afford help. The girl ahead of me in line knelt down to button her boot, and as she did the clerk behind the counter said, "Next, and don't be all day about it neither."

The girl who was buttoning her boot looked up and said, "you go ahead, then." It was just such a twist, a click of a peg on a lottery wheel, and I was placed with the Burtons.

Their house was on Prytania, just past Melpomene Street. They were a young couple, the husband a businessman of some class who was active in the Confederate government, the state Treasury, I believe. The wife was a lovely enough looking woman who would have been more so, were it not for her pinched face and righteous demeanor that made her look like a bird in some respects. Of course, self-righteousness doesn't look good on anyone, does it? We stood in the front parlor as she looked me up and down.

"Can you read?" Mrs. Burton asked me. The look on her face was like that of a hen eyeing a beetle and deciding if she could nab it.

"Yes ma'am," I said. "I can read quite well."

"Hmmp," she snorted. "Read this. Do you know what it says?"

"Holy Bible," I said.

She softened a little.

"All right. Open it and read something."

I opened it and read from First Samuel. *"Reaching into his bag and taking out a stone, he slung it and struck the Philistine on the forehead. The stone sank into his forehead, and he fell face down on the ground..."*

After a good minute or two she stopped me.

"Mr. Burton and I are planning a family, if God in his infinite wisdom grants it. We'll need a nursemaid to look after the child...the children," she said as she expanded her plans hopefully.

"'Tis a favorite of boys," I said handing the Bible back to her. "The story of David and the Philistine giant. They like stories of giants and swords and battles, ma'am."

"We'll want someone to read to them. It's why we don't just go down to Mr. Banks' Arcade and buy a darkey."

"Yes ma'am," I said.

"Do you attend the papist Mass?" she asked me next. Her gaze was down her nose and inquisitive, as if this was the most important question to be asked.

"No, ma'am," I said, and it was true for I hadn't attended Mass in years, not since Colleen died. I waited for her to ask me where I did attend church, but she didn't. I supposed she cared more about where I didn't attend than where I did.

If she had asked me, I would have been inclined to tell her that I attended services on Sunday afternoons with the darkeys in Congo Square and that they knew more about the joy of being alive and being a creature of a loving God than any piss-pious church that I knew of.

But she didn't ask me where I went to church.

And I didn't have the chance to give her a smart answer.

And I was hired.

And, of course, it changed everything. All because the girl ahead of me stopped for a moment to button up her boot.

Jan. 26, 1937

I reluctantly spent the night at home, if you can call it that. I think it best that Ellie and I not be under the same roof. In the morning, I went back downtown again to see Ellie and Miss Fenerty.

"She's still asleep," Miss F said. "She's had quite an ordeal, you know."

Ardeal, ye knoo, she said it.

Instead, we sat, and Miss Fenerty told me more about her employment with the Burtons, speaking in a low voice. Eventually Ellie came downstairs, which is really what I was hoping for. We sat and listened to Miss Fenerty, Ellie's legs pulled under her with her hands tucked between her knees.

When we were done, Ellie suggested we go fix the Packard. Her throat is the faintest yellow-green now, the bruise only recognizable if you had seen it at its worse. Miss Fenerty had sent for a doctor who came and took out the stitches.

We walked the few blocks to Market Street where the Packard sat parked. Ellie asked again for the symptoms it had. She kept asking as she folded the hood back to the side and peered into it. Her artist's hands reached into the engine like the nose of a hound probing a hole for a rabbit. She rose up on the balls of her feet to peer further, shading her eyes under her blonde bangs with a hand that was smudged black now. Her brown wool skirt fell over her hips. Her feet toed inward as she rose up on them. I don't think I've ever seen a woman in a ballroom gown look more lovely.

"Think I know," she said.

She disappeared under the Packard. As she lay in the street, her legs protruded from under it.

"There's usually a cotter pin near the clutch arm. Way it is on a model T Ford, at least…tends to wear out or lose its shape." Her voice echoed around the motor and found its way out through the wires and hoses and engine block.

Ellie's legs jiggled as her unseen upper body worked at something. She grunted, and it echoed, too, filtering up through the engine.

"You have a pair of pliers?" she asked, and then she said, "No, wait, I got it."

Something under the hood made a sound like metal ridges being pulled through a hole. She pulled back from under the car and when she did her white blouse came untucked and rode up over her creamy pale midsection dimpled by her navel. She stood and the blouse fell haphazardly, half tucked, half untucked, back down over her skirt. She flourished a piece of metal that looked like a giant bobby pin. She held it up triumphantly with a hand stained black with grease. There was a clean break in one of the limbs of the pin.

"Yep. Cotter pin. Why your clutch wouldn't catch."

The men of the machine shop had filtered out from their jobs, some of them smoking in the great doorway.

"I'll be damned," one of them said.

Ellie turned to them and held up the pin. Ellie and the men were all mottled black with grease. They looked like they were all the same tribe of people, and she was their priestess holding up an icon.

"You boys got somethin' or 'nother like this?" she asked.

"Believe I do," one of them said. He disappeared into the depths of the shop and reemerged with a shiny new cotter pin that was an exact match but intact. He handed it to Ellie, who held the two up to the sky.

"Yep," she said. Then she looked at the man and said, "You got a wrench?"

"Crescent or monkey?"

"Either'll do," she said.

He disappeared again and came back with the wrench.

"I can do it for you," he said.

"Thank you, but so can I," Ellie said as she took the wrench.

She disappeared under the Packard again. The whole shop of men had gathered on the sidewalk, along with several other men and women who happened to be passing. Ellie's blouse pulled tight against her chest as she slid under the car again. As the men looked on, I was relieved for her that she had worn a brassiere today. There was a tapping and then the same catching sound that the other pin had made when it came out.

"Miriam," she called to me, "mash on that clutch now."

I got in, and the clutch felt like it did before, like it was supposed to, firm, responsive.

She slid out from under the car, and now her blouse was completely untucked. Her face was smudged, her rosy cheeks mottled with grease. The crowd that had gathered on the sidewalk dispersed. The men of the machine shop applauded quietly, and one of them from within the darkness joked, "Will you marry me?" to which the other men laughed.

Ellie shook her head and grinned at the pretend proposal. She handed the wrench back to the workman. I opened the door for her, went to the driver's side, and got in. I checked traffic in the side view mirror and pulled out. It was a little odd to be driving again.

As we headed down Market Street, I asked her, "Where did you learn to do that?"

"From my daddy," she said. "Remember, I was raised on a farm. Got to know how everything works. Going to town is too far and too expensive. If you get me spare headlights, I can replace those for you, too."

As we waited for the light at Market and Marshall, the black Cadillac turned onto Marshall Street. It glided away among the other traffic on Market Street. Mixed in with the other autos, it was conspicuous only to me. I watched it and then realized that Ellie was snapping her grease-black fingers in my face.

"You look like you just saw a ghost," she said.

Jan. 26, 1937, FWP, Transcript of Bridget Fenerty

Polly Rourke. The name of the girl who was buttoning her shoe, 'twas Polly Rourke. She ended up working for a pair of bachelors who lived on Napoleon Avenue. Two dapper men, they were. Rumors were that they kept to the same bed, but Polly Rourke never said a word about it. She kept her mouth shut, as a good servant does. Secrets, no matter how salacious, how juicy, keep themselves to the house.

I, of course, was working for the Burtons. From my quarters upstairs, I could hear them downstairs, the sounds of their love. Every month, I waited for the announcement, we're having a baby, isn't that just grand? But every month, there was no news and then a year went by and there was no news. The nursery upstairs stayed decorated but vacant. It was becoming apparent that my mistress was barren.

In the meantime, war was beginning to assert itself with grandiose promises and military music and flowery prayers published in the papers so that an angry God, *our* angry God, could smite theirs and so prove the point of the righteousness of our cause.

Mr. and Mrs. Burton were ardent proponents of Our Righteous Cause and read the papers and attended the rallies religiously, hanging on every printed and spoken word of every politician, every bishop, every general. Sheet music was sold in the music shops in the city, songs that were learned and sung in the saloons and coffee houses and, when the weather was nice, in concerts given in the public squares.

To hear the Burtons talk, you would have thought that Jefferson Davis had written the Fifth Gospel and published it in the Richmond papers. Mr. Davis says we should do this; President Davis says we should do that. If Jefferson Davis had made a decree that we should dance naked in the moonlight, well, they would have peeled off and done it, I'm sure. He was their Lord and Savior, Jefferson Christ, whether they wanted to admit it or not.

Patch heard all the flowery nonsense as well and was sucked into it like so many others. Of course, it didn't hurt that the police were beginning to get suspicious that Patch was involved in Monsieur Vauborel's disappearance. For some reason, they didn't suspect Ned, and in that they were correct as it was Patch who'd done it. Put the knife in him, I mean.

And so, as the spring moved on toward summer, Patch finally enlisted in the Confederate army. Curiously enough, it was in a coffee house with the ironic name of The Olive Branch, on Erato Street. The young men were signing up for the usual reasons, glory, honor, fear of censure, peer pressure, a paycheck, adventure. No one signs up to be maimed or killed. No one would if they thought about it.

They marched them out to the Metairie Race Course, where Monsieur had spent so much leisure time and money. They had renamed it Camp Walker after one of the officers. The city would go out to watch them drill, often bringing picnic lunches, though it was a rainy spring, and the ground was soggy, and the air smelled like wet horseshit. Most ate in their carriages as the men milled about and endured the shouts of the sergeants and lieutenants and other officers. I would go, too, trying to spot Patch in the lines and columns of men who marched with sticks and shovels and rakes as if they were rifles. They got those later when they went to a camp near Mississippi. Maggie never went, and I often wonder when it was that she saw him last.

Perhaps a little tea, then?

Jan. 27, 1937

Another letter from Irving. I read this one, which asks what I thought about the last one. I'll have to find the first one and read it. His attempts at the romantic are clumsy, like erotic poetry written by a ninth grader. I'll reply but not in the steamy vein that he would like.

Ellie is back to her old self, though putting off talking to Lemurier who I don't think has noticed her absence, but then again he doesn't notice much anyway.

I told Ellie about the Cadillac. She wonders if it's someone from the government interested in Lemurier's political views or perhaps a creditor or someone sent by creditors. She doubts it's anything to do with Irving.

Jan. 27, 1937, FWP, Transcript of Bridget Fenerty

Spring was well established when news reached us of the first battles in Virginia. Of course, it caused quite a bit of excitement. It wasn't long after that that they marched them from Camp Walker to the train station to take them to some other place, I forget the name.[27]

Ned was somewhere on the river, though traffic was slowing as the northern men put up a blockade. Bales of cotton and barrels of sugar and all classes of other goods were stacking up on the levee with nowhere to go. People with tastes for the finer things imported from Europe were forced to develop a taste for the domestic.

When I told the Burtons that my brother was off to the war, they seemed pleased and gave me half a day to see him off. On the days I was off from the Burtons, I was sharing a room with Maggie, though I rarely saw her. On the day that Patch left, she was there in our room, however. She was doing her hair up and putting on rouge like the Creoles across Canal did.

"Are you coming with me to see Patch off on the train to the war?" I

---

[27] Most likely it was Camp Moore in Tangipahoa Parish, Louisiana.

asked. 'Off to the war' in those days had the same significance as 'off to a picnic' or 'off to see Grandma and Grandpa in the country.'

She seemed preoccupied and continued to dab at her face.

"Aren't you coming?" I asked her again.

"I have an appointment." She smacked her lips a single smack into the mirror.

"An appointment? What sort of appointment?"

"I'm going to see a gentleman." She leaned into the mirror and applied something to her eyelashes. "About a matter." She paused. "A job. Employment." She dabbed at her face again as she and her reflection made faces at each other.

"You're not going to see brother off? Your own brother?"

"He told me himself he wouldn't be gone long. Just a few months. Back by harvest time, the farm boys say."

Farm boys? Where had she met farm boys? I thought. I gave up and went down to the station by myself.

Later, Maggie would have other excuses for her so-called appointments. A business matter. Discuss employment. Discuss a job. Always dolled up. I didn't understand it then, perhaps because I didn't want to. I do now.

So I went down to the station at Baronne Street. It was a foggy morning, so dense that the second stories of buildings were hidden. I waited with the sea of other families and well-wishers who were there under bonnets and top hats. We heard men singing and the shuffle of feet like an army, which it was, of course.

Everyone hurrahed and waved handkerchiefs. The men were drawn up in line, and then an officer allowed them to fall out and see their loved ones. I couldn't see him, my brother, and I was becoming worried I wouldn't get to see him before he left. And then I felt a hand on my shoulder. There he was.

"I shan't be long," Patch told me.

And then they stepped up into the cars, handing up their knapsacks and belongings up to each other. One man brought a pet raccoon on a leash with him. Some still had sticks, still getting into the part of carrying guns. The men hadn't been given any yet; they would get those at the next camp up near Mississippi, so they'd been told.

They were the best and the worst the Irish of New Orleans could provide: stevedores, screwmen, draymen, barbers, bank clerks, store clerks, altar boys. Brawlers, drunkards and their bartenders, cut-purses. The low elements of the town. Give them all guns and a flag and they all become heroes. Patch among them.

He hugged me, smelling of the nickel shave he'd just treated himself to that morning. Then he said, "Don't worry sister, we'll be back before you know it," and he kissed me on the cheek. His cheek was as smooth as mine. And then he was up and into the car, his friends pulling him up. They started singing a song about what they would do to Abe Lincoln if they came across him, and there was hurrahing and laughter and more singing. All under a dome in the white fog. Further up and down the train, the same scene was happening with other families, the sound of it similar to our scene but muffled.

The whistle blew, ghostly in the white mist, and then the train lurched forward, and there was a loud cheer the length of the train. The wheels of the train were big like the lids of cauldrons, and they began screeching and squealing and squeaking on the rails. They galloped into a rhythm, and a thought ran across my mind of the day that Ned Hennessy and I fell beneath the train after swimming.

I began walking with the train and then running, filtering around people in the crowd, clutching my skirt. The rustle of it as I ran fell into the rhythm of the train, the crossties under the rails rocking gently. I looked up, and there was Patch and his friends singing a song about the virtues of Jeff Davis and the southern man in general. My brother and the rest of them smiling, their mouths open like a big fish about to swallow a minnow, singing at the top of their voices. Patch winked and waved, and his car slid into the fog, and I stopped and watched it.

Their car slipped away, out of the dome in the fog, and another took its place, and it slipped away, and another and another, fading into a thicket of wet cotton fog. The rhythm of the train kept up and then quickened its pace until the last car exited into the mist, the white covering over it.

Only women and children and old men remained. Our boys were gone, my brother Patrick among them. The air was muffled by the fog, and it was such a contrast, the quiet after all the hullaballoo of bands and singing and shouting. No one said a word. We all went home leaving the train station empty and quiet. Soon all the boys of the city would be gone. Then, later, in a year or so, the streets would be filled with northern boys. But I would be gone as well by then.

Jan. 28, 1937

The Packard runs now but still needs the lights fixed before it can be safely driven at night. We took the Jewella bus west to see the lake at sunset.

"One of the prettiest things you'll see," Ellie said.

We got off after a trip up a street the bus is named for, Jewella Avenue, all the way to where it dead ends into the far western end of Milam Street. The driver announced end of the line, and Ellie and I got off. There was a small dimple in the yellow weeds where a trail disappeared into the gray of the winter woods. The failing light played on it, and it all seemed to glow. Under the skeletal branches, there was a litter of leaves, a lumpy carpet of every possible hue of brown. The carpet covered things on the forest floor, fallen branches and logs. My eyes were focused on the ground beside the trail looking for things under the leaves that might have their eyes on my ankles. My heels were making it a little hard to walk, but it was too cold to take them off.

"This is about where they found that girl a couple of years ago," Ellie said.

"What girl?" I asked as I balked at a puddle, wondering if Uncle Jack Hennigan was right about there being a snake in it.

"A girl that was raped. Then murdered," Ellie said as she took my hand and helped me around the puddle. "It was in all the papers down here. Even the Texas ones."

"Did they find out who did it?"

"They did. Some drifter from Georgia who made paper butterflies that he sold to people. They hung him in the courthouse downtown. They say it'll be the last one. Electric chair from now on."

I must've gotten quiet. The light had fallen a little more, and I was formulating in my mind how spooky the walk back to the bus stop would be in the dark after the sun had set. Ellie was still holding my hand, leading me, and I liked the feel of my hand in hers.

"I'm sorry," she said. "I didn't mean to scare you. I just thought the journalist in you would appreciate the story."

She was right. It was a story, not a ghost story. A journalist is interested in the former.

The trail flared out to where the railroad tracks ran in a sweeping curve, and we walked on them. The rails were cold and hard, parallel and orderly in the chaos of nature. We walked on opposite rails, still holding hands. The woods thinned and fell away, and then there it was. The sun was poised above the far horizon, leaking orange and gold onto the surface of the water. Against its light were the black outlines of cypress trees, old and ancient in the new lake. It was spectacular, something worthy of an Impressionist's paintbrush, a blur of color. I knew I'd want to come back one day.

"Is there a shorter way?" I asked.

"Just up that hill if you have a car. The bus don't-*doesn't*-go that way. From the bus it's quicker like we just came. If you had lights and could drive at night, we could park up there and just come down the hill." She pointed to a light up on the hill where there was a square little tavern sitting in the twilight. The music from inside murmured.

We were sitting side by side on the rail with our hands by our sides, palms pressed into the cold steel rails. The light on the lake was changing moment by moment like a kaleidoscope, some colors I'd never seen before, colors I couldn't begin to describe. It was turning cold, and our breath was beginning to steam into clouds.

"I can fix your light for you," she said. I didn't follow her at first. I was transfixed by the sunset.

"What's that?" I asked. I turned, and she was looking at me. The unexplainable, indescribable light was over her face and her smile.

"I can fix that light on your car," she said. "Easy fix."

I drew near her on the rail, and we leaned into each other. Our shoulders pressed into each other, and I put my head on hers. I tried to will the sun to stay in the sky just a little while longer, but at last it fell. We rose from the rails and ascended back up through the weeds to the bus stop.

Jan. 29, 1937, FWP, Transcript of Bridget Fenerty

It had begun in the years of working with the Vauborels. Maggie's nervousness, I'm speaking of. It was at that time that she turned to laudanum. You could buy it in the drug stores then, under a variety of names. Slowly, surely, quietly, like the squeeze of a jungle snake, she became what they called then an opium eater, though most of those what took it just drank it in a tea, which is what she did. And when she had turned to opium, by necessity she turned to the world's oldest profession.

There were evenings when I returned from the Burtons to the room that Maggie and I shared to find her and one of her 'gentleman callers' as they were sometimes called then. Once, I walked in, and there was a white arse above Maggie, working like a fiddler's elbow. She looked over his shoulder and jumped. The fellow fell off her and pulled the covers over them.

"Bridget, aren't you supposed to be at the Burtons?" she asked.

"I'm off for the night," I said, eyeing the man who was hurriedly slipping himself into his trousers as if he had been caught by his missus.

Later, I would knock and, when there was no reply, go in. But still, I would often find her with a man. She would be on top of him or on her knees before him with her blonde hair laid out on his legs while the man leaned back with his hands on the bed and his head back with his eyes closed. A different man every time. The next time I made sure I knocked louder. I finally stopped visiting altogether and stayed in the small quarters that the Burtons provided.

She was prettier than I was, my sister, Maggie. I was a pretty girl who turned the heads of all the boys, but as pretty as I was, she was twice as pretty. My hair was copper red, but hers was fairer, yellow. The color of piss, I would tease her. But I was only jealous, you see.

She had a voice that was like the pleasant patter of a spring rain, gentle and pure. Inside her, though, there was turmoil. Troubles swirled about in her. But when Patch left for the war, she was the only family I had, not counting the Burtons who were no family at all.

A month went by that I hadn't seen her, and I began to worry about her, so one evening I went looking for her. The room we used to share on Chestnut Street was empty, the water in the basin evaporated out to dry enamel. It was a foggy night that was lit by a full moon somewhere up in the sky past the fog. Everything was illuminated like the prolonged flash of a photographer's bulb. The mist of the fog was like a thin school of tiny fish, a fizz in the moonlight.

I wandered the streets, up Carondelet until I came upon a girl of the night, Mary O'Meara, a lewd woman as they said. I says, "I'm looking for Maggie Fenerty. Have you seen her?"

"You must be lookin' for some girl-to-girl love," she says, "and she'll do it for you, she'll do most anything."

"I'm her sister," I says, and the girl's smile vanished, and she says, "Oh. She's further up, corner of Camp and Gravier, most nights she is."

And there I found her. Her cheeks were sallow, and her hair was greasy, the pupils of her blue eyes tiny dots. Her gaze wavered, and her smile was idiotic. She was flirting with two soldiers. The city was full of them then. At the start of the war, it was southern men, and then later, I'm sure, northern men, but by that time I was gone.

She looked up to me, and I'll never forget it, her face fell and she said, "Bridget, sister, what are you doin' here?"

One of the soldiers said, "This your sister? Why don't the four of us go have ourselves a time?"

I told him to feck off, and the two of them laughed, but Maggie didn't. I told her, I says, "You come home, come home now, and I'll make us tea and maybe I'll sing for you." By then I had a lovely voice, like Da had had, and Maggie loved to hear me sing.

But she tried to smile, and she told me, "It's not your sort of tea I crave."

There was a regret in her eyes, a sorrow so intense that it almost hurt me to look at her, like she was looking at me from the inside of a cage. And she turned down Gravier Street with the two soldiers.

And that was the last time I saw her alive.

Someone found her in a room above the druggist on Poydras. The examiner's verdict was opium intemperance, but how can you be sure?

Jan. 29, 1937

It was out there today, the black Cadillac, the man smoking and eyeing the house. He stayed pulled up behind the Packard for most of the morning. It was disconcerting, his patience, his single-mindedness. All morning, sitting and smoking, sitting and smoking. Just before noon, he pulled around the Packard and vanished down the street.

Now that the Packard is fixed, I have no excuse for not going out into the countryside. Ellie thinks we should go see if Gladiola Longhat can give us any history. It might be interesting to someone.

I spent the day answering letters. I sent one to Leonard (Lennie), one to Mother, one to Father, even one to Uncle Sol and Aunt Gertie.

All day I've thought of what Miss Fenerty said of her sister: it's not yer *sart* of tea that I crave.

Jan. 30, 1937, Sabbath

This morning, I caught a glimpse of her headed down to the river. I visited with the other Jews on the steps after temple, keeping one eye on her as she walked down Cotton Street. As I watched her, there was talk of backyard gardens, what to plant in them and when, and last year's gardens and what did well and what didn't and what did you do differently? In short, conversations you don't hear on the steps of Emanu-el in Manhattan.

When I found a pause, I excused myself and followed her down Cotton Street. She disappeared through a break in the weeds, down toward the river. I pushed through the grass and tiny yellow flowers, the very first harbingers of spring, to where Ellie lay. She was stretched out in the sun on a blanket, reading a book on the sand bar by the river's edge. The red-brown water drifted hurriedly by, drifts of bubbles riding on the surface in the current. The railroad bridge loomed over our heads, just downstream from us.

"What are you reading?" I asked.

She jumped.

"Sorry," I said. " I didn't mean to startle you."

She looked at the cover of the book and then said to me, "Radclyffe Hall, *The Well of Loneliness*."

"Is it good? I've heard of it, but little more than the title."

"May be one of the best books I've ever read. A lot of libraries have banned it, though. I found it in the trash at the diner when I went for California."

"The trash? What's it about?" I asked.

"It's a love story," she said. She started to say something else. But her words faltered, and she changed the subject. She does this sometimes.

"And what are you doing?" she asked. A train was puffing over the bridge above us, headed east across the river.

"I came to see the river. Close up."

"Not much to see, is it?" she said. "Muddy. Too wet to plow and too muddy to drink, I think the saying is"

"Very muddy. Murky," I said. I must have tilted my head to see the title of the book better because she seemed ill at ease and placed it near her satchel, a little tan one made of canvas with leather straps. Her bare heels were dug into the pale sand of the bar. Her calves were speckled with grit and freckles. She was wearing a light cotton dress today, white with a print of small tulips on it, knee length. When she moved to put the book away, it pulled against her, and I could tell she wasn't wearing a brassiere. Her breasts are neither small nor large, but tilt up optimistically under her dress. She brushed sand off her legs and sat Indian style. The river slid by the muddy color of cocoa.

I picked up the book and read. After a sentence, I read out loud. "You're neither unnatural, nor abominable..." I wish I could remember it all.

She stood up and wiped the sand off her backside.

"Let's see if Mr. Wray has those lights for your car," she said.

He did, and it took Ellie all of ten minutes to fix them. Then we went to see if Miss Fenerty would continue her story.

Now I know how an Irish girl ends up in Shreveport from the bogs of County Roscommon. What I don't know is why a New York girl and a girl from the Texas panhandle end up here.

[Patrick, here is the passage I read that day by the river. I remember it clearly. I still have the book, The Well of Loneliness, by Radclyffe Hall, so I'll copy the quote here. -Aunt Miriam:

"You're neither unnatural, nor abominable, nor mad; you're as much a part of what people call nature as anyone else; only you're unexplained as yet--you've not got your niche in creation. But some day that will come, and meanwhile don't shrink from yourself, but face yourself calmly and bravely. Have courage; do the best you can with your burden. But above all be honourable. Cling to your honour for the sake of those others who share the same burden. For their sakes show the world that there are people like you and they can be quite as selfless and fine as the rest of mankind. Let your life go to prove this--it would be a really great life-work."]

Jan. 30, 1937, FWP, Transcript of Bridget Fenerty

By Christmas of that year, it was beginning to look like six months wasn't going to be enough time to hold a war, and, when our boys didn't make it home for the holidays, it cast a gloomy spell on everyone and everything.

The Confederate government passed a law that said all men between the ages of eighteen and thirty-five were to be compelled to serve in the army. Ned had finally come to the city to stay and had joined the Navy before being conscripted so as to get the enlistment money. I didn't particularly like him joining, but it did keep him in port as the Federal men had a stopper in the river down below the city and above it. Goods were stacked everywhere, a reminder that you couldn't eat cotton.

It was a week in April that year that changed everything. The northern men were coming upriver and were threatening the forts below the city. When the wind was from the south, you could hear the small, distant boom of the big guns way off in the distance. Along the levee, ships were being readied to repel the invaders. Ned was on one of them, a tugboat whose job it was to wait until nightfall and tow a barge of flaming pine knots into one of the northern warships.

Ned had sent word that he was to be off at daybreak, and I was again granted time off by the Burtons to see this young patriot off to do his duty. I went down to the river and looked for his boat. It was the Musher or the Mouser or something like that, I can't remember it now.[28] The sun was just coming up over the river where it took the right turn past the city. A man with red whiskers was bustling on the deck. I called to him, I says, "Is there a Ned Hennessy on this boat?"

He called down below, "Hennessy! Someone here to see you."

A soot covered man came up from the hold, and when he smiled, I knew it was Ned. He scrambled up the side of the boat and down the gangplank. He seemed as giddy as when he was a boy, like he was playing a part in the spectacle, as if it were a play at the Olympic or the Varieties, where the young, honest Irishman follows his duty and will surely triumph in the end.

He pulled something from his pocket, fifty Confederate dollars, his bounty for enlistment in the Confederate navy. He gave it to me. "Keep this," he said, "and when I come in, I'll take you to see Father Mullon, and we'll put the money on a house."

I took the money, five ten-dollar notes drawn on the Bank of Louisiana, and put it in my pocketbook. I was smiling so hard I could feel myself doing it. Then he says, "I would have asked you to marry me ages ago, if I had thought to save the money for a house. I won't have me wife and family living in a rented house. I wish I had been wiser with me money."

It was just at that moment that I realized how proud he was, and I felt bad

---

[28] The ship was most likely the *C.S.S. Mosher*.

for him, and my smile evaporated.

"Ned," I says, "I'd have married you and lived in a rented house. Surely I would have."

"A girl as fine as you deserves more than a St. Thomas flophouse. She does."

The red whiskered man called for him, "Hennessy!"

"Two or three days," Ned said as he cast a glance behind him to the boat. "Captain says we'll be back in two or three days after we deliver a surprise to the Yankees."

Beneath the layer of soot, his whole face grinned, eyes included. I noticed that he had new boots on and that the whole crew were sporting the same kind. They'd all been given fifty dollars' bounty and new boots. He tried to kiss me and I wanted him to, but he was all grimy, and I was clean for inside work. So I blew him a kiss, and he smiled and reeled his cheek back like it had struck him hard. He always did that. And then he got on the boat. He scrambled up the gangplank and waved and then saluted me with a solemn look. The boat's engine bubbled black smoke out of its stack as it backed out into the current and went down the river.

There, and now he'd finally said it. I was excited to be Mrs. Ned Hennessy when he returned, excited to have a house of our own, maybe with a garden spot and a milking cow. The two or three days couldn't pass fast enough. Through the day that was filled like all the others, with laundry and cleaning and the market, I kept whispering to myself, "Bridget Hennessy, Bridget Hennessy," for I liked the sound of it.

Night fell, and we in the city could hear it and see it, small thunder from the southeast and the flashes of explosions on the horizon. People gathered on the levee and on rooftops to see it, women assembled under parasols in small groups, gazes fixed on the southeastern night sky. The horizon would flash orange and then a second later the rumble and then the oh! of the people gathered. I looked to see rafts of fire, but it was too far away, and then the crowd on the roof drifted away to their houses and their beds, and I was left alone up there, leaning against one of the brick chimneys that pierced the flat roof.

A day or two later as I was expecting Ned, I read about it in the paper. It was in all of the papers, under screaming headlines that the northern men were in the river negotiating with the mayor, a man named Monroe who kept delaying them. The news was horrible and especially horrible for me.

That night, Ned's boat had pulled a raft of fire into one of the northern ships, which shot the tug full of holes, and it went down with all of them, including Ned, my Ned. All of them in their new boots.

Their names were listed in the paper, the men who were on the boat, and halfway down the list, Ned Hennessy. I read it in the *True Delta*, and I didn't believe it, perhaps 'twas a mistake, I thought. Perhaps 'twas a different boat. Or perhaps it was the right boat, but rather than sink, it had made the bank and the men had escaped to the countryside, and soon Ned would appear in the alley with a loud stage whisper like he always did, "*Pssst...Bridget!*"

But then I read it in the *Bee* and the *Picayune* and the rest of the papers, all varying accounts of the same occurrence. The Muster or whatever the name of the boat was had gone to the bottom of the river with a crew of young men who weren't so much brave as they were excited and agitated.

Mrs. Burton said, "How proud you must be! Your boy is a real hero to Our Righteous Cause."

If I hadn't been in such a fog, I would have told her I didn't give a fiddler's fart about Our Righteous Cause, that it had been dreamed up by small mob of small men with their little alter egos erect at the prospect of pomp and violence. But it was as if I was sleepwalking then. I had lost my best friend and my future husband and lover. It would never quite sink in that I had.

I've come to believe that when the ones you love die, they don't leave you. They just follow you around like silhouettes, transparent and empty. No, they never leave you. Not completely. And Ned Hennessy hasn't. I carry him with me yet, and I always will.

The mayor's hocus pocus and double-speak couldn't keep the northern men in the river forever. He did keep them there long enough for the Burtons to make plans and escape. Mrs. Burton scurried around the house, directing men to pack things. Armoires, bedsteads, sideboards, the harp, the pianoforte, all were crated up and taken in mule-drawn wagons to a steamer hired by the Confederate government. The treasury was brought on board as well with armed guards who sat and played cards on the crate while they babysat it.

Stories circulated of the abominations that would be committed upon us by the northern brutes, rapes and murders and the sacrifice of children, the emptying of warehouses by armed companies of Negroes and their Yankee overlords. The Philistines would soon be in the camp of the righteous Israelites, thirsty for blood and whiskey and cotton and the curvy smooth skin of southern women.

And so when Mrs. Burton asked, at the last moment, if I would accompany them to Shreveport, I said yes. Ned was gone. Maggie was gone. Patch was gone and with every report of every bloody battle it seemed like he would be gone forever like Ned and Maggie. Everyone was gone, and I was alone. Going with them was the natural course.

I just never thought that we might go by the river. It didn't occur to me. I was just nineteen at the time and short on details about things such as that. When the steamer was packed with Confederate officials and their families, and their servants and other belongings, I was the last to board. Mrs. Burton called from the deck, "Are you coming or not, Miss Fenerty?" I balked like a mule would, my feet shaking over the gangplank as I lifted my skirt over my boots. The hungry water slid under me. I felt my legs shaking and rubbery as I scurried over the short section that separated the bank and the levee from the boat. Once on board, I took up a position deep inside the forest of crates and boxes on the lower deck.

Through a break in them, though, I could see the city diminish in the twilight, and I thought of that day when we Fenertys, all six of us, stepped out into it like strangers in an Arab bazaar. Now we were all gone from it, every last one of us. The light fell, and the smell of burning cotton and sugar rose with the fires on the levee. The shadows of people seemed to dash in and out of them. A mob was raiding the government warehouses, carting off things to use instead of letting them burn or fall into the hands of the Yankees.

I would never have gotten on the boat if I hadn't been so stunned with grief. Part of me wished that our boat would go down as well. I sat within the crates, and at last I cried for Ned. I sat on the deck with my face in my hands, and I sobbed loudly, but it was all drowned out by the noise of the boat. The thump of the steam engine like the deep beating heart of an athlete, the arm that turned the paddlewheel like the long sprung leg of a grasshopper. The hull of the boat would smash away tree trunks that were washing downriver. The engines kept hammering away like large feet stamping the ground, and the steam kept hissing over and over again like the exhalation of an enormous beast, like a dragon, perhaps.

The next day, it became too hot for them to stay in the cabin, and the Burtons adjourned to the covered deck. They delighted themselves in looking for birds and alligators and other wild creatures. The water terrified me, however, and I couldn't look past the rail of the ship.

"Oh, Bridget," Mr. Burton would say, "There's a bobcat prowling in that thicket. Do you see it?"

"Oh yes. Just look at it," I said, just to satisfy him, but I hadn't seen it at all. I hadn't seen anything. I couldn't look out and see so much water.

The carcass of a horse, brown and swollen as big as an elephant floated past us. We covered our noses as it moved downriver, an island for flies with an atmosphere of stench. It rotated slowly as the wake of the boat kicked it about, and then it receded past us and down river. Willows lined the low, sandy banks, scrubby trees no taller than a house.

During the long days, I read the optimism of newspapers now a week old and from another era, or I wrote letters to Patch in Virginia. I hadn't received any from him, save for a few terse, boasting lines from Camp Moore in Tangipahoa. About his regiment, the Sixth Louisiana and its flag, two red stripes and a white stripe with *Let Us Alone* and under it, *Trust in God.* About camp life, about a joke someone played or a peculiar mascot a company had or who had the best regimental band and what airs they played.

But it didn't matter. It was my duty as a sister to send him letters to keep his spirits up, and I resolved that I would do it until such time as he might return or I might receive notice of his death. It was a ritual, and such rituals keep us alive sometimes.

Nights were a bit of a relief. A basket of fire lit the bow and the path of the boat and flickered orange off the black night water. The breeze across the deck cooled to a more pleasant temperature. The Burtons slept in their cabin while I slept on a pallet of quilts on the deck, well away from the edge and within the fortress of crates.

During the day, it was a different matter altogether. The river was swollen from the spring rains, the limbs of trees that were once well away from the edge now drooped in the current that tugged and nudged them downstream. Every once in a while, the water would scour away the roots of a tree, and it would crash into the water and head downstream with it. It was terrifying, though perhaps only to me, one who was well aware of the power of water.

The fields were sugarcane for days on end. Then one day we slowed, the big thumping engines grunting mechanically and the forward motion of the boat turning to the left. Off the right side of the boat, the starboard, they call it, I saw the broad channel of the Mississippi, and I felt sick, terrified of the broad silver shimmer of it. I felt as if it had a magnet in it, a magnet for me.

I staggered to the very middle of the deck, in the shadows of the towering crates, deep in a dark space within them. I sat down on the deck and rocked and rocked with my hands in my skirts between my knees. I struggled with my breath, feeling the water yearn for me. I stayed in that little alcove there in the shadows of boxes until I regained myself. Then I took the inside stairwell up to what they called the Texas deck, a place where I could see the riverbank but not the water, and I convinced myself that we were on a train or just floating above the land.

Mr. Burton joined me. There was a breeze blowing that played with his hair and lifted the lapel of his black frock coat. His hand rested on top of his hat to keep it in place. He raised his voice over the noise of the engines.

"We're in the Red now. See out there?" he said down his outstretched arm and finger, "Cotton. Just what the Yankees are after."

To Mr. Burton, the war wasn't about freeing Negroes or States' Rights. It was about greedy Yankees who merely wanted our cotton, such was his reasoning. Some people are like that, they have the logic of an animal, like a dog guarding a bone that they think all other dogs want.

Green plants stretched all the way from the river to the distant green tree lines, a stippled sea of green leaves. Lone trees grew up in little islands of shade. Negroes were scattered in the leafy sea, the adults up to their knees and hunched over it with hoes, the younger ones up to their waists. On seeing us, they straightened up and waved. I always waved back, though Mr. Burton never did.

The sun rose every morning on cotton fields and set every evening on cotton fields. The moon and stars shined at night over cotton fields. Embers twisted out into the air from the twin smokestacks and whirled into the night air that lingered over cotton fields. In the morning, the sun rose yet again over cotton fields as we made a bend to see more cotton fields.

Bales of cotton sat uncollected under sheds and in the doorways of barns and on the levee. With the river being closed at New Orleans, there was no way to get it to England, and so it just sat while more grew in the fields. Occasionally, though, there were pecan and peach orchards, and cattle in the fields. It was calving season, and the little black and brown calves stood close to their mothers or nosed under them to get at their udders and the milk. In the heat of the day, they all gathered in the shade of the isolated trees.

We passed Alexandria, and such a fine town it was, a pretty little place. The northern men burned it a year or two later.[29] Much of the government was being set up there, but the treasury was being sent up further, to Shreveport where so much of the war material, especially foodstuffs, cattle and corn from Texas, was coming in. We continued up, and the noise of the engines droned on, and we were all used to it. We stopped at little landings to take on wood or to transfer passengers or freight. In the lull, we found that we shouted at each other having become accustomed to the hullabaloo of the engines.

Mrs. Burton stayed in the cabin, citing a headache as her trouble or some other illness, a different one every day, it seems. I would bring her water and things to eat and drink from the galley. Their cabin opened up to the river, and I was careful to keep my eyes away from it.

Above Alexandria, we met the Great Raft, a tangle of tree trunks and debris with a channel kept cut into it. The hull of the boat kept bumping into debris, and there was a great deal of shouting up to the pilot in the pilothouse from crewmen down at the water line. The men had big poles with hooks they used to parry away tree trunks and limbs. Whenever a particularly large trunk would bounce off the hull, the men would shout, *G-D-!* to the dismay of the women on board.

It took a day or two to weave through it, but the raft was a relief to me as it seemed more like solid land than water. At last, we were through it and to open water again, and then one morning, there it was on a small bluff above

---

[29] Alexandria, Louisiana was burned in the spring of 1864 in the ill-fated Red River Campaign. Each side blamed the other.

the river on the left bank, red brick buildings, church steeples, warehouses flanked by bales and bales and bales of useless cotton.

Shreveport. It was a town that smelled like mud and wood smoke and fresh-cut pine and cow manure and cottonseed.

Shreveport. And here I am yet.

Jan. 31, 1937

Quiet Sunday. Church bells distant downtown. I suppose that E has gone to the Baptist Church, but I'm not sure. Spent the day reading and cataloging disks.

Nice piece in the paper on Champ Lockett, though to read it, it seems he did everything but make his daring dash over water.

My housemates spent the day like two animals in a den, snarling, growling, copulating.

Part IV
February, 1937

February 1, 1937

Today was Miss Fenerty's birthday, and Ellie and I made her a cake. We asked her what kind of cake she wanted.

"Make any kind ye like," she laughed, "and surely *(shorely)* I'll eat it."

It's a good thing that Ellie is here, as Nina is due any day. Her size no longer hides her status, her stomach pushing out past her large bosom. She was there today, however, and gave us pointers on baking. I think I had more flour on me than the cake had in it. We had our cake (chocolate with chocolate icing) and sang happy birthday to Miss Fenerty, a small cone of a hat on her head, held in place by a string under her chin. We set one candle in the brown frosting, and she took three tries to blow it out.

"If you'd put the proper number of candles on it, you'd get a visit from the fire department, then wouldn't ye?" And then she laughed that laugh, so warm and comfortable.

Ninety-five. Will I live to be that old? Will Nina? Will Ellie? And if we do, will we be as alive, as vital, as Bridget Fenerty?

I left Ellie at Miss Fenerty's. She brushed flour off me, and her touch made me close my eyes and sigh without meaning to. She stopped abruptly, and we made a quick goodbye, as if we were warily skirting a whirlpool, afraid we would be pulled into it.

When I returned home (Stephenson Street, I mean), there was a letter in the mailbox from Mother. I opened the door and backed through it as I opened the letter. I looked up to see that Lemurier was painting Mirlette, working on his next *tour de force*. She was sitting on a stool, nude and unashamed, smoking a reefer, setting it down smoldering into an ashtray as she resumed her pose in the bitter smoke. Neither she nor Lemurier seemed to notice me or care. I went upstairs and closed the door to my room and read the letter.

Dear Miriam,

I received your letter and the money you sent. The amount surprised me. Where did you get that kind of money? Never mind, only know that we're glad to have it just now…

The letter goes on to tell me how everyone is doing. My little cousin's bat mitzvah. Aunt Gilda was ill but is better now. There was talk about flowers, receptions, and so forth. She said that once we set the date, the wedding will be on a small scale. She adds that it's a shame, that Father wishes he could put on a bigger celebration. She hopes I won't be disappointed.

I won't tell her where the money came from. I can't tell her. It would break her heart. I won't tell anyone. I'm ashamed of how I got it. I can't even write it here.

Feb. 2, 1937, FWP, Transcript of Bridget Fenerty

The government set us up in a house on Fannin Street. Negro men carted the crates up from the river, and everything was unpacked, crowbars prying nails out of planks with a squeezing sound and the slap of wood sides falling away like blossoms to reveal household items: the armoires, the bedsteads, the pianoforte, the harp, missus' sewing table. She had stopped sewing children's clothes; they had given up on having children, and I never heard them in the act of trying for them in that house on Fannin. Before, they were loud with their passion, but now either they were quiet about it or had nothing to do with each other. A servant notices these things, soiled bedsheets and so forth. Instead, Mrs. Burton spent the days playing hymns on the pianoforte, missing notes and not seeming to notice or care.

I was in a new town, and even mundane things like going to market were complicated, held up by small details. What street is the butcher on? Where does one buy fresh produce? Is the fish fresh here, or is there somewhere else to buy it? The town was full of strangers, and the only two people I knew were the Burtons, who I didn't care for at all, of course. Well, thank goodness for being Irish.

I acquainted myself with everyone in the City Market. The woman who had the fresh corn, the fishmonger who sold the catfish that were as big as a hogshead of molasses, the old couple who sold the pears and peaches and had the little dog that slept at their feet under the table. Oh, I knew their names once and the names of their families, but time has taken them from my memory and left me with only their faces. Their smiles specifically.

Food and supplies were much more available in Shreveport as it was so close to Texas, which was largely unaffected by war at that point. I made friends in all the shops and thought it might indeed be an entirely pleasant place to live. The men my age were all away with the army, and the only ones left were either very young or very old or infirm in some way. There were a couple of theaters, my favorite among them was the Gaiety, though there wasn't near the selection of them as there was in New Orleans.

Life began again there on Fannin Street as I began a new chapter. I mourned Ned as I still do, and I still thought of him when my hands were busy on my work, and I'll admit, sometimes myself, and my mind stretched and flitted in random thoughts. No, go ahead and record that, Miriam. God already knows it, and I'm old enough now that I don't give a fiddler's fart who else does.

It was a day just a few weeks later. The summer days were getting longer and hotter. I was wiping down the kitchen on a midmorning. The house had an indoor kitchen, which was a novel thing then. My mistress was away, and I was thinking of Ned's lips on my neck and his hands on my breasts, and I sorely wished he were there, and I was sure that if he were, he wouldn't have to take me to see a priest to get permission.

He came in the kitchen and crept up behind me. My mind was still on Ned when he put his hands around my waist, and he started kissing my neck. I admit, it was lovely, to feel a man's lips on the softness of my neck, but I certainly knew it was wrong.

Mr. Burton, I said.

He answered with his breath. And then I was turning my neck this way and that, and then I felt his hands on me. I fell with my elbows on the kitchen table. His hands were on me through my skirt, pressing between my legs, his breath heavy and labored. My own breath joined with his, rapid and shallow. I whimpered as my skirt came up, it seemed by itself, and then he was jerking my drawers down as I leaned on the kitchen table, and my will struggled and failed.

Mr. Burton, I said again, but it was feeble. His belt jangled and then I saw his trousers around his feet and then he was inside me, and truthfully I wanted him there, though I knew he shouldn't be, and he grunted and slapped into me and then he stopped and only the part of him inside me moved. His soft, money-stained hands were over my mouth, just under my nose. It had all taken a minute or less.

It was silent except for our panting and the afternoon sounds outside through the window, dogs barking, the rattle of wagons and the distant shouts of the men coaxing their teams, the sounds of commerce, of business. Children playing a few blocks away in the schoolyard, small shouts on the breeze that stirred the ivory lace curtains in the kitchen window. You could almost hear the world turning.

He separated from me and pulled up his trousers. I was still stunned at how quickly it had happened. As he left the room, all he said was "Fix yourself."

That was it.

Fix yourself.

He never again said much more than that to me, and he never touched me again, though perhaps I would have let him. No, he rarely spoke to me, and we couldn't look at each other. Perhaps he was infected by shame, Mr. Burton was. The powerful, tangled roots of it grew inside him and choked him.

Something else grew in me. The most beautiful thing I've ever seen.

Feb. 3, 1937

The telephone rang, and she answered it. I waited, but she happily talked with the person on the other line, and finally I turned off the recorder. She was receiving belated birthday wishes.

When she hung up the phone, she wanted to talk about the latest issue of *National Geographic* which included a pair of articles on Berlin and Hitler. I found it was odd that I had no interest in those things and wanted to know what had grown in her. She doesn't have children that I know of, though that had to be what it was. What else could it have been? She didn't say but excused herself for an afternoon nap, teetering on her cane, her steps heavy in the hall. I spent the afternoon reading.

Ellie returned from the Y, where her mail is still being delivered, with a letter from her family. She sat on the couch and told me that one of her brothers is sick in a hospital in Bakersfield, California. She had found her paycheck waiting for her also but had cashed it and sent every penny she had. She's decided she'll have to go back to work for Lemurier.

We returned together on the trolley past the frosty lawns of Line Avenue to Stephenson where in *Chez Lemurier* another sink sculpture had been erected. They do that from time to time; no two are ever the same. Pots, pans, silverware at random angles, plates and bowls on edges, smeared with whatever has been eaten that day, or if I'm not around, the last few days.

He was in his undershirt and trousers, smoking on the couch while Mirlette scratched around in the kitchen, looking for a clean plate to bring him the sandwich she had made for him.

I won't go into the specifics of Ellie's conversation with him. It would just make me angry all over again. But simply put, he blamed the lack of any progress on Ellie, that if she had not been away, then so much, *so much!* could have been accomplished. *It ease a shame!* he said.

Foolishness.

"I am thinking of telling the man in Washing-tone about theece!" And then to justify it, he added, "It is *I* who report to the man in Washing-tone."

In the end, he took her back. I suspect it's so he'll have someone to put the blame on in the end when nothing is ever done. It hurt me to see her have to deal with him. Ellie finally left for the trolley stop and downtown, probably still biting her tongue.

So this evening, at random intervals, I've gotten up and looked through the blinds, announcing from time to time, "Oh, there it is, the Cadillac," even though the street was vacant. He would jump up and come to the window, and then I would say, "Oh, false alarm. It was just the neighbor."

Then I said as I peered through a crack in the curtain, "It's him this time, it's him, it's him!"

It caused him to scramble up the stairs and finally stay up there, leaving

Mirlette sitting on the stool, naked and indifferent, obtuse with wine and reefer.

I look up from my writing here to tell her, "I don't think he's coming back down this time."

She grinds down the butt of her 'Can o' bees' cigarette, shrugs her shoulders, and slinks upstairs.

Delicious mischief.

Feb. 4, 1937, FWP, Transcript of Bridget Fenerty

A young woman's body can't keep a secret for long, can it? I tried to pretend that it didn't happen, that it wasn't going to happen. Everything would go on just like it had. But suppers were delayed as I broke free to tend to my weak stomach. I was fatigued and frequently overslept. Of course, there was no monthly, and in fact, I never had another. By the fall, my dresses were tight around the middle. And then there was the matter of Mrs. Burton.

She knew. I don't know how, but Mrs. Burton knew. She knew I was expecting, and possibly she may have known that it was Mr. Burton's, but she knew. As I look at it, years later, her ease with the situation makes me think it had all been planned. They had both raped me.

To have a baby out of marriage in those days certainly occurred, but it was a sinful, shameful thing, a secret you crawled out of town with until the thing happened. If a girl was got with child out of wedlock, there were no prospects for her. She was turned out shamed and destitute.

I awoke one day from an afternoon nap I shouldn't have been taking to find Mrs. Burton's face right above mine. A sharp nose flanked by accusing eyes; her face could be a scary, pinched thing, especially when you saw it close. She smiled thinly and lifted her chin slightly like someone who knew a delicious secret.

"I know the truth of what's going on with you," she said, though I wasn't sure if she knew who the child was for. Nevertheless, she said, "Mr. Burton and I will raise it. The child," she added, her thin lips tight over her teeth as she strained to keep from smiling broader.

I didn't try to lie to her. She never asked me who the father was, though there were times that I thought she might know but refrained from saying so to avoid embarrassing her husband or herself along with him. Society people never risked being sullied in such a manner as that. Instead, Mrs. Burton made a deal with me. "Let's us both stay inside until your time comes," she said, "you and me, and I'll say it's me that it's going to happen to." How was I to say no?

We stayed in that fall and winter, and 1862 became 1863. I was locked inside and longed to go to the market, just to walk in the cool air, but my secret was obvious, and the whispers would prompt the Burtons to turn me out, pregnant and with no prospects. They brought in a Negro woman to help me with the cooking and cleaning and then, as I got further along, to do it for me. She was threatened with violence or something much worse, being sold from her family, if she told anyone.

Mr. Burton would leave the paper for me when he was done with it, used and folded up. I read about the battles, particularly in the east where Patch was. All the news was whitewashed, sanitized. Every small victory was magnified into an epic triumph, every crushing loss diminished into a minor skirmish. With every report of a great battle, the town would brace themselves for the news in the papers that would come a week or so later, the lists of the dead and wounded. And then there they would be, sure enough, things like:

John Smith, arm.

Jim So and so, chest, mortal.

Tom So and so, leg, status unknown.

Winter passed that way. The Negro woman, whose name was Tarvie, I believe, kept the house hot, and Mr. Burton scolded her for using so much firewood. Coal was a thing of the past, as it couldn't get into the interior of the country any more than cotton could get out. Mrs. Burton couldn't stand being under her own self-imposed house arrest and began going out with a melon under her dress, saying that she needed the fresh air. Such an elaborate lie from a fine Christian lady. But I was happy, for when she left, it was just Tarvie and me. We cleaned together, and it was a joy for me to stay busy.

"White women, they sits on they bottoms when they's in the family way, but slave woman and her swole up belly pull a hunnert pound cotton sack down a row," she said as we worked side by side. I was glad for her company and glad to be useful.

But in the evenings, when the Burtons were home, I was forced to play the role of a hen incubating an egg. I read a great deal that winter, all of Dickens and anything else I could get my hands on. The little fellow inside me kicked and stretched and kept me company the whole time. My stomach grew in size, a cantaloupe, a pumpkin, a watermelon until finally, it happened.

It was in March. The trees were leafing out into yellow sprouts, and the azaleas were budding into pods that were on the verge of opening. We had a warm spell, and I wished I was allowed to sit on the back stoop, which Tarvie would have let me done, but Mrs. Burton was home, and I was forced to sit in a chair while the hall clock ticked patiently.

My appetite had slackened quite a bit, and I was more tired than usual, and there was a mild turning in my side which I attributed to the baby. Then I noticed a discharge on my drawers, blood tinged, like the first day of a monthly. My stomach was tightening, and the little person inside me seemed to be balling up and then stretching.

Well, let me tell you, Miriam, childbirth is everything they say. It rolled in like waves, and then my water snapped within me, dampening everything. Within a few minutes, it all became unbearable; I heard someone shouting from a mile away, and then I realized it was me. Mrs. Burton slapped me and told me to be quiet.

Of course, I could do no such thing. It's impossible, or at least it was impossible for me. The pain from her slap was nothing compared to the pain within me. When she saw I couldn't be quiet, Mrs. Burton began adding theatrical screams or groans in her own voice, aimed to the window for the benefit of those who might be passing by. It would have been something worthy of an Irish comedy, something that would have been shown at the Varieties Theater on St. Charles to a house full of guffawing Paddies.

The clouds grumbled, and it sounded like something was breaking, tearing, crumbling. The laundry on the line in the yard behind the house lifted and fluttered and fell. Lifting, fluttering, and falling, like this. I thought, I must get the laundry in before it rains. I was becoming delirious, and I thought that if I got up to see about the house's errands, all this labor business would change its mind, and life could go on as before. But every time I lifted from the sweat-soaked bed, Mrs. Burton and Tarvie would push me down or pull me to the center if I tried to slide off the edge to the floor. A pair of white hands and a pair of black hands guiding me.

I tried again, and finally Tarvie said, "She need to walk. Let her walk some." They let me up, and I nervously paced the floor a time or two, but then I went down to my knees on it and then all fours, rocking back and forth, my belly and my breasts swaying in my gown. I was fidgety, restlessly waiting on each wave of pain, each worse than the last. The afternoon shadows grew and gathered together into darkness. The rain began falling hard outside, and lightning painted everything in a sudden crash of gold that fell to blackness again just as suddenly.

At times such as those, a woman finds herself intensely alone with her pain. I desperately wanted Maggie or Ma or Colleen or Madame Prudhomme, or even my Da. My pains twisted through me, all through the day, and then night fell, and I paid no notice to it. The Negro woman lit a lamp, and the orange light gave the room another aspect of the theater. The pains were wrenching, and my stomach clinched itself tightly into knots and then expanded. It was strange to hear Tarvie boss Mrs. Burton around: Get sheets. Boil some water. *Ball*, she pronounced it.

Sometime during the night, Mr. Burton came to the door, smiling nervously like a dog that's been caught in the middle of shitting. Tarvie threw a sheet over me and told Mr. Burton to kindly excuse himself, that this was a private moment. And he was so nervous that he let her talk to him like that.

Late that night, my bottom began to hurt. It felt as though it was full of something, and I struggled to get up again. "I need to go to the privy," I panted.

"No, chile, that baby right there," Tarvie said.

Mrs. Burton had long since given up on her pantomime labor sounds and was sleeping fitfully in a chair. The Negro woman looked at my bottom confidently, but when Mrs. Burton awoke and looked, she seemed shocked, repulsed. Her face looked like a baby bird waiting for a worm.

"They he go," Tarvie said with her confident, uneven smile, and the urge to push out what was inside me was overwhelming, and I screamed as loud as I can ever remember screaming, and this time Mrs. Burton didn't shush me. Her mouth was agape. And then I heard him cry.

He was born an hour before sunrise on March 14, 1863. His cry began when mine ended, a rapid whimper, one after the other as he pushed air into his little lungs. My hair was matted with sweat, and I blew it back off my forehead. I smiled; it was over, a relief, and there fat and wet, swaddled in a blanket, was a part of me.

"Can I hold him?" I asked Tarvie. Her smile was missing teeth and looked like the keyboard of a pianoforte. "Show," she said.

"Nonsense," Mrs. Burton said as she intercepted him from the brown arms that held him.

"Please," I asked, but she cradled the little bundle next to herself and jiggled it and flitted around the room with it.

I pushed the hair away from my forehead and felt something wet on my forehead, thicker than sweat and smelling of metal. I became aware that I was in a puddle of something that extended halfway up my back. I put my fingers to it and held it up in the first light of day. 'Twas blood. My blood. That was the first time I saw Tarvie upset. Up until then she seemed confident.

"Miz Nancy, we gone have to call a doctor dis instant. She bleedin' rat smartly," she said. My arms and legs were heavy, and I was thirsty, and the room seemed far away, Mrs. Burton and the baby and Tarvie blurring, voices distant. A shout for Mr. Burton to fetch the doctor. A muffled roar in my ears, the shuffle of blood struggling to keep up.

I woke up a few hours later in the morning light. I say a few hours; it was really two days. A doctor in a top hat was at my bedside. He was white-headed with a droopy white moustache and a white van dyke beard; he looked rather like a billy goat with glasses. All the city's younger physicians were at war. He was fussing at the Burtons.

"This girl needs whiskey toddies, three times a day. Rye whiskey, not bourbon, rye. Got that?"

"Yes, doctor," the Burtons said.

"My word," the doctor said as he shook his head and put on his coat. He said it with the disgust of an honest man who had been drawn into dishonest business. A woman as dark as night and wearing a bonnet sat next to my bed, rocking and singing low to the baby in her arms. It wasn't Tarvie, but some other woman with skin as dark as the tombs of Egypt.

"Let me nurse him," I insisted. The dark woman looked to Mrs. Burton, who nodded, and then the baby was handed to me. I struggled to sit up in bed. The perfect little weight of him nestled into my side and molded to me. He looked up at me and then shut his little eyes and waggled his wide, open mouth over my breast, at last finding the nipple and latching onto it. But as much as the little boy tried, there was never any milk. I felt I had failed him.

Mrs. Burton never nursed him, either. That was left to the Negro woman. Well-to-do women never stooped to such things as nursing. As soon as I was up and around, it was Mrs. Burton who took to bed, dressed in a beautiful dressing gown with a high collar, receiving the wives of the mayor and the leading citizens of the town, including the wife of the Governor, Mrs. Allen. Mrs. Burton received their compliments for the beautiful baby boy she had delivered, the boy named Frank Burton, Jr.

My baby.

February 4, 1937

When she finished her story, my blood was boiling. If hers was, she didn't show it. I'm guessing that her anger had long since burned down to a cinder that the wind had blown away but that it was a cinder that had singed her and left a scar, a pale, painful thing hidden somewhere deep. She was only twenty-one when she had her baby, one year younger than I am now.

But instead of even a breath of bitterness, she took me into the kitchen to show me how to make Irish soda bread. She tottered between the counters, asking me to reach a bowl up in that cabinet there, or here in one of these drawers there's a set of wooden spoons. She kept up a pleasant soliloquy as she spread a kitchen towel on the counter, preparing it to receive the bread and pausing to ask me a question or make a point about baking in general and soda bread in particular.

"Mrs. Haughery in the Channel made a fortune (*fartune*) with it, and many an orphan (*arphan*) was raised on it."

We sat as it baked and filled the house with the rich, tan smell of love and abundance. She asked me about my family and then about my engagement. I wonder if she could sense my reluctance about it. Time vanished, and when she opened the door to the oven, the bread was done, two brown-domed rectangles. She sent me home with one of the loaves, wrapping it first in cheesecloth and then in a linen towel. It sat in a sphere of warmth on the seat next to me in the Packard.

I found the door of Stephenson Street unlocked. In his studio, Lemurier was smoking and staring into the line where the ceiling and the wall met. As I got to the foot of the stairs, glad I had avoided any discourse with him, his voice met my back. I was cradling the bread like a football player about to cross the goal line.

"You fascinate me," he said as he contemplated me.

I turned around.

"Thank you," I said warily, without a smile, without any emotion. Miss Fenerty's bread warmed my hip. I clutched it tightly, trying to keep it to me without crushing it.,

"I wish to paint you," Lemurier said in his haze of smoke and sweet pomade. He examined his fingernails.

I said nothing. Instead, I stood there. I should have gone upstairs.

"Take off your clothes, please," he looked off to where he had been staring.

"I beg your pardon?"

"Take off your clothes."

My mouth dropped open at his impertinence.

"Certainly not," I said.

Then he laughed, a sneering, derisive laugh as if he had been joking about painting me in the nude and wouldn't do it if I begged him to. I was so incensed that I left him sneering and leering in his 'studio' and went upstairs and locked the door.

Feb. 5, 1937, FWP, Transcript of Bridget Fenerty

It wasn't three weeks after his birth when the Ladies' Aide Society held a ball. Mrs. Burton threw a tantrum to attend. There were sharp words behind closed doors, a discussion of appearances, and how would it look, and people will be aware. In the end, however, Mr. Burton gave in, and they attended the ball, a benefit for the soldiers. The talk of the town was what a dramatic recovery she had made from her delivery, and wasn't that just the fortitude of southern womanhood? Why, if women were allowed to fight, then the Yankees wouldn't stand a chance, they'd be whipped within a month! And then laughter all around. That sort of nonsense.

Champ Lockett returned later that year. He slunk into town and told us Vicksburg had fallen, which was no news at all to us, as we had found out months before.[30] The leaves were yellowing, and autumn rains fell that clipped them from the trees. You know the time of year, don't you, Miriam? The air is cool and wet, and the earth has that smell to it? He emerged off the ferry at the foot of Texas Street, a bearded, ragged, barefoot scarecrow with tattered clothes on his back, hardly what you would think of when you imagine a hero. As he walked up Texas Street, a clot of people formed around him and followed him until they stopped at the courthouse. A widow named Willis pressed to the front of the crowd, still in her mourning black (and she wasn't the only one, sure) and asked him if he was there when her son Charlie had gotten shot and killed.

"Did he die a man?" she asked. Her sad face sagged between the black muslin curtains of the mourning bonnet she wore. I hadn't seen her since before Frank Jr. had been born. She seemed to have aged twenty years. Champ Lockett and the Willis boy had been great friends, inseparable it seems, before the war, and they had volunteered together. They hunted and fished together, drank and played cards and courted girls together.

Well, Champ Lockett mumbled something about being a prisoner and not seeing it. He had been handsome and a town favorite, everyone said, a boy with a quick wit and a quick mind, but now he seemed exhausted and dull, not the vibrant lad who had marched off. He also seemed taken back by the reception he got and ill at ease by the hugs from his mother and the widow Willis. From that day on, Mrs. Willis always treated Champ like her son, too.

My son, my little boy, grew quickly, and what a jolly thing he was, that little baby. They named him Frank Jr., Frank Burton, Jr. after his father. We were perfectly enthralled with each other, the little fellow and I, as you would expect, smiling and cooing at each other. I loved the way I could make him smile on one side of his face like babies do, you know. I would read to him and tell him stories of his grandpa, his real grandpa, and what a kind and decent man he was, and how proud he would be indeed to see his grandson, his own flesh and blood, despite the circumstances of how he came into the world. I would sing to little Frank, and he would look at me in wonder, twisting his face as if he were trying to see my voice.

In the year that followed, little Frank began to grow, taking his first shaky steps like a little monkey holding his arms above his head for balance. I let him bang on the keys of the pianoforte with his open palms, a rumble of tinkling sounds, until Mrs. Burton complained of her ears. I always let him resume when she left for an auxiliary meeting or a benefit for the troops. He squealed

---

[30] *The Shreveport Southwestern* records Champ Locket's return as Oct.12, 1863.

with delight at the sounds, looking at me with a *how-do-you-like-that?* look and then doing it again.

The boy and I had plenty of time together, as Mrs. Burton was frequently away at various civic organizations and Confederate auxiliary functions and do-gooder clubs, the Ladies' Aide Society and the like. It was just fine with us; it gave the two of us, him and me, more time together. From a safe distance, we would go watch the boats come and go, and I would point and say "boat" and he would say "boot," and I would laugh and he would laugh and say "boot-boot-boot!" and I would kiss him all over his face and make noises like the whistles of the steamboats into his neck.

People around town would comment on how much we looked alike, and we did, of course. I wanted so much to exclaim, *yes, yes, he's mine, he's my son!* But instead, I told them of my old belief from childhood, that if someone spends a lot of time working with something or someone, then they take on a common resemblance. Like the man who works with horses, remember?

Oh, but they grow so fast, changing at such a pace that it amazes me that they don't make a squeezing sound while they do it. I was there to pick him up when he fell, to stay up with him when he felt poorly, to explain things to him in a gentle voice. So much more than his so-called mother, who used him more as a prop or a trophy in her world of small-town society.

When he was two or so, I took him down on Texas Street to the Star and Pelican Gallery to have our photograph made together. I'd saved up enough money to do it. I could see him beginning to grow and change, and I wanted to capture the moment of him as he was, a memory of time.

Well, then. Speaking of time, would you look at the clock, then?

Feb. 6, 1937

She confided in me that after the birth of Frank Jr., she never had another monthly and that someone named Elias told her that he had seen this before in women who had come near death in childbirth. He told her that a woman could stop having monthlies because of the loss of blood.

This morning when I came downstairs on my way to temple, Lemurier was looking through the blinds.

"Have you noticed the black Cadillac?" I asked him. He jumped, and it gave me a certain glee to have startled him.

"I do not know of what you are speaking, " he said disdainfully as he let the slat fall. He feigned nonchalance as he lit a cigarette, but his hand shook almost imperceptibly, like it was responding to a slight tremor at the very center of the earth. He shook out the match and slumped back forcefully into a chair.

"You and my assistant, you are lovers, are you not?"

My face fought hard to conceal my shock at his impertinence. For one thing, how could he consider Ellie his assistant? What business of his was it? What makes two people lovers, the act or the longing for the act? Either way, his knowing anything of our relationship was disgusting.

"What makes you say that?" I asked.

"I see how the two of you look at each other," he said down to the ashtray as he tapped an ash into it. The smoke curled up from it, tracing a fancy curve. "It ease a common thing in Paris, two women."

He tapped another ash and waited, but I said nothing.

"Her position is in danger, you know," Lemurier said as he pulled again on his cigarette. "The boss-man is unhappy with her lack of progress on ideas for the Fairgrounds mural."

It was ludicrous, his capacity to put all his sloth on Ellie.

"I have decided to tell the man in Washington about your friend," he announced. "She deserted me and him and the project of the great mural on the building of the state of Louisiana. It is, after all, her fault that we have been delayed."

"Are you out of your mind?" I said.

"Are you out of yours?" he shot back. He contemplated the cigarette in his hand as he continued.

"I can put in a word for her, to the man. For her to keep her position."

I didn't know if I believed him, but I was afraid not to. I had no reason to doubt his connections. Still, I asked him, "What is the name of the man in Washington? Your boss and Ellie's boss?"

"I do not have to speak his name to you," Lemurier said as he blew smoke up to the ceiling. He wiped his free hand on his trouser leg. His palm must have been sweaty. "But I will call him. I will call him now."

He lifted himself from the chair as if he weighed a thousand pounds. His steps sounded equally heavy on the stairs. From the landing, I heard the dial of the phone rattle. His voice was small.

"O-pear-a-ture, Washingtone, D uh C. Monsieur, eh, Mister..." his voice lowered. There was a pause and then the murmur of a conversation I couldn't understand, a small garble of French accented discourse, though the only part I understood was Lemurier saying, "There ease a problem I need to discuss with you, about the girl Eleanor, Ellie she is called." The conversation, Lemurier's half, descended back into murmuring again. Then the closing salutation, "*Très bien-merci-au revoir*-thank you-goodbye."

When he came back down the stairs, I was standing at the window. I turned from it and faced Lemurier. He looked past me as if he wanted to see through the blinds, as if something interested him. A short silence followed as he looked at me, or past me to the overlapping layers of the blind-covered window.

"Well?" I finally gave in and asked.

"He says for me only to say the word, and she is finished." He touched his nose and pondered me as if he had just said, *checkmate.*

I turned to the blinds and lifted a slat and said, "There he is again" though it was only the mailman. I looked back, and Lemurier had scurried upstairs. The door to their bedroom shut abruptly. I left for temple.

Mr. Levy was cantor again. Such a voice.

Feb. 7, 1937

Last night, I awoke from a troubling dream that I couldn't recall, other than the theme was that of Ellie and me being separated again. I got up and read from *The Well of Loneliness*:

"I am one of those whom God marked on the forehead. Like Cain, I am marked and blemished. If you come to me, the world will abhor you, will persecute you, will call you unclean. Our love may be faithful even unto death and beyond-yet the world will call it unclean."

I can't lose her again. My friend, my best friend, I keep telling myself.

I'll let him do it, let him paint me.

I went downstairs to tell him. He was still up from the night before; he seemed to be keeping a vigil, his silhouette smoking against a window full of the impending aqua blue sunrise. There was no jazz musique on the phonograph. The lights were low, and the smoke drifted around in the dim heat.

"I will let you paint me. With clothes," I said, "If you give me your promise that you'll give a good word for Ellie to the man in Washington."

He seemed unmoved, only watching the ember of his cigarette. When he pulled on it, his face emerged in yellow light from the darkness only to fade into smoke and disappear into darkness again. He pushed the butt into the ashtray.

"Very well," the silhouette of his lips said. His tone was such that it seemed as if I had begged him to paint me. "It will be as you wish. I will speak to him after you have sat for me. We will do it later, this afternoon. The light is better." His finger waved to the room he calls his studio like a conductor giving the orchestra a final flourish.

A muffled rumble announced an auto on the street. Lemurier arose and approached the front window, lifted a slat, and put an eye to the wedge of light. His finger dropped the slat rather quickly, feigning nonchalance but clearly flustered. There was a rustle of thin planks as the blinds slapped against the window and the sill. Then he ascended the stairs, two steps at a time. The door to his room shut, and the lock added an exclamation point.

I lifted up a slat and peered out. Under the street light out front, the black Cadillac was parked right behind the Packard, out front in the orange sunrise. I waited for almost two hours before he finally drove away.

Feb. 8, 1937, FWP, Transcript of Bridget Fenerty

Well, of course you know how things turned out. The newspapers tried hopelessly to put a happy face on the plight of the southern cause. The northern men threatened the town once but were repelled just south of here, around Mansfield. None would say, but most knew that it was only a matter of time.

News reached us that Lee had surrendered in Virginia and that it wouldn't be long for Johnston in the Carolinas. I wondered if Patch was still alive, and I worried that he was cold or hungry or maimed. But there was no word. He was the only family I had left, and I had sent letters to him on a regular basis, but never received a single word. I was resigning myself to the fact that he might be dead, too.

A week later, news reached town that Lincoln had been shot, and everyone's spirits rose. They all supposed that we might be left alone now. The assumption was that perhaps now the northern people would be demoralized in some fashion and all go home. Of course, nothing of the sort happened. If anything, it only made things worse.

Then there was talk that Jefferson Davis was retreating into the countryside, and possibly to another country altogether, to form a government in exile. All that talk came to an end in May when Mr. Davis was caught in Georgia. The newspapers said he was wearing petticoats and a dress and a bonnet, trying to disguise himself as a woman. Perhaps it was true, though it may have been an invention of a northern journalist. No offense, dear.

Mr. and Mrs. Burton fell into a deep hole of depression. The end of the world was upon them. They were sure that they and, perhaps every one of us, would be hung or shot or both or marched away to work in camps where Negroes would guard us with bayonets. Such foolishness. Such paranoia.

It was on a day in late May or early June, though to be sure we could go up to the cemetery and check the date on the tombstone. Mrs. Burton was out on errands and had taken little Frank with her. Her errands, as she called them, were merely opportunities for her to parade him about to society. Mr. Burton was home, as there was no more government for him to work for. He had been burning boxes of documents in a small bonfire in the backyard and smelled of smoke from it a good bit of the time. Up in smoke, the treasury archives of a government that no longer existed.

He was in their room when I came in from the market. I could hear his pen scratching at his desk as if he were putting a lot of effort into what he was writing. I was putting things away in the kitchen, the indoor kitchen that was one of the first in town then, something Mrs. Burton had urged him to have put in, even though she would never have to work in it. I was happy to have it, of course. My little boy had a high chair in the corner, and I would sing to him while I cooked.

Yes, well, I was putting things away, and I heard Mr. Burton call from behind the closed door.

"Nancy, is that you?"

"No, Mr. Burton, it's me, Bridget."

"Where are Nancy and the baby?" His voice was muffled through the door.

"I just saw them at the market," I says, "and missus said she was going down to the river with the boy to watch the boats."

"All right," he said through the door. I heard a sound, and, as I look back, it was blubbering, a wet, sloppy cry. I kindled the fire in the big square cast iron stove. I stopped to listen again as I went to the cistern for a bucket of water for the cooking. Chicken and dumplings, I believe it was. After about ten or fifteen minutes, I heard the shot.

At first it didn't occur to me what had happened. I paused, and the only sound was the fire popping quietly in the belly of the stove and the water beginning to boil for the dumplings. I wiped my hands on my apron and approached the door to their room, which was adjacent to the kitchen.

"Mr. Burton?" I asked through it.

There was no answer.

"Mr. Burton, are you all right, sir?" I asked again.

No answer.

So I opened the door.

The first thing I saw was a spattered blotch, a starburst of red on the wall. He was on the floor, and he looked up at me. He blinked once, and his lips moved as if he were going to say something. Then his eyes stopped looking and went blank, open but empty. There was a note on his dresser, and I started to read it then, but I was flustered, I suppose, and I just put it in the pocket of my apron without reading it. I knew that Mrs. Burton would be home any minute with the boy, and I didn't want her to see him this way. I paced back and forth and finally ran next door holding my skirt up, running to send the neighbors for the police.

They came and got him, and then it was I who had to tell Mrs. Burton. And then it was I who had to console her. And then it was I who had to clean things up. I swept up bone and hair and brains, and then I mopped up the blood.

And then it was I who kept the baby during the funeral, jiggling him and shushing him to keep him quiet. They buried the man in Oakland Cemetery, there behind Texas Street. Sometimes I visit his grave. He was the father of my baby, after all. We'll always be connected by that.

Suicide doesn't take away the pain; it merely gives it to someone else, and it was Mrs. Burton who got it. She became a flurry of black lace, a mound of black taffeta that rustled as she moved through the house, a voice that spoke without lips behind a veiled face with indistinct eyes. She moved around the house like a shadow, frantic, moving to and fro, while I shushed the baby and sang him to his nap in the afternoons.

She spent a lot of time going back and forth to the telegraph office, floating within her mourning clothes like a black cloud. I fixed supper in the evenings, but there was always too much with the loss of Mr. Burton's appetite, and the laundry didn't take near as long without his clothes. There was a void, an emptiness. For me, the emptiness would get bigger.

Feb. 9, 1937, Tuesday

I was exhausted, exhausted by her story and exhausted by what I had to do. Concentration was becoming impossible, and finally I begged my leave.

"Just as well, dear," she said, her old eyes peering over the lenses of her glasses. "You remind me of a lid rattling on a boiling pot."

The drive down Line Avenue was a blur as I kept thinking of how much Ellie, and her family I've never met, needed her job. And how much I needed Ellie, as a friend at least, someone who celebrates my strengths and endures my faults. I don't want her on the road in the cold, at the mercy of lecherous cooks and truck drivers. I took a big gulp of air at the door of Stephenson Street and knocked, too distracted to be annoyed at having to knock to enter my own dwelling. He cracked the door and, when he saw it was me, opened it only enough for me to squeeze in sideways, and then shut it again.

"Where shall we?" I asked. I had to calm my breathing. My upper lip was sweating. He sat in a chair and leaned forward over the coffee table and a saucer. He calmly and lightly dropped a boiled egg, the shell quietly crunching as it fractured. He peeled away the shell without answering me; I think he was enjoying my anxiety. Finally, he spoke.

"There." He gestured with his head to the stool where Mirlette sits for him. His fingers peeled away the tattered shell of the egg. A lock of his slick-sweet hair dangled on his forehead as he tilted his head to a bottle of champagne that slumped over in a bucket of ice. The gold foil had been ripped back and the cork removed.

"*S'il vous plait*," he said. "Help yourself. It will help you relax."

I poured myself a coffee cup of it. It was flat and tasted bitter, but I had a cup anyway. My senses were dulled with anxiety, and my courage needed help. So did Ellie, I told myself.

"You will need to remove your coat," he said.

I had forgotten to take it off. I shed it from my trembling arms and then straightened the line of buttons on my blouse and tugged my skirt into better shape.

"With clothes," I reminded him.

I think he nodded. It was a gesture so subtle, so nearly imperceptible. He looked at me, and, though I still had on a skirt and blouse, I felt naked. He looked as though he saw what was most horrible about me and was about to paint it, expose it, and that it gave him great satisfaction. He put the last of the egg in his mouth with all of the grace and finesse of a snake swallowing a mouse and wiped his fingers on his shirt. He lit a cigarette and reached for his pallet and brushes.

"You are a Semite, no?" he said to his pallet as he mixed paint.

"Pardon? You mean Jewish? Yes. Yes, I am."

"Like Salome, the painting by Regnault," he muttered with a cigarette in his lips. "Sit up more straighter, *s'il vous plait*." His brush tipped the canvas, his eyebrows raised at what had been wrought by it. "Are you familiar with it?"

"I've seen it," I said, and I realized my speech was slurred. I took another sip of champagne from the coffee cup.

"Lift your chin," he said. I tried, but my head seemed heavy. My chin wouldn't lift and only sagged toward my chest. He sighed in mild exasperation and set his pallet down and transferred his cigarette from his lips to his hand. Then his other hand was under my chin, lifting it. His fingers smelled like pomade, sweet, and like egg, a rotting yellow like sulfur as he lightly lifted, his soft fingertips pressing into the angle of bones under my chin. I thought of Regnault's painting of Salome in the Met, gold and yellow tones, Salome with a cascade of thick black hair. I've always thought her to be a little mannish.

I struggled to keep my chin up, and I thought of what Father would tell me at a setback: *Keep your chin up, Miriam.* It became more and more of a struggle for me to sit straight. My spine felt like it was made of wax and melting. Time was melting. The clock said an hour had passed, and the light and shadows concurred. But it felt like it had only been a few minutes.

"Now your true beauty, your essence, your pride," Lemurier whispered, and it sounded hollow, a voice rising from a well. His hand was slinking into my blouse, like the tentacles of a sea creature probing the surface of something in the dim, cold depths of a lightless ocean, prehensile, smooth, sweaty, echoing the curves of my body, my powerless body, feeling the contours beneath my brassiere.

Where is Mirlette? I kept thinking. Does it matter? Would she care? He lifted another coffee cup of flat, bitter champagne to my lips with his free hand, fingers smelling of eggs and pomade and cigarette smoke.

There was a chill, and I felt my top half bare, the tips of my breasts responding to the cold. Then he was fidgeting with my skirt. I felt his hand run under the hem and unhook my stocking. I swatted at his hand under my skirt, but he ignored the feathery, ineffective blows and rolled down my stockings, his thin mustache on my neck, the wet sliding, glancing touch of a sea creature on my throat, a snail, an eel. My head was swimming. How many leagues under the sea? Ten thousand? Twenty thousand? Yes, that's right, twenty thousand leagues under the sea. Jules Verne.

There was a knock again on the door, far away, but insistent. My hand made a knocking sound on my skirt as I batted at the hand under it, and then I realized the knocking was separate, someone was knocking on the door. A small voice from above the surface of that underwater world: *I'm gonna knock this goddam door down!*

A clicking and a sudden force behind the door. Shouting accents competing in an invisible whirlwind. Something thrown over me. Footsteps hurrying up the stairs. A whirling, blurry vision of Lemurier slipping his suspenders over his shoulders with the footsteps. Ellie's voice, and another voice, a stranger with a southern accent, different from Ellie's.

I woke up later in the day with a terrific headache and a dry mouth. There she was, golden hair spraying from under her knitted cloche. A concerned smile within her kind, lightly freckled face.

"Ellie?" my dry lips asked. "How did you get in?"

"Key under the mat," she said, holding it up, something small and brass between her fingers. "Probably been there all the time."

"I'm sorry," I said. I was sobbing like a grade school child. "I'm sorry I'm sorry I'm sorry" I whimpered. It was a disconsolate, irrational cry, fueled by whatever was in the champagne. She held my head under her chin, and I felt her kiss the top of my head. She shushed me, tenderly, pressing her cheek into the crown of my head, cradling my twisted face into her neck. I kept blubbering.

"I don't want you to be fired. I don't want you to be fired. I want you to stay here." I wept as bitterly as I can ever remember; it was something in the champagne, it had to be. I felt like I had tried to save her, but instead, I had betrayed her.

"What are you talking about?" she asked with a puzzled face.

"He said you would be fired if I didn't let him paint me."

"Fired?" she asked, and then she pulled a letter out of her sweater pocket. "I got a letter from Washington. It's him that's got a problem with the man, not me. He's the one with his ass in hot water."

She gestured upstairs with a movement of her head. It was then I realized that he had fled with the canvas of me. The easel was empty. It was odd; I felt as though he had made off with part of me.

I was on the couch with a sheet over me, a canvas drape mottled with stray paint from one of his masterpieces. I drew it around me, then looked within it to discover that the only articles I had on were my step-in panties and my stockings, rolled down to my ankles. The rest of my clothing, my blouse, my skirt, my brassiere, everything else was in a pile by the stool I had been posed upon.

She pulled me up from the couch, and I wrapped the sheet around myself. She guided me up the stairs, one shaky step at a time. In my room, she pulled a gown over me and lifted the sheets of my bed. I slipped in, and she pulled the covers up to my chin. When I awoke, she was there reading silently from *The Well of Loneliness.*

"What happened?" I asked.

"I came in, and he had you half undressed. You looked weak as a kitten. Well, anybody could see what he was about. We started arguing, and, while we was arguing, *were* arguing rather, the man in the Cadillac stopped and knocked on the door, and that made Lemurier skedaddle upstairs. I opened the door, and he asked to speak to the man of the house. I told him the truth."

Ellie had told him that there was no one here that you could truly call a man.

Feb. 10,1937, FWP, Transcript of Bridget Fenerty

She began talking of us three going to Texas, and I thought it a grand place to be. Plains and cattle and Indians, and handsome cowboys, you know. I attributed her franticness to a preoccupation in making plans for us to make our way west. She bustled about like a teakettle set to boil.

I awoke one morning and realized the baby hadn't woken me up in the night. At first I was elated that my little boy had made a milestone, sleeping the whole night through. Then I felt the silence of the house, something that was felt rather than heard, a vacuum, an emptiness. I dressed quickly, at last pulling on my apron and tying it behind myself. I was afraid that my mistress had risen before me, something that is never to happen, not to a good servant.

I checked her room. The bed was unmade, of course; she never made it herself. I always did that. My heart began to race as I scurried to the nursery.

He was gone. They were both gone.

I thought perhaps they had gone down to the market or to see the boats on the river or to look in the shop windows along Texas Street. I tried to calm myself, so I went to the dining room to shine the silver. It was what I did when I needed to calm myself: keep the hands busy, you know. There I saw the note.

Miss Fenerty, it said,

I'm terribly sorry to have to leave you, but the authorities won't be looking to hang you or put you in prison. You were just a servant. Frank Jr. and I are headed to South America, Brazil or Argentina.

I have left you a week's pay and the hope that the Invaders will treat you favorably when they come to ransack the city. May the God who is currently testing us not find us wanting, and may He watch over you.

Mrs. Frank Burton, Sr.

There in a separate envelope was a week's pay, ten dollars in now worthless Confederate script. Five two dollar bills with a picture of Judah P. Benjamin in the corner and the promise to pay the bearer when a treaty of peace was signed at the conclusion of the war. Worthless, and she knew it. I sat down as my mind tried to sort through this strange collection of facts:

Still in black, my mistress, Mrs. Burton, had packed their bags during the night, gotten up before dawn, and taken our baby to South America.

I felt my heart fall out of me. I cried. No, the truth of it is, I howled. I have never wept so bitterly in all my life. I retraced my steps through the house. Perhaps if I went back to their rooms, I told myself, they would be there. So I did, and, of course, they weren't.

In those days there wasn't a train to Houston and Galveston like there is now. There had been pieces of a line, but the Confederate Army had pulled parts of it up and melted it down to lob it at the northern men. All we had then was the stage that ran that way. So I ran to the station where the coaches departed, the hem of my skirt just above the dirt of the streets. Perhaps the stage was delayed, I thought, I hoped. I leaned into the ticket window where a man was reading the newspaper. I asked the man there, I says, have you seen the widow Burton with her boy, Frank?

"Well, yes ma'am," he says, "She was kinda secret-like about it. Finally said she was going to Galveston, gonna take her boy Frank to see relatives somewheres," he says.

"How?" I asked. "How was she going?"

I felt like grabbing his lapels and shaking the answer out of him. But he told me anyway with a surprised look on his face. Perhaps it was from the look on mine. I suspect it was the wild look of a banshee.

"Gonna catch the packet out of Logansport, down on the Sabine, then across from Orange to Houston and Galveston."

My demeanor must have eased up, likely because I was stunned by his news. It was true, they were leaving their collapsing country, their nation that was now a non-nation. As I lost my composure, he regained his.

"Yessum," he says, and he pulled a watch out of his vest pocket and looked at it. "Left about an hour ago. Headed to Logansport to catch a boat."

As I walked to the edge of the road, I felt the wood planks of the platform under my feet, and I realized that I had neglected to put shoes on. No one could tell because the dresses we wore then went to the ground so that we would have to lift the hems out of the mud. I stood on the edge of the platform and leaned over the twin ruts and looked down them. They converged to a single point away in the distance.

My boy was gone, gone on a chase that I had no funds to pursue.

I suppose I could have sued for my child, intercepted them with a telegram in Galveston, if they were really going that way at all. But if I could find them at all, it would've been hard to prove, you see, as a woman like Mrs. Burton carried such weight, the widow of a Confederate official. The world was in such a state of chaos then. Our government had collapsed. And who would take the word of an Irish Bridget against that of a woman such as her? It was no use. And it broke my heart to know it was no use.

I stood there sobbing on the empty platform for the boy who I wouldn't see grow up to a man, the boy that might hold me in a special place in his heart, not as his mother but as something very much like it. But I was learning that it was true what Ma had said, that pity for yourself is useless and serves no one, least among them yourself. So, I went for a handkerchief to dry my eyes, and when I felt in my apron pocket I found the other note, the one Mr. Burton had left. It was written in his flowery script, the writing of an educated man:

Dear Nancy,

I can't live under Yankee tyranny, and I won't be dishonored by being hung in front of my wife and child.

You see, he was afraid he would be hanged as a traitor to the United States government; a lot of people were. Well, the note says,

There is $3,000 in silver coins in a false compartment in the back of the bureau. Take Bridget and our son and get away, to Mexico or the Caribbean or Cuba, anywhere safe from these Godless men and their Negro minions.

Remember that I have loved you faithfully and will do so from beyond the grave if permitted by the Almighty.

Your loving husband,

Frank

I ran home, clutching the note on the creamy paper. My bare feet drummed on the wood floor as I made my way through the house to their room. The empty house gasped with a dreadful silence. I pushed the bureau away from the wall, and it scraped across the floor with a sound like thunder in the distance. There was a little dust behind it, and the housekeeper in me was appalled for a moment that it was there. Then I saw it, a panel in the back of the bureau with a small circular hole in it where you could put your finger in to slide it to the side.

There it was, and could you believe it, then? Three thousand dollars in silver coins, just like he said. Too heavy to lift all at once. Certainly it was money embezzled from Our Righteous Cause, funds of a government that no longer existed. It was a lot of money, then and now.

I scratched out a few coins and put them in my pocketbook. I pushed the bureau back against the wall, over the dusty floor, and then I packed a bag quickly with a change of clothes. I locked up the house before I realized that I still hadn't put on shoes. I unlocked the house and found my shoes, thinking of Ma always insisting we keep our things in order. There they were at the bottom of my chifferobe. I only fastened the top and bottom buttons, the shoes then had so many buttons, you see. I locked the house again and ran to the station, and I bought a ticket for Logansport.

And then I sat.

Every moment was crushing, every small hope fading with every second. The next stage for Logansport was three hours later.

Now, a Negro man wearing a dark green frock coat and a brown felt top hat with the crown busted open came riding up in a carriage. He was newly freed, of course, and he had decided he would try his hand as a hack. He had a secondhand carriage with two sorrel geldings, fine looking horses, and he was proud of them. He had moved to the city as a refugee from further south, brought along as property with a fleeing master. He had spent the war years driving Mr. Rusk the owner around, and when the owner Mr. Rusk died, his estate stipulated that Mr. Rusk the property was free and had use of the carriage and horses.

He was a man with a face like a potato, brown and lumpy. His lips were pressed together in a look of pleasant exasperation, and he had one eye; the other was missing, and the lids drooped over its emptiness. I never knew what happened to it; he didn't like to speak of it. There was a small tuft of a graying beard, much like the pictures of Jefferson Davis himself. He pulled outside the coach station waiting for the next stage to come in, to take a fare into town or wherever. He tipped his tattered old hat and introduced himself as Solomon Rusk.

I said, "Mr. Rusk, can you take me to Logansport?"

"Yes ma'am. I knows it. It's a ways, now. Pretty far."

"I'll give you twenty dollars, silver," I said.

"It ain't twenty dollars' worth of far, now," he says. "But I'll take you."

We rode out on the Keatchie Road, through there and then on to Logansport, which took most of the day. He tried to make conversation, and, for once in my life, I found myself unable. His amiable questions over his shoulder fell without meeting a mate of an answer from me. At last, he fell to silence, except for when he shouted a word or two to his pair of horses.

When we got to Logansport and the Sabine, there was a steamboat, a sternwheeler called the *Uncle Ben,* pulling out. The beat of its paddlewheel was stirring the water into small waves that were washing the shore, up and around the knees of the cypresses. I leaped out of Mr. Rusk's buggy and asked the man in the ticket window, whom I could barely see, "Is there a Mrs. Burton and a young boy on that boat?"

I could hear him scratching inside as he looked at the manifest.

"Why yes," he says. "Bound for Orange and then Galveston. I can flag them down and row you out to them in that johnboat yonder if you want to go with them."

There are moments in our lives such as that one, when our fears jerk us back like a dog on a chain, and we strain against them and find we can't do it, we just can't do it. I looked out to the *Uncle Ben* which was thirty or forty yards off the dock. Before it, the Sabine River stretched out for several hundred yards before bending behind cypress trees and out of sight.

All that water between us. All that water. If only I'd had the courage then. How differently things might have turned out.

"No," I told him. My voice sounded so far away, it sounded like someone else's. "I'll meet them in Galveston."

I asked Mr. Rusk, who was sitting patiently on the buckboard of his buggy, "Have you ever been to Galveston?"

"No ma'am, ain't never," he says.

"I'll give you sixty dollars in silver if you take me."

"Sixty dollars?" he asked, a question more for himself than for me. "How long you speck it'll take?"

The voice of the man in the ticket office answered him.

"Two or three days, depending on your weather and your luck."

"How long do you think it'll take the boat?" I asked.

"Day or two to Orange, stage through Beaumont to Houston, then ferry to Galveston," I could hear him figuring. "Two or three days, depending on their weather and their luck," he repeated like an echo the time he had quoted for my trip by stage. The *Uncle Ben* was sliding away on the green water between the cypress trees on either side of the channel. The day was creeping toward evening, and the trees on the right were beginning to throw shadows over the Sabine and the *Uncle Ben*. The boat belched an immense black puff into the sky above them.

"Well, I reckon we better get, then," Mr. Rusk said. He helped me up into the buggy and called to the ticket man. "Which way Galveston, suh?"

"That road yonder, boy," he called back, even though Mr. Rusk was at least twice his age. "Center, then Nacogdoches, then Lufkin, then you'll have to ask."

Mr. Rusk tipped his hat and shook the reins. We left Logansport, crossing the Sabine over an old wooden bridge, and I put my hands over my eyes when we did. When I heard the sound of the buggy's wheels change back from the hollow, wooden sound, I knew we were on solid ground again. I uncovered my eyes to find Mr. Rusk looking at me with a sidelong glance. I thought he might say something, but he didn't. The woods opened up into cotton fields, green plants studded with pink blossoms on the verge of opening.

"Lawd, but I'm show glad to be done with cotton," he said as he shook his head at the sea of dark green bounded by distant tree lines. The sun hovered in the west and threw an amber light over them.

We made the town of Center, Texas by nightfall. Mr. Rusk stopped and lit the lanterns on either side of the buggy. In the middle of the night, we were in Nacogdoches. We stayed the night there, or what little night was left. I wanted to continue on, but Mr. Rusk insisted the horses needed a rest, and I knew he was right. I took a room for a few hours pacing the floor and lying staring at the ceiling, while Mr. Rusk slept in the livery stable with his horses and team. It was how it was then and still is in a lot of places, though there are more hotels that cater to the Negro now than there were then. Even if he had been granted a room and a bed, I think he would have still slept with his team for fear of having them stolen. Horses were in short supply after the war.

A handful of hours later, in the early morning, I came down to find Mr.

Rusk sitting on the front steps of the little inn. He had brought us a basket with breakfast from the hotel kitchen lady, biscuits left over from the morning before, and we were on the road again. I sat on the buckboard next to him. The road had been cut between the banks of red clay that loomed over our head like the Red Sea. I was tired of the silence. I thought maybe he had a wife and family, children and grandchildren, back in Shreveport who might be worried, so I asked.

"Are you married, Mr. Rusk?"

"Yes ma'am, I was," he said, and then he paused, "and in my heart I always will be. But she done passed."

"Any children?"

He shook the reins and made a loud ticking sound with his tongue to encourage his team. The wheels rumbled quietly beneath us. He cleared his throat and gave the reins another little shake.

"We did at one time. They all passed or got sold off."

He said it as though there had once been a sting to it, but now it had been softened and could be told as a fact and not an emotion. I sat with him on the buckboard as we rode in and out of dappled sunlight. He sang hymns and short bits of other songs, a deep rich voice. Later in the heat of the day, I got in the back of the carriage and took a nap to the rhythm of horse hooves and the creak of the buggy's wheels. Tree limbs with green leaves and blue sky floated past.

Small towns passed by while I slept, and more small towns while I was awake. The sun set again in a silent blast of color in the west. The wind picked up in our faces, and that night the rain began, and Mr. Rusk stopped to pull the top of the buggy up and over me as if I were in a baby carriage. Meanwhile the rain beat on him in his oilcloth slicker, but he continued to sing, and Tom and Jerry, *Jay-ree*, he pronounced it, continued to pull, side by side, their flanks shifting on either side of Mr. Rusk's silhouette. Lightning would crack, and Mr. Rusk would flinch and then shake the reins to keep his team pulling. Hooves and wheels stirred the slurry of mud, but we drove through the night rather than rest.

The next day, we met a group of men, young boys and old men, driving a herd of cattle to market. We pulled onto the side of the road and let them pass, the backs of the cattle just below us, black and brown, white mottled with gray, all of them with glassy eyes like polished black stones, wide noses with short bristles, bellowing as they pushed against each other's flanks and through the narrow gap our buggy created. All with mud brown feet as if they were in stockings.

The muddy roads impeded our progress. The cows had left their mark as well, and the air was fragrant with it. I barely noticed. I was formulating a plan to free little Frank from Mrs. Burton, all sorts of foolish diversions, all equally implausible. After I captured him back, I thought, perhaps I would flee out west with him under an assumed name, maybe somewhere in Texas or Nevayda. Or San Francisco.

The road descended into a dense forest of thorny trees that repeated themselves back into blackness. A spindly, prickly gray and black cloud of limbs and trunks fading off into the blurry distance.

"This here must be that Big Thicket they talk about," Mr. Rusk said looking about himself. His hands held the reins lightly while his forearms balanced on his knees. The woods seemed to collapse on us, and midday was as dark as dusk. Mr. Rusk seemed to hear something and kept jerking his head in different directions, his one eye narrowed, his lips pursed upward. Tom and Jerry plodded on.

And then they were upon us. Dingy white men in ragtag uniforms, or really pieces of uniforms. There were four of them that I could count, though there may have been more further in the woods. The lead one had a slouch hat with a turkey feather in the crown. He held up his hand, and Mr. Rusk slowed the team to a stop. He tipped his hat and then set it down on the buckboard.

"Aft-noon," he said.

"Afternoon," the man said. He peered in the back of the carriage at me and moved his horse close enough to run an admiring hand over Jerry's flank. "Where y'all headed?"

"Galveston, suh," Mr. Rusk said.

"Galveston?" the man asked quietly into the woods as if he were disinterested. The reins of his horse were drawn up in one hand on the pommel of his saddle. He spat away and wiped his mouth with the back of his hand. "What for, may I ask?"

The men to his back, a couple of them barely teenagers, sat resting with their hands before them on their saddles. One of them was shoeless, his bare feet curling over in the stirrups. One of their horses snorted quietly and shook his head. Another pulled with big clumsy lips at clumps of grass. One of the men, a boy, really, had a flannel plaid shirt with suspenders. What caught my eye, however, was a large knife, a Bowie knife, tucked in his trousers at the side. I was wondering if the boy had ever killed with it when Mr. Rusk spoke.

"My mistress, here, she got to get to Galveston," Mr. Rusk said.

"That right?" the man said as his tongue probed one of his teeth.

There was an odd, silent moment. Finally, the man pulled off to the side of the road, and his followers opened ranks, and we were allowed to pass. After a minute, I was finally able to harness the courage to look over my shoulder. They had disappeared.

"Home guard mens," Mr. Rusk whispered over his shoulder. "Ain't got no more deserters to round up."

After an hour or two, the thicket opened up, and there was salt in the heavy breeze. Then, after an hour or two more, there it was again. The thing I was most afraid of.

Feb. 11, 1937

We ate at the diner downtown where the cotton ball-bearded Santa had once been. Now Valentine hearts with arrows through them floated over the glass of the window, outlined with dainty wisps of cotton. A lumpy cupid hovered among them with his bow drawn and a fiendish look on his toothy-smiled face. Ellie and I sat near the window and shared the Thursday special, chicken fried steak with sawmill gravy, mashed potatoes, and green beans. Ellie sawed off a piece and gave it a twirl through a drift of white gravy speckled with pepper.

"Why don't you see if Miss F would put you up, too?" she mumbled as she chewed.

"No, "I said, "I'm paid up, and I wouldn't ask for my money back, and besides, I wouldn't want to take charity from her. I guess I am my father's daughter. Lemurier gave me a deal if I paid through March in advance. I'll just be extra careful from now on."

I didn't tell Ellie, but, of course, the real reason is more than that. Ellie and I under the same roof would be too volatile. I feel it every time I look at her lips. At one point, she had a spot of gravy on them. I watched it bob as she talked until finally her tongue corralled it.

"What about the man in the Cadillac? What was he like?"

"Had a southern accent. Pale blue eyes, middle-aged, forty or so I guess..." she stopped talking and followed my gaze.

I looked out through the array of tempera painted red hearts that drifted like balloons in the window, and then there it was, there *he* was, the Cadillac and the man with the dark glasses. He took them off, and his eyes looked almost pupil-less. He took a final pull from a cigarette and threw the butt of it into a garbage can. Then he went down the alley away from us.

"Well, speak of the devil. I say it's high time we meet this feller," she said, and before I could object, she was through the door of the diner and across the street.

I watched her through the window as she looked down the alley where the man had disappeared. She looked back to me and shrugged her shoulders, but then put her hand to the glass of the Cadillac. She looked under her palm into the front seat and then into the back seat. She took another look down the alley and then back to me. Another shoulder shrug. She waited as traffic crossed on Milam in both directions and then trotted back across. She sat down and put her napkin in her lap.

"Do you want any more?" she asked.

"No," I said. My appetite had departed when the man arrived. Ellie continued eating. Her appetite was unfazed.

"So?" I asked. "What did you see?"

"One of those file folders with a name on it. A briefcase, sort of a valise, kind of fancy." She speared a trio of green bean, flecked with onions.

"Was there a name on the folder?"

"Yeah. Higgins or something like that," she said.

"Hickey?"

"Yeah, that's it," she said in a voice tinted with wonder, a voice that asked how I knew, though she didn't ask me how I knew. Instead, she said, "And something else."

"What?"

She paused. She swallowed. She looked at me and thought. She spoke.

"A gun. One of those nickel plated numbers. Daddy had one just like it to shoot snakes back home. It was a real nice one. He got it after we'd had a good year."

When she was finished, we walked back to see Miss Fenerty, who continued her tale about her journey to Galveston with Mr. Rusk. Then with great effort I returned to Stephenson Street.

Received a letter from Irving. Why don't you write me? he asks.

Feb. 11, 1937, FWP, Transcript of Bridget Fenerty

It was the first time I'd seen the ocean since it had killed the Prudhommes and spared me, spitting me out like the whale spit out Jonah. It advanced on us in a brushing, fading rush and then retreated into itself in a second of silence and then advanced again, roaring monotonously under voluptuous clouds and quarreling gulls. I bowed my head and stared at the planks under the buckboard. Mr. Rusk looked at me in wonder.

"You scared a that water, now ain't you?"

He put his arm around me. "That's alright, now. We all got things we scared of. Even the most bravest ones of us. Yes ma'am, ever body got somethin' what hangs outside they window at night or sleeps under they bed. Jess close your eyes, now."

There was a long bridge over the water to the city of Galveston, the railroad and carriages and wagons all shared it. The hurricane in 1900 washed it away, I've read. Well, we proceeded over it, the wheels of the carriage grinding into the planks, the hooves of Tom and Jerry clopping on it like mallets. My eyes were shut tight; I was curved into a ball in the back of the buggy, listening to the wheels and the small waves that slapped the bridge pilings and the gulls squawking over us. Mr. Rusk began singing a song about Moses parting the sea and the Israelites and the land o' kingdom come, humming the part I knew was about the pharaoh's chariot being swallowed by the sea.

Then I heard the sounds of the city, the sounds of other carriages, and the sound of our carriage on cobblestones instead of planks, the snap of canvas sails in the wind, the shouts and singing of stevedores. The buggy and Tom and Jerry clopped along the streets. My eyes were shut tight. Gulls laughed overhead, and the surf came and went, and I decided it was only gusts of the wind, not the sea.

The blockade had been lifted, and ships were beginning to call on the port again. We rode down the quay that paralleled the shore. Cotton bales were marching up gangplanks under men who maneuvered them like ants, and cotton bales hovered from pullies over ships' holds before disappearing into them.

"I'm gone need you to tell me which one of these mens you need. I can't read none, not a lick," he said. I opened my eyes slowly as if I thought the sea had a hand up and was ready to slap me. Signs were everywhere, for boarding houses, dining halls, hotels, saloons. Along the quay, however, was the one I needed:

Portmaster, Port of Galveston, it said in the letters that were used on signs then, letters with big block feet. Mr. Rusk helped me out of the buggy and stood behind me playing the part of a respectful servant. His brown fingers rotated his hat as he held it over his stomach. The sea breeze tugged at the gray tuft of his beard.

The port master was an old fellow with a beard like a goat and little round glasses that perched on the tip of his nose. He was scribbling in a manifest.

"Help you, ma'am?" he asked without looking up.

"I'm looking for Mrs. Frank Burton, Nancy Burton, and her son. I'm to meet her here," I said, which was a lie, of course. The port master looked through the manifests of the ships that were due to leave that morning. There were four ships total that were embarking, and he took his time going through each ship's manifest, his old eyes following his finger down the page, looking, looking, no particular hurry, as if he were reading the Sunday paper. He found a name and said, "Why, old Colonel so and so, why, my nephew in Tyler served in his regiment at the start of the war!"

He continued on, at last getting through the fourth and last manifest. His fingers massaged his snowy beard, perhaps as an aid to his concentrating. At last he looked up, and his white mustache and beard flopped up and down with his answer.

"No ma'am, don't see 'em."

"Would you look again?" I asked him. He stifled a sigh and looked again. And then he found it.

"Mrs. Frank Burton, Sr. and son. Right here. Missed it the first time. I had crossed the T over the R and it looked like Button instead of Burton."

He laughed a single hoot at his oversight, tickled at how it could have happened. I could have killed him with my bare hands and perhaps I would have, but he hadn't told me what I wanted to know yet.

"Which one, sir?" I asked impatiently, and he gave me a look meant to question my civility.

"The *Halcion*," he said.

"Which one is the *Halcion*?" I asked as I scanned the ships lined up and down the quay.

"That one right there. Off to Rio de Janeiro. That's in Brazil!" he said proudly as he pointed out to sea. I squinted, and then I saw it.

A speck on the horizon, beyond the golden shimmers of ocean like scales on an enormous fish. It was so far away as to seem not moving at all. The port master began reading the names of those on it, announcing 'how about that!' and 'my stars!' with each notable person who was absconding on the *Halcion*. I didn't hear any of them. I was watching the sea as the ship taking my boy became a smaller and smaller speck and then the horizon flattened it. The next ship to Rio was the following week. Too late.

I took a hotel room, and I cried for two days and two nights, so much that a physician was sent to see me. I found out later that Mr. Rusk had asked the hotel manager to send for one. I barely remember any of it. When I awoke, however, I knew that the one thing that was too horrible to be true was true. My boy was gone, borne away by the person I considered his stepmother.

February 12, 1937

I now sleep with a chair propped under my door knob, and I don't drink anything that I don't open myself. If I hadn't paid the rent in advance, I'd be back at the Creswell. I can't ask Miss Fenerty, and besides, being under the same roof as Ellie would be like putting the earth under the same roof as the moon. There would be a collision.

I have very little money left for the month. I sent most of what I had to Mother. A letter from her arrived today thanking me. It helps, and don't worry, she says, I just deposited it so your father won't know. You're right, Miriam, he would have to accept it, but it would be a blow to his self-worth.

But it's a relief knowing we won't have to move again.

Mother won't come out and say it, but I think they were close to being evicted. She all but said that Father is paying off a debt that Mr. Gaudette accumulated. I'm beginning to realize it. They work so hard and live so frugally, no wonder they don't make any headway.

I've been wondering what happened to the painting of me, and I was beginning to think that I had imagined the whole thing, like a drug-induced hallucination. But then I heard the sound of a nail being hammered. I waited for his footsteps, heavy and hungover, to recede downstairs before I slipped the chair from under the door knob.

Peeking through a crack in the door, I see it. The hall light is on (I paid the bill myself), and there it is. He's put it on the wall on the landing and added naked details. Within the cheap frame, I stare back at myself, at an unflattering sneer on my face, at my body, naked despite my insistence to the contrary. He imagined what I looked like without my panties and painted that, too. It's beyond vulgar.

I tiptoed into the landing, removed it, and put it in my room.

Behind the desk.

Facing the wall.

As I place it, I noticed he's signed the back: *Jos. Lemurier.*

Feb. 12, 1937, FWP, Transcript of Bridget Fenerty

At last, we plodded home on the road to Shreveport, seeing the things that the night had concealed from us on the way south. We passed a field in which two men and two mules pulled on a stump that angled up and out of the ground, tilting with their exertions. The field was littered with dozens of other stumps and huge piles of burning brush, and I imagined a Hell such as that and populated it with people such as the Burtons, minus little Frank, of course. To me, he would always be a Fenerty. Mr. Rusk gave the field-clearing only a passing glance and then turned his gaze to the twin ruts of the road again. I was sitting beside him on the buckboard, my palms pressed into the plank that had been smoothed over the years by countless bottoms.

"Did you ever see any of your children again?" I asked him.

He looked up from the road and to me, and then he looked at the road again.

"No ma'am," he said, and I heard the pain in it. Neither of us said anything for a while as we shared the same gnawing pain, the pain at the loss of something loved exquisitely, something irreplaceable. And then I leaned into his shoulder, and I began crying, sobbing, shaking and heaving like they say the ground does with an earthquake. Without the slightest hint of shrinking away from the pressure of my face in his shoulder, Mr. Rusk shook the reins and sang a hymn to the twin rumps of Tom and Jerry.

We spent four days getting back, traveling in fine early summer weather beneath a blue sky filtered by long green tunnels of leaves. We camped together rather than me take a hotel and him sleep in the stable. Across the campfire, his face stared into the fire with one eye; it was a comfort to me. He whittled small figures and then threw them to the fire.

At daybreak, the mist lingered among the trees until midmorning when it was burned away by a bright summer sun. I stayed in the shade of the buggy's canopy that Mr. Rusk had pulled over me, listening to him sing and shout to his team, pausing to clear his throat and spit and say, *yes, lawd*, to the surrounding countryside as it passed.

Once he said, "well, looka heh," and we stopped to pick blackberries in a thicket of them. The thorny canes were spotted with black and red.

"Careful a Mister No-shoulders, now," he said as he filled up his hat, holding the flopping crown closed by cupping his pale-skinned palm under it. Snakes, he meant, that was what he called them. I pulled the hem of my dress into a sort of bowl and filled it, unconcerned with Mr. Rusk seeing my ankles. My fingers reaching among the thorns to gently pluck the sweet black pods from among the bitter red ones.

My appetite returned a little, and back on the road we ate blackberries. The pads of our fingers were stained black by them as we sat side by side on the buckboard. The buggy jiggled us, and Tom and Jerry shook their heads and snorted. The peaches were coming in, and later we paid a farmer for a hat full and an apron full. If it hadn't been the worst time of my life, it would have been the best.

I asked Mr. Rusk how old he was, and he said he was born when ole Tom Jefferson was president and that he remembered when he was a very young man or a very old boy when Louisiana became a state. He lived around Coushatta then. He remembered fixing a cotton gin while a long line of wagons waited and the white men being amazed that a black man could do it, could figure it out, that is. He recited the Psalms he knew, the Twenty-third, the Ninety-first, and some verses from Proverbs. Occasionally he would spout out something, bursting forth with a line from a sermon he had heard, perhaps, or a snippet of scripture.

"Yessuh! Pilate washed his hands. The people shouted for Babbas..." – how he pronounced *Barabbas*- "and Pilate washed his hands! Yea, verily, I say to you, brothers 'n sisters, jess as you sow shall you also reap."

He thought for a moment and then he said wryly, "I guess I ain't the onliest person what preaches to horses' asses. Heh-heh. And just like them other preachers, when I'm done, they still horses' asses!"

I laughed despite the great pain, and I told Mr. Rusk, with a sentiment like that, he would make a fine Irishman.

"You think I would?" he said, and in such a way that I wasn't sure if he took it as a compliment or a slight, but I believe that he was touched.

When we returned to Shreveport, there it was flying in the sky against the blue sunshine, and how strange it was to see it after four years. The stars and stripes lilting in the breeze there above the courthouse. People walked around with their gazes turned down and their hands in their pockets as if they were ashamed to look at it. They felt they had betrayed it, and they had.

Night was falling by the time we reached the house on Fannin, a house that was now haunted by memories of my little boy, padding along in bare feet. His memory would float through a room in a wispy daydream and then vanish as it crossed into the next room, a memory so intense I would get up to look for it but instead only find the next room and the whole house empty.

I thanked Mr. Rusk and settled up with him, even giving him a small tip in addition to the sixty I had promised. I paused at the door, and he took off his hat. He squinted at me with his eye and said, "Don't be sad, no ways now. I'll be by tomorrow to check on you."

He started for the street and his wagon where Tom and Jerry stood shaking their heads lightly in the twilight, lifting up their hooves and clopping them impatiently. Then Mr. Rusk stopped, and he looked back at me, and he said, "That baby's yours, ain't it?"

I stood there at the door with my bag in my hand and the key to the house in my other. I set the bag down.

"How did you know?" My question admitted the truth. And another followed it. "Was it our red hair?"

"I seen you round town with the little feller before, and I know how a mama looks at her baby. I know what love looks like when it sees itself."

He climbed up into his carriage, tipped his hat, and shook the reins, and Tom and Jerry, *Jay-ree*, he said it, shook their heads and cantered down Fannin Street. Mr. Rusk sang a song up into the night air. The song faded as the distance and the darkness took it.

The house yawned around me. A rain fell, a cold rain for that time of year. It had that sound, the sound like something sizzling in a skillet, that crackling, popping, rustling sound, that made it seem that it was raining over the whole of the earth. I sat in the center of that big house by myself, listening to the silence. It was overcast for what seemed like weeks. The days began with gray mornings which became brown noons which faded to gray evenings then black nights.

Everything was clean. There would be no more meals to cook for anyone. There would be no more clothes to clean, dishes to wash, lullabies to sing, stories to tell little asking eyes. The silence was overwhelming. The rain fell on everything, and steam rose from the warming earth, and the earth cooled again. I sat in the dark until at last, I remembered the money and went to check on it. I lit a lantern and pulled the bureau away from the wall again. It was still there, of course.

Now I know what you're thinking. Did I owe Mrs. Burton an attempt to find her? Would it be right to deprive a man's widow and orphan of the money? Certainly I could've tried to find them somehow, I could send a telegram to Rio De Janeiro, and the money would get their attention, or would it? What would you have done?

Well, I'll tell you what I did. I went right down to the Mr. Talley's bank, and I opened an account, and then I deposited it, a little at a time, to avoid suspicion and besides, it was too heavy to carry all at once. After a few days, the man across the counter and through the bars asks me, he says, "Where do you get this money, if you don't mind my asking?"

I told him my brother was in the silver fields in Nevayda and had struck it rich.

"Well, I guess it's your lucky day," he says.

"Yes it is," I says. "It certainly is."

And I never gave the money another thought.

Feb. 13, 1937, Sabbath

Went to temple this morning. Mr. Taylor was cantor. The weather was beautiful, the air crisp and alive, metallic, electric. The florists downtown were bustling with activity for Valentine's Day tomorrow. I bought carnations and then some chocolates at Woolworth's.

The two of them, Ellie and Miss Fenerty, were on the front porch when I arrived. Ellie was sitting on the steps, her bare calves in a patch of sunlight, her fingers seining her blonde hair into neat shocks of wheat as she quietly sketched a street scene. Miss Fenerty was deeper on the porch, propped in the swing with a folded over copy of *Life* magazine in her lap. Her stockings sagged down onto her ankles like little circular hats for her boxy shoes. The swing moved shallowly in a pendulum motion, like a creaking metronome. They looked up together, Ellie and Miss Fenerty, and closed what they were doing. Smiles met me as my feet tapped the steps up to the porch.

"Well, then," Miss Fenerty said. "A beautiful flower with beautiful flowers."

Ellie took a carnation, a red one, and put the stem behind her ear. The red blossom deepened into a darker red against the soft straw of her hair. I gave her the box of chocolates. She opened it and presented it to Miss Fenerty who peered through thick ovals to make a selection. I put a white carnation behind Miss Fenerty's ear, and she said "oh!" with a smile as her fingers patted the stem nestled over her ear.

"Thank you kindly," Ellie said as she chewed, putting fingers over her mouth as she spoke. She swallowed and said, "I was thinking." She swallowed again. "I want to paint your picture for you. As a gift."

"Could you paint anything prettier, then?" Miss Fenerty chimed in before I could say anything. "And I have a perfect spot. On the upstairs balcony, among the camellias."

She took us upstairs to a part of the house I'd never been to before, a balcony on the side of the house. A dense wall of waxy, dark green leaves hemmed in the balcony, creeping over the white railing with explosions of red blossoms embedded in the green. The city beyond the thick foliage was only a vague idea.

Miss Fenerty tottered over to a white wicker chair, consulted the sky for sunlight, and straightened the chair. From the way she slowly moved it, it seemed heavier than you would think for a wicker chair. I looked down. I still had on my brown wool skirt and white blouse and sweater from temple.

"Should I wear some sort of hat?" I asked. "Should I change?"

"I say just wear what you have on, dear," Miss Fenerty said. She was holding the box of chocolates like a book, her fingers curled under the edge. She watched as Ellie had me sit and then as Ellie arranged me. She looked on me beatifically like one would watch a sleeping child. It was almost adoration.

"Well, Ellie," she finally said. "You've got your work cut out for you to capture the beauty here." Then her old expression changed, the flaps of skin at the angles of her jaw reformed, and she turned, slowly pivoting as she adjourned to "me nap," as she calls it. Miss Fenerty's cane tapped down the hall to silence.

Today was a brisk day that had embedded in it a promise that spring did in fact occur here and that it occurred in a big way. It was a promise whispered in the sunlight. I sat in a blotch of that sunlight, a careless smudge of it, warm in the cool breeze that only occasionally lifted the tops of the oaks and brushed through the dark, shining green camellia leaves. Birds flitted in and out of the leaves and branches, rustling with small shakes and chirps. I watched one tilt its head and scratch its neck in a blur of a claw.

"That face," Ellie said. "That's the look. When you were watching that bird. Imagine you're watching birds in the camellias."

I tried to recreate it.

"Yes," Ellie said. She kept her eyes on me in my pose as she backed to her easel and the canvas. She used a series of fluid brush strokes to outline me, or I suppose that's what she was doing. Beyond the wall of camellias, the sounds of downtown life rumbled, autos, conversations, commerce, business. Only murmurs.

I sat silently as Ellie worked, looking at me, looking into me. The faces she made as she studied me. I wished that I could paint her instead. The silence was holy, blessed and intimate. Something so magnificent that it can't be endured for long. At last, I asked Ellie as she painted, "Do you have a favorite painter?"

"I like the Spanish. El Greco, Velasquez. Especially Goya. *La Maja Vestida* and *La Maja Desnuda*. Same woman, same painting, really, painted clothed and naked. He painted clothes over one version to avoid scandal. Somebody, the church, I'm thinking, or maybe his patron's missus, objected to the nudity so he painted a version with clothes. I've read the patron had one on a pulley so he could 'put clothes' on her. Lower her down, see. When company came."

"I've never heard that story," I said, trying to keep still, staring at the camellias blooming in the green growth, brilliant bursts of red and white against the glossy dark green leaves, the small birds, snowbirds, flitting in and out of the branches and leaves. There was silence again. Down on the street, there was a distant, muted conversation between two men walking by. I heard one of them use the term, 'middlin' cotton,' and then a breeze obscured their conversation, rattling and whistling through the camellias. It chilled me, and I had to pull my sweater around me.

"Sorry," I told Ellie. "The breeze was cold."

"No problem, I've got you sketched in," she said. "All a matter of color and shade and nuance now." She looked down her nose at her brush and the canvas and made a mark. Then she spoke.

"Paintings don't get painted all at once. They emerge, the same as a photograph develops, little by little."

She turned her head to check something on the canvas, the play of color and light.

"My daddy and I loved baseball, still do," she said. "Used to go on Saturday nights to Perryton to the general store where they had electricity and a radio. On clear nights, we could get the radio station that broadcast the St. Louis Cardinals, KMOX. Me and my daddy and all the men in town sitting around on barrels and boxes in our overalls, eating peanuts and listening to the play by play."

A thought struck her, and she paused her brush and pulled her chin in and imitated a male voice, "*This is France Laux, KMOX, voice of the Cardinals!*" She smiled and dabbed a spot onto the canvas. I couldn't see, but I assumed it was something on my face.

"Baseball…" she paused as she dabbed another spot of me on the canvas "…baseball is an interesting game. It is. Everyone wants to hit a homerun, but it's the singles and the walks and the stolen bases and sacrifice bunts that win games. Little by little." She dabbed more paint. My hair, I think. The color was raven black.

"You know, Miriam, there are quite a number of women reporters in the panhandle. A few women editors. Granted, they're not covering the White House or Wall Street, but they're reporting the truth, or the truth as they see it. They report what matters to people as well as what they think *should* matter to people. It may or may not be a man's world, Miriam. Maybe it's just the world, the plain ol' world and you want to go straight to the part of it you want to. Swing for the fences, hit a home run right off the bat, so to speak. You may have to work your way there, though. But it's possible. Amelia Earhart is flying all over the world. Nellie Ross was governor of Wyoming a while back. It's possible. But you can't hit a homerun your first time at bat."

I didn't say anything for a long time, and neither did she. I just sat there, watching her smile as she contemplated me, her gaze quick from me to the canvas and back. Eventually, the light began to fade, and we adjourned.

When I returned to Stephenson Street, there were a dozen red roses for me, wrapped in green tissue paper, with a note on creamy paper. I was excited to get them until I found out they were from Irving, wired to and delivered from a local florist.

"Happy Valentine's Day. Miss you something awful, my southern belle. Love, Irving."

And that has me feeling wretched.

Feb. 14, 1937, FWP, Transcript of Bridget Fenerty

I may not have given the money another thought, but I did give my boy another thought. I thought of him on every holiday. And I still do. I made a cake for him on his birthday every year, March fourteenth. And I still do. I dreamed of him, cried for him, longed for him. And I still do. I would see boys his age playing, and I would have to pretend a sneezing fit to hide my tears. I pitied myself, and I alternated between asking for God's wrath on his mother for taking him and His aid in helping her raise him.

But the boy was gone, and though I had the money to pursue Mrs. Burton for a time, South America was too big, and besides, she could have taken him anywhere in the world. It was a hopeless, useless feeling. And it still is.

At last, I reasoned that I must move along in some fashion or wither away entirely. I had no need for money, but I had a huge hole that begged for the company of others and to be useful to others. I sat in the empty house that was like the mouth of that hole, listening to the clock tick in the parlor. But pity serves no one, least among them yourself. Statements such as *why me?* and *it's not fair.* A bottomless pit, they are, sure.

Around this same time, the last of the Confederate potentates had fled or resigned themselves to prison or the noose, but I don't know of any who got it. Before they dispersed, there had been trouble among the Confederate army, and most walked off without a band to blow brassy tribute to them, without a hurrah, without so much as a whisper. Off they went to their homes, fading away like the mist on a spring morning.

Most had left just a bit before the men in blue came into the city, hundreds of them, gray trousers, blue jackets with brass buttons. I imagined at the time that it was like Jerusalem being occupied by the Romans, Romans with rifles and mules and wagons plowing through the mud of Texas Street. The citizens of our city were a conquered people, sullen, sulking, brooding, humiliated. School boys amused themselves by shouting insults at the conquerors and running down alleys or writing crude slogans on the flanks of their horses tied up on the street, the paint and brushes given to them by older boys as a dare. The horses twitched their hides and looked off, oblivious to the joke played upon them, literally.

The northern men, on the other hand, seemed perplexed at their new duties, ready for another insurrection but only finding a few shouted insults and painted horses. Everyone fell into a new routine. The market and stores sold goods. River traffic resumed. Steamboats began arriving and bales of cotton began heading south again.

Of course, our men came home from the eastern places, too. And if there was one maimed man, there were a dozen. What a sad, miserable lot they were. Empty sleeves and trouser legs, crutches and eye patches. One man was chinless. One man wore a white canvas hood over his head with eyeholes. Several who had marched off proud and bold and upright came back with lurching strides that would have been ridiculous and comical had they not been the true gait of the man. One of them was missing an arm he claimed he got in battle, saving the regimental colors from the enemy. Others knew better and word floated about that the man had tried to steal the wrong Maryland farmer's chickens. The farmer had been hung for it.

I waited for Patch, though I knew he would go to New Orleans to look for me. I put an announcement in all the papers there. It was surely one of many, all along the lines of, "Anyone who knows the whereabouts of..." and "information regarding..." The paper was littered with them, family looking for soldiers, soldiers looking for family.

That October, when the weather turned cold, I went to Silver Lake which was south of the city then, before the raft was taken out of the river and the water went down. Some of the men who hunted ducks trained their dogs to retrieve there. Mr. Rusk and I would go watch them. The dogs were always so eager to jump in the frigid water, the men shouting terse commands to them.

It was on a morning that brought the first frost, the roofs and the ground glittering white with it. Mr. Rusk and I were sitting on the buckboard of his carriage eating biscuits and molasses, watching the dogs splash grinning into the water. In between tosses, they would stand in water up to their bellies and nose through the frosty weeds along the bank.

"Do you think it bothers them, the dogs, the cold water?" I asked Mr. Rusk as I stared at the dogs and their antics. Their coats were slick with the frigid lake water. They pranced through it, happy and oblivious.

He took a bite of a biscuit and a quick swallow of milk from a jar we'd brought. Then he wiped the moustache of milk off with his sleeve. He was eyeing the playful work of the dogs as they splashed.

"Oh, I'm show it's painful, that cold, cold water. But they don't suffer from it, no ways. They stay too busy and too happy."

Pain but no suffering, I thought. Just then a dog barked happily and jumped in with a splash. I decided then that pain is put upon you, but suffering is another matter altogether. Suffering you choose.

When we returned to town, I placed an ad in the *Southwestern*, advertising myself as a domestic, with a particular knack for the care of children. Within a day, it was answered by a Major Lundgren, Quartermaster with the occupying Federal army. He was one of those perplexed northern men, unsure of their new role in this place that was like Judea was to the Romans. He had been with the army quartermaster the whole war, passing out tents and boots and hardtack. As far as I ever knew, in four years he never fired a single shot.

He was not one for conversation, the major. We had one, a conversation, that lasted a minute or less, and, with a nod, I was given the job of housekeeper. And, on a cold November day, Mr. Rusk got a wagon and moved what things I cared for to Major Lundgren's house on Crockett Street. This very house.

Feb. 14, 1937, Sunday

I asked her whatever became of the Burton's house. She said it was razed and a livery stable was put up not long after. Then that burned down, and it became an overgrown field that was a popular trysting spot with the young people. Now it's just a parking garage.

Ellie joined us for the end of today's interview, and, when we were finished, the two of us adjourned to the balcony, and she worked on my portrait again.

Feb. 15, 1937

Obituary in the paper for Savannah Wilkins who, it says, died last week of a 'lengthy illness.' Cirrhosis, no doubt, same as Father's old partner Mr. Gaudette, the one who ruined us. The paper says that she was only seventy-three.

Ellie has given up on Lemurier and is submitting proposals directly to Washington now. The feedback has been good.

Plaintive letter from Irving. I'll have to reply, I suppose.

Feb. 15, 1937, FWP, Transcript of Bridget Fenerty

A taciturn man he was. Major Lundgren, I'm speaking of. As intense and humorless as if he'd been made out of clay. And white clay, too, for he was a pale man with a bowl cut of white hair. It wasn't white because he was old; he was just incredibly fair. Clean shaven and with a wan look on his face, like this, as if he were listening to something humming in his head. A quiet man who read in the evenings in Greek and Latin and French, and from the Bible on Sunday afternoons after he attended the Presbyterian church, there being no Lutheran church in town at the time. It was a long, quiet fall and winter.

I kept house for him when I decided that work was what was needed, and a quiet, lonely sort of work it was, too. The tapping clock made more noise than the major did. Sometimes I would sing to break the silence, and he would thank me to stop. He enjoyed the quiet, he said. I would have enjoyed some commotion in those days. I tried to imagine the chatter of the Prudhomme children. Even the sniping and arguing of the Vauborel children would have been an improvement. But it was like a funeral parlor, truly it was.

The whole house seemed to sag under a suffocating silence that made you hunger for air, made you yawn. It was so quiet that the brush of the curtains in the breeze sounded like a stampede of cattle, and when the major sneezed, it was a blare of horns; when he coughed, it was like an elephant trumpeting. And then the silence, the insistent, covering silence crept in again.

He had an office on Levee Street, what Commerce Street was called then, and was in charge of keeping the occupying Federal Troops supplied and paid. He also had something to do with getting the abundance of cotton downriver and to market. The men who worked for him called him 'Glum-gren,' it was said. He probably wouldn't have cracked a smile if you'd told him the devil was dead.

That first winter after the war was over, at Christmas time, he let me put greenery about the house. I thought the fresh green smell might revive some happy memory. But on Christmas day, there were no visits from any of the other officers in town, and the major and I sat in separate rooms and ate the dinner I had prepared as a sleet rattled on the house. He sat eating alone in the light of the festive candles, his elbows held high as he cut away at the goose I'd prepared while his nose dipped into a book he read while he ate. It could have been a time of celebration, of joy, as it should be, but in truth it was an evergreen scented vacuum, a candlelit emptiness.

It was Mr. Rusk who kept me from losing me crackers those long months. We would lounge on the front porch here when the weather was agreeable. He would rest and listen to me read, then he would nap with his hands laced together behind his head as he waited for the boats so he could go down and pick up a fare or two. Whenever he heard the bellow of a steamboat whistle, he would open up his eye, stand up, and scratch his belly. Then he would say "Well, Miss Bridget, mule can't pull while he's kickin' and can't kick while he's pullin'," and he would hobble down the steps and pull the reins from one of the hitching posts the city had on the streets then. The carriage would squeak and shift with his weight as he climbed up to the buckboard, then his tongue would click out the signal, and Tom and Jerry would follow the dribble of people headed down to greet the boat.

Mr. Rusk was taking great pride in his new line of work, and, when passengers made their way down the gangplank, they would usually seek him out. He had a fine pair of sorrel geldings, Tom and Jerry, *Jay-ree*, he said it, of course, and he had a wonderful gift of song and conversation. I always told him he would make a fine Irishman, and he would chuckle and say, "Well, maybe I would, then."

The carriage needed a little work, as it was rather old and plain. So one day Mr. Rusk and I went down to Buckelew's where Champ Lockett sat on the front steps in a chair with a wicker-caned bottom and talked to a knot of men and boys there. Inside, Mr. Rusk and I selected the colors. He painted his carriage a dark, deep green and asked if I would put his name on the side. We decided on gold for it, and I carefully printed his name in the big-footed block letters so popular in those days, *S. Rusk, Carriage for Hire*. I could feel him watching me with pride at seeing his name in print and perhaps feeling regret that he couldn't write it himself. It was just a day or two later that he appeared on the porch. He knocked, and, when I opened the door, there he was with his hat in his hand.

"Ma'am, got something to axe you." That's how he said it, axe.

He shifted and hemmed and hawed and stammered. I thought he needed money, which would have been odd, for he was a frugal man with few expenses

"I was wondering if you wouldn't mind...wouldn't mind...ma'am...teachin' me to read. A free man needs to be able to read if he means to stay free."

So, every day when the major was down at his office on Levee Street, and Mr. Rusk and I waited for the steamboats to arrive, we had our reading lessons, right here on this porch. I'm sure I sounded so much like the Misses O'Riorans in me Channel days, going over McGuffey's primer and the other books for children with simple words and simple sentences. Of course, at first he stumbled over them like a man walking on a path of uneven stones. But, by and by, he became quite proficient, which was a wonderful thing because he had a fine, rich voice.

In those months following the war, men were returning from the battlefields and from the Union prison camps, Camp Chase, Camp Lookout, and others, returning with the names of the ones who wouldn't be returning. A few would trickle in every week, and I kept up hope that my brother would be one of them. I would ask the returning men, I'd say, did you know of a Patrick Fenerty, from New Orleans? Sixth Louisiana regiment? Some of them would answer with a 'fraid not,' and some of them with a just slow shake of the head. No one could say for sure if they had known him, and of course no one could say if he was alive or not.

And then just a few would trickle in every month, and then just every so often, and then there were no more. I had given up hope. I was sure that I would never see my brother again.

Feb. 16, 1937

I wrote a long letter to Leonard (Lennie! Ha.) and let Ellie proofread it. She said it was good, but that it sounded like a commencement address, full of advice and encouragement. Don't you want to tell him you're proud of his hard work? she asked.

Of course I am. So I added that, and then I sent it.

Feb. 17, 1937, FWP, Transcript of Bridget Fenerty

During the day when the major left for his office and after the house was put in order, which never took more than half an hour, I read or knitted or sang to myself. But as much as I would try not to, sometimes I would walk down to Fannin Street and gaze at the Burtons' house, our old house. The history of the house, Mr. Burton's putting an end to his own life in it, hung over the place, and, despite the booming of the city's economy, no one wanted to buy it or rent it. After a year or two, someone bought it and razed the house for the lot under it. I think they put up a livery stable, didn't I say?

Well, it was early spring, a dank, white day when a cool steam of fog crept in from the river and met a fog that had crept in from the lake. They seeped in over the streets and suppressed the smell of mud and manure and the sounds of conversing men and rattling wagons and the boats on the riverfront, all made invisible by the mist. I was walking down Texas Street on my way to the market with my wicker basket on my arm and singing a song under my breath. There before me was a gray shape in the white mist, and, as I walked down the planks of the sidewalk, I saw who it was. I ran to him and embraced him.

He smelled awful; he was skin and bones. As I pressed my cheek into his bony chest, all he could say was, "Sister."

It's over a thousand miles from Virginia to Louisiana, I looked it up in *Funk & Wagnall's Encyclopedia.* Patch Fenerty had walked every step of it. Sleeping in barns and the rain, scraping something to eat from the bare, bony, exhausted countryside. Every rule he had lived by for four years had disintegrated, dissipated like a vapor, leaving him weightless, without guidance.

I held his shoulders and looked into his hollow eyes that seemed to regard me as an apparition, a specter from his past. He seemed to be wanting me to be there but couldn't allow himself the possibility. I pulled him to me again, pressing my face again into his chest and my hands into his back between the bare plates of his shoulder blades, never mind the smell. Then I examined him as a mother cat or dog would examine a lost and found kitten or puppy. There were scars on him, including one on his cheek. I shuddered at how a turn of his head to load his gun or shout to a comrade might have saved him. But worst of all were the scars on the inside, the invisible, terrible ones.

I rented a room for him from a widow woman on McNeil Street. The room was simple, but had a fireplace, and I heated water in a kettle and poured it into a tub. He sat in a chair with his forearms on his knees, staring at things I couldn't see and frankly didn't want to see. When I had the tub full, I told him to peel off. I turned my back as he took off his clothes. His movements were deliberate, slow and forced. Then the tinkle and slap of the water as he got in the tub.

"Are you in?" I said to the wall, just to be sure. We had grown up bathing together, but those days, of course, were long gone. He was a man now, though a broken one.

"Yes," he murmured.

I turned again, and he was in the tub up to his chest. I scrubbed his back and washed his hair. And I tell you, Miriam, the water turned a brownish black with all the filth that came off him. The dirt of seven states. I gave him a rag and told him, "Go ahead, wash yer business," and I turned my back again.

"We can be happy, now," I said to the wall, and then I went to the stove and got another kettle of hot water and poured it into the tub. He was staring into the water.

"Happiness," he snorted. "Don't look for happiness…"

"…'twill only break yer heart," I said with a smile at the memory we shared. "Uncle Jack Hennigan used to say it."

"True, that he did," Patch said. "And 'twas the only truthful thing he ever said."

"Oh, I don't know about that, brother," I said.

He seemed to slump forward in the water. His bearded frown was mirrored in it.

"It's a world of blood and shit and deceit. Lies, every bit of it, lies. I've seen every bad thing earth and hell have to offer. All of it."

He seemed to want to sob but couldn't. His tears dripped into the bath water, the tip of his beard dipping in it, meeting the tip of the beard of the reflected man. Both with a face as sad as the devil.

"I've killed, sister. Not just Mr. Vauborel, who deserved it. I've killed the innocent. Poor young, creamy faced boys who had lives ahead of them. I've killed them by the dozens. To preserve myself. And sometimes for the pure animal joy of killing. As cold-blooded as you please, young boys like me, I looked into their eyes, and I killed them, as cold-blooded as you please."

It was the first time we had ever spoken of Mr. Vauborel. "Oh, Patch," was all I could say.

"They deserved to live, sister. 'Twas I that deserved to die."

To this day I'm not sure why, but right then I slapped him. Right on the face. And despite the thickness of his beard, it was hard enough to make a sound.

"You're never to say that again, you hear me? You deserve to live as much as anyone."

Outwardly, Patch was whole, but it was inside that he was maimed. In the days that followed, if a man suddenly struck a board with a hammer, Patch would dive behind the nearest post or tree or under the nearest wagon. He drank heavily and found a hard time holding a job. I found him work at Mr. Lewis' shoe factory, the butchers, Levy and McCoy, the carriage factory on Travis, all of them I was on good terms with and were happy to do me a favor. But each would pull me aside and confide to me that Patch would either show up drunk or not at all, and each would ask me, could I persuade him to move on to spare him the embarrassment of getting himself fired?

Late at night, he would knock on the major's door, looking for me, drunk to hell, taking issue with my working for a Federal officer.

"I can't believe yer workin' for a Yankee bastard," he slurred as he swayed under the influence of the creature.

"The war's over, have you heard?" I told him, trying to keep my voice low due to the hour. "It was in all the papers."

I would lift up the candle to see his face, our face, for we resembled one another strongly. His eyes were wild and glassy, the lids drooping in his state. His belches were strong with beer and whiskey.

"Me own sister," he mumbled.

With that, I would shut the door on him, hoping he hadn't woken the major. Then my brother would stagger off to the room I rented for him, for if I didn't, he'd be like old Uncle Jack sleeping under someone's eaves or in the graveyard. The dead drunk sleeping with the dead.

Mr. Rusk would look after him as well, fetching him from one of the saloons on Texas Street after the last call, gently leading him out of a fight he'd gotten himself into, or lifting him out of the street he might have passed out in, covered with mud and manure. All the while, Mr. Rusk patiently enduring the torrent of rude names Patch called him, most pertaining to his being a Negro, until Patch ended up blubbering over the things he had done in the service of our dearly departed country.

After several months of this sort of business, Patch and I had a sharp conversation. It was on a morning when you could tell his head was splitting. His eyes were red, and he looked like he would be sick at any moment. He held onto his skull as if he expected it to pop open suddenly.

"Listen to me, brother," I told him. I was right in his face, and his breath was fetid and sweet from the drink. "You've got to get a hold of yourself," I says. "We all commit sin, big ones, little ones. Sin is inevitable. It's redemption that isn't. You've got a week to get a job and a month to hold it, or I stop paying your rent, and I turn you over to the world."

They were spoken words equal to a slap in the face. I turned and left him. It was one of the hardest things I've ever done.

Well, it must've done the trick. He stayed sober for a day, then a week, and then a month. Then, with Mr. Rusk's help, he landed a job as a mud clerk on a steamboat line running the Red to New Orleans and back. Mr. Rusk knew the captain, a Mr. Cheney, from their dealings on the landing, and he knew the captain to be a man who was hard but fair. So one day, Mr. Rusk rode my brother down in his carriage to the landing. Approaching the captain, Mr. Rusk said, "Captain, this man here need a steady job."

The captain of the boat, the Lewis something or other,[31] took him on, and for encouragement, I gave Patch a watch I bought from Mr. Burnside on Texas Street. It had a lovely inscription on it in Latin, which neither of us could read. 'Twas lovely all the same.

Feb. 18, 1937

Miss Fenerty said once that if you give someone enough rope, he'll hang himself. Well, Lemurier appears to have finally hung himself. Not literally; that would be too much to hope for.

The man in *Washingtone D uh C* has finally had enough of his sloth and dismissed him. Ellie received a letter telling her so. It also told her to hold on and keep working on ideas for the State Exhibit Building mural. Lemurier is dismissed, it says, and a man named Albrizio will be coming to town when he completes a project elsewhere in the state.

If the man in the Cadillac is someone from the WPA or the FBI keeping tabs on Monsieur, then perhaps his job is done, and he'll leave now. If he doesn't leave, then maybe it is a man sent by Irving. Or maybe it's someone from the government interested in Lemurier's political leanings. I just wish the man, whoever it is, would leave and stop haunting me.

Of course, to observe Lemurier's lethargy, it would be hard to tell he's been fired. The same amount of work gets done. None.

Feb. 18, 1937, FWP, Transcript of Bridget Fenerty

It occurred to me that perhaps the major was lonely. I myself certainly was. He wore a wedding ring, so surely I thought that there must be a Mrs. Lundgren somewhere up north. I never saw any letters from her, but then again he got his mail down at his office on Levee Street. And, of course, he never spoke of her. He never spoke of anything.

If we could send for her, I thought, perhaps we would both be a little less lonely. So I went down to see the general in charge of the occupying army and told him that I was worried about my employer, that I believed he was suffering from melancholia.

The office of the commander was on Levee Street, which is what they called Commerce Street in those days. The corner of Levee and Milam, if I

---

[31] The boat was likely the *Louis D'Or*, which ran from Shreveport to New Orleans and back during the time the subject indicates. The captain was a man named Cheney Johnson. The *Louis D'Or* was used in the service of the Confederacy and, after the close of hostilities, ran until 1867 when it was dismantled.

remember correctly. A couple of Negro soldiers flanked the door which faced off to the river across the way. They sat on bales of cotton and leaned into their rifles, looking bored out of their wits. I passed through the doorway without a word or glance from either of them.

The front room was a sort of receiving room There were a couple of petitioners ahead of me, one claiming lost property, the other begging for the freedom of a family member caught in some sort of questionable business. They made my request seem noble.

A lesser officer scribbled in a ledger on a simple slant front desk like a plantation overseer might use. I sat with a loaf of bread wrapped up in a linen kitchen towel in my lap, and the smell of it mixed with the smell of sacks of cottonseed propped in the corner, like the smell of melting butter. It was a cool day, unpleasant enough for us southerners to wear coats, but many of the northern men were in shirtsleeves with the windows half open. I sat patiently. Out on Levee Street, harnesses jangled, and men shouted quick bursting messages to their teams whose hooves clopped to the squeak of wagon wheels, wagons that were piled impossibly high with cotton bales, last year's crop waiting for transport to New England or Old England.

A breeze brushed in through the window, carrying with it the odor of the cattle that the men from Texas drove down the street named for them. Through the upper panes of glass, the far off smokestacks of a boat floated downriver, pushing twin furry black serpent clouds up into the air. The distance of the boat made its bellow seem disconnected from its image.

The door opened, and a woman who was pleading mercy for a man, her son or husband, I assumed, came out dabbing her eyes with a handkerchief and thanking the old officer in the room she was exiting. I supposed her petition had been granted. The man at the desk scratched out something, and the officer signed it.

The general, or colonel, perhaps, whose name escaped me long ago, was a jowly sort of man in a blue coat with the two rows of brass buttons like the Union men wore. He looked like a pig in a jacket, and I wondered if he might have grown up tending hogs. He stood in the doorway of his office and smiled a porcine, lardaceous smile with an arm extended to usher me in. I gave him the loaf of soda bread, Mrs. Haughery's recipe from New Orleans, wrapped in a kitchen cloth, and he received it, peeking under the edge of white linen, his mouth on the edge of salivation. He stared at it a moment and asked what he could do for me.

He pointed to a chair, and I sat down and then he sat himself down behind his desk, leaning back and forcing his chair to give up a groaning squeak. He seemed amused with me, the way older men are with younger, pretty girls. Which I was, then, still in me twenties with thick red hair and deep green eyes. And just look at me now, would you, then? [*laughter*]

"I'm worried about my employer," I says. "Surely 'tis a case of melancholia." And then I painted a portrait of the major's hidden misery and loneliness, but of course 'twas mostly a self-portrait. The officer, General or Colonel Somebody, seemed moved by such a selfless request in the steady stream of people requesting selfish favors.

"He has a missus," I said. "Perhaps it would cheer him some to have her here."

He pressed his fingers together like two spiders pushing their legs against each other as he pursed his lips and thought.

"I think we can arrange this," he said as he tore off a small corner of bread and stuffed it in his mouth. Chewing and brushing his fingertips together to rid them of crumbs, he stood and took my small hand in his hands. As I left through the buttery aroma of cottonseed, he was dictating a letter to the lesser officer in the receiving room.

Feb 19, 1937

There was a knock from outside, and we concluded today's interview. It was a Mr. Eaves at the door. He was a well-dressed, nice looking man with rugged Hollywood looks, a square chin and sharp nose. He wore a gray wool suit and had a dignified drawl and gracious manners. He said he thought we had met before, and I said that I believed we had, on the bus.

As he entered, Miss Fenerty exclaimed *goodness gracious* and reached her old arms up to him. He addressed her as 'Miz Biddy,' kissing her old cheek when she gave it to him with a smile. He turned to us, Ellie and me, and said, "Heidi, ladies."

Miss Fenerty sat forward leaning her chin on her cane. It was clear she adored him, though I think she looks at Ellie and me in the same manner. We got up and kissed her cheek, Ellie and I, one after the other, her old hands closing over our hands and releasing them, and then we excused ourselves to let them visit.

We made our way down Crockett Street to Commerce and rounded the corner where we first met. I wonder if Ellie feels as nostalgic for that spot as I do, the view of the old iron span bridge over the Red perched on stone pillars.

"This was called Levee Street," Ellie said, interrupting my musing. "I wonder which building it was." She stopped to put her hand up to a pane of dusty glass, peering into the dark.

I stopped and did the same, looking into an abandoned building to see only the dim shape of a cast off chair in the darkness. "At the corner of Levee and Milam, didn't she say?" I said as I turned from the window and looked further down Commerce.

"That's right." Ellie said as she wiped dust from her hands.

We found the building at the corner of Levee/Commerce and Milam. It was abandoned, with a window raised open. We peered into it with our forearms pressed into the sill.

"Smell that?" Ellie said. "This must be it. Cottonseed. Seventy years later, and it still smells like cottonseed."

We leaned into the window of the darkened room, our shoulders pressing into each other, side by side. To the left near the rear, there was a doorway that lead to another room.

"I bet Commander Somebody's office was there." My voice echoed into the empty room. I could imagine it moving in the same space where Miss Fenerty's had echoed, on that day in the early years of Reconstruction.

"I bet so," Ellie said.

I replayed the scene in my head. Pretty young Bridget Fenerty sitting patiently with a loaf of warm bread in her lap, waiting for an audience with the Union commander of this conquered place. Apparently Ellie was doing the same.

"I can still see her as that age. Clearly. I can still see her young like us."

"I can, too," I said.

We turned from the building and its memories. I looked over to the river that was empty of twin chimneys and paddlewheels. Instead, a train chugged over the bridge that Ellie had painted that day we first met. We walked up Milam toward the court house, bumping shoulders playfully, veering as we altered each other's course. Out of the corner of my eye, however, I kept looking for the Cadillac. I haven't seen it for a while. Maybe now that Lemurier has been canned, the man in the Cadillac's work is done.

Feb. 20, 1937, FWP, Transcript of Bridget Fenerty

As it turned out, the major not only had a wife, but three daughters up there somewhere. I never would have known it. He never spoke of them, but of course, he never spoke of much. I never would have guessed he was married at all if not for his wedding ring.

On the advice of the general and the purse of the United States Army, the major sent for them all. I thought surely they would give the old house some life. The prospect of a family to care for gave me hope. It certainly wasn't that I was wanting for money; I just needed someone to love and someone to need me, the most basic human requirement of all, slightly ahead of food and shelter

They arrived a couple of months later, sometime around March or April 1866. We waited on the levee, the major and I, the broad expanse of the river stretching over to the Bossier side. The major stood like a marble statue watching downstream with his hands clasped together behind his back.

And then there it was, the twin stacks and the puffs of black above them rising up into the sky between the riverbanks lined with willows and cottonwoods. The major took off his blue slouch hat at the sight and held it at his side as the steamboat got larger. At last, we could see the bow of the boat pushing a furrow in the brown water, like liquid brown glass, it was. On the side of the boat were fancy, big-booted letters in black against the white background, the *Caddo*.

Up on the hurricane deck, there they were, and let me tell you, Miriam, they were the palest sort or people you could imagine, at least as pale as the major. Snow white children dressed in lily white summer dresses, all flounces and bonnets. They even had a little white, fluffy dog named Millicent, perhaps the most foul-tempered little dog I've ever known of.

When the girls saw their father on the bank, they began jumping up and down, and Millicent started barking. The major put his hat on his head, and then took it off again and waved it at his family. It was the most emotion I've ever seen from him, like a statue grinding on its base and coming to life. The girls ran down the stairs of the *Caddo*, hands on the banister, watching their feet, big smiles on their faces. The crew could scarcely get the gangplank down before the girls ran down it with the dog barking at their heels.

Mrs. Lundgren stood on the deck near where the gangplank began its slow decline into the muddy bank that marked your welcome into the city in those days. Men put planks of wood into the mud, but the mud always seemed to creep up over it, so you had to be careful. Mr. Rusk got quite a reputation as a gentleman by helping women off the boats, holding their hands to steady them while saying, *watch that step now, ma'am*, or carrying their small children in his arms and placing them lightly in his carriage.

Mrs. Lundgren seemed very little amused with the present situation. She was very pretty, with a perfect nose and perfect cheekbones and a fine, lithe figure under her fancy dress and bonnet. A statuesque woman, a tall porcelain woman with three china doll children. Perhaps the second prettiest woman I've ever seen. Maggie was and always will be the prettiest. Ah, you should have seen her, Miriam, my sister Maggie.

Mrs. Lundgren tiptoed her way down the gangplank, three strips of wood about this wide, holding her arms out, balancing as if she were walking over Niagara Falls. In her hand, she had a fancy parasol decorated with organdy roses. She stepped off the gangplank as her girls clung to their father's legs, and he pulled the smallest, Klara, up into his arms. The little girl threw her arms around his neck, and his smile made him look like a different man altogether. The major and his wife exchanged a kiss, a small, pointed, peck on the lips.

The middle girl, Elsa, they called her, said, "Mama, it's as big as St. Paul." Elsa had a peculiar way of talking at the time as she was missing her front teeth and waiting for the replacements to push through. Sort of a whistling.

"Oh, I don't know about that," Mrs. Lundgren muttered as she lifted her hem up and stepped carefully through the mud. "But it's certainly hotter."

Just you wait, I said to myself, and I thought of how Uncle Jack had said it twenty years before on the levee in New Orleans. Stevedores loaded the baggage onto a wagon, and the family loaded into Mr. Rusk's carriage, Mr. Rusk smiling proudly and saying, *'welcome, welcome,'* and *'step up in here, be careful, now, missy.'*

The oldest girl, Ingrid, a gangly thing on the edge of womanhood, and the middle daughter, Elsa, didn't I say, held hands as Tom and Jerry cantered toward Levee Street and then Crockett. The girls' little heads looked this way and that as they surveyed the town. They were named for Major Lundgren's old Swedish aunts somewhere up north. Their hair was so blonde as to be silver or white, pale blue eyes, creamy northern complexions. So fair that at first glance it appeared they didn't have eyebrows or eyelashes; you only saw them when you were right up on them. With the fair complexions of their parents, it's no small wonder they weren't transparent altogether. They were as pale as ghosts, little friendly ghosts.

Well, now that you ask, Miriam, the truth of it is, I've only seen ghosts once, and I saw them all at the same time. In New York, it was. But I was speaking of the Lundgren girls, then, wasn't I?

Their mother, Fanny, kept them indoors a great deal of the time, something some people call hothouse children. The girls never got a chance to run and jump. Not until they were under my care.

As the weather warmed and then grew hot, Fanny Lundgren kept to her dark room, fanning herself and praying for a breeze. By June or July around here, the breezes have all played out, and the air sits and clings to you as if it wants to get inside of you. She was a nice woman, Mrs. Lundgren, really she was, and perhaps a little more effervescent than the major. I pitied her, of course, as she was unaccustomed to the heat. She stayed stretched on the bed in her dressing gown, the barest, flimsiest of fabric clinging to her porcelain skin. Her blonde-white hair clung to her head as she stared to the open window waiting, wishing for the air to do something other than just sit there. I would bring her ice-soaked cloths which she would thank me for, but she kept to their room until the sun tired of tormenting us and moved off west to do it to the people over that way. Then she would come out and try to make up for her absence.

By then, I had the girls fed and dressed for bed, reading to them as they piled up next to me, even the oldest, Ingrid. We read Stevenson, Dickens, all of them, for an hour or more at a time, keeping a pressed flower, a gardenia usually, in the book to keep our place for the next night. My missus would be up and around just in time to say their prayers with them and tuck them in. But the next day when the heat was on us good, it was as if their mother didn't exist any longer or became a creature hibernating in a den, a thing that wasn't to be disturbed.

"Shh," I'd tell them, "let your poor mother rest, then. The heat has got her something awful."

Then I would make a game of the four of us, tiptoeing through the house toward the outside, prancing with our hands up like this, in a manner suitable for the Gaiety Theater. Heat or no heat, children need the sun to shine on them, the rain to beat on them occasionally. You can't stop living simply because you're uncomfortable.

Patch would be in, usually for a day as his boat prepared to return to New Orleans, and goodness but how he was turning out, happy, sober. He had a purpose, a work he enjoyed, sailing the river like Ned Hennessy had done. The water still terrified me, as it still does, and I worried for Patch and his safety. But he was content on it. How could I persuade him from it?

Especially when his returns to the city were the cause of such joy for the Lundgren girls and me. For some reason, those three took a shine to my brother. They brought out something wonderful in him as only children can. He would bring them trinkets from New Orleans and Memphis, presenting the small gifts to them in simple magic tricks, candies and small figurines and bracelets appearing from ears or from the hand opposite the one they chose.

When he was in, they would run to him with their arms up, hurrahing, and he would scoop them up and say, "Well, I've sailed up and down the river and right here in Shreveport I've found the prettiest girls in all the world."

His watch was a particular object of their fascination, and they would ask to see it. Little Klara would run her tiny, soft fingertip over the inscription in Latin and ask what it meant.

"Not sure," he would say, "but it's certainly pretty, now ain't it?"

He sounded like a riverman. I think he had decided it was who he was. To find out who you are and accept it is a wonderful thing, truly 'tis. Patch had changed boats by then, the old one which had served in the war was taken out of service, and he'd gotten on with another boat that was part of a line owned by the Kouns brothers, a local firm. All of their boats had two white rings around the chimneys and announced themselves with two long whistle blasts. Patch's boat, the *Era No. 8*, had a big elaborate eight on the side. He got on with another one a year later, and what a stroke of bad luck it was for both of us. 'Tis a shame what luck hands you sometimes.

Well, they began calling him 'Uncle Patch,' as they had no uncles of their own, only aunts and them far away. He and Mr. Rusk would go fishing, bringing back stringers of green bass with jagged black lines on their sides; blue, green, and black bream with orange bellies; sliver gray catfish with slippery white paunches. The girls running down Crockett Street to greet them, touching the fish with their fingertips. And then Patch and Mr. Rusk, laughing in the backyard as they cleaned them. Patch would move the gaping fish mouths, making them talk in voices for the girls.

If you throw me back, then I'll give you three wishes.

I can't throw you back, Mr. Bass. What'll we have for supper, I ask ye? And what more could a fella wish for than supper?

Then the girls would laugh until they watched in amazement as the inner truth of what a fish is made of was revealed by the knife, little faces agape at vessels and guts, pale flesh and spiky bones.

The youngest, Klara, soon decided that she wanted to go fish with them, and they took her. They had the patience of Job with her, untangling her line, baiting her hook, wading out into the current to unsnag her line off a stump, removing a fish, wriggling and contorting in reversing J-shapes. She sat on an overturned bucket, her legs dangling from it, her bare feet just above the sand. The tip of her pole faltering toward the water as she brushed her hair out of her face with the back of her hand and contemplated the far bank. "Got to keep your pole out the water, now, missy," Mr. Rusk would say patiently.

The two of them, Patch and Mr. Rusk, built a racer out of scrap wood, barrel lids for wheels, and took them to a hill on the edge of town here, Mr. Rusk pushing them down and Patch catching them and slowing them to a stop at the bottom, then pulling the thing up to the top again before racing back down to the bottom and waiting for them. Those two men, one gray-headed, one red-headed, doted on those children as if they were uncle and grandfather.

And when Patch left for another tour of the river, the girls and I always went to see him off in the afternoon heat. He was certainly shaping up as a man, and beginning to court a little, though his history of troubles with the drink marked him for life in this town. And anyway, his itinerant work made it difficult to settle down, and so those Lundgren girls and his work became his true loves. He was promoted to first clerk from mud clerk, with hopes of making pilot one day.

When he was out on the river, the girls and I picked blackberries with Mr. Rusk, who warned them to be *careful a Mister No Shoulders, now.* We splashed in puddles, the girls and I, and I showed them how to do the wash. On rainy afternoons, we baked soda bread and ginger snaps, and as they baked, we sat and read aloud. I would give each girl a paragraph to read, and then I would pick up and read my bit. The youngest, I would only give a sentence or two to read and a little coaching with it.

On sunny days, we picnicked by the river and watched the steamers arrive and depart. Mr. Rusk taught them how to ride, the small little towheaded things perched high on the flanks of Tom and Jerry. Two on Tom, Elsa with her little arms wrapped around Klara, and Ingrid sitting proudly by herself on Jerry. The horses trying to peek around their blinders at the small weights on their backs.

Some days, I let them make pancakes for lunch, little Klara standing by the stove on a footstool with a spatula in her hand like a little soldier, staring at the disks in the pan. "Wait for the bubbles, dearie," I would have to tell her. "Wait for the bubbles on top before you flip them."

And every year on March fourteenth, on my boy's birthday, we would make a cake for him and wear little hats and sing happy birthday. The girls asked *who's little Frank?* and I told them he was a boy about their age who would be delighted to have them at his party even if he himself couldn't be. That was explanation enough for them.

In the fall, the girls began school. In those days, there was a place called the Shreveport Institute for Young Ladies, a school on Edwards Street run by a Mr. Ford and a man with the apt name of Mr. Horn who taught vocal lessons as well as the melodeon and the pianoforte. Mr. Horn also gave lessons in French and German, for those who thought they might need such a thing.

In the evenings, when the Lundgren girls studied by the fading light of the day and Mrs. Lundgren was in her room beginning her daily toilet, Mr. Rusk would be there also. I read to him pointing to the words and having him sound them out. The girls would read with him too, patiently moving their fingers along and looking up and saying "very good" when he stumbled through a particularly difficult word. Kind little blue eyes under hair that was all soft and blonde, almost white.

One evening, Klara, the youngest asked, "Mr. Rusk, what happened to your eye?"

Ingrid pounced on her with a shhh. Mr. Rusk seemed perplexed by the question. It was clear to me that he didn't know what to say. He seemed stuck for a good answer.

"Yessum, that eye." He chuckled nervously. "Yes, that eye yonder."

"Perhaps we shouldn't ask such personal questions, ladies," I said wiping my hands on a kitchen towel after finishing the evening dishes. Honestly, however, I wanted to know about the eye as much as they did. He never spoke of it, and I never knew.

"Now, here, Mr. Rusk, read us a bit from *McGuffey's Primer*."

He stumbled through it, very little inflection in his voice, but it was passable.

Oh, but the questions those girls asked. They needed to know how everything worked, in this world and the next. How does a steam engine work? Does God sit on a chair or just a cloud? Does He wear shoes or is He barefooted? Do they really have a lot of tea in China, or is it just a saying? Their little minds never stopped. Several months later, we were at the table after supper, and I was putting away dishes.

"Miss Bridget, do dogs and cats have souls?" Elsa asked. We had just had to bury their fluffy ill-tempered, ankle biting beast of a dog. Mr. Rusk had helped us and had even preached a short sermon and had each girl deliver a quick tearful eulogy, the oldest going first and then the youngest giving the shortest, a tearful, lip-quivering "And may God bless Millicent, and I hope she doesn't bite Jesus."

Now, on the matter of dogs and cats having souls, I said that I believed in general they did, though I left out that I wasn't sure about this particular dog. I changed the subject before they could ask about her particular case.

"Mr. Rusk, could you read to us from the Ninety-first Psalm?" I asked him.

He did, and it was a thing of beauty, the way he read it. Perhaps even better than King David himself could have sung it.

Feb 20, 1937, Sabbath

We sat in the parlor in the radiance of the gas heater. Outside, the Saturday afternoon was dampened by a cold drizzle. I realized that I still had on my nice dress from temple this morning. I felt so comfortable. The recorder was put away, but I asked her more about Mr. Rusk and his voice.

"Oh, 'twas rich and deep when he got his confidence under him. It got so he would read on the river banks, especially the newspapers. Tom and Jerry patiently grazing as the three of them waited for the boats to come in with passengers to be taken into town. The horses clipping the grass on the levee, and Mr. Rusk sitting on the buckboard of his carriage, a handsome dark green with *S. Rusk, Carriage for Hire* in the gold letters that I had painted there meself. Sitting there outlined against the Bossier shore as the cocoa colored river sped by, the eddies and currents spelling out letters and partial letters, his top hat propped on his gray head, his elbows propped on his knees, his brown hands on the dingy white of the paper. A free man reading the papers. A content man who had crawled up out of his circumstances.

"He would ask the captains and boat agents and clerks for the New Orleans and St. Louis and Memphis papers, whatever he could find. I've always thought that he would have made a fine orator, if he'd an opportunity to learn to read earlier in life."

I was about to ask whatever became of Mr. Rusk when the phone rang. She got up, but it must have rung another dozen times before she finally got to it. I could have gotten up to answer it, but I think it was important for her to answer it herself.

"Can't ye see I'm coming?" she scolded the phone, and she chuckled as she picked up the receiver.

"Hello, whozit? Oh, wonderful, just wonderful. A boy? Is that so? And how's Nina? Glad to hear it. Thank you reverend, and my best to Nina, and I can't wait to see the little fellow. Perhaps you and I can celebrate with a cigar. Ha ha."

She replaced the receiver back on the base.

"'Twas the reverend, Nina's husband. They've had their baby, a boy. All's well."

I left her with the good news and promised to take her to the hospital to see the new baby and mother when they're allowed visitors in a few days. As I drove down Line, I thought about Uncle Patch and his fair little nieces, a man who chose to be part of their lives. He could just as well come into town for whores and booze and sleep, but he chose those girls instead.

I think that Lemurier and Mirlette have slept the whole day. They seem to be active only at night, 'like two possums,' Ellie says. On the table downstairs are the January issue of *New Pioneer* and a pamphlet entitled, *The Workers [Communist] Party, What It Stands for and Why You Should Join,* by someone named Ruthenberg. I don't think Lemurier will qualify. You apparently have to be a worker to join.

Wrote a letter to Uncle Sol tonight. I should have written him sooner.

Feb. 21, 1937, FWP, Transcript of Bridget Fenerty

When the weather cooled, October generally, 'tis around here, Mrs. Lundgren would take shorter and shorter naps. She gradually rejoined family life, like a flower blooming or a creature coming out of hibernation, a beautiful creature nonetheless. In those days, we would enjoy the concerts given on the courthouse steps by the various regimental bands of the occupying army. There would be barbecues and suppers on the courthouse lawn. We would go down to see Mr. Brewer, the confectioner on Texas Street, for lemon drops and the like, and admire the things that Mrs. Wells had at her Millinery and Fancy Goods Store, or at a place called the Missouri Store, a place that sold all manner of things and had a sign with two bears on either side of it.

But the next summer, as regular as the tilting of the earth, Mrs. Lundgren would take to her room for the heat of the day, a longer time with each longer day, her slip clinging to her like a second skin, outlining her body's secrets, and the poor woman unable to worry about the exposure as she lay there listless, fanning herself and wishing for a northern summer.

She endured another summer, the summer that we had that first outbreak of fever, the lesser one.[32] She missed things on those hot days. She missed Ingrid becoming a woman in that monthly way. I attended to that. She missed Klara losing teeth. I attended to that. On hot summer days, May until October, it was if she ceased to exist. It pained Mrs. Lundgren, too, for she wasn't necessarily a lazy woman. When the weather was tolerable for her, the two of us would frequently work side by side. The summer evenings for her were more in that way that you might oversleep only to wake and find that something you were to take care of had been taken care of by someone else. She was embarrassed that the heat put her down as it did.

We all enjoyed the winter and the half of the spring and fall you could consider pleasant, but, as soon as the days lengthened and became sweltering, she retreated into her sanctum.

Well, it was just after the president had been impeached by the Senate but acquitted. The newspapers were full of talk of it, plenty of barbs aimed at the Republicans, who were seen as conquering devils. Louisiana and several other states had been readmitted into the Union that month, though there was very little about it in the local papers. That sort of news was spread word of mouth. It seemed to me that the papers didn't want to admit we had left in the first place.[33] And of course, the heat was on us good again, and she, Mrs. Lundgren, I mean, had had enough. I heard them argue, or discuss, rather.

"I can't spend another summer in this heat, Peter, I can't," she said behind the door. And then she fell into sobbing, and I suppose her crying was what settled it for the major.

"All right," he sighed. "All right."

As much as you might like them to, apple and cherry trees don't grow well in the Louisiana heat. Many have tried it, but it's just too hot. Nor did Mrs. Lundgren believe do little girls with apple cheeks and little cherry voices. Mrs. Lundgren wanted them to know about northern things, rhubarb, the northern lights, snow, and toboggan rides in knit caps and mittens. To be around old aunts and uncles, to hear stories told by grandparents of life in Sweden and Norway. She wanted them away from the threat of summer fevers, which were

---

[32] In 1867, Shreveport experienced an epidemic of Yellow Fever. Over a hundred died that year.
[33] President Andrew Johnson was impeached but acquitted on May 26, 1868. Louisiana was readmitted to the Union on June 25, 1868.

always a real possibility. The year before there had been an outbreak of Yellow Fever that lasted into the fall, but none of our household got it.

Plans were made for Mrs. Lundgren and the girls to leave. It broke my heart, but it had been broken before, and I knew it would be painful. But I also knew that it was up to me whether I chose to suffer or not from it. The pain I could manage.

That summer there was a drought building, and the water was dropping in the river on account of it. There was fear for the corn and the cotton and the general livelihood of the town. For Fanny Lundgren, there was fear of being stuck in the city for another long, hot summer. In those days before the railroad was built up, the river was still the main way in or out.

With reports of the river falling as much as a foot a day, they left on the last Saturday in June, 1868 on a boat with the ironic name of the *Monsoon*. It was a market day, when the population of the town swelled with wagonloads of whole families arriving fresh off weekly baths in their best clothes. The ground right down to the water's edge was packed and fissured, and any scuff of a hoof or a shoe brought up a cloud of dust.

I'd made a trip down to Hyams & Kennedy on Texas Street and gotten them all stationary so they could write us, me and Uncle Patch and Mr. Rusk. I gave them the little gifts that would turn into little gifts back to us when we received them in the mail. The girls nodded and blinked away tears with their little bottom lips pushing out.

They moved up the gangplank, slower now than on the day they had scampered down it to see their Da. The major stood there with his hands in his pockets, watching the *Monsoon* plow downriver, puffing on his pipe like the boat. Little Klara, her face red while she bawled like a banshee, her sisters crying too, though more quietly. Then he turned away and went back to his office, even though it was a Saturday. Mr. Rusk and I stayed perched on the buckboard of his carriage and watched them disappear.

The major gave no hint of what he was going to do, caught between his duty and his family, each at odds with the other. He had a commitment with the army through the following spring, and he was the sort of man who kept promises, no matter how painful. What finally decided it for him was when Mittie Stephens came to town in February of 1869 and took the two favorite men of my life and replaced them with another.

Feb. 21, 1937, Sunday

I had to know, so I asked her, and she told me.

"Oh, they made it back to St. Paul," she said, "and I kept up with them for a long time. I still keep up with little Klara. The other two have passed on.

Ingrid lived until just a few years ago."

But they were just girls, I thought, but of course they were *just girls* in the 1860s. All the same, on the heels of Miss Fenerty's telling of it, it was just strange to think of them as old women and not little girls. I told Miss Fenerty so.

"'Tis the way of things," she said, "and who can do anything about it, I ask you then? Get up and live each day, whether it's one of ten thousand or one of fifty thousand."

Driving down Line Avenue, I wondered who this Mittie Stephens was. Why would she come and take men from young Bridget Fenerty? Was she some kind of rival?

I'm upstairs writing with plans on a little reading in a few minutes. Lemurier is downstairs, listlessly

(later)

I smelled smoke in the house and ran downstairs toward the source. It was different than cigarette smoke or reefer smoke. It smelled like something was on fire. Downstairs in his studio, I found Lemurier burning letters addressed to someone named Hickey. He had accumulated a bundle of them from an address on Fortification Street in Jackson, Mississippi. None of them were opened.

"That's someone's mail," I said incredulously.

"No it isn't," he said, letting the flames advance up to his fingers before dropping it into a bowl of some half-eaten something. "Not anymore."

"It's against the law to destroy someone's mail," I said.

"It's also none of your focking busy-ness," he said. He made that haughty, exasperated noise he makes. Then he took a long pull on his cigarette and threw himself back into a chair.

Feb. 22, 1937, FWP, Transcript of Bridget Fenerty

We were speaking of Mittie Stephens, last time, then, weren't we?

She appeared in the river that morning, traveling upstream on her way from New Orleans, gliding through the mist that hovered over the water in the sunshine. Her twin stacks pushed upward through it; her bow cleaved the water into two wet ridges that separated behind her. She was stacked high with hay bales, shaggy with straw, and I knew that somewhere on one of those decks was my brother. It was a February day, a cool, hard day, plenty of sunshine, the world with spring on its mind but not doing anything about it just yet. The river was coming up with the winter rains, tugging and pushing at the new green willow branches that drooped down into the current.

Patch was part of her crew, the boat, the *Mittie Stephens*. He had changed from the Kouns Brothers' Line because it was a faster path towards pilot, though he still had a year or two left before he would be allowed in the pilothouse, such is how it worked. It ran from Jefferson, in Texas, down to New Orleans and back, stopping to land at Shreveport on the way.

Mr. Rusk was waiting with me on the river bank. He stood there gazing downstream, dressed in his nicest livery suit, a royal blue jacket and a black top hat, black Wellington boots. You see, he had business in Texas.

He'd heard from Patch, who heard from a man on the Dallas Street Warf in Jefferson, who heard from a farmer somewhere out in the countryside that there was a man named Ben Rusk who was born in Louisiana and sold from his family as a boy. The farmer said that this man Ben Rusk lived in County Upshur just north of Jefferson with his family.

Well, it was a long shot, but the prospect of a family, his own flesh and blood, had him spinning. He'd planned on taking Tom and Jerry, and his carriage, his name and livelihood written on the side. But after the boat landed, and we greeted Patch, the horses balked at going on board. They straightened their legs and shook their heads up and down as Mr. Rusk pulled on their bridles and a couple of deckhands pushed on their rumps. In the end, when the *Mittie Stephens* departed with Patch and Mr. Rusk aboard, I drove the carriage and team back up to the house on Crockett, put away the carriage, and boarded the horses at the Eclipse stables.

I still had my misgivings about the water, of course, and especially about the trip to Jefferson, which had the reputation of being equally treacherous whether at low or high water. But over those years of my brother safely coming and going, I was beginning to trust it again. Looking back, however, I should have known when Tom and Jerry wouldn't board. Even with all those bales stacked on it like a palace made of hay, I think they knew. I should have trusted their animal intuition, their horse sense, if you like.

My birthday had just passed. Mr. Rusk had gotten us a metal bucket of oysters from Lem's on Market Street as a treat, as it was February, a month with an R in it, in accordance with Uncle Jack's sensible policy. Mr. Rusk had also gotten a sack with some other eatables, including a cake from Mr. Brewer's Confectionary.

After we ate, the three of us sat lounging about on a blanket spread out just off the river. Mr. Rusk was reading out loud from an article in the *Southwestern* about the prospect of paving Texas Street and possibly Milam and Market, as well, with something called the Nicholson Pavement, and there was talk about establishing a charity hospital in Shreveport. In the sunshine and out of the wind, it was a pleasant day, the hour or two when you tell it wouldn't be long until spring. The horses, having asserted their will, grazed on the new grass where they were tied to a bois d'arc tree. It was a pleasant afternoon and nice to be among family, Patch, of course, and Mr. Rusk, whom we considered equal with an uncle.

I was grateful for the two of them, as once the girls left, the house fell into the same sort of mausoleum it was before, with all the cheer of a funeral parlor. On those painfully quiet days, you could hear the dust falling as the clock ticked for no one. The summer had slipped into fall, fall had slipped into winter, and then winter held fast. The major himself celebrated another bland, humorless Christmas. Miserable, despite all my attempts, empty and miserable.

On that day in February, Patch sat eating an apple, watching the river coast by, and waiting on the *Mittie Stephens* to make steam again. He threw the core over to the horses, who nosed each other away from it, necks wrestling until one of them got it. Then Patch checked his watch, anticipating when he would need to board and resume his duties. He saw Mr. Rusk looking at the watch and handed it to him to examine.

"Well, looka yonder that watch. Now ain't that somethin'? *'To Patrick.'*"

Mr. Rusk turned it over and leaned his head back and peered down his nose with his one eye.

"Now what's all this fancy writing?"

He handed it back to Patch.

"I've always wondered myself. It's Latin, but that's all I know," Patch said as he put it back in his waistcoat pocket. "Do you know, sister?"

"I've no idea," I said. "Surely a priest could tell you. Or perhaps the major."

With the way he admired Patch's watch, I thought I might give Mr. Rusk one, too. Money was no issue, and I thank you, Mr. Burton, sir.

Patch got up and helped Mr. Rusk up, and they brushed off their backsides at the same time, almost like father and son. Mr. Rusk went to re-hitch Tom and Jerry so I could take them back up the hill. He had resolved that he would see to a horse in Jefferson. Patch pulled me up from where I sat in the style of an Indian, and he embraced me. Such a strange thing, too, when you look back, when you realize it was your last embrace. He kissed me on the cheek.

"I tell you a secret, sister. I may be closer to cub[34] than I thought I was, but shhh, don't tell anyone just yet."

"What marvelous news," I whispered, and it was, especially considering how low he had sunk just a few years before. The river had been good to him.

---

[34] Apprentice pilot

Mr. Rusk hitched up Tom and Jerry, and I sat up on the buckboard holding the reins in my hands in the folds of my skirts, as it was getting late in the afternoon and turning cold again. Long shadows fell out onto the river and the *Mittie Stephens*. Mr. Rusk was standing on the Texas deck, one of the highest ones, his royal blue jacket brilliant in the fading sun. He took off his black top hat, waved it to me, and set it back on his gray head. Just then Patch emerged from a gap in the hay and waved. They put their arms on each other's shoulders and squinted into the sunlight behind me, and then they waved to me. The *Mittie Stephens* clacked out into the channel and then huffed and grunted upstream. The ferryboat paused for her, slowly veering from her path and then bobbing in her wake. When the *Mittie Stephens* made the bayou at the north edge of town, she turned into it, a floating castle of hay bales. The distance and the failing light obscured them from me, and I shook the reins for home.

I found out about it the next day, when I was at the market. A boy came running out from the telegraph office. The agent had sent him with the news.

"The *Mittie Stephens* done burned! The *Mittie Stephens* done burned!" All up and down Texas Street, like this, you know, hands in the air, his coat flying open to show his red flannel shirt. His hat flew off, and he paused from his role as the town crier to go back for it.

"The *Mittie Stephens* done burned!" he says.

Well, my heart dropped. We gathered around him like things drawn into a whirlpool. A small knot of grownups formed, and then the knot grew around the boy.

"What's this?" a man asked. "Where?"

"Up on Caddo Lake," the boy panted, "'Way to Jefferson."

"All safe, I pray?" a woman asked.

"No ma'am," the boy said, shaking his head as he gathered his breath. "Plenty dead."

He pushed through the crowd with *excuse me's* and resumed his errand, all the way up Texas to McNeil, and then over to Milam, "The *Mittie Stephens* done burned!"

The waiting was like the war all over again, waiting, waiting. I didn't sleep, nor did anyone with a loved one on the boat. Lists of the dead and the surviving were printed, incomplete at first, dashing hopes, for some temporarily, for some permanently. I sat on the porch right outside there and waited. I waited for word one way or another.

Well, a boat called the *Dixie* was down a few days later with some of the bodies of the dead and some of the survivors. The published lists were still incomplete. I still had no definite word concerning Patch or Mr. Rusk. That afternoon, a man knocked on the door and introduced himself as a Mr.

Williams. He asked if I was the sister of Patrick Fenerty. I said I was. He had bad news, he said.

"I'm afraid your brother is dead."

I didn't believe him, or rather, I couldn't believe him. I refused to believe him.

He says, "I was on my way to Jefferson with the payroll for the troops there. I had just fallen asleep in my cabin when I woke to the sound of Sam Underwood, the watchman, going down the line of doors, hitting each with a double rap and two words, 'Warn far!' he said. Each door was louder until he came to mine. I was half asleep so it took me a moment before I realized he wasn't saying *warn far* at all, but *we're on fire*.

"I opened the door to see the whole forward end of the boat on fire and people, men, women, children, jumping into the cold lake. The captain had turned the boat to make for the shore, but the water was shallow, and she couldn't make headway. Many who jumped in the water were beaten by the paddlewheel.

"I jumped in aft of the paddlewheel so's not to be sucked into it. Then I managed to swim out of the way of the wheel and to shore. There was a family named Sproul who had a farm there, and that's where the living and the dead were being collected. Miss Fenerty, I saw your brother. He was badly burned."

Mr. Williams lifted his eyes to look at me and then looked to the floor again.

"I asked, I says, who is this man? Does anyone know his name? His family? We were all asking questions like that. Do you know who this is? What about this lady here? That little boy there? Well, Mr. Lodwick says, why, that's Patch Fenerty. Irishman. Got a sister back in town, Shreveport."

I sat and looked away, down Crockett Street. The more I began to believe it, the further away Mr. Williams' voice seemed.

"When the light come up the next day, we commenced to burying the dead in a trench there. He's not alone," he said, as if it would console me.

"A rain was falling on us, turning the soil into mud. As the dirt was hitting them, I noticed the watch chain in his pocket. I jumped in and pulled this from his pocket. I figured his family might appreciate a memento. It might help you, might lessen your grief in some way," he said as he reached into his pocket and unfolded his handkerchief.

I still didn't want to accept the news. Until I saw it and held it in my hand.

It was the watch I'd given my brother, *To Patrick*, engraved on one side, and on the other side the inscription, something written in Latin. The watchmaker, Mr. Burnside, had several of them. I'd had him add the inscription to my brother. The watch had stopped five minutes past one, one in the morning.

"There's also a Negro man says he knows you, a Mr. Rust," Mr. Williams says.

"Rusk, you mean?" I corrected him. "Alive?" I asked him.

"Yes ma'am, alive but real sick. Liked to drowned."

Well, I sent for him, trying to salvage part of my life, my family. Two days later, he rolled up in the bed of a wagon, and there was no mistake about it: he was gravely ill. Old men shouldn't jump into cold water. And if they do, they should get right out, not keep going back in to fetch people. Leave that to others. Someone, some kind someone, had taken his wet livery clothes, the ones he was so proud of, and put him in an old nightshirt and wrapped him in a blanket. He looked up to me.

"He was dead when I found him," Mr. Rusk muttered. "I'm sorry, Miss Bridget. He was already passed."

We put him in the guest room here, and the major called for a physician who made the diagnosis of pneumonia, brought on by jumping into the cold February water of Caddo Lake. And then when the major left for Minnesota a few days later, I moved him into the major's old room. He left, you see. Perhaps the major had a sudden reevaluation of his priorities. He resigned his commission, and he left, and when he did, I moved Mr. Rusk into his room.

He lingered for several weeks, in and out of his wits. There were days he seemed to be on the verge of recovering, or at least I fancied that he was, and then those days were fewer and fewer. On one of the last of those lucid days, he had me read a verse from Proverbs. He said it reminded him of his wife. Here, Miriam, let me get it. I'll read it to you:

"Strength and honor are her clothing; and she shall rejoice in time to come; she opens her mouth with wisdom; and her tongue is the law of kindness. She looks well to the ways of her household, and eats not the bread of idleness. Her children arise up, and call her blessed."[35]

"That was her favorite, that'n right there from the Proverbs," he murmured. "She used to get the preacher to read it to her."

And he opened his one eye and put it on me. "Miss Bridget, if you ever see one of my children, or grandchildren, or they children, well you tell 'em ole Grampa Rusk is show proud of 'em. Tell 'em to live tall and walk straight, cause we all take our first steps on this earth, and we all take our last."

That was the last coherent thing he said to me, other than asking for water and things like that. He lingered a week or so more after that, sleeping most of

---

[35] Proverbs 31: 25-28

it, babbling some of it, and on the first warm day of the year, the first one you could keep the windows open, Mr. Rusk died peacefully while I sat in a chair by his bed and sang him to his rest. The doctor taking care of him was Elias Gramhar.

February 22, 1937, Monday

It was if she thought that, by continuing to talk, she could avoid the tears, the sadness, but at last, her story today was interrupted by a visit from Hank Eaves. Miss Fenerty took care of him and his brother when they were growing up some twenty years ago or so. Ellie came downstairs, and the four of us talked like we were family.

"We were just talking about Klara Lundgren, Klara O'Mara, now, of course. That child's been married fifty years, and I still call her by her maiden name." Miss Fenerty rapped her spoon on the edge of her cup of tea. It made a ting-ting-ting, a cheerful little noise, but it was a noise that made a memory flash across my mind, the sound of a knife on the rim of a water glass in the dining room of the Waldorf the night Irving proposed. I drifted for a moment with that memory.

"How's Miss Klara doing?" Mr. Eaves asked as he put his lips on the edge of his hot coffee and sipped.

"I got a Christmas card from her. Doing well. Eight grandchildren and three greats, last count."

"Well, my goodness," Mr. Eaves said. He spoke like her knew her well.

"Klara O'Mara!" Miss Fenerty exclaimed as she put up her finger as if she were about to touch something invisible. She does this sometimes when she's about to make a point. "While it's been said that 'greater love hath no man than to lay down his life for a friend,' I myself believe it's equally true that 'greater love hath no *woman* than to marry a man whose last name rhymes with her first name.'"

We all laughed, a laugh so deep and genuine and good that we looked to one another as we laughed. When I looked at Ellie, we stopped laughing and smiled at one another. We spent the rest of the afternoon in each other's company. After Mr. Eaves left and Miss Fenerty went upstairs to bed, Ellie and I sat up talking for a while in the blue glow of the gas heater.

She said her brother has fully recovered and has been dismissed from the hospital in Bakersfield. We talked about our families then, about Mother, Father, Lennie. She asked me where my engagement ring was. "You never wear it," she said holding up my naked ring finger with her thumb and forefinger.

"Oh, it's around," I said. "I just hate to lose it."

I think she knows I'm lying.

Feb. 23, 1937, FWP, Transcript of Bridget Fenerty

After Mr. Rusk died, I sent word on the telegraph to Jefferson asking about the whereabouts of one Ben Rusk, or Rust, or Rush, anything close. If he did have family there somewhere, I wanted them to collect his body so that Mr. Rusk could be among his descendants. But no one seemed to know anything about him. I had him buried myself.

I also thought of leaving then, going to Texas. I had read of it in the *Texas Almanac*, what some called the Texas "free and easy ways about town." Or perhaps to California, or to New York or Baltimore or Boston. Anywhere. I had a little money, you know.

But my roots were sunk here. I was nearing thirty, and starting over somewhere else seemed so daunting. Little did I know that I'd live as long as I have. I might have made a go for it.

There was another reason. It was clear that few if any would get the noose or prison for treason to the United States, and I had a hope, a small and sad but persistent hope, that Mrs. Burton would bring my boy back. I was afraid that, if I moved on, she wouldn't be able to find me. It was a foolish hope, of course. He would soon be six, my boy would, showing glimpses of the man he would be perhaps, a little redhead among all those dark haired people in Brazil.

Instead, the house was sold to another northern man, and I was retained as housekeeper. He was a physician, a surgeon, who had served under General Grant in Mississippi in the siege of Vicksburg, and then in the Red River Campaign under General Banks in a regiment that called itself the Greyhound Regiment[36], I suppose for its marching speed, though I never knew for sure. He'd had some sort of personal disturbance then after the battles down below town[37] and resigned his commission. Some sort of emotional trouble. Rather than return home, he stayed, first in Natchitoches, and then when the war was over, in Shreveport.

He was the only child of a man in Cincinnati, a native Kentuckian, who was a copperhead.[38] Elias' mother had died having him, which was the first of many hammer blows between father and son. It culminated in Elias leaving the medical practice they shared in Cincinnati and joining the Union Army as a regimental surgeon. It was the final straw between them, the end result of a

---

[36] The 83rd Ohio Volunteer Infantry

[37] The battles of Pleasant Hill and Mansfield, both Union losses in the spring of 1864.

[38] A northerner sympathetic with slavery and the southern cause.

hundred smaller quarrels. Elias' father fiercely supported slavery on account of it being condoned in the Bible, in the Old Testament. A case of someone reaching into scripture to pull out the piece that suits them, as if they're looking for a spare part or a particular item in a tool box, a hammer for some people.

As a northern man in a conquered city, Dr. Gramhar was a bit of an outcast, like a Roman in Judea. He could only get patients from the lower reaches of society, the whores and the saloon brawlers, poor whites and Negroes. But he treated them like they were kings and queens. He was a fine man, a good man.

And he was far better company that Major Lundgren, though that's not much of a ruler to measure it by. Elias and I discussed poetry and art and music. It got so we sang together. His voice was awful, but it didn't stop him. He was handsome enough, in an abstract sort of way, sandy haired, boyish, but with a beard about so long. Well taller than me, over six feet. Kind gray eyes that looked at you when you told him something. Eyes that listened.

I found myself enjoying his simple, quiet company. As much as Major Lundgren was indifferent to my society, Elias seemed to crave it. We were two people that the world had left to be alone, with no family to speak of. At first, I left him to take his meals by himself, as I thought that might be the way of northern men, having had contact with only one of them. The papers had always portrayed them as barbarians and vandals, coarse men with very little capacity or desire for refinement. But it became apparent that it was different for Dr. Gramhar. I would be in the kitchen attending to things, hungry and waiting for him to finish so I could eat, and he would call to me from the dining room.

"Miss Fenerty! Well, they've gone and done it. Who would ever have thought it possible?"

"What, sir?" I asked as I came into the dining room drying my hands.

"Why, they drove the golden spike[39]," he said, folding up the paper and placing it near his plate. "Now you can travel from New York to California. By train!"

"'Tis so?" I'd ask.

"Yes," he said. "Fix yourself a plate, and I'll tell you about it."

I would sit down, nervously at first, crossing my legs and arranging the folds of my skirt across my knees. He would ask me what I thought about things in the news, questions such as, 'what do you think ought to be done?' and 'have you ever thought about such and such?' He was very companionable.

---

[39] The ceremonial "Golden Spike" was driven by railroad baron Leland Stanford at Promontory Point, Utah Territory, on May 10, 1869, to connect the Transcontinental Railroad.

Or, another time, "Miss Fenerty, it says here in the *Southwestern* that old Dickens is ill.[40] Have you read much of his work?"

"Yes," I said, "'tis one of my favorites. *'A wonderful fact to reflect upon, that every human creature is constituted to be that profound secret and mystery to every other,'*" I quoted.

"Ah, yes, *A Tale of Two Cities,*" he said, and then he closed his eyes and said, *'I wish you to know that you have been the last dream of my soul.'*"

"Ah, but that, 'tis a fine one! And how about, *'There is a prodigious strength in sorrow and despair,'*" I replied.

And so we would talk about literature, and art, current events. And religion, which he said he could no longer subscribe to. He wouldn't say why, only that he had seen too much. Though I hadn't been to church in years, it pained me to hear him talk in such a way as that.

The short of it is, over the first few months, we became friends, he and I, something that Eliza Leslie would have frowned upon. Perhaps Miss Leslie saw that befriending the master of the house was akin to fraternizing with the enemy. But he was interesting and had a kind way about him. He was good company, and I was sorely in need of it.

He may have been an amiable companion during the day, but there were nights when I woke to him shouting in the other part of the house. Angry, anguished questions that would echo through the house. *When? When?* he would shout, rousing me from a deep sleep, causing me to run upstairs in my robe and sleeping cap to see to him, only to find him asleep in a tangle of bedsheets. Or I would find him sleepwalking, pacing the upstairs hall looking into the rooms and asking, *where are we to put them?*

I think he was relieved on the nights he was called out, stumbling out the door in the cold or the heat or the rain, some nights. Under an umbrella, drawing up his collar with his black bag at his side, off down the street, down to St. Paul's Bottoms to see to someone, off to check on a brawler who'd been knocked out and had taken his own time to come to again. Elias seemed happy to be up and occupied, leaving his nightmares to occupy themselves.

As the summer rolled forward, we tended a small garden during the day, working a row across from each other, sweating together. It was in the garden one day that I showed him the watch. I kept it in my apron in those days. It was a sort of magical thinking, that if I had the watch in my pocket, I would have my brother near. A sort of proxy, a talisman.

I asked Dr. Gramhar if he knew much Latin. He said he did some, mostly diseases and symptoms, anatomical terms. His shirt sleeves were rolled up, and

---

[40] English author Charles Dickens fell ill on April 22, 1869 at a book reading in Preston, Lancashire, and was advised by physicians to discontinue his farewell book reading tour.

he braced himself on a hoe, sweating under the brim of his hat, the blue slouch the Union men wore, the officers did. He only wore it for gardening. He reached out and took the watch from me and examined it.

"Virgil, the *Aeneid*," he said as he handed it back to me. I slipped it carefully into my apron pocket and asked him what it meant. He took up his hoe again and began chopping the ground around a tomato plant. He seemed lost in thought, pondering the watch and the soil.

"Well?" I finally asked. I put a handful of tomatoes in my apron next to the watch.

"Too much mud on it," he chipped away at the crust of the earth. Finally, he said, "Can't make it out. Maybe we'll take it down to Mr. Frank's and have it cleaned up. I was always better with Greek, anyway," he said.

But such is the way of icons and treasures: to take the mud from them would be to take some of their value, their history. It would be a bit like sanding down the Cross because it's rugged. After some time passed, I finally put the watch in a drawer and kept it just as it was.

It was on a day we were working in the garden that I finally asked him. I had been curious from the start, but politeness had kept me from asking.

"If you don't mind my asking, is there a Mrs. Gramhar? Or was there?"

He stopped pulling weeds and straightened up.

"There almost was."

He threw a handful of ragged shoots to a pile and knelt again. I didn't say anything. I just waited, and the silence must have pressed the rest of it out of him. His jacket was off and his white shirt had sweat under the arms and on the sleeves where he would wipe his forehead occasionally. He spoke from under his blue slouch hat with the US Army on it as his hands stayed busy gathering and pulling.

"Her name was Kate, Kate Crittenden. The ones that the county is named after. We were engaged to be married until I went to be a Union man."

He threw another handful off down the row.

"I left and went off to war, expecting to return to her. Then one day in camp, I get a letter. 'I release you,' it says."

He pulled on a shock of weeds, and they made a wrenching, crunching sound as their roots relinquished the earth. He threw the handful on the pile, then put his hands on his hips and straightened up to stretch his back. "It happened so fast that it makes me think she already had another."

"I'm sorry, sir," I said, and I was.

He smiled wryly and moved a plant down.

"So there's no other?" I asked, and it embarrassed me that I had. I felt I had pried. Which I had.

"No, army life is conducive to neither the romantic nor the domestic," he said. "And no one here in this city wants to be known as consorting with the enemy, even though the war's over."

We worked quietly for a while. Then he changed the subject.

"That man that holds court down at Buckelew's. I think I've seen him before. I know I've seen him, unless he has a doppelganger, as the Germans call it."

He always had a sense for the truth, Elias did.

Well, let's give Mr. Roosevelt the rest of the day off, shall we my dear?

Feb. 23, 1937, Tuesday

How does one tell a lover that his or her affections are no longer desired and not have it sting? Is there a way to build a scaffold around them, a bracing so that they aren't crushed by the truth? An anesthetic, perhaps? Does a shot of brandy help? Is rye whiskey preferable to bourbon? How does one accomplish such a thing from so far away?

Feb. 24, 1937, FWP, Transcript of Bridget Fenerty

It was an evening that the sky turned from brilliant blue to gray, and then a cold rain fell, and then ice and sleet rattled off the roofs and porches. Snow fell thick and then rose from the ground until the clouds moved off with a brisk cold wind, and the moon made it all glow, glowing around the black trees and the black houses. The house was cold, and I kept a fire going in the hearths of his room and mine.

He was a restless sleeper, Elias was. Most nights I could hear him shout in his sleep, though I could never make out what he was saying, only that it sounded anguished, the sound of someone traversing a private hell. I think he was glad on the nights he was pulled from bed to pay a call on someone who was sick.

We get snow here once a year, on average, and it's like a holiday with no set date. It just shows up unannounced. Well, on that night, the night that the snow fell, I was in his room putting wood on the fire when I heard him rustle, and then he threw the sheets and blankets off. He curled himself up in a ball and then straightened out with his hands over his eyes and said, *"Good God, how many more?"*

He seemed awake for a moment. He looked up at the ceiling at the smudges of shadows and light that echoed off the fire in the hearth, and I had such pity for him, you see. He seemed alone, alone in this world and in his dream world. I knew what alone felt like, and my heart was breaking for him.

I pulled the sheets and quilts up over him again. He was weeping. Fast asleep and weeping. I couldn't leave him in such a state as that.

That was the night that I got in bed with him.

I got in bed with him and held him. Nothing else happened, I just held him, the same as I would do for a child in the midst of a bad dream, which he was. I held him as he trembled, shivering against the cold and the past that stalked him. I held him until I heard his breathing dissolve into snoring, and then I slipped myself out of his bed and went and got back in mine. But I clutched a pillow, trying to recreate the feeling of how good it is to feel another's warmth against you.

I listened in the direction of his room as he slept quietly the rest of the night. The next morning, he came down for breakfast, and he seemed to have no memory of any of it. I eyed him as I flipped the bacon and spoke above the sizzle of it.

"Good morning to you. How'd you sleep, sir?"

"Never better. Like I slept when I was a boy," he said.

It was gratifying to know he had slept so well, but I also realized how much he had comforted me without knowing he did, and I had enjoyed the physical closeness of his body next to mine. After all, we were a man and a woman at the heart of it, weren't we now?

And that's how it began, with simple, easy cuddling. I suppose that's how it often begins, isn't it? A closeness that's not meant to be anything else. A well-meaning, innocent intention.

The night terrors didn't stop, of course. He had accumulated enough in four years to last him the rest of his life. They returned, accompanied by his shrieks and groans, shouts out into the house in the night, sleepwalking, searching, searching, looking through the house, completely unaware that he was asleep. I was afraid he might fall down the stairs in his sleep, so I would gently take his hand in mine and lead him back to his bed, lying with him until good sleep overcame fitful sleep. I never spoke to him when he was in his state, afraid he would wake and be embarrassed.

I couldn't bear to hear him tortured so. And, of course, as I said, if the truth be told, I enjoyed feeling him in the bed next to me. Houses got cold back then, before the gas heat, when fireplaces were all there were to warm them. I was always careful to get up after he fell into a deeper, peaceful sleep and before I myself went to sleep in his bed. It was only a matter of time that I would slip.

And so it happened. I woke one night to see his face looking at me. It looked different in the moonlight, older perhaps.

"Miss Fenerty, how did you get here?"

"Sorry, sir. You were having a terrible nightmare."

I flipped the covers back and moved so as to get out of the bed as the cold poured in around me, but he gently took me by the shoulder.

"No. Stay," he said.

I settled in next to him. It was awkward, resting shoulder to shoulder, our hands clasped over our chests. Next thing I knew, it was morning.

From that night on, we fell into the habit of sharing a bed together, with the flimsy excuse of warmth, sure, but for the companionship, the closeness of one human being for another. When the weather began to warm in the first days of spring, we kept to the same bed, shedding altogether the excuse for warmth. His nightmares were fewer when we slept next to each other, which was most nights. It was only when we knew a call was likely that I slept in my own chambers, to keep from arousing suspicion.

I know what you're thinking, Miriam, and let me tell you this: we were chaste for quite a long time, longer than you might imagine. And then as you might also imagine, one night I found myself atop him, my gown cast aside and my hair and my breasts hanging down toward him, his hands and his manhood reaching up for me. It was all so dreamlike, like a trance, a scene that plays out behind a screen of thin white muslin cloth.

The next morning, I awoke to find myself alone in his bed. I hurriedly put on my gown and dressed in my room. I looked for him downstairs and heard him in his study, the squeak of his chair as he read. I peeked in and could see his pants legs and shoes, already dressed for his day. I put on my apron and got to work.

I was in the kitchen reaching for something in a high cabinet, suddenly aware of how my blouse and apron pulled against my breasts, aware of how my skirt fell over my hips. I retrieved whatever it was I needed, and, when I looked over, I jumped. There he was waiting for me in that apologetic way of his, the same manner he had when he had to tell a loved one bad news, a dejected, pained look. Arms to his side, a stare that falters toward the floor, a wilting look.

He was a man of great skill, and I sometimes accompanied him on his rounds, watching him set a broken leg or a broken arm, stitch together a deep cut, the same beefy red under the skin, whether white or black. Maneuver a stuck baby out of a writhing woman, or, just as deftly, maneuver the story out of how someone who was sick or injured. But just then he looked awkward.

"Miss Fenerty, I wanted to tell you..." he said to the floor.

I set the article down, whatever it was, and used the back of my hand to sweep a stray lock of auburn hair out of my eyes. It was still red then. I tucked it under my white cap.

"You've got nothing to tell me," I said. "I have no misgivings about what we did for each other. And the truth of it is, I don't expect a wage if we're to live in such a manner as we did last night, which I would be altogether willing to do. I don't want you to feel as though I'm a kept girl or a woman of easy virtue. Just keep the roof over our heads. Just provide for us, that's all I ask," is what I said.

"Yes," he said, and he cleared his throat. "Yes, of course."

From that night forward, behind closed doors, we lived as man and wife, though not in the eyes of any church or courthouse. There was one thing that he had to make clear, however. He was worried he would get me with child.

"I don't think it's possible," I said. "I haven't had a monthly since-"

I broke off my sentence. It was impossible to lie to the man, no one could. The truth would just bubble out while he looked at you and waited on it. Perhaps that was part of his skill, his gift.

"-since the baby," I muttered.

There, I'd said it, and then I told him all of it while he sat and crossed one leg over the other, his hands clasped together over his knee, waiting for the truth.

He didn't say a word in judgment of me, or the Burtons, or anyone. He merely said, I'm sorry for your suffering. Then he said it was well known in the medical books, something called Simmons Disease.[41] Then he said it was unlikely I would ever have children. I'm sorry, he said. And then he pulled me to himself.

At the end of that week, the week we first enjoyed the blessing of making love, the question of my wages came up again, and I'll have you know that I refused them. It freed my conscience for the enjoyment of our intimacy, on nights when we watched the rain bead onto the window, small crystal pebbles made amber by candlelight, his arms around me, his weight behind me, pressing into my back. My breasts lounging onto his forearms, or the feel of his beard on my chest between the soft, suppleness of them or his beard on the skin above my navel and then the skin below. You can see how, even when the passion that two share fades with time and age, the simple memory of it keeps them bonded for the rest of their lives.

In public, I continued to play the role of housekeeper, dressing and acting the part, but, in the evenings, we sat side by side in front of the fire or lay exhausted in its shimmer. I longed to hold his hand in public, something I never did, or flirt openly at the market like any other couple, or attend programs side by side at the Gaiety Theater or Talley's Opera House. Many days, he would come home, and, as soon as he was in the door and it was closed behind us, he would gather me into him, and I would press my cheek into his chest and he would put his big arms around me. We shut the door on

---

[41] Very likely Simmond's syndrome, or now more specifically described as Sheehan's syndrome.

them, a city of clucking hens and strutting roosters. We shut out their judgment.

To become a couple suitable for public display would mean a trip to a church, and neither of us could believe in a God that would cast such heartache on a world he created, and neither of us could take up the hypocrisy of saying we did. We had seen too much. So we left things as they were.

There was a man named Allen[42] who was an architect and had a band that gave concerts for the town's amusement on the courthouse lawn in the summer months. Elias and I would sit just far enough apart to avoid suspicion, but I yearned to able to hold his hand or lean my temple into his shoulder as the band played "Her Bright Smile Haunts Me Still" and the other popular airs of the day.

My thirtieth birthday arrived for me, and he put a sign on the door, *Please See Dr. Cutliffe on Milam Street*, and we celebrated by keeping all day to bed, while outside a cold February drizzle shut out the rest of the world. Eating in the kitchen, wrapped only in quilts, reading quietly in bed side by side, waiting for the next wave of passion to boil up in one of us.

To feel your body, your sex, strain for another person's. What a gift, what a blessing, as natural as the first breath of a baby. We're all born with it. On days such as that, my thirtieth, when the weather was cold, I would watch as he would leap from under the covers to put another bit of wood or coal on the fire. I would admire his naked figure as the firelight played upon it, and his shadow trembled on the wall and the ceiling to the dance of the flames. His bearded silhouette making him look like one of the gods in the books the Prudhomme children read. When it was my turn to stoke the fire, I stood there for a moment, perfectly aware he was looking at me, the play of the amber light over my curves, my hair let down on my shoulders for the night. My body was beginning to billow at that age, which was considered alluring, the ideal in those days. I would turn around in my nakedness and see his smile in the yellow-orange light, his hands laced behind his head. Then I would jump back under the covers to the warmth again.

What a strange and happy thing it is, to hold someone close and feel the silent electricity as your bodies burn calmly in the wake of shared passion. To feel someone's fingers stroke the nape of your neck or the small of your back. To run your fingers through their hair as the two of you breathe deeply, and you nudge into the small hollow of their chin and chest. What a strange and happy thing.

When the weather was pleasant, we would travel to the country side and spend the day and then the night there, leaving his patients in the care of Dr.

---

[42] Shreveport architect Capt. N. S. Allen

Cutliffe. There was a town in those days called Ananias, and Elias knew of a spot on the lake, Caddo Lake, where the sun would set over the far bank, bearded black cypresses against an orange sunset. Under the starry sky, we lay on a blanket while the locust droned out chorus after chorus. The boiling vibrations of insects in the night treetops. The embers of lightning bugs, floating and dashing above us as we reclined panting after our love. There in the wilderness, we could be free to be a couple and enjoy the simple arithmetic of how one plus one can equal everything else. How it can equal the whole world.

Oh, the phone is ringing. Let me get it.

February 24, 1937, Wednesday

The phone rang, and, as she answered it, I thought of the exquisite loneliness of loving someone and not being able to display it. How many are there in the world, people who are in love with someone of the wrong sex or race or station or religion? Are there people who continue to love that way but keep it secret? Or give up their true love and take up a lie that's more convenient?

I heard Miss Fenerty's voice from far away.

"'Twas Nina. The baby's awake, and she'd like for us to come see him. Would you drive, dear?"

"Gladly," I said.

As we exited the house, I noticed the shed out back. People in the Hamptons would call something like it a 'carriage house.' The doors were paired and made of vertical slats, painted white with green trim, but in need of another coat of both. Dusty windows hinted at the darkness inside. She saw me looking to them.

"Take a quick look if you like," she said, and she handed me the key to a padlock holding the doors together.

She stood by the Packard, leaning on her cane as the doors creaked in response to my opening them. Inside, it was dark and dusty like the tomb of King Tut. The detritus of three quarters of a century lurked in the shadows. There were boxes, old horse collars and other tack no longer needed. Cast-off furniture, crates with cheerful labels, *Ruston Peaches, Tangi Brand Louisiana Strawberries, Blackburn's Cane Syrup Jefferson, Tex.*

"There's a fine difference between a junk store and a museum," she mused. "A lot of those boxes contain Mrs. Taylor's clothes. She had quite a collection, a real clothes *harse*. Enough to feed a swarm of moths for months."

"What treasures," I said as I squeezed down a small alley between rows of articles. High chairs where generations of children had sat and been coaxed to take a bite. Trunks with clothes long since out of style. A pair of bicycles, tires dry-rotted and flat. A canvas bag with *Excelsior Laundry* written on it lay on its side.

"That punching bag made out of a laundry sack, that was Morris'," she said from the sunshine outside. In the middle of the menagerie, covered with cast off things, was a carriage, big-spoked wheels and the limbs where a team of horses had once pulled. I knew right away the names of them.

Tom and Jerry, Jay-ree, I thought. And then, wiping my hand across the side, a swirl of dust erupted. There it was, *S. Rusk, Carriage for Hire* in gold letters on a pine green background. On the buckboard, horse hair stuffing pushed out from a crack in the leather covering.

"My brother's watch is in there someplace, in a box somewhere," she said into the dark as I rubbed dust off my hands and looked in wonder at the artifacts. "Some of Mr. Rusks' things, the Eaves boys' bicycles."

I was mesmerized by all the history in the shed. Everywhere I looked was something else of interest. Her voice summoned me, and I emerged from the shed and shut the doors. They squeaked back into place, and I locked the padlock.

"Well, we better be off if we're to catch the baby awake. Never awaken a sleeping baby."

"Did Miss Leslie's book say that?" I asked as I gave her back the key.

"That's just common sense, dear." She playfully wrapped me on the backside with her cane and smiled.

We drove west, past the Methodist temple at the head of Texas Street, down the hill to a part of town called St. Paul's Bottoms. Her little old head peered out, just tall enough to see out the window, the white hair on it seeming to be in the process of evaporating.

"The brothels were all down this way," she said casting her finger in a line back and forth at an area out the window. "Either the valley of sin or the garden of delight, depending on who you asked. Bea Haywood's place was right over there. Annie McCune's was down that way. Oh, you should have seen the crowds of young men on Saturday nights."

Negro children played in the street, jumping rope, pigtails bouncing with colorful berets, boys running off like a flock of birds taking flight. Brown faces singing, brown hands clapping out rhythms. She waved to them, and they waved back and returned to their play.

"What are these purple trees?" I asked, looking up through the windshield at the magenta blossoms.

"Redbuds," she said proudly, happily. "The first sign of spring. Won't be long now."

Nina and her husband the reverend live in the whitewashed parsonage of the Ezekiel Baptist Church. The reverend met us at the door, grasping our hands in the two of his, and thanking us for our visit, holding Miss Fenerty's arm and helping her up the steps. He was in trousers, starched white shirt, and suspenders with a tie, having just returned from 'visitation.'

"Easy now, Miss Biddy," he said.

Inside, Nina was as big as ever but holding a small bundle of an infant that seemed even smaller next to her size. Miss Fenerty tottered over to them, and Nina smiled up to her with pride and pulled the edge of the blanket away from a little face.

"Ah, but would you look at him! Isn't he a right handsome devil? Oh, angel, reverend, angel, surely, 'tis."

"Have you named him?" I asked.

"Not yet. We're still trying to figure out who he wants to be. He's gonna wear that name a long time," Nina said as she smiled into the face of her baby. "We're thinking Benjamin, after his grandpa Ben."

We took turns holding him. When it was my turn, Reverend Beannock eased him down to me, and I took the little weight uneasily. I was afraid I would hurt him.

"He won't bite you, dear," Miss Fenerty said. "Just relax. Hold him to you."

I realized that I've never held a baby before. Not once. I marveled at how good it felt, like a new, warm loaf of bread. What a blessed thing, to hold a new life close to you, little eyes behind flimsy new eyelids, dreaming blank dreams, clean and new and untroubled by a restless world. Having children never made sense to me before. It's always seemed like an illogical proposition, until today.

A conversation spun itself into the room, but I barely noticed. I was enthralled with the child who might be named Benjamin Beannock, we'll see, for he'll wear it a long time, with God's good grace and help, according to the reverend. When they took him from me and gave him back to his mother, I felt a small sting, a mere splinter compared to the beam of a crushing blow that Miss Fenerty must have felt when her baby was handed to Nancy Burton.

On the way back to drop off Miss Fenerty and return to Stephenson, I scoured the streets for the Cadillac. There's been no sign of it for several days. I'm beginning to allow myself to believe that he was sent by Mr. Alsberg to look in on Lemurier, and now he's gone for good.

I received three letters today, all unsettling.

One: Irving threatens to come to Shreveport, so I wrote him to say that I stay incredibly busy, and it would be a bore and a waste of his time.

Two: Mr. Alsberg asks me what progress has been made and wonders if

I've interviewed anyone other than Miss Fenerty. He has a position back east in Sag Harbor on Long Island, several Union army veterans, and men who served on whaling ships. Six months ago it would have been perfect. I have no desire for it now. I've already sent a letter declining.

Three: Mother wants to know about flowers and a specific date in June so she can reserve the synagogue.

I can't keep putting her off.

Feb. 25, 1937, FWP, Transcript of Bridget Fenerty

Gossip and masturbation are the two simplest forms of human entertainment, but isn't it so, then? I ran into one of them at Mr. Ripinsky's store. Gossip of course 'twas, not the other. [*laughter*]

A lady, whose name I won't mention because she has descendants, and prominent ones, still living in this town, began spreading stories that Elias and I were more than employer and employee, a fact that was the truth, of course, but it was no one else's business. I overheard it in Mr. Ripinsky's store, the whisper of it and then the gasp of the woman's companion. I knew who it was; she had a very distinctive voice, a high-pitched voice that didn't lend itself very well to a whisper, apparently. It was a fluty, birdlike warble.

I waited on the bench outside the store, an old church pew that was set out there under the awning. When Mrs. X came out, she was shocked to see me, the very object of her juicy morsel. Well, if you want to get someone's goat, pay them a compliment they know they don't deserve. It's like handing them a burning hot coal.

I complimented her dress and her hat and then spent several minutes complimenting her on her children, the true source of a woman's pride. What well-behaved things they were, angels worthy of sainthood. In reality, it wasn't the case. They weren't bad children, really, they were just children, no better or worse than anyone else's. But every mother wants to hear that hers are extra special. As noble as the saints, as sacred and pure as the baby Jesus.

Well, she took the bait and ran with it, cooing, oh you think so? And, well so nice of you to say! And she added small anecdotes about each one to verify my praise.

I asked her if she would like to take refreshments down the street at the Tea Room, and she said, well, yes. She was well in the net at that point. We even walked arm in arm down the sidewalk as men tipped their hats to us and wagons mumbled down the street.

We took our tea, she in her dress with fancy blue satin skirts and black bodice, me in my plain white muslin dress. She had a hat in the style of the times, a small blue thing that perched on her head, with a couple of black feathers on it. When our tea arrived, I casually changed the subject. I leaned in as if I were telling her a secret, watching my spoon as it stirred around slowly in my cup.

"Tell me, Mrs. X," I said, "which do you believe the worser sin, adultery or gossip? I've thought on the matter, and I'd like to know your thoughts."

I tapped my spoon on the rim of my cup, and it made a ring like the bell before a round in a boxing match. I laid it on the saucer as she sat silently with a look on her face as if I'd betrayed her. I kept going.

"Now, it seems to me that adultery is the harder of the two sins to pull off, as it takes a bit of deception and another willing person. Gossip, however, is much easier, as it only requires a black heart, a quick tongue, and a willing ear."

The ice man and his assistant were delivering just then, through the front door. He struggled with a wet crystal block as big as a cornerstone, flecked with sawdust and dripping in the big tongs they used. He passed our table, excusing himself as he did, and took the block of ice to the back. His assistant followed him with one almost as big. Each block sent a breath of cold air over our table as it went by. Mrs. X absently stirred her tea. I think her hand was shaking a bit. She remained silent, flustered with the turn in our conversation.

"You know, Mrs. X, I've heard it said, in such a way as to believe it, that you think I'm no better than one of Miss McCune's girls and that Dr. Gramhar keeps me in the same manner as one of them, paid for special favors." I leaned back and sipped my tea with a smile.

You see, there was a lady, Miss Annie McCune, who ran one of the biggest brothels in town back then and did so for decades. All legal but kept hidden at the edge of town. But I think I may have told you that already.

Mrs. X shrank back in hearing what I had to say. To hear your own gossip flung back at you will do that. It's much more unpleasant coming back at you than it was going out.

"Well, I-I-" Mrs. X stammered, all the speech she could gather. I knew what I wanted to say, so I said it.

"Well, of course, if it were true, it would be none of your business, then would it? Especially to you who call yourself a Christian lady. And isn't gossip a sin, then?

Then I leaned in again and looked her straight in the eye and said, "Perhaps the question you should ponder isn't *'Is Dr. Gramhar's Bridget kept like one of Miss McCune's girls?'* but rather, *'Is Mr. X one of Miss McCune's boys?'"*

That one hit home, I suppose, for she gathered up her hat and gloves and said, "Thank you for your hospitality, ma'am, but I should be leaving now."

She made her exit so quickly that she dropped one of her gloves and just left it. I suppose that her husband *was* one of Miss McCune's boys and she suspected it was so. She trotted to the door, pushing her bird's nest of a hat back up on her head. Her steps beat on the planks of the sidewalk outside and down the street.

There was never any trouble after that. Either they kept shut or were more careful with their whispers.

February 26, 1937, Friday

This morning, I woke from a dream in which I had had a baby. No labor, no pain, just suddenly I'm holding a baby. It began pleasantly enough, but then, in the dream, I felt I should return it to Irving, and I couldn't find him. Then I got sidetracked in that way of dreams, forgetting my original purpose until I looked down to find that my baby was reduced to a loaf of bread. I woke both relieved and disappointed, and it made me think of Elias Gramhar's nightmares. I wonder if she ever found out their content.

Lemurier and Mirlette are apparently still here. They must have come in very late in the night, as there are dirty dishes in the sink, and their door is closed.

Feb. 26, 1937, morning interview, FWP, Transcript of Bridget Fenerty

You were asking me if Elias ever told me about the content of his dreams. Well, the truth of it is, it took a couple of years for me to even bring it up. It was the spring that somewhere Frank was turning ten, the spring that there were troubles down in Colfax[43], something to do with the election for governor, I believe. Old Mr. Antoine[44] was the Lieutenant Governor. Of course, he was a young man then.

It was on a Sunday morning when we were lying in bed, listening to the bells summoning the rest of town to church. He had been out late the night before attending to some of the town's gadabouts who had gotten into mischief and then mayhem, a frequent combination.

"Your nightmares, you never speak of them," I said. My head was to his

[43] The Colfax Massacre, also referred to as the Colfax Riot. On Easter Sunday, 1873, in the Grant Parish town of Colfax, white Democrats clashed with Republicans and blacks over the disputed gubernatorial election. The courthouse was burned, and over one hundred Negro men were killed, many reports say after they had surrendered.
[44] Caesar Antoine, a Negro from Shreveport, was elected Lieutenant Governor in the disputed election of 1872.

chest.

"How did you know I had nightmares?" he asked.

"You sleep a bit restlessly at times," I said, which was a gross understatement, of course. Poor man. He was so immersed in them, he had no idea that I knew. They were just that private. In fact, he turned his back to me to tell me, and I curled up into it. He pulled in a big breath and sighed and told me, going slow as if he was trying to remember them. As if telling me all of them might make them go away. They all involved battlefield dead. The worst ones involved his old professors at the medical college in Louisville.

They would begin with battlefield sounds, which made sense to me since they seemed to be worse on rainy nights when the roll of thunder mimicked cannons in the distance and the rain on the roof sounded like the rattle of rifle fire. He would find himself in some makeshift hospital, a barn, or a lady's fine parlor or dining room with the mahogany table used for operations. Blood would be dripping onto the sort of fine floors that had been polished on hands and knees with beeswax before the war, on days that no one could imagine how they would be sullied later.

In his dream, he would look in a trance at the blood dripping on the floor, drops cleaving slowly and falling and then hitting the floor in a small, shattered circle. He would find himself unable to move, unable to attend to his task on top of the table, mending the broken. Finally looking up, he would find himself in the surgical amphitheater in Louisville with his professors in the front row of seats. He named them. A Dr. Gross. And a Dr. Yeager or Yardell, or something like it, I believe.[45] Sitting behind them, rising up in row after row were dead soldiers, blank gazes and open mouths staring down at him.

His professors would ask questions with no space for him to answer. The questions would come thick. Their voices were hollow, a waterfall of echoes, one question after the other.

Name the three symptoms of lues tarda. What are the manifestations of Pott's disease? Of scrofula? What are the measures taken against typhus? Tell me, doctor, tell me. If a man has an arm taken away by cannon shot, what is to be done? Can a head that's been severed by a bayonet be reattached? Pray tell us, Dr. Gramhar.

The room would revolve, dead faces spinning, laughing without smiling, and then a blanched face from a stack of bodies would suddenly be wide-eyed and animated, saying *Good God, out with it, man!*

The next part I knew, for that was when he woke, and I heard the response to the questions he had been asked in his nightmare.

I don't know! Elias would wake with a plaintiff howl, an anguished cry, *I*

---

[45] The University of Louisville College of Medicine faculty in the 1850s included a Dr. Samuel Gross and a Dr. Lunsford Pitts Yandell.

don't know! and I would hold him, his eyes blinking in terror as he gazed over my shoulder into the darkness. It hurt me to know that he had had to endure the terror for years, alone, prior to meeting me. I put my arms around him and kissed his back and stroked his hair, sandy and with the first strands of gray.

Well, in those days, the cattle drovers would bring their herds down Texas Street to the river. It wouldn't surprise me at all if there was a thick layer of bullshit below the pavement. *[laughter]* Anyway, they'd get paid and then head for the saloons and brothels, Miss McCune's or Nell Jester's place or one of the others, there were plenty, sure. And of course, if you combine young men and whiskey and guns, then you know what's bound to happen.

Two of the drovers got in an argument over something, something that probably would've been forgotten by both of them the next day. It was the usual order of events, the liturgy of fighting: names were called, punches were exchanged, and then pistols were drawn, and shots were fired, but not mortally in this case.

It occurred right there in front of Buckelew's hardware store, where Champ Lockett sat like a wooden Indian, drawing folks in to shoot the breeze and get invited in to spend money. Elias was in his office down the street, and, when he heard the first shots, he ran down the street without a coat or a hat, just with his black bag. He was there, even before the last shots were fired. One of the boys was grazed off the shoulder, requiring very little other than a bandage. In applying it, Elias saw Champ Locket looking out the window of Buckelew's, absolutely terrified.

Elias told me that, as he reached the scene, stray shots clipped the wall beside the bench, and Champ Lockett scurried inside and hid behind a stack of No. 2 washtubs, only coming out when the street was quiet.[46] Elias said that it all came back to him when he saw the look of terror on Champ Lockett's face. He was almost positive he'd seen the man bolting through the hospital camp of the Greyhound Regiment, the same hell-bent for leather look of horror on his face.

"Are you sure?" I asked Elias.

"Not a hundred percent, but when I saw him with that look, that look of terror, it brought back that memory. 'Look at him go,' someone said that day, 'he's fast enough to be one of ours.' All I know is that there was a man who looked just like him, with that exact same look of terror, running through our camp at Vicksburg, the way deer would come through suddenly, spooked by

---

[46] Champ Lockett's daughter Susie Lockett Breag gives a different account of that day in front of Buckelew's: "Daddy was at his post in front of Mr. Buckelew's that fateful day, and when the shots rang out, he did not hesitate, did not shrink from duty, but subdued one of the men while reasoning with the other, preventing further issuance of blood." *Memoirs of a Confederate Daughter, Vol. III.*

the enemy. In fact, we waited for the rest of the rebels, but he was the only one."

So I'll let you be the judge, Miriam. They say everyone has someone who looks like them. Perhaps there's an old woman sitting in her parlor in Cork who looks just like me, or a young woman walking in a plaza in Seville who looks just like you, or a young woman in Harlem in New York who looks just like Nina. Everyone has a *doppelganger*, as the Germans call it. Well, perhaps 'twas so with Champ Lockett.

The summer advanced, and let me tell you, it was hot. Dogs followed ice wagons and stood in the water dripping from them and caught the drops that fell in between the seams of the floorboards. Everything in the distance shimmered in the hot air, a watery sort of effect. No one ventured into the direct sun for any length of time. It was the time of year that household secrets sometimes escaped through the curtains of open windows, as mundane as who was having mutton chops for supper and as serious as whose marriage was in trouble. Those sorts of things were generally already known, as gossip was as big a form of entertainment as the theater and administered under the innocuous heading of *"Have you heard the news?"*

Well, despite the heat, another form of entertainment, the circus[47], was coming to town, and it was a big event for us. The children of the town were all excited, and, if the truth be told, most of the adults were, as well. Later, all of it was blamed on the circus or the traffic of strangers coming off the river or the boat that had gone down with a load of cattle in the bayou. Those were the suspects for what happened that summer and fall.

Three men had died in an alley off Market Street, and it was thought to have been from drunkenness as they were river men who lived hard. The city fathers swept the deaths under the rug, and my apologies to Monsieur Vauborel for putting it that way. Then one night, there was a knock on our door. It was late, a little after midnight. Elias was sound asleep next to me, and I was studying the moon through the window, a pale yellow thing hanging up there past the night heat. The covers were thrown off, and the silver light of it made us glow white, my breasts luminous with pale circles on them, his back gleaming next to me. When I heard the knock, I jumped and hurried to get my clothes on.

A Negro man, a servant of one of the well-to-dos, was there. He'd come requesting the services of Elias, which was a strange thing, too, for Elias rarely attended to the upper crust of town. Later, it became apparent that quite a number were quietly falling ill, and the town's physicians were beginning to stretch thin. A couple of the town's doctors had left with their families,

---

[47] The Transatlantic Circus visited Shreveport in the summer of 1873.

abandoning the town to the fever. All of it had been hushed up to protect the town's reputation. Progress was calling, and they didn't want us to be bypassed in favor of Marshall or Minden.

Elias saw to them, the families of the small town aristocrats, people who normally wouldn't request his services. People of that station were having to make choices such as that. I accompanied him, as I did sometimes on nights when sleep escaped me. He treated them all, indifferent to their class.

We arrived at the house, which was walking distance, a big house set on a hill near the foot of Cotton Street. It's gone now and has been for years, but it had gaslights that burned all night, an advertisement of luxury in those days. The servant who had come for us opened the door and ushered us in.

The old aunts were seated around the parlor like hens in a henhouse, ensconced in the dim gaslight. A younger woman stood in the middle of the room, clutching a lifeless child to her breast, jostling him as if she were only trying to get him to sleep. The aunts seemed to know that it was too late but were afraid to get up and tell the woman, the child's mother. The child's father was braced against the door frame with a hand behind him and the other cradling his forehead.

Elias gave me his black bag. Then he touched the woman's shoulder and said quietly, "Ma'am? May I?"

She stopped her jiggling of the child and turned her shoulder to let Elias see his face. In the low light, it appeared that the child was only sleeping, but, when he pulled up the boy's eyelid, the stare was undeniable. The child was dead. And he was as yellow as could be.

Elias looked to her and said, "I'm sorry, ma'am. Nothing can be done. The boy is gone."

She jerked the child away from him, and I'll never forget the look on her face, the look of pure indignation. She yelled at poor Elias, who had only told her the truth.

"You lie!" she screamed. "You lie, you lie! You! Lie!" and she collapsed on Elias' chest with the child between them. Her crying was muffled into his shoulder as she sobbed bitterly.

The child's father pulled her back by her shoulders and said gently, "Come now, mother." The father took the child, and the mother collapsed in a ball on a settee. At last, the old aunts rose from their nests and surrounded her, stroking her hair and clucking and cooing.

At home the next morning, we sat quietly in the parlor. I had made biscuits and bacon, but neither of us had much of an appetite.

"You know what this is, don't you? What the child had? You've seen it, haven't you?" he asked.

"Yes," I said. "I know. I've seen it."

'Twas the way of the fever, you know. One case, then a day without, then a few, then half a dozen or so, then a few less. Someone always wants to blame it on bad potato salad or spoiled milk, usually the Merchants' Committee or the Chamber of Commerce trying to keep the town's reputation clean, but then the day comes that a dozen get it, and then two dozen, and no one can deny it. And so it was that summer.

All traffic to and from the city was stopped, no boats, no trains. We were becoming locked in, and I tried to convince Elias to leave. But, once I said it, I knew that to even entertain the possibility that he would leave was an insult.

"Certainly not," he said, never looking up from the textbook at his desk. "I took the Oath of Hippocrates."

The weather stayed hot, as it does here well into September and sometimes October. People began dying faster than they could be buried. Wagons rumbled down the streets, about the only sound now that the sounds of commerce had been silenced. No trains huffing, no steamboat whistles shrieking. Most people who went out wore masks, though some didn't. We still didn't know it was the mosquito what brought it. Not the circus. Not dead cattle in Cross Bayou. The mosquito.

Well, there's nothing like an epidemic to show you whose lifeboat you'd get in and whose you wouldn't. Many spent long days and nights tending the sick, including most of the clergy who would end up preaching funerals for their patients when they were unsuccessful in nursing them to health.

Elias and I were among those making rounds. Horrible sights, whole families taken, or perhaps worse, all but one taken, leaving the one left to contemplate why they were spared. Everyone wore black despite the heat.

It was on an evening when we had just returned home and were sitting on the porch together, wishing for the air to stir a little.

"Perhaps it's time we should marry," Elias said.

We had avoided such talk all those years. Maybe we were scared of changing our world by doing it, but now the world was changing anyway.

"All right," I said. Ordinarily, I would have been moved to a great show of happiness. But happiness had been cancelled for our town.

Now there was a Judge Hall[48] who was as close to a friend as Elias had in town, a man who had served in the Confederate Army, a man who had seen enough hatred for a lifetime. Perhaps they would have been better friends if the sore heads of the town had allowed it.

Well, we stopped at Judge Hall's house, which was on McNeil, I believe, though I may be mistaken. The judge said he would be honored to marry us when the town was right again, but his wife was sick, and he didn't feel his

---

[48] Judge Henry Gerard Hall

heart would give it the joy it deserved until she recovered. Well, his wife ended up dying, and one of their children, and then the judge himself would die the next month. The fever, all of them.

September rolled on, and still we waited on cooler weather. Boats stayed tied up in the river, silently watching our struggle. We spent long days and nights, doing what little we could for the sick and dying.

In the four years that he and I shared a roof, Elias Gramhar rarely slept past five in the morning, even after a night of being up. He was a man of regular habits in that way and in many ways. When he kept to bed that morning, I knew something was wrong.

I had put the last of the coffee on, waiting for him to come down for it. I went upstairs after a time and found him still asleep. There was an enamel basin at his bedside. As I went for it, my footsteps must have woken him.

"I'll get that," he said from the bed, though he made little effort to get up.

There was black vomit in the basin.

He spent the rest of the day in bed, though he attempted to rise through the gnawing waves of his nausea, getting only as far as sitting on his bed with his head in his hands, his fingers weaving in his sandy brown hair. The night was worse. A man whose wife was sick came for him a little after sunset, and I had to tell him the doctor himself was ill. I sent him away with a promise that we would stop by the next day when the doctor had recovered.

But in the morning, if anything, he was worse. I sat by his bedside, washing his face. His beard was flecked with clumps of black, and, under the yellow-brown whiskers, his cheeks were hollow and pale. He had purple circles under his eyes.

"I should have married you when I had the chance," he mumbled. "I should have made a will. At least you'd get the house. But too late now."

"Shhh! Such nonsense," I whispered to him as I dabbed the sickness out of his beard. "This is the worst it'll be. By tomorrow, we'll have you sitting up in a chair, we will."

"Run and fetch the priest," he muttered. I didn't want to leave him to do it. Besides, I wasn't sure if there was still a priest in town. Four priests had died, and the last one was sick. All of them Frenchmen. All of them from yellow fever.[49]

Of course, he was right. By the next day he could barely speak.

His face was tilted back to the headboard, and his chin toward the ceiling. I pushed my arms under his chest, into the dampness of the bedsheets, and put my ear to his chest. I could hear the air rattle inside, and his kind heart labor.

At last, he whispered to me. He said, "You're the only one who ever..."

---

[49] In all, five French priests died in the Yellow Fever epidemic in Shreveport in 1873.

I'm sorry, Miriam. I've never spoken of this to anyone. Not in sixty years. Not ever.

He said, "You're the only one who ever made…"

I'm sorry, dear. Give me a moment.

"He said…he said…you're the only one who ever made me want to believe in God again."

Yes, dear. I believe you're right. That will be enough for today.

Feb. 26, 1937, Friday, midday

She cried this morning. Not the weeping, keening cry of the mourning Irish, but a slow, smoldering cry, a cry borne out of uselessness and frustration, a cry that seeped out of her. Tears pinched themselves out of her eyes and found the channels in the wrinkles on her cheeks. It was a cry that had certainly occurred before, many times before, and it seemed to know what to do with itself, like a river knows its way to the sea. I stayed until she had cried all she needed to, until a smile emerged like the sun behind rain clouds that have spent themselves.

"Sorry to tear up, dear." She seemed amused at herself for having done so. "Sometimes the sadness needs to get out and stretch its legs a bit." She grinned and wiped her eyes with the back of her old spotted hand. Then she said, "Come back this afternoon, and we'll talk some more for Mr. Roosevelt. I believe there's a nap in me that needs some attention."

Feb. 26, 1937, second interview, FWP, Transcript of Bridget Fenerty

He died later that day, the first day of October, and was buried in a common grave with all the rest that died that day and the day before and the day after. Lieutenant Woodruff was one, and the man who ran the ice plant. One of the French priests, as well, the one who came from Monroe.[50] Close to a dozen. His body was laid in next to several people who wouldn't have given him the time of day in life. I found it odd that they would spend eternity together.

A month later, it was all over. The air was cool and brisk and stayed that way. In the end, almost a thousand were dead, one of every four persons. Some of the ones who survived left, most of them for good. I stayed. And this time when I stayed, I knew it would be for good. My memories were here,

---

[50] The subject is referring to Lt. Eugene Woodruff, US Army Corp of Engineers, Charles Horne, engineer at the ice works, and Father Gergaud.

and they would keep me here.

Among those who left were the troops. The government withdrew them not long after. I suppose they felt they had done all they could with us and that any further effort would be futile. The town watched in silent celebration as the blue uniforms with black faces, most of them, filed onto steamer after steamer. There was no cheering as I remember.

The house was empty again, quiet except for the silent echoes of the shouts and giggles of the Lundgren girls and Elias reading poetry to me. They were painful memories, sweet ones, but painful all the same. But, as Mr. Rusk said, I didn't choose the pain, but I could choose whether or not to suffer from it. I stayed and put on a mask of cheerfulness to hide the devastation inside. There was simply no other choice.

Money wasn't the issue. I still had plenty of it, thanks to Mr. Burton and his gift, but I had no one to love and no one to do for, and it left an awful hole. Elias had died intestate, that is, without a will. Poor, optimistic Elias. He had seen people die on a weekly basis and never thought it would happen to him personally. Of course, it'll happen to all of us. We all take our first steps on this earth, and we all take our last, as Mr. Rusk said.

The house was sold at a sheriff's sale, as he had no heirs and there was no will. It was bought by a mysterious man no one ever saw, a person who went by the name of Ned Hennessy.

Yes, Miriam, you know why I'm smiling. 'Twas me, of course, acting through a lawyer who had an office off Milam Street, a Mr. Herndon. Ned would have been so pleased to have held the title of such a house as this one. From that day forward, the mysterious Mr. Hennessy rented the house with the condition that I came with it.

A house is one thing, but to have it animated with life is another, so Mr. Herndon and I put an ad in the paper. House for rent, housekeeper included. It sounded better than 'boarding house.'

Well, a man who went by the name of Taylor responded to the advertisement in the paper. I say his name was Taylor, but it had been something else, a hard slurry of consonants beginning with a K, something from the countries around Russia, not a soft sound in it. He said it to me once, and it was the sound of a shovel pushing into gravel. It had been changed quickly on Mr. Taylor's father's arrival at the port of New York.

The clerk had asked him, he says, "Name?" and old Mr. K-something's English was poor then and besides he was tired and nervous. I could remember the feeling fresh off the boat, your body still leaning this way and that, still full of the motion of the sea. Well, he had thought the man had asked profession, and so he responded "I am tailor."

And the clerk wrote down *I. M. Taylor*. Old Mr. K-something, now a newly minted Mr. Taylor, didn't want to cause a stir so he stuck with it. With a new language to learn, it was easier to write down Taylor rather than that other one, K whatever it was, and, of course, it made blending in better. Nevertheless, I thought it sad that the family's proud name, handed down lovingly from father to son to son, the name that had fought the Cossacks and endured the pogroms of the Tsars through decades, centuries perhaps, was struck down in three seconds with the stroke of a clerk's pen.

The Taylors were Jewish. I had several other offers, but I felt a bond with the children, you see, as Elias had delivered them both, difficult breech deliveries, and I had been there when they were born, both of them, holding them as their mother napped after their birth. There were two of them, Leah was the oldest, and Morris the younger, a girl and a boy. By the time I went to work for them, in seventy-three, they were both toddlers. A delightful age for children if you ask me.

Isaac Taylor was a slight man with thick spectacles. He worked late into the night, most nights, struggling to keep up with the bills generated by the lifestyle of Mrs. Taylor. He was a man who walked with his arms straight down to his sides, as if the life was being sucked out of him or as if he was being beaten by invisible spirits. If you knew Mrs. Taylor, you would have an idea why.

Her name was Bathsheba, Bathsheba Taylor. She went by the name Battie, which didn't have the meaning it does now, but it could have. I don't recall anyone ever calling her by her first name except for Mr. Taylor, and then it was only once or twice. She was always Mrs. Taylor to me and to everyone else in town. Mr. Taylor usually called her Shama or something like that.[51]

I'll tell it to you plainly, Miriam. She was a verbally cruel woman, a caustic woman, capable of cutting remarks delivered with a smile and a high-pitched, shrieking laugh. She had a gnawing need to belittle, as if there were a rat inside her and if she didn't turn it on others, it would devour her. Her head and chest were small and out of proportion to her teeth and her arse, which made her look like a horse or a rat or both. In those days of the bustle, Mrs. Taylor scarcely needed one. She had an exaggerated sense of her own importance and had to be the 'bride at every wedding and the corpse at every funeral,' as the saying was.

I've never met anyone who could spend money like her. It seems I was constantly changing out curtains for them. Furniture would arrive in crates on the steamers from New Orleans after a journey across the sea from London and Paris. Decorating the house was left up to my mistress. Keeping it clean was left up to me. It was easy, too, as things rarely stayed long enough in the

---

[51] Neshama, 'darling,' or literally, 'soul.'

house to collect any dirt or dust.

Mr. Taylor worked long hours, deep into the night to sustain his wife's domestic tastes. New furniture, new dresses for the Purim Ball the Jewish folk held in those days. Hats, dresses, shoes. New hats, new dresses, new shoes. Newer hats, newer dresses, newer shoes. Mr. Taylor always saw to it that she had the latest fashion, or, I should say, Mrs. Taylor saw that Mr. Taylor saw to it.

And despite all her spending, she always found a way to short me on my pay, and Mr. Taylor knew it. He would come in late, slump in a chair and ask me, "How much are you owed, Bridget?" I always told him how much, never any more than I had coming, and he would count it out, peering through the small glass circles of his thick spectacles. His fingertips were speckled where he had stuck himself with pins in the course of his long day.

The children, Leah and Morris, were two lovely things that had gotten all the goodness of their father, angelic things who napped in the afternoon together on a settee in the parlor, their heads at opposite ends with their feet together. They were three years apart, the girl older than the boy, but both of them beautiful, beautiful children, their eyes closed like little lambs sleeping, their lips parted and the air nudging them slightly.

The boy, Morris, wasn't yet privy-trained, and of course it fell to me to do it. He would stop his play and put his hand to the back of his britches and say, "Oh, Miss Biddy, it comin' out!"

I would grab his little hand, and we would run, the little fellow half running and half dancing, trying to hold it in. We would laugh and run, and I would say, "Stay in little mud cake, don't come out yet, don't come out!" and he would parrot me, "No, no, no mutt-kick, don't you come out!" Then I would sit patiently beside him on the plank in the dark and then show him how to clean himself. I had him trained within a week. I trained many a child like that, sitting with them, singing songs and telling stories while we waited for them to do their business.

The girl and I liked to bake together on Saturday afternoons, gingerbread or sweet rolls and the like, the house smelling warm and inviting, especially on cold rainy afternoons like this one. She would set at least two aside for her father who was working at his shop, *one from me, one from brother*, she would say. We would place them in a basket with kitchen towels around them, and she would write in her little girl handwriting, backward Ps, "For Papa." I could have corrected her, but I knew he would be amused by her spelling and besides, the note was from her heart rather than mine.

Within a couple of years, the girl made the age for starting school, and Mrs. Taylor enrolled her at St. Mary's Convent School. They took all denominations and besides, it was where all the best people were sending their children, and that was all Mrs. Taylor needed to know. It broke poor little brother's heart on the mornings she left for school without him, so I would give him tasks to keep him occupied. He was so earnest, just like his father.

On Saturdays, I would take the children to see their father in his shop. The walls were lined with bolts of fabric, grays and blacks and blues for winter, beige and whites for summer, stacks of bowler hats, waistcoats, cravats on hangers. Their father would always be hunched over a sewing machine with a tape measure draped about his shoulders, his foot working the treadle as the whole apparatus made a thack-thack-thack sound, his spectacled eyes on the seam, the tip of his tongue at the corner of his mouth, his hand on the wheel at the side of the machine. The children would run up to him, *Papa, Papa, Papa*, and he would look up and smile wearily and straighten his back as if it took great effort, which I suppose it did.

We returned in the evening with his supper, which he took in the light of a lantern, chewing absently and watching his children from behind lenses so thick his eyes looked big. His children poked about his shop, examining everything like children will do. He would let them make small things from scrap, little Leah cutting with the scissors as they crunched through the fabric, her tongue tip resting at the corner of her mouth in concentration just like her father. Morris watching her in the ridiculous outfits Mrs. Taylor had me dress him in.

"One day, vhen you are a leetle older I vill make you a suit fit for a young man, a gentleman," Mr. Taylor told his son.

"It's how she has me to dress him, sir," I muttered to Mr. Taylor.

He nodded his head slowly with a grim look on his face. It was a look that said there was nothing we could do about it.

His shop flourished due to his industry and skill. He knew how to make a suit that made a man seem an inch taller. He would quietly boast to bachelors that if they didn't want to be a groom within six months, then they should shop elsewhere, for the ladies would certainly begin noticing them in one of his suits. And it wasn't an idle boast.

I have here somewhere a clipping from the paper of the day. Let's see. Here it is.

[Patrick, I still have the clipping she gave me. I'll include it here. —Aunt Miriam.]

Isaac M. Taylor

Keeps on hand a full assortment of cloths and trimming for gentlemen. Particular attention given to the manufacture of clothing made to order, and a fit is guaranteed. Corner Milam and Market.

Feb. 27, 1937, Saturday

After she found the clipping, we called it a day and gave Mr. Roosevelt and his recorder a rest. We visited a while longer, and then I returned home with leftovers: roast, rice and gravy, all smelling heavenly on the front seat of the Packard. That was last night.

Went to temple this morning, and Mr. Taylor was cantor. I got the giggles imagining him holding his pants and warning mutt-kick to stay in as he ran to the privy in his finery. I had to excuse myself from the quiet reading of the Torah and have an extended belly laugh on the steps on Cotton Street.

I went from there to the Western Union office to wire flowers to my parents for their anniversary, which is sometime around now. I should know it exactly, but I don't. The light bill will have to wait.

Their anniversary is this time of year because I remember Father coming through the door in the winter dark of early evening in his heavy overcoat, a spray of flowers in his hand. He would always hand them to Mother, who would take them with her fingers over her mouth in a Vaudevillian blush, and they would recite their running joke in over-the-top, Yiddish accents. They did it every year, the annual repetition of it making it into a tradition, something of an oddity for a man who joked very little:

Father: Happy Adversary, *Neshama.*
Mother: You mean Anniversary. *('anna-voice-ery')*
Father: Like I said.

They would laugh and kiss, and Mother would put the flowers in a vase where they would be a small outpost of spring in the grip of a New York City winter.

On the card with the flowers, I had the Western Union man put: *To an excellent team.*

Then I wrote a note separately to Mother and mailed it, telling her how much I admired her frugality and industry. *You and Father really do make an excellent team*, I said, *and I'm lucky to have your example.*

Afterwards, I went to hear what became of old Mr. Taylor. I reasoned that he had passed on, but it's a shame he died so young.

At the old house on Crockett, daffodils seemed to have sprung up overnight. They were blooming around the perimeter of the house, small cheerfully petaled faces, yellow leaves on green stems that bent slightly in random directions like a line of school children waiting to reenter the building after recess.

I just saw Lemurier, the first time in several days. He was jumping the fence, backlit by the neighbors' back porch light, his breath a cloud from the cold night air and from his cigarette, which he clinched between his teeth as he vaulted over. He disappeared down the side of the neighbors' house to the street in front of their house, Linden, I think. No telling where he's going.

Out front, on Stephenson, sits the Cadillac. It's not the WPA that's interested in Lemurier. They've already gotten the goods on him and let him go. Who is it, then?

Feb. 27, 1937, FWP, Transcript of Bridget Fenerty

The way Mr. Taylor worked always reminded me of a mule pulling around in a circle, a heavy gait with shoulders sagging, his eyes blank, measuring, cutting, sewing, measuring, cutting, sewing. Round and round, small eyes peering through small lenses, daylight coming through the window facing Market Street, lamplight going out of it at night. He would march off before sunrise and march back after sunset, heavy steps on the porch out there, a cough at the door that sent the children running down the stairs to greet him.

It all unraveled suddenly on New Year's Day of that year, one of the biggest snowfalls I can ever remember.[52] Snow fell all that day and into the night, New Year's Eve. Mr. Taylor was working late, which he frequently did, and we all went to bed thinking nothing of it, waiting on the new year and more snow and Mr. Taylor's return in the morning. The new year and the snow made it right on time. Mr. Taylor didn't.

He always put his coat on a coat rack when he came in late, but when I got up the next morning, it wasn't there. I thought perhaps he'd fallen asleep at his shop, something that happened occasionally on nights when he worked particularly late. So I prepared him some biscuits and jam, lastly pouring him hot coffee in a thick earthenware cup with a saucer over it to keep it hot. Then I set off for Milam and Market Street in the snow, thinking how excited the children would be when they woke to see it.

I let myself in under the sign that said, *Isaac M. Taylor, Finest Gentlemen's Attire*. The bell on the door jingled, and I stepped into the small world of familiar scents, of wool and flannel, linen and leather. I set down his breakfast and coffee and wished him good morning as I took off my coat. The fire had gone out in the night, and the shop was cold. He was asleep at his sewing machine, his glasses on top of his head, the bridge of them over the spot where his hair had thinned to shining, flesh-colored skin. There was a note on the

---

[52] January 1, 1877 brought close to a foot of snow in Shreveport with accumulations of two feet in surrounding areas.

table next to the machine, an old Singer. It was written in a jagged, wavering, shaking hand:

Miss Fenerty, please raise Morris to be a man.

He hadn't signed it. It was then I knew he wasn't asleep. And I knew that he had known his moments were numbered. Fabric was in the machine under the little silver foot, gray flannel trousers, a seam still incomplete.

I ran in the snow to tell the town constable, who came with Dr. Schumpert who verified that Mr. Taylor was dead. Then they went and told Mrs. Taylor. I've always been grateful to them that they did; I couldn't have done it. I think it was the beginning of her descent into her own personal troubles, a fuse that was lit for an explosion that occurred years later. For Mr. Taylor, the coroner's verdict was acute indigestion, what they nowadays call a heart attack. I believe he'd just worked himself to death.

In the Hebrew's Rest section of the Oakland Cemetery, the snow was scraped away and the frozen earth chopped open with picks, and I thought of the song Uncle Jack used to sing in the alley, *ten thousand Micks, they swung their picks.* The ground was opened for him as the men who were hired to do the work muttered under their New Year's Day hangovers, their breath clouding up in the cold, gloved hands on picks and shovels. The hard, shuffling sound of their tools punching the earth.

The family was assembled, for of course, as you know, the body had to be buried before sundown. Leah and Morris crying and shaking under a blanket, Mrs. Taylor staring blankly with tears in her eyes at the rectangular hole in the dirt, like a cellar door in the earth. Around them in black dresses and suits was the congregation, bundled against the cold. The winter wind rustled now and again, sifting snow out of the branches of cedars and scaring whorls of blackbirds out into the white sky.

Afterwards, they sat shiver[53] for him that week, strange chanting in Hebrew, though really, little different from the chanting in Latin that Catholics have. Morris and Leah sat on the floor, and Mrs. Taylor sat on a short stool someone from the temple brought for that purpose. One of the ladies from the temple had me to cover the mirrors and place a pitcher of water near the front door here. Someone else from the temple brought a long candle that was kept lit for a week it seems, and the family, the three of them, wore ribbons, a black button with a black ribbon attached. I drew no baths, as no one bathed that week, and I did very little cooking. Food was brought by the congregation, but the Taylors had but little appetite.

---

[53] Shiva, Jewish ritual of mourning

How unlike death in the Channel. There was no loud wailing, no keening, no telling stories, no passing of a flask among brothers and sons, uncles and nephews. No toasting the dearly departed and no *may God rest their souls and all of the souls of the departed then.* There was no singing, no old aunts thumbing beads, and, of course, no mumbling the Rosary. Everything was quiet except for the low murmur of conversation now and again and the crackle of the fires in the grates when I put a new log on them.

They sat and waited for there to be ten of them, and, when old Mr. Kahn arrived taking off his scarf and hat and gloves, the Kaddish began, the Hebrew sounding like a song. The family kept to the house for a week, and no one bathed, or read, or sang, or anything. Everyone sat quietly and mourned. If Mrs. Taylor said something, the other mourners from the temple would engage her in conversation, but otherwise, nothing, silence. On leaving, however, visitors would tell her the same sort of blessing in Hebrew.[54]

The children endured the muffled shouts outside as down the street their friends played in the snow, a rare treat for southern children. To their credit, Leah and Morris never whined, never breathed a word of it. I think their father would have been proud. By the time the days of mourning were done, it had all melted, even the patches under the trees.

Isaac M. Taylor, Finest Gentlemen's Attire was taken up by Mrs. Taylor, who initially had a flurry of enthusiasm, plans on expansion, both geographically into the stand of the merchant next door and into the realm of ladies' apparel, but those projects fizzled, and she became disinterested quickly enough. She found it hard to keep workers for any length of time as her mercurial temper and her scattered ways kept driving off the best and most talented seamstresses and tailors, leaving only the ones with lesser talent. Leah and Morris were drafted to work after school and on the weekends, including Saturdays, the Sabbath, which I knew would've broken Mr. Taylor's heart. He was a stickler for the Sabbath, Mr. Taylor was.

Isaac M. Taylor, Finest Gentlemen's Attire continued on as the name of the place at Milam and Market, wheezing along under a fading name and a faltering reputation. With time, six, eight years perhaps, the status of the shop had waned almost completely without Mr. Taylor's attention to detail, and, by the time Leah was thrown out by Mrs. Taylor and Morris was on the edge of manhood, the shop had declined completely, mostly selling readymade garments shipped in from elsewhere.

A decline in income had no effect on Mrs. Taylor's ability to spend, however, and soon creditors began to call. I suppose I could have stepped in and fixed it all, as I still had money in the bank, but I knew that to throw

---

[54] Likely it was, *"May God comfort you among the other mourners of Zion and Jerusalem, and may you have no more sorrow."*

money to Mrs. Taylor would only give me the opportunity to throw her more. Even the nicest of people will spend money as long as you give it to them, let alone people of Mrs. Taylor's sort.

I kept the children and their mother fed, and Ned Hennessy kept a roof over their heads (me also, of course), but I refused to pay the bill to keep the latest fashion draped over Mrs. Taylor's ample hindquarters. Years went by, and the four of us kept time as her debt escalated slowly but surely. The cycle of holidays revolved, Hanukkah after Hanukkah, Passover after Passover, the cycle of our birthdays.

Leah made her bat mitzvah the summer that the president was shot and died after a few months.[55] I remember there was talk of it among the adults in attendance. She was twelve or thirteen about then, and so in a month or two she also became a woman in the monthly way, and I had the talk about monthlies and womanhood and the regularity of the moon, and then the talk concerning the strange facts about men and women and the urges that they might feel for one another. We're made out of flesh and blood, aren't we all, and who can deny it, I ask you, then? Mrs. Taylor was either too embarrassed or too busy to give the talk herself. This may surprise you, Miriam, but very little if anything embarrasses me. *[laughter]*

Leah and Morris were working in the shop after school, the public school on Edwards Street, as the Taylors could no longer afford the Convent School. It was at the Edwards Street School that Leah met Will McShan.

He was a boy who had a strong sense of fairness, a swarthy young fellow, a short, dark, powerfully built, kindhearted fellow who, like Leah and Morris, was a child of modest means. The key difference was that he had always been poor; it wasn't suddenly thrust on him the way it was for Leah and Morris. Will worked afterschool and weekends as a stable hand at the Eclipse livery. In fact, he had cared for Tom and Jerry after Mr. Rusk's passing until the horses took their last steps.

More than once, he came to the rescue of Morris, whose mother still insisted he wear his finery, more of a costume than clothes. Will would step into the circle of taunts and shoves that Morris found himself in and scowl and push back against the boys who were tormenting Morris. His intercession on Morris' behalf was in part due to his sense of fairness and the rights of the underdog, but in larger part due to his admiration for Morris' sister.

Leah was becoming a pretty young woman, a lot like you, Miriam, though not quite as tall. Her hair was dark and wavy like yours, and we kept it in curly trellises and bangs which was the way of the times. She was blossoming and the boys were taking notice, and it didn't matter if they were Baptists or

---

[55] President James A. Garfield was shot on July 2, 1881 and died September 19, 1881.

Methodists or Catholics or Jews. No boy with a beating heart gives a fiddler's fart about religious differences when it comes to the fairer sex. A young person's body knows its truth and will hear no other.

It began simply enough, a glance, a word, a small trinket, a token of affection. Hand holding on the porch swing outside, and then arms around one another, and then long walks, and then longer, more secluded walks. Empty errands, I've heard them called. Just two young people enjoying the company of one another. They were fifteen or so by then.

I would happen upon them as I went to take clothes down from the line, their hands wandering over each other as they embraced behind the shed, the looks on their faces. Bewildered with themselves; enthralled with each other. In a state, as they say. The look on her face, the wonderful, worried look of passion rising. I knew it because I had felt it as well. I had felt it as my face put it on, that same look, those years before with Ned, and with Elias. I was afraid where it was headed, afraid of Will and Leah having to deal with the consequences, for, of course, I was acquainted with those, as well.

"Leah," I took her by the shoulders one day when we were alone in the kitchen. "The druggist sells some things," I said in a whisper. "Some protective articles. For Will to wear."

"Oh, Miss Biddy," she said dismissively, in the way of a denial. But I knew. What was I saying then, about a woman's body and its secret?

The months revealed it as it pushed its way out until it was apparent to us women of the household. Dresses no longer fit around the middle and became tight in the bosom. Morris had little knowledge or interest in these things. He probably thought she had been eating too much of Mr. Stoer's Ice Cream or that the old saying about swallowing a watermelon seed was true.

Well, I'll tell it to you plainly, Miriam, for there's no dressing it up. That woman put her daughter, her only, lovely, daughter on the train with a bag. Just one bag. That's it. Of course, many did it that way then, and still do today, some of them, in cases such as that.

Mrs. Taylor wore a green and black day dress made of silk that day. I can see it now; it had a fitted bodice. Hadn't paid the rent in years, a fact that Mr. Hennessy, me really, directed Mr. Herndon to forgive more on behalf of the children than Mrs. Taylor, but she was always, always dressed impeccably. She faced her daughter on the train platform, Leah wearing a white organdy flounced dress with a pink sash around the waist, a matching bonnet with a wide brim and a pink silk ribbon around the crown. I can see it clearly, fifty years later. She would have looked like she was ready for a parlor portrait were it not for her red, wet, swollen eyes. Mrs. Taylor faced her daughter, putting her hands of the girl's trembling shoulders as passengers scrambled by with bags and boarded.

"Esau sold his birthright for a bowl of soup," Mrs. Taylor hissed to her, and then she moved her lips to her daughter's ear, but I was close enough to hear it. "I hope you enjoyed it, dear." And Mrs. Taylor gave her daughter, now the girl she considered her ex-daughter, a smile. An evil, sarcastic smile. The smile faded as she added one more thing.

"From this day forward, you are dead to me."

Leah gave her brother a long hug and sobbed, and the she stepped onto the train, dressed in finery, but with a face as sad as could be. I watched her appear in one window of the train and then the next, until she sat on the side facing us and looked out. She took off the bonnet and set it in her lap. Her sad face was framed by the window of the train.

"Why is she so sad, Miss Bridget?" Morris asked me. "She's only off for a short visit, isn't she? She'll be back soon, won't she?"

I had to choke back my own tears. The boy didn't understand, but I didn't feel it my place to explain.

"Oh, I'm guessing she just loves you so much she's going to miss you while she's away."

What an awful, pitiful explanation, I thought to myself. But I put on a sad smile and waved to Leah, and Morris did, too. Mrs. Taylor made a point of looking away, over the tops of the other cars of the train, off in another direction.

"Where's she going, Mother?" He asked Mrs. Taylor.

"To see Aunt Sally," she told him as she looked down again and stared a hole in her daughter's face, a portrait of shame framed by the casement of the train window.

"Aunt Sally?" Morris asked. "I didn't know we had an Aunt Sally."

You don't have an Aunt Sally, you poor boy, I wanted to tell him. *It's what they call it.*

"Who's Aunt Sally?" He looked up to ask his mother.

"The girl's off to see her Aunt Sally," Mrs. Taylor said under her breath. She had resolved never to utter the name of her daughter again. How hateful. How wretchedly hateful.

The engine began huffing, and the big grasshopper arm began to tilt up and down and back and forward. I looked at the poor girl in the window, her eyes blinking tears. She raised a palm to me and her brother, and perhaps her mother. The conductor leaped onto the steps as the train began to move, *Texas Pacific* in gold writing on the black metal. The conductor blew a whistle with his free hand and shouted, *'Board.* Then the girl and the train and the conductor and the gold *Texas Pacific* letters and the steps, they all slid away.

Leah Taylor was sent away, and for what? Being young? Being human? Answering her body when it called for her? For being in love? I tell you,

Miriam, death cut me off from my family, but it was life, the little life within her, that cut Leah off from hers. 'Twas a shame. I don't know who was more upset, Morris Taylor or Will McShan. He would approach the house, Will would, and ask me if Leah was home.

"No, son," I would say. And then, just when I was about to tell him why, Mrs. Taylor would shoo him away. "Go vay, you're not velcome here."

As weeks passed, Morris realized that his sister wasn't coming back. I think it finally dawned on him when he asked Mrs. Taylor, "Mother, when's Leah coming home?"

"I don't know who you're talking about," she had said.

"Leah, my sister," he said, puzzled by his mother's response.

At that, Mrs. Taylor pounded her fists on the table and screamed, "I don't. Know. Who you're…talking about!"

Morris didn't ask again.

Yes, I think it was then that he finally realized it. He ran up to his room and shut the door, and I could hear him crying. Such loneliness, brought on by spite, pure spite. And it broke my heart, surely it did. I knew what that boy needed was a little love.

So's I went down to the city market where a pack of stray dogs loitered about. I stood there and observed the social order of the dogs. Then I picked out not the biggest nor the smartest nor the quickest but the sweetest looking one, and I lured her home with a leftover biscuit and I fed her on the sly there under the Taylors' house. I went up to Morris' room and whispered for him to come downstairs, that outside there was something I wanted to show him. He looked up with red eyes and followed me down the stairs and out the back door.

"Well, look who's here to see us, would you then?" I said as if the dog had just appeared under the house. She daintily took the biscuit I just happened to have in my apron. I gave one to Morris, and she almost apologetically took it from him, that way some dogs do, you know.

"Well, I think she likes you," I says.

The boy and I named her Queen Victoria, after the English queen, but he didn't know that. We called her Queenie for short. She was a class of dog I can only describe as a hound, a sad-eyed dog who smiled easily and rarely barked.

They became inseparable, Morris and Queenie, rolling on the ground together, playing tug of war with a stick or an old rag. Mrs. Taylor tried to shoo the dog away, frantically shouting *go vay, go vay, go vay!* but the dog wouldn't stay gone long, not with the biscuits that would keep appearing under the house. Like a pure biblical miracle, it was! She finally stopped trying to keep the dog away. The boy and I had won that one.

Morris Taylor spent more time with that dog than any other creature. She would trot at his heels as they walked down Crockett Street, looking up at him, silently asking, "Where are we going now, my boy?" Funny isn't it how a child can learn more about love from a dog than from his own parents? Or from most of the clergy for that matter. I like to imagine God as having the loving heart and temperament of a dog.

Well, you ask about Leah, so's I'll tell you. The boy and the dog weren't the only two that I lured together.

A good housekeeper isn't to spy on her master or mistress. Miss Leslie's book[56] clearly says so. But believe me, Miriam, I've read it, cover to cover, several times, and I don't recall there being anything in it saying that if a servant comes across an article of information in the course of her straightening up, say, an address for a certain home for unwed mothers in Fort Worth, Texas, on a certain street that's two blocks off the train station, that's she to forget about it completely. And there's nothing in Miss Leslie's book prohibiting a good servant from giving a train ticket to a certain boy Will McShan, an honest and handsome and earnest boy who's in love and whose heart is breaking on account of it. And Miss Leslie is completely silent on the issue of writing addresses for those homes for unwed mothers down on scraps of paper to be given to certain boys such as Will McShan.

No, Miss Eliza Leslie doesn't mention that at all in her book.

Feb. 28, 1937 Sunday

Miss Fenerty says that on Sunday mornings in this city, and perhaps most cities, everyone is either in church or hungover or both.

I'd ridden downtown to have breakfast with Ellie and Miss Fenerty and ended up walking with Ellie to church. The streets were covered in a cool wet blanket of fog, and we walked in it. There was a colorful glow in the whiteness, and when we got near it, I realized it was the marquee of the Strand Theater, still lit up from the night before. *The Good Earth, starring Paul Muni and Luise Rainer* glowed out from it. One of the theater people was on a ladder that leaned up against the marquee and into the fog.

"Morning," he said down to us, and we said it back up to him. It was the same man who takes tickets.

We turned onto McNeil, our ears listening for sounds on the cross streets, Milam, then Texas. Down on the courthouse lawn, a granite Champ Lockett anchored to his granite pedestal leaned on his granite rifle and looked north. The moist air fizzed around us.

---

[56] *The Ladies' Guide to True Politeness and Perfect Manners, or, Miss Leslie's Behavior Book*

We walked without a sound, an intimate silence in our traveling sphere of fog, Ellie in a white sweater over her "Sunday-go-to-meetin' dress," she calls it, her black leather bound Bible clasped to her hip by a white-gloved hand. There's a hole in the knuckle of the index finger of the right glove. The things you notice, the things you remember. The walk itself had seemed like church to us, something spiritual, something sacred. And, though neither of us said anything, I think we both knew it.

At Travis and McNeil, the steps and columns of the Baptist Church rose and were made incomplete by the fog. Nicely dressed people, Baptists, were ascending the steps or visiting on them, greeting each other with slightly canted heads and handshakes, *how are yew doin'?* Ellie turned to me.

"I'll see you at Miss Bridget's," she smiled, and she turned and went up the steps two at a time. A man in a navy blue suit greeted her and then others behind her as they filed in. She cast one more glance-and-smile to me and then disappeared inside as an organ began playing some type of powerful prelude.

I turned on Texas Street to get a closer look at Mr. Lockett's likeness. I paused as he towered up into the fog. I looked up to him as he looked out to something in the soggy, pale air. If he could talk, I wondered, what would he say? If the statue could part his stony lips and say a truth, what would it be? Be kind to others? Love your neighbor as yourself? Your father shouldn't have trusted Mr. Gaudette? Go ahead and marry Irving, it'll be easier? Don't marry Irving, do you really want to be heiress to the kosher packing fortune? Is that who you are?

I turned, intent on going down Marshall Street to Crockett Street and Miss Fenerty's, and then there it was, there *he* was. The front of the black Cadillac peered out of the fog at the corner of Edwards Street. The mist glowed from red to green, and he turned onto Texas Street.

I panicked, the instinct of a rabbit as the fox approaches, and slipped around the corner down Marshall Street, across the street from the Slattery building. Behind me I heard the squeal of brakes and then the rev of his engine. He'd seen me.

I cut across the south lawn of the courthouse, my shoes clopping on the pavement and then falling silent on the grass. On Milam Street, there he was, trolling slowly, steadily, the Cadillac now a dim white shape in the mist, the engine ticking patiently. I tripped on a tree root, gouging a hole in my stocking, but I scrambled up quickly and ran toward McNeil Street again, barely missing a lamppost that appeared suddenly out of the fog.

"*Oh Miss,*" his voice rose over the quiet rumble of the Cadillac and dug into the wet air. "*Like to talk to you, ask you some questions.*" His voice was southern. He pronounced 'you' like 'yew' and 'questions' like 'querstions.'

An alley appeared to my left, and I sprinted down it, frightening a cat into a darting blur and screeching yowl. The echoes of my steps rattled off the dingy red brick on either side of me. My haste knocked over a trash can, and it gave a metallic crash like the rattle of a cymbal.

"*Just a couple a quer-stions,*" the voice surged musically down the alley and off the underside of the fog. I ran trying to make the voice smaller.

Suddenly the alley opened up onto Common Street, just down from the Methodist Church, where the organ was droning out a thunderous hymn for the Methodist voices to accompany, *Lord our God to thee we raise, this our hymn of grateful praise...*

To the left down Common Street was the old Creswell Hotel. I ran to it, almost tumbling down the hill in the process. The clerk looked up in askance. I claimed to need the restroom, what some here call the *necessary* room. He looked up from the Sunday comics and pointed to it. I locked myself inside and waited.

I'm exhausted, and my hand is shaking too much to write anyway.

Part V
Spring and Summer, 1937

Mar. 1, 1937, Monday

I finally feel calm enough to record the rest of what happened yesterday.

From inside the bathroom of the lobby of the Creswell, I heard him.

"Young lady just run in here? Real pretty?" he sounded genial, like a kind uncle giving advice to a favorite nephew.

Behind the simple door, I sat on the lid of the toilet and trembled. I was panting so hard that I put my hands over my mouth to dampen the sounds of my breathing.

And then inexplicably, I heard the clerk's voice:

"No sir. Purty quiet, act-shly."

I could've kissed him, thrown open the door and kissed him.

"All right," the Cadillac man said, and then I heard the door open and close, the tingle of the bell on it, and the engine take off down the street, west down Texas Avenue. There was a knock on the door.

"He's gone," the clerk said.

I opened the door to a quizzical, bookish, bespectacled look.

"Thank you thank you thank you," I gushed.

"Listen, ma'am. It ain't none a my binness, but whatever you got yourself involved in, you just might want to get yourself out of it."

I thanked him one more time and left. I wound a crooked path down Milam, then Louisiana Avenue, onto Crockett, then past the Strand where the man had extinguished the lights of the marquis and removed part of the movie title. He'd apparently taken a break, and only *The Good* remained on it. Every few steps, I cast a glance over my shoulder. The fog was lifting as I got to Miss Fenerty's. I took a deep breath and straightened my hair, and then I knocked. Old steps shuffled inside, and the door knob rattled.

"Miriam," she said as she opened the door, "You can just come in. You don't have to knock anymore."

Then she looked up from the threshold and into my face.

"Good heavens, dear, you look like you've seen a ghost."

"The fog was creepy," I muttered, which wasn't near the whole truth.

She looked at my knee and the hole in my stocking and then pointed at it with her cane.

"And what happened, might I ask you?"

"I tripped on a root on the courthouse lawn." That was truer.

I slept upstairs most of the afternoon yesterday, missing Ellie coming in and making Sunday dinner, fried chicken with mashed potatoes and mustard greens. She fixed me a plate when I arose, embarrassed to have slept most of the afternoon. I ate quietly, and Miss Fenerty and Ellie let me. Finally, I claimed to be feeling 'under the weather' and returned to Stephenson.

On Stephenson, it was another raucous side show of an evening.

Lemurier and Mirlette had another huge fight in the middle of the night. This one was the biggest yet. I awoke from a deep sleep to hear them shouting and the thud of objects against the wall. As my consciousness returned, I heard Mirlette's voice shriek:

"You will kill us *Wheel-ard*. You keep smoking in the bed, and you will kill us!"

Something heavy slammed on the floor, and Mirlette shrieked again. A man's voice shouted.

"Never. Ever. Call me that again. You hear me? Never."

It was angry, and it was distinctively southern. There was a slap, and Mirlette shrieked again, a shriek that dissolved into a sob. Their door slammed, and there were heavy, quick thuds on the stairs, and then downstairs the front door opened and slammed. Mirlette continued to sob. Lemurier's smoke hung in the air, and then the door to their room slammed shut. The smell of his cigarette and Mirlette's crying had long faded when I finally went back to sleep.

Mar. 1, 1937, FWP, Transcript of Bridget Fenerty

Will left as soon as he found out where Leah was, which left Morris to fend for himself when it came to the taunts of the bullies on the schoolyard. Mrs. Taylor still dressed him, or rather had me dress him, in knee pants and stockings, and a shirt that was more of a blouse with an elaborate white collar, a frilly thing. He looked like little Lord Fauntleroy. As I straightened his ruffles and combed his hair, I wanted to whisper to him, "I don't like it either," but that would be going behind my missus' back. But all the same, I pitied the poor boy.

I pitied him because, of course, it made him the object of derision for the other boys, and he took some beatings on account of it. Along with the frilly collars and knee pants, he frequently wore a black eye or a busted lip. He would sit on the steps with his head propped on his hands and Queenie sitting with her head on his knee. Twain said that children have but little charity for one another's defects, and isn't it so, then? The taunts, the name calling, all followed by shoving and arm twisting and punches.

It was then that I felt it was time for him to learn the fine art of boxing, the "sweet science" as it's called,[57] as practiced in the Channel by the greats like Paddy the Bull and Cornelius Horrigan, Sam O'Rourke and John McLaughlin. I was raised with it and, when I was a young girl, practiced it from time to time.

We filled an old canvas laundry bag with river sand and hung it behind the privy. I showed him the footwork that I knew and a few combinations and the

---

[57] The subject is referring to 'the sweet science of bruising,' a term from a series of articles called *Boxiana* by 19th century British journalist and sportswriter Pierce Egan, an Englishman borne of Irish parents.

like. His strikes against it were tentative at first, barely making a sound against the canvas, all arm and no body, and it's the body that makes a punch something beyond a weak slap.

"Put some pork in it, boy! Keep yer hands up! Don't let the other man in!" I urged him on.

We would work until we were both sweaty, Queenie yelping and bowing and leaping sideways at our feet as she enjoyed the spectacle of what she perceived as her boy's play. Then the both of us would return to the house, Queenie smiling as she trotted at our feet. The boy and I would wash our hands and faces side by side from the basin on the stand by the back door. His knuckles were red from the punishment he was learning to give to the bag.

I was afraid that Mrs. Taylor would notice and say something, but she was getting more and more self-absorbed, her behavior more and more erratic. She began applying makeup, thick and theatrical; her clothes became more and more of a spectacle. Looking back, I could see it was the beginning of the new phase of her descent, her fall into mania, as they called it then.

Well, the day came that a boy challenged him, and Morris refused to back down. 'Twas the McKerran boy, I think, one of his principal tormenters. A mean spirited boy, a coarse sort of boy, a boy with crooked teeth that peeked out from behind his sneer. A boy from the 'West End' that blocked alleys with arms crossed and hurled insults at boys who fled.

It was in the alley off McNeil Street, and let me tell you the truth of it, then, Miriam. My Morris beat the stew out of him. I watched the whole thing from a distance, as it was his fight, not mine. The McKerran boy was little more than a bag of river sand. Body blows, head blows, each one the McKerran boy failed to answer, his hands falling with each one, opening him up even more.

But at last I thought Morris would kill the boy or maim him entirely so that the boy would never be fit for anything other than begging, so I intervened. I held Morris away and told the boy, who was bloodied on the ground, "Run for it, boy! Run before he sets on you again!" knowing full well that the act of running from a fight would be the icing on the cake for the McKerran boy's reputation.

Of course, a crowd of other boys was there in the alley behind McNeil Street, and they saw the McKerran boy jump up, wiping the blood from his nose, and run down toward Texas Street, elbows pumping and flying in his haste. He took off like a scalded ape, as some around here might put it. The crowd of boys looked to Morris and then to his fleeing opponent and then back to Morris in his mother's feathery finery, sullied a little by the struggle. He was in fine feather, Morris was, and so he wiped his nose on the sleeve of his frilly shirt and asked the other boys, he says, "Anyone else care for a go?"

They all shook their heads and drifted away. And my boy never had any trouble after that.

March 2, 1937, Tuesday

So it's set. June 8, a Tuesday and the new moon, Rosh Chodesh. An auspicious day for a wedding.

I finally sent the telegram to Mother. The questioning face of the Western Union man waited for more of a message than, "WEDDING DATE JUNE 8 TUES."

"Okay. That's all, nothing else. You can send it," I said with a sigh I hadn't intended.

I sat on a bench outside the courthouse under an umbrella and the last of the passing rain. I looked up at Champ Lockett, waiting for words of advice. He was silent, of course, just staring north and waiting. The rain stopped as it grew dark, and the wind shook the leaves of the live oaks on the courthouse lawn.

I decided that, while I was downtown, I might as well go back by Crockett Street and ask Ellie to be my Maid of Honor. When I got there, Miss Fenerty had already gone to bed, a little earlier than usual. The front room was dark except for the glow of the gas heater. Through the window, I saw Ellie in her nightgown staring into the light of the flames.

She jumped when I knocked lightly. A rhythmic trail of her footfalls pattered inside as she got up and answered the door. "I was just thinking about you," she said.

We sat on the couch facing each other, and I asked her. I thought we might have grasped hands and squealed like I'd seen girls do under the columns of Milbank Hall at Barnard. But instead, she nodded a small, brave, tentative yes with her head tilted a little, blonde bangs shaking over a sad smile.

"Sure. Sure, I'd be honored." She put her hand to my cheek, and I thought from the way she looked at me that she might kiss me. She did kiss me, but it was a chaste kiss on the cheek opposite her hand. I turned to her, to look into her eyes, her lips, but she dropped her face, down and away. Then, after a moment, she looked up and nodded again, saying only "Congratulations." She seemed to try to force out a bigger version of her smile, but it was weak and became even less of one.

I wanted to pull her to me, to feel her against me, her silent energy and mine, intertwining. And so I did, and we allowed it, we enjoyed it, for a moment, a brief moment, feeling her press against me and me against her, our hands pressing one another together, moving softly over each other, exploring the geography of each other's bodies, our geometry, describing the sweep of the arcs, the rise and fall of our curves. And then we kissed again, on the lips, a moment I've been dreaming of and dreading.

But then she released me, and I turned to the mantle. When I turned around, her head was in her hands, and then she moved her fingers over her temples. Her attempts at a smile had failed now. She stood and put one hand to her forehead and the other to the hollow where neck meets chest. Yellow light glowed from the blue and orange jack o' lantern grin of the gas heater under the mantle. The room was dim light and shadows, nothing else.

I sighed a weary murmur, "I think it's best if I head home now."

"I wish you'd stay. I worry about you over there." She paused as she gathered herself. Then without conviction she muttered, "Yes, you're right."

I opened the door to the cold. A wind was pushing in from the north, and it had gotten colder since I'd come in. The front door balked against my closing it, and I had to lean with my weight to pull it closed. Through the window, I saw Ellie go upstairs, her hand leaping and bounding up the bannister.

Driving home down Line, I felt as though something was burning between my hips, something almost pleasurable, almost painful. I stopped for the light at Kings Highway. My mind painted a picture of the two of us together, in a world where anything was possible, a moving picture of us, vivid colors of desire, vibrant longing, soft pastel tenderness. I closed my eyes to it, to look away from it, but I only saw it more plainly. I opened my eyes again and looked up to see the intersection bathed in yellow light. I sped through it as I realized that I had sat through an entire red and green cycle.

I was alone on the night street, the lights that Ellie had fixed shining out, bleeding yellow-white off the slick pavement of Line Avenue. No one had been behind me to disturb me. Could they have? I was disturbed already.

When I arrived on Stephenson Street, I vaulted up the steps and squatted to retrieve the key from under the mat. I dropped it twice trying to fit it into the lock. I felt myself burning and fluid, my body seemed to be pressing against my clothes. I left the key in the lock and the door ajar. I flicked the light switch but remembered that I had used the money for the light bill to send flowers to my parents for their anniversary. I hurried upstairs to my room, missing a step in the dark and tripping momentarily. I couldn't tell if L and M were home, and I didn't care. I did, however, manage to put the chair under the doorknob. If Lemurier had walked in on me, I would have been helpless.

Afterwards, my shaking hand lit a candle, and, in the fading aftermath of my private ecstasy, I began crying because the facts are clear. My true desire is at odds with what is proper, what is expected by society, what is advantageous to my family's well-being. These fantasies I entertain can't be. They just can't be.

Now, it's morning, and I just went to retrieve the key from the door. It's gone, though the door is still ajar. I know I didn't take it up with me.

Someone else has taken it, Lemurier or Mirlette, I'm assuming.

Mar. 3, 1937, FWP, Transcript of Bridget Fenerty

Well, a little success kindles the small flame, and isn't it the truth, then? Morris continued to box, spending long hours behind the privy, letting the laundry bag full of sand have it. In a matter of a year or two, he grew from welterweight to lightweight to middleweight. I struggled to keep him filled up. He had an appetite equal to that of an entire regiment.

It was in the days that the city began supplying the water, and people were filling in their old wells and cisterns. The streets were being paved, beginning over on Texas Street and then Market and the others. The city had installed a pumping station for fresh water and sewer lines for spent water, and everyone in the city gave up on cisterns and privies. There was talk of electricity and telephones.

That wasn't the only progress. Leah and Will had married and were expecting their second child in Fort Worth. Morris was beginning to enter boxing matches in Texas, and Leah and Will would come to Marshall and Tyler to watch him. I don't know who was more proud, Leah or Will. After each bout, smiling with his sweaty hair plastered to his head, Morris would pick up his new nephew, Ike, Isaac after his grandfather, they'd named him, holding the little fellow to his muscular torso, so proud to be an uncle. Old Mr. Taylor had asked me in his dying moments to make sure I raised Morris to be a man. I was happy not to have let him down.

I also got Morris a suit, the kind a gentleman wears, and Miriam, you should have seen the look on that boy's face. I say boy, but he was a man now, surely, and you could really see it when he put on the suit and saw a man looking back at him in the mirror at Levy's. I had to get it from Mr. Levy's place, as Taylor's was on its last legs. It was also about this time that Mrs. Taylor finally went altogether crackalty[?].[58]

I had passed forty about then, and it occurred to me that I had outlived my parents, and it seemed odd to me that it should be so. Little Frank would be twenty-five, which was odder still. Through the papers, I still kept up with the goings on in Brazil. They had abolished slavery there, the last nation in the world to do it. Emperor Pedro abdicated the throne the next year and moved on.[59] I wondered how the changes in his new country affected my boy. Was he well? Was he alive? Did he marry? Did I have grandchildren somewhere?

[58] Possibly "*craiceáilte*," an Irish term for crazy
[59] Brazil abolished slavery in 1888, and was in fact the last country in the world to do so. It was in part due to the efforts of old Emperor Dom Pedro II, who voluntarily abdicated the throne in favor of a republic in 1889.

And simpler questions. Was his hair still red? Did he speak Portuguese?

Well, we were speaking of Mrs. Taylor, then, weren't we?

She was denied credit at one of the few shops on Texas Street where she still had it. It was on a day that she was in front of a mirror trying on a succession of bonnets that the salesgirl handed to her. She was tilting her head this way and that with her white-gloved hands on the brims of each one, giving a scalding critique of each hat before deciding to take them all anyway. The chief salesclerk, an effeminate fellow named Campbell or Camden or something like that came and interrupted her primping and told her something in a low voice. Mrs. Taylor exploded.

"I happen to be the wife of one of the finest tailors in the state, and, when he finds out about this treatment, you will have his wrath!"

The clerks and shop girls all looked up from helping other customers and looked at each other. Mr. Taylor had been dead for ten years by then, of course, and as far as I knew never had an ounce of wrath in him, anyway.

"Are you feeling well, Mrs. Taylor?" one of them said.

"Why shouldn't I be feeling well? Just because the state has bank auditors taking money from my account at night when the town's asleep, why shouldn't I be? Why, Governor Nicholls told me himself!"

Her agitated eyes were wild, and her speech curled and twisted out of her, making very little sense. At last, she exited the shop, throwing off the bonnet, sales tag attached, and slamming the door behind her. In the next few days, she worsened, making preposterous statements, pronouncements, declarations. She slept very little, blathering on from one topic to the next, all of them unrelated except to her. Her eyes were piercing when she was in one of her states, and her gaze seemed like it wanted to squeeze you. She went days without sleeping, until finally it caught up with her, and then she wrote letters of apology to the merchants she may have offended and had me deliver them. And then, after a week or two of sleeping, it was all repeated.

She would go for days without rest, still up when I arose, which was early by habit. She was dressed and waiting, ready to go out and take up a quarrel with someone, anyone, usually over her being denied credit. People were stealing from her, she said, the list growing longer all the time. She threatened to take the train to Marshall or Monroe where the merchants would be happy for her business.

Finally, she accused me of selling her silver. And that did it for Morris, that was the last straw. He was just a teenager then, so he consulted with Mr. Levy and Mr. Kahn, who sent a telegram to St. Louis to Mrs. Taylor's sister. When she arrived a few days later, they came with her and Morris to the house. The governor had just commuted the sentence of Gus Logan to life, and the two men were discussing it quietly; the whole town, and especially the Jews, were unhappy. Logan had shot and killed one of the Jewish merchants.[60]

"Morris, where are your clothes?" Mrs. Taylor asked as she scanned him head to toe looking for the fussy apparel she preferred on him. Her hair was in a distracted state, her stare intense. Her own clothes were garishly mismatched as if she had dressed in the dark. Her sister, a Mrs. Bernheimer, had gently tried to direct her, but Mrs. Taylor had refused. Finally, Mrs. Bernheimer had let her sister dress as she pleased. But Morris gently balked at Mrs. Taylor's idea of his clothes.

"These are my clothes, Mother," Morris said quietly, trying not to agitate her any more than she was. He was wearing a gentleman's suit, the one I'd gotten him from Mr. Levy's. A sharp, gray flannel suit with the waistcoat and pearl buttons. He was so proud of it.

Mrs. Bernheimer had me pack a bag for Mrs. Taylor who was insisting that she also be allowed to bring enough steamer trunks and hat boxes to rival Napoleon's army. Mrs. Bernheimer pretended to allow the porters to load them on the baggage car but instead gave some Negro men some money to return them to the house.

"She won't be needing all that," she confided to me.

Mrs. Taylor was accompanied onto the train by the conductor, who held her forearm and smiled at her, telling her, *'watch your step, we wouldn't want to ruin your shopping trip to St. Louis, now would we?'* Her hair was disheveled, and her vigilant eyes made her look like a wild animal that had just spotted a wilder, larger animal.

Mrs. Bernheimer stood with us for a moment as we watched her sister, Mrs. Taylor, being put in her seat. Then she turned to us, Mrs. Bernheimer did, and she gave us a look of sorrow so profound it seemed to scent the air or make a small sound, like a buzz, perhaps. Then she put her white linen palm to Morris' cheek and smiled at him regretfully.

"I'm sorry, Morris, that I was never able to keep up with you and your sister. She would never let us, your uncle August and me. The worst thing of all is, I could see this day coming when we were girls, just children. To some extent, she was always this way. I always hoped your father's goodness would improve her, but she was always this way."

Mrs. Taylor sat on the train, framed by the window, looking straight ahead with her chin up, a tight, determined look on her face. She probably felt that she was escaping this small city and its hard-hearted people who would no longer give her the credit, literally, she deserved. *Just wait until they see me returning with all the fine things I'll bring back from St. Louis,* I'm sure she was

---

[60] In 1888, as his term of office expired, Governor Samuel D. McEnery commuted the sentence of Gus Logan from death to life in prison. Logan had been convicted of killing Jewish merchant Nathan Goldkind in a backroom card game at Goldkind's store in Shreveport in 1885.

thinking.

Mrs. Bernheimer looked to her sister's image through the window. Mrs. Taylor was already engaged in an argument with the conductor. It was silent behind the window glass, though still animated by a frenzy of hand gestures.

"I told her I was taking her back to St. Louis to take her shopping," Mrs. Bernheimer said, her face a kinder, more reasonable version of her sister's. "I'm afraid I lied to her. I'm taking her to an asylum. Forgive me, Morris, but that's what it has to be."

It was obvious, of course; we all knew it. Morris embraced her, the aunt he had never met. There were tears in their eyes. She withdrew from the embrace and took my hand in her white gloved hands, pressing mine between her two.

"This boy is a man because of you," she said. Then she shook the hands of Mr. Levy and Mr. Kahn, who were there. Mr. Kahn kept nervously looking at his pocket watch, palming it closed with a snap, putting it back in his vest pocket, and then taking it out again to repeat the whole process. Mr. Levy waited patiently on the platform with his hands clasped behind his back.

Mrs. Bernheimer climbed the steps of the train car as steam boiled out from between the cars and under them. The wheels began to squeal and turn, but there was no 'all aboard.' The other conductor had been summoned to deal with an unreasonable passenger. And you know who it was.

She left on the Vicksburg railroad, the train sliding back through town and over the new bridge they'd built a few years before, the first one over the river. I put my arm around my boy as we walked away, and he stopped and fell into sobbing, and I felt his manly frame tremble. I turned and I held him, there on the platform. Mr. Levy and Mr. Kahn put a hand on my boy's back, and then drifted away without a word. When I looked up, the train had cleared the bridge and was gone. All that was left was the whistle in the eastern distance.

Under the tutelage of Mr. Levy and Mr. Kahn, Morris took over the shop, which was a gracious act as they were both competitors. Morris changed the name from *Isaac M. Taylor, Finest Gentlemen's Attire* to *Isaac M. Taylor and Son, Clothiers*. He took out a loan from Mr. Jacob's bank and hired men from New Orleans and Memphis. He also immersed himself in the trends of gentleman's fashion, working with the tailors he had hired. Together, they slowly nudged the town's sense of style toward that of London and Paris and New York.

The Norfolk jacket found its way to town, along with sack suits, wider lapels, tall collars, four-in-hand ties and bow ties. Waistcoats made from contrasting fabric, cut low to show off more of the fine white linen shirts. And though Morris may not have been the best tailor himself, he knew how to motivate others with an encouraging word or a hand on the shoulder. Morris was on top of it.

He continued to box, and, though it was illegal, it was largely overlooked. He had gone from fearing physical confrontation to enjoying it, as long as it was in the context of sport. He studied it, reading Egan's *Boxiana* and the sporting magazines of the day. In the evenings, he still practiced with the laundry bag, moving it from behind the privy to a tree limb in the backyard. There used to be a big sycamore tree back there, but we lost it to a storm years ago. He wore a circular path around it, stalking it, his feet scattering the big dry sycamore leaves with a rustling sound as his fists fell heavily in rapid succession on the bag.

When Leah and Will came for visits, little Ike would watch his Uncle Morris work the bag or do calisthenics, preparing for his next bout. Morris would lift up the little fellow, who would slap away at the bag, and then Uncle Morris would say, imitating me, I'm sure, "That's it, Ike, put some pork in it me boy!"

Leah and Will were frequent visitors for Morris and me. They would come in from Fort Worth where Will was working in the stockyards. It seems like every time they returned they had a new baby boy. First there was little Ike, then Abram, then Aaron. Most of the time, it was just Morris and me in the house, until he married the Levy girl, and they had a family of their own.

The state legislature had legalized boxing that year, the year after the Chief of Police in New Orleans was shot, a man named Hennessy, just like Ned. It was in a time that the Italians were coming into New Orleans in big numbers, just as we Irish had done fifty years before, and they were organizing into gangs just like the Irish before them. They tried a couple of dozen for Chief Hennessy's murder, but the jury found them not guilty, so a mob broke into the jail and lynched all but a few of them. It was in all the papers.[61] People were as wary of the Italians as they were of us fifty years prior.

Morris won the city middleweight championship and decided to enter the state championship to be held in New Orleans. Earlier in the year, Bob Fitzsimmons had knocked out Jack Dempsey there in New Orleans for the championship. They didn't box at the fork of the Bayou Road anymore, they boxed at the Olympic Club in New Orleans with gloves instead of bare knuckles like they did in the old days. There was a purse for the winner, and Morris wanted to apply it to his debt.[62]

He was scheduled to fight the New Orleans city champ, Bruno Messina,

---

[61] New Orleans Police Chief David Hennessy was shot on October 15, 1890. Italian gangs were thought to be responsible for Chief Hennessy's death, as his last words were reportedly 'Dagoes done it.' There is no evidence that he was related to Ned Hennessy.

[62] Some sources, including the minutes from the Olympic Club, put the prize money at close to $1,000, a tidy sum in those days.

and quite a fighter he was. Undefeated in thirty something bouts, ten or twelve knockouts or something like that. Most of them were from the time that it was illegal and practiced behind the closed doors of places like the Olympic.

Morris and I rode down on the train. I spent most of the trip silently reminiscing about my Channel days, wondering how much the city had changed in thirty years. I found that the accent was different by then, less of Auld Ireland in it and more like, well, like yours, more like New York. For one thing, now Fenerty rhymed with Kennedy.

When we got to the river to cross, I pretended to sleep as the ferry carried us over, though I thought my heart would race right out of my chest. I peeked at one point to see Morris leaning into the window to regard the wide river, the Mississippi. I shut my eyes tightly again.

"Goodness, just look at it," he said in wonder.

"Yes, isn't it something?" I said behind my eyelids and my palms.

Well, we got off the train, and there was a lot of taunting from the start. *Well, it looks like you brought your grandmamma with you,* and *you better step lively and watch yourself, there, Jew boy,* and *didn't know anybody could fight up there in Shreveport,* and so forth.

There was a Negro featherweight they called "Little Chocolate[63]" who offered to spar with Morris the day before the fight, and they had a light workout, footwork, mostly. At the close of it, he and Morris tapped gloves, and he wished Morris well.

It was a long night for both of us. I could hear Morris pacing next door in his room, then the flurry as he went through his steps and combinations. The bed would creak as he lay down, then creak again as he got right back up, then more pacing. So restless.

At six the next morning, there was a knock on Morris' door so loud that it would have woken me up next door had I not already been up. It was a telegram from Leah and Will in Fort Worth wishing him well and telling him they were all proud and that if the next child were a boy they would name him after his Uncle Morris. It seemed to cheer him some, but he was still very, very nervous.

We left the hotel that morning and hired a hack to take us down to the Olympic Club out on Royal in the old Second Municipality and what a crowd there was, let me tell you. At first they wouldn't let me in, but one of the men was sympathetic and let me pass, but they wouldn't allow me in his corner and arranged for a man to attend Morris. It wasn't a place for women, they said.

The bell rang, and it was a fiasco from the start. Morris kept looking up into the galleries jammed with people, mostly men, and letting his hands drop,

[63] George Dixon was a Negro boxer who was known by the nickname "Little Chocolate." He was from the town of Africville in Nova Scotia, Canada and was at one time the featherweight champion.

and the Italian kept letting him have it. The referee wore a swallowtail coat and kept prancing, hop-stepping around the action, reaching in to separate them when they locked up, then stepping back and prancing again.

To my Morris' credit, he lasted four rounds. Just before the fifth, I'd had enough and I pushed my way to his corner. At the end of that one, he was slumped back on his stool, his arms stretched out on the ropes. His lip was fat and bloody, his hair sweaty, his left eye swollen almost shut. He slouched back into the turnbuckle.

"Morris. Morris!" I shouted, and I don't think he heard me. Finally, he turned his head to me, slowly as if it took great effort. The eye that wasn't swollen focused on me.

"That's enough, Miss Biddy. That's enough. I'm done. Finished," he muttered.

"It's fine with me if you pack it in, son," I said.

The referee came to Morris. Across the ring the Italian was up and ready. He had a mark or two on him but nothing near the punishment that Morris wore on his own face.

"Up, son," the referee said, and I could hear the brogue in his voice. His name was Duffy, I seem to recall, but they called him Professor. "Up for the next," he said.

"Are you sure?" I asked Morris. It sounded like a whisper against the roiling excitement of the crowd.

"Done," he said.

I took the towel from the shoulder of the corner man and threw it in the ring. A roar went up in the club, and men climbed in the ring and lifted Messina onto their shoulders. He smiled weakly but then motioned for the men to put him down in front of Morris, who had gotten to his feet though he was supported by the corner man. Messina looked up into Morris' face and said some things in Italian. Messina's corner man translated.

"He say you hit a hard. Thassa longest he ever gotta fight." Then Messina put his arm around Morris' shoulder and leaned his forehead into Morris'. The crowd roared its approval and lifted Messina up again. Then it bore him away, just like that day that they carried off Cornelius Horrigan so many years earlier, and gradually the room was empty except for the men hired to clean up. And then I put the robe over my boy, and we hired a hack to take us back to our hotel. Morris shakily climbed the steps of the brougham as the cabbie and I supported him. At the hotel, I ordered a bucket of ice and some towels for him.

That evening, we went to eat at Tujague's place, and men would stop and shake his hand and give him compliments and tell him how much they admired his pluck. Someone even paid for our meal. On the way back to our hotel, we ran into a woman I recognized vaguely. She appeared to be in her forties or fifties, a woman of easy virtue still plying her trade at such an age.

"Miss Bridget?" she asked.

I studied her face behind the rouge and eyeliner before I recognized her. It was Monique Vauborel.

I asked about her family, and she answered with the candor that a woman of the night has. They seemed to have fallen into the same lifestyle as their father. Monique had been a cheating wife, then a beaten wife, then a destitute wife, and finally a whore. Her brother Guillaume a whoremonger, a drunkard, a gambler, and a wife-beater who had been shot to death by a jealous husband in one of the last duels in Orleans Parish.

As much as Monsieur Vauborel had demanded piety and pretense from the children and their mother, Mass on Sundays and all the Holy Days, the Rosary before bed as he himself slipped out onto the town, he had failed to demonstrate it himself, and, upon his widow's death right after the war, his children had been taken in by what he did and disregarded what he preached to them. All that kneeling on rice as an Act of Contrition and praying the Rosary, all for naught. So I suppose it's true what they say, then: the things you do speak so loudly, I can't hear what you say.

I didn't have the time or inclination to tell her what had happened to me, so I only told her that Morris had fought for the state title but lost.

"Well, then," she said, running the back of her fingers over his cheek, the one that wasn't bruised, "Perhaps I can be your boy's consolation prize."

'Twas a shame to remember her as a little girl in her ballet skirt, pink gauze and fitted bodice and tights, a saucy little thing, even then.

"I thank you, ma'am," I says, "but what this boy needs is a good night's rest."

Well, I believe Mr. Roosevelt's ears may be tired. Let me make us a little supper, Miriam.

March 3, 1937 Wednesday

I had supper with Miss Fenerty tonight, hoping to see Ellie, hoping that she hadn't left town again. I asked Miss Fenerty where she was.

"Something's bothering her," Miss Fenerty said as she rattled around in the kitchen. "Kept to her room all day yesterday, then got up and went to the fairgrounds to sketch. She's been gone since this morning."

I found myself worried for her, worried for her on the bus at night in the west end of town. I waited around for a while, hoping to see her, but finally I went home to an empty house. I thought I might have to find a window to go through, but I found the door unlocked and ajar. The squeaking door seemed to ask a question, and I asked my own to the darkness:

Lemurier? Mirlette?

Silence answered.

I took a candle and looked through the house. Their room was empty. They only go out at night, and then only infrequently. I chalked up the open door to their alcohol and/or reefer induced inattention. I had no idea where they'd gone, and, though the house was dark, I was happy to have it to myself. I dressed in my gown and then went down for a glass of water, carefully picking over the stairs.

From the kitchen window, I saw a light in the greenhouse. The ceiling panels were illuminated yellow except for the cardboard replacement panel, opaque like a missing tooth in a smile. At first I thought that L and M had gone out there to copulate outdoors, but then in the glow of the flashlight I saw him.

The light moved over the ground as it approached the back door. I set down my glass and backed out of the kitchen in the dark, bumping into the door jamb and stifling an exclamation. From the landing, I heard the back door open, lightly, barely, like someone who has practiced stealth. Hardly a noise.

Below me, steps creaked on the wood of the first floor, and I saw the sector of light from the flashlight shine over the floor, illuminating the paintings on easels and making them even more grotesque than they are in daylight. He held the flashlight under his armpit and made notations in a small notebook, then moved on.

I eased up the stairs, as quietly as I could. The flashlight paused as he listened. I paused. My heart was pounding so that I thought whoever it was might hear it. I eased air in and out of my lungs, slowly, silently. I had perhaps ten steps to the top and the door to my room. I held up the hem of my gown as if it would help mute my steps.

I slipped into my room and slowly put the chair under the door knob. The smoky smell of the blown out candle wafted in the room, and I wondered if he would be able to smell it.

The flashlight illuminated the door. The knob turned but bumped against the chair. I was plastered to the wall behind it with a lamp in my hand, not for light, but to use as a weapon if he gained entrance. The light retreated from the crack under the door, and I could hear him in the bedroom across the landing, L and M's. I heard the squeak of their door. Thank goodness it's theirs that squeaks and not mine.

I had to make myself breathe. I heard the flash of a camera and, in a quick, silver line at the crack at the bottom of the door, I saw the flare of its bulb. Footsteps eased away down the stairs, and then the distant creak of the front door.

And then I saw him, the glare of the flashlight on the front lawn. He clicked off the flashlight and then walked down the street. Moments later I heard the rumble of the Cadillac, parked down there, somewhere. After he had gone a while, I walked down the stairs, my breath a vapor in the cold, dark house. The key was back in the lock.

Mar. 4, 1937, FWP, Transcript of Bridget Fenerty

Well, you seem a little rattled this morning, Miriam. Are you sure you're up to a long winded tale told by an old woman? Very well. All right.

The town greeted us at the train station. Some felt disappointed in Morris, that he had let slip the chance for the state's second city to land a blow on its big brother, New Orleans. Some even went so far as to nickname him 'No Mo', but most of those people had never thrown or taken a punch in their lives. For most, he was hero, though a minor one compared to Champ Lockett. If he had won the fight, perhaps he would have been almost as big.

I was turning fifty, and, in the mirror, my shoulders and hips were spreading, my breasts were beginning to respond to gravity, dipping below the water when I took my bath. When I tied my apron about me, there was less string leftover. Gray hairs were beginning to line up with the auburn ones, like leaves changing color in the fall. You look in the mirror and say "Imposter! That's not me at all. I'm but a girl still!" But of course you know 'tis true. Old age will come for us all.

Morris came home to the debt he had inherited from his mother. I could have helped him with it, though he had no idea I could. I always kept that secret from him, and he still doesn't know. And besides, a boy becomes a man on the day he pays his own bills. Until that day, he's just a boy, and to pay them off for him would be to sentence him to more boyhood, the equivalent to keeping him dressed up in frilly frippery.

Instead, I watched as he applied himself with the same zeal he had when he was training for a bout. His shop became the place for young professional gentlemen to clothe themselves, the young cotton factors and attorneys and lumber agents of the day. To conduct business properly, a man had to be wearing one of Morris Taylor's suits. Men began coming in on the train from as far as Marshall and Tyler to get attired. It was a rite of passage for a young man to come and get fitted for his first suit at *Taylor and Son*. The pews of all the churches and the Hebrew temple were filled with his suits.

It took the better part of three or four years, but, when he finally retired most of the debt, he began courting one of the Mr. Levy's girls, a pretty thing with sleepy eyes and lovely brown hair that she wore up on her head like they did in those days with the high collars and the puff sleeves. Lovely, just lovely.

He asked me for advice on marrying, and I told him, "Son, you can take or leave this piece of advice from someone who's never married and likely won't. Don't marry someone who can't make a sacrifice, and don't marry anyone if you can't make one yourself."

"That's all I needed to know," he said

"Go speak to her father, then," I said. He put on his hat and his coat and went out the door to speak with old Mr. Levy. I watched him walk down Crockett Street. It was a bittersweet moment.

Permission was granted, and he married the Levy girl, the youngest one, Sophie. She was and is a wonderful mate, an industrious woman who wasn't above hard, cheerful work. They worked side by side in the shop, putting in long hours. Mr. Levy gave them a house on Jordan Street and a dowry, which paid off the last of Mrs. Taylor's debt.

When the first of the children came, Sophie Taylor stayed home to raise them. I was the equivalent of a grandmother to them, a position I shared with Mrs. Levy. Sophie's mother, old Mrs. Levy, was an elegant lady who had the slightest of accents and who wore pleated blouses with high collars. She and old Mr. Levy considered me Morris' mother. They'd seen the pains I'd gone through in raising him. We all became an extended family, all united by our love for the same children and then, grandchildren.

But on that day that they married and moved to Jordan Street, it left this house empty. Oh, I'd take the trolley down Louisiana Avenue to Morris and Sophie's house on Jordan Street where they still live, though the children have grown and Morris and Sophie have grandchildren. But it wasn't the same as having a family to care for, a family under the same roof.

So, Mr. Hennessy, me of course, had Mr. Herndon, Jr., put an ad in the paper, and I got on with the Randolphs, or rather, they got on with me. It was in the last years of the old century. Mr. Randolph was a manager at the Victoria lumberyard on the riverfront. He was one of Morris' customers, a man who was tanned from outdoor work, a man with tired blue eyes with swags of skin under them, a man who smiled and smoked nonstop. His name was Cyril or Cyrus or something like that, but most called him by his nickname, Woody. He and Mrs. Randolph had a house full of children, all boys and one little girl. Strong, handsome, bright children. Keen, shrewd, intuitive children who were delightful to be around. But, of course, children such as that are a handful most of the time.

Mrs. Randolph was a plain, blithe woman who went along with her husband on whatever he said as if he were a merry whirlwind, and she were a leaf. She laughed at all his jokes and brought him his toddy in the evenings after dinner, which he took on the porch with a cigarette in his hand and his heels on the railing, rain or shine, cold or hot. Then, when his glass was empty, he left to go on what he called his constitutional, his footsteps receding down the street with his cough.

He was a man with an active social calendar, card games, evening skull sessions with the other managers, Knights of Pythias dinners at the Phoenix Hotel, Hoo Hoo meetings.[64] On Saturday evening, he gave Mrs. Randolph her due and took her to the Vigil Mass and then to the theater, the *Majestic* or one of the others on Milam in those days. The other nights of the week, he would leave after the bourbon he took on the porch, taking a last pull from his cigarette and putting it out on the bottom of his shoe and throwing the butt into the azalea bushes. Then, putting on his hat and his coat, he left for his nightly errand. He always went up Crockett Street this way, up toward Common, not toward Spring Street where the Hoo Hoos met or where the Phoenix Hotel was. I suspected it then, but it was none of my business.

The street would grow dark, and the lights would glow in the windows of our house, shaking with footsteps and the shouting of children, up the stairs, down the stairs, chasing after one another, giggling, and the shouting of adults telling them to keep their voices down and don't run indoors. They were some wonderful years for the Taylor and Randolph children, two houses full, constantly on the Louisiana Avenue trolley, back and forth between this house and the house on Jordan Street. The majority were boys, with a few sisters who played as rough as their brothers. And, on certain weeks, especially in the summer, the Texas cousins would come in on the train, the McShans, in from Fort Worth, and then, let me tell you, it was a free for all. What a tribe of wild Indians they were!

They grew up like cousins, three families linked through me. They enjoyed each other's company, stuck up for each other, a quarrel against one was a quarrel against all. They learned the things you only learn from cousins, when to take a dare and when not to, how to lift a cookie from the jar without making a noise, how to play 'Champ Lockett.' How to shoot a slingshot and ride a bicycle, which was something new then, the bicycle. None of the adults knew how to ride one.

They taught each other which moves to use in wrestling, and they speculated on whether there was a secret move that could kill a man if you used it, and they asked each other, if you knew it, would you use it on someone? I recall they were split on the matter. Half said never, and the other half, yes, but only if it were a bad man like Jack the Ripper or Jesse James.

And as I put up linen in the upstairs closet, I would hear them in their room discussing whether or not there were ghosts and who had seen one, and that there were naked women in the windows of the brothels down in St. Paul's Bottoms, and that there was a woman in one of the upper windows at Bea Haywood's place that would blow you a kiss and lift up her skirts for you, and sometimes she would be wearing drawers and sometimes she wouldn't. Delightful, whimsical, earnest little conversations to listen in on, each assertion

[64]The Concatenated Order of Hoo-Hoo, a lumberman's fraternal order.

punctuated with *nuh-uh* and answered with, *uh-huh, is so.* The Taylors and the Randolphs and McShans grew up raised as one family, Jew and Gentile making very little difference. And on the weekends, there was what we called Camp Taylor.

When Morris and Sophie had first married, a man had come in his shop needing to sell a hunting and fishing camp quick on account of debt, and we got a good deal, fifty cents an acre on close to four hundred acres. Morris had paid off his mother's debt, and there a little left over. So, he and I went in fifty-fifty on it, land north of town, a retreat to hunt and fish and camp on. It was the year of the panic, the economic panic,[65] and if you kept your ears and eyes open, you could get things cheap.

Steamboat traffic was falling with the river, ironically from the clearing of the raft, the very thing that was opened to get the boats here in the first place. Trains were taking their place, and a train line up toward Kansas City was completed that year, 1895, and a stop was included on it for a fishing camp called the Ananias fishing club, a joke among fisherman as Ananias was a liar in the Bible and many a fisherman prides himself on the ability to stretch the truth or discard it entirely.

The years around Mr. Bryan's second visit[66] to Shreveport to court the vote were the glory years of Camp Taylor. The Randolphs were Catholic and took the Saturday vigil, and we would all come up on Sunday mornings on the train and spend the whole day there, and sometimes the whole week when the weather was nice. The Texas cousins would come when they were in town, which was at the very least three or four times a year.

Morris would spar with his brother-in-law Will as they cooked together over a barbecue pit by the porch of the camp house, laughing as each landed a tap on the other, both wearing aprons stained with sauce. Then they would pause to flip the chicken quarters and resume their boyish tussle. Mr. Randolph, smiling with sad blue eyes, lounged on the porch watching them, smoking and sipping bourbon. Children would run by in a chase, and the wives would sit and swing side by side in the hammock like sisters. The smell of cooking meat and the fresh breeze off the lake and the sweet aromatic scent of the cypresses.

We had a fine time, camping with the boys, all considered cousins, the men and the older boys hunting squirrels and deer and rabbits, everyone fishing, even the girls. The Louisiana cousins and the Texas cousins and the Randolphs with Morris and Will rowing in old johnboats, or the little fellows swinging on muscadine vines, running and playing like a tribe of wild Indians. They would poke around the shallows of the lake, and I would warn them to

---

[65] Of 1893.
[66] William Jennings Bryan made campaign visits to Shreveport twice, in 1892 and 1900.

be careful of Mr. No-Shoulders, now. Or they would chase through the flats where the cypresses grew in groves on flat, sandy ground with palmetto ferns at their bald knees.

In the evenings, there would be dinners of lemonade and potato salad and barbecued chicken or fried fish, even catfish, though it wasn't kosher, lacking scales, of course. Campfires in the evening, me singing for everyone while it crackled and the sun set blue and orange and pink across the lake.

Once they talked me into a walk through the woods down to a spot, a beautiful spot where two cypresses grew. Then I recognized it. It was the exact place that Elias and I used to tryst twenty years before. I knew it because there were two cypress trees with trunks twisted about each other, a rare thing for that sort of tree as they tend to grow straight. I think he would have been pleased to see all these children running around enjoying the place.

Those were some wonderful years in the days before the discovery, days of hard, happy work and the shouts of children. Scraped knees, cuts that only needed clean water and a kiss to heal, bumps and bruises from playing 'Lockett' with cypress balls. Old Queenie lounging on the porch of the camp, old and fat and content at the end of her days. Randolph and Taylor and McShan children pausing from their frenzied play to stroke her belly and ears before running off the porch with a drumming clatter of young footsteps and into the cypress flats again. The slap of the screen door as the youngest and last in line struggled to keep up with the chase.

The four hundred acres that Morris called Camp Taylor on the banks of Jeems Bayou on Caddo Lake was as pretty a spot as you could imagine. A place where the only care was whether or not the fish were biting. It was a magical place in those days, simply enchanted.

And what a boon it proved to be when the town of Ananias was renamed Oil City.

Shall we end there for the day, dear?

March 4, 1937, Thursday

I finally did it today. I was tired of slinking, running, hiding. At first, I thought I would go to the police to report that a stranger had been in my house, but then I thought, what if he *is* the police? Now, I know who he is and what he's doing here.

After I left Miss Fenerty's, I walked down to the diner and was having coffee by myself as the waitress decorated the window with leprechauns and flowers that announced that *Spring Has Sprung*, though everyone says it may be another few weeks. Lime green shoots are dotting the branches of some of the trees, however, and the azaleas are putting out green buds that are beginning to bulge a little with a hint of color within.

A rumble on the street announced him, and then there he was, sitting behind the wheel of the Cadillac, looking at a notepad that he held against the upper margin of the steering wheel. He looked over at me, and I held up a hand, somewhere between a wave and a salute. He just nodded his head. I thought of what Ellie might say:

"Come on, enough of this. Time to face your fear, Miriam. You can't be so chicken shit and expect to get anywhere."

I told the waitress, Francie, that I was going across the street to talk to the man sitting in the black Cadillac, and I asked her if she would mind keeping my coffee for me. Just to be sure, I also asked her to watch for a moment, that the man was a stranger to me, and I wasn't sure how much I trusted him.

"Sure, hon," she said, and she stood at the window holding a tin coffee pot among the flowers and the leprechauns and bunnies with Easter baskets. She watched as I crossed the street, pausing to let a couple of cars pass by.

As soon as I exited the diner and came across the street, he got out of the Cadillac and leaned against it on the sidewalk side with his forearms on the hood. The brim of his hat concealed his face as he looked in the notepad in his hands. The shine of the hood held his dim counter-image, as if there were another version of himself trapped within it that moved when he moved. He didn't bother with a hello; he just put the notepad in his coat pocket. And though he didn't look up at me, he knew I was there. I kept his car between us.

"Why are you following me?" I demanded, though my voice tried to crack and falter, dipping like a bird on a downdraft. He didn't answer my question. He simply asked a question of his own.

"The man in the house with you. Your husband?" His fingers toyed with an unlit cigarette.

"No," I said. If I hadn't been so scared, I would have been disgusted at the thought of it.

He lit the cigarette, shielding the match from the wind with his cupped hands, then pushing his hat down on his head with one hand as the wind nipped at it. The other hand flicked the spent match away.

"Boyfriend?" He mumbled the word around the cigarette in his lips and exhaled it out into the wind. The smoke dissipated quickly leaving no trace of it except the faint aroma. Chesterfields, I think.

"No," I said again. "We're just housemates. Share the rent."

"Painted a naked picture of you, though, didn't he?"

He said naked like nick-ed. There was something unrelenting about him, something dogged, strangling, like the rolling twist of a python squeezing something. My mouth opened, but I was too embarrassed to say anything, so he did.

"Has your housemate ever mentioned the name, Mildred Hickey?"

He looked up for a fleeting moment, a glance. His eyes were a pale blue, almost translucent, an eerie color. He seemed reluctant to make eye contact with me. It was almost as if he thought he would hurt me if he looked at me for very long, and he didn't want to hurt me.

"No, never," I said. He was looking at his fingernails as he pried dirt out from under them with a toothpick. Finally, he looked up again, and I looked into his eyes and had to turn away. His eyes bore into me. They were the color of thick ice, a blue that was fading into aqua, the color of the sea. When he looked up at me with them, it made me recoil. It was the color of something unmistakably ancient, something that had always been, something as old as the earth or older.

"Do me a favor," he said. "I'm staying at the Youree. Bellman knows which room. Call me if you hear him speak of Hickey or Jackson."

He never said hello or goodbye, nor did I. He just gave me his card, *G. H. Firinne, Jackson, Miss.* He put his head down, the brim obscuring his face again. He flicked his cigarette into the gutter and got in behind the wheel. The Cadillac roared to life, leaving me standing speechless on the curb. I had to sit down on a bench.

Now I remember the name on the letters from Jackson.

Hickey.

March 5, 1937, FWP, Transcript of Bridget Fenerty

At first, everyone thought that it was a joke or that someone was lying, for in the Christian Bible, Ananias and his wife were struck down for it,[67] a story that children in town were told as a precaution against the practice of bearing false witness. Many of the adults seemed to have forgotten that story, of course, and were willing to take their chances.

Everyone here had always figured that the riches of the land were on the surface of it in the form of cotton and lumber, not under it. Not buried like the gold in California and the Yukon or the silver in Nevayda.

The first ones, the first wells, came in about the time that the courthouse monument was dedicated, Sergeant Lockett sitting with the notables who extolled his virtues and the righteousness of the failed southern cause.[68] The speaker used words like 'magnanimous' and 'alacrity,' words that sailed over the heads of most of the people who sat there batting at the heat with fans, including Mr. Lockett, who sat in a suit at the dais with the other dignitaries

---

[67] Acts 5:1-11. Ananias and his wife Sapphira sold land, and, instead of giving all of it to the common good of the church, they lied about it and kept a portion of it for themselves.

[68] The monument on the Caddo Parish Courthouse lawn was dedicated in 1906.

and examined his fingernails like he wished he were somewhere else, as if he were embarrassed by the attention. The band played "Dixie" and "The Bonnie Blue Flag" and so forth and the massive sheet draped over the statue was pulled down, and everyone sighed and clapped. And then the band played "Dixie" again.

I was there with the crowd. Morris had driven me in his motorcar, one of the first in town. We sat side by side as the last of spring's pleasantness ebbed away, one of the last days before it would be too hot to do anything but sit on the porch. Birds flitted and chirped in the branches of the live oaks, tiny piccolos against the great tubas and trumpets of oration at the podium. The service closed with bowed heads and a fervent prayer, a supplication that seemed to go on for hours, days, centuries, everyone's bladder straining, children fidgeting, old men yawning and nodding. Wives nudged the shoulders of sleeping husbands when the damn thing was finally over. Then everyone left, and the Negro men picked up the wooden folding chairs, the slap of them closing in the distance at our backs. As we got up and shook life back into our sleeping legs, most of the men were talking about the same thing. Oil.

Oil fever was about us, the topic of every other conversation in town, talk of barrels and gushers and derricks and wildcatters. There was a sudden interest in geology, sand and rock and whatever else was under the earth. Things like that had been of little or no interest a year or two before. By the time Caddo Parish declared prohibition -ten years ahead of the rest of the country, and let it not be said that Shreveport has never been ahead of its time- quite a number of wells had been drilled and were producing.[69] It was about that time that our wells came in. Those of Morris and me.

Motorcars were beginning to appear in the streets, competing for space with wagons and teams, mules veering slowly and uncontrollably to the side, nosing to the curb and then staying there frightened by the noise as their masters yelled from the buckboard and shook snapping waves of leather at them with the reins, all to no effect. Gradually, the streets began smelling less and less like manure and more like the fumes of the auto.

Around this time, there was a man who came in for a new suit. Actually, he came in for two new suits and paid for them in advance with a roll of bills that bulged in his trouser pockets like he was glad to see us. He struck up a conversation with Morris as Morris' man, a Mr. Wembley, measured him. The customer's name was Hughes[70], not the aviator and film producer, but his father. Well, he said he had some new class of drilling bit he'd invented. He

---

[69] By a narrow and contentious vote, Caddo Parish went dry in 1908.

[70] This is none other than Howard Hughes, Sr., inventor of the rotary drilling bit which revolutionized the oil and gas industry. Hughes once said, "I never held a public office except that of deputy sheriff and postmaster at Oil City, La. Therein I lost my religion."

said it would revolutionize how oil and gas were got out of the ground. Morris said that he and a good friend had some land up near Pine Island on Caddo Lake and that we might be interested in giving the new bit a try.

Well, it worked. Our wells came in faster and out-produced those around us. Morris' shop became a hobby, a tradition, a homage to his father, something to do during the day. And my keeping children became something of the same, though really it had always been that way, and I thank you again, Mr. Burton, sir.

But the oil changed things for us. For one thing, the quiet of Camp Taylor was shattered by the clacking away of the pump jacks and the flare of gas at night. Oil wells, salt wells, gas wells. One well, not one of ours but one on an adjacent tract, burned for six years and could be seen for miles. The peaceful sounds of croaking frogs and the bellow of alligators and the flap of ducks taking off were obscured by the roaring of gas wells exhaling messy spirals of deafening flames like dragons.

When a gusher came in, oil and dirt blew out skyward in a foul mud that covered the men working there, explosions that mangled some men and made others filthy rich. You could hear it when it happened, when a blowout took place, the shake of the ground and the boiling plume of mud up into the air and back down, clattering down on the earth with a smacking, wet sound. Somewhere below the din, almost silent by comparison, was the hurrahing of men turned slick and black by the downpour.

So many wells were flaring off natural gas that it was said that, even miles away, you could read a newspaper at night. We would sit out at night, on the nights we went out to Camp Taylor, just sit out there and watch the flames from far away, dancing, twisting yellow orange tongues of fire up into the night sky, the reflection of it at night in the black surface of the lake, which had taken on an oily sheen. You could even see the fires from all the way in the city if you looked off to the northern horizon. It seemed something like Sodom and Gomorrah, and I felt as though at any moment I should be turned into a pillar of salt like Lot's wife.

It changed Ananias, too, not just in name but in temperament, as well. If the sleepy whistle stop of Ananias was Dr. Jekyll, then Oil City became Mr. Hyde. Up east of town a place sprung up called Reno Hill, a boozing place with every vice a young man with pockets full of money could want, a place on the Kansas City line where conductors would advise passengers to pull down the shades as the trains passed through to avoid getting an eyeful. A place with a tree in the middle of main street where drunks were shackled until they sobered up, a place where murders occurred so often that only a fraction of them made the papers.

The other thing that changed was Mr. Randolph. He, like so many others, was lured by the prospect of riches, wildcatting as the oil field was discovered north and east of here, Haynesville, Homer, Smackover, El Dorado. The Randolph children were uprooted from their lives and from me, and so was Mrs. Randolph. He gave up the lumber business and the Hoos Hoos and his friendly card games and the rest of his social calendar and took his wife and children to live lives in clapboard shanty towns in the piney woods among tent cities of single men who brawled and whored and gambled, all in the name of making a small fortune.

We all would have traded it for how it was before. Some things like peace and quiet and camaraderie you can't put a price on.

Let's stop there, shall we?

March 5, 1937, Friday

Miss Fenerty said that she still heard from the Randolph children and from Mrs. Randolph, whose health was poor. "Mr. Randolph…" She looked to me and stopped in midsentence. "You seem someplace else, dear."

"Oh, I suppose. I've got a wedding to arrange. Maybe that's it," I said. (I just got another letter from Irving. I think he's aware of my reticence.)

"You never speak of your fiancé," Miss Fenerty said.

"Oh, I guess there's not much to say," I said. "He lives so far away, is all."

She didn't say anything but only smiled and offered tea. We sipped it slowly while listening to Pagliacci on the gramophone, our eyes closed as the disk revolved with an undercurrent of static from the needle. Ellie had gone to take dinner to Nina and her husband and to see the new baby. Ellie makes herself scarce now, anyway, thinking of errands to go on when she knows I'm coming.

Caruso sang "*Vesti La Giubba.*" His voice was fine and regal and soaring even though it emerged tinny and scratched from the wax it was trapped in as the record spun under the needle. The words in Italian whirled out in invisible agony: *Put on the suit, clown, and laugh, laugh even though you just found out your wife has been unfaithful. The people have paid, so put on the costume and laugh.*

I thought of Irving, a successful man but a simple man, a good man, really, who deserves more than what I can give him. I felt in a trance as I watched the label of the record spin, concentric revolving circles of blurred letters. My mind put Irving in the white silk clown suit with three black pompom buttons and a wide circle of a collar, spitting out a frowning laugh.

Miriam?

Miss Fenerty's voice was accompanied by the ticking skip of the needle on the record.

"Well, you certainly floated away there, now, didn't you dear? I'd give a penny for your thoughts, but I think you may have a dollar's worth or more."

"If you had it to do over again…" I began to ask her. She stopped me abruptly.

"No one gets to do it over again, not one of us," she said, rather sternly. "You do the best you can, and if you fail you only get the next moment to start over in and that will have to be enough. The past is past and always will be."

I've sent for more blanks for the recorder, as I'm down to just a few. They should have been here by now.

March 6, 1937, Sabbath

Well, now. What an interesting day it's been.

I overslept this morning and missed temple, so instead, in the way of a spiritual experience, I went to watch the sunset over the lake this afternoon, and what a beautiful thing it was. I parked near what appeared in the daylight to be an abandoned building that advertised itself as the Lakecliff Bar. I eased the Packard under a billboard next to the cinderblock edifice. The evening light fell on the face on a billboard, an advertisement, a doctor with a head mirror and a white smock. He held out a pack of cigarettes in his hand as if offering one to the viewer. *More Doctors Smoke Camels* was written across the top of the ad. Dry yellow winter weeds sprouted around the bases of the pilings of the billboard.

A trail heading down the hill to the lake had been beaten, and I followed it to the dam and the water's edge. Railroad tracks ran along the top of the dam, and I sat on the smooth, metal coolness of the rail and watched the sunset. The air was pleasantly cold, and I wished again for a cup of coffee or hot cocoa and someone to enjoy it with. The evening light serrated the surface of the lake, golden, orange, shimmering, glistening. At last, the sun was a semicircle and then a sliver. The horizon glowed orange like the long, last closing note of a symphony, and then the lake water was black under the night sky.

I trampled back up the hill through the weeds to where I had parked. I found that the failing light was the signal for the Lakecliff Bar to come to life. Lights were beginning to shine from the windows and around the door as laughter and music escaped whenever patrons arrived and entered through it. From behind the building, the smoke and the smell of cooking meat filled the air.

I stood by my car and watched the little watering hole like a scientist might. It was alive with activity. Above me, the Camel-smoking doctor smiled out beatifically over the bar and its patrons and the parking lot. His grinning face was up-lit by electric lamps at the base of the billboard.

Suddenly, inside the bar chair legs scraped, and there was shouting. The door opened and became a rectangle of light. Two men threw another man out into the night, and he landed in a heap at the perimeter of the darkness in a skittering of gravel. One of the men shouted.

"Get on away from here! And don't think a comin' back until you can pay your tab and keep your hands off a the waitresses!"

He was a big man who wore an apron that was stained a dingy beige. The other man was smaller and slimmer with a rail-thin body and baseball bat-shaped head. His pants were hitched high, and the belt holding them up was overlapped by a short, wide tie. Both men were smoking; the billboard doctor seemed pleased. Behind them, the rectangle of light was a pale smoky yellow. Laughter and the clack of billiard balls escaped from around them and through the doorway. I approached the parking lot, and the light shifted behind the big man and the skinny man, and they became mere silhouettes.

I paused at my car with my key in my hand just steps from the altercation. The heap of a man on the ground sat up and braced himself on his hands in the gravel of the parking lot. Inside, music continued playing, some song I didn't know, but there was a shout answered by a cheer, and I took it that the song was a favorite. The man in the parking lot finally spoke back to the shadowy men in the doorway. As he stood up and dusted himself off, I recognized him.

"Y'all ain't right...peckerheads," he said as he got up, but he fell silent when he saw me. I stepped forward, away from the Packard and toward the men and the light. Yes, it was he, Monsieur Lemurier, *le muraliste.*

"Well, I declare," I said, making sure that my southern accent was as affected as his French one. "I do believe that you're acquiring a southern accent after your sad exile here in the South. Or is it a homecoming?"

He glared at me, and taking up a French accent again he hissed, "You go to hell, Madame."

He turned and headed down the street into the night, toward the bus stop.

"Hey!" the big man with the apron shouted. "Look a here! That ain't no way to speak to a lady, mister. You get the hell on your way!"

As Lemurier slunk away, he made a crude gesture to us without turning around.

"Some fellers sure got balls...oh, uh, sorry ma'am, no offense," the man with the high pants and baseball bat-head said.

"No offense taken," I said. "No offense taken at all because you are exactly right. I couldn't have said it better myself."

They went back inside, and, as they were closing the door, one of them asked, "You comin' in?"

"No," I said, "I'm headed home."

I moved away from the door, and the men shut it against the chilling night air. The sounds of billiards and music and laughter and conversation were muffled. I got behind the wheel of the Packard, and it rumbled to life, its two bright eyes shining into the darkness.

349

I passed Lemurier. In the rearview mirror, I saw him making his way down the shoulder of the road. Within his silhouette, a small dot of ember glowed from the cigarette in his mouth, and, above his shoulder, the doctor on the billboard appeared to have given it to him. The dark outline on the side of the road exhaled, and the smoke rose up mystically over the smiling physician in the cigarette ad. I turned onto Milam Street and left the man, Lemurier, or whoever he really was, walking.

Mar. 7, 1937, Sunday

When Ellie left for church, Miss Fenerty asked if I would walk with her up to the cemetery. She carried a handful of daffodils in one hand and her cane in the other. It probed the sidewalk, rapping slowly with each step. I offered to drive us if she preferred.

"Oh, I'd prefer to walk while I still can," she said, as if it were a personal maxim.

Behind the tall stained glass windows lined up along the flanks of the church, the Methodists were singing in joyful, soaring blasts, the organ sawing and snoring and blaring and honking with them, leading them: *God-in-three persons, bless-ed trin-i-ty...*

A warm wind stirred from the south, a soft, downy wind that promised rain. It pushed at our backs, urging us down Common Street as the flags that strained against the pole over the Central Fire Station rattled and popped. Firemen were taking advantage of the weather to wash the engines out front. Wet, soapy clouds of bubbles coasted down the concrete, drifting and weaving around and under their rubber boots.

At the Milam Street entrance of the cemetery, she nudged the iron gate as if she had done it a hundred, a thousand times before. The wind nudged it, and it groaned a metallic complaint and then fell silent. Her cane tapped and crunched in the gravel lane that came to a halt a few yards into the cemetery, a stopping point for hearses. She wandered in among the lanes dotted with granite and marble and cedars. I tarried for a moment to watch her, imagining the countless times she had been among the mourners, outfitted in black with a veil behind a horse-drawn hearse. She turned and made a rolling motion with her old hand, and I trotted to catch up.

We weaved among the gravestones into the interior of the cemetery and came to a large area with a simple marker, "Yellow Fever Mound." She paused, braced herself on her cane, and leaned down to place a yellow daffodil near the center of the clearing, which was flat, no longer a mound. She straightened up with quite a bit of effort; she smiled without the least bit of it.

"Elias is in there, his body is. Such a comfort it was, lying next to him on those nights," she said. "Sixty years and more. Can it be that long?"

I took a daffodil from her bunch and laid it with the first, crossing the stems. She stared at them as if in a trance, surely her mind chewing on some happy memory.

"Well, let's go pay a call on old Mr. Taylor," she said brightly as she surfaced from her daydream.

His gravestone was ornate with a Star of David on it and the date of his birth, *May 30, 1838, Plotsk, Russia,* and the date of his death, *Jan. 1, 1877.* Between the two dates, there was writing in Hebrew that I recognized as *Beloved Father.* There were several others like it in this area of the cemetery, a section called Hebrews' Rest.

"Mrs. Taylor?" I asked.

"Long gone. Buried in St. Louis on the grounds of the asylum."

The wind filled the silence. Clouds were floating hurriedly to the north, racing against the sky blue sky. Traffic was picking up on Texas Avenue where it veered away in the direction of the state it was named after. A car honked a quick salutation to another, distracting us from our revelry. We turned and rambled up the hill. I asked her where Mr. Rusk is buried.

"Up here," she said as she puffed up the incline.

"There are Negros buried here? Not separately?"

"Oh, yes. We never had that sort of thing here like they do in Alabama or Mississippi. We could be buried together; we just couldn't drink from the same fountain when we were alive."

She brought me to a secluded spot among a grove of massive cedars, a prime looking spot that seemed separate, more peaceful. She leaned forward and reverently touched the headstone, a raised rectangle of granite with the inscription, *Solomon Rusk, a free man gone home.* Under it, *Thy word is a lamp unto my feet, and a light unto my path.* Her old hand grasped a weed sprouting from the base of the stone and pulled it from the ground. She shook the dirt from the roots and tossed it away as she straightened up.

"Elias and I planted these cedars," she said. I laid a daffodil by the marker and snapped off two dandelions, one for her and one for me. We both knew what to do. Giggling like two girls, we closed our eyes and pushed our breath, and white tufts scattered to the breeze, racing away on the south wind. We snatched another breath and rotated the tiny green stems and blew again, watching the tufts take flight and disappear, as invisible as the wind. The sky had become almost solid white, clouds creased into folds.

We made our way arm in arm across the rows of stone, some big, some small, but all of them marking a memory. Names appeared on them and then faded with our passing as they had faded with the passing of the sleepers beneath. We came to an obelisk that tilted slightly. It was a mottled marble, about chest high. On it was inscribed, *Frank O. Burton, Sr.* Under it was a hand with a finger pointing heavenward and under that, *He died with his country.*

There were dried flowers in a marble urn at the base, what was once a healthy bouquet of expensive flowers. Miss Fenerty removed the old dried ones and set them at the base of a cedar.

"The birds like to make nests of these old stems," she said. Then she put the daffodils in the vase and looked up to the sky, which had begun turning from powdery white to dingy gray. "The rain will put some water in there tonight. 'Wind from the South has rain in her mouth.'"

She stood and contemplated the monument. I couldn't tell if she was praying or just thinking. At last, she said, "Strange, but sometimes, every once in a while, there are flowers already here. Chrysanthemums, Mrs. Burton's favorite. He didn't have any relatives here, not that I knew."

I had to ask.

"Why do you put flowers on his grave after what he did to you?"

"'Tis simple, really. It's the only connection I have to my boy. I wonder if he's still alive somewhere." She looked around as if somehow he might be near. "I wonder if he remembers me. He would be seventy-four next week. A day doesn't go by that I don't think of him."

A trolley went down Texas Avenue grinding metal wheels on metal rails. It rumbled to a stop, dinged a couple of times, then rumbled off after the door shut with a slap. I turned to look at it, and the wind pushed my hair into my face, and I turned my face directly into it. When I did, the rush of air pushed my hair completely back; I could feel the warm moist breath of it, the wind, on my bare forehead and cheeks and chin and neck. I shook my head and pulled a stray strand of black back behind my ear. The tepid breeze felt good after a winter of cold winds. I closed my eyes and asked a question.

"What does it stand for?" I asked.

"Pardon?" she asked me back.

I turned to the marker. "The O, what does it stand for?"

"Ovid," she said, "like the Roman poet."

We stood and looked at the granite marker as the wind gently pushed at us.

"*Bear and endure...*" I began to recite the little Ovid I remembered, but I faltered as my mind reached for the rest, and a silence ensued, the bare, hard kind of silence one only finds in a graveyard. Her old voice quietly broke into it.

"*...for this sorrow will one day prove to be for your good,*" she finished the quote as she tapped the O on Frank O. Burton, Sr.'s marker with her cane and said, "Ovid."

She turned with a smile, pivoting on her cane and tottering down the row, examining the names of people she had known, or known of, when they were alive. I held her arm as she stepped carefully through the graveyard, over the roots of cedars and small sinkholes. As she passed some monuments, she would say, *good morning, Joe* or *how are you, Mary?* And then she would chuckle to herself. We approached a rusted iron fence with two stones within it.

"Well, Miss McCune. Still flat on your back, I see."

She said it as if she and the woman had known each other as friends and enjoyed a delightful, intimate banter. Perhaps they had. I read the name on the monument.

"Annie McCune. The madam?" I asked.

"Yes. That's her. I used to bring dinner to her girls once a week. I got in the habit of it when Elias was alive. He attended the girls. Took care of them, I mean. After he died, I continued to pay them a call, to help look after them. I would come with a noonday meal, Wednesdays, usually. The girls would filter down from upstairs in their fancy underclothes, half-dressed, women who were used to being naked a great deal of the time. It did me some good to show the girls some kindness. When you show someone a kindness, you save their life just a little."

Miss Fenerty didn't say, but I'm sure she clung to the hope that someone had shown her sister Maggie a similar kindness. She turned slowly, carefully and eased up to a nearby block of granite.

"Let's have a seat on Mr. Reynolds's headstone," she said. "He was a nice man; I don't think he would mind a pretty girl's bottom resting on it." She laughed, and the cemetery almost seemed a happy place because of it. I smoothed my skirt and sat down on it as I made room for her, and she sat next to me. Her hands rested one on top of the other, both of them on the crook of her cane. Next to Miss McCune's monument was a smaller one. Both were enclosed in the same rusted iron fence. I read it out loud.

"Ada Mary Carlile. Carlile without an S."

"Annie McCune's married name at the time of the little girl's birth. Later, for some reason, she went back to McCune. The girl was the baby of one of her girls, a pretty, sandy haired girl with brown eyes. She was from somewhere out in the countryside, like so many of them were. She went by the name Lorelei, though I never believed it was her real name. They rarely used their real names and instead took on fancy ones."

Miss Fenerty smiled up into the dark green branches of a cedar tree where a blue jay landed with a slight recoil of the bough. She looked at the gravestone again. The blue jay took off and left the cedar bough swaying gently. The spring breeze kept it moving with a rushing, brushing sound, the tree shimmying in aromatic green waves.

"Well, Lorelei had a regular caller, a married man who got her with child. They took her out west of town for the alternative, but it failed. So Miss McCune put her up in a separate place when the girl's time came. It was what she did with them when that sort of thing happened. The moans and groans of labor would interfere with the gay, lighthearted feelings of the other sort of moans and groans. Elias delivered more than one of them, to be sure. Well, it lasted a day, a night, and another day. Little Ada Mary here lived, but her mother died. Miss McCune, Carlile at the time, took the baby to raise as her own, little Miss Ada, as the girls of the house called her. The little thing was a pet to them.

"Well, 'twas on a Wednesday that I brought dinner, and there on the landing of the stairs was none other than Mr. Randolph. Holding the little girl. The baby was less than a year old then. To see them there, the faces of the two of them next to each other, same sad blue eyes, father and daughter. Oh, there was no denying it, who the girl's father was. *Miss Fenerty*, he stammered.

"I winked at him and his secret and put my finger across my lips and said, 'Well, how sweet of you to come and help out with the baby.' But I knew. And he knew that I knew and that I wouldn't tell anyone. It would have only broken up a family and caused more heartache."

She looked up into the branches of a sapling growing behind Miss McCune's obelisk. It was dotted with small green buds.

"Ah, poor little Ada, she was a sickly little thing. Lived a few years and died of scarlet fever."

Miss Fenerty squinted as she read the date on the stone. "April twelve, nineteen hundred. Yes, I thought it was on a spring day. The girls put azaleas on her grave." She put her chin on top of her hands, which were still draped on top of her cane.

"After the little girl died, scarlet fever or some such-there were plenty of things to die young from then-Mr. Randolph seemed distant after that, tormented by his secret, his shame. One after-dinner bourbon turned into two and then three. I think he moved his family as much to get away from the memory and shame of Lorelei and Ada Mary as to make a fortune."

"You said you hear from the Randolph children and their mother. Do you ever hear from Mr. Randolph?" I asked.

"He was killed a few years after they moved, killed in an explosion up near Smackover. Hit right in the chest by one of the big beams of the derricks. Something broke loose in him, his heart or a big vessel, I suppose. Crushed his chest. Their wildcat well had finally come in dropping oil on them like shiny black pudding. He had literally died a rich man without ever getting to live as one. Mrs. Randolph became a wealthy widow and remarried. She lives in El Dorado now, though I hear her health isn't good."

Her tale at an end, we rose, and Miss Fenerty said down to our headstone-seat, "And I thank you kindly, Mr. Reynolds, sir, and I trust that a gentleman such as yourself didn't peer up our skirts."

She chuckled, and I could almost imagine Mr. Reynolds blushing or chuckling himself. She tottered down a row of graves, her arm on mine. She paused when she got to a gravestone of another man she remembered.

"This man was one of the ones who used to sing in Mr. Zwally's barbershop. Did I ever tell you about that? Let's go back home, and you can wind up your recorder, and I'll tell you and Mr. Roosevelt. I believe the rain will be on us soon, anyway."

Mar. 7, 1937, FWP, Transcript of Bridget Fenerty

The house got big and quiet again after the Randolphs left. Mr. Randolph shook hands with Morris with his right hand and then put his cigarette to his lips with his left, looking around and exhaling nervously. The wives, Sophie Taylor and Mrs. Randolph, embraced and then held each other at arms' length with melancholy smiles and moist eyes.

The new Ford model T truck Mr. Randolph had bought was jammed with their household items, bedsteads and so forth, Mrs. Randolph's nice chifferobe, all of it packed in behind the cab and lashed with ropes as if they were going over the sea, though the roads then may have given a similar experience. Children were in among the family's belongings with a couple of the smaller ones up front on the bench seat of the cab where Mr. and Mrs. Randolph would take their seats. The old truck had sides in the back like a chicken coop, wooden slats that bulged with their household, both children and goods. Faces of children peered out from the dark spaces between chairs and trunks. The sad faces of children who had been uprooted.

The model T sputtered down Crockett toward the river and the ferry at the foot of Texas Street. The Taylor cousins watched from the porch that day in 1909, or perhaps 'twas 1910, well, no matter. They stayed overnight with me and then through the weekend, but had to return home to Jordan Street Sunday night to go to school Monday morning. This house was big and quiet. Empty.

Morris offered again to put me up with them, but your own house watches you live and secrets away your memories for you. It absorbs them into its wood and plaster and paint and reminds you of them. You see the doorframe with the marks of the height of children, you step on the floorboard with its squeak where their little steps have hit randomly for years, you smell Elias' pipe and Mr. Randolph's Camels on the porch. You catch the memory of Old Mr. Taylor's shadow sitting in the parlor chair early and late, or the sunlight that fell on Elias sitting there reading. Even though they can't be heard, the sounds of the celebration of Christmases and Passovers still haven't stopped reverberating in the corners. The house keeps them for you, the memories, like companions, and you don't want to abandon them. So, the mysterious Ned Hennessy, the man no one ever saw, had Mr. Herndon, Jr. find new tenants.

The family's name was Eaves, a tow-headed family of such energy that I'm surprised the house didn't hum and levitate or glow at night. Mr. Eaves was an architect with Mr. Neild's firm.[71] There was a lot of building in the city then, as there is now, oil driving commerce, which drove construction, which drove commerce again, a lot of it in the last twenty years on a black tidal wave of oil. The Slattery Building, the new Courthouse, all put up here in the last twenty or so. Of course, it meant a lot of the old family homes had to be put down.

Well, I'll tell you, Miriam, the Eaves' household, this house, was wall-to-wall, floor-to-ceiling, threshold-to-threshold enthusiasm. Everything was an adventure, everything was interesting, a house full of books and paintings and discussions and singing. All sorts of drawing and musical instruments. A joyful household and a noisy one. Someone was always playing a violin or a trumpet or the piano. The joy spilled out the back door and into the back yard, where, after the circus came to town one year, Mr. Eaves constructed a pair of trapezes and a net, and Mrs. Eaves sewed fanciful costumes for the children as if they were circus performers. She even made a little cape for the dog, Ol' Susanna, an old long haired red dog who played the role of every animal she was asked to with a good natured smile, though she was too sweet to make a very good lion or tiger. Children coasted back and forth along the arcs of the trapezes, shouting to me, 'Watch this, Miss Biddy' before tumbling to the net below. I would clap vigorously, of course. Those rascals even knew how to dismount the net by grabbing the edge and flipping themselves off it. They'd seen it at the circus. Nothing escaped them. Little daredevils.

There were three of them. A big sister, Lola Mae, followed closely by brother Hank and the youngest, John. John-John, they called him. All curly, wavy blonde, constantly smiling, constantly reading, asking, poking, prodding, taking apart, putting back to together (mostly), running, jumping, shouting, singing, inspecting.

Their mother, Aurelia Eaves, not only endured it all, she enjoyed it all. A placid, peaceful woman, a small woman with big eyes, a big smile, and a little voice which she never raised. A petite little thing with a smile that was never bigger than when she leaned into her husband with her arms around him. Mr. Eaves towered next to her with his big hand on her little shoulder, a man with a quick handshake and eyes that really looked at you and ears that listened earnestly. He was a thoughtful man who truly wanted to hear what you said.

Mr. Eaves was a tall blonde man with a moustache he waxed to small yellow points. At home, he usually wore Turkish slippers and peculiar hats, a fez, or one with little projections with tassels on them. Frequently, he added

---

[71] Edwin Neild was an architect active in Shreveport, responsible for the new Caddo Parish Courthouse, among other buildings.

shiny gold pantaloons like a sultan. He was part ringmaster and part husband and father. An eccentric, a golden-haired, golden-hearted eccentric. I think he would have dressed like a Turk around town had Aurelia not put her foot down with a kiss and a teasing, "Honey, I don't want the other girls honing in on my man." So he wore a suit, a *Taylor and Son* suit, like every other fashionable professional man in town.

Although they were Catholics, Mr. Eaves also subscribed to *The Christian Science Monitor* and kept a statue of the Buddha in the parlor. He liked to make the rounds of the churches, Mr. Eaves did. After his attendance one Sunday, the Presbyterians congratulated themselves on having rescued a lost soul from the clutches of the Roman Dictator, only to find out Mr. Eaves was spotted the next week wearing a yarmulke in the Hebrew temple and the week after that singing in the choir with the Methodists. He called it going on a spiritual pilgrimage for a 'second opinion.'

Well, they were happy years, watching the Eaves children, having them animate this house. Airplanes were becoming the things then, and Mr. Eaves and his boys had a particular fascination with them. The rare and random sound of one droning in the sky would send the three of them running to catch the trolley with the crowds going to watch them land at the fairgrounds. There, having landed, there was talk about horsepower and fixed wings, and the boasts of the pilots, who held court like royalty, that they could achieve a top speed of over a hundred miles an hour. Some speculated that they may even be used if war was to come in Europe.

There was talk of war in Europe in those days, same as there is now. Wilson had been inaugurated the year before, having beaten the big fellow. What was his name? Oh, I can see his mustached face, jowly character. Tate? Ah, at my age, the memory belches and forgets sometimes. Yes, that's right, Taft. An enormous fellow, surely he was.

Well, there was a man named Henry Zwally who had a barber shop on Texas Street then, and it was there that I used to take the Eaves boys to get their haircuts. Women generally weren't welcome there, or perhaps they had no interest in going, but they tolerated me as I sat and watched the boys get their hair cut. They were small fellows then, six or eight years old, I suppose, sitting on empty crates Mr. Zwally put in the chairs. Their little heads protruding up through the black capes that covered them.

The boys loved going to get their haircuts, and the men enjoyed listening to the stories the boys told about little boy things. There was a Negro man named Walter who was forever sweeping hair into a pile and then calling for the boys, telling them, "You boys come see this rat we killed this morning in that back room yonder."

The boys would go with him and marvel at the pile of hair which was really about the size of a dog. One of them would push at it with the toe of his shoe, and then they would run back to me.

"Gaw, Miss Biddy!" They would say. "Mr. Walter killed a rat as big as Ol' Susanna!" That was our old dog's name. "Come see it."

Of course, I had to get up and marvel over the size of it, and Walter and I would wink at each other.

"That's the biggest one yet," I would tell him.

"Yes ma'am, it show is. I don't rightly know how they keep gettin' in here. I kilt this one while he's gnawin' on a chicken bone he got out the garbage." And that made the boys' eyes get big. Walter and I winked at one another again.

Meanwhile, the men would talk about the prospect of war with the Hun,[72] and politics, and the weather. The subject of weather had three subheadings: weather of the past, weather of the future, and then the worst weather ever. Blizzards, floods, droughts, hailstorms, combinations of them, sometimes occurring within hours of each other. Everything except tongues of fire from heaven and swarms of locusts.

Then there were cotton prices and hog prices and oil prices, and then baseball, which was becoming the rage then. The scissors clicked, and the straight razors slapped against the leather straps. And then more talk of politics. The men of Henry Zwally's barber shop tended to be devout Democrats like most Southerners. And, when they ran out of things to talk about, they would sing, and everyone would listen. I couldn't help but think how much Ned Hennessy would have loved such a life as that.

And so it was one day that the men had fallen into singing. They sang "You're the Flower of My Heart, Sweet Adeline" and "Down by the Old Mill Stream" and "Let Me Call You Sweetheart," a new one then. And then some others, and it was very lovely, very enjoyable.

One of the Eaves boys says to Mr. Zwally, he says, "Mr. Henry, our Miss Biddy can sing. She can sing real good."

It was always so lovely, so heartwarming to be referred to as 'Our Miss Biddy.' His brother, who was sitting in the chair next to him, concurred.

"That's right," he said. He winced as the other barber, a Mr. Malcolm, pulled a comb through his hair. "She sings like an angel."

"That right?" Mr. Zwally said as he elevated the chair a little by pumping the lever on the side. The chair rose with a gulping sound. "Sing us something, then, Miss Biddy."

He took up the comb and scissors again as he kept his concentration on the little head of blonde curls before him. I could tell he was doubtful. I think I was blushing, but I remembered what Ma used to say: sing loud and make God sorry for the voice he gave you.

---

[72] Germany

"Sing the one about Kathleen Movin'," John-John said.

"Yes ma'am, that one," Hank seconded it.

Kathleen Mauvorneen, they meant, the popular song sung by Catherine Hayes in the old century.

I began singing. And all the haircuts stopped. And all the jaws dropped open. When I finished, there was a silence, and all you could hear was the sound of the trolley passing and automobiles sputtering by outside and a breeze moving down the street.

Mr. Zwally moved over to the door and shut it to keep out the noise. All he could say was, "Another, please."

Despite my blushing, I sang "My Wild Irish Rose," *[singing] the-sweetest-flower-that-grows*, and "I'll Take You Home Again, Kathleen," some of the songs made popular by John McCormack, "I Hear You Calling Me,"

I hear you calling me.
You called me when the moon had veiled her light,
Before I went from you into the night;
I came, – do you remember? – back to you
For one last kiss beneath the kind stars' light.

Now, there was a man named Mr. O'Hare,[73] and he was responsible in some way for the Grand Opera House. He ended up moving to New York, and perhaps he had moved at that time and was merely down for a visit-he had married a girl from Marshall, you know. But regardless, he was in his office which was a block away. Mr. Zwally sent Walter to fetch Mr. O'Hare.

Mr. O'Hare arrived with the napkin still tucked in his collar; he had been at his lunch. He sat in an empty barber chair and pulled the napkin from his shirt and put it over his shoulder.

"So I hear you can sing," he said. I recognized him as a man who had once lived a few doors down from us on Crockett Street during the Randolph years. He was a mustachioed man with his hair swept back.

"I do passably," I said.

The men all guffawed, and one of them said, "Why, she's a regular songbird, that one is."

"Sing something for me, then," Mr. O'Hare said as he looked down at his lap where his hands were folding the napkin he had taken off his shoulder. He looked up again with a smile and a look of concentration on his face.

I sang "Jeannie with the Light Brown Hair."

---

[73] W.C. O'Hare (1867-) is a composer active from the turn of the century onward. He was an instructor at the Kate Nelson Seminary, a boarding school for young ladies on Texas Avenue, and manager of the Grand Opera House in Shreveport around this time before leaving to compose full time in New York.

Before I was finished, he interrupted me.

"Have you ever sung in public before?"

And so began my life on the stage, at age seventy, no less. The next week I sang at the Grand Opera House. The lights were hot and blaring in my face, the audience only a vague idea in the darkness. I remembered the day Ned and I watched Jenny Lind from the rafters of the St. Charles Theater in New Orleans. I comforted myself thinking that perhaps he was up there now watching me, nodding and smiling, saying, *go on, now Bridget, go on, me garl.*

I had a new dress, and Mrs. Eaves had done a magic trick or two with my thinning hair. I looked up to the balcony, and there was Miss McCune and her girls, the madam herself in a special double wide throne of a chair. She was an enormous woman, especially as she grew old. Up in the front row, close enough where I could see them distinctly, were the Eaves and their children, patiently waiting and smiling, all dressed nicely as if for Mass or temple or church.

I went through my repertoire, songs I knew by heart having sung them for decades to myself in kitchens over cooking pots and tables of clothes being folded. Songs I'd sung to baseboards being scrubbed, children being tucked in, sheets being hung on lines. My time on stage passed by effortlessly, more so with each round of applause after each song. Afterward in the lobby, it seemed no one had left, and people I scarcely knew were gathering about to congratulate me.

"Why, we didn't know you could sing, Miss Fenerty," and "lovely, Miss Fenerty, simply lovely." Rapturous looks on the faces of the women, handshakes from men who had been marched in by their wives and then found they had enjoyed it.

It was well received, written about in the papers, and people would stop me on the street, people I knew only through someone else. *Such a lovely voice, ma'am. Why, I didn't know we had a God's honest angel living among us!* That sort of thing.

Well, the short of it is, I became a regular at the Grand Opera House and occasionally in the outlying towns, Monroe, Marshall, Longview. After the city declared prohibition, the theater was one of the only forms of entertainment. That and fistfighting. Oh, yes, the brothels, too, of course. You could buy love, but you couldn't buy a drink.

I was in acclaim, singing all these different places, singing at weddings like Da had done, as a gift to the bride and groom. And, if they insisted on paying me, I quietly gave the money to charity.

My health was good, and, as the stages got bigger, fame fed on itself, getting larger merely from fame. But it lures you, fame does, and you follow it when your courage tells you the time is right. It takes you places and shows you things, good and bad, delightful and dreadful. 'Twas the same for me.

We all say we want simple lives, humble lives of contentment. But what we really want are marching bands to spell out our names, statues of ourselves in museums, thunderous applause as we stand above the footlights. We all claim to be humble, but none of us really wants humility, then, do we Miriam? We only want humility for others.

So fame seduced me, and despite being an old woman, I succumbed to it. It took me on a trip halfway across the country and almost took me halfway across the world. It showed me the big city, and it showed me something else. I think I told you before that I've only seen ghosts once in my life, and I saw them all at the same time.

Well, look at the time, will you, then? Let's take a little tea. I believe that Jack Benny is due on the radio.

March 8, 1937, Monday, rainy

We listened to Jack Benny and Rochester, and then I bid her adieu, wondering about her seeing ghosts but not asking her. The recorder was turned off, and I wanted to wait until a time I had it turned on, to capture it for posterity.

The rain came in on a stiff south wind last night, coming down hard as I got in the door at Stephenson Street and continuing on and off through the night and all day today. It seems to have washed quite a bit away and revealed a truth. It all makes sense now.

I was cleaning the kitchen while the man who calls himself Lemurier took a nap on the sofa, and Mirlette did the same upstairs. They're like a pair of housecats, lounging around all day in odd places. The last plate was in my hand to be put in the cupboard when there was a knock on the door and then another more insistent one. Lemurier slept through both of them.

I put the plate away and went to the front door as Lemurier stirred, scratching his belly which I now know is a prelude to him getting up. I looked through the window to see a rather stout woman standing outside on the porch. When I opened the door, she looked at me and then nervously past me. Her eyes widened when she saw Lemurier.

"Hi, ma'am, I'm...Willie!" she cried out. "It's you!"

My housemate was up and off the couch. He had an unlit cigarette in one hand and a book of matches in the other. He stood at my back, and I felt uncomfortable. We looked too much like husband and wife standing together like that. I moved out of the shadow of his hair pomade and over to the window.

"That detective we hired, Mr. Firinne, he found you! He sure did!" the woman exclaimed as she moved forward to embrace him. "It took almost ever cent we had, man with fancy clothes and a fancy black car, but by God he found you. By God's honest truth he did! A regular Dick Tracy!"

She paused when he evaded her embrace.

"Willard, son, where've you been? Your brother, Jasper, you remember him, don't you, son? He misses you so. He always looked up to you. Billy Adcock said you weren't in that trench, and I knew it. A mama knows these things, Willard. Come on home, Willard. Come on home, Willie boy."

"Don't call me that. Willard Hickey died in a trench, ma-madame." I think he almost said mama. "Joseph Lemurier crawled out, alive, stronger, reborn like the Phoenix. Godlike."

Mrs. Hickey pursed her lips and knitted her brow like one would do when seeing an oddity in a tent at a state fair.

"Son, you're talkin' crazy now. Your family wants to see you. Your sister, your brother, your mee-maw. Tell him," she looked at me. "Tell him he belongs at home."

"Woman, it is *you* who are talking the crazy," he said, his accent thick again. "Go away from me! Go away for-ever!"

He slammed the door on her, and I watched her through the front window. She stood for a moment contemplating the door as if it had shut itself. Slowly, gradually, she began weeping, her massive chest heaving. Then she turned and went toward the street, wiping her eyes as she wandered. The rain pattered on her, teasing her. She looked to the house again and then got in a car, an old Dodge. A man that I couldn't see well was behind the wheel. It moved a few feet, and she held her palm up to the driver. She looked up to the house and at me in the window, and I raised a palm to her, some sort of salute that I felt I owed her. She began crying again, and the car moved forward again. It disappeared down the street.

I turned to see Mirlette standing at the foot of the stairs. When Lemurier, Hickey, I suppose now, turned, he approached her, looking for solace, I assumed. He found none.

"You said you had no family, Wheel-ard!" Mirlette shouted, and Lemurier-Hickey slapped her cheek, and her argument stopped suddenly.

He got drunk this afternoon and beat Mirlette to the point that I was on the verge of calling the police when he slowly stopped like a windup toy at the end of its spring. He fell asleep on a chair downstairs, slouched back with his arms and legs splayed. I came down for something, and she was sitting on the couch smoking. I was about to go back up when she spoke.

"*Son français est terrible, vous savez,*" Mirlette said suddenly in a low voice.

I wasn't prepared for French, and it took me a moment. My Barnard College days and its continental French seem like decades ago.

"*Pourriez-vous répéter?*" I asked as I sat on the couch.

She spoke slower, but still in French.

"His French is horrible. He barely speaks it. He only pretends."

Hickey's mouth was open, and he looked like a fish, a fish head you would see at a market. A slack-jawed, snoring fish. His neck was exposed; he needed a shave.

I waited for Mirlette to speak. It was something they taught us at Barnard: sometimes just a little patience, and the story will jump in your lap. It did, still in French:

"To turn your back on your mother. It is unforgiveable," she said. I waited again. "He's not who he says he is." She sounded as if she were giving me a warning. Her hand trembled, but the smoke from her cigarette calmly reeled out from the end, reeling out like her story.

"I met him in Saint-Dizier, in France, where I was raised. He was an American soldier, and I was a just a girl, widowed at eighteen. So many of us were then." She switched to English. I suppose it had the words she needed for the bitterness she felt:

"Just eighteen *fucking* years old."

She switched back to French as her lip pulled at her cigarette and let the smoke go. Her legs were crossed, and her foot jiggled nervously. She glanced again at the man who said he was Lemurier.

"He appeared in my village. He told me he was an American soldier and that he had deserted. He would occasionally tell the truth in those days. He said that he wasn't a hundred meters from his trench when a shell hit, and it caved in. All his childhood friends lost to the earth. Apparently, all but one, that boy his mother spoke of, this Billy Adcock." She pronounced Adcock like Ad-cook.

"Willard said he was a housepainter before the war in a place called Jackson, Mississippi."

Jack-sown Me see see pee, she said it.

"He said he could provide for me. He was handsome. He was persuasive. I had no other prospects. He took on the name of my late husband, Joseph Lemurier. The name, and the clothes and the bed."

Her cigarette had burned down, and she lit another from the stub of it before she pushed the butt into a saucer on the end table. She leaned back into the sofa and blew smoke up to the ceiling.

"We traveled France and Belgium, I speaking for him as he claimed to have lost his hearing due to artillery. He also claimed great skill, or rather, I claimed it for him, and towns would pay us in advance to create murals in their public places, anything for beauty in those shattered days after the war. Everyone wanted something beautiful then.

"We would collect the money in advance, and he would spend a week or so on the scaffolds painting on some public wall, one of the free cigarettes he demanded from the town hanging from his lip as he painted up there. The murals were awful, as you might imagine." She gestured to the paintings around the room.

"The townspeople would question the work as he painted, and he would say, through me of course, *'just you wait'* and *'don't bother an artist while he creates.'* As soon as he had painted something passable, or as soon as he became bored, or as soon as we felt the anger of the town building against us, we left. Usually, it was in the night and unannounced. As soon as we left, the town would pay to have his work painted over.

"His reputation, or I should say, *our* reputation, for his pulled mine down, began to follow us. And then our reputation began to greet us in the next town, and he could no longer find work as a *muraliste*, as he calls himself." She rolled her eyes and scowled.

"He sent telegrams announcing himself to America as the great French muralist Joseph Lemurier, the man who had re-beautified the French and Belgian countryside after the war. An ad was placed in the papers." She snorted and put the cigarette to her lips again.

"A wealthy socialite in New York responded to the ad and paid for our passage to America. It didn't take long, however, for Willard's lack of talent..." She looked at him as he slept on the couch and then scowled at him and whispered, "Wheel-ard Wheelard Wheelard Wheelard," taunting him as he snored indifferently. She ended by pursing her lips at him derisively.

"Oh, I forgot," she wagged her head as she said facetiously, "*Monsieur Lemurier*, it didn't take long for his lack of talent to be discovered. So, instead of murals, we traveled the country painting advertisements on barns. For shaving cream, tobacco, and what have you. He was passable at that, at least. That," she lifted her cigarette to highlight her point, "That was honest work. But a dishonest man can't do honest work for long, can he?"

She put the cigarette to her lips again and ran her other hand through her hair. I realized then that she was older than I had thought, in her late thirties now, but I still saw her as a girl. She was still beautiful.

"He craved attention, attention as an artist. Adoration is his drug, or one of them. Work painting barns trailed off as *l'economie* failed, and he saw in the paper a call for painters and writers. He inflated his credentials, again, this time in English, so I didn't have to lie for him, and here we are.

"To see the anguish of his mother, to see him reject her...it is unforgiveable. *Unforgiveable*," she said to the sleeping man in a whisper.

"I can no longer do this, Miriam."

It was the first time either of them had called me by my name. I was beginning to think that they had forgotten it.

"I have been saving money, putting a small amount away in a bureau. He skims the rent from you, you know? The government has paid our rent. You have owed nothing. As soon as I have enough, I will go back to New York and then to France one day. To restart my life. I will repay you then."

Lemurier, just Willard Hickey now, awoke in a fog.

"What are you two talkin' about?" he said blearily.

I will never hear France in his accent again, as much as he may try to affect it.

March 9, 1937, Tues

Last night I had a dream, and, when I awoke this morning, I realized that I'd had the dream or variations of it before. In it, I was sitting in the waiting room of the newspaper in Chicago, waiting to be interviewed, and I was totally nude. I was aware of my nakedness and shifted forearms and hands and knees to cover myself, but no one else seemed to notice. Savannah Wilkins was the secretary. Her crusty pink face gazed thoughtfully at the papers she shuffled and the typing that her old, jeweled fingers clattered out. There were other people in the waiting room, and, though I never really saw them in my dream and couldn't identify them, I could feel their eyes on me.

At last, a buzzer on her desk rang, and she said Mr. Moses will see you now. She escorted me and my nakedness into an office where sat Moses Cotter. I sat and realized that I had a string of pearls on but nothing else.

When Mr. Cotter spoke, he was surprisingly erudite, and I wondered if he had been this sharp before he was slowed by age. I asked him what he had meant by his comment to me, "White boys…they don't get theyselves none." He chuckled and said, "You know, I did say that once."

Then I woke up. I write this now so I won't forget it.

(later)

The whole city is abuzz about the First Lady's visit tomorrow. Talk is of little else.

I went today to interview a new subject, a former prostitute who worked for Nell Jester. When I arrived, the address on Caddo Street was in the process of becoming an empty lot. The house was being dismantled after having sat empty for a number of years.

I returned to find out that, while I was out, Hickey got in my room and hung my nude portrait on the wall of the landing. I just look away from it rather than engage him in a battle of wills.

Mar. 10, 1937, FWP, Transcript of Bridget Fenerty

The first telephone call I ever received was from New York. I had the thing put in a week before, but few others had one, so calls were few and far between. When it finally rang, it startled me into some impolite language.

Well, it was an operator, then another operator, and then another, and then finally Mr. O'Hare, in New York City as I said, and he had a proposition for me. He was looking for a singer to book in New York, and was I interested, he asked. Irish singers like John McCormack were quite the thing then, very popular. I consulted with Mr. and Mrs. Eaves, though I knew what Mr. Eaves' answer would be.

"Well, it sounds like we're going to New York!" he exclaimed.

The *Times, the Shreveport Times,* ran an article with my picture, announcing that I, Bridget Fenerty, The Irish Songbird, would be traveling for a month's worth of engagements in New York City. It was on the same day that the papers ran the news of the arrest of Mary Mallon[74] and the departure of Champ Lockett to Atlanta to attend a Confederate veterans' reunion. The article with Champ Lockett ran on the front page.

The Eaves came with me, as did Morris, though he had to get the shop in order and took a later train. The Eaves children were like little rubber balls bouncing from one side of the train to another and looking at all the interesting sights, every barn, house, field. When we got to Vicksburg and the river, they said, "Look, Miss Biddy!"

There it was stretching north and south, wide and threatening, bottomless, licking its banks waiting for me. There wasn't a bridge then, though I understand there is one now. They loaded the cars of the train onto a boat and ferried them across. The engines of the train fell silent, and those of the boat picked up with a clanking rattle, rotating slowly in the current before the engines created enough momentum to propel it forward again. Though my eyes were closed tight, I could hear the swish and slap of the water against the side of the boat, smacking its lips as if it were salivating for just such a morsel as me and the ones I loved.

"The Mississippi! That's Indian language. It means the father of all waters!" Lola Mae said with her face pressed up against the window. Her brothers were on either side of her, three little blonde heads side by side.

"Oh, just look at it," I says, though I wasn't looking at all. I was afraid I might piss myself or throw up or both. The children ran to the back of the train to catch a better glimpse of it. Mr. and Mrs. Eaves followed them, giddy at another great experience their children were enjoying. I just sat there, my hands on either side of my face to block the chance of any view of the river.

"Ma'am?" someone asked.

I looked up from my shoes, and who should be there but Champ Lockett. He looked out quietly at the town of Vicksburg as if retracing his memory over it. For such a celebrated man, he was also a shy man, a quiet man. While several of the other old veterans wore their old gray uniforms with the curving

---

[74] Irish domestic "Typhoid" Mary Mallon was put in quarantine on Mar. 27, 1915.

lines of piping up the sleeves, he simply wore a plain gray wool suit.

The train crossed the river and was brought on the tracks again. As it moved through Vicksburg and passed the monuments on the eastern edge of it, the two of us fell into conversation, about his children, about Buckelew's Hardware store, about the weather. Everything but his dash. He seemed relieved to have something else to talk about and was softening a bit, and I was glad to put him at ease. It's always been a gift of mine, to put people at ease. We talked about the merits of apple versus peach pie, whether we preferred ham or lamb on Easter, things like that.

Finally, after we had cleared Jackson, he said, "I want to tell you something, if you promise you can keep a secret. I need to tell someone." He seemed to be straining under a burden that always tried to come to the surface, no matter how lighthearted and pleasant the small talk.

"Surely," I said.

He leaned in toward me. I thought perhaps he was going to pay me a compliment such as what pretty green eyes you have, or something of the like. Such is the way of a person's conceit, I suppose, even at seventy.

He cleared his throat and stammered, "Well, well, uh, that day they say I…"

Just then some men entered our car and called for him. They were Mississippi men, veterans who had boarded in Jackson. White-headed, white-chinned, a couple of empty sleeves, grinning like boys on a lark.

"Champ Lockett! The hero of the Great Redoubt at Vicksburg! Come have a cigar and a drink with us in the gentlemen's lounge. The younger boys want to serenade you, and then a toast!"

He looked at me regretfully, as if there was something he needed from me. He looked over his shoulder at them and then at me and then at them again, back and forth, me and them.

"You can tell me later," I said, not wanting to deprive him of his moment. "Later, perhaps."

"Certainly," he said, "Yes ma'am." Then he got up and followed the men into the dining car, holding onto the backs of the seats as the train rocked us all. As he got to the forward door of the car, he looked back to me. I smiled, and he smiled back, but his was weak and pitiful. Up ahead, the engine whistled from the back of its throat as the crossties clacked below us.

I never got a chance to talk to him, and perhaps he changed his mind on what he had to tell me. I saw him the rest of that day in the company of other veterans and their sons and grandsons, enjoying cigars in the smoking car with whiskey toddies in their hands. The next day, the whole menagerie of Confederates got off in Atlanta singing "The Bonnie Blue Flag," old heads with thinning hair and mouths full of false teeth. Through the window, I saw him on the platform, and our eyes met, two old people. The train pulled out with a long hoot, and his gaze followed me through the window as if I were taking something important with me. He slid away into the distance, and I continued on to New York with the Eaves.

The Eaves children became the mascots of the train, old women drawling, "Well, aren't they just precious," and the porters saying, "Now, ain't them chirren somethin'!"

News circulated that I was on me way to New York to sing, and so I was persuaded to give a little concert in the club car. People closed their eyes and smiled as I sang, without accompaniment, and then there was applause, the clapping of the bare hands of the gentlemen and the white-gloved hands of the ladies.

At night, a single berth was shared by the boys, and Lola Mae had her own. But it was empty, as she appeared from behind the velvet curtain soon after their bedtime, crawling in with me, claiming to be scared. Which I knew was a ruse, those children weren't scared of anything. She slept with me both nights, the grinding of my snoring playing a duet with the whistle of her night breathing.

As we neared New York, I began to worry about the expanse of water, the Hudson, for I had inquired and learned that it was as big as the Mississippi. Well, I waited, and then suddenly we were in the city. We had gone under the river! A tunnel they had!

We arrived at Penn Station, a beautiful place, a busy, bustling place, and Mr. O'Hare was there, his hair swept back and his mustache resting on his upper lip like a little pet. He had us put up in the Waldorf-Astoria, the first one, the one they took down when they built the Empire State Building. I met a Mr. Frohman[75], a friend of Mr. O'Hare's, and several other theatrical personages.

Mr. O'Hare showed us the town. We ate at Shanley's Lobster Palace, run by some brothers from County Leitrim, and the Vanity Fair Tea Room. We rode the trains that traveled over the streets on iron girders studded with rivets, on the subways that went under them. The Eaves children were, for once, speechless.

Easter Sunday fell that first week and, along with it, the Easter parade on Fifth Avenue, and we watched the men and women strut like peacocks and roosters with elaborate hats, the men with gold handled canes and the white wingtip shoes that were the thing then. I could see Morris taking inventory of everything with plans of slowly introducing it to our little city. He knew to do it as quietly and gradually as possible so as not to 'spook the herd,' as he liked to joke.

Later in the month, Mr. O'Hare treated us to a baseball game, the biggest

_____

[75] Charles Frohman, (1856-1915), Broadway producer

crowd I'd ever seen, at a place called the Polo Grounds. The Yankees were playing the Washington team as a big crowd of men watched from a bluff perched above right field. Mr. O'Hare said you could watch the game without paying, and I laughed to myself thinking that's exactly where Ned and I would have watched it.

But, of course, I was there to sing, and that I did. Over the course of the next few weeks, I sang at several places, at Webster Hall, the Carnegie Lyceum, the Hammerstein. The reception was warm, the crowds a little larger every time, and it was easy as I told myself I was singing for my families or for the men in Mr. Zwally's barber shop. Or to baseboards or into stewpots or sheets hanging on a line in the backyard on Crockett Street. The only moment I felt the slightest bit overcome was the night I sang in the Hippodrome. It held five thousand, and, though that night it was only half full or a little more, it was a huge crowd nevertheless. Crowds didn't scare me; people didn't scare me. I was only scared of one thing.

Well, the night I sang in the Hippodrome, I had run through my typical repertoire and was enjoying the waves of applause, when suddenly there was a tidal wave of it, a large roar louder than its predecessors, and who should appear onstage with me but John McCormack.[76] The crowd roared its approval, I had no idea what for, as I didn't see him at first, and then he was there, walking in from the wings. He took my hand, and we lifted ours together, and we took a bow. Then he said in a low voice in my ear, just above the murmur of the crowd, "How's about we do 'The Last Rose of Summer' for them?"

"All right," I said, smiling at the honor of it, and then we stood as the crowd simmered down to a silence, and then we began. I had sung along with him on his gramophone records so many times that singing with him in person was no different. The crowd roared for us and begged for another, and then we sang "Molly Brannigan" and "I'll Take You Home Again, Kathleen," and then we joined hands and raised them and took a bow together as the crowd rose to its feet. The heavy red velvet curtain with the gold trim came down, and then we walked off the stage together. I looked up and imagined Ned applauding and whistling with his fingers in his mouth from the rafters backstage. I couldn't help but to wink at the memory of him up there.

"'Twas lovely," Mr. McCormack said, and he shook my hand and pecked it with a kiss, and then he was gone through a backstage door. I stood there and looked around. I looked for Mr. McCormack, hoping he would return, and we would cut our way between the separation of the curtains to the bubbling of the crowd and make it boil over again. Adoration is like that: you get a little and you want more, and then, if you can get that, then you want

---

[76] Irish tenor John McCormack.

more still.

But I couldn't find him. Instead, I found Mr. O'Hare waiting for me in a backstage office with another big surprise. Mr. Frohman had heard me sing and wanted me to accompany him for a set of dates in London.

London, England.

Across the sea.

The ocean.

The one with all the water in it.

I was speechless. He thought it was from the honor of it, but of course it was from terror.

"You'll accept, of course!" he said merrily, his mustache dancing along his upper lip. "I'll send the telegram telling them the good news!"

As he marched off a back hallway, he said in a voice that diminished with the distance, "I'll book you and Mr. Frohman passage on the next voyage!" Somewhere down the hallway, a door shut on his footsteps and his whistling, "I'll Take You Home Again, Kathleen," and then it was quiet. Outside the curtain, the crowd had also fallen silent.

I thought of my home, Shreveport, and how pleased everyone would be to have me put them on the map, the map of the world, the Irish Songbird from Shreveport, Louisiana, in America, singing in the Royal Albert Hall in London. *The* London, the one in England. The one with all the water in front of it.

Morris had arrived a few days after us and was there in the lobby of the Hippodrome in a tuxedo with the ends of a scarf draped over each lapel and a top hat on his head and a cane in his white-gloved hands. He always thought there was nothing I was afraid of, nothing. I was his heroine, the woman who had taught him to box and stand up for himself. Word had already reached the lobby, and he was so proud of me.

Well, in celebration and anticipation of my trip to London, he took me to some of the finer shops on Fifth Avenue and the Ladies' Mile, B. Altman's, Bergdorf-Goodman's, Lord & Taylor, and so forth. I had a trunk full of new clothes for my trip to London. And I was petrified.

The night before the scheduled embarkation, I lay in bed there in the Waldorf watching the waning moon veil and unveil itself with passing clouds high over the Woolworth Building. There had been warnings in the papers, ads put taken out by the German consulate warning travelers going through English waters to be mindful that there was a war on, and certain things might happen. I had no trouble feeling terrified on my own, without such a notice as that. I didn't need any help from the German consulate.

I told Mr. O'Hare that such news troubled me, but he told me that Mr. Vanderbilt and Mr. Frohman would be on board, what could possibly happen?

And a Mr. Kern[77], who was a friend of Mr. O'Hare.   Mr. O'Hare was persuasive, exuberant, and I resolved that I would go.

The morning of the voyage, he hired a taxi to take me and my trunk to the dock on the Hudson, Pier 54 with *Cunard Lines* in big letters next to the ship. The ship was a long, black thing, enormous, gigantic, four red funnels topped in black perched above a long white building on the deck that looked like a wedding cake. Morris had ridden in the cab with me, and he hugged me, told me he loved me and to have a great trip and to knock 'em dead in London and break a leg and all that.

Men on the dock took my trunk to stow with all the others below deck, a great horde of men rushing about the pier like ants pushing morsels of baggage down into their mound. I walked up the gangplank as a band played on the pier, a number from one of Mr. Frohman's Broadway shows. My legs shook, and I balanced myself on the handrails of the gangplank. When I arrived on deck, one of the stewards, a young man with a Cork accent, said, "Are ye all right, mam?"

I nodded my assent, though I wasn't at all sure. I looked to the center of the boat, anywhere but the water. I told myself that I would stay below deck for the week we were out to sea, and everything would be all right. I kept my gaze to the middle of the deck. But then I heard my name.

"Miss Biddy!"

It was the Eaves and their children, shouting and waving to me from the pier among the throng of people. The travelers on board shouted and waved to the crowd on the pier, one side waving to another, handkerchiefs fluttering in the air like two fields of white flowers in the breeze. I felt like I would be sick. What happened next I can't explain. Twenty years later, and I still can't explain it. Perhaps it was the rich meal Mr. O'Hare treated us to the night before.

Well, I think I told you that I've only seen ghosts once, and I saw them all at the same time. I say ghosts, but what are ghosts, then, but embodied fears? And what are angels, I ask you, but embodied hopes? Perhaps, 'tis all they are, fears and hopes.

I looked down on the deck to keep from looking at the water, and I saw a pair of new boots, familiar but not of this era, but from an earlier one, new boots hastily made of cheap materials. I followed the trousers up, and there's Ned. Ned Hennessy, I'm saying. "Ned," I said, but as I said it, the face faded into just one of the sailors on the ship, not Ned at all. The sailor said "Welcome aboard, ma'am" and undid one of the big ropes from a cleat on the deck. It clearly wasn't Ned; my troubled mind had played a trick on me.

Everyone on the boat and on the dock kept waving handkerchiefs at each

---

[77] The composer Jerome Kern

other, the ship's band and the band on the dock playing one for the other, people blowing kisses and saluting from across the gap of water. The ship brayed an enormous, tubular note like the deep call of a dozen locomotives. My breath was short, and I inhaled deeply trying to calm myself. Just then, two boys ran past me and down the deck, one chasing the other, then a third one followed, and he stopped the chase and looked at me.

"Dan? Brother Dan?" I asked him.

I thought it was another mind trick, but the boy said, "Hi Bridget," and resumed the chase on the deck, following the boys around the funnel, dodging through the crowd.

I was determined to face my fear, to summon my courage, and I looked down in the water. The current was stirring between the ship and the dock, clear water fading down to a dark emerald green. Then, up from the depths came a face, a face in a cloud of bubbles, a face with eyes closed, indistinct at first, rising, rising from the deep, hair waving around it, closer until I saw it clearly. The face had a scarf tied under the chin where the neck would be. It was about to break the surface when I recognized it, the face with its scarf. From so many years before, one of my first memories.

Da.

The current washed over it, and it disappeared for a moment, but then the eyes opened and looked at me as the lips moved. Then it disappeared entirely.

I grabbed my handbag that I had put down by the railing, and I pushed past people on the deck, struggling to get to the gangplank. I scampered down it as one of the stewards called to me.

"We're about to make way, ma'am," he said in something just under a shout. I waved my hand back to him, lacking the courage to look. Morris had pushed through the crowd to greet me at the gangplank. He knew I was upset. Mr. Eaves and Mr. O'Hare were right behind him.

I'm sorry-I can't-I'm sorry, I said to them. "I thought I could put our town on the map, on the map of the world. But I can't do it."

Well, they all looked bewildered, including Mr. Eaves, who never looked anything but resolute and optimistic. Morris shushed me and held me and said "Don't cry, mama, we still love you."

I think it was all hysteria, not ghosts at all, but pure hysteria. I felt silly on account of being played by it, my own panic. Terrified, sure, but silly all the same. That is, until a week later when the world got the news. It came as a cable from London and then exploded across every paper in the world.

Ah, the phone again. No, no. I'll get that, dear.

March 10, 1937, Wednesday

She got up to answer the phone and then returned after a brief conversation.

"That was Mr. Herndon. I need to meet him at the courthouse for some business. If you go with me, I'll treat you to a movie afterward at the Strand. Errol Flynn has a new one out, and he's certainly a charmed man in the way of his physical appearance, wouldn't you agree?"

I agreed, though really I find Gary Cooper to be more handsome. She put her blue tam over her thin steam of hair, drew her sweater over her shoulders, and took her cane. We made our way down McNeil Street, walking side by side, her cane clicking out the same note on the pavement.

"The ship?" I asked, though I was pretty sure which one.

"'Twas the *Lusitania*," she said. "And you know that story. Torpedoed right off the coast, near the teardrop of Ireland."

I realized that I was only a year old at the time of the story, that our histories, our lives, overlapped from this point on. We were living at the same time, walking the earth together, though I was toddling it. Both of us on the sidewalks of New York. Would I have remembered seeing her? When does one develop a memory? When are our first memories? Her quiet voice and a chuckle tinted with irony summoned me.

"A whole trunk of new clothes, at the bottom of the Atlantic, off old Kinsale."

We went to the courthouse, slowly up the steps and through the big brass-framed doors. In the lobby was a blind man who manned a little kiosk where he sold pencils and chewing gum and that kind of thing. She put a dollar in his basket.

"Howdy, Miss Bridget," he smiled with a vague, sightless stare, off behind us to the opposite wall of the lobby.

"How'd you know 'twas me, Raymond?"

"Your footsteps. Everybody got their own tune, their own rhythm. Besides, your money always rustles when it goes in that basket. It don't clink or nothin', but I can hear it."

She laughed and said, "Very astute you are, as usual."

She and I walked away, arm in arm.

"That's very generous of you," I whispered to her as we made our way down the hall. She cast a glance back to Raymond who was smiling and staring across the unseen distance.

"We're all beggars before God, every one of us," she whispered back. "I believe 'twas Father Mullon in the Channel said that and old Martin Luther before him."

Then she disappeared behind a door with translucent glass to meet with Mr. Herndon. I sat and waited, looking at my naked ring finger. Typewriters clattered and clacked in offices, the heels of secretaries clicked up and down the halls. I contented myself with a copy of the *Times*. Shreveport, not New

York.

After a half an hour, she returned, Mr. Herndon in shirtsleeves and a vest and tie opening the door for her. He leaned down to hug her neck and then waved to me.

"Y'all goin' down to see Mrs. Roosevelt?" he asked us.

"Oh, no," Miss Fenerty said. "We're off to see the picture show. Not so crowded today."

Then she and I went to a Shirley Temple movie at the Strand, *Now and Forever*, co-starring Carole Lombard and Gary Cooper. Her treat. Sorry, Mrs. Roosevelt, maybe some other time.

Mar. 11, 1937, FWP, Transcript of Bridget Fenerty

Well, do you have your ears on, Mr. Roosevelt? In more than eighty years of reading to children, it's something I've always asked them when we sit down to do read. Children, do you have your ears on, then? They never fail to pat the sides of their little heads and nod seriously as if they might have forgotten to put them on, as if they might be on the top of their dressers or hanging by clothespins on the laundry line drying out after a wash. *[laughter]*

We were speaking of my one and only trip to New York, then, weren't we?

Well, we left Manhattan the next day, the second of May, the big city with its bristling, smoky skyline, its nervous, bustling streets. The train began to slowly descend into the earth, under the Hudson. This time I was well aware of the water above us when we went in the tunnel. As Mr. Eaves and the children marveled at the spectacle of it and its technology, I excused myself and went to my berth and cowered below the weight of all that water I knew was above me. I pulled up into a ball, alone behind the red velvet curtain with my palms tight to my face. I stayed there until I felt the train ascending and then until I was sure there would be daylight outside the train.

I came out again to find the Eaves, all five of them reading, the children looking at a picture book of the city that Lola Mae held on her lap, Mrs. Eaves reading a romance novel of the sort one could only get in New York City at the time. I recall she had a satchel of them and was unashamed to be reading them out in the open. Mr. Eaves was reading a book on the architecture of ancient Greece and Rome.

Morris was a few seats behind them, watching New Jersey as it slipped by, the grimy red brick buildings of the cities slowly giving way to the countryside and the green of May. I sat next to him, and he smiled at me. We rode quietly as the train rocked us like a mother does her children. I know he wanted to ask me why I'd bolted off the ship. But he didn't. Perhaps he knew that I could never explain it, or perhaps he knew how embarrassed I was by it.

"I'm sorry," I told him again. "I feel I've let the whole city down. It was our chance to be on the map."

He took my hand in his, and I noticed that it was showing signs of becoming old and spotted like mine. He said, "Shreveport's already on the map. You remember what you told me when we returned from the state bout in New Orleans twenty-five years ago, mama?"

He's always called me mama. Of all the children I've raised, he's the only one. Even his sister Leah calls me Miss Bridget.

"Yes, I remember," I said.

He put his arm around me, and I put my head on his shoulder and neither of us said a word for a very long time. Dinner was served, and he asked the steward if we could take our meal separately away from the other passengers. He didn't want me to have to deal with questions. It was arranged, and we ate quietly, just the two of us.

When we arrived home, there was some consternation about me not going to London. That is, until a few days later when news of the sinking got out and circled the earth. Like a slap, the news exploded that Germany had sunk a vessel full of civilians, men, women and children. My detractors fell silent, eyeing me suspiciously, as if I were some sort of gypsy fortune teller.

The news gave me a reputation as a clairvoyant, one who 'had the goods' on people, though in reality I had merely been a nervous, panicky old woman who had guessed correctly. People in town eyed me as if I knew things about them, and honestly it made me as uncomfortable as them. I finally told everyone that I had left something I needed with Morris and that I had rushed back to get it. I had simply 'missed the boat,' and I wasn't clairvoyant at all, just lucky. And isn't it the Irish who're lucky? I told them with a laugh which may or may not have been convincing.

A few days later, a picture ran in one of the New York rags, one of the low brow sheets, and a furious Mr. O'Hare shared it with me. 'Twas a grainy one of me leaving the Lusitania's gangplank with the title "Rats Leaving a Sinking Ship." It was in incredibly poor taste, of course, both to me and to those who perished. Morris was outraged and wanted to bring action against them, but I laughed it off and told him it would only become what Uncle Jack called a pissing contest, one in which nobody wins, but everybody gets wet. Let it go, I told Morris.

Well, when Germany sank the Lusitania, war drums began to rattle. As is usually the case, older men fanned the war flames with newspapers, and young men began to enlist to impress young women and each other. The Kaiser had swatted the wrong hornet's nest, had kicked the wrong dog.

The Taylor boys and the McShan boys all enlisted. Ike McShan, Abram, Aaron, and little Morris McShan, who was now bigger than his namesake, his

Uncle Morris, their little brother George, and their Taylor cousins, Morris' boys, Ben and Simon, all of them went for a soldier's life. Little Morris and his cousin Ben were on the same transport and got to within sight of France at the time the Armistice was signed, but never set foot there. Abram and Aaron never left Fort Dix in New Jersey. Only one of the cousins ever heard a shot, Ike, and that was when a teamster had to put down a lame mule. Fate had spared the ones I loved, and I felt grateful and relieved. They all felt cheated of a grand adventure. I knew they'd been spared one.

When they returned, the city had closed down the Sporting District in St. Paul's Bottoms. Bea Haywood, Nell Jester, Annie McCune. Dott Maydwell. All turned out, the fine things in their houses sold at auction, the girls having to learn honest, upright work, pun intended, of course. Miss McCune died a few years hence, after her leg was removed on account of diabetes. She had gotten enormous.

The Eaves moved out to the South Highlands to a house Mr. Eaves had designed for them. They wanted me to move with them, but I didn't want to leave this house and the memories that had seeped into it. So I sat for people here and there, but my house here has always been so filled with friends and children of friends.

The cry of war had drowned out the other cry that had been going on for several years: the cry of suffrage for women. There was a Mrs. Comegys[78] and a Miss Lavinia Hartwell Egan,[79] among others, who crusaded for a woman's vote. And, as you know, it was granted us, the Nineteenth, in 1920. That's it, isn't it? Nineteen twenty?

Since then, my biggest concern for our country isn't the Nazis or the Tagalogs or the Apaches. My biggest fear is the vote of those who are illiterate and illogical, those who have no idea what the Constitution says or means. Those who couldn't pick the three branches of government out of a list of four. Or worse, those who have no sense of kindness for others and who vote that way. When you have people who are easily swayed by the papers, and now, the radio, then men get elected who would rob the milk out of your tea if the price went up a penny, and then the capitol building and the statehouses become the devil's toolbox, and the country goes to hell on account of it. The enemy from afar would never have to lift a finger.

---

[78] Mary Elinor Foster Comegys was President of the Shreveport (La) Woman's Club. She once wrote, "I want men to stop calling me a queen and treating me like an imbecile. I have a head as well as a heart, common sense as well as intuition. I am tired of the bullet business. Are men who are exempt from military service disenfranchised? If not, why not?" -*The New Woman of the New South*, Josephine K. Henry.
[79] Lavinia Hartwell Egan (1863-), Shreveport native, journalist, story writer, and suffragist.

So yes, when you ask me if I voted, yes I did. I read the papers and thought about it, really thought about it, and then I voted, as I still do, regularly, though there have been times I've been tempted to vote with a clothespin over my nose.

How did I vote, you ask me?

My conscience, girl. I voted my conscience.

Well, how's about a little tea?

March 12, 1937, Friday

I write this still smelling of smoke. I will put this very plainly: I almost died last night.

I was dreaming that June Longhat was the queen of England. She was sitting in a kitchen, in a chair with the icebox at her back. She had a beaver pelt hat on her head. And then, suddenly the scene changed in that nonsensical way of dreams, and June was seated on a throne in front of a fire in the middle of the woods. Two men, their features hidden by masks, brought in a doe which pranced in on tiny hooves into the circle of light. The doe had a wreath of flowers around her small head. Dim forms pranced around the light, chanting and hitting sticks together that made a cracking, crackling sound, and the fire grew brighter.

The smoke woke me up. The smell of it, I mean, and then I saw the haze illuminated by the flash of murky orange and yellow flames.

I grabbed my robe from a hook behind the door and put my journal in the pocket. I glanced at the portrait of me that Lemurier had done. I don't know why, but I started to pull it off the wall and take it with me. It gazed back at me, sneering through a veil of liquid flames, but I left it.

On the landing of the stairs, I looked back to their room, Lemurier and Hickey. The door was merely an upright rectangle framed with a thin rim of yellow and orange. Smoke boiled from under it, an updraft of it, a linear curl like a wave breaking not downward but upward. I staggered to the door and rapped on it with my knuckles. I put my bare palm to it and instantly recoiled from the heat. I called to them. Lemurier! Mirlette! I even called the name I knew would infuriate him.

Willard! Willie Hickey!

There was no response. I began to feel weak and short of breath. The air was thick with smoke but thin with anything nourishing. Flames boiled along the ceiling. I got low to the floor. Isn't that what you're supposed to do? I thought.

When I got to the top of the stairs, I sat there; I had to rest for a minute. I sat on the landing with my hands on my head, my elbows on my knees, pulling for air, my chest never quite expanding enough for a satisfying gulp. I lay down; it seemed to me that, yes, that's what you did, you got down low because that's where the air is, down low. The heat was becoming unbearable, but at the same time I was becoming indifferent to it. I thought of the story of Shadrach, Meshach, and Abednego and the king's fiery furnace. I looked up and someone was there.

I was woozy and the figure made me think of Miss Fenerty's Negro angel in the marsh after the Last Island hurricane. He approached as a dark outline. He scooped me up, and I felt myself high above the stairs, like I was levitating. He brought me down the stars as effortlessly as if I had floated down. I felt limp and helpless in his arms. We exited the house through a window that had been shattered open. His boot crunched in the broken glass, and he lay me down on the front lawn and the cool earth under it. He took off his hat, and it was then that I saw it was a fire helmet. His face was swarthy with bold features like an Indian or an Italian or an Arab. His voice was gravelly.

"Ma'am, are you all right? Are you still with us?"

I must have nodded or blinked because he smiled briefly.

"Two others," I mouthed the words.

"Too late," he said as his smile disappeared.

We sat on the front lawn as the red lights whirled and flashed under the trees and the water from the hoses arced through the air and splattered off the house and hissed into the fire. The neighbors came out in their housecoats and slippers, and we watched the house dissolve into a cube of liquid yellow and orange. The fireman knelt beside me on one knee and held a black mask of oxygen over my face, the smell of rubber competing with the smell of smoke. Finally, I pushed it away, and he turned off the dial on the metal cylinder. I sat shivering under a borrowed quilt that someone had put over me.

"Sugar, do you have somewhere to stay?" someone asked me.

"Yes," I said.

The fire chief drove me downtown as I watched the sleeping houses on Line Avenue slip past in the night. I realized that I didn't know where the recorder was. Had I left it in my room? Or in the trunk or back seat of the Packard? I began to panic at the thought of all that history lost.

We pulled up to the house on Crockett Street. The chief got out and ran around to open my door. As we walked up the steps, the porch light came on. The door was already open.

"Why dear," the voice was cheerful for that time of the morning, "Why, I woke up thinking about you. Come in," she said. She turned to the fire chief and said, "And I thank you, Harry. She's like a niece to me, surely she is, and a favorite niece at that. A fine girl."

He touched the bill of his cap and left, and we sat on the couch. I nestled right into her and put my head on her chest, and she put her old arms around me. I began shaking and I cried and she didn't say a word. There were no adequate words. But, of course, she knew this.

Ellie appeared on the stairs in her nightgown, plain, sturdy white linen, something in keeping with a Texas childhood. Soft only from repeated washing. Her hands were on the bannister together, and there was a look in her eyes of both excitement and relief. She went upstairs, her feet drumming on the wood, and she returned with her spare nightgown, identical white linen with a smocked top.

I don't remember getting dressed in it. I just remember sobbing uncontrollably, forcefully, trembling and crying loudly into Miss Fenerty's shoulder and feeling Ellie's hand on my back. Finally, I cried all I needed to, for last night at least. As I drifted off to sleep, I saw the recorder on the tea table across the room, and I remembered that's exactly where I had left it. Ellie was sleeping curled up in the chair next to it.

March 14, 1937, Sunday

They let me sleep in yesterday, through the Sabbath, and then this morning, as well. I vaguely remember Ellie leaving, dressed up for church and then the smell of a pot roast, the smell of Sunday dinner driving away the lingering smell of smoke.

I found a stack of newer clothes, nicer than what I'd brought down, from Rubenstein's and courtesy of the First Baptist Church and Temple B'nai Zion, Miss Fenerty says. I dozed again but committed to getting up the next time I woke up. When I did, the smell of pot roast had been joined by another smell, the mellow smell of butter and vanilla.

They were making a cake downstairs. It took me a moment before I realized it was little Frank's birthday. I did the math in my head. He would have been seventy-four. I dressed in the new clothes and shook out my hair in front of the full length mirror in the corner of the bedroom. My hair made me look like Ruth in a story book I had when I was a girl.

The two of them were downstairs. Neither said anything; they just smiled. I ate as if I hadn't in two days, which was the case. Miss Fenerty joked that I put it away like I was coming off a hitch in the oil fields. After my second plate, we had cake. Ellie asked me if I was up for a ride. I said I was.

We took Miss Fenerty in the Packard, Ellie driving as I was still too wobbly. We parked in the parking lot of the Lakecliff Bar, where a handwritten sign curled at the edges announced, *Close Sunday.*

Ellie and I worried over Miss Fenerty the whole way down the hillside, through the dry yellow weeds that were awakening green again as the first dragonflies darted around, big-eyed and four-winged.

Miss Fenerty seemed to be having a grand time. We climbed the embankment of the dam as the lake hinted at itself, more with each step. I led her up, and Ellie propped her from behind as her cane made circular impressions in the soft spring earth. She stepped over the rails that ran atop the dam, and I wondered if she was thinking of Ned Hennessy and the near-miss-adventure of almost ninety years ago. I was.

At last, she looked up, and Ellie and I looked at her regarding the sunset, the surface of the lake orange and yellow and white like shattered glass. The sun hovered above the lake as if it were a swimmer testing its temperature before settling into it.

"Well, my, isn't this just spectacular," she said at last. "Leave it to the two prettiest girls in town to find the prettiest sights. Reminds me of the view from Camp Taylor on Jeems Bayou." Her mind seemed to be scrolling backward. "Or the view from Milneville on Lake Pontchartrain."

Ellie and I sat side by side on the railroad tracks that ran over the dam, watching the sunset. Miss Fenerty stood propped on her cane.

"Seventy-four," she said suddenly, in little more than a murmur. Her old eyes were transparent and green in the sunlight. "He'd be seventy-four. I wonder if he's still alive."

"I think he's aware of you," Ellie said as she leaned her head into my shoulder. "I really do."

"That's sweet of you to say, dear," Miss Fenerty said, and then she fell silent again looking west, just standing and looking west as she leaned forward on her cane. Then she looked away from the sunset and to us, Ellie and me, sitting holding hands like two sisters might, Ellie's head on my shoulder.

"There are times, I've come to believe," Miss Fenerty said, "when you see the one you love not as male or female, black or white, fat or thin. Gradually, you see them as just themselves. And then, I suppose, you begin to see them as the other part of you."

She looked again to the sunset, and the light illuminated her eyes. I can't explain it, but, for a moment, she looked like she was our age.

Mar. 15, 1937, Monday

Getting back to work today, and I have to say, it feels good to be doing something. Ellie is expecting a man named Conrad Albrizio any day now. He's an art professor at the university in Baton Rouge and has done several murals for the WPA. He's offered to come take a look at Ellie's ideas for the mural at the State Exhibit Building. Right now, he's in a town called DeRidder south of here painting a mural in the post office there. The most interesting thing? He's a New Yorker.

Ellie said she went to the scene of the fire to see if any of my belongings survived. She said they didn't, and I'm not surprised. I asked her if she saw any trace of Mirlette and ~~Lemurier~~ (old habits die hard, I guess) Hickey. She paused as if she didn't want to upset me, but I was adamant that she tell me what she found.

"No," I insisted. "I survived. They didn't. I need to hear it."

She said she got there and found two firemen and a man in a coat and tie, an inspector, she supposed, poking through the blackened ruins. The timbers of the house were burned down to rows and columns of charred squares. One of the firemen came running toward her, high-stepping through the rubble to intercept her.

"Miss, you can't..." he began. Just then, the other one whistled a quick burst, and the three of them gathered around something in the smoldering ashes and blackened beams. They stood staring at a spot in the rubble. The man in the coat and tie put his hands on his hips inside his jacket and looked up and away. One of the fireman made the sign of the cross.

The firemen got two canvas bags from the trunk of the inspector's car and put the remains in them. As the firemen carried them off to their truck, the man in the coat and tie asked Ellie if she knew them.

I did, she said.

She told the inspector their names, and then they were sent to Jackson on the train c/o Mildred Hickey to be buried as Willard Hickey and Mirlette Lemurier. It was the truth. It had finally caught up with both of them.

I received two letters today, actually a letter and a handwritten note.

The note was delivered by a boy in overalls who took off his cap when I opened the door and handed the creamy envelope to me as if he thought it would shatter if he dropped it. The stationary had an embossed *SLB* on it:

Miss Lewiston,

Daddy has expressed a rather adamant desire to talk to you. Please drop by anytime tomorrow morning at our home on Mertis Street at the corner of Lakeshore Avenue.

Sincerely,

Susie Lockett Breag
Secretary-Treasurer, General Richard Taylor Chapter
United Daughters of the Confederacy

Thankfully, I have one or two blank disks left for the interview.

The letter is from Mr. Alsberg. He makes no mention of my request for more blanks for the Presto. He does, however, have another position for me and hints that if I don't take it, my assignment with the FWP will be at a close.

March 16, 1937, Tuesday

381

I would have thought their home to be a little more palatial, but it was rather plain. Not an antebellum mansion with two-story columns, but a squatty one-story bungalow with trapezoidal posts. The camellias at the four corners of the house clung to stems in shades of brown, blooms well past their time and devoid of any hint of redness. A woman who was more black that brown answered the door wiping her hands on her apron. She shouted to the back of the house, "Miz Susie! Company here!"

Susie Lockett Breag met me at the door as the servant retreated back into the house to resume whatever chore she was in the middle of. I lugged the Presto in, bouncing it off my knee, and we made our way down a hallway. She paused at the door of a bedroom and spoke into it.

"Daddy? Company for you. Do you feel up to it?"

I heard him spit into a metal basin, making it ring, and then his old voice, gravelly, phlegmy.

"Yes."

Time had been cruel to the handsome young man, the optimistic model for the courthouse monument. He was a man with jaundiced skin and a swollen belly, a midsection that looked like it had settled on the wrong man, a man with skinny legs and arms. His hair was thin and stringy, failing miserably at covering his head. He held the fingertips of one trembling hand to his forehead where they lightly danced as if he was trying to determine the shape of his skull by feel. His stare was far away, off into the far corner of the room. When I entered, he looked to me.

"Who is this purty girl come to see me?" he said without a smile, though it seemed as if there had once been a time when he did say it with a smile.

"Oh, Daddy," his daughter, said. "There you go a-flirtin' again."

"About all I can do anymore is flirt," he exhaled regretfully.

"Oh, let a handsome young man flirt with a girl," I said as I set up the Presto. Setting it up has become second nature.

"Heh-heh," he wheezed out a chuckle. "Now ain't you the sweetest thing, too. You Roosevelt's gal come to see me, take my witness?"

"Yes sir, " I said, as I arranged the recorder on the side table. "Champ," I said, "that's quite a nickname."

"That's not my nickname. That's my Christian name. Daddy give us all names like that. Homer, Champ, Laurel, Victor."

"Well, it's fitting. I understand that you're a hero."

Any good humor he had suddenly evaporated. He frowned and looked toward the wall.

"Susie, will you excuse us?" he said, his voice rattling with phlegm.

"Surely, Daddy."

When she had left, he said in a low voice, which was really the only volume he had, "Shut the door, will you?"

I shut the door, and he turned to me.

"Hero," he huffed. "I've lived my whole life on that lie." He looked down at his bloated belly. "The doctor says I got a cancer." He pronounced it 'cane-ser.' "Started in my gut. Says it's in my liver now. That's why I'm yeller. Don't have long."

To look at him, you would have known he was right. His belly pushed out from under his pajama shirt, straining at the white buttons on the thin, pale yellow fabric. His skin was sallow and swollen. It appeared as if the raised moles on it were clinging precariously.

"I want you to know something."

I was switching on the recorder. The stylus arm paused above the spinning disk.

"Excuse me?" I asked.

"Turn that thing off," he said, like a man who had seldom been told no. "Let this be between you and me."

I lifted the arm off the blank and turned the knob. With a click and a tiny recoil, the blank disk on the recorder went from a blur to a distinct disk again. The clock in the hallway clicked in the silence that floated between us. Then he spoke up to the ceiling.

"I ran that day, but not for help. I ran to save myself."

I listened.

"They elected me sergeant. Not on any ability, but on popularity. How they did it then. We was at Vicksburg, like you probably heard." His trembling finger scratched the side of his nose. "We was under siege. Food was scarce. We looked like an army of scarecrows."

The fingertips of one of his old hands rested on his forehead. He cleared his throat. It was like a saw cutting through lumber.

"The Yankees was testin' us, tryin' to see where we was weakest. They tried us one day, *that* day. Our line gave a little, and I guess they thought they'd try us a little more. The fightin' was a-gettin' hot. They was all over us before too long. Boys was cussin' and cryin'."

He stared at the ceiling, his eyes searching it for something. The whites of them were yellow.

"I ran. I ran because I was little more than a boy. I ran because I was hungry and scared. And I only ran because I couldn't fly."

He stared up to the ceiling as if he was telling his story to the light fixture. His fingers wandered over his nose like someone groping for something in the dark.

"Charlie Willis was there, right there next to me. I said 'Charlie, I'm gettin' the hell outta here.'"

Champ Lockett turned his gaze from the ceiling and looked at me.

"Excuse my language, miss," he said. I smiled and nodded at him.

"'Yer yeller,' Charlie says. 'Champ Lockett, yer yella and a coward.' Bullets was spatterin' in the ground around us. Charlie kept loadin' and firin', loadin' and firin'.

"Well, I didn't care if I was blue, yeller or gray. I took off between them lines, no thought of where I was goin', just somewheres else. Anywheres else. Bullets was whistlin' past my head. I ran, pantin' and blubberin' and callin' for my mama. I ran until the sound of the battle was far away. I ran through sticker bushes and brush, waist deep through creeks, past snakes a-sittin' up on logs. I ran and I hid."

His tongue gave a passing try at wetting his chapped lips and failed. He exhaled a rugged, serrated, staccato breath.

"I slept in a tree hollow that night. And then I kept there in the woods for several months, livin' like a wild man. The barns that the armies hadn't burned were empty, empty of anything you could eat or sleep on.

"One morning, probably late August or so, I was cornered by an old woman in one of them barns, raised out of a dead sleep. She saw my gray uniform and said, 'Best you get on way from here. The Yankees done took Vicksburg.' I knew then that the war was about over. In the west, at least.

"I crossed the river with a group of boys the Yankees had paroled. That's when I found out Charlie Willis had got shot and kilt. Right through his heart. Must've been right after I run off. And that's when I found out that I was a hero.

"Well, it just so happened that a lieutenant in our regiment, just before he died, swore he saw me headed through a hailstorm of bullets over to where the Alabama boys was. He figured it was to bring a message for them to close up with us, close up and maybe we could keep from gettin' whipped. They say that's what the lieutenant said as he died. I don't know why he thought that's what I was doin'. Maybe because I was runnin' toward the enemy and not away. Really, I was runnin' right *through* their lines. I didn't give a hot damn about Alabama troops or Union troops or no kinda troops. I ran to save myself."

Someone was doing something in the kitchen, a rattle of pots and pans. When I heard Susie Breag's shush, I knew it was the hired girl in the kitchen.

"Ever body said it saved the day, my dash through the lines did. It saved that particular day, at least. But it had nothin' to do with me. Alabama boys was headed into the gap anyhow, without nobody tellin' 'em."

He coughed a wet rattle and spit into a metal basin that his trembling hand held.

"Word had traveled ahead of me that I was a hero. A whipped nation needs its heroes more that the winners do. I became the local hero around here. I wandered home and made up a story about bein' held prisoner and escapin', and nobody questioned it.'"

He fell silent for a moment, and the clock in the hall clicked twice in the pause before he resumed.

"Mr. Buckelew gave me a job at his hardware store. In sixty years I don't think I sold so much as a piss jar. I was supposed to sit there on the porch in the summer and by the stove inside in the winter to talk about the weather and tell tales and then later have my picture struck with people. They would put their children on my lap like I was Moses. Like a damn wooden Indian. They always wanted me to say a word on the courthouse steps, right next to the statue made in my likeness, on Confederate Memorial Day ever June, and on my birthday and on Dash Day, May 22, ever day since Adam was a boy as they say, but I never said much. I certainly never said nothin' about that day at Vicksburg when I ran, and Charlie Willis got shot through the heart. Everybody said, 'aw, just look at his modesty, would you?'

The clock in the hall clicked and popped. I could hear it chime through the closed door.

"People are amazed I've lived so long," his fingertips kept playing lightly over his forehead like the dainty steps of a spider. He looked to the closed door and then to me. His voice lowered.

"This lie's been like an anchor, holdin' me from goin' anywheres else. I'm shackled to this earth by it. The reason I stopped goin' out in public was that I couldn't keep my lie straight no more."

He coughed again, so hard and deep that I thought he might spit out his heart. The door opened a crack, and his daughter's face appeared in it. He raised his hand and shook his fingers at her to send her away. The crack narrowed again, and he watched it close over her face.

"Pilate asked Christ what truth was, and I tell you, ma'am, the truth is like havin' your bare feet on solid ground. You might feel soft green grass or grass with stickers in it or sand like velvet or hard jagged stones, but the truth is feelin' it whether it feels good or not. The pain and pleasure of the truth beats livin' your life floatin' around unsettled. You ain't no kinda man if you ain't livin' the truth."

He turned his gaze to me. His yellow eyes looked into mine.

"You can let it out now if you want. My posterity has enjoyed the lie long enough, bein' the child or grandchild or great-grandchild of a great hero, enjoying the status of local royalty, my wastrel sons and grandsons gettin' it for free at Miss McCune's on account of it, my lie. My daughters and granddaughters enjoyin' discounts at all the shops. You and I know it ain't so." His voice collapsed into a sob as the corners of his mouth tried to twist themselves out of a powerful frown. His lower lip quivered as he looked away to the opposite wall. "And Charlie Willis. He knows. He still visits me in my dreams and calls me yeller."

At that moment, that intimate moment of an old man weeping regretfully, I wished he hadn't asked me to come. He took my hand, and I held it in mine. His was golden-hued from his disease, sickly and brown-spotted. Mine was creamy, fresh, elegant. He moaned a small, desperate moan as his fingertips caressed his forehead. There was a knock on the door, and it cracked open.

His daughter appeared and smiled at us. I tried to separate my hand from his so I could leave, but he held tight. Through our connected hands, I felt his need. So I sat there.

We sat with him a long time, his daughter Susie and I. Lunch time came and went, but I wasn't hungry. We sat on either side of his bed, listening to the hired girl sweep and vacuum and mop somewhere else in the house. Below us, the earth turned quietly.

He looked at Susie and mouthed the word *water*. She took the glass from the bedside table and lifted it to his lips. His knobby throat bobbed up and down, and then his lips closed on the rim. She held the glass, half full or half empty, in front of him, and he just said *bless you, darlin'* in a thin strand of a voice. She set it down on the nightstand. He dozed for a while, and Susie tried to make conversation with me about New Yo-ork Cee-ty. I'm afraid I answered her tersely; I found it hard to make eye contact with her.

Later, he opened his yellow eyes and scratched the yellow skin of his swollen belly. He mouthed a word to me that I couldn't make out. He looked to Susie with a wisp of recognition, and his crooked finger pointed to something unseen in the air. His chest rose and fell, and Susie went to use the telephone in the hall to summon someone, the doctor I guessed.

His grip on my hand loosened.

The doctor arrived and looked under the patient's lids at the lifeless eyes. He glanced at the watch he produced from his vest pocket and then closed his eyes and nodded with an expression of regret. The hired girl, the young woman with shining black skin, opened the long case of the clock and stilled the pendulum. Then she covered the mirrors with sheets. And Sergeant Champ Lockett, a lesser hero of the siege of Vicksburg, was unchained from his lie and taken up into history.

Mar. 17, 1937, Wednesday

Ellie and I were planning a trip to interview a VIP, a Mrs. Birdie Lee Houston Etheridge, in the town of New London, Texas today, but my monthly arrived which has made life too miserable. We've put it off until tomorrow.

Miss Etheridge claims to be the great-niece of Sam Houston, the first and only president of the Republic of Texas. She's said to have many vivid memories of her 'Uncle Sam' and wants to share them. Hopefully, it will satisfy Mr. Alsberg. If not, I have one blank left for the Presto. Ellie insists on going; any descendant of Sam Houston is considered Texas royalty.

But instead, I stayed in bed this morning, and Ellie brought me some aspirins and a toddy of brandy.

"Mama always took brandy for one purpose and one purpose only: female trouble. Only way a Baptist woman can imbibe."

She mixed my toddy, something with lemon and honey. As she eyed the brown liquid coursing into the glass she held at eye level, she said, "You know something? I like to think that Mirlette has made her peace with St. Peter." She stirred the glass with her finger and then put the finger in her mouth. She handed it to me and said, "And I shouldn't say this because it's wrong to speak ill of the dead, but I bet the devil can't get a lick a work out of Hickey."

Later today, I went downstairs in my robe and slippers. Ellie and Miss Fenerty had different sections of the paper, quietly, comfortably reading on different ends of the couch. Miss Fenerty reads the paper cover to cover, while Ellie likes the serials and goes straight to them. The *Times* has started a new one called *Playgirl* by someone with the pen name Julie Anne Moore. Or maybe it's her real name.

"It says here in the paper that Mr. Lockett, the hero of Vicksburg, died," Miss Fenerty said as she wet her finger and turned the page.

"While I was painting, they broke into *Jack Armstrong* to announce it on KWKH," Ellie said into her paper, her finger following her story line by line.

"Well, may God rest him, and all the souls of the departed, but that means I'm the oldest person left in the city. And isn't that the luck of the Irish, on St. Patrick's day in the morning?"

Suddenly, outside and away in the distance, there was the sound of metal reverberating on metal, like an iron rod banging an iron kettle, the same sound as the bell at summer camp on Lake Winnipesaukee, summoning us from our play, the make-believe games of children, us girls running laughing and screaming toward the dining hall in the main square of camp.

Bells joined bells, and we walked out on the porch, the three of us, Miss Fenerty, Ellie and I. On the porch, outside, the bells were louder, ringing sky blue and lime green. Flags were half-mast, Confederate flags, and oddly, American flags.

The bells frightened clouds of blackbirds out of belfries and bell towers and trees and into shapes with meanings known only to birds, things only birds know to be true. The bells kept pealing away, peeling the glossy lie away from the inner, brilliant, bitter truth:

"Raaan...raaan...raaan..."

I am the only one who knows it. And Charlie Willis. He knows, too.

March 19, 1937, Friday

It's three a.m., and I just made my first deadline for my first big article for a newspaper. What an odd sauce of emotions, what a tragic tangle of events. What a horrible thing. What a horrible day. Yesterday, March 18, 1937.

We were running a little late, and, as it turned out, this was fortuitous, at least for us. We were to meet Mrs. Birdie Lea Houston Etheridge right after school was out. Though close to eighty, Mrs. Birdie Lea still teaches Home Economics, as she has for decades.

Children were beginning to filter out of the school, which was a showcase of a building, a million-dollar school recently built from the proceeds of the oil and gas fields around it. As it turned out, the gas fields that built it were also responsible for bringing it down. And it happened in seconds.

The walls suddenly bulged out and then in, and in a matter of moments the whole thing was rubble. Debris flew by the Packard, which was miraculously untouched. At the sound of the explosion, Ellie and I ducked down below the dashboard. When we looked up, people, mostly young people, were looking back at the spot where the school had just stood, pausing in disbelief at the immense cloud of dust there. Then they began running to the rubble. So did Ellie and I.

Workers from the oilfields came in and were there within half an hour. Parents were crying, calling out for children, crying when small recognizable fragments were found, his favorite shoes, her favorite skirt, the schoolbook with her name in the front. Burly oilfield roughnecks cried with store clerks as each passed debris down a line. Mangled young bodies were uncovered.

Ellie and I were helping. We came to one body, and I won't describe it but to say that I turned and vomited into the rubble. I felt Ellie's hand on my back

"Miriam, the world will know about this, and it'll need to know soon so it can grieve, the sooner the better. Tell them, Miriam. Tell the world. There are plenty of strong backs here to pull up the wreckage. Texas and the world need to know."

Then she paused with an enormous chunk of concrete in her hands, and she told me this as the sweat of her exertions trickled down in a rivulet in the dust on her face:

"My daddy told me something when he sent me to Shreveport to paint for Mr. Roosevelt. I wanted to go with them, out west, to California. I didn't want to be separated from them, especially my daddy."

She passed the concrete to a man in khaki work clothes that were dark under the arms and neck with his sweat. He still wore his tin helmet from the oilfield. He threw the jagged block effortlessly, and it made a hard, hollow sound as it hit and tumbled down to the base. Then he scurried over a mound of rubble where he had spotted the corner of a student's desk.

Ellie turned back to me and said, "Daddy told me that a dream will stay just that if you wait for someone else to make it come true."

She ran stumbling over the mound of debris with the oilfield man and began helping him uncover the desk. They removed another block of concrete, and I saw a dust covered hand.

Without a word, I staggered back to the car and got my pad and paper. The page is stained with blood from my hand; I had cut it on a piece of iron that was protruding from a block of concrete. I sat on the running board of the Packard and composed the story.

I ran down the road to a store and called the paper in Shreveport, and I asked to speak to someone. An associate editor, a Mr. Tiner, got on the line. I told him what happened.

"Oh, sweet Jesus. When?" he asked.

"Just now," I said.

I told him I had the story, and he was welcome to use it.

"Tell me what you know," he said.

I read him my story, over the phone, from my notebook. He read it back to me, and then he praised my succinctness, he praised my style, he made over the completeness.

"You sound like you've been born to be a reporter," he said, his voice distant and crackling over the phone. It was only then that I let him know that it was my training, and that I was a graduate of Barnard College in New York City. I left out the part about being the top graduate.

"This'll make this evening's *Journal*," he said. "Do you think you can give us a longer version for tomorrow morning's *Times*?"

I said I could.

He said something that I didn't catch over the ambulance sirens.

"Excuse me?" I said.

"When can you start?" he asked again. "We'd be honored to have you full time."

March 22, 1937, Monday

First day in the newsroom. A lot more to it than I thought, both the newspaper business and this city. So much more goes on under the surface than I was aware of. I am exhausted, happily exhausted.

Today, I sent my resignation to Mr. Alsberg along with a thank you note for the opportunity of a lifetime.

March 23, 1937

Irving arrived within an hour of his telegram:

MY SO. BELLE IN TOWN MARCH 23 QUICK TRIP DAY OR TWO
THEN HOME BEFORE PASSOVER CANT WAIT SEE YOU
SURPRISE

Surprise all right. I paid the Western Union delivery boy and put the message in my desk. I'm glad it wasn't a singing telegram. I resumed working on a piece about Mayor Caldwell's attempt to set up public health clinics.

A little later, Irving appeared in the newsroom with a briefcase of salamis he presented as gifts to my coworkers. They held them up to their noses and sniffed, and then smiled politely and thanked him in that southern way, "Thank yew, sooo much."

"Say," he said. "Why don't you show me where to eat in this berg?" He was eyeing me in my new professional clothes and my haircut, shorter and up to date thanks to the ladies in the salon at the Youree.

"Well, I'm working late on a couple of stories," I said as I watched his face fall. "Mr. Tiner really went out on a limb for me. I want to give him my best."

"Sure. Okay," he said. "I'll just go back to the hotel and grab a nap or something."

"There's a place called Herby K's on Pierre Avenue. Really good sandwiches and beer. Mr. Busi would be great company for you. It's on the Allendale trolley line."

"Sure." His shoulders slumped, and his chin fell a little. His body language was screaming and wailing, *rejection*.

"Tonight," I offered him. "Tonight I'll take you to dinner." I raised his chin with my finger. "My best guy."

He brightened a little. "All right," he said

"I'll come by the Washington-Youree when I'm done this evening."

He kissed me and brushed his hands near a couple of secret places. It was unexpected, and I shuddered. He turned and left, taking with him the smell of garlic and fat. The typewriters and conversations came to a boil again. I hadn't realized they'd stopped.

March 24, 1937

Last night, we went to dinner on the rooftop of the Washington-Youree Hotel, up at the level of the belfries and steeples and the top of the courthouse. It was a beautiful spring night, just cool enough to wear the wrap I'd gotten from Baird's. A small splurge.

Irving wore a nice suit, though no nicer than the ones *Taylor and Son* has. He kept brushing my ankle under the table, and I kept retreating, a game of cat and mouse under the white linen cloth and silver and crystal as the house band,

Glenn Lee and his orchestra, played popular tunes of the day into the night air. Irving ordered us champagne and then reminded me in a whisper that he had a room downstairs. I whispered back that we should wait until June, and anyway, I was on my period.

Yes, a lie.

He said that he was glad that I moved out of the house with that Frenchman. Then, as we talked, I became aware that he had no idea that the house had burned. I had almost died, twice if you count the school explosion, and I had neglected to tell him. It was an enormous revelation to me.

The orchestra thanked us diners and requested a short break with a promise to return very shortly and *we thank you kind folks*, and the sound of polite applause rose like the flutter of wings into the cool March sky leaving the murmur of conversations to fill the air.

We had another glass of champagne as a silence seemed to restrain us. I tried to bring up the subject of the Yankees and their prospects for 1937, but he pouted, his finger toying with the base of his champagne flute, tersely answering each question I posed.

Finally, he said, "That Frenchman. He never tried to…you never…did you?"

Before I could even think, I slapped him. Irving put his hand to his cheek. Conversations stopped, silverware silently paused above plates so that all that was heard were distant sounds of automobile accelerations far below on Market Street. I realized what I'd done and blushed with the stares of the other diners.

"Sorry," Irving said in a low voice as he put his palm to his cheek, maybe to feel it, maybe to soothe it, maybe to hide any redness from the other diners. "Sorry," he repeated. "That was uncalled for."

"No, I'm sorry," and I made myself add, "-*sweetheart*. It was an honest question. No, no we didn't." Then I told Irving a truth, though it was a stunted, twisted one, a half-truth.

"My heart never belonged to him. He never had a chance with me."

Irving smiled, a vague, wan smile, as if trying to verify that he was the one that my heart belonged to.

And Glenn Lee and his orchestra returned early from their break to hastily fill the silence.

March 25, 1937

Irving left this morning, back to New York on the train. I let him kiss me, and I even indulged him in a couple of surreptitious caresses, finally pulling his hands away with a whispered *Irving, we're in public.*

He grinned like a schoolboy and mounted the steps. Through the window, he blew me kisses, and I blew one back to him. The train slid off for the river and beyond, and I exhaled.

I called Mother today for her kugel recipe. She asked why I was suddenly interested. I told her I was attending Passover with the Taylors. I could almost feel her pride over the phone.

Father made a point of getting on the phone to tell me how proud he was of me for getting my first newspaper job. Then he said, "I love you, now get off the phone, you're costing yourself a fortune." Good old, practical Father.

March 27, 1937, Passover

Attended the Passover Seder at the Taylors'. Miss Fenerty sat in a place of honor next to Mr. and Mrs. Taylor as the candles were lit and the story was told of the release of our ancestors from the slavery of the Pharaohs. Faces glowed in the candlelight, mine among them. I feel that I'm finally old enough to truly appreciate the story, the story of escaping bondage.

My kugel was okay but not like Mother's.

March 28, 1937, Easter Sunday

Easter dinner with Ellie, Miss Fenerty, and a revolving door of well-wishers in Easter pastels, the very youngest with white baskets and chocolate smiles. Little girls in white stockings and Mary Jane's and white sweaters, little boys in miniature blue seersucker suits with bowties. The Eaves boys and their children were there, a flurry of names, none remembered. The Taylors and their children, dressed the same way in solidarity with the gentiles, I suppose. The McShans, Will and Leah and their children and grandchildren, all in on the train and staying with the Taylors on Jordan Street.

We ate all day, it seems. Both ham and lamb were served, with green beans, sweet potatoes (Ellie: 'taters'), rolls, peach pie, ambrosia, a carrot dish called copper penny. That's what I can remember; there was much more.

March 30, 1937, Tuesday

The AP wire had a story on a triple murder in Turtle Bay, NY. Dead are a mother and daughter, strangled, and their deaf butler, stabbed, just a few subway stops from Mother and Father. I fear for them in that neighborhood.

March 31, 1937

Letter from Irving telling me, "'your' not going to believe where we'll honeymoon. Guess where? Here's a hint. Parlee voo francie?"

Poor guy. A good secretary would spot the grammatical errors in his notes but would blush like a thermometer if she had to read them. It still bothers me that he never asks me about my new job.

April 3, 1937

Sabbath. God of Israel, give me strength and right judgment.

April 4, 1937

Color is everywhere here, every conceivable shade of green with explosions of magenta and red and white. Lavender wisteria on arbors. A yellow-flowered, fragrant vine called Confederate jasmine. Tulip trees erupting into rounded, rosy clouds, just over housetops, thousands of blossoms opening upward, the detonation of something pink and white against the straight blue sky. Magenta-pink redbud blossoms wander in a mist around gray, smooth-barked trunks. Birds fly from one to the other as if unable to choose.

Miss Fenerty has gone to Fort Worth to see the McShans, and who knows, she said, maybe for the last time. "Of course, I've been saying that for twenty years," she added with a laugh that made the whole thing seem like a grand joke.

The house on Crockett has been empty this week with just Ellie and me. Ellie came in, her sweater tied around her waist, the weather having warmed quickly since she left for church, her arms bare, the hint of a farmer's tan still lingering from the prior summer. We puttered around the house like an old married couple, cooking side by side, dusting, doing dishes, even scrubbing baseboards. All in the intimacy of shared silence.

We were looking over the paper, the Sunday *Times*. Ellie was laughing about something Dixie Dugan said when suddenly I got an idea.

"Paint me," I said.

"What? Again? Or you mean paint you like a house? Would you like to be white with green shutters?"

I laughed but insisted, "No, silly. Paint me. Again. On the balcony. With the azaleas in the background this time."

She folded the paper and put it on the end table on top of the sports section, the "*Realm of Sports.*"

On the balcony, I sat in the white wicker chair where behind me azaleas were bursting out of an uproar of green leaves and surging into a brilliant red and white crescendo. My hands were in my lap as I waited for Ellie to get her easel and paints set up. Neither of us said anything until she said, "Unbutton the very top button of your blouse. Here." She pointed to her own neck.

I unbuttoned it. Then I did the next. I paused, then did another. Then I undid all of them. My hands were shaking. I looked up, sheepishly.

She left for a moment, and I was afraid I had made a misstep. I felt very alone and silly with my blouse completely unbuttoned and the white of my skin and my brassiere showing. In a moment she returned with a white bedsheet.

"This is a classic pose," she said. "An ancient one, as ancient as Rome. The first men and women to be portrayed this way all spoke Latin."

I undressed as she looked off into the thick green leaves of the azaleas, speckled intensely with red and white blossoms. Beyond them was a world where nothing of any importance was happening, a world so inconsequential to us that it was as if it didn't exist. Shreveport, New York, Paris, Constantinople, none of them had any relevance to this balcony and this small, sacred place.

I sat in the white wicker chair feeling the rows of small cords press into the curves of my bottom, my soft skin. I draped myself with the sheet, or really half-draped myself, and said "Okay."

She turned around and found me with a look on my face that I'm sure was embarrassed, shy, nervous, reticent. Hesitant.

"Is this okay?" I asked her.

"Yes. Perfect."

She sketched me first, hurriedly, as if she saw something painfully beautiful but fleeting, something temporary. Red blossoms with occasional bursts of white echoed my nakedness, skin creamy against the white of the sheet, but still pale and elegant and smooth against crimson-nippled breasts and the hint of the black tangle wedge where my torso met my legs, one leg crossed over the other.

She worked quickly, more quickly than I've seen her work. At last, she turned the easel to me. The background of deep greens and explosive reds and brilliant whites was unfinished at the margins, but my image in the middle was complete. I could hardly believe it was me, but I was complete.

I stood. I let the sheet draping me fall, and I stood before her. She took my hand in hers, flecked with spots of paint, rose and red and white and green, and we went inside.

And that's all I will write on this subject. There is no need to write down something you will have no trouble remembering forever.

April 7, 1937

Irving called at Miss Fenerty's. He wants to know if I'll quit this Podunk town and just move home. He finally asked about my job at the *Times*, but only speaks of it as if it were a hobby.

"There's more to this town than you think," I told him. "Full of generous, cheerful, interesting people, mostly. I few soreheads, like anywhere else, but good people."

"Ha," he said, and I could have slapped him through the phone. When I hung up, Ellie said my jaw was clenching like I was about to bite through barbed wire.

BF returned this evening from Fort Worth on the T & P. Good to have her back, though E and I have returned to separate bedrooms.

April 13, 1937, Tuesday

Flowers and chocolates from Irving, wired to a florist here in Shreveport, and a letter from Mother bubbling with wedding excitement. She's found a secondhand dress and will need me to come up before the wedding so she can alter it. It's something she's always dreamed of, she says, me in my wedding dress, her altering it before the big day and giving me honeymoon advice.

I'm sorry, Mother. I'm so, so sorry.

April 20, 1937

Left newsroom early today, about six pm. Got into the eighties again with some rain.

April 24, 1937

Sabbath today, which Mr. Tiner insists I take off. The weather was nice with a high temperature of only (!) seventy. Ellie is working nonstop with Mr. Albrizio, who's suggested fresco for the mural, a technique he learned in Italy. She's excited to learn it. I'm glad to see her working and happy.

After temple, I took Miss Fenerty to the lake again. She seems to have returned from Fort Worth a little frailer, but she insisted on going. The sunset is occurring a little later every evening, which is good because the days begin early and end late at the *Times*.

I brought two wooden folding chairs that have stenciled black letters on the backs, "Ezekiel Baptist Church," courtesy of Rev. Beannock. Their legs rested in the coarse gravel of the railroad right of way, just off the tracks. We sat and admired the sunset. Her hands were draped across the top of her cane, a shawl over her shoulders, her blue tam over her wispy white hair. Her gaze was on the setting sun.

"Ah, but if I had known 'twas this pretty, I'd have come out when me health was better." The fading sunlight melted into glitter on the lake's surface, advancing across the lake as if reaching out for us as it eased itself into Texas.

I watched her as she watched the sunset, and I asked her silently, why are you so happy? So content? But the question I really wanted to ask her was, *why are you my hero?*

What I asked her instead was, "You've had some hard luck in your life. Why aren't you bitter?"

"Choose bitterness, and it will choose you right back, Miriam, and then the two of you, you and your bitterness, will have a long unhappy life together. A shame, too, for it didn't have to be that way. It was simply your choice. Uncle Jack was only partially right. Don't look for happiness. You'll never find it if you look for it. But I say be still, and it will find you. It will find you, sure. Just be still."

She smiled into the setting sun and the mark it was leaving on the water.

When we finally returned to the car, our long shadows fell before us, equally tall and thin, equally dark.

April 28, 1937

Irving called just as I was getting in from a long, difficult, satisfying day and about to slip into the tub for a good soak. Ellie took the call, and I could hear her talking baseball with him. At last I heard her say, "Well, maybe it'll be your Yankees and my Cardinals in the fall." Her voice was cordial but less animated than usual.

Then I heard my name through the door. I wrapped up in a bathrobe and went out to take the call. Ellie handed me the phone with a look of embarrassment on her face. I think we both want to believe that he doesn't exist. When he calls, that belief is shattered.

There's a hesitation in his voice now, in both of our voices, I suppose. He still insists that my job with the paper will be temporary. I didn't argue with him, but I didn't agree either. Instead, I steered the conversation to latkes, knishes, and the Yankees.

April 30, 1937

Miss Fenerty says the paper reported that a Mr. William Gillette died yesterday. He was the actor famous for playing the role of Sherlock Holmes.

"Well, he was supposed to be on the Lusitania with me, but overslept or something like that."

Weather "fair to middlin'" as they say here.

May 6, 1937

The wire announced that the Hindenburg exploded today in New Jersey. Several dozen were killed. What horrible news for those families.

Work going great guns. Journal entries suffering from it. Sorry, my little companion.

May 8, 1937

Wedding one month from today. My stomach boils, and my throat swells every time I think about it.

May 10, 1937, Monday

Mr. Tiner may be sending me to New Orleans to cover the closing of the last Chinatown there. He says then I'll be getting a few days off for my hard work. He says I've exceeded his expectations, which were substantial to begin with.

May 14, 1937, Friday

Back in Shreveport. I wrote the Chinatown article on the train back. Everywhere I looked in New Orleans, my mind saw young Bridget Fenerty.

May 15, 1937, Saturday

The Victory Natatorium opened for the summer season today. It was built to commemorate the victory in the Great War and dedicated in 1919, a saltwater pool with a handsomely designed bathhouse. The weather was warm, just warm enough to justify a swim.

Ellie and I swam in our clothes, as we have no suits, and the shops haven't started carrying them yet. Mine is back home in a drawer in my parents' apartment. I don't think Ellie has ever owned one. She tells me she swam in her slip like Miss Fenerty did in the river, except that Ellie swam in the big round metal livestock trough under the windmill of their farm in north Texas.

Miss Fenerty was with us at the natatorium, sitting on the steps well away from the edge with her cane between her knees.

"Is it cold?" she called to us.

"Not to a girl from the north," I shouted back.

"Or a girl from north Texas," Ellie said, and we dove together underwater. In truth, it was almost painfully cold, but we were happy, happy to be together with her. Happy enough that we chose not to suffer from the cold.

We came up together. Ellie lifted herself dripping onto the edge of the pool and padded up the steps, still dripping a trail of drops that darkened the concrete of the pool deck. Her blonde hair was wet and close to her head. She took Miss Fenerty by the arm.

"Come with me, Miss Biddy. Just your feet. It'll be nice, just see."

Ellie pushed golden wet hair out of her face so she could watch Miss Fenerty's steps for her. She held onto Miss Fenerty's old arm as she worked her way down the steps, two feet at a time on each step, her cane reaching out for the next lowest. At the edge of the pool, I took her cane and laid it down and put my arms out to her like someone receiving the first steps of a toddler, that *come-here-I've-got-you* pose.

Ellie and I removed Miss Fenerty's shoes. Then we sat her on the edge of the pool and put her feet in. "Ooh! 'Tis cold!" And she chuckled.

Ellie and I eased against the edge of the pool, flanking Miss Fenerty, as the three of us watched the other bathers. A young woman with a svelte figure and curly blonde hair executed a complicated dive, hitting the water with barely a ripple. She came up and saw Miss Fenerty dangling her legs in the water and swam over to us, a practiced stroke, effortless and graceful. She pulled into the breaststroke as she neared.

"Hi, Miss Biddy!" she said.

"Goodness," Miss Fenerty squinted with her hand over her eyes. "It's my Lola Mae!"

The girl submerged and reemerged next to us.

"Lola Mae, this is Ellie and Miriam," Miss Fenerty said. And then she said something that would have been strange had it not made perfect sense.

"Two of my other daughters."

"Hi, Miriam. Hi, Ellie," the girl said. I say girl, but really she was older than Ellie and me.

"Now, did I see your wedding banns published in the *Times*?" Miss Fenerty asked.

"Yes, ma'am. Took me long enough, but I found the right one."

"Well, it probably took him just as long. What will your last name be?"

"Smith. Plain ol' Smith. Might have to hyphenate it like the English."

"Well, wouldn't that be something, then? What will the ceremony be? Hindoo?" Miss Fenerty joked.

Lola Mae laughed and rolled her eyes and put her hands on her hips in a fake admonishment. "Well, no ma'am! Catholic, of course!" Then she paused and said, "Daddy couldn't get the Hindoo Temple. It was booked."

The four of us laughed like sisters, the four of us with nothing in common except each other.

And that we were all four in the water. Even Miss Fenerty.

Somehow, by talking nonchalantly while she did it, Lola Mae had eased her into the water where it came up to her waist. Miss Fenerty stood there stroking the water back and forth as if it were a cat. Over her head was the word VICTORY spelled out in an arch.

May 17, 1937, Monday

I took her to confession, *first time in eighty years*, she said somewhat proudly. I waited for her in the back of the church and looked at all the iconography, the sagging Christ that the Klan and the Pope said I was responsible for killing, the rows and columns of candles under the statue of Mary, the Blessed Mother. Each one representing an anguish or a gratitude, large or small. A draft moved in the church, and the flames leaned one way and then the other like a flock of birds moving with a sense of communal direction. On the ceiling on either side of the main aisle, angels were painted frolicking among clouds and red silk ribbons that concealed their nakedness.

I thought she would come out red-eyed and wet-faced. But no, she came out with her head high and smiling. The priest came out a moment after her, and I couldn't tell if he was on the verge of tears or laughter. He nodded to me and walked to the front of church and exited through a door.

Miss Fenerty took her cane and pointed to the ceiling. "Naked angels cavorting in heaven." And she laughed a single, hooting laugh.

May 19, 1937, Wednesday

We're on the train, the overnight to Houston and then Galveston. The train shakes the thin mattress in my berth like I'm being rocked by a hand with a tremor, and I roll slightly from one side to the other with each jostling movement. The whistle up ahead is muffled by the thick curtain of the sleeping space and the heavy night air of East Texas. What isn't muffled is her snoring. She's in the berth below me, and I can hear her as she sleeps, and I hope she's dreaming of the ones who have left this world, the ones she's loved most of all.

Earlier this evening, we were sitting side by side and had just cleared the outskirts of Shreveport. The train tossed us lightly, rocking us tenderly like a mother trying to sooth a child. Farm houses and fields were slipping by as the train rattled out a rhythm on the tracks, and the whistle warned the world that we were coming. Sunlight-shadow-sunlight-shadow-sunlight pulsed past the windows as the pleasant spring air rushed by. The green velvet of the seats changed from dark to light to dark with each passing flash of sunshine. People napped crumpled into the corners of their seats or read newspapers that trembled with the movement of the train.

We passed a crossing where a flatbed truck waited. The back of the truck carried a farmer's children, all of them with shimmering blonde hair. Their faces moved to watch those of us in the train pass by. I watched them slip away, and I wondered, what do they know of me? What will they ever know of me? That I'm Jewish? That there's a world beyond these piney woods and cotton fields? That there's art and music and beauty?

And then I thought, what will I ever know of them? That there are families in these woods that work hard and love one another and sing in church on Sundays? And marry their neighbors and have children and live lives of honorable contentment, never venturing twenty miles from home? Standing firm and proud between the ground and God?

I was lost in these questions when Miss Fenerty's voice startled me. She was peering through her glasses at a magazine she'd bought from the kiosk in the train station.

"But what a fine looking man that Errol Flynn is. I knew some Flynns back in me Channel days. Not near as good looking."

She wet her finger on her tongue and turned the page smiling in amusement at each new page, each one brought into focus by the tiny glass ovals of her spectacles. Finally, she closed the magazine, placed it in her lap, and folded her hands over it. She looked out the window as the blurry world raced by.

"You and Ellie, you're more than just best friends, aren't you?" She asked the question to her reflection. The train lightly shook us; the engine hummed and grunted up ahead barely audible over the cadence of clacking crossties under us. One after the other after the other after the other after the other and then the hoarse, distant hoot of the whistle far up ahead.

Her question was so sudden, so unexpected, that I didn't have a chance to even think about whether or not I wanted to lie, let alone what lie I would concoct. The facts flowered from inside me, beautiful and fragrant.

"Yes," I said.

She smiled an admiring, thoughtful smile.

"The truth, your own truth, can be uncomfortable. 'Tis like a pebble, a small stone. Hard to lie upon by itself, but if you put layers of time or lies or both atop it, like cushions, well then, most anyone can endure it. But of course, it's a bit like *The Princess and the Pea*, remember that one? Deep down, it's still your truth, not anyone else's. And lying is a sin, isn't it, then? Especially when you lie to yourself."

The train clattered in the short silence that followed. She turned to me, and her pale green eyes were on me.

"So, I'll tell you this, Miriam. Lead your own life, or someone else will surely lead it for you."

She turned to the window as her reflection turned to her, and they smiled at each other. The sun had set on the dark green of the late spring leaves, and it was dark except for a few orange patches of sunset light in the woods. We crossed the iron span over the Sabine as up ahead the engine brayed low and hollow. We were in Texas.

May 20, 1937, Thursday

Schools will be out in a week or two, and the beach will begin filling up, I'm sure, but today it was deserted, not a soul in sight. We stood there together looking out into the sea, and I became distracted watching a ship steaming in from the south and into Galveston Bay, just gliding over the surface in the distance. The Gulf wasn't heaving or restless, but sleeping like a giant or a monster, the waves rhythmic like a quiet snore under an air that was heavy and briny. The gentle surf yawned and sighed, over and over, as gulls laughed high squeaking, squawking laughs. I got caught up in watching the undulating flap of their wings, the glide over the air currents, the flap again.

When I looked over to Miss Fenerty, she had taken off her clothes, not a stitch on, as they're fond of saying down here. They were in a pile in the sand behind her with her cane.

"If I'm to go in," she said, "I'm going in the altogether, like a Tahitian wahini swimming out to greet Captain Cook." She looked behind herself and then in front of herself at her old skin, her old, collapsing body, and she began laughing. Her eyes were squinted, and her teeth were exposed.

"It appears as though me arse has melted away," she paused with laughter that kept her from continuing, "and me tits are all dejected about it," she chuckled.

Her breasts did look like they were staring down at her feet, and I must have smiled, because she laughed again, a single laugh, a hoot. And then she looked out to the sea and down at her feet where the brown water was advancing and retreating, the surf murmuring and testing them. She took a step like the first step of a long journey, and then she waded into the Gulf, carefully, slowly until the water was well over her knees and just under her sagging cheeks. The sea was calm, just the gentle roll of it, the small waves wetting and smoothing the sand at my feet.

She turned to me and said, "Are you coming in, then? If you're worried, I don't think a policeman will want to get within a hundred yards of this old body."

"Yes," I said, and I took off my clothes, too, shorts and a blouse and my underclothes. My body young and crisp compared to hers, everything high and in its place. It struck me that one day it would be like hers and that hers once was like mine, when all the handsome young lads of the Irish Channel in New Orleans would die for a kiss from her, when she was young and vibrant and didn't give a fiddler's fart what anyone thought.

We stood there in our naked truth. She reached her hand out and I took it, and we waded in up to her shoulders, and I squatted in the water to cover my breasts, still fearful that someone would happen upon us. A wave lapped over our faces, playfully almost, and we tasted the saltwater, and I used my free hand to push my hair out of my face.

She regarded me with a smile, a radiant, beatific, Irish smile and said, "Ah, but I was young and lovely once, too."

We turned and looked to the horizon, presumably to Mexico out there somewhere, or further, Brazil, maybe. We held hands under the water, her old hand in my young hand somewhere under the murky Gulf. We stayed that way for some time, each of us made lighter by the force of the water and swaying with it like seaweed in the sea's invisible current. A pelican, sandy brown, flew in with great hinged wings and a bill like a ridiculously long yellow chin. It hovered, flapped a few times and rested on a piling set to mark the shipping channel. It shifted from foot to yellow webbed foot, tucking in its wings.

"A remarkable bird is the pelican. His bill can hold more than his belly can," I said quietly.

Miss Fenerty laughed in peaceful wonder.

"Old Uncle Jack. God rest him," she said.

Over to our right, where the shoreline receded away from us, the sun was dropping, wavering and orange. Dropping carefully into Texas.

May 22, 1937

Arrived this morning from Galveston, but missed temple. I've composed a letter to Irving, and in sending it I feel lighter. I also wrote Mother, to tell her as well. And that's the one I feel worse about.

Ellie is working long days with Mr. Albrizio on the mural. He says that she's working so hard that she's wearing him out and that he needs a day off for rest. I've suggested the same for Ellie, maybe a drive in the countryside.

May 23, 1937, Sunday

Ellie and I went down to Keatchie this afternoon to see Gladiola Longhat, to see if she could remember much about her grandmother. Not for Mr. Roosevelt; I'd just like to know. I'll admit here that I was more interested in the girl's welfare than I was about any story concerning her grandmother's past. Looking back over the last few months, I realize I've thought about her from time to time, and now I feel I've failed her by not stopping by to check on her. The Packard's clutch was just a convenient excuse.

The little cluster of antebellum buildings of Keatchie greeted us in cheerful white clapboard, and Ellie commented that they would make interesting subjects to paint. We came to the fork in the road, and I remembered the difficulty I had that day. I chose the right road this time.

The way was even more tangled than before, however, and I was glad to have Ellie's company. A couple of times, we got out to scout the woods for signs of the road's imprint on the ground, and then finding it, we continued on. At last, we came upon the house.

A riot of spring green underbrush was knee high in the yard. Pine saplings were growing in the solitary gutter that ran along the front of the house. The gutter itself had been struck by a limb and crumpled into a shallow V. Kudzu raced along the eaves of the house, and wisteria boiled up the sides like a green house fire.

There were no old dogs sleeping beneath the house. There were no chickens strutting and muttering in the yard. The only thing alive there now was the surrounding forest that was advancing on the house at a rate that I would have never thought possible.

I walked onto the porch, carefully testing each step. The front door was open. The wall where the painting of the blessed virgin had been hanging was blank. The rocking chair that June Longhat slumped in that day was the only thing that remained. That and the silence.

I heard Ellie's steps behind me and then felt her next to me. Her quiet drawl explained what she knew of the way of these things.

"In a year, it'll be a heap, the roof caved in," she said. "In five, nothing, just woods. Just cedar trees, and in the spring, daffodils and jonquils will come up. Year after year, just cedar trees and daffodils."

May 27, 1937

Phone call from Father. He says they received my letter and for me to do what I think is right. He'll cancel the temple and the rabbi, he said, but he just wants to make sure it's what I want to do. He says mother can't talk to me right now. Just give her time, he says.

May 31, 1937

This is the letter I sent to Irving upon returning from Galveston. He's returned it.

Dear Irving,

I wish you not only happiness, but a true, honest happiness.

That's why I can't marry you, Irving. I encourage you to move along and find someone you can share your dreams with, someone who wants to go where you go.

I am simply not that person.

I am embarrassed to tell you that, some months ago, I pawned the engagement ring you gave me and sent the money to Mother and Father, as they were in great need of it. They have no idea where the money came from.

I am truly sorry, and you have my promise that I will eventually repay you for it.

Sincerely,

Miriam

Written in the bottom in big letters: **NO! NO! NO! NO! NO!**

June 3, 1937

Today, I covered Confederate Memorial Day for the *Times*. Bunting and flags were everywhere, but there were only a few slumped bodies with white beards and canes, all from outlying towns in Louisiana, Arkansas, and Texas. There are no more Confederates living in Shreveport.

In other news, cotton beginning to 'boll.' Hogs up three and a quarter, corn down a half.

Ha! Just listen to me.

June 5, 1937, Saturday

He appeared in the front yard late last night.

I was sound asleep upstairs, with the window open and the rain falling, pattering off the new leaves of the trees outside my window. I was half-awakened by a sound outside that seemed to emerge from the sound of the rain. The air was cool, wet and metallic, scented by the wire mesh of the screen. I lay there for a moment, trying to imagine Maggie Fenerty's voice in the spring rain, dripping and popping off the leaves through the open window.

"Miriam," the rain said.

It pattered again, dripping off the leaves just outside the window. The air was almost unpleasantly cool, just enough to make me bundle under the blankets.

"Miriam?" The rain questioned me this time.

"Miriam!" The rain shouted my name, and I arose from a nameless, forgotten dream to see what it wanted. I drew my robe around me and nosed my feet into my slippers. Through the screen of the front window, I saw a figure in the front yard. His arms were limp at his sides. The rain was beating down heavier now, and I strained to see who it was.

Irving. Irving Glickstein.

"I know you're in there, Miriam." He motioned to the Packard parked on the street. "New York plates, Miriam. I know it's you."

Fearing he would wake Miss Fenerty, I hissed out to him.

"Irving! It's...." I looked at the dial of the clock on the bedside table. In the darkness it was only a circle of luminescent numbers that floated in a small orbit around the minute and second hands. "It's three a.m.!"

"Let me in, Miriam!" he shouted so loud that a dog down the street barked into the night.

"Hush, now." I was surprised to hear this southern word come out of my mouth. "I'll come down."

I opened the front door and saw him still standing there. He had a bottle of liquor in one hand, only an inch of amber tilting in the bottom as he swayed. In the other hand was a revolver.

"Irving?" I said as I looked at the revolver.

"I love you, Miriam," he said. His eyes were red from crying and drinking. "I love you and I can't live without you. I won't live without you."

The rain rattled down on him and formed a curtain like chains around me on the porch.

"I can't marry you, Irving." The pattering tick of the rain again. "I'm sorry, but I can't."

His face contorted, his eyes squinting, his lower lip bulging. He pulled the gun up and put the muzzle at his right temple. The black end of it wavered as his hand shook.

"Don't Irving," I called in a low voice, just above the rain. "You have so much to live for."

"What? What do I have to live for? A world without you? A long, empty life without you?"

He stopped his blubbering and gulped a big swallow of air, as if it would be his last. He looked at me. His thinning hair was plastered down on his head. His clothes were clinging to him. Desperately, hopelessly.

The porch light came on, and I could see Irving clearly now, and he could see me. Behind me the door opened, the clunk of the heavy front door and then the wheeze of the screen door. I didn't want to take my eyes off Irving, but, in the corner of my vision, I saw her cane before I saw her. It probed the boards of the front porch until she stood even with me.

"Good morning," she said as if she was genuinely glad to see him at three in the morning. "I was just about to make tea. Come in and have some with us."

Her voice was pleasant, playful, cajoling.

"Come in, son," she said. "Come keep an old woman company for a while."

Irving's eyes opened from their squinting, and his lower lip fell from its contortion.

"Don't keep me waiting, now," she said. "You may have your whole life ahead of you, with plenty of time in it, but I'm an old woman."

And then she laughed that laugh, gentle and loving, inclusive and mischievous.

His hand and the gun wilted down. The rain slackened with his arm. Miss Fenerty smiled and made a rolling gesture with her old hand.

And Irving Glickstein dropped the whiskey bottle and came inside.

He ascended the steps in his soaked gray flannel Fifth Avenue suit, clinging to him and pulling against him as his legs wobbled. His tie, an expensive Italian one, hung loosely around his neck. Miss Fenerty reached for the revolver, and Irving let her take it.

"Miriam," she said, "fetch us some towels and a bathrobe. Closet at the top of the stairs. Thank you, love."

I scampered up the stairs, glancing in Ellie's room. She was twisted up in the sheets, blonde hair on the pillow, everything in gray tones in the dim light. I came downstairs, looking over my bundle for each step down, finding Irving shivering over a puddle in the front parlor floor. Miss Fenerty was lighting the gas heater under the mantle. It came to life with a rush of blue and orange light. I gave her the towels and the bathrobe.

"Now go and make us some tea, will you? Strong tea. This handsome young man could use a cup of strong tea, I'd wager."

I went in the kitchen and put the kettle on, and, when I returned with the two cups of tea on a tray with the little white sugar bowl and the creamer, Irving was out of his wet clothes and in a bathrobe. It was one of Miss Fenerty's, with small pink roses over it. Irving's white, hairy legs protruded out from the bottom of it. He and Miss Fenerty tried to hold a conversation despite the liquor and the emotion. The revolver gleamed under the yellow light of the lamp on the end table. Irving's eyes closed and his head sagged forward, and it was clear that the whiskey had finally caught up with him.

"Fetch a blanket, dear," Bridget told me, and I went back upstairs to get one. When I returned downstairs, Irving was lying on the couch, snoring, and Miss Fenerty was smiling and admiring him the way one would watch a newborn baby sleep.

I put the blanket over him, and a stray note of regret came over me that perhaps it would be nice to have someone to care for like this, someone to watch over. But I still knew that I didn't love him and that I would never love him near enough to marry him.

Miss Fenerty stood up and took the revolver gingerly as if she didn't want to touch it any more than necessary. I followed her into the kitchen, and she opened a drawer and found a paper bag. She slipped the gun into it, folded the bag over several times, and put it in a drawer behind some kitchen towels.

"Ma always said that the pistol is the devil's right hand," she said.

All that happened last night. This morning, I woke to find Irving and his wet clothes gone, the blanket neatly folded, and the puddle of water on the parlor floor evaporated to just a few scattered drops. I began to wonder if I had just dreamed it all.

Out on the front lawn, however, was a whiskey bottle, empty and on its side.

June 7, 1937, Monday

Mr. Tiner called me into his office today. He said I need to speak to you about a story of yours we ran.

Though Dash Day wasn't held last month (May 22), out of respect, Confederate Memorial Day was held again last week. My assignment was to cover it, and I had this piece published:

Confederate Memorial Day Observed; First Without Hero Sergeant Lockett

SHREVEPORT, June 4, 1937- The city celebrated Confederate Memorial Day for the first time without local hero Sergeant Champ Lockett. Mr. Lockett passed away in March. His likeness still graces our courthouse steps, facing north towards the direction of his adversary, like so many do on courthouse lawns across the South.

Put them all together, all the farm boys, shopkeepers, and schoolteachers whose stony likenesses stand on courthouse lawns and stare north. Put them together, and you would have a regiment or perhaps even a brigade, men who never had the means or inclination to own another man but who were made afraid through the printed and spoken word, baited into fighting an army of strangers who, they were told, were coming to occupy their land and everything else that was sacred. The men in these counties and parishes were apprentices, stevedores, and river men who only wanted new boots, a uniform, and a rifle, as well as a chance for adventure in an otherwise mundane life. They were men stirred into action by a threat that was fanned by others, and just like most wars, it was the journalists who fanned the flames to their hottest.

I had the privilege of being the last person to interview Mr. Lockett. He was a truly a gentleman and a hero, not because of his battlefield exploits, but because he was a simple man who hungered for the truth. His dying wish was that people would look to the future and not stay mired in the past. May God rest his soul and all the souls of the departed. -MRL

I didn't expose his secret. I believe it will die of natural causes.

Mr. Tiner sat on the edge of his desk in seersucker trousers, suspenders, and white shirtsleeves rolled up. He set down the paper with my article in it.

"We've gotten a lot of response from your story," he said. "Some of it good, and some of it not so good."

I worried that I was going to be 'fussed at' as they say here, but instead he just laughed.

Then, he shook my hand and said, "Congratulations, Miss Levenson. Some hate you for your story, some like you for your story, but no one loves you for it. But at least you've inspired them, made them think. It looks like you're a real journalist, my dear!"

I like it when he calls me 'my dear.' It's from the heart.

June 8, 1937

What a strange feeling. I would've gotten married today.

June 13, 1937, Sunday

She wasn't herself today. Nina had come by for a visit with the baby. At first everything seemed okay.

"Oh, would you look at this little one, then, would you?"

Then she fell silent as Ellie, Nina, and I talked. She seemed to stare across the room at something far away, and then she exclaimed, "Nina? Did you hear? They've shot Senator Long. Down in the capital. Baton Rouge."

"Yes ma'am. But that's been mostly a year or two ago, Miz Biddy."

A fog seemed to lift from her. She seemed to be trying to recalculate time.

"The year after they shot Bonnie and Clyde and hung the Butterfly Man." Miss Fenerty added, probing as if using additional facts to re-orient herself.

"That's right," Nina said reassuringly.

"Oh. And who are you?" Miss Fenerty asked me.

"I'm Miriam, Miriam Levenson."

"Oh, that's right. I remember now," though I wondered if she really did.

"I babysat a few times for the Longs, you know," she said. "When they lived in Shreveport. On Atkins Street, it was. That Russell. So serious. Not at all like his father."

She fell asleep in her chair, as she's become accustomed to doing more and more. When she was finally deep asleep, Nina said, "Miz Biddy always told me that if she gets so she don't know nobody, get the priest in here. Before she goes."

Nina got on the phone and placed a call. Miss Fenerty woke, her old eyes opening like the rising of the sun, and Ellie and I escorted her to her bed. She complied with us, napping after we got her settled.

Father Van Haver came by the house directly after Sunday Mass. He prayed with her and asked if she would like to take the sacrament. She answered with a weak voice.

"Yes, Father."

She struggled, trying to right herself into a sitting position in the bed. Finally, she held out her old arms as if they were flightless wings.

"Maggie, Colleen, will you two help me up?" she asked Ellie and me in the same small voice. We pulled her up to a sitting position, a Jew on one side, a Baptist on the other. Father Van Haver held the full moon of a wafer before her and looked into her pale green eyes and said, "Corpus Christi."

"Amen," she mumbled, a childhood ritual resurrected after being dormant for eighty years. She opened her mouth, and he laid the ivory white moon on her tongue.

June 17, 1937

"Listen."

He put the rubber earpieces in my ears. His voice became small, and I cast my eyes upward to follow his lips.

Do you hear it? It's called a gallop.

I had hoped to hear the whispers of memories, voices of the ones she'd loved, kept there. Instead there was a buzz, a loping, floppy gait of a heart that had been broken, healed, and broken and healed again, over and over. Her old, big, kind heart was headed down the homestretch for the finish line. I took the earpieces out of my ears and gave the stethoscope back to him.

"Dropsy," the doctor said as he coiled up his stethoscope and tucked it into a corner of his bag. "It means her heart is failing."

It seemed impossible to me that a heart as big and strong as Bridget Fenerty's could fail.

"That can't be," I said.

"I'm not sure if you're aware of it, but Miss Bridget is an old woman," he said with a wry smile. He rolled his sleeves back down and pulled his tie out of his shirt. As he put his arms into his coat, he said, "Best we can do is for me to keep her comfortable, and you all to keep her company."

When he left, Nina and I sat and visited while Miss Fenerty slept crumpled in the chair she insisted we help her into. Ellie is out at the fairgrounds with Mr. Albrizio. They're looking at the State Exhibit Building going up.

The sounds of children shouting as they played in the warm afternoon sunshine moved out on the street. We listened to them as they receded. There's talk of closing the last school left downtown. How long before the concrete of downtown will be free of the distant banter and shouting of children freed after a day of confinement? Certainly it's been music to the ears of this old woman.

As Miss Fenerty slept away the day, Nina and I sat listening to the radio. After a while in silence, I casually asked Nina why she named her baby Benjamin.

"That's a good Jewish name," I said.

"Benjamin was my grandpa," she smiled as if the memory of him had warmed her.

"What do you know of your family?" I asked her.

"I was a Rusk," she said. "Before I married Reverend Beannock."

"Rusk?" I asked. What were the chances? I thought.

"Yes, my people were from down around Coushatta. My great-grandfather was owned by a man named Rusk."

I cautiously asked the question, cautiously as if I had to be careful in asking it so it would be true.

"By any chance, was your great-grandfather's first name Solomon?"

She looked straight at me. "Yes, it was," she murmured in wonder.

"And he had one eye?"

Her face was locked on mine, waiting for something, listening as if I were speaking an ancient language that only the two of us knew. The radio had been playing low, and she kept her eyes on me and reached over to shut it off as a commercial began: *Friends, it's common knowledge that a man has to dress sharp to feel sharp. At Jordan and Booth...*

"That's the family story," she said, "but I never met him. My grandfather was sold away by old Mr. Rusk, and when he did, great-grandfather Solomon fought to keep it from happening. Old Mr. Rusk put out my great-grandfather's eye with an ember and said, 'Boy, you challenge me again and I'll put out the other one, and then we'll see how far you can run.' And my grandfather, Ben Rusk, said that's the last he ever saw of his daddy. None of us have ever seen him, not even a picture, but we've heard the stories. Old Grandpa Solomon had a fine voice, and he could fix anything, wagons, cotton gins, you name it."

The clock tapped in the hallway and then chimed. Motes of dust swirled in the afternoon sunshine.

"Just a second," I said. I opened the case of the Presto. My hands shook as I hurriedly rummaged through the disks and examined the notes I had made on the cases. There it was. I held it up and squinted to make sure. I loaded it onto the spindle of the Presto and turned the knob. The disk revolved in a perfect circle as I lifted the arm and carefully set it down. The stylus made a zipping sound and found a groove. There was Miss Fenerty's voice, and, from time to time, mine in the background.

I listened for clues as to where in the story she was, her story, our story. I lifted the arm of the stylus and set it down further and further ahead catching a little more of Miss Fenerty's voice, lifting it up and setting it down and listening, more of her voice, up and then down again and her old voice. Nina looked at me with a puzzled look. And then at last, her great grandfather's words, told by Miss Fenerty's voice with a background of static:

"...Miss Bridget, if you ever see one of my children, or grandchildren, or they children, well you tell 'em ole Grampa Rusk is show proud of 'em. Tell 'em to live tall and walk straight, cause we all take our first steps on this earth, and we all take our last..."

I looked up to Nina. Her fingertips were at her lips. "That's exactly what my grandpa Ben used to say."

June 20, 1937

Why do these things happen so slowly? Why does someone, something, so wondrous and magical have to be lost to the earth and to mankind?

We take turns turning her, cleaning her, bathing her.

She's slipping away, and my heart is breaking.

June 21, 1937

Mr. Taylor sat with her today. I went into work but found it hard to concentrate. Mr. Tiner finally sent me home. The Eaves boys were just leaving when I returned. Hank had his arm around John, who'd been crying. Lola Mae emerged from the back of the house, crying also.

June 22, 1937

She was more lucid today. She remembered me, and we held hands. At last, she smiled at me and said, "May your joy and purpose meet and become the same. And then happiness will find you, sure." Will it be the last coherent thing she says to me?

I thought all day on what they used to tell us at summer camp. If you ever find yourself lost in the woods, don't wander around, just stay put, or you'll just get more lost otherwise. Stay put and you'll be found.

You'll be found, sure.

She rambles now, mumbling. This afternoon, she clearly said 'Patch'. Then later she may have said Elias, though I'm not sure.

Father Van Haver came by to give her Last Rites. She was oblivious.

411

June 23, 1937, Wednesday

She died today.

June 24, 1937, Thursday

This morning, Ellie and I went with Mr. Taylor to make arrangements. Mr. Herndon had directed us to a plot she'd reserved in the Oakland Cemetery. Mr. Tiner put this announcement in the paper, morning and evening editions, with her picture:

Fenerty Rites to be Held

A funeral Mass for Miss Bridget Fenerty will be held this Wednesday at Holy Trinity Catholic Church, Marshall and Fannin Streets, the Reverend Monsignor Francis Van Haver presiding. Miss Fenerty was a native of Ballinlough, County Roscommon, Ireland, and resided in the city since its early days.

Many in this city will attest to her giving spirit and her lovely voice. She sang professionally for a time as 'The Irish Songbird,' both here and as far as New York City. Her angelic voice was frequently heard at weddings as well, and she never charged a dime, preferring to render her services as a gift to the bride and groom.

She is preceded in death by her parents and siblings. She is survived by those who loved her, of which there are many, including the children she helped raise through the decades. At her request, the Joyful Mysteries of the Rosary will be said thirty minutes before services begin. Internment in Oakland Cemetery to follow.

June 25, 1937

When Nina, Ellie, and I arrived, he was there on the steps of the church. He must have noticed my stare as we walked up because he quickly took one more pull on his cigarette and dropped it and stepped on it. His hair was white, but he had a nose that was familiar, the same spot of a nose that I'd seen on someone else.

Nina and Ellie filed in as an usher held the door for them, but I stopped for a moment. I know I was staring; I couldn't help it. He leaned in courteously and gave me his hand. The movement was gracious and practiced.

"Have we met? I'm Frank DaSilva," he said.

"Miriam Levenson. Nice to meet you, Mr. DaSilva," I said.

"Oh, you can call me Frank, or even my nickname growing up, Ruivo, if you'd rather. Means redhead in Portuguese. Mine was red at one time. Now it's turned white, what hasn't turned loose." He smiled and asked me, "Do you live here?" He must have heard my New York accent.

"Yes," I said. It was strange for me to admit, but yes, I live here.

"Do you?" I asked him in return.

"Oh, no. I grew up in Brazil, though I was born here in Shreveport. I live in Texas now. Houston. Have for years. But I come here every so often on business. I'm an engineer with Texaco. Yes ma'am, seventy-four and still working. I've always had a need to be useful. Being useful means being alive, now doesn't it?"

"You know, someone told me that once," I said. "How did you know the deceased?" I asked him. It felt strange to refer to Bridget Fenerty as the deceased. She was the most alive person I've ever known.

"Strange thing," he said, "I saw her picture in the paper with her obituary, and it triggered a memory, a memory from a long time ago, my very first. The barest wisp of a memory, like a flash on a screen. The kind of thing that might be forgotten if ever remembered at all. I remember sitting in her lap, pulling her nose and her laughing about it. Clearly."

From his coat pocket, he pulled an old photograph, and there she was, young Miss Bridget Fenerty. On the back was stamped, *Star and Pelican Photograph Gallery, No. 30 Texas Street, Shreveport, La.* She looked exactly as I pictured her: full head of red hair photographed as gray and pulled up under a cap, a white smock apron with frills on the edge. She was holding a baby, a version of her in miniature. The picture was frayed on the edges like it had been carried all over the world.

"I found this among some pictures when Mama was dying. I asked her who it was, and she would only say it was our housekeeper when we lived in Shreveport. She couldn't remember her name, only it was Finnegan or something like that. But the picture stirred a memory for me."

"What do you know of your childhood? I mean here, in Shreveport?" I asked, and then I took a long look at him. There was no mistaking who his mother was.

"We left when my father died in the last days of the Confederacy. My mother took me, and we fled to Brazil. She met my daddy there, my step-daddy, when I was ten or twelve. He adopted me when they married, and that's how I became a DaSilva. I was born Frank Burton, Jr."

413

I couldn't say anything. Nothing. So he did.

"I often asked mama about my daddy, my real daddy, and she would only say he loved his country more than life itself and gave his life for it. I've always assumed he was a soldier. I put flowers on his grave when I'm in town. Someone else does, too. I've never seen who, though. Some relative, I guess."

His accent was thick with Portuguese, but when he said 'daddy' I could clearly hear the South in it.

"After mama and daddy died, my step-daddy, I mean, I moved back to the U.S., to Texas." He looked at me with that same kindly smile I'd seen almost daily for months and asked, "How did you know Miss Fenerty?"

"She was my friend," I told him. "And she spoke of you when you were a child. Of all the children she helped raised, I'm sure that you were her favorite. I'm sure of it."

His mouth shuddered and trembled and twisted, and his eyes watered, and he reached in his pocket for a handkerchief.

"Excuse me, miss. This is silly of me. I didn't even know her." He was crying in earnest now. "But at the worst, lowest, most trying times of my life, I've always remembered her, that first memory and her smile."

I didn't say a word to him about his origin, his true origin. That his grandfather was a decent man who died on a ship on a journey to save his family, and his body was slid into the sea, or that his grandmother worked long hours until her feet ached, just to keep her family together. Or that the woman who bore him was one of the most remarkable people I will ever meet. He was too old to start questioning who he was and where he had come from. So I told him a delicious truth I knew he could digest.

I told him that she spoke of him often and that Bridget Fenerty loved him like he was her own son and that she would be proud to know he was here, at her funeral. The old, pale man sobbed, his white hair shaking, and I felt bad for having told him. Or maybe having had to tell him, for as I look at it now, hours later, I had no choice. Not telling him would have haunted me the rest of my life.

I thought of the irony of it, that this old man had been raised by a woman who wasn't his mother and a man who wasn't his father.

And Frank DaSilva, Frank Burton, Jr., was crying because he'd never gotten a chance to know her. I was crying because I had.

We chatted a few more moments, trying to regain our composure before going in. The congregation inside was chanting the Joyful Mysteries together. As the door opened, I heard Father Van Haver's voice monotone, *And the word became flesh*. Outside, Frank DaSilva spoke proudly of his beautiful Spanish wife *of fifty-five years*, once with beautiful black hair like mine, now gray-headed like him, and their children and grandchildren, and a great-grandchild on the way in Galveston.

Finally, we entered the church and filed by the casket. I tried to convince myself that she was only sleeping and was on the verge of waking and telling a joke or a story. Or that she had been reunited with the ones she loved, and we would be united with her one day, because she loved us, too.

We took a seat with Nina and Ellie, but not before I surveyed the crowd. Will McShan and his wife, Leah Taylor McShan, had come in from Fort Worth with their children and grandchildren, all of them, as did the Eaves boys and their children. The littlest ones wiggled and fidgeted in the pew like a line of baby birds on a wire. Lola Mae was there with her fiancé. Although old Mrs. Randolph was too ill to attend, she sent her best through her children, who were there.

Also there was a tall, pale woman, Klara Lundgren O'Mara with her grown granddaughters, Bridget, Ingrid and Elsa, all named after old aunts.

Morris Taylor was there with his children, and their children. We were all there, her friends, as well as shopkeepers, store clerks, delivery men. And all their children, friends of their children, people whom she had wished good day and Merry Christmas, people she had smiled at once. Every one she had blessed. The church was packed, people standing four and five deep at the back and along the sides under the stained glass windows commemorating the French priests who died in the epidemic of 1873. Naked angels cavorted in the sky-blue, cloud-white heaven painted on the ceiling.

Ellie and Nina had saved me a seat. Frank DaSilva and I squeezed into it together. As the service progressed, Nina, Ellie, and I remained seated, but Frank Burton, Jr. followed the liturgy. Surely he had been raised Catholic by his stepfather. A papist, his mother (his stepmother, really) might say. How ironic. How fitting.

Father Van Haver recited the litany of saints:

St. Mary.
Pray for us.
St. Joseph.
Pray for us.
St. Peter and St. Paul.
Pray for us.
St. Bridget.
Pray for us.
St. Patrick.
Pray for us.
All you holy men and women of God.
Pray for us.

The priest gave a homily about Miss Bridget, and he seemed unsure of what to say. He hadn't known her very well, though you could tell that he wished he had. I did know her well, and in that I am lucky. At the end, he made the pronouncement that death has been swallowed up by victory.

I realized today that death will come for all of us, in its own time. There may be angels with harps reclining on clouds or peering down from the moon, or endless feasts and happy reunions. I only hope that, when it comes for me, the afterlife will be simple, merely simple. Peacefully, ecstatically simple.

June 26, 1937

After the graveside service, we adjourned to the house on Crockett Street. It was markedly different from sitting Shiva. There was an abundance of food and conversation. Miss Fenerty would have hated to miss a party like that. But, in some way, it felt as though she were still among us and very much so. Maybe because *we* were there, and she had left her mark on all of us.

I asked Frank DaSilva to come by, but he had a train to catch back to Houston. He has a great-grandbaby due any moment, his first, and he didn't want to miss having a cigar with his grandson to celebrate the new arrival. I wished him well, and I made sure to get his address. I told him I'd love to keep in touch with him. He said he'd like that, and he gave me his hand. I embraced him instead.

The house stayed full all afternoon, until evening when the crowd dwindled to just a few dozen, still so many that we were piled in two or three to a chair, five or six to a couch. The younger ones were lined up on the stairs, looking through the bannister, laughing and smiling with the reminiscences traded by men with ties undone, women reclining with shoes off. Teenagers sat on the floor, looking up at the adults. A wine bottle orbited around the room between the grownups, and I think I saw a flask get passed as well.

Hank Eaves told a story about her. "We were talking a few years ago about the TVA, and she said, '*Hank*,' she says," he imitated her mannerisms perfectly, and everyone recognized them and laughed. "*If the government could figure out how to generate electricity from self-righteousness, well, then they wouldn't be damming up the Tennessee.*"

We laughed, and someone said, "Now don't that just sound like her?"

"It does," someone else said. "It sure does."

Klara O'Mara spoke. Her shoes were off, and her stockings were rolled down in the room full of strangers that were family somehow because they, we, had been touched by the same person. Her voice was sharp edged with the Midwest, and it made me think about my own accent and how it didn't matter here.

"This was probably sixty years ago," she said as she reached down to rub her ankle. She carefully held up her wine glass as she did. "We had this little white dog. Its name escapes me right now-"

Millicent, I thought to myself.

"It never cared for me," she continued as she reclined back and took a sip of her wine. "It was more my older sisters' dog than mine. That dog hated everyone else, other than Elsa and Ingrid, and the dog especially hated Miss Fenerty, probably the only creature that ever did. Well, one day when Miss Bridget was coming in from the clothesline with a basket of laundry, the dog scrambled up to her and started nipping at her heels, biting her ankles. Would've drawn blood if the shoes in those days didn't go up over the ankle. Well, Miss Fenerty says, she says..."

Klara O'Mara fell into laughter recalling the story, putting her fingers over her mouth, squinting and shaking. She had to set down her glass of wine and bend forward. She rose again like she was coming up for air.

"She says...*feck off, beast*."

Everyone laughed in a sudden collective howl.

"Well, she thought she was alone, but I heard it through the screen door, and when she came in I asked her, Miss Bridget, what does feck off mean?"

Another gust of laughter from those of us who called ourselves mourners.

"*Well, dearie*," Miss Klara's version of Bridget Fenerty's accent wasn't a replica. It was a duplicate.

"*Well, dearie, 'tis an Irish blessing of a sart, but in reverse, ye see. And yer nivver to repate it until yer a groon woman and then oonly to the sart of payple who need it the moost. Doont warry, dear, you'll knoo who they are. And yer sartainly nivver to repate it to yer ma and da, as it might cause the fairies to cast a spell on an innocent parson.*"

Everyone laughed again in another fine burst, some bending forward, some wiping tears out of their eyes. Klara continued, but in her own voice.

"Well, the dog died later on of old age or meanness, and we buried it, Miss Fenerty and old Mr. Rusk and my sisters and me."

Nina was pressed in next to me, and I reached over and squeezed her hand. The room was full and quiet as Klara O'Mara continued.

"My sister asks her, 'Miss Bridget, do dogs have souls?' Miss Fenerty said, 'generally, yes, they do.' Then she said, and I'll never forget it, 'but the truth of it, 'tis really the other way around. We don't *have* souls, we *are* souls, and that we merely *have* bodies.'"

And our glasses went up with that.

Morris Taylor had been silent most of the afternoon. He was clearly having a harder time with this than everyone else. But finally he spoke up.

"It was, uh, it was the time we were, uh, riding back on the train from the state championship bout. I still felt sore about losing. I felt I had let the whole city down, that New Orleans had gotten one over on us again. Well, she said, and I'll never forget it, she said, 'Greatness is just for a few. Aspire to goodness, for we all have a chance at that, at least.'"

The men and women lifted their glasses to each other and took a sip.

"If she told me that once, she told me a hundred times," Hank Eaves said. His tie was loose around his neck, and his sleeves were rolled up. His wife Lucy was on his lap, leaning into his chest.

Morris' spirit seemed to lift itself up.

"She would hand me my yarmulke on Saturday morning before temple and say, 'don't forget your halo.'" Everyone laughed, and Morris smiled.

Klara said, "Oh, I've heard that before." Then the whole room, teenagers on the floor and behind the bannisters, adults on the sofa and in the chairs said in unison, *"off to polish yer hay-los then, are ye?"*

They had all heard it.

I left the gathering and sat out on the porch in the swing. The sound of laughter and conversation and the glow of light inside the house warmed me. Ellie followed me out, and we sat together. We watched the moon come up in the east, as usual, as always.

I was thinking of the epitaph that Keats had wanted, *Here lies an English poet, his name writ in water.* I shivered as I thought about it.

"Do you want me to get your coat?" Ellie asked.

"No. No, don't leave me, stay here."

Instead of leaving to get my coat, Ellie took her sweater off and put it over me. As she did, she said:

"The Navajo believe," she adjusted the sleeves over my shoulders, "that a person can die three times. The first time is when their heart stops beating. The second time is when they're buried. The third time is when those left behind stop talking about them and forget them."

Under the dark blue sky, a dog barked in a faraway back yard, and a city trolley's tether slapped sparks out of overhead lines somewhere. Over the Slattery Building, the slow-rising moon was full and white.

June 28, 1937, Monday

Morris appeared in the newsroom in a seersucker suit. He was behind the glass in Mr. Tiner's office with one white wingtip shoe crossed over his knee. His ivory-colored hat was on the corner of Mr. Tiner's desk, and Mr. Tiner was sitting on the other corner. I don't think I've seen him sit in the chair behind it once. Morris got up, and they shook hands. Then he came and spoke to me.

"Had to get permission from the boss man," he said. "Mr. Herndon wants us all to meet down at his office at the courthouse."

As we exited the *Times* office, Mr. Hanley was headed down to the basement to prepare the press for the evening run. Outside on Marshall Street, the ink truck was parked.

The ink man said, "Afternoon, ma'am. Boy howdy, it's hot ain't it?"

It was. This is what Uncle Jack was talking about when he said *just you wait.*

As we walked through the heat, Morris said, "Mr. Herndon has some news for you. Says it's important."

We skirted the sun and its heat, staying under the awnings where old people sat fanning themselves waiting for the trolley. We ascended the courthouse steps across the bright hot sun and stepped into the cool lobby of the air-conditioned courthouse. As we passed his pencil-and-chewing gum kiosk, Raymond smiled to the elaborate molding up and across the lobby, "Hey, Mr. Taylor."

"Hey, Raymond."

Ellie and Nina were waiting there. Ellie was in paint-stained overalls, random orange, blue, and yellow drops and smudges on the denim. Nina waited in a light linen dress, voluminous on her large frame. The reverend's mother must've been keeping the baby.

Mr. Herndon came in with a satchel. He wore the same type of seersucker suit as Morris, but in a peach tone. He fished his keys from his pocket and said, "Sorry I'm late. I had to go to court upstairs to get Judge Samuel to sign off on this. We got to talking about Miss Fenerty and ran a little over."

We assembled in his office as he took off his coat. Nina, Ellie, and I were allowed seats. Morris stood. Bookcases were on all sides of us, identical dusty spines of *Louisiana Revised Statutes.*

"Miss Fenerty left a will. I'm not sure if you were aware, but she was very well off, though she gave quite a bit away when she was alive. Thanks to Old Miss McCune, no child ever went without shoes, and thanks to Miss Fenerty, no child ever went hungry. The two of them saw to it."

We looked to each other. Morris smiled and looked down, shaking his head. "She never said a word."

Mr. Herndon produced reading glasses, opening them as he looked to the document before him. He slipped them on. They were perched on the end of his nose.

"All right," he said. "Nina Beannock. Nina?" he looked over his glasses. Nina looked at us with embarrassment and raised her hand slightly.

"Says, 'to the Ezekiel Baptist Church, for the new sanctuary fund, new choir robes, an endowment for a scholarship to go to a deserving young boy and girl every year to attend college.' She also adds a note that there's a little left over if you want to buy a camel for your living nativity."

We laughed. She was gone and still making us laugh. Mr. Herndon was laughing with us as he swung his attention back to the document.

"She says for me to just show you the amount. Says you're real modest." He swung the paper over for Nina to see. She straightened it so she could read it. Then she put her fingertips to her forehead and said only, "Sweet Jesus!"

"Ellie…Schultz?" Mr. Herndon asked.

"Schultis," Ellie said.

"All right," Mr. Herndon affirmed, then he read, "One hundred and sixty acres of land in Bossier Parish on the Sligo Road for the family of Ellie Schultis to farm. Rich, wet river bottom land that will never dry out," Mr. Herndon looked over his glasses at Ellie. "She's written here, '*Sligo is a county in Ireland, you know.*'"

It was the first time I've seen Ellie cry.

At last, he came to me, and I was embarrassed to have been included. She had already given me more than I could ever repay. It was a princely sum, too, more than enough to pay off an unjust debt incurred by a drunken stock broker and rescue a floundering family in New York City, and still with plenty left over.

"She says that she's died still in your debt for the love and friendship you gave her."

Morris pulled his handkerchief from his pocket and gave it to me.

There was one more thing. There were several boxes of photographs and mementos that were locked in a bank vault on Texas Street. Mr. Herndon said that after the house fire on Stephenson Street, she had them moved from the shed behind her house for safekeeping, fearing a similar occurrence.

July 4, 1937

The smell of meat cooking has been on the air all day. I spent the holiday with Morris and his family on Jordan Street. Ellie and Mr. Albrizio, the Eaves, everyone was there. Finally, Nina, Ellie, and I came back to Crockett Street, leaving everyone, including Rev. Beannock and the baby. Little Ben Beannock has been held and cooed at by adoring faces all day.

The task of sifting through the archives of a life has been left to me, a curator of memories. Ellie and Nina have agreed to help me. The boxes sat on the floor of the parlor like cardboard treasure chests.

Today, in Miss Fenerty's belongings, we found a Bible, the kind that Nina says Christian families use to mark lineages and events. Miss Fenerty has filled in her parents and her siblings. They're all there: Mary (Maggie, she added in old, jagged print), Dan (drowned), Colleen (fever), Patrick (Patch-steamboat accident, Mitte Stevens [*sic*] Feb. 1869).

Bridget, *me*, she writes, born 1842.

And under it where the names of children, one's descendants, are to be placed, she's written the names of every child she ever cared for and every friend she's had. At points, she simply writes:

There were more. Memory fails me.

A page and a half and another two pages folded to fit fall out. More names of friends. And the families she chose for herself.

We came to three shoeboxes of photographs, filled with pictures of people in now out of style clothes. Each of us took one. Even though I had never met them, I knew who most of them were. Near the bottom of mine, I found one that made me pause, and then another that went with it.

"Nina," I said. Both Nina and Ellie put down their shoeboxes and came and looked over my shoulder.

It was a picture of young Bridget Fenerty and an old one-eyed black man. In the first, they were perfectly still and looking at the camera. In the second, they were laughing, and the movement made their faces and upper bodies blur into white as if they were becoming like angels.

"Here," I said. "Miss Bridget and Solomon Rusk. Your great-grandfather."

Nina had been chattering, keeping up a running commentary as she sifted through her box. She fell silent and touched her fingertips to the old man in the picture as she muttered his last words: *Live tall and walk straight.* Then I gave her a handkerchief from my purse. When she was done crying, I wrapped the two pictures in the handkerchief and gave them to her. And then we went to the shed. I had forgotten about the carriage.

July 5, 1937, Monday

A letter from Mother:

Dear Miriam,

You'll never guess what happened. It's a miracle, manna from heaven.

Mr. Vann at the bank called your father today and said that someone claiming to have had a debt to your father has paid it, just deposited into his account. Your father, as honest as he is, at first refused to accept it, but there's no way to send it back, as the person didn't identify themselves other than the name Ned Hennessy. Your father is certain he's never met anyone by that name, and he's certain that he would remember being owed this much money. It's quite a sum.

He's going to use it to pay off Mr. Gaudette's debt and reestablish a firm, his own firm this time, one that will operate soundly and honorably. I haven't seen him bounding with such joy since we were children, making plans, phone calls. He bought himself a new suit. Your father! A new business suit!

That's all I can write for now. My heart is filled to overflowing.

Love,
Mother

July 7, 1937

Here is a rough draft of a letter I'm composing to Mr. DaSilva in Houston:

Dear Mr. DaSilva,

Enclosed is a cashier's check for $3,000 which I believe is owed you from long ago. I will give you no more details than that.

You may keep it, invest it, spend it on your grandchildren, donate it to charity, anything you like. Please accept this as I'm sure that Miss Fenerty would want you to have it.

I want to reiterate that, of all the children she raised, you were her favorite, by far. She spoke of you constantly and even celebrated your birthday every year. March fourteenth, isn't it?

I again send you condolences and assure you that I share your grief for one of the most remarkable people I have ever met.

Sincerely,
Miriam Levenson

July 10, 1937, Saturday

Some men from the Ezekiel Baptist Church came and cleared out the shed, including the carriage, which they plan to use during church functions, picnics, and so forth. It disappeared west down Crockett Street, turning left on Texas Avenue on the back of a flatbed truck in the early morning haze.

Ellie and I have rented a house on Egan Street for now. The city has answered the siren call, the duet of Commerce and Progress, and made good on its promise and come for the house on Crockett Street and the lot it sits on.

Mr. Herndon regretfully explained to us that Miss Fenerty had agreed to let the city have the house, or really just the square of land it sits on, upon her death. The papers were drawn up; he said there was no point in arguing.

So it was this morning, a Saturday morning when the air was uncomfortably warm, that it came for the house on Crockett Street. One of the oil companies wants the lot for an office building.

Ellie and I watched from a bench across the street as a big truck pulling a bulldozer on a trailer parked out front. A man with a cigarette hanging off his lower lip climbed into the driver seat. He turned a switch, and the bulldozer grumbled off the trailer belching blue smoke from a pipe through a flap that gave way with each snort. The machine raised its plow as if shielding itself from some force in the sky and then dropped it on the ground with a thunderous blow like a challenge to the house. The sound of it reverberated off the sides of the buildings nearby, and then the flap on the pipe opened again and blue-white smoke erupted as the bulldozer rumbled over twin conveyor belts of tracks.

The front porch took the first blow, crumbling inward and snapping. The bulldozer retreated a few steps, pivoted and advanced again, splintering the next column. The corner of the roof gave way, and the bulldozer scooped up scraps of wood and shingles and dumped them in a pile in the front yard, near where Irving had dropped his whiskey bottle a few months before.

My vision blurred, and Ellie pulled me toward her and cradled my head under her neck. I shook with my crying, and she kissed the top of my head. I felt my face contorting, and I hid it into her shoulder. I could hear the men and machines continue their work, but I couldn't look.

Finally, Ellie said, "Sugar, let's just go. You ought not have to see this. Let's not look at it again and just remember it as it was."

So we did. When I looked around me, most of the crowd that was there with us had left also. Ellie drove; I couldn't.

Part VI
2005

Journal of Miriam Levenson
November 15, 2005

I haven't written in this journal in seventy years. And I haven't seen it since our last move, back to New York. I stopped writing in it shortly after I became a real journalist for the *Times, The Shreveport Times*, in the spring of 1937.

That summer, Joe DiMaggio hit his first career grand slam, Amelia Earhart and her navigator disappeared over the South Pacific, Japan invaded China, and the Nazis opened Buchenwald. The Marihuana Tax Act was passed that essentially made marijuana illegal. *Gone with the Wind* did in fact win the Pulitzer. The Duke of Windsor married the woman he abdicated the throne for, Wallis Simpson.

And Bridget Fenerty died at the age of ninety-five.

Knowing her was an honor that was unexpected and undeserved, meeting her was a gift without an occasion. And in seventy years, not a day has passed that I haven't thought about her. Not a single day. I've prayed to her regularly as if she were a Catholic saint, my intercessor before God, that I would be a good friend, a good aunt-daughter-sister, a good co-worker. A good person. God and those I leave behind will judge me on that.

Ellie and I stayed through the completion of the Louisiana State Exhibit Building and its mural. After a few years in Shreveport, my career took off, and Ellie and I moved to San Francisco, where I wrote for the *Chronicle*. It was hard to leave Shreveport; we had so many friends there. When war broke out, I was offered a position with the *New York Times*. Men were hard to find then, and women filled the gaps. With time, I became the White House correspondent with the southern manners, the Irish wit and gift for conversation, and the New York accent. When I finally met Mr. Roosevelt, I thanked him for the opportunity he gave me. He said you're welcome, though he seemed to have only a vague idea of the program.

Ellie painted and made a name for herself, exhibiting paintings on both coasts and in Europe. The Met has in its collection a pair of paintings, *La Camellia Vestida* and *La Azalea Desnuda*, both painted on a balcony in Shreveport, Louisiana in 1937. They'll be exhibited together after I'm gone. Having one's nude portrait displayed isn't in keeping with being a two-time Pulitzer winner, which I must say, I am, once for a story about the Berlin wall going up, and the second about the Berlin wall coming down. And a lot of near misses for Pulitzers in between which I took with a humility I didn't have until the winter of 1936-37.

We returned regularly to Louisiana to visit Ellie's family. To them, I'm sure we were just two old spinster friends, sharing the same "Boston marriage" as some called it. Two women who just couldn't seem to find the right man. LOL is how they put it now. Ha! is what we said then. We would always make a stop by Herby K's for a Shrimpbuster, which cost more than the fifteen cent sandwiches we ate in the thirties.

And one December night in the Fifties when we were in for the holidays, Ellie and I went out to the Lakecliff Bar to hear a young musician play. His name was Elvis Presley. Nobody knew who he was then. What a polite young man he was among that rough crowd of oilfield men and mechanics, and the rowdy women who attended them.

Morris and Sophie Taylor, the Randolphs, the Eaves boys have all passed on after giving to me and receiving from me a lifetime of friendship. We all take our first steps on this earth, and we all take our last, Mr. Rusk said. Their families were like my family. I always enjoyed entertaining them when they came to the big city.

Irving Glickstein returned to New York and began courting Hannah Blomberg and married her six months later. A year after that, they had the first of five children, a string that would only be interrupted by his time in a Japanese POW camp after he was captured in the South Pacific when his plane went down. Our victory liberated him, and he came home and had four more children. Each of them grew to be beautiful and gracious.

He was a good man who got the life he deserved, a hero to me not because of what he did in the Pacific, which was certainly heroic, but for deciding to continue on when his heart was broken and bleeding in the Louisiana rain. He and I were good friends until his time came, the time that was natural for him, not the time he chose for himself when he thought a pretty young Jewish girl was the whole world, and he couldn't live without her. Which most certainly was not the case, then or now.

We never spoke of that rainy Louisiana night when he came within a breath of departing early, and an old Irish voice called him in for tea at three in the morning. What we did speak of was how he would think of her as he squatted low in a grass hut eating rice with his fingers out of a bowl and drinking weak tea out of another as Japanese soldiers with kepis and rifles stood watch over him and the other POWs. Irving told me once that he would hear Bridget Fenerty's voice, "How's about a good strong cup of tea for a handsome young man?" It was a joke among the American and Australian prisoners in the camp, said in an Irish brogue, a cause for small laughter and hope.

Several times, I offered to pay him back for the engagement ring I pawned, money from whose sale kept Mother and Father from being evicted that winter. It had bothered me from the moment I accepted the money from the man on Common Street and continued to bother me for years. I offered to pay Irving back for it, but he wouldn't let me.

"I'll just consider it tuition for a valuable life lesson," he smiled.

Ironically, one of Irving's sons was the doctor who pronounced Ellie dead after her breast cancer returned and claimed her. He held me as I cried in his arms at a nurses' station at Columbia Presbyterian, and he whispered to me, "She was lucky to have you. She put up a good fight to stay with you."

I left a black smudge of mascara on his starched, white shoulder. He looked at it and smiled and drew me to him again.

"My father always thought the world of you," he said as he patted my back.

Young Dr. Glickstein had no idea how close he came to never being born at all. But life squeezes through a hole in the fence where death can't pursue it or waits trembling while the shadow of it passes over and away. Then life moves on and flourishes again. It is simply too strong for us.

February 16, 2006

Forgetfulness has put me here. I resisted the efforts of everyone, all my family, until the day that I almost lost Miss Fenerty's tam.

It was on the Number Six train headed uptown. I was coming back from the library when I became distracted by an old memory, but of course, at my age, they're all old memories. Across from me on the subway was a young man, a construction worker, headed up to Harlem or the Bronx. He looked African American or Dominican or somewhere in between, wearing work boots and a hard hat under a gray hoodie. He closed his eyes in fatigue, thinking or sleeping, perhaps.

The royal blue tam had gotten wet in the gray Manhattan mist, so I had taken it off and put it in my lap. When the train stopped at 68th Street, I got up, forgetting about the tam in my lap. It must have slipped to the floor, and I shuffled off the train. When I got to the top of the steps and onto the street, I felt the cold on my head. I put my hand there and realized I didn't have it.

I scrambled back down into the subway. I nervously searched the steps, the platform, under benches, everywhere, even the tracks themselves, but it was gone.

A woman in a business suit and a trench coat was waiting, and I asked her if she saw it. Just then the roar of a train on the opposite track filled the air, and then a train approached on the near track.

"Excuse me?" her lips said without a sound. Then, thinking I was panhandling, she reached in a clutch purse and gave me a couple of crumpled up dollars. I was so stunned, I took it. The doors opened to the train, and she stepped onto it. They closed, and she was gone. They were all gone, everyone in the train and on the platform. And the tam. Gone.

I sat down on the bench, and I just wanted to cry. So I did, for a moment. Then I realized what Miss Fenerty would say:

"Oh, dear, it's just a thing. Let it go, then."

I made my way up the steps without the tam, my head cold. When I got to the top, I saw the construction worker across Lexington Avenue. He saw me and waved to me with the blue tam in his hand. I stepped off the curb and a taxi honked at me, and I stepped back on.

The man, whose name was Hector Ramirez, motioned that he would bring it to me. I waited, and when the light changed, he brought it over with a big smile. I cried in relief, and he put his big gloved hand on my shoulder.

"Don't cry, *abuelita*," he said. "You dropped it on the subway, and I picked it up for you. We were at 103rd Street before I realized it."

I tried to give him money, but he wouldn't take it, so we went into a Starbucks, and I bought him a coffee with the money the young woman had given me. He thanked me and said he had to get home to the Bronx to sit with his baby while his wife went to work. He left me sitting in Starbucks with Frank Sinatra playing overhead and the royal blue tam in my hand.

Then I thought, 103rd Street?

He had ridden three stops back downtown, dead tired after a day of work in the cold, wet outdoors, anxious to get home and see his wife and his child, just to give an old woman her hat.

God bless him, I thought.

Sept. 11, 2006

My neighbor and best friend here at the retirement center is Mervin Washington. He and I jokingly call this place the Dinosaur Ranch, though, for the most part, we like it. They let us keep our pets here. Francie stays curled up with Mervin's little orange mop of a dog whom he's named Elmo after the Sesame Street character.

Tonight, the television had a special on the five-year anniversary of 9-11. I remember watching the television in horror as a plane crashed into the first tower and then from my window as a second one crashed into the second tower. Then I waited nervously for my great-nephew Patrick to call, which he did. He was okay, but he lost a lot of friends. He's like a son to me.

Mervin and I sat and watched the special, each of us getting angry all over again. Finally, Mervin said, and these are his words and not mine, "How *effed* up you gotta be to think of something like that and pull it off?"

Even in the dimmest of times, Mervin always makes me laugh. I hope I go first. I can't imagine a world without him. I've said goodbye to so many.

Let someone else say goodbye to me this time.

From the desk of Patrick Levenson

May 29, 2007

She rides in the front seat, blinking her eyes in the green dashboard light and watching the signs go by as if she's reading them. Maybe she is. Her small head with its small ears watch each white-trimmed green sign flash by, and then she looks at me.

The cardboard box with the ceramic urn is on the backseat. Written on it in Sharpie is *Miriam Ruth Levenson.* No way would I put it in the trunk. She rides up here with us, Francie and me.

South of Raleigh, about halfway to Charlotte, I've finally driven as much as I can, and we stop and get a room. It's a room with two doubles, all they had, but the dog wants to sleep curled up at the foot of my bed. I prefer it that way, too.

I call Jeannie and tell her where I am, and she asks one more time if I'm sure I want to do this alone. She could fly into Atlanta or Charlotte and meet me. I would meet her at the gate, and she would be wearing the blue tam.

No, I say, and I thank her. I miss you, but this is a job, a duty, for me and Francie. Then Jeannie and I tell each other we love you again and we mean it again and we say good night.

The old dog wakes me up at one a.m. to go outside.

I scramble on a FDNY sweatshirt over my pajama bottoms and nose my feet into slippers. My graying hair is askew, I'm sure, but I leave it. She sits patiently as I put her on her leash, and we take the elevator down to what is delicately called the "Pet Relief Area." There's a post with disposable bags next to the sign.

I let her go, and she noses around the patch of grass hemmed in by a generic iron fence. The wind pushes the tops of the pines and makes them brush out a song against the Carolina starlight. They bend slightly and recover upright again and then bend when the next wind pushes high in their tops. The sound of the surf up in the green boughs, here over a hundred miles inland.

I think of Aunt Miriam on her maiden journey south, and I wonder if the buck she saw that night in 1936 moved on to sire a fawn from a different doe when the object of his desire was struck by a 1928 Packard driven by a pretty young Jewish girl on her way to the only job she could get.

And then I think of my namesake, Patrick Fenerty. Perhaps he camped under pines like these one hundred forty years ago when he was a private in the Sixth Louisiana, headed north on a six-month adventure that became a four-year horror, part of an army that marched and cheered and shouted and fought and coughed and shit together. They camped together on nights when it rained hard and cold, and on nights when it rained hot and steamy. And on perfect nights like this one when the air is neither cool nor warm and is whipped gently and lovingly into a breeze that sways the highest parts of the trees.

And when the war was over, Patrick Fenerty walked every pace of it back to Louisiana, sleeping under trees much like these, perhaps, listening to the brush of them against the midnight blue Carolina sky. Sleeping with the ghosts of the ones who would not come back, as the pines swayed at the top and shushed the drowsy countryside to sleep. Hush, now. Hush.

I look up to the waxing moon, oblong but filling out, just a night or two from becoming a perfect white disk mottled with slate blue smudges.

I feel a nudge against my hand, and it's Francie. She's relieved herself and sampled every scent the small Pet Relief Area has to offer and left her own. We walk slowly between the cars parked in orderly rows painted in the asphalt, Francie leaning sweetly into my leg and loping along with the slinky gait of her breed. Her claws clack when we move from the asphalt of the parking lot to the concrete of the entrance way. The sliding doors open for us, and we pass through, and the dog's claws fall silent on the carpet. In the industrial cold of the lobby, the night clerk is absorbed in his cell phone, thumbs bouncing off the tiny screen. The dog and I wait for the elevator as the canned music plays softly overhead, something contemporary and non-confrontational. When the bell dings, we quietly get on and ride upstairs.

Days Inn
Meridian, Mississippi
May 30, 2007

Television lawyers have commercials here like in New York, each one trying to out-badass the other, except with southern accents. They point at the camera and scowl, some wearing ridiculous hats like cowboys. All of them are just trying to be memorable.

In between them, the weatherman says that the rain is moving in. I click off the television after the weather and sports. She's looking at me, looking for Aunt Miriam, the lifelong companion of the dog's comparatively short life. Francie slept the whole drive curled up in a ring on the front seat, only occasionally rising to look at the road before curling up again.

I wake to the flash of lightning and the distant muffled sound of thunder a few seconds later. The dog is under the covers with me, nestled in close with her head on my chest. I pull the comforter back and there's her small head, eyes blinking in canine embarrassment. Something primal inside of her is terrified by the sounds of the weather. I get up and close the curtains, but the weather still flashes behind them as the rain flies in sideways and clatters on the window.

I was dreaming of Scotty Morelli, an eager, fresh-faced probie who was gaining a reputation in the department for his dependability and in the station for his Bolognese. The dream is one I have often, of him headed up a stairwell in his bunker gear while people are filing down past him. Like a fish swimming upstream. It was the last time I saw him alive.

I reach under the lamp on the bedside table and turn on the light to look at the map of Louisiana and Mississippi again, the states like Siamese twins hugging the same river like a shared organ. Tomorrow I'll make the final leg of the trip. I should be in Shreveport well before sunset. I'll find Cross Lake and the dam, and I'll set out two canvas lawn chairs, one for me and one for Francie. I'll have a glass of Pinot like Aunt Miriam liked, even though I prefer Guinness, and I'll feed Francie treats, as many as the old dog wants. This is a special occasion.

Then, as the sun slides under the bridge and is about to dip into the lake and Texas, I'll spread Aunt Miriam's ashes in the water, along with the ashes of the letters to and from Ellie. But I'll hold onto the vase and keep fresh flowers in it like she asked, daffodils if I can get them. And I'll keep her memory.

And then, when it's dark, I'll turn our lawn chairs to the east, into the night sky, and check the watch that Aunt Miriam left me, the one that was Patrick Fenerty's watch given to him by his sister Bridget. It keeps perfect time now, now that the man down on Lexington Avenue has cleaned out the Caddo Lake mud from the inside of it and polished it so that the inscription from Virgil's *Aeneid* is clearly legible.

"Nulla dies umquam memori vos eximet aevo."

No day shall erase you from the memory of time.

The internet says the moon will rise at 8:26 pm in the east, a full moon. There are footprints there, footprints that are only a memory now, unseen but surely still there in the windless moon atmosphere. Footprints that weren't there in 1937 when Bridget Fenerty and Ellie Schultis and Miriam Levenson looked up to it.

Tonight, I'll look up into that moon and see if there's anyone looking back.

Metropolitan Museum of Art
Accession Number 7.28

Child's doll. Loose cotton, canvas, copper, wool thread.

Made on a transatlantic crossing from Galway and Liverpool to New Orleans by Maggie Fenerty of Ballinlough, County Roscommon, Ireland for her younger sister Bridget, most likely in the late winter of 1847. Take special notice of the twine bindings and the small details of the doll's facial features. The eyes, made from copper tacks tarnished to green, and red woolen thread smile and hair are testimony to the maker's creativity with only a modicum of materials.

Gift of the bequest of Miriam Ruth Levenson, 2007

Metropolitan Museum of Art
Accession Numbers 7.65 and 7.66

La Camellia Vestida and *La Azalea Desnuda.*

These paired paintings were made by American painter Eleanor 'Ellie' Schultis of her friend Miriam Levenson, the Pulitzer Prize winning journalist. The titles of the paintings are plays on the titles of Francisco Goya's famous paired masterpieces, *La Maja Vestida* and *La Maja Desnuda,* which are displayed in the Prado in Madrid. Schultis is thought to have painted *La Camellia* and *La Azalea* in the spring of 1937, just before Levenson began her newspaper career with *The Shreveport Times.* The clothed version was very likely done first, as the camellias are in bloom in the background. The pose is identical in each work, and the gaze of the subject is at once soft and intense in both portraits. The nude version, however, contains a background of blooming azaleas, and there is an inner vulnerability that goes beyond her nudity when compared to the clothed one. Notice how the red and white flowers are echoed in the skin tones of the subject. The paired paintings are exhibited here for the first time, which was the wish of Miss Levenson.

Gift of the bequest of Miriam Ruth Levenson, 2007

Acknowledgements

I've drawn on a number of books in preparing this novel. Father Niehaus' *The Irish of New Orleans*, a wonderful description of antebellum New Orleans, when the Big Easy was essentially an Irish city, home to twice as many Irish as French; Goodloe Stuck's *Shreveport Madame*, the story of Annie McCune, an Irish immigrant who ran the most notorious brothel among the dozens of brothels in turn-of-the-century Shreveport; John D. Winters' *The Civil War in Louisiana*; Bill Dixon's *The Last Days of Last Island*; and *Wicked Shreveport* by Bernadette Polombo, Gary Joiner, Chris Hale, and Cheryl White.

Miss Eliza Leslie wrote several books regarding housekeeping and "female deportment" that were considered the ultimate authority of the nineteenth century. Among her titles were *The Lady's Receipt-Book: A Useful Companion for Large or Small Families*, and *Seventy-Five Receipts for Pastry, Cakes, and Sweetmeats*, and *Miss Leslie's Behavior Book*. They give a wonderful, valuable look at nineteenth century life.

Radclyffe Hall wrote *The Well of Loneliness*, the story of the love between two women in a time when it was tacitly, if not overtly, forbidden. She had previously published a successful novel, *Adam's Breed*, but risked "the shipwreck of her career" in publishing *The Well of Loneliness* in 1928. The editor of the British paper *Sunday Express*, James Douglas, said of the novel, "I would rather give a healthy boy or a healthy girl a phial of prussic acid than this novel." Well, Mr. Douglas, censorship is the equivalent of prussic acid.

And of course, there's Eric Brock and his collection of books on the history of Shreveport. He died young, and it's a shame. I would have loved to have visited with him. May God rest his soul and all the souls of the departed, then.

Oakland Cemetery holds Mr. Brock's grave, along with those of Annie McCune, Nathan Goldkind, quite a number of Levys and Kahns, and the Yellow Fever mound. Ada Mary Carlile was only four when she died in 1900, though there's no convincing information on who her mother and father were. She is, however, buried in Oakland Cemetery within the same wrought iron fence as Annie McCune, who most definitely was a real person and a notorious madam, along with Nell Jester and Bea Haywood. You're quite unlikely to find the graves of Isaac Taylor, Frank O. Burton, Sr., Solomon Rusk, or Bridget Fenerty there, though.

The historical events happened much as I've described, including the translocation of the Confederate government to Shreveport after the fall of New Orleans, though it stayed a brief time in Opelousas and Alexandria. Shreveport was an occupied city after the war, and the Yellow Fever epidemic of 1873 killed a fourth of the population and drove many away for good. Just after the turn of the century, oil was discovered north of town, and beautiful old homes downtown were brought down by prosperity, and new ones were built in South Highlands.

First lady Eleanor Roosevelt did in fact visit Shreveport in March of 1937, and it's quite possible that she was accompanied by her very good friend Lorena Hickok, who was a journalist assigned to cover her. There are some who say that both FDR and Eleanor had girlfriends, and surviving correspondence hints at this. But in those days, you didn't march in the street under the rainbow flag. Most just kept quiet and hoped their own personal truth didn't gnaw a hole in them. In some states they could've gotten arrested; in some countries, they can still be put to death.

The Caddo Parish Courthouse has a monument on its north side, the Texas Street side, a remarkable thing if you view it as art and history and not politics and philosophy. It was sculpted by a Texan, Frank Teich, out of Texas granite. The model for the young man on the pedestal is unknown to me, though I imagine it was a young relative of the sculptor. Will people see Champ Lockett up there from now on? If so, then my apologies to whoever the model really was.

The New London, Texas school explosion of March 18, 1937 remains the worst school disaster in American history. The *Shreveport Times* carried the story with a headline in large font, and the story was picked up by the *New York Times* as the news was spread around the world. Among those who sent their condolences was the chancellor of Germany. Yes, him.

Ma Fenerty said that the pistol is the devil's right hand. Actually, Steve Earle said it in his song of the same name.

Gratitude

This book was born into a family of first readers who crowded around it, held it, praised it, scolded it, and saw to it that it grew up. Thanks to them, it got better:

Gina Lobue, Shawn Kleinpeter, Dawn Jelks, Gloria Thudium, Nan Murtagh, Lindsey Fontenot, J'on Blumberg (who checked my facts on Judaism, particularly southern Judiasm), Flavia Lancon, Steve Feigley, Julie Abadie, and Liz Parker. And, of course, Katie Schellack and Emily Aucoin. If you enjoyed this story, you can thank them.

When I think of the teachers I had growing up, I think of Mark Twain's quote about his mother: "My mother had a great deal of trouble with me, but I think she enjoyed it." And so I thank the men and women who dedicated their lives to the task of educating me and the rest of us. Of course, when I think of having trouble with me, I think of my own parents as well. Thanks, Mom. God rest you, Daddy.

Thanks to my wife, St. Catherine of Louisiana, *pray for us*, my children, Tom, Patrick (Patch), Rosie, and Rebecca (Boots). The Chinese blessing says, "May you live in interesting times." I can't imagine more interesting people than my family with whom to spend those times.

C.H. Lawler is a Louisianan from his first steps. *The Memory of Time* is his second novel. The first, *The Saints of Lost Things*, is also set in Louisiana and the South. He has a blog on Goodreads.com and has been a guest blogger for *Southern Writers Magazine.*

More information and discussion can be found at::

www.facebook.com/chlawlerstories/

and

www.facebook.com/The-Saints-of-Lost-Things -818005771597745/

and

https://www.goodreads.com/author/show/10362089.C_H_Lawler

Made in the USA
Coppell, TX
27 October 2023

23468105R10260